# Falcon Night

## Book Three of The Falcon Trilogy

### Stphan & Melodi Grundy

TLS

ISBN13: 978-1-959350-05-7

Set in: Georgia 11pt/Concetta Kalvani 27pt, Farmhouse 36pt

©The Three Little Sisters
USA/CANADA

# Chapter One

Nikolaus sat in his own chamber, the keening night wind lashing pellets of sleet against the little glass panes of the arrow-slits. It was foul weather, even for the end of October, and the room in Burg Fürstensee's old tower - built more for defense than for comfort, unlike some of the later-built parts of the castle - was always a little chilly, even when the fire of his stove roared at its full strength. He stretched his stockinged feet out towards the stove, letting the warmth soak deep into his frozen bones: even his heaviest boots could not keep out the cold of his cavern-sanctum, and he had been down there long that night, speaking again with the ghost of Graf Günther.

So Priestess Margerite has brought challenge to Princess Ortlieb, he thought. The knowledge brought him some relief after the long months of worry, of carefully phrasing his Order reports so that there would be no hint of his failure in watching over her - and, worse, in holding the demon in his elder brother's body under control. He had not guessed at the power that the eclipse would lend it, enough to wrest free of the carefully crafted bonds that kept Christoph acting closely enough to himself that none would blame his vagaries on anything more than grief and strain. Yet, Nikolaus consoled himself, he had won mastery over it again, without even the aid Günther's ghost had given him in calling it up, and that was sufficient to prove him worthy of the Order's onyx ring, though he would have to be most circumspect in demonstrating his skill.

Wrapping his hand in cloth against the metal's heat, Nikolaus lifted the silver pitcher of Glühwein from the top of the stove, pouring out a gobletful for himself. He blew hot steam from the drink, sipping carefully at it: strong red wine, honey, a touch of precious cinnamon, all fit to restore the warm humours of his body after a night of speaking to the dead in the cold. If Margerite had chosen, as was any Order member's right, to call challenge on Ortlieb, then Nikolaus was no longer responsible for her actions: should she succeed in slaying the Light-Bearer Princess, Margerite would wear Ortlieb's ruby ring on her finger thereafter; while, should she fail...she, and her son, would be Ortlieb's responsiblity.

And am I, then, to lose such a prize? Nikolaus thought angrily. With an effort he calmed himself: as unfitting for a magician of the Order of Light-Bearers to let himself be mastered by fury as by any other feeling. Order ranks and rights might, to the initiated, supersede the ranks and rights of law; but they could not overturn them. While his father Graf Heinrich still drew breath, Margerite was bound by law to Burg Fürstensee; until her son Wolfram reached his majority, she would be regent in Burg Falkenstein - now held by men who were Nikolaus' in truth, though they believed that it was still Christoph who ordered them while his father was incapacitated.

As well, that I did not slay my father straight off, but have taken care that he remains alive, though he can neither speak nor move. Nikolaus allowed himself a brief smile: always trusting that Ortlieb did not simply dispose of her, Margerite belonged to Burg Fürstensee; and Burg Fürstensee belonged to Nikolaus. And soon she will belong to me more directly: the Pope shall grant my request, for it costs him nothing and gains him monies that he needs desperately - and she shall no longer be my stepmother, but free to wed me.

But what drove her to seek out Ortlieb? Nikolaus rested his elbows on the polished table-top, staring at the gold haloes of the two candles reflected in the shiny dark wood as though he might see some answering vision there. Ambition, perhaps: Nikolaus had heard that Margerite's father was a poor Ritter holding a little border keep; having leapt from Ritter's daughter to Gräfin of Falkenstein to Gräfin of Fürstensee - did Margerite now seek a higher place yet, as Landgräfin of Niederwald, hardly a step beneath the wife of Kaiser Karl himself?

Nikolaus could credit that easily enough, for he had heard of how swiftly she had seized her rights as mistress of Burg Falkenstein after Graf Ruprecht's death, and here in Burg Fürstensee she had wasted no time in gathering the reins of what power she could into her hands. Once Margerite had overcome those vestiges of squeamish sentiment that still seemed to plague her, she would be worthy indeed of the ring Ortlieb wore - if she could overcome the magics of the Order Princess.

An unequal battle that might be, like a new-made squire lifting his sword against a knight belted for twenty years; but Graf Günther assured him that there was more to Margerite than her short half-year of Order learning hinted at. And she would have help: Graf Günther's, limited though he might be by the bounds that had been set upon his spirit in punishment for his failure at Wolfram's birth; Nikolaus' own, as much as he could give...and, it might be, the aid of their Master, Whose son had grown within her womb and nursed now at her breast. The gardens of the Bishop's courtyard shimmered pale with Martinmas frost beneath the morning sun, ice glazing the stone seats and shining mirror-bright from the surfaces of the little pools.

Her son cradled warmly under her fur-lined cloak, Margerite stood between Georg and Eva, with Bernhardt discreetly on the squire's other side; the Bishop and several churchmen were there as well, and Father Etienne standing slim and straight in his black robe and rolled canon's hat, ready to lead the celebratory Mass. Before them, Arnmut knelt in front of Ritter Gottfried.

In spite of the cold, the squire's fair head and white feet were bare, though otherwise he was dressed as befitted a young man of knightly birth, in thick woolen hose and a blue doublet of fine wool trimmed with black velvet. Ritter Gottfried's black velvet doublet bulged over the bandage that wrapped his shoulder; he had untied the plain dark tail of his hair, its loose silken shimmer softening the severe lines of his sharp face, and he smiled down at his Knappe with a look of rare joy, though it seemed that his cold gray eyes watered a little in the winter brightness.

"Arnmut von Eisenstein," Gottfried said, his strong baritone voice rough - with the sting of tears? Margerite wondered. For something precious was ending: Gottfried must soon take another Knappe, as Arnmut would have a squire of his own, and the two of them might well be parted by their duties when they came back to Burg Fürstensee. "Well have you served me as Knappe, through many dangers and hardships; well have you proven yourself in battle, by the strength of your arm and your honour. I offer you now the oath of a knight. Will you swear this day, before these nobles of the Church and of this world, to raise your sword in defense of the defenseless..."

Margerite could not help glancing sideways at Bernhardt. His face was still as he listened to Gottfried speaking. Once Bernhardt had knelt as Arnmut did, and sworn the same vows: how many of them had he been forced to break, in the harrowing course of his long exile?

That is over now, Margerite reminded herself. Whatever Bernhardt does after this, he shall do in his own name as knight and nobleman, and no longer have to cloak himself in a lesser evil in order to strike a blow against the greater. Beside Bernhardt, Georg trembled a little with eagerness, his blue eyes shining beneath the shadow of his deep red hood. Margerite needed no spell or talisman to tell her the youth's thoughts. Georg was thinking of the day when he, too, would take that oath, and no doubt hoping that it would not be long.

He had shown his mettle as surely as Arnmut had, carrying Bernhardt's standard in that desperate battle with Ortlieb's troops: the neatly sewn wound that slashed down the side of his freckled cheek stood as proof of his bravery. If only Christoph... but surely it would not be long before Father Etienne turned homeward with them, to free Heinrich's eldest son from the demon that raged within his flesh! Then, Christ willing, Christoph would be able to name his own Knappe as knight, and surely would do when he heard of Georg's bravery.

The sunlight flashed blue from the polished steel edges of Gottfried's sword as the young knight drew blade, tapping Arnmut's broad shoulders and shining hair. Despite his wounded arm, Gottfried's hand flickered out so swiftly that Margerite could hardly see its path, striking Arnmut's cheek hard enough to rock his head back.

"Let that be the last blow you take for which you do not give answer," Gottfried said proudly. "Arise now, Ritter Arnmut." He took the new knight's square hands in his own thin ones, lifting Arnmut to his feet and embracing him tightly as he kissed the young man's fair cheeks. Arnmut clung to Gottfried in turn, as if they had been lovers long-parted, and Margerite swallowed hard against the lump rising in her throat.

It ought to have been one of Arnmut's kinswomen, or his lady, who girded him with the belt of knighthood: but they were far from Burg Eisenstein, Margerite was wedded, and Eva was...almost spoken for by Christoph. If she can still bear to have him - Margerite thrust the thought away hard. So it was Gottfried who buckled the white belt about Arnmut's waist and fastened the spurs upon his heels.

Bernhardt embraced the new-made Ritter in turn with the kiss of brotherhood, and Margerite found her eyes closing for a moment: while Heinrich drew breath, she would never feel Bernhardt's lips upon her own skin, nor the solid strength of his body warm against her own. Indeed, it might be that they must soon say their farewells for a while, for Bernhardt had his battle of law to fight against his brother, and Margerite had...her own duties.

The thought dogged Margerite through the celebratory
Mass, shadowing the brilliant play of colours through Bishop
Otto's stained-glass windows and dulling the brightness of
the beeswax candles in her mind. Even when the Bishop
lifted the Host, the gilded plate on which the bread rested
flashing the windows' rays of red and blue, purple and gold,
like clear light broken through water into rainbows, she
found it hard to turn her thoughts to the Mystery of Christ's
Body and Blood; nor did the deep smooth gleam of the
thumb-sized amethysts set about the bowl and foot of the
silver chalice soothe Margerite's mind, though she knew that
to be one of the virtues of Jupiter's stone.

Bishop Otto had ordered up a fair feast, celebrating
Martinmas and Arnmut's knighting at once. Three great
roasted geese stuffed with apples and chestnuts held pride
of place on the Bishop's table, their crackling brown skin
glazed shiny with honey. The best pure white salt glittered in
the shell-shaped silver cellar; rich cheese pastries steamed
upon silver dishes, and the dry spicy white wine from France
flowed freely into the silver goblets.

The heavy weight of Kobolt's furry side leaned against
Margerite's leg, and when she was not quick enough to slip
a sliver of goosemeat down from the table, she would feel
the cat's paw upon her thigh and the delicate touch of claws;
she noticed, as well, that Eva's hand dropped from her plate
every so often, and guessed that Kriemhilt was serving her in
the same manner.

"It has been a delight to have you here, Gräfin Margerite,"
the Bishop said politely to her.

"I thank you for your kindness to us, your Grace,"
Margerite answered. "Surely you have treated us with every
charity and honour, and I hope that someday we shall be
able to repay you."

The Bishop waved a heavy hand, the amethyst of his episcopal ring glinting. "You have done far more for the good folk of Niederwald by your part in bringing down the Landgräfin's evil." He shuddered, his ruddy face paling for a moment as if he were recalling the horrors he had seen in Ortlieb's wain. "Be sure that all Christians in this land would thank you, if they knew what you have done! But now I would ask what your plans are, so that I may better aid you. Do you think you will need much longer to recover from your ordeal, or do you mean to start southward before the snow blocks the road? You will assuredly be welcome here for as long as you choose to stay - yet I know that it must grieve you to have been so long away from your husband, in his sorrowful state."

Margerite started. She had not expected this choice to come on her so soon; and the temptation to stay with the Bishop for the winter, here in his court where she and Wolfram were safe from the Order of Light-Bearers, safe from Nikolaus' machinations...and from the sounds of hoofbeat and hunting horn through the night-storms, for Burg Fürstensee was not, after all, so very far from Burg Falkenstein...was very great, like the temptation to stay snuggled deep in a warm featherbed on a morning when a crust of ice glazed her bowl of washing-water. Yet there was still Christoph to think of; and beyond that - she tried to press the thought down, but could not - there was no way to know whether Heinrich still lived: Margerite could be a widow even now, and free to marry...

Bernhardt's head was bent doggedly over his plate, as if he feared to meet Margerite's gaze. His hair still looked odd, a finger's-length of brown showing above stark walnut-dyed black, as if the Landgraf's son were only slowly pushing away the soldier of the Free Companies; still, better for him to look a little strange than to crop his head like that of a peasant or criminal. But Father Etienne was staring straight at Margerite, his pale sapphire eyes piercing through her own, and his sternness goaded her on as surely as the brightness of morning light reminding her that it was time to arise from sleep.

"It does, indeed," Margerite told the Bishop. "Though I shall be sad to leave you, it were best for me to be going within a few days, no longer."

Bishop Otto inclined his raven-black head, his face calm. "And your companions, save for Herr Bernhardt and Father Etienne, shall undoubtedly go with you?"

Etienne's eyebrows went up, and Margerite saw his long fingers tighten on the slim hilt of his eating-dagger. "Your Grace, I had thought to go with the Gräfin as well," the canon broke in. I have been her confessor for some time, and..."

"You are needed too badly here," Bishop Otto said, his deep voice quiet, but ringing with authority. "I have not dealt with the Inquisition among my flock before, nor am I the man who can explain these dire matters to them. I am sure that these two noble knights - " his brief smile flicked over Gottfried and Arnmut - "and this brave young Knappe can see to the Gräfin's bodily safety, while there are many holy shrines among the way which can tend to her soul."

Etienne frowned, his lower lip thin and pale as if he were biting it to keep his words back. Of course: he could not speak to the Bishop about Christoph's possession, nor was there any plausible urgency which would override his need to stay in Niederwald and await the Inquisitors who would examine Ortlieb's dreadful baggage and ask their questions of Hedwig and Oda - if the Order Princess' assistants lived long enough to be interrogated.

O dear Maria, Margerite thought, if only I had not spoken so quickly! Now I must go back without Father Etienne; and having failed against Christoph's demon once, it will be sure of its strength against me. The scabbed wound down Georg's cheek stood out raw and livid against his sudden pallor as he, too, realized what the Bishop's words must mean, and Eva brushed the sign of the Cross swiftly over herself. Bernhardt was frowning as well; only Gottfried and Arnmut, who had not seen the demon for themselves, and had been chafing quietly since hearing what had come to pass in Burg Fürstensee while they were gone, looked eager to set out.

"Your Grace," Margerite said, "though I had not forgotten about the Inquisition, that brings me to another question. I am surely likely to be called as a witness: though I am eager to be home, I would not leave what I have done unfinished, for the sake of all those whom Ortlieb's evil harmed. Should I, then, stay here until the matter is finished with?"

Bishop Otto looked at Father Etienne. "Etienne, you know the Inquisitorial procedure well. Shall they, do you think, require the Gräfin's presence at once upon their arrival, or is the case likely to be drawn out for some months?"

Father Etienne's mouth worked as though he were swallowing down the aftertaste of a bitter morsel: Margerite could guess that what he wanted to say and the truth he must tell the Bishop might not be the same thing. "The Inquisition does not move swiftly, for the power vested in them and the grave matters with which they deal requires the greatest caution, that the strength meant for good does not do evil in its haste. There may well be much for them to do before Gräfin Margerite is called in to give her testimony: that will almost certainly take place towards the end of their investigation."

The Bishop smiled heartily at Margerite. "Then, Gräfin, you are free to go home as you please! Do have some more of the goose; it is by no means gluttony for a woman who is nursing a strong son to eat as well as she can, especially when feasting in the honour of such a saint as the holy Martin."

"I see no way out of it," Father Etienne sighed later, sitting in Margerite's chambers with the rest of their little company gathered around - even Arnmut, though the new knight's eyes were heavy from the rich meal following his sleepless night of vigil. "Bishop Otto rules his episcopate with such a firm hand, I had not guessed that he would quail before the thought of dealing with the Inquisition; but he was badly shaken by what he saw of Ortlieb's wagon, and has little liking for matters that go beyond his usual compass."

"Yet Margerite cannot go back alone to face a demon!" Bernhardt protested. "If you cannot be with her, or even I, though I can aid only with my sword..."

"I shall be with her, and Ritter Arnmut also," said Ritter Gottfried, turning his cold stare on Bernhardt. "As the Bishop said, there is no need for the Gräfin to fear for her bodily safety: I will trust my sword and my faith to stand between her and any spirit of darkness."

"Except," Father Etienne added gently, "that the demon possesses the body of a man who, I believe, has no part in its evil. Though some failure of faith or mind is needed for such a spirit to creep in, no son of Adam is without some chink in the armour of his soul, nor is there any reason to believe that Christoph invited or knowingly assented to his possession. Therefore even the most steadfast sword shall be of little avail. You would not, I believe, willingly bring about the death of any man within a demon's embrace, unshriven and unable to repent of his sins - much less the death of Graf Heinrich's son, who may indeed be the lord of Fürstensee already, if Graf Heinrich has perished in these last months."

Gottfried shook his head slowly, his thin features pinched and pale.

"What can we do?" Georg asked, his honeyed tenor sharpening with urgency. "If you will not come with us, Father, and we cannot lift blades against the demon for Christoph's sake, how then can he be freed?"

The tiny lines around the priest's blue eyes seemed to deepen, his forehead furrowing. Margerite guessed that Father Etienne was struggling sorely: his duty as an exorcist, and his knowledge of Christoph's torment, balanced against the Bishop's orders - and perhaps the need to guide the Inquisitors carefully away from those things they must not know, as well as make clear to them those things they must.

"I shall do what I can," Father Etienne said at last. "Though the foes of the Order are not neatly ranked, nor always known, yet I have many strong friends and allies on whom I can call at need. Christ willing, I shall be able to send someone who can aid you in Christoph's exorcism as well as I can myself, and as discreetly. I can ward all of you as well, to hold you as safe as may be from the demon's power; though I warn you, its worst weapon is not its magical might, but the words which may bring you to self-hatred or despair, if there is anything within the depths of your souls which you have not already met and mastered." Father Etienne looked straight at Gottfried as he spoke.

The severe young knight did not turn from the canon's gaze, but a faint flush of pink blossomed on his stark cheekbones...and whatever Ritter Gottfried has said to the Father in his confessions is a matter for himself and God alone, Margerite reminded herself. But she remembered how Christoph's demon had used her night with Heinrich to taunt her, and terrified Georg by another means: she could well imagine what words it might use to a chaste and deeply pious young man.

"Then we must trust in Christ for aid," Ritter Gottfried said. "When shall we ride? And what of the men of the Bear's Paw, who fought beside us? Shall they stay here with Bernhardt, in case Landgraf Gerhardt chooses to forget the inviolability of Holy Church, or go back to Burg Fürstensee with us - or do you mean to pay them now and send them on their way?" Gottfried's voice betrayed no hint of which choice he thought best. Though Margerite knew how strongly he disliked the Free Companies, the knight did owe his life, or at the very least the use of his arm, to Jochanan's skill as a physician; and the Bear's Paw's loyalty and fierceness in the fight must have impressed him as well.

"I do not think Bishop Otto would thank us for keeping them here any longer than we must," Bernhardt commented dryly. "Nor will it be to my credit when these matters are looked into, if I kept a Free Company as bodyguards in the Bishop's court. Perhaps it would be best to pay Hauptmann Paul off now and let him seek a commission elsewhere... Yet, Margerite, I would feel safer in my mind if I knew that there were a number of strong men in whom you could trust utterly either in or near Burg Fürstensee, should things go ill. It was by Mother Maria's mercy alone that you managed to live through your last escape, and I do not wish to think of you taking to the road thus again."

"And we cannot set off from here too quickly," broke in Arnmut. "My...Gottfried's shoulder is still far from healed. Surely you will not leave until he is fit for hard riding again?" The new knight looked anxiously at Margerite. Though the shadows of his night's vigil blurred purple beneath his clear blue eyes, they only underscored his youthful fairness; and it touched Margerite that, even though Arnmut wore belt and spurs of his own now, his care for his knight had not lessened in the slightest.

Gottfried moved his shoulder, rotating it beneath the bandage. "I am well-healed enough now. I could ride, and fight, tomorrow if it were needed."

Margerite paused, torn. She was sure that Gottfried ought to rest longer, for it was but a week and a half since he had taken his wound, and two days less since the battle around Ortlieb's wain had reopened it, bringing him to the very threshold of death. And the longer she stayed at the Bishop's court, the longer it would be before she had to say farewell to Bernhardt - dear Maria, it had been such pain to part from him before; how could she bear to do it again? Yet there was no telling what state Burg Fürstensee might be in now, how openly Nikolaus had taken the reins of power into his own hands or what damage might have been done between the Light-Bearer and Christoph's demon.

"I think we shall let Jochanan be the judge of that," Father Etienne said firmly. "When he says that you are fit to ride, then you shall be. But be assured, Margerite shall not set on her way without you."

It was then Margerite realized that Eva, usually so outspoken, had not said a single word since the discussion began. The blond maiden sat quietly with Kriemhilt in her lap, petting the cat and looking into her green-gold eyes as if the others were not in the room with them at all, let alone speaking of the fate of the man who was almost her betrothed. But Margerite could see Eva's hand trembling against Kriemhilt's gold-dusted black fur: she knew - from her years as virgin helper to the Light-Bearer abbess of the Convent of the Holy Cross, perhaps better than any of them - what it would mean to dwell in a castle where a demon walked free in its ruler's flesh, however warded against its powers they might be; and Eva would have the added pain of seeing the void of corruption in the eyes of the man she had loved.

Yet the girl made no protest, nor did she plead for even a day's delay in their return to Burg Fürstensee. Was she wise enough to know how much worse fear became when sharpened by anticipation, or too resolute to risk the chance that her own faintness would sway her comrades? Margerite did not know, but she felt her respect for Eva strengthening.

"That is settled, then," Margerite said, her voice as brisk and strong as she could make it. "Since we must go, we shall go as soon as Jochanan pronounces Ritter Gottfried fit for the journey. Now I mean to go to the chapel and light a candle to the holy Martin, in hopes that he will aid Father Etienne in finding someone who can perform Christoph's exorcism for us, and I think it would be well for the rest of you to do the same."

Now that they had made the firm decision to leave the Bishop's palace for Burg Fürstensee, Margerite did not know whether it was a mercy or a torment that Gottfried's wound was slow to heal. In spite of the young knight's bravery and indifference to pain, he could not make his flesh knit any more swiftly; nor could she and Jochanan convince him that testing a wound's limits daily in hopes of pronouncing himself cured was not the fastest way to make his arm sound. Gottfried fretted and paced, chafing more each day against his confinement, and only the company of Brother Sigvrit and Arnmut's faithful tending could quiet his eagerness to be armed and horsed again.

Margerite and Bernhardt seldom had more time to themselves than it took to clasp hands and perhaps brush a kiss across each other's lips or whisper a few words of love in passing: it was maddening, to be so close and yet unable to embrace, to have done the deed that should have brought them to their goal and yet to know that there would be months, maybe years, while the Inquisition and the Emperor looked into the issue, with no surety of victory at the end of the wait. But Bernhardt's seal ring hung warm on its thin golden chain between Margerite's breasts, his pledge and her hope nestling above her heart like a falcon chick beneath its mother's feathers, though only the two of them - and Wolfram, whose little hand Margerite had to pull away from the chain before he broke it at every nursing - knew that it was there.

Often Margerite walked out across the snow-banked flagstone paths, sitting on a freezing stone bench and staring at the ice-locked pool in hopes of finding some peace in her soul. But ice did not draw the mind as a running fountain did, nor soothe it like the gleaming ripples and depth of a pond. Sometimes, when the snow fell white and silent from the heavy gray sky, Margerite could let its softness ease and slow her thoughts; but more often, she was distracted by Kobolt and Kriemhilt, rolling in the snow until their long shiny outer coats shimmered with little crystals, leaping up to bat at mothlike snowflakes - as if, Margerite thought sometimes, they have become jesters to try and make me laugh. But darker spirits distracted her thoughts: knowing that she must face Christoph's demon again, she had been studying the Black Book to see how Order members dealt with the most dangerous and untrustworthy of their allies.

Despite her disgust, Margerite could not help feeling a germ of grudging respect towards those who had gained the onyx ring: she, sustained and protected by her faith, had not managed to fully hold against Christoph's demon, while the Order members who dealt with such beings faced them with nothing save wit and will to set against the vile malice of servants who would sooner betray their masters than their foes. It troubled her that the Light-Bearer rites should lodge so easily in her mind - and yet, if it came to using the means of constraint written out so carefully in the Black Book or seeing Christoph's demon harm Wolfram, there was not a moment's doubt in her mind as to which she would do. Yet at least, as in the hallowing of her magical tools, Margerite had subsituted the names and titles of God for those of Lucifer: she hoped thus to taint her soul less - and she would not trust the power of the Lord of Lies to defend her from his own angels, however readily they heeded threats in his name.

Margerite was also more troubled daily by her thoughts of Oda and Hedwig, bound in their cell to await the Inquisition. Though the two Order women were treated far better than she and her companions had been through their brief stay in Ritter Hermann's stable, Margerite knew how it was to be imprisoned. And she had been locked up but from Friday to Sunday, with no worse before her than the quick jerk of a hangman's noose: what must it be like to know that imprisonment would last for months, perhaps years, and end not in swift death, but in slow and lingering pain - or in whatever fate the Order of Light-Bearers reserved for those who betrayed them?

There was no doubt that Oda and Hedwig deserved their suffering, but Margerite felt the weight of what she had brought about all the same. Yet that might not have been enough to drive her to look into their faces again, to listen to Oda's weeping and Hedwig's arrogant defiance - save that Margerite could not push away the tantalizing feeling at the edge of her thoughts, the sureness that they knew something which was hidden from her. As often as she told herself that the Order women could bring her nothing but betrayal, or worse, seduction, she could not stop thinking about them.

"I would speak with the prisoners," Margerite said finally to Father Etienne as they sat in the library.

The bright colours of the stained-glass windows were dulled by the gray morning sky outside, but the patterns of dribbling snowflakes gleamed through the rainbow hues as the storm whipped around the Bishop's palace. It was but three days before the first Sunday of Advent; and Margerite could not help remembering back to a year ago, when she sat in the besieged Burg Falkenstein...It was beginning to seem to her that her safety in Bishop Otto's court seemed all too much like that: hidden behind secure walls, but with a dwindling store of strength, while the foe waited outside for the will of those within to weaken...

Etienne held his silver mazer in both gloved hands, sipping at the steaming spiced wine within - though coals glowed in brass braziers about the library, it was still cold enough to wear gloves and cloaks inside. His blue eyes flickered about to see who else was there, but they were alone. Even Brother Sigvrit, who spent much of his time with his bad leg propped up as he worked slowly through Latin texts, was not there - most likely going over the palace guard, or doing something with Gottfried and Arnmut.

"Why?"

Faced with the question, Margerite could not put her feelings into words. She shifted Wolfram from knee to knee beneath her cloak - he was growing heavy now. At last she fell back on an easier answer: "I put them there: I should not forget what I have done."

Father Etienne regarded her for a long time, watching her cooly. "I do not think you shall forget. I trust you have remembered to pray for their repentance and atonement?"

"Yes, I have. But..."

The canon swirled the dark wine in his mazer, the little frost-puffs of his breath melting into the steam that rose from the silver vessel. "Then there is no more you can do for them, and further speech with them would only imperil you. Indeed, at this time, I would keep you away from all contact with Order members: I have already spoken to your companions regarding your return to Burg Fürstensee, so that they will do their best to make sure that Nikolaus never has a moment alone with you."

Alarmed, Margerite clutched Wolfram more tightly to her breast, swathing him in folds of cloak like a mother bird wrapping wings about her chick. "Do you think they will harm me in revenge for Ortlieb?"

Father Etienne frowned, brows lowering to shadow his gaze. "I did not say that. Nevertheless, I think you stand in worse peril than you have for some time, and I can but call it the grace of God that Gottfried's wound has kept you here so long."

"Father! If I am in peril, should I not know of what, and why?"

The canon lifted his head, looking up at the window. St. Catherine, gowned in flowing crimson robes, stood there; the black glass of the great wheel beneath her hand gleamed dull as polished iron in the gray light. At last Father Etienne reached into his belt-pouch, bringing out a little bag of black silk. "For your soul's sake," he murmured, "I suppose it is better that you learn this from me."

He dropped the tiny black pouch into Margerite's palm. It was heavier than she had guessed, her hand lowering beneath the unexpected weight. As if in a dream, she untied the silken threads that held it closed and looked within.

The first thing Margerite saw was a red glow, burning like a small coal in the bag. At her feet, Kobolt miaowed, standing on his hind legs to hook his claws painfully into her thigh. Before she could falter, Margerite tipped the bag, her waiting palm prickling painfully beneath the hot rush of tainted power.

Margerite knew the ring at once - as she had first seen it in a dream, then upon Ortlieb's hand: the great smooth ruby in its golden setting, and graven around it the familiar, dreaded words EX TENEBRAE LUX. Hastily, as if scraping away the clinging slime of a slug, she picked it up with the silken bag, knotting the threads at the top tight. Even with the ring wrapped so, Margerite thought she could still feel it pulsing like a tiny heart in the concealing darkness of a ribcage, and she shuddered, wiping her palm against the nubby brocade of her skirt.

"Why have you given this to me?" Margerite whispered. "I do not know how to deal with such a thing..."

Father Etienne's ascetic face was remote, calm and pale as a saint carven in stone. "As you said, it is best for you to know the danger in which you stand. I expect the Order to send one of their folk to seek into this matter. Hopefully, they will believe that you chose to challenge Ortlieb, and managed thus to overcome her and take her place - Princess."

Margerite felt the blood dropping from her face, her fingers chilling to lumps of ice inside her fur-lined gloves. The light from the stained-glass window swirled in her eyes as though St. Catherine's wheel had begun to spin; her arms were weak and numb, and fearing to drop Wolfram, she tightened her embrace on him until he began to wail.

Maria, I wish that I had never asked! Margerite thought. For at once she realized how much power she would have as an Order Princess - how much power to keep her son safe, even to influence the doings of Church and court. As one of the great among the Light-Bearers, she might well be able to ensure Bernhardt's victory over his brother, to bring about a swift annulment of her marriage with Heinrich without fear of where the Order might give her next...she could give Bernhardt all that he yearned for, most of all herself.

But would he want such a tainted gift? Margerite asked herself in horror, and felt a deeper shudder at the answer: He would never have to know.

Etienne watched Margerite dispassionately. The lightlessness behind his eyes reminded her of what she had seen, that night she had flown out seeking him so desperately - the castle walls rising too high and sheer to scale, the moat dropping down to fathomless black water. Why is he shutting me out so?

Her hand shaking so badly that she could hardly hold the silken bag with Ortlieb's ring, Margerite laid it down carefully upon the tabletop. "Take it," she whispered. Wolfram let out a louder wail, and Margerite began to rock back and forth in her chair, murmuring soothing words to her baby.

"There is no turning back from knowledge," Etienne answered, his voice equally soft. "No more than the sons of Adam can walk back through the gates of Eden...I would have kept this from you as long as you let me."

The library door opened. Hastily Margerite snatched the black silk pouch from the table, hiding it in the folds of her cloak before Gottfried or Arnmut could see it. Arnmut's fair cheeks were pink in the cold, and a light flush overlaid the pallor of Gottfried's thin-angled face; melting snowflakes dewed the shoulders of their cloaks, bright as tiny crystals against blue and deep red wool.

"Frowe Gräfin, Jochanan says that I shall be ready to ride and fight within the week, if you are willing to travel in the snows," Gottfried told her.

Margerite felt her heart beating rapidly beneath her ribs, light and fast as the wings of a panicked lark struggling to escape a sparrowhawk's talons. She forced a smile onto her face, saying, "God be thanked that you are healed at last! But surely this weather shall not be kind to travellers, and with a babe to tend..." She pulled back a fold of her cloak, as if the sight of Wolfram's face would lend weight to her words. Ritter Gottfried, though, was looking at her hand rather than the child.

"Have you hurt yourself, Frowe Gräfin?" the thin knight enquired.

"Hurt myself?" Margerite repeated. Despite the cold of the room, she could feel a thin chill film of sweat beading on her forehead.

"There is blood on your hand."

Margerite feigned a smile, hiding her hand in her cloak again before - she hoped - Arnmut could see what she saw: her hand white and smooth as it had been before she began her labours in Schloss Niederwald, with no smear or trace of gore to be seen. "Only a scratch from one of my pins, nothing more," she said lightly.

Yet when she could get away, on the pretext that Wolfram needed feeding, Margerite hastened back to her rooms to murmur the purifications of Water over her washing-bowl, immersing the hand that had held Ortlieb's ring and scrubbing it as hard as she could in hopes of cleaning off the invisible stain.

Once Gottfried had spoken of the blood on her hand, she
had seemed to feel it, clotting damp and slimy upon her
skin; she thought she could tell when she was clean at last,
but a lingering unease prickled at her nerves. The simple
silver Order ring on her hand had burned her with its cold
when she faced down Christoph's demon, so that her will
had wavered - what of Ortlieb's ring, steeped as it was in all
the Order Princess' deeds?

I must learn what I am to put on, Margerite thought.

Her back to the door so that no one could see what she
was doing on first entry, she opened the chest in which
she kept her magical tools and the Black Book. Briefly she
wondered what Ritter Gottfried would see if he looked upon
the smooth, fine-grained leather that bound the Order book,
and thanked Christ that she shared his sight only when she
flew forth as a falcon.

The Black Book seemed to fall open in answer to
Margerite's will, upon the very pages she was seeking.
The Order of Light-Bearers did not spare its members any
knowledge, once they had given their irrecallable oath: their
dreadful path was charted before them from the silver ring
of a Priest or Priestess to the Imperator's adamant. Silver
for a novice; gold for one who had learned the techniques of
magic; onyx for demon-summoners. A human sacrifice was
needed to gain an Order Bishop's amethyst - Ruprecht wore
that ring when we met, before he murdered Gertrude.

Whose life did he buy it with? Margerite felt the dizzying
faintness buzzing in her head again, but she breathed deeply
to calm herself, the slow measured breaths of the trained
magician, and the spots faded from in front of her eyes,
leaving the neatly penned words clear upon the parchment
leaves. The rite by which Ortlieb had won her ruby ring was
worse than anything Margerite had seen in the sorceress'
wain: it was meant to prove, as it did, that no scrap of feeling
was left in the worker, nor could the aspirant's senses or will
revolt at the foulest horrors a human could perform.

Maggoty dead flesh, with a demon gazing from decaying eyes, Margerite thought, choking down her gorge. Thanks be to Maria that Bernhardt will never know the fullness of what he lay with in his innocence! And a thousand more thanks to the kindly Virgin, that Ruprecht had not yet gone so far into darkness when we were wedded. Shaken as she was, Margerite forced herself to read further. The adamant ring alone was always won by challenge, unless its wielder chose to give it up in favour of one more worthy.

But, the book's neatly scribed characters spelled out, lest the great should grow soft in their power, or forget that each breath must be a battle of the will, any rank may be taken thus: the stronger shall overcome the weaker, as is fitting, and the slayer wins the power and the burden of the slain. Margerite's hand went to her mouth. The little black pouch with Ortlieb's ring lay on her bed like a dead thing; Margerite knew that the silk held its power quiescent within, but, having touched it once...

And if I put it on my finger? She wished now, with all her heart, that she had not pressed Father Etienne so closely for an answer he had not wanted to give. Christ forgive me: I am guilty of the sin of Eve, and my penance is upon me even now. Carefully Margerite picked the bag up by its knotted threads, dropping it into her chest. She would not by choice have had it so close to her magical tools, but they were wrapped in silk as well, even as the Black Book was, and there was no other safe place for such a thing.

Perhaps on the way back to Burg Fürstensee she could find a goldsmith to destroy it, to melt and cleanse the metal with fire, to heat the great ruby and strike it with a hammer until it cracked to powder. But it could be a very useful thing to keep, the thought came creeping to her. Nikolaus would have to obey my commands; I could even force him to release Christoph. Margerite heard the footsteps echoing down the stone corridor and shoved the Black Book into her chest, slamming the lid down and pushing it under her bed. By the time the door opened, she was bending over Wolfram's cradle where Kobolt lay with his front paw over the baby's body as if to protect him from harm.

"Is all well, Margerite?" Eva asked softly.

The laugh strangled in Margerite's throat. Only the greatest effort of will kept her face calm as she turned to look at the younger woman. The clothes the Bishop had ordered provided for them were a hasty mixture: plain, if good-quality, wool and linen, covered by brocaded and fur-lined cloaks, as if they were well-off servants trying on their mistress' outer garments.

But it was more to be wondered at that he had been able to find women's clothing that would fit them and not be shameful to wear; and her days on the road had made Margerite more than grateful for whatever was well-made and clean. The pale blue wool brought out the rich gold of Eva's hair, the pinkness of her cheeks against her creamy skin; and if the dress was a little tight in the waist, it curved fetchingly about the maiden's wide breasts and rounded hips.

"There is nothing wrong," Margerite answered. But her conscience pricked at her like blackberry thorns, and she knew that she would be doing Eva no good service to keep what had happened from her - she would never tell Bernhardt, or Gottfried, but she remembered Eva saying, If you were a knight, and I your Knappe, you would not bid me stay behind.

And it seemed to Margerite that, though they had sworn no oaths - perhaps women needed binding words and laws less than men - that Eva stood in a squire's stead to her all the same, and she could not keep their danger from her. "No: forgive me, that I lied to you. I pressed Father Etienne for knowledge, and he gave it to me, and something worse with it."

Eva frowned, her hands clasping each other tightly. "What might that be?" Though her voice was staunch, Margerite could hear the tremors behind it.

"Ortlieb's ring."

Eva heaved a deep breath, closing her eyes a moment. "Dear Christ. Surely...surely he cannot mean for you to wear it! Do you know how she...?"

"I know," Margerite said grimly. A wave of deep anger welled up in her breast: it was bad enough that she had needed to learn of that Order rite, but that Eva should have come upon it before she had even passed from childhood - that was almost beyond bearing.

Margerite remembered the frightened wretch who had first been presented to her as a servant at Burg Falkenstein, shivering in a coarse habit that stank of damp piss; then she had felt little beside contempt for Eva, and now she could not name her admiration for the girl's strength in surviving her days at the Order-ruled abbey with will and mind intact. For she must have been the virgin helper at that ritual, for some Light-Bearer Prince or Princess.

"And yet the day will come when I may have to put it on, for all our sakes. More: Father Etienne took two onyx rings from those women - from Hedwig and Oda," Margerite added reluctantly, for to deny the Light-Bearers their names was to admit that she could not face the consequences of her own judgement. "It may be, as well, that you shall have to bear one of them, and play at being my apprentice in order to convince our foes that I chose to challenge Ortlieb for her place, according to the Order's own rule."

Eva's skin had gone gray-white as ash, and it seemed to Margerite that she could see the bones standing out beneath the pretty curves of the girl's face, as though she looked through a dark mirror at Eva's old age. The younger woman breathed deeply again, breasts straining at the pale wool as though her body were swelling to bursting point. Margerite wanted to comfort her, to speak some word of kindness, but this was no time for such things: for all their sakes, Eva must master herself as Margerite had.

"Can you?" Margerite said, the whiplash of her voice as harsh as if she were, in truth, an Order Princess challenging her subordinate. She nearly broke into tears herself then, but something - anger, or pride, Margerite could not tell which - flared in Eva's eyes.

"If you can bear it, be assured that I shall not falter!" Eva flung back at her. "I am not so weak as you seem to think me."

She is, indeed, worthy, Margerite thought. And then, But worthy of what?

In two steps Margerite crossed the distance between them, embracing Eva tightly. Eva stood rigid in her embrace, strong muscles knotted, and Margerite's tears began to fall at last. "I did not mean to speak so to you. Forgive me, for it is a dreadful thing that I ask of you; and if we take up the Order rings in pride and wrath, I fear that it will not be long before we are no better than those who won them."

Then Eva was weeping too, her arms going about Margerite as she leaned her head on the shorter woman's shoulder. "I am sorry, Margerite. I know you have by far the harder part, and such a burden would sharpen the tongue of a saint."

"That, at least, I am not," Margerite replied. "But I thank Maria for sending me such a trusty companion in this. I could not tell Bernhardt..."

"Oh, no," Eva breathed.

"And you have seen far more of the Order from within than I: I shall need your help, if I am to carry this through."

"I shall give it gladly, though it were to cost me my soul."

Margerite shook her head, her tears dampening the blue wool of Eva's dress. "No. Never that, not for anything, or else we have lost our battle already."

Bishop Otto's table was set especially finely that day, as if to strengthen the Bishop and his household for the austerities of the Advent abstinence with its twice-weekly fasts - though Margerite, having seen what the episcopal kitchens could provide by way of meatless and milkless dishes, did not think that anyone there would suffer too much while they waited for their Christmas hams and geese.

Still, there was no harm in enjoying the good food, especially since she knew how much work had gone into it - the chessboard pie, with its squares of ground meat tinted bright red and gold separated by savoury pancakes, the red squares flavoured with a tingle of pepper and the gold rich with saffron and cheese; the tender slices of roedeer, lightly grilled and sauced with a mixture of verjuice, wine, and ginger beneath a precious dusting of cinnamon; the little pastry cases filled with sweetened pork or chicken or beef mixed with marrow and spices; and the coin-sized rondels of veal shimmering through an amber wine-jelly.

Margerite had just allowed Ritter Gottfried, next to whom she was seated, to cut her a generous slice of the meat jelly when the great doors of the dining hall opened and a man was shown in by two servants. Her breath hissed silently in through her nostrils as she looked at him: she knew that pleasantly open face, the lively blue eyes and slicked-back dark hair, and recognised his smile at once.

Damiano! she thought. How dare he come here, to the Bishop's very palace? But when they had first met, the Order's messenger had spoken of guesting in Avignon, and talked of several cardinals as though he knew them well. I should not be shocked: I knew that the Order has many members within the body of the Church. But Margerite desperately wanted to know whether Damiano had come alone, whether she should rush out of the hall and clutch Wolfram to her, lest she come back to find an empty cradle once more...

At least the Bishop's hall is well-guarded: surely no one would be able to walk out of here carrying my child, Margerite told herself. But she did not believe it: she knew herself how easy it might be to turn a guard's sight away for a few moments, to pass unseen as the wind through hallways and gates.

O blessed Maria, guide me for my son's sake! she thought. Yet it came to her that Wolfram's safety was guaranteed for the moment by something darker - by the ruby ring that lay hidden in the casket with the Black Book.

"Your Grace, greetings," said Damiano, walking swiftly over to bow and brush his lips across Bishop Otto's episcopal amethyst. "I am sorry to have interrupted you at your meal..."

The Bishop waved a square hand, brushing the apology away. "If I am not mistaken, you have come with some news of importance: why else should a messenger from Cardinal Fleurs arrive here so close to Advent?"

"As always, you see deeply, your Grace," Damiano replied with another smooth bow, sweeping back his marten-edged cloak to show the fashionable long dags of his scarlet sleeves - in spite of his long journey, he was as elaborately dressed as he had been at the dinner in Freiburg, though his particoloured doublet was cut closer and more daringly, as if he took inordinate pride in having tightened up the slight sag of his belly. "But this is hardly the time or place to speak of such things, and my news can wait."

The Bishop nodded to the servants who had brought Damiano in, and another place was quickly set for him. Margerite could not miss the quick flicker of the Italian's blue eyes towards her hands, and it was all she could do to keep them from shaking as she neatly spooned up a bite of jellied veal - Dear Maria, dear Christ, so soon? Beside her, Ritter Gottfried stared hard at Damiano, his eyes gray and cold as the snowy sky outside. If the hatchet-faced knight's intense scrutiny bothered Damiano, he did not let it show, favouring Gottfried with a sly grin as he stripped off snow-damp gloves to show the onyx gleaming upon his hand.

"Well-met again, Father Etienne," Damiano said, and to Margerite's surprise, Etienne smiled back at the Italian.

"Well-met indeed, Damiano. How goes it in Avignon?"

Damiano raised his eyebrows in that peculiar way of his, the inner ends tilting quizzically upwards, and shrugged his broad shoulders. He seemed about to speak when his gaze passed over Bernhardt - then back again, eyes widening as though he could not believe what he saw. Bernhardt met his look firmly, strong jaw set as though he were holding back harsh words and a dangerous gleam in his hazel eyes.

So the Light-Bearers had not yet guessed that their Free Company soldier Bertram was the same man as Bernhardt von Niederwald! Margerite thought. And then, with cold certainty, But now they do. Blessed Maria, help Bernhardt to speak no more than is wise - let him keep his tongue with a bridle while the wicked are before him. For she knew that she would have no help from Bernhardt if she tried to go forward with her masquerade: his time of disguises was done, and he had suffered too much in seeming to be the Order's man.

But to Margerite's relief, neither Bernhardt nor Damiano spoke - of course: Damiano could hardly acknowledge before the Bishop that he knew the former Bertram, any more than Bernhardt could speak up to denounce Damiano as a worm in the Church's body. The moment of recognition snapped; Damiano looked back at Father Etienne. "

It goes...poorly enough, after the paying of Bertrand du Guesclin's ransom." He shook his head. "At least those ruffians are readying themselves to march across the Pyrenees, and Avignon shall be troubled with them no more - for a time."

Bishop Otto's florid face reddened farther: du Guesclin's name spilled choleric humours into the Bishop's blood more surely than any leech's treatments could do, and, having heard him speak on the subject before, Margerite knew that it would be some time before anyone else was expected to join in the conversation again, or before the Bishop paid the least bit of attention to his dining companions. Hence, she allowed herself to look at Bernhardt a little longer than might be proper.

The muscles at the squared-off edges of his jaw were twitching, his big scarred hands clenched tightly on the handles of eating-knife and spoon like those of a rough soldier expecting a tavern brawl to break out - but the light in his eyes and the strength of his clean-shaven features gave the lie to that: he had the look of a Crusader about to couch his lance for battle, ready to ride through whatever stood between himself and his high goal. Maria, I love him! Margerite thought. He is magnificent - but please, please, Blessed Virgin, help him to stay silent a little longer.

The meal dragged out maddeningly long: the fine meat dishes were replaced with a creamy syllabub, followed by hardened sugar-lumps spiced with cinnamon and cloves. As was proper, Margerite held hers in her mouth until it melted, as though she were flavouring her breath for a lover - she could not help thinking of Bernhardt's kisses warmed with spice, the heat of his mouth on hers tingling with the faintly burning sweetness of the little comfits. But the pleasant dream melted more quickly than the sweets, for Bernhardt's gaze went to Damiano more often than to Margerite, and though his brown beard was cropped short and his hair neatly trimmed into a nobleman's shoulder-length curls, his face was as steel-hard as it had ever been as a guard captain's.

At last the Bishop rose from his table, his heavy features settling into the mask of a powerful man faced with an undesired duty. "If you will come with me, Damiano, then we shall talk about the news you have brought. Is there any other who should be present?"

"I believe it concerns Father Etienne and...Herr Bernhardt...as well," Damiano answered smoothly. "As for the rest of your noble guests - not yet, at any rate."

"Come, then," ordered Bishop Otto, his eyes meeting Etienne's and Bernhardt's for a moment. The three men left the room; out of politeness, the others lingered a little while before departing.

Though Margerite knew better than to run, driven by restless worry, she strode ahead of her companions, her skirts swishing about her legs. As she entered her room, she drew a deep breath of relief: she could hear Wolfram's happy gurgles, and the loud purring of two cats, Kobolt's deeper note harmonizing with Kriemhilt's higher voice.

"Who was that man, Frowe Gräfin?" asked Georg as soon as the door was shut. "He wore an onyx ring such as Ortlieb's servants had - and it looked as though you recognised him."

"So I did," Margerite said, her voice grim. "He is a Monsignor of the Order, indeed, and I have had some slight dealings with him before."

"He is one of their most trusted messengers," Eva broke in, her voice hard and clear as rock crystal. "I know him better than I should like, for it was he who delivered me from the Convent of the Holy Cross to Burg Falkenstein. He was not allowed to assault my maidenhead, but he treated me as no freeborn woman should be handled."

"Shall I bring challenge to him, then?" Georg said fiercely, the fresh pink scar down his freckled cheek reddening as if the wound had split open again. "You have only to say the word, and I will not hesitate a moment; that I swear by Christ and St. Michael and my own good sword."

Eva's cheeks flushed suddenly, and Margerite realized with horror that the girl might be seriously thinking of accepting Georg's offer. "Those are such things as cannot be dealt with before other eyes!" Margerite snapped at the two of them. "Have you forgotten where we are?"

Georg dropped his gaze, but his thin hand was clenched white-knuckled about the hilt of his weapon. "Nothing need be said of the Order; it is enough that a messenger of the Church abused his trust so," the Knappe argued. "And what manner of knight would I make, did I let my...a lady's honour be treated in that manner without a blade raised in argument?"

"Georg speaks rightly," Ritter Gottfried agreed, his strong baritone voice clear and confident. "If this man cannot claim the Church as his sanctuary against challenge, then I, too, stand ready to meet him with my sword."

"And I," said Arnmut. "I think it would be well-done for my first deed as a knight to be the lifting of my blade in vengeance for a noble frowe thus mishandled."

Another young man struck by Eva's charms? Margerite wondered, amused in spite of herself. But no, Arnmut was looking at Gottfried as though he were still the older knight's squire, waiting for his approval, and rewarded by the faint smile of pride touching Gottfried's thin lips.

"As Ritter Gottfried says," Margerite told them firmly, "there is every likelihood that Damiano can claim to be a churchman, and hence inviolable. As for the ill he has done, it shall be judged in due time; but I think that the judgement cannot be carried out by your blades. Therefore calm yourselves, for I mean to ride for Burg Fürstensee tomorrow, and we should be making our preparations towards that - and as far as Damiano is concerned, at least we shall not have to look upon him any longer."

I am defending Damiano, Margerite thought in amazement as she spoke. Why? But she knew why: he would be the mouthpiece of her deception, for it would be he who bore news back to the Order that she had knowingly challenged Ortlieb.

"The Church's inviolability was surely not meant to allow wrongdoers full freedom of deed," Ritter Arnmut argued. "If we cannot challenge Damiano, can the Bishop not judge him by ecclesiastical law?"

Margerite shook her head. "It would be no more than one word against another, and we have heard that Damiano has powerful friends..."

"Very powerful," whispered Eva, picking Kriemhilt up from Wolfram's cradle and cuddling the dark tortoiseshell cat close to her breast, as if she feared to catch a chill. No one but Margerite seemed to have heard her; and so Margerite went on, "If he is known to be a cardinal's man, as he seems to be, I think we will have little luck in convincing Bishop Otto to punish him on a woman's word, the more so since Eva was brought to Burg Falkenstein as a maidservant."

"Still, I mean to pay this debt if ever I can!" Georg vowed fiercely, flushing to the roots of his bright red hair when Eva smiled at him. Margerite was sure that the girl knew her power over the young Knappe full well, and suspected that Eva was getting some enjoyment out of it: she was almost tempted to slap her, but that, of course, she could not do.

"At the moment," stated Margerite implacably, "it is enough for us to know that Damiano is our enemy, and a spy from the Order of Light-Bearers. I believe that he is here to investigate what has happened for them - and perhaps to try to either free Hedwig and Oda, or slay them before they can speak to the Inquisition. Hence, Ritter Gottfried, I would ask you if you think you can make an offer to keep guard on their cell without rousing suspicion."

Gottfried's gray eyes narrowed, his sharp-arched brows drawing together in thought. "I believe that I can. As Brother Sigvrit is in charge of the guard detail, he will, I think, find it praiseworthy that I ask to take on a share of the work."

"And I, as well!" Arnmut said passionately. "If there is like to be trouble, I shall not go from your side."

Ritter Gottfried favoured Arnmut with another of his rare smiles. "Of course you shall not, nor would I ask you to. Come, then: Damiano cannot stay closeted with the Bishop forever, and we do not know whether he entered here alone. Frowe Gräfin, Frowe Eva, Georg, I bid you good day." Gottfried made a stiff little bow of courtesy to them, Arnmut mirroring his gesture more smoothly, and the two young knights left the room.

"Do you wish me to guard as well?" Georg asked. "Though I have not been knighted, I have shown, I think, that I can fight as staunchly as you could want."

Margerite shook her head. "Two must suffice; three would look suspicious. And," she added, mindful of the Knappe's pride, "the men of the Bear's Paw are quartered too far away for any call to reach them in time, and if Ritter Gottfried and Ritter Arnmut are watching over the prisoners, then who but Bernhardt and yourself are left to be sure that nothing untowards happens to Wolfram and Eva and I?"

The new scar down Georg's homely face twisted his wide grin into the look of a cheerful gargoyle. "You may rely on me utterly, Frowe Gräfin."

"I know that well. Take care, though, not to be too obvious. Keep to your chamber for the most part; but come out when you hear footfalls in the corridor - and hold your ears open for any sounds of distress or struggle, for if there is trouble, you shall be needed at once."

"Of course!"

When Georg had left, Eva sighed deeply. "Margerite, do you really think there will be fighting this night?"

"No. But would you have told Georg that he is not needed here, when he is so eager - and when he should have received his knight's accolade together with Ritter Arnmut?"

"I see what you mean," Eva said slowly. "Still, I wish he did not hang on everything I do quite so obviously, since he is far younger than I and barely half my size."

Margerite laughed. "Georg is less than a year younger than you are, I think; and though he has not matched your height yet, he has begun to fill out his bones since we set out from Burg Fürstensee. And it is well for a Knappe to have a frowe for whom he can play Minnesinger without fear that either of them may be led too far into temptation."

Then she sobered: her own words had suddenly cut too close to the bone, as though she had been playing carelessly with a fresh-sharpened carving knife. Ruprecht's squire Wolfram had been just such a Minnesinger to Margerite; and she had given him the draught that eased the pain of his mortal wound...into the sleep of death, guided only by her husband's Light-Bearer blessing: Margerite prayed that Christ might have mercy on his soul.

As if in answer to his mother's thoughts, the babe Wolfram suddenly began to wail, a steady high-pitched sound. Margerite's milk-full breasts panged sharply in answer: how had she been so caught up in worries as to neglect her son? Eva was at her side at once, helping her to unlace her bodice so that she might give Wolfram suck as she stroked his soft golden hair and murmured to him, "There, there, Mutti is with you, everything is all right. I did not mean to leave you hungry so long, but I have plenty of good milk for you - drink, my dear son, and grow joyful and strong."

Kobolt leapt onto Margerite's lap as well, snuffling hopefully at her other breast and kneading hard with his paws. Caught between laughter and embarassment, she tried to push him away, but he snagged her dress with his long hooked claws, purring and rubbing his head against her. "You are not a kitten, sir, and I am not a mother cat," Margerite said sternly to him, but the great black tom paid her no mind.

Eva waited quietly until Wolfram had drunk his fill and Margerite sat bouncing him on her lap to burp him. Then, without warning, she said, "Margerite, do you know who Cardinal Fleurs is?"

Margerite shook her head.

"He is the one who wears the adamant ring - the Imperator of the Order of Light-Bearers."

Margerite sucked in her breath in shock, gasping as though Eva had struck her in the pit of her stomach. "Then Damiano..."

"Will bear whatever news he can find back to the head of the Order."

At dawn that day Margerite had felt no more than a vague unease, a sense that there was, perhaps, some need for knowledge tugging her on. Now it seemed as though the siege had suddenly broken, the thick walls of the Bishop's palace shattering beneath the iron onslaught of a thousand great guns. And she had found her safe-conduct that day - but was it by the grace of God that she had Ortlieb's ring and knew what it must mean for her within the Order, or was it a cunning snare of the Devil, to give her the Order Princess' emblem just as the time struck when she must choose to claim or deny it, before she could meditate or seek advice from those wiser than she?

Kobolt jumped from Margerite's lap with a reproachful purring chirp as she stood abruptly, holding Wolfram tight against her bosom. "Come with me to the chapel, if you will, Eva. I do not know if prayer can aid me now - but I think Father Etienne will be closeted with the Bishop for some time, and I know of none other save the Virgin and Christ who may give me counsel in this."

Before Eva could set her own cat down, Kriemhilt leapt from her lap, crossing the floor in two great hunter's bounds and disappearing under the bed. Margerite spared no moment of pity for whatever vermin the cat had heard rustling: she would much rather have it in Kriemhilt's furry belly than in her own hair. The two women were almost to the door when they heard the clinking of something hard rolling across the floor and the rush of tufted paws as Kriemhilt and Kobolt raced for it.

A glint of gold, a deeper gleam of black - the cats were batting a ring back and forth, a heavy ring set with a smooth onyx. Margerite and Eva stared at each other, frozen, then down at the toy that Kobolt had just hooked with outstretched claws, tossing it in the air like a mouse and swatting it away for his daughter to chase.

"I do not think they mean us ill," Eva whispered.

"Never that," Margerite agreed in equally hushed tones. "But..." But Kobolt is an earth-spirit, knowing nothing of salvation or damnation: I think it would mean nothing to him whether I became a cloistered nun, or joined the Light-Bearers in truth.

Yet neither Kobolt nor Kriemhilt should have been able to get through Father Etienne's wards, unless he gave them leave, and he is not such a man as to leave Order rings unguarded. If the onyx ring is here for Eva, it is by his will.

"It were best if you took it, I suspect," Margerite said, her voice ringing hollow in her own ears. "I think we have just gotten the advice I sought." Unless the Light-Bearers have somehow managed to guess at our plans, and will give us all the tools we need to work our own damnation in the guise of deceiving them. For the first time, it seemed to Margerite that she truly understood what drove men and women to enter the monastic life under the harshest Rules: when it was so hard to guess between sin and virtue, between God's aid and traps laid by the Devil, what safer place than a cloister where all choices from waking to sleep, from prayers to silence, were laid out in immutable trustworthiness? But while they lived in the world, sooner or later contemplation must end and action begin.

Eva might have been thinking something similar: at least, she bent decisively and scooped up the ring from beneath Kriemhilt's paws. "Should I put it on now?"

"I shall put on the other - but let me at least ward us both from them as best I may, and we shall pray to Christ with good hearts that He keep us from the temptations they offer, and deliver us from their evil."

It was a relief to Margerite that the Bishop usually ate his modest evening supper alone, so that his guests were not required to gather in his dining-hall as they were at dinner-time. Even though her wards had dimmed something of the ruby ring's power, as though she wore an invisible glove of silk beneath it, she could still feel it pulsing hot and foul as a corrupting boil on her finger - and she would put off, as long as she could, the moment when Bernhardt had to see Ortlieb's jewel on her hand; if Maria had mercy, Margerite would have a chance to explain the matter to him before a chance meeting while she was wearing it caught him unawares.

But she did not dare take it off now, for she was sure that Damiano would find some chance to speak with her alone, or with only Eva present, that night. Bernhardt, Bishop Otto, Father Etienne, and Damiano spoke for a long time in the Bishop's private chambers. Bernhardt said no more than he had to: the Order man's sly glances at him said, more clearly than words, that Damiano thought the Light-Bearers had the power to use his past in the Free Companies to break him forever in Kaiser Karl's eyes.

For his part, Damiano addressed little speech to Bernhardt. Instead, with the smoothness of a practiced diplomat, he deplored the dreadful news in Etienne's missive, even while the quirking of his back-slanted eyebrows suggested his skepticism - and, by implication, that of Cardinal Fleurs - regarding the very elements of the report which Bernhardt had already guessed made Bishop Otto most uneasy. Bernhardt admired Damiano's performance as he would admire the sleek sudden uncoiling of an adder and its eyeblink-flicker into long grass.

It took a cunning man to deliver three messages at once without speaking any of them aloud: for Bernhardt, the message of the hold the Order of Light-Bearers still had upon him, or could have if he allowed himself to fear their political influence; for the Bishop, the message that the matter of Ortlieb was perhaps not so grievous as he had feared, and trying to play it up would make him seem, at least in Cardinal Fleurs' eyes, like the kind of superstitious young priest he disliked; and for Father Etienne...Bernhardt could not tell, but he could guess by the grave look on the canon's ascetic face that something more than simple speech was passing between priest and Light-Bearer.

"Cardinal Fleurs also wished me to see the Landgräfin's two attendants for myself," Damiano said offhandedly when the conversation had turned at last from Ortlieb to the doings of the great in Avignon. "In truth, I had almost forgotten; but the Cardinal is a man to pay attention to every least detail, and he would not be pleased with me if I did not send my own report of each particular to him."

Bishop Otto frowned, shifting uncomfortably on the cushions of his great carven chair. To the best of Bernhardt's knowledge, the Bishop had not gone to see Oda and Hedwig since they had been brought in, though Father Etienne went to their cell each day.

"They are accomplices to murder, at best," the Bishop began slowly. "As to whatever else they may be, is that not a matter best left to those appointed by the Church to deal with such things?"

"Nevertheless," Damiano insisted. "I have my own orders, and surely there is no reason why Cardinal Fleurs should not receive as full a report as he expects of me?"

Your own orders, indeed, thought Bernhardt, trying not to shake his head. I wish that I had run you through when we first met on the road those years ago: you are a small serpent, but a very troublesome one - and, worst of all, smug about it.

"I suppose not," the Bishop conceded, inclining his dark head towards Damiano. "Father Etienne has been acting as their chaplain, though that grace seems to have done them little good as yet. I expect that he shall be willing to go with you."

Damiano's smile was not quite broad enough to be a smirk; to ignorant eyes, it might almost have seemed a look of relief. "I am honoured, Father."

"A sensible man," Bishop Otto said to Bernhardt when Damiano and Father Etienne had left. "It is easy to see why Cardinal Fleurs places so much trust in him."

Bernhardt could not keep from scowling: years of grimness, with unwanted expressions hidden behind his tangle of beard, had left him ill-practiced in the schooling of his face as a Landgraf's son learned to do. Fortunately for him, Bishop Otto misread the look.

"No, I think you need not fear that Damiano will speak against you. Nor have I ever heard ill of Cardinal Fleurs: he is said to be a great scholar and a man of honour, fair and just in his dealings - as, alas," the Bishop added, lowering his voice, "is not always to be said even of those whom God has set above us in the Church. You may be sure that with the good Cardinal on your side, you shall find this tangle easier to escape from."

Bernhardt stared searchingly at the Bishop. Otto's blue eyes were open and honest, his ruddy broad face showing nothing but a look of fatherly concern. But what he had just said - Was Father Etienne wrong? Bernhardt wondered. Is our Bishop, too, a Light-Bearer, hiding the evil that Ortlieb paraded so brazenly? For a moment he desperately wished for the camouflage of bushy black hair to hide his naked thoughts. But that was shameful cowardice: he would not have turned back to be Bertram the free soldier again, even if he could have - not least, because Margerite deserved better of him. Bernhardt took in a deep breath and let it out slowly, letting his features fall into the pleasant neutrality he had learned in speaking with his father's peers.

"It is good to know that I may have such an ally,"
Bernhardt said carefully. "But is Cardinal Fleurs, then,
associated with the Inquisition?"

Bishop Otto shook his head, the gray light through the
windowpane gleaming on the violet silk of the simple cap he
wore when ceremony did not call for his mitre. "Not to the
best of my knowledge. But I am told that even Pope Urban
listens with careful respect when he speaks."

Christ preserve us, Bernhardt thought in disgust. Perhaps
the End Times are indeed near, when the Imperator of the
Light-Bearers can advice Christ's vice-gerent on Earth!

The Bishop leaned forward in his heavy oaken chair,
his amethyst ring flashing as he patted Bernhardt on the
shoulder. "I know it is a daunting thing, to have some of the
highest-set men of the Church concerned suddenly with
your life," he said in a comforting manner; but beneath his
mask of calmness, Bernhardt felt his jaw tightening in a
sudden flare of resentment. I was son to the Landgraf von
Niederwald, and squire to Landgraf Friedrich von Thuringia.
Why should I be daunted by the thought of dealing with
cardinals? - They may be Princes of the Church, but I was
raised to be the equal of any prince in Europe.

Yet Bernhardt knew better than to speak so rudely to his
Bishop, who moreover might be one of his staunchest allies
- if he is not, after all, a man of the Order! Though only long
watching will prove that, and by no means with any surety.
So he contented himself by saying, "Your Grace, I count it
rather as an honour, and not one undue to the gravity of
the situation, when such a realm as my father's hangs in the
balance."

Bishop Otto nodded, his face thoughtful. "That is the answer I should have looked for from the young man I knew. I wish that this matter were solely one for the Church to decide: we should have a swifter resolution and, I think, a better one. But there is no telling how secular authorities will deal with it - though, Christ be thanked, Kaiser Karl is a pious man, and not such a ruler as to set himself against the Pope for pride or gain: we may hope that he will at least take our rulings into account when the time comes for him to give his judgement."

Again Bernhardt's head whirled, as he tried to guess whether or not the Bishop's words held a Light-Bearer's layers of meaning. *Perhaps, after all, my long struggle has left me unfit to rule honest folk, if I see ill so easily where-ever I look!* But even as he thought that, old training spoke through his mouth, saying politely, "I hope that it may be so, and I thank you with all your heart for my help."

"There is no need for you to thank me, when I have seen more than I would have liked of the evil from which you freed your father's realm!" the Bishop said fervently, the florid hue of his cheeks brightening. "Believe me, I shall give you all the aid I can."

"It is most welcome, your Grace. And now I have a favour to ask of you. I would pray in silence: will you let me do so within your private chapel?"

"Gladly, Herr Bernhardt."

As when Bernhardt had seen it before, the Bishop's chapel glowed warm with beeswax candles, the scent of frankincense hanging sweet in the air. Alone, he went to kneel before the altar, turning his gaze up past the fine embroidered silk of the altar cloth to the gilded crucifix hanging on the wall, and the statue of the Virgin beside it.

Perhaps Father Etienne - or Margerite, little as Bernhardt liked to think of her doing such things - might have been able to feel whether the chapel was truly hallowed: Bernhardt had no such dangerous lore, but he had seen the subtle twistings that the Light-Bearers could give to holy art, a curve of the Virgin's lip making her seem cruel or wanton, a slight mis-proportion of limbs and head turning Christ into a crucified jester-dwarf...

Here, all was in harmony, Maria's painted eyes gazing kindly down at him, and the exalted nobility of Jesu's face proclaiming His triumph over the agony of His wounds and death. Maria, forgive me, Bernhardt prayed silently. Christ, forgive me. Blessed Virgin, Holy Mother, let your waters flow for me: help me to cleanse my soul of the darkness that stains it yet, that I may not dream evil thoughts in the hearts of good men, nor see my own wickedness mirrored in those who are innocent.

And help me to cast out the pride that guided me to my downfall; for I had thought it dead these many years, but now it springs up again in me like a beheaded thistle flowering anew from old roots...And most of all, forgive me, that I yet find such hope in Graf Heinrich's illness, that I cannot turn my mind from Margerite and my desire for her. Forgive me, that I have been so glad to keep her beside me for these weeks, though it was at the cost of a good man's pain: it shall break my heart to see her ride away tomorrow, and yet every day that she lingers here, I come closer to yielding to temptation again. Forgive me and help me, as you have done so long, though I am little more worthy than I was before. Salve, Regina...

Ritter Gottfried stood braced easily at one side of the door that locked Oda and Hedwig in, with Arnmut - Ritter Arnmut, Gottfried reminded himself with a warm glow of bittersweet pride - keeping watch on the other side. They had been there since that afternoon, with only brief pauses when one or the other must go for a chamber-pot or food; though the moon was deeply shrouded in clouds, so that no glimmer of light showed through the corridor's windows, Gottfried guessed that it was nearing midnight now.

Still, he was not tired: rather, he felt more alert, as though the wind that whipped spatterings of sleet against the darkened glass blew cool over his skin, tingling through all the tiny hairs on his arms and at the nape of his neck. The two young knights had hardly spoken to each other since Brother Sigvrit gave them leave to take the watch at the prisoners' door, for they were sure in their duty, and no words were needed between them - as though they had campaigned together for twenty years instead of a twelvemonth.

Though he did not let his awareness of the corridor fade - the glow of the candles in their niches reflecting blurred gleams of colour from the stained-glass windows, the silence broken only by the sounds of himself and Arnmut breathing and the slight jingling of their hauberks when one or the other of them shifted his stance - Gottfried found himself thinking, wondering how much Brother Sigvrit had guessed of how matters stood with their prisoners and the Order Monsignor who claimed to be a cardinal's messenger.

The old Teutonic Knight had told Gottfried and Arnmut a great many things that he had seen in Lithuania, things that Gottfried would have doubted, save that he himself had looked upon, and indeed been wounded by, stranger; if the younger man had not been there when the Bishop came to examine Ortlieb's wain, Gottfried thought that Brother Sigvrit would not have spoken so freely to him.

There were a few men like you and Father Etienne in our Order, though our Rule never acknowledged it, the Teutonic Knight had said, stretching his maimed leg out on his footstool as Arnmut rose to fill Brother Sigvrit's battered pewter mug with wine. And I owed my life to one several times over.

You would be welcome in the Brotherhood, no doubt of it. Though Gottfried hardly thought that he could be classed with Father Etienne - his sole talent of that sort was the uncertain blessing of his sight, and he knew nothing of the great prayers that had so awed him when Father Etienne had given his protection against Ortlieb's magics - still it was comforting, to hear himself judged worthy by a man who had lived and fought and taken his crippling wound as one of Christ's warrior-monks.

And it was yet more comforting, to have the Teutonic Knight's words assure him that the things he had seen in the past month were not the dazed dream of his half-blindness, as it had almost begun to seem, but true and real enough for a hard-bitten campaigner such as Brother Sigvrit to speak of the sorceries of the pagan Lithuanians in the same breath as he spoke of their arms and tactics.

Gottfried stole a glance sideways, looking at the clean lines of Arnmut's shadowed profile against the dim candlelight. His former Knappe had never doubted him for a moment: when Brother Sigvrit began to talk about the things he had witnessed, Arnmut had said at once, "I see what Ritter Gottfried cannot for him, and he sees what I cannot for me."

Those words of trust had filled Gottfried with such joy that he had almost wanted to weep. Yet it was joy woven on a warp of sadness, for Arnmut's knighting had drawn the day when they must part a little closer. Arnmut would take a squire of his own, and Gottfried would find another; and then, someday, one of them would have to leave Burg Fürstensee for good, going back to the duties demanded in the keep of his father or elder brother.

It does no good to weep over sorrows to come, Gottfried reminded himself sternly. Only God knows what shall come to pass: a good Christian should trust in Him, and be thankful for His blessings and tests alike. Still, he could not keep from glancing at Arnmut again. In the shadows of the candles' steady flames, the new-made Ritter's face seemed pensive, golden brows drawn close and finely moulded lips pursed slightly, as though he wished to speak some thought that he could not shape into words.

At the end of the corridor, the candlelight flickered in the wind of an opened door. Though Gottfried was already standing perfectly straight, and he knew better than to lock his muscles, he could still feel himself bracing a little tighter, ready - for what? There was no guessing what the Order man might try, here in the Bishop's very palace; but that was why he and Arnmut were standing guard.

Gottfried could see no more than a dark man-sized blur moving slowly down the passageway towards them, but Arnmut, though he stood as alertly as his companion, seemed to see nothing.

"Who is it?" Gottfried whispered softly.

"Where?" Arnmut whispered back, blue eyes widening suddenly as he followed the direction of Gottfried's gaze. "I see nothing!"

The new knight's hand went at once to the hilt of his sword; Gottfried's was already halfway out of its sheath when an Italian-accented voice said, "Why are you so nervous, good knights? Surely you have nothing to fear from a pair of fettered women?"

"Greetings, Damiano," Arnmut replied steadily as the Light-Bearer drew nearer. "You startled us coming so suddenly from the shadows, at an hour when the Bishop's folk are mostly in bed."

Gottfried heard the rustle of Damiano's cloak, and thought that the Italian shrugged. "I did not mean to affright you," Damiano said, and now Gottfried was sure that he meant to mock them - to rouse their anger? Why? "But I remembered that there was another question that Cardinal Fleurs wished me to ask these women, and I thought that rather than disturbing the rest of the good Father Etienne, it would be simple enough for me to come by myself."

"I fear that you shall have to wait until morning," Gottfried said firmly. "Our orders are to let no one in or out here without the leave of the Bishop, and we must hold to that."

Gottfried wished he could see Damiano's expression: the Italian was yet too far away for his face to be more than a pale blur. But his voice was calm enough as he said, "This is only a little thing I have to ask. If it will make you happier in your duties, one of you may come in with me to be sure that your prisoners stay secure."

"Those are not our orders."

Damiano made a sound that might have been a light cough, or a muffled laugh. "Your orders," he repeated. "But I could have sworn that I saw you seated near the Bishop as honoured guests at his dinner-table, and that I recognise the belts and spurs of knights upon you even now, though this candlelight may deceive my eyes. Surely Bishop Otto does not give orders to his knightly guests - nor dine with his guards, though it may be Christian for the great to sit as equals with the lowly? That would be a tale worth telling in Avignon!"

Gottfried heard the restless clinking of Arnmut's chain hauberk, and knew that the Italian's mockery was setting his companion's nerves on edge, though whether Arnmut was growing angry for Brother Sigvrit's sake, or for the good Bishop's, or his own, there was no guessing. But though Arnmut was knighted now, Gottfried was still the elder, and it was still his duty to set the pace for his friend.

"Neither is the case. Rather, out of respect for Brother Sigvrit, who commands the Bishop's guard, and in thanks for the Bishop's hospitality, we chose to offer our services here - a small repayment for the kindness we have received, perhaps, but a token of honour nevertheless."

"Ah," Damiano said. "And answer me this, then: do you think you do the Bishop any service by thwarting the messenger of Cardinal Fleurs, for whom I believe he has the greatest respect?" The man's voice was infuriatingly smug, as though he believed he had just set down a chess-piece in the final move of a well-plotted checkmate.

"It is hardly for us to judge such matters," Gottfried answered. "But we have the orders given to the Bishop's guard, and we cannot do other but fulfill them. However, it is the Bishop's custom to rise for matins, and even if you must ride out at dawn, I do not doubt that he will be glad to see you in here himself. And if you are leaving so early, I should advise you to get a good night's sleep."

"You would not do badly to follow your own advice... Herr Ritter," replied Damiano, waving his arm as if he were painting an illumination of his words in the air. The streamers of his long scarlet sleeves flowed like battle-pennants, and candlelight flashed dark from the ring on his hand, but Gottfried could not see well enough to follow the Italian's gestures as he went on smoothly, "See, the eyes of your comrade-at-arms are drooping already, and you have been standing here for a long while. You were best to settle yourself in a warm featherbed and sleep deeply...sleep sweetened, mayhap, with dreams of a woman wrapping you in white arms and white thighs..."

Shocked, Gottfried said sharply, "That is hardly a proper thing for a churchman to speak of! I do not know what manners are like in Italy, but I assure you that such things are not said here."

At the sound of his voice, Arnmut started up at once, blinking hard and glancing wildly about himself as if he had, in truth, fallen asleep at his post. Damiano's waving hand halted in mid-air, and he snapped out, "In Italy, we do not answer so rudely when a man of no small importance offers us good advice and good wishes! Perhaps you would prefer another sort of embrace: that is hardly my concern." Damiano added a word in Italian that Gottfried could not make out, then spat, "Good night to you, Herr Ritter," as he turned on his heel and stalked off.

"Is he gone?" Arnmut said in a small voice when the sound of the door clanging shut at the end of the corridor had faded from the stones.

"So far as I know, and good riddance to him."

"I did not mean to fall asleep, but the flashing of his ring caught my eye, and suddenly I could not hold my lids up any longer. Forgive me, my Ritter, for this disgrace."

It seemed to Gottfried that his companion was near to tears, and he leaned over to pat the cold linked rings covering Arnmut's solid shoulder. "There is no disgrace, for I believe he may have used some magic of the sort Brother Sigvrit talks of in order to lull us to sleep."

"But...but you did not fall, and I did..."

"Only," Gottfried said gently, "because I could not see what he was doing. There is no great virtue in that: it is no more than God's grace that he could not ensnare us both in the same trap."

Arnmut sighed, a great shuddering breath. "I shall light a candle in thanks for that tomorrow."

"I, as well," Gottfried agreed. "As Brother Sigvrit says, these are no easy things to deal with. And yet we may be grateful to Christ that He has sent us a battle in which His will and His foes are so clearly made plain, when it is not always so." For Gottfried shuddered yet when he thought of how close he had come to bringing down Herr Bernhardt, who fought for God as surely as any Crusader, though no mortal man could have guessed it when Gottfried and Arnmut had set forth from Burg Fürstensee in search of the fugitive guardsman.

"That is true," Arnmut said, his voice very soft. The light was too dim for Gottfried to see his companion's sweet smile clearly, but he knew the curves of Arnmut's fair face well enough to recognise the youth's look of gratitude.

The two knights lapsed back into silence then, watching and waiting. After a time, Gottfried found that his thoughts were turning to the two women behind the door they guarded - most particularly the fair one, Oda, who had ridden beside him on Ortlieb's hunt. He could not recall her face, but he remembered the sound of her voice clearly, and her pretty tinkling laugh as she spoke to him.

Thinking on her words now - O, the Landgräfin said that you had never learned to play courtly games with women, so perhaps one should take it upon herself to teach you...Every knight should have a lady...Gottfried supposed she might have been flirting with him: no woman had ever spoken to him thus before, so he did not really know.

He remembered little of the next time he had seen her, bound in Ortlieb's wain, for he had been half out of his head with fever, trying to fight back the dizziness and pain so that he could ride to the Bishop's palace as a knight ought, though even at a gentle walk, every hoofbeat had seemed to send shards of glass splintering out from his shoulder.

The poor, wretched woman, Gottfried found himself thinking, and envisioned, almost against his will, Oda with heavy iron fetters on her hands and feet, her shining golden hair matted and filthy around a face drawn by starvation, rat-bites standing out red against the chilled bluish skin of her bare feet...

Gottfried shook his head. He was quite sure that rats did not run freely in the Bishop's palace, and the chamber where Oda and Hedwig were locked was hardly a dungeon. As for starvation and ill-treatment, he had seen two of the Bishop's guardsmen bear in a perfectly good, if penetential, supper of bread and brined herring that evening, complete with a little pot of water and plain napkins so that the women might wash their hands: even in the face of their appalling crimes, the Bishop had not forgotten that they were of gentle birth. Now Christ help me against the deceits of the Devil, Gottfried prayed silently. Brother Sigvrit had spoken of how Satan gave the pagan sorcerors of Lithuania great power to cloud the mind: it would be no surprise to Gottfried, if the Foe had bestowed the same gift on those who worshipped him in Christian lands.

"Arnmut, what are you thinking?" he asked.

Arnmut blinked, but answered at once, "I am wondering if Damiano will try another means of reaching the prisoners. Is there a window in their chamber?"

Gottfried's brow furrowed a moment in thought. "I do not think so, for one of the guards who brought their supper was carrying a candle, though it was full day. We guard the only way by which living flesh may enter that room - and as for other things, it would be my guess that Father Etienne has barred the walls there by means more powerful than our swords."

"That is well. But - Gottfried, what brought you to ask after my thoughts? Is something amiss? You looked troubled..."

"Aye," Gottfried said slowly. "I think that it were best if you kept speaking to me - it makes little matter what, so long as it busies my mind."

"Well then, have you thought much on the road we shall take home? The Frowe Gräfin and Herr Bernhardt seem set on having the Bear's Paw travel with us, but I must say that it would be asking a great deal of any castle's lord to let such a rough band within their walls: if my father were to see them, he would bar his gates and ready his bowmen at once."

"As would mine," Gottfried replied. Any man, looking on Captain Paul's company, would recognise them for what they were at once: the mismatched armour, scrounged from battlefield after battlefield, without so much as a tattered surcoat to hint at any allegiance; their irregular habit of march - they could fight in a disciplined formation well enough, but Paul the Bear had wasted no time on making his men hold line and step beween battles - and something beyond that, some air of cheerful defiance blustering over the grimness of men who lived by slaying others for pay, marked the Bear's Paw soldiers in a way that even Gottfried, short-sighted as he was, could see whenever he looked upon one of them. Still...

"It would take a long time," Gottfried mused, "to make even the simplest tabards for forty men: alas that we did not think of it before. Yet we took the arms and armour of Ortlieb's guard, and they were well-equipped: that will make at least some of the Bear's Paw look less ruffianly. Before God," he added with a sigh, "I never thought that I should be trying to make a Free Company seem more respectable for travelling with us, but just as Christ found souls in publicans and sinners, so, I suppose, we have learned that there may be good men among mercenaries."

"Even so," Arnmut agreed cheerfully. "I have often given thanks to Christ that He sent us a physician skilled enough to heal your arm, when at first I feared that you might lose it."

Gottfried shifted his feet uncomfortably. Jochanan was a Jew: forbidden by law to bear arms - let alone, Christ help it, to wield the dreadful might of guns. As a youth, Gottfried had heard the more dreadful tales that sprang up when the Death first walked: how the Jews of Neustadt, as one of their community, the physician Balavignus, had confessed, had poisoned the wells; how cities across Europe had risen up against the plague's agents in turn when the black boils began to swell on Christian bodies and the death-carts to roll through the streets.

He had heard rumours of Hosts desecrated, even of Christian children kidnapped and eaten at Jewish feasts, and of the many signs of Satan on the flesh of Jews, that they cunningly kept hidden...but Gottfried had never met a Jew himself, nor, he thought, had many of those who told such stories over their winecups. Now Gottfried knew that Jochanan hid no cloven hoof beneath his boots, for he had seen the gunner's feet stretched out to a fire to dry the wet wool of his stockings, and there were certainly no horn-buds under his hair, since he did not wear a cap as Jewish men were always said to do.

Out of modesty, Gottfried had refrained from looking when Jochanan chanced to piss on a nearby tree, but a man who trusted in hearing more than sight could not help picking up the sounds of gossip, and he was quite sure that if Jochanan bore any deformity other than the snipping of his hood, someone would have mentioned it when men spoke of such things.

After what he had seen of Ortlieb's doing, Gottfried thought that he had a much clearer idea of where evil worked than he had before - and it was not through the good man who had cleaned and stitched and salved his shoulder: if he doubted his own wisdom in that, he had only to trust in Father Etienne's.

Yet Gottfried could not forget that his silent acceptance of the falchion at Jochanan's side- the only fit answer he could give in gratitude for that healing - set him against all Christian countries' laws, and that chafed him as surely and irremediably as ill-fitting boots on a long journey.

"Christ's ways are often hard to understand," Gottfried said, as much to himself as to Arnmut. "But if He wished me healed, there must have been some purpose to it, and I am grateful."

Gottfried and Arnmut talked softly through that night until dawn began to brighten the coloured glass of the windows and two more guards came to take their place.

"Let us sleep while we can," Gottfried said to Arnmut as they walked to their chamber together. The night had told more harshly on him than he would have guessed: his eyelids slid grittily over his eyes whenever he blinked, and the deep scar through his shoulder muscles was beginning to throb with each slight movement of his arm. Blue shadows under Arnmut's eyes showed his tiredness as well, and his voice was hoarse when he answered, "I think that would be well. The Gräfin can hardly mean to leave too early this day, if indeed she goes today at all, now that the Light-Bearers have cast their first die here."

Margerite had stripped down to her shift for bed, but could not bring herself to blow out the candles and lie down in the dark with Ortlieb's ring on her hand. She did not know what it was she feared - whether some lingering malice of the woman she had slain would come upon her in her sleep, or whether it was only her dread of the dreams she had earned by putting on the emblem of a Light-Bearer Princess.

Wolfram slept peacefully in his cradle with Kobolt sitting guard at his feet, sable tail-plume draped over the child's body and golden eyes gleaming like pools of candlelight in his black fur; Eva lay in bed with Kriemhilt curled beside her, but Margerite could tell from her soft breathing that the girl was not so much as drowsy.

"I think it must be past midnight," Margerite said. "If we mean to ride before dusk tomorrow, you ought to sleep." She knew she was talking to herself as well as Eva, but it comforted her to address the younger woman.

Eva's eyes opened at once. "The same is true for you," she retorted. "At least I am in bed, while you are sitting up worrying. But Damiano has not come yet - and if he does, you outrank him in the Order's eyes. If he is foolish enough to disturb you, then you have the right to send him off with a curse and a cuff on the ear; I often saw the Abbess do as much with others of his rank."

Margerite swallowed her answer, for she truly had not thought the matter through. By the Order's rule, she did have that right, just as if she were a princess in truth and Damiano merely a servitor: he could no more complain if she struck him in the face than she had been able to when Ortlieb's ring had cut her own cheek. Indeed, Margerite realized, her heartbeat quickening as she thought of it, Damiano really ought not make the first approach without her permission. If she did not give him the word, he was meant to keep his silence: and why should she not judge speech on Order matters too dangerous within the Bishop's palace, surrounded as they were by priests and monks and guards?

That knowledge relieved much of her heaviness of mind, and Margerite knew then that she should take her own advice, and go to sleep. Margerite's shift was half off when she felt the chill creeping through the room: she thought at first that it was merely the cold of the air against her bare skin, but then she heard Kobolt's hiss, and Kriemhilt's echoing it, followed by Eva's soft gasp. Skin prickling up in goosebumps, she pulled the plain linen garment back down, turning to look at the corner of the room where the candles' light did not dim the shadows...where the shadows were darkening, thickening and curdling like a charred sauce.

A breath of something cold and foul reached Margerite's nostrils, its taste gagging in the back of her throat. I should have my wand, she thought: but it was too late to scrabble in her chest for it, lest the desperate movement should bring her fear rushing up from her swift-pounding heart to break through the banks of her will - and the thing drawing shape from the shadows was closer to Wolfram than she was.

Margerite lifted her hand, pointing at it with her ruby-ringed finger. "O thou wicked and disobedient spirit," she said, fighting hard to keep her voice calm, lest its least tremor should unleash the tainted power building before her.

"Because thou hast come here unbidden and against my will, know that I have the power to bind thee in chains of adamant, and beneath the eye of Lucifer thy master to cast thee into the eternal lake of fire, where thou shalt burn in pain for a thousand years. And by the power and dignity of the Omnipresent and Immortal Lord God of Hosts IHVH Tetragrammaton, the only creator of Heaven, and Earth, and Hell, and all that is therein, who is the marvellous Disposer of all things both visible and invisible, I shall curse thee, and deprive thee of all thy office and joy and place, unless thou at once appearest to me in a shape which is pleasing to the eye and without offense to any senses, and tellest to me fully and clearly why thou hast come here, without offering any threat or doing any harm to myself or others, human, animal, or spirit, in this place. Behold thy confusion, if thou refusest to be obedient! Behold the person of the exorcist in the middle of the exorcism, she who is armed by God and without fear. Wherefore make rational answer unto my demands, and prepare to be obedient unto me in the name of the LORD. Bathal vel Vathat super Abrac ruens! Abeor veniens super Aberer!"

To Margerite's surprise, she found that the words of the ritual calmed her burgeoning terror, even as the thickening shadows churned more frantically in answer, and it seemed to her that she suddenly understood one of the things written in the Black Book: To master demons is to master yourself as well: it is the same Will which forces the unruly spirit to submit to control.

The shadows thickened as their writhing quieted; but Margerite could not have said when the man's figure became recognisable in the corner. A glimmering of golden hair, a flash of blue eyes, the lightening sheen of a green velvet doublet: the glimpses coalesced from the darkness like a shape coming nearer through the fog. But when she saw the face clearly, a wave of faintness rolled over her: she was looking upon Ruprecht as she had first seen him, young and fair and unstained - or was it Ruprecht as he had come to her from his dreadful ritual with Gertrude, the star-glow of Hell's light searing from his eyes?

Not letting her gaze drop for a heartbeat, Margerite bit her lip hard to keep her thoughts from wavering. The Black Book had warned that demons would play such tricks, in hopes of distracting the mage for a vital second; and she knew better than to command it to take another form, for then it would know that it had found a weakness.

"Ask, and I shall answer, beloved," Ruprecht said lightly, in the familiar voice that Margerite had not heard for eleven months.

Margerite had to summon all her will to remind herself that this was not her first husband, neither living nor even in his damnation - Keep to the ritual: do not let it distract you! Looking on Ruprecht as dispassionately as she could, she replied evenly, "Speak not to me with such familiarity, unclean spirit, but tell me thy true name and rank among the host of fallen angels, and tell me who sent you to me and for what purpose."

"My name is Bifrons, and I am an Earl among the hosts of Hell. I was sent to you by Monsignor Damiano, who hoped to take you unawares or find you weak, and thereby that I might overcome you so that he should be able to claim your place within the Order of Light-Bearers, as you took it in your turn by slaying Ortlieb. That was a deed which made all of us joyful, for she was a cruel mistress, who tormented us for her sport, and I think you will be kinder to me - will you not? I shall serve you well, and if you wish proof of that, I shall gladly rend Damiano for his trespasses against you."

If Margerite had not been half-numb from the shock of the demon's appearance, and forcing herself to calm with every second that she looked upon Ruprecht's shining face, the news would have taken her harder. As it was, it seemed to her almost as if she were watching Bifrons from the height of an icy tower room, her thoughts keen and cold as the edge of a fine steel sword. The woman the Order thought her to be would have sent the demon back to Damiano at once with the orders to slay him as quickly as it might, and if the Light-Bearer coveted her ring, his death was by far the safest thing for her - but am I to become Ortlieb so swiftly? The Blessed Virgin preserve me from that!

Ruprecht's eyes were still looking at her with desperate pleading, and she could not help hearing his last words in her thoughts. Margerite, I have wronged you, but I would make it up...

Quickly, before her memory could betray her to this false reflection of the man she had loved, Margerite concentrated all her mind upon the rites she had read and reworked for herself, speaking to the demon in the stern tone she would use for a sluggard scullion.

"In the glorious and incomprehensible names of the True God, the creator of thee and of me, and of all the world: I do by the power of these names the which no creature is able to resist command thee, in and by these names of GOD, ADONAI, TZABOATH, ADONAI, AMORIAN, to depart unto thy proper place, without causing harm or danger unto man or beast or spirit. And I further command thee, being exorcized and constrained by the sacred rites of magic, to come never again to Damiano's call, nor to work his will in any manner, neither for his benefit nor for his deceit, nor to tell any being, man or beast or spirit, of what has passed between us, lest I chain thee by such curses as I have spoken before, and bind thee to the depths of the Bottomless Abyss to remain until the Day of Judgement, where thou shalt be burned in the immortal fire and buried in immortal oblivion. In the name YHVH and by the power and dignity of these three names, TETRAGRAMMATON, ANAPHAXTEON, and PRIMEUMATON: shouldst thou disobey me, all the company of Heaven shall curse thee; the sun, the moon, and the stars shall curse thee; the Light and all the hosts of Heaven shall curse thee into the fire unquenchable and into the torments unspeakable. Go now, and withdraw peaceably and quietly, and the peace of God be ever continued between thee and me! Amen."

Margerite did not blink, though her eyes stung with water; but between one heartbeat and the next, the shape in the corner was gone. Then she staggered and would have fallen, save that Eva caught her arm and bore her up, supporting her to a chair and pouring her a goblet of wine mixed heavily with water.

"Drink this, for you need it," Eva muttered in a hoarse croak. "I wish that there were some food here for you as well, but I suppose there is nothing we can do about that. By Christ, Margerite, you dealt with that magnificently!"

Margerite shook her head, blinking her eyes clear. "I thought at least the ruby ring would give us some safety of body, though it imperiled my soul. Maria help me, what dangers more have I taken up?"

"Nothing that you cannot face, by the look of it," Eva said comfortingly. "Even the Abbess could not have handled a strange demon any better."

Margerite did not hide her horrified look, and Eva flinched back; for a second, her face was that of the terrified child Margerite had first met. "I did not mean that as it sounded," Eva apologized hastily. "I think Father Etienne would be proud of you. As for Damiano, when he sees you alive and cheerful tomorrow, if he has any sense, he will realize that you are too mighty a fish for his line, and grovel in gratitude for his life."

"If we had been sleeping when he sent that..." Margerite heard the shaky tears in her voice, but could do nothing to hold them back.

"Not when we have such watchers as Kobolt and Kriemhilt," Eva asserted. As if to support what she was saying, Kobolt leapt from Wolfram's cradle, walking deliberately over to the corner where the demon had manifested and backing up to it. Margerite heard the hiss of the cat's urine striking the stones, and a whiff of the acrid smell seared her nostrils as Kobolt scraped at the floor with his paws in a pretense of covering his puddle. Eva laughed. "There: that is what Kobolt thinks of it, and of Damiano as well, I have no doubt."

Still, Margerite did not sleep that night: she sat awake, burning the candles one by one so that she need not fear that they would all have guttered out before morning. Sometimes she would rise, taking Wolfram from his cradle and hugging him to herself - Maria be thanked, that he had slept through the visitation! She whispered songs to him, and murmured prayers into his ear as he tangled his fingers in her unbound ash-blond hair; and when she wrapped him up and laid him in his cradle again, Kobolt took up his post by the child at once.

Yet even Wolfram could not distract Margerite from the truth of what had happened: Damiano had tried to kill her, and despite Eva's comforting words, Margerite could not trust that he would not try it again by a different means. Yet, silly as it might seem, she found that she was more outraged than frightened - she was a noblewoman, a mother of a young child at that, and it was not right for a man to seek her life. If Bernhardt knew what had taken place, Damiano's claim of Church protection would not save him from a swift sword-blow, Margerite thought with a sudden vindictiveness. Or Ritter Gottfried or Ritter Arnmut - even Georg would not hesitate a second to prove Damiano's wrong on his body.

But for that very reason, Margerite could say nothing to the men. Even when the taint of having taken seeming power within the Order was set aside, if Bernhardt slew a cardinal's messenger, that would forever end his hopes of being granted his father's lands. Nor did any of the others deserve what would fall upon them for such a deed; if they escaped imprisonment, then excommunication might easily follow at Cardinal Fleurs' whim.

But Paul the Bear could do it without any new condemnations, and would, if he knew that my life was in danger, the tempting thought whispered to Margerite as she stared at the single beeswax candle on the table before her. The flame did not tremble with her breath, but slowly the golden pool of molten wax welled higher around the black wick, until at last a weak point in the candle's thinning edge gave way, and a trail of pale liquid spilled down its side, thickening into a long solid dribble before it reached the polished brass plate cupping the candlestick's base.

Though Margerite had not slept that night, she began to pack her few belongings as soon as the first light of dawn glimmered through the window. It was not long before Eva began to stir as well, sleepily stretching her long limbs and rubbing her eyes with her fists like a drowsy child before she climbed out of the bed and bent over to pull out her chamberpot. Margerite turned her back, bending over Wolfram's cradle. Her son was awake already, reaching up for her, and she put him to her breast before he could begin to cry out his morning hunger.

"Best pack what you have now," Margerite said to Eva. "I think it is time for us to be gone from here - since we must go, I would not have waited so long."

"But do you not think yourself safer here, in the Bishop's palace and close to Father Etienne? I fear that Damiano may not be the only one to think that your ring may be easily won."

"Whoever thinks that shall find it is not so," snapped Margerite. Her head ached from lack of sleep and staring too long at candleflames against the darkness, and she was in no temper to be patient. Eva looked as though she might be about to answer just as sharply, but in the end she pressed her lips hard together and went about gathering her clothes.

By tierce, the travellers' horses were saddled and their
gear all loaded up, Kobolt draped over Margerite's cantle
and Kriemhilt sitting on one of Eva's saddlebags. The Bishop
had given them their farewell blessing already, adding that
he would offer his prayers for Graf Heinrich's recovery, and
that he would always stand ready to give whatever help he
could if any of them ever needed his aid.

Father Etienne lingered until the Bishop had gone back
inside: then he came up to Margerite, so close that she could
smell the fresh bread on his breath and see the tiny silver
strands frosting the close-cropped line of dark beard along
his jaw.

"You know the dangers of your choice," the priest said
softly, his light sapphire eyes staring down into Margerite's.
"May Christ give you the strength and the wisdom to come
safely through them." Clumsy as it was for him to take her
hand while she held Wolfram snuggled warmly beneath her
cloak, pressing something small and hard into her palm.
"Should you need me, this may make it easier for you to
find me than before; but if you are in peril of losing it, then
destroy it if you are able."

Margerite closed her hand about whatever he had given
her. "Pray for me, Father," she stammered. "Damiano
already..."

"I know," murmured Etienne. "You did well - but do
not try the same against a demon housed in human flesh!
Where-ever you are, even camped upon the roadside, do not
forget to ward yourself more thoroughly than you did in the
Bishop's palace. And be warned: Damiano has ridden out
already. Though I do not think he will dare challenge you
again, do not be surprised if you meet him along the road
and find that he is riding the same way as yourself."

"Should I turn him away?"

"That can only be your decision. Be aware that he is a
messenger and a spy - and think on what you want the Order
to know and believe of you." Father Etienne's black-gloved
hand moved smoothly in the sign of the Cross. "Dominus
vobiscum, Margerite."

"Et cum spirito tuo, Father."

Etienne likewise exchanged a few words with each of Margerite's companions, blessing them separately, before he also retreated inside. Thereafter, Margerite could only wait, hoping that Bernhardt would come out and that she could steal a few moments' speech with him, that she would have time enough to explain, in a few words, why she must bear Ortlieb's ring - for after Damiano's attack, she did not dare to put it off: the Light-Bearer must know that he had no hope of overcoming her - and time, if kind Maria granted it, to hear Bernhardt say, "I love you," that she might wrap the sound of his words about her heart like a warm cloak as she rode away from him in the snow. Margerite knew that she could not look for Bernhardt too obviously, but she thought Arnmut gave her a sympathetic glance whenever he noticed her casting about for the one who was not there. At last she dared to say straight-out, "Ritter Arnmut, do you know where Bernhardt is?"

The young knight smiled warmly at her - were she a painter or sculptor, Margerite thought, she would ask Arnmut to stand as an earthly model for an angel: it was not fair that a man who was hardly old enough to shave should have such flawless skin, as well as features a maid might envy, though there was nothing effeminate about his broad shoulders and sturdily muscled build. Some woman will be very glad of that man someday, if he has not pleased his share already, she thought.

"Frowe Gräfin, I believe that he has gone out to make sure that the men of the Bear's Paw are ready to ride with us, and looking as near to respectable as a Free Company can."

Margerite smiled back, thinking that she heard an echo of Ritter Gottfried's sternness in Arnmut's last words, though the younger knight's voice had no sting in it.

"I am sure Herr Bernhardt will be in time to bid you farewell," Arnmut added. "He is too courteous a lord to let you go without his blessing."

Troubled as she was, Margerite almost laughed, thinking of Bernhardt as she had known him first. And yet she had not really known him then; whereas now, his true nature was brought forth for all to see. Or at least his manners and habits have changed again: though he behaves now as though he had never left the Landgraf's hall, Bernhardt is hardly the youth who fled Ortlieb's curse eight years ago. And Margerite would not have had him so: she preferred the man she had grown to love, whether he wiped his fingers with a napkin after every bite or swore like the rudest of the Bear's Paw Company.

For a moment Margerite debated with herself whether she should ask Arnmut to see if Bernhardt would come and speak to her now. But Arnmut was Heinrich's man, and she was still Heinrich's wife by law and oath. And her hands were gloved thickly against the cold: Bernhardt would not even see Ortlieb's ring, and if Father Etienne told him of it later, at least the matter would be properly explained.

"I would give him my blessing as well, for he shall have no easier work here than we shall have at home - but, as you say, he will no doubt be there to bid us farewell."

Georg checked the girths of all the horses, leaning his full weight on the straps to tighten them. "I believe we are ready now," he announced.

Gottfried passed by the steeds, feeling quickly at their straps as if he had just taken Georg on as his own Knappe. "Well-done," he said. "Frowe Gräfin, may I help you to mount?" Margerite nodded, handing Wolfram over to Eva while Ritter Gottfried bent and cupped his hands for Margerite's foot to boost her up into the saddle. When Eva had passed Wolfram back to his mother, Ritter Arnmut gave her the same courtesy; the men vaulted lightly to the backs of their own horses, and Margerite nudged her steed into a walk.

The Bear's Paw Company was assembled outside the gates of the Bishop's palace. Their breastplates, hauberks, and helms were scoured clean, but nothing could hide the battered look of dents beaten roughly out of metal, nor the piecemeal nature of their gear. Still, Margerite's heart lifted as Paul's horse ambled over to hers and a grin split the mercenary commander's red-stubbled face.

"Ready to go at last, Gräfin?" Paul the Bear asked.

"I believe so."

Paul turned, bellowing loudly to his men. "Bear's Paw - move out!"

"Glück!" the answer thundered back from forty throats. The mercenaries began to move, but Margerite, seeing Bernhardt at last, hung back.

Though Bernhardt's hazel eyes were clear, their rims were reddened as if he, too, had slept ill that night - perhaps even, in the privacy of his chamber, given way to his sorrow at parting from Margerite again. Margerite thought that his lips trembled as he looked up at her, as though there were words that he could not speak, even as she could not say how she loved him here before witnesses, nor bend down from her horse to touch her mouth to his. But she touched her breast above his hidden signet ring, and Bernhardt nodded, brushing his own fingertips over the slight lump in his gold-brocaded black doublet where Margerite's falcon-necklace rested.

"Fare you well, and come back safe," Bernhardt said. "You know that my blessing goes with you." And my love: he might have spoken the words, so clearly did Margerite seem to hear them.

"And mine with you," she murmured.

Bernhardt bowed his head, taking her hand to bestow a last kiss: a gesture of courtesy, and only they would know how truly it was felt.

Then his fingers tightened bruising-hard on hers and his eyes snapped up again, his face suddenly, shockingly white. Margerite knew at once that he had felt the ring beneath her glove, and known it - had he touched it thus upon Ortlieb's hand, on some cold winter day eight years ago?

"Ortlieb's ring?" Bernhardt breathed.

Margerite might yet have lied, but she could not. She only nodded, watching him in dread.

Slowly, never letting go of Margerite's hand or letting his gaze drop from her, as though her free hand might flick out a dagger at any moment, Bernhardt reached back behind his neck, unfastening the clasp beneath the gold-patterned brocade. The necklace she had given him came free, spilling into his palm in a pool of red and violet and rainbow-clear glimmers, as though one of the Bishop's stained-glass windows had suddenly shattered into tiny shards.

"You shall need this more than I," Bernhardt said, his words thudding dead against Margerite's ears. He released Margerite's hand, pressing the necklace into her aching fingers. Numbly she closed her fist on it, watching him turn and walk away.

The other horses were moving past her now, and - in the way of horses, who could not see another steed go without wanting to follow - Margerite's gray gelding began to walk as well. Needing the reins little while her horse was with the others, Margerite was able to fumble the necklace one-handed into her belt-purse, but she kept her face turned away from her companions for a time: she might have mastered her fear and the demon Damiano had sent to slay her, but she could not trust her self-rule to keep the tears back from her eyes.

# Chapter Two

The snow began to fall again after a time, first only a scattering of few wide flakes through the bare ice-covered branches of the trees, then thickening to a soft drifting blanket that blurred the figures of the farthest riders. Though the Bishop had provided Margerite with thick fur-lined boots as well as gloves and cloak and hood, it seemed to her that the only warmth she could feel was that of the horse beneath her legs and Wolfram nestled against her body. She did not dare to shed any tears now, for she felt as though their water would glaze her eyes with ice; but the numb thought repeated itself over and over in her brain like the refrain of a clumsily-written verse: He gave my token back.

But at least he did not ask for his own in return, Margerite told herself, chewing on that one scrap of comfort like a toothless beggar-woman mumbling over the hard burnt crust of a bread-trencher. She could make little of it, though. There had been scant time at their parting, and many eyes; Bernhardt might simply have been too deeply shocked to think of the ring he had given her in pledge.

O, my love, Margerite thought, her face twisting in tearless pain, why could you not have trusted me? Surely we have borne enough together for that! But beneath her grief, like the deep throb of infected bone under a scabbed-over wound, was the worse aching of guilt: if she had trusted Bernhardt enough to tell him about the ring at once, then he might have understood - he might not have recoiled from her as though he had suddenly seen Ortlieb's ghost shadowed in the bones of her own face. Agonizing enough, that Bernhardt had turned from her; far crueller, to know that it was at least in part her own fault...

The company did not stop for a mid-day meal, for in such weather, it was best to keep men and horses both moving until they came to somewhere a little warmer: they chewed dried stockfish and passed about flasks of ale and wine on the move, stopping only briefly a few times when Margerite had to suckle Wolfram or change his soiled cloths beneath the warm hut of her cloak. The Bishop had told them of a guest-house in the village of Würfenstein, which they should reach before dark if they kept to the road.

And he had spoken truly: in spite of the thick snow underfoot slowing both horses and marching men, and the gusts of snow-laden wind beating against them, the white and gray world was just beginning to dim into a deeper twilight when Margerite saw the first houses looming as dark shadows against the snow, and the welcoming warm glimmer of a lantern through an upper window.

A thick glaze of ice-crystals hid the emblem on the guest-house's snow-capped sign; but the snatches of song floating out through the door were unmistakable. The two knights and Georg dismounted first, helping Margerite and Eva down; Ritter Gottfried opened the door for the ladies.

As Margerite stepped inside, she could feel her face flushing with the sudden warmth, and discreetly snuffled into a handkerchief as her nose began to drip. The inn's main room was thick with the smells of smoke and dogs and food, its benches already crowded with men dressed in rough gray and brown wool - the lodgings would be a long way from the Bishop's clean featherbeds, but Margerite was aching and exhausted from the day's ride, and thought she would be happy enough with a straw mattress that was not too filthy.

Seeing the fur-edged brocade of the women's cloaks, a tall thin man hastily set down his tray of tankards and hurried over to them, the firelight gleaming from his bald crown as he bowed deeply. "Noble frowes, how may I be of service to you?"

"We seek lodging for the night, for ourselves, two knights and a squire, and some forty men-at-arms," Margerite told him.

The innkeeper clutched at his heart with a swollen-knuckled hand. "For yourselves and the noble knights, I can easily find rooms. But forty men-at-arms? Forgive me, noble frowe, but I can hardly sleep them all in here. Perhaps if some were willing to stay in the stables for the night - I would charge you but half for their lodgings, if that pleases you."

Margerite glanced back at Paul, who had crowded in the door behind Georg. The mercenary commander shrugged his thick shoulders. "A quarter seems fairer, since you won't be lighting a fire in the stables, and we'll be sleeping in the smell of horseshit - sorry, Gräfin," Paul added to Margerite. The innkeeper's fire-reddened face flushed brighter as he heard Margerite's title and he bowed again, so deep that Margerite could hear the joints of his spine creaking.

"Forgive me, forgive me, frowe Gräfin," he babbled. "I have nothing fit for you here, neither food nor beds...I shall clear my own chamber for you, but I am a poor man..."

Margerite held up her hand to silence him. "Good innkeeper, we have ridden long in the snow. So long as our rooms be clean and warm, I think I shall find nothing to complain of. Now bring us hot wine, or hot ale if you have no good wine, and food." She looked about the crowded room, but the innkeeper was already hurrying over to the table nearest the fire, shouting, "Hai, you lot, find other places, for there is a most noble frowe here who shall have this seat!"

The men seated there did not grumble, but hastily grasped their tankards and melted away. By the time Margerite and Eva had reached the bench, Kobolt and Kriemhilt were already sitting by the hearth, busily licking their paws and smoothing away the dew of melting snowflakes from their fur. Thanks be to the Virgin, Wolfram seemed content to lie in his mother's arms, bright eyes looking happily about while the Bear's Paw men pushed their way in to find seats among the villagers. Georg was still outside - mindful of his duties, he would be seeing to the women's and knights' baggage and horses, no doubt.

Jochanan settled himself beside Gottfried, pushing his dark hood back from his rumpled black hair. "How is your shoulder?" the gunner asked anxiously. "Have you felt any pain from it this day?"

"Nothing worth speaking of," replied Gottfried. "I have told you before, it is full-healed."

Jochanan clicked his tongue. "You have told me that since it first scabbed over. Still, I shall have a look at it later if you don't mind."

Ritter Gottfried shrugged - one-shouldered, Margerite noticed. But the thin knight was not looking at Jochanan: he was staring at someone across the room, frowning in the stony concentration that had so unnerved Margerite when it was first turned on her.

"Is something amiss, Ritter Gottfried?" she asked.

"I thought I saw a flash of scarlet cloth, such as a man of wealth might wear, and wondered if I might recognise who it was, or be recognised, if it was someone who had been at Ortlieb's banquet. But the man I was looking at was too far off for me to make out his features, and I think he has turned away."

"Well, even a farmer may get hold of a little bright cloth if his crops prosper, and if there is someone else of good birth here, he is likely to come over and greet us before the evening is out."

It was not long before the innkeeper brought out a pitcher of steaming ale with a floating nut of butter melting on top of a froth of apple pulp, pouring the drink carefully into the nobles' cups and Paul and Jochanan's tarred leather jacks. He had not skimped them: as well as the butter and sweet cooked apple pieces, the hot ale was sweetened with honey, and it seemed to Margerite that she could feel warmth and strength flowing back into her veins as she drank.

"I should travel with you more, Gräfin Margerite," Paul declared as he lowered his mug, wiping froth and bits of apple from his red-gold mustache. "Free Company men don't get this kind of treatment often: it's cold beer and day-old stew for us, often as not. Do you need a full-time guard at your castle?"

Gottfried looked icily at him, and Margerite remembered that, as long as the young knight had been gone from Burg Fürstensee, he still held the post of the Hauptmann's second - and she very much doubted that his tolerance for her unlikely allies would reach as far as offering them posts in the castle.

"We shall see how matters go," she said swiftly before Ritter Gottfried could speak. "Since we do not know how things stand at Burg Fürstensee now, I can hardly say."

Gottfried's thin lips parted, then closed again, a shuttered look in his gray eyes. Margerite guessed that he was going over the men he knew, wondering, perhaps, who could be trusted if Christoph were still under his younger brother's control.

"If Christ has not granted healing to Graf Heinrich or gathered him to Himself," Gottfried said finally, "then the Frowe Gräfin is the ruler of Burg Fürstensee, and she may order her guard as she pleases, at least for now." He went no farther; but Margerite was surprised to have gotten so much of a concession out of him - or was that Gottfried's way of admitting that he thought it would be best if there were men at Burg Fürstensee whose first loyalty was to its Gräfin?

The innkeeper returned with bread and a wheel of white cheese veined with the green of crumbled herbs. "You must have travellers' dispensation not to keep the Friday abstinence?" he said. "Alas, that I have but fish to serve you for dinner, but they are good fish, pike and carp, and I can make you a cheese sauce to go over them."

"That will do nicely," Margerite declared, pulling off her gloves. She moved her ringed hand under Wolfram, lest Gottfried should notice Ortlieb's ruby - or the stain he saw before, when I had merely picked it up without putting it on. "Ritter Gottfried, if you will please cut me some of the bread and cheese?"

Gottfried raised a sharply arched eyebrow, but then his gaze fell on Wolfram in her lap, and he seemed to think better of whatever he had meant to say. Still, despite their undeniable dispensation as travellers, he did not take any cheese for himself, nor, following his example, did Arnmut, though the younger knight seemed glad enough to cut Eva's portion for her; and Margerite could not help being conscious of every bite she ate, as if she were indeed flouting the Church's rule of Friday abstinence.

By the time Georg came to join them, the Knappe's long nose was almost blue with cold, but he was grinning cheerfully. "I have taken care of everything for you," he announced. "The rooms here are not so fine as they might be, but I think we have slept in worse. At least it is not a stable."

Eva shuddered prettily, as though Georg were merely exaggerating for effect, but Margerite could not help thinking of Merlin - wondering if the Welsh peddler was drinking in a warm inn that night, or huddled alone in his cold wagon with only the clothes and costumes of his dead family for company. Maria, look after him, she prayed wistfully. Few scoundrels are such good men.

As the innkeeper had promised, the fish were good: roasted with a sprinkling of verjuice tart and savoury beneath the smooth richness of the cheese sauce. Unfortunately, Margerite had only eaten a few bites before Wolfram started wailing and her fingers felt the beginning of a telltale dampness soaking through his cloths.

"Georg, where is our room?" she asked, rising to her feet. Kobolt leapt onto the bench and had his muzzle in her plate at once. With her hands full, Margerite could not push him away, and Ritter Gottfried's tentative movements were hardly enough to discourage the cat - the knight still seemed uncertain of Kobolt, and Margerite wondered briefly what the tomcat looked like to him. "And we shall take Kobolt with us, I think."

Georg picked up the black tom, who let himself be draped across the youth's shoulders as the Knappe took a candle from the table and led Margerite up the stairs. The innkeeper's chamber was small, his sheets and blankets patched, and the small stove in the middle of the floor leaked a trail of smoke; but it was clean and warm, with four fresh tallow candles on the windowsill ready for lighting, and Margerite's bags stacked neatly beside Eva's.

"Thank you, Georg. I think you can put the cat down and go now, unless you wish to learn a skill that few knights ever find a use for."

Georg grinned, letting Kobolt leap from his arms and touching his candle-flame to the wicks of the lights on the windowsill. "I shall do well enough without, I think."

Margerite changed Wolfram's cloths swiftly, wrinkling her nose as she tucked away the soiled ones in the separate bag she had brought for them. She would have to ask the innkeeper for washing-water that night and hang the wet cloths over the stove to dry, or perhaps his wife or one of the two serving-maids she had seen carrying ale about downstairs would see to it.

"O, Wolfram," she said. "What a brave boy you are, to endure such long journeys as a babe. You shall be a hardy man when you are grown."

Wolfram bubbled out a little laugh, and Margerite tickled him as she dabbed his mouth clean. Kobolt jumped up to the bed, flicking his tail towards Wolfram as if he expected the boy to pounce on it like a kitten. Wolfram let out a cry of delight, grasping for the black plume and tugging on it, so that Kobolt lay down and purred for him.

"Be joyful while you can, Wolfram," Margerite said sadly. "For someday you shall love - God grant you never have such sorrow of it as I have." Though she knew it was no more than salting her wound, she opened her pouch and took out the necklace Bernhardt had given back to her, stones and metal icy in her bare hand as though it had lain in the snow all day. The gold falcon's sapphire eye stared coldly at her, beads of ruby and amethyst glimmering dark beneath the golden reflection of candlelight in the small crystal spheres, their light seeming to catch the deep red glow of the stone on her finger. "I wish that I had cast you into a smith's fires before this day," Margerite said, and she did not know whether she was speaking to Ortlieb's ring or her own forsaken necklace. She was alone at last, with no one to see her weep - and yet the tears would not come: her eyes burned with cold pain, as though they had been seared out with an icy brand, but no water swelled to ease their ache.

Witches cannot weep, Margerite thought in sudden alarm. And where is mercy, when tears cannot flow?

Margerite's head jerked up as a knock sounded on the door. Hastily she tidied the necklace back into her pouch, standing up and straightening her clothes.

When she opened the door, Margerite felt her heart clenching within her chest. Gottfried had not been mistaken, even if his bad eyesight had betrayed him. Damiano wore another scarlet-sleeved doublet, though the body of this one was a stiff golden brocade figured closely with tiny red swirls, and his hose were half yellow, half red. A deep blue cloak hung loosely off one shoulder, and his pleasant face was framed by an ermine-edged blue liripipe, its long tail trailing down his back.

"Ex Tenebrae, Lux, Princess," the Order man said, smiling down at Margerite. "Did you receive my message last night?"

Margerite almost welcomed the flare of fury that sprang up in her heart at his words, for it drove away her thoughts of Bernhardt for a moment. "Your message, Monsignor?" she answered coldly.

"Aye, I thought it too dangerous to come to you myself in that place, so I sent one of our special messengers to you."

Even distracted as she was, it did not take Margerite more than a second's thought to understand what had happened. She had ordered the demon to tell her why it had come, and it had done so - leaving out the whole of whatever Damiano's pretext for sending it had been, in hopes that the loss of that knowledge would mean harm to one human or the other; and that it could do without fear, for Margerite had not known the right order to give it. Christ be thanked that I came to no worse harm than I did in dealing with such a being! Margerite thought.

"You would do well to couch your orders more carefully in regards to such creatures, as your ring shows that you should well know how to do," Margerite told him. "The more so when the one to whom you send your servant has no cause to expect it: had I not thought that your hand might be in the matter, Bifrons would be bound in torment for a great deal longer."

Damiano paled visibly, the tip of his tongue licking nervously at the corner of his mouth, though, to his credit, he did not quite drop his eyes. *So he knows, then, that I am aware of what he meant to do!* Margerite thought. Before the Light-Bearer could recover his equilibrium, she spoke again. "Now I would hear your message from your own lips, and it had best be worth the annoyance you have put me to, or you shall find out swiftly that I have no more patience with men than I have with demons."

The Italian swallowed hard, his liquid accent coming through more strongly as he spoke. "Princess, many of us were doubtful that one who had been in the Order for such a short time should challenge Ortlieb, and concerned lest some harm should come to you and your great talents be wasted, but it is clear that you judged your strength well. Truly, I sought only to find out what your intentions are now, and to make it known to you what help the Order can give you, as well as I can. There are many names that you need to know, and our Imperator tells me also that you must be brought into the Council of Princes as swiftly as possible. Madame du Guesclin has offered to stand as your Guide there: she wishes you to contact her at the appointed time, and come to meet her in Avignon as soon as you are able."

*I should not have taken the ring,* Margerite thought. *I should have done something... claimed my ignorance, or admitted that I had not the strength yet to wield it: the Order does not punish its members for knowing their limits. But now it is done: Maria help me!*

"Did she say how I am to contact her?"

"She knows of your skill in taking the shape of a falcon. She herself is able to travel in the form of a great cat; and she says that you shall find her in the forest of the Auvergne on the first night of Advent."

"Indeed," Margerite said, raising an eyebrow. "Well, tell me what more you have to tell me, and then be gone from here, for I have many things to see to yet, and I expect that you will be on your way to Avignon tomorrow."

Damiano smiled shiftily. "I, too, have many things to see to before I return to the Imperator. In fact, my journey will take me the rest of the way with you, since one of my duties is the training of young Nikolaus, and I understand that he may soon be ready to take the onyx ring."

Margerite drew a deep breath, letting it out in a semblance of an exasperated sigh. "Not unless his control is far greater than it was when I saw him last. And I have some doubts about you journeying with us. Though my companion Eva is herself of your rank, there are those in my close company who know nothing of the Order, and would ask questions about why a cardinal's messenger is suddenly accompanying us to Burg Fürstensee, after having been sent to enquire of the Bishop of Niederwald concerning a most serious affair."

The Italian shrugged, the gold embroidery edging the long dags of his sleeves winking and glittering in the candlelight. Kobolt hunched down, the end of his tail twitching; Margerite was just a moment to slow to catch him before he launched himself from the bed, claws snagging in a streamer of red cloth before the cat's weight ripped him free. Damiano's face darkened, and he drew back his foot as if to aim a kick at Kobolt, but Margerite's glare stopped him. With a visible effort, the Light-Bearer recovered himself.

"I gather you mean that scrawny little knight and his pretty catamite?" Damiano asked.

The unexpected rudeness of the Italian's attack on Ritter Gottfried staggered Margerite for a moment in turn, but not so much that she could not snap at him, "You will not speak that way of Ritter Gottfried and Ritter Arnmut! They are not among the illuminated, but they will fight for me. As for their friendship, Ritter Arnmut was until lately Ritter Gottfried's squire, and there is nothing unseemly about his loyalty to the man who trained and knighted him."

"I know a pair of sodomites when I see them," Damiano muttered, but Margerite could see him wilting beneath the force of her anger. "Anyway, what business of theirs is it if my orders lead me to travel with you? And as far as that goes," he added, "why did you not tell them to let me in to see Hedwig and Oda last night? You know full well what must be done about those two."

"Be sure, I have already made certain of Ortlieb's apprentices, and by far more subtle means than I think you would have used. There will be enough unwanted attention drawn to this case without someone who was not there when they were taken bungling the way they are handled."

Damiano bowed his head. "As you will, Princess," he said - but there was something in the meekness of his submission that Margerite mistrusted: it reminded her somehow of the ready obedience of the demon he had called. Enough rope to hang myself, she thought.

"But if you must travel with us, then I suppose you must, so long as you behave yourself properly and do not do anything whatsoever that might draw attention to us. Do you understand?"

"I understand, Princess."

"Now, as I said before, tell me what you have to tell me." Margerite sat down on the bed, but did not invite Damiano to sit: let him be uncomfortable. Kobolt leapt into her lap and purred as she stroked him, though she could feel the tension in the heavy muscles beneath his soft fur as he stared at the Light-Bearer with the gaze that she had sometimes seen the tomcat use on large and fierce mastiffs.

Margerite was hard put to it to show no reaction as Damiano listed the names of the great Order members from Cardinal Fleurs downward. There were two more cardinals in the Order, and the Archbishop of Trier wore a Light-Bearer amethyst as well as the one that covered the fragment of the True Cross in his episcopal ring. It did not surprise her to hear that Bernabo Visconti was one of the Order's Princes, nor that Bertrand du Guesclin was ranked a little below his wife.

But the astrologer and advisor to the king of France, Thomas de Pisan, was also an Order episcopus, as was Joanna of Naples and Sicily. Nor was Kaiser Karl's court free of the Light-Bearers' taint, though the Kaiser seemed stauncher in resisting the advice of the Order than was the French Charles or even - oppressed by the huge sums of money that first , then Bertrand de Guesclin, had forced from him - Pope Urban V. The Order had its men in Florence and Venice, whereby their riches thrived and grew; it was no wonder that Ruprecht had been able to borrow so much to fight his war with Heinrich.

They had their dealings with the Saracens as well, and maintained an uneasy equilibrium with the Turks, for the Turkish threat was a useful means of pressure, but a Turkish invasion would bring as much destruction for the Order as for good Christians. Nor, as Damiano made clear, were the men and women he named by any means the Order's only notable members; but the full count of those bearing the rank of Princeps were known only to the Council of Princes, and only the Imperator knew the identities of all the Light-Bearers - for no matter how high one might rise, the Order was always watching for signs of weakness or failure or betrayal.

"And if you are successful in gaining Niederwald as your own, then you will be able to carry out the policies Ortlieb should have enforced," Damiano concluded. "She was a great magician, but sadly, less able in matters of politics and finance. It is the Imperator's hope that you will do better in Niederwald, as it is a powerful and well-placed land."

"I expect that my triumph speaks for itself," replied Margerite. "Have you any more to tell me? Be sure that if I am caught unawares by something I should have known, you will suffer far worse from it than I ever could."

"I have told you all that I can, Princess."

"Then go, and do not let me see you until tomorrow. No: wait." As Damiano turned to go, Margerite remembered sharply what Eva had said of him, and her contempt and wrath blazed up like aqua vitae cast into a fire. "Do you remember the girl you brought from the Convent of the Holy Cross to Burg Falkenstein?"

Damiano touched a finger to his clean-shaven chin. "I may...She was a snivelling servant of some sort; I dare say you or Ruprecht disposed of her quickly enough?"

"She is my apprentice and companion now," Margerite answered. Even the shaking of fury had died down in her limbs, so that she felt a strange calmness in her hatred. "And I believe I have a debt of hers to pay you." With great satisfaction, as though she were striking at all her frustration and sorrow and anger at once, Margerite drew back her foot and kicked Damiano squarely in the crotch.

The Italian doubled over, gasping for air, his face red and twisted with pain. "Get out of my room," Margerite said. "Remember this, and if you dare to so much as speak to Eva when it is not needful, it will be a harder foot than mine that kicks you for it. Ex Tenebrae, Lux," she added vengefully.

"Ex Tenebrae...Lux," Damiano wheezed, hobbling painfully out. Even in his agony, he closed the door carefully behind him, so that Margerite would not have the least thing to complain of.

But as soon as he was gone, Margerite felt her stomach rising in trembling heaves. She barely managed to scrabble the chamberpot out from beneath the bed before the bread and cheese and ale came up in a clotted mass, long strings of ropy saliva hanging from her mouth as she retched again and again.

Dear Maria, dear Christ, what am I becoming? Margerite asked silently. I never gave a servant worse than a slap across the face, or, when it was truly needed, ordered five strokes with the end of a rope: I was never cruel without clear reason.

Damiano tried to kill me, she answered. And he mishandled Eva when she could not defend herself; he deserved far worse than a foot in his groin. We shall all be the safer on this journey because he knows now, in body as well as mind, that he has reason to fear me.

But I think...I think I did it not for the sake of justice, or even safety, but because I dislike him and I could do it. O, Father Etienne, why are you not with me when I truly need Confession and a penance?

And perhaps...Margerite could hardly form the thought, even in her own mind, but she forced herself to do it: she had seen already how a demon could throw in her face the thing she was least ready to acknowledge. Perhaps Bernhardt was right to turn away from me, if this is what I am becoming.

At that, the dam that had held her tears in her courses broke like a tangle of logs swept away by springtime flooding, and Margerite wept hard, hugging herself and rocking back and forth as though she were comforting Wolfram. Aroused by his mother's distress, though he had slept peacefully through Damiano's recitation of names and offices, the baby began to wail as well, and Margerite caught him up in his arms, crying into his soft golden hair. "O, Wolfram, Wolfram. Maria help me, I fear I am hardly a fit mother for you now."

But Father Etienne's words came back to her, and she found a painful comfort in them: Even had Wolfram been in the hands of the Order from birth, he would still have had a chance to choose salvation; and even were he raised in a holy cloister, the chance of damnation would still have found its way to him. No matter how deeply Margerite was mired in sin, she could still have hope that it would not taint Wolfram, even if the hand that changed his soiled cloths and lifted the breast to his lips bore the Light-Bearer's ruby ring.

When at last Margerite went downstairs again, her fish was cold, and she barely had the heart to eat more than a few bites, picking delicately at the bones with her fingers and slipping pieces down to Kobolt and Kriemhild whenever she thought her companions were not looking. At least Damiano had not been bold enough to force himself on them here: he was sitting hunched on the other side of the room with his back to them. Still, Eva was very quiet, and Margerite wondered if she had recognised the Order messenger.

Wrapped in her own worries as she was, it took Margerite a little while to notice the scowl on Georg's freckled face. Though Paul the Bear was telling one of his campaign stories, which the Knappe usually delighted in, Georg's blue eyes were fixed on Eva; and she, for her part, was not meeting his gaze, but sat with her hands clasped tightly in her lap.

He must have seen the ring on her finger, Margerite thought, and almost in the same heartbeat, At least she is not in love with him.

But when the women went up to bed, their cats scampering before them, Margerite could tell that Eva was in an ill humour. She forebore to say anything about it, though she could hear the girl's angry snorts of breath, and finally Eva burst out, "What a little fool Georg is!"

"What has he done?" Margerite asked calmly.

"He saw that I was wearing the Order ring, and he started glaring at me and did not leave off for the whole evening. You would think, if there were a brain in his carroty head, he could have figured out that I would not do such a thing without good reason. A proper man would have realized it at once."

"Maybe not," said Margerite, the bitterness bursting like a hare's gall-bladder on her tongue. "But you can explain it to Georg easily enough, for we have many days of riding ahead of us." Whereas I...

"That may be so," Eva muttered, as though she did not wish to smooth her rumpled feelings that easily. "But I think it will be an unpleasant ride. Before God, I almost wish that we were back in Merlin's wagon!"

"Is something else wrong?" Margerite asked, making her voice as gentle as she could.

"Travelling with Ritter Gottfried is like wearing a hair shirt: good for the soul, no doubt, but prickly and uncomfortable. Just because I flirted a little with Ritter Arnmut to take my mind off Georg's sulk, and asked him if he yet had a lady to dedicate his deeds to as a knight ought, Gottfried stared at me as if I were the very Whore of Babalon, and poor Arnmut was too frightened to say anything to me. You know that I am as chaste as any woman, but that is no reason for me to behave as if I had taken a nun's vows."

Margerite thought of how uncomfortable Gottfried's silent reproach had made her feel while she was eating the cheese, and she could not help but smile ruefully. "Some men are too pious for this world," she agreed. "Still, that is better than many other faults - I suppose one should not even call it a fault. And we cannot blame poor Gottfried that his father will not let him join the Teutonic Knights, though he would be happier among them. Do not let his strictness worry you. As long as your own conscience is clean, what he thinks is hardly something for you to worry about, unless you have suddenly taken it into your heart to make a husband of him."

Eva laughed. "I think I should have a better chance of becoming Father Etienne's wife! Though if I were not already pledged to Christoph - half-pledged, anyway," she added softly, "I might give more thought to Ritter Arnmut: I have seldom seen such a handsome man. And anyway there is no harm to a few courtesies between men and women, which Ritter Arnmut ought to learn if he is to be a proper knight in the feasting hall as well as on the field."

"Ritter Arnmut is a fine and brave youth, and you could no doubt do worse. If Christoph..." Margerite stopped, unable to go on.

Eva looked down, twisting her hands in her skirt, then up again. Her rosebud lips trembled; she cleared her throat, but her voice was very tight as she said, "Margerite, you wear the ring of a Princess, and you cowed the demon that Damiano sent. Can you not command Christoph's freedom? Please, if you can - I beg it of you!" To Margerite's horror, Eva sank suddenly to her knees, bowing her head before her companion as her tears fell freely on Margerite's boots.

Margerite reached down, clasping Eva's hands in her own and trying to haul her up. But Eva would not come, and she both outweighed Margerite and outmatched her greatly in strength. "Eva, please!" Margerite said. "Eva, get up!"

Eva only clung to Margerite's legs, her wide shoulders shaking and generous breasts heaving with her sobs. "Can you? Have I ever begged anything of you before? For all the sake of our friendship, Margerite, for the months I served as your maid - for the love of Christ, Margerite, can you free him?"

"Eva! Before God, I do not know. And I do not know how far each thing I do in the power of Ortlieb's ring puts my soul in peril, and..."

"Not so much peril as Christoph is in!" Eva avowed passionately; and Margerite could not deny that. "Margerite, will you swear to try? For all the ill these Order rings have brought us already, they may as well serve for at least one work of good, or why else did we take them on?"

Margerite wanted to give voice to her doubts, to tell Eva of how, it seemed, the very act of pretending to be a Light-Bearer Princess had brought her to behaving as one in truth. And yet she knew she would not scruple to use that power for Wolfram's sake, if she had to: how, then, could she justify leaving Christoph in his demon's thrall? O, if Father Etienne were here, that he might tell me whether I am struggling back up along the road to Hell, or following it further downwards even as I seek to turn about!

"I will swear," Margerite said, the words falling heavy as stones from her lips. "By Christ, and Maria, and my hope of Heaven - whatever power I may have, I shall use it as best I can to win Christoph's freedom."

Eva stood, embracing the smaller woman so tightly that Margerite could almost feel her ribs creaking beneath the girl's strength. "Thank you! O, Margerite..." Eva laid her head on her friend's shoulder, sobbing hard, and Margerite could only hold her and stroke her hair, murmuring meaningless words of calm to her as she would to Wolfram, until Eva's body gradually ceased to shudder, and at last she took a handkerchief from her belt-pouch and blew her reddened nose hard.

"It shall not be so hard to bear the journey back to Burg Fürstensee now," Eva said hoarsely.

Should I tell her? Margerite wondered. But...better to be warned than taken by surprise. "That is good to hear, for you shall have another burden in your companions. Damiano is here in this inn, and he insists on travelling with us, in spite of everything I told him; it is in his mind to visit Nikolaus, and he is within his rights, for Nikolaus is his own student."

"God rot his bones!" Eva burst out. "That bladder of foulness tried to kill you last night, and now he wants to travel with us? Why did you not just kick him from the door like the mangy cur he is?"

"O, I did," said Margerite. "I kicked him in the groin." Eva's eyes met hers, and suddenly they both burst out laughing, laughter as hysterical as Eva's weeping a moment before, that left both of them with aching bellies and tears streaming down their faces. "Still, I am ashamed of it," Margerite went on when her helpless giggles had subsided at last.

"Ashamed that you were not wearing pointed steel boots, I hope," gasped Eva, and began to laugh again. Margerite waited patiently until her companion had quieted.

"No, I did it because I had the power to, and I wanted to strike out at someone. And perhaps because of what Damiano had done to you, and tried to do to me...but still..."

"I wish only that we could set the men on him. It would not be hard to make him disappear on the road," Eva mused, a steely cold settling behind her blue eyes.

"No," Margerite said firmly. "We are beset with evil enough, without becoming its agents ourselves. You heard what the demon said last night: it would have been glad enough to murder Damiano at my command - but I will not have his blood upon my soul, unless it is a matter of life and death."

Eva heaved a deep sigh, but her face had grown thoughtful as Margerite spoke. "You are right, I suppose. Still, it is a difficult task, to set ourselves against foes who are bound by no such concerns when we are hampered thus."

"Not hampered, but - please God - strengthened by faith and trust in Christ, Who is more powerful than any of our enemies," Margerite told her. She did not know whether she was trying to convince Eva, or herself; but to her surprise, she found that her own words were calming her heart.

"May it be so," Eva agreed gravely. But Margerite could hear the doubt in her voice: after all, Eva had known only a few months of peace between Ruprecht's death and Christoph's possession; most of her life had been spent in terror of Satan, with his power made clear in a number of ways that Margerite, thank Christ, yet knew only from her readings in the Black Book.

"It is so," Margerite insisted. "Have we not overcome far worse foes before now? Graf Günther and Ortlieb were dragons in the earth; but neither Damiano nor Nikolaus is more than a small serpent. And Christ is with us, and we have strong men beside us where earthly swords are needed: how then should we fail?"

Eva bowed her head once more. "May Christ forgive me, but I am still afraid. I do not know if I dare to look on Christoph again, and seeing Damiano's demon reminded me of all that I had to do for the Abbess." The muscles of Eva's left cheek were beginning to tic, jumping nervously beneath the skin, as though her will to hold her body together were beginning to fail. Margerite patted her shoulder reassuringly.

"Of course you are afraid. So am I. But you are a strong woman, and together we shall make our way through this dreadful maze."

Eva said nothing; but a soft chirp came from her feet. Kriemhild stood up on her hind legs, pawing at her mistress' skirts, and Eva bent down to pick her up, smiling wanly as the cat began to lick her tearstained cheeks. "I begin to think that maybe we shall. Thank you, Margerite."

"You shall do as much for me someday, maybe. And I thank the Virgin that neither of us has to endure this alone!" Perhaps I should tell her about Bernhardt, after all, Margerite thought. But her shame choked the words in her throat: how could she confess such a dreadful mistake now, just when Eva needed her to be wisest?

Forcing her thoughts away from Bernhardt - the shattered light of my necklace in his hand, the broken look of sorrow on his face - Margerite remembered the warning Father Etienne had given her that morning. "Now pet your cat and calm yourself a little while I feed Wolfram. And then, if you have the strength for it, I shall need your help in warding this room before we sleep, lest another evil come upon us in the night."

Georg held his tongue until he had closed the door of the chamber he was sharing with the two knights, but then he could not keep from bursting out, "Herr Gottfried, did you see that there was an Order ring on Eva's finger? What is happening? Has she deceived us?"

Gottfried's mouth tightened as he looked at the Knappe, and Georg felt the blush rising to the roots of his hair. I should learn to hold my tongue, he thought. But he remembered, all too clearly, when he had last seen such rings; though his shameful dreams of Ortlieb had ended with her death, sometimes the shadows of the three women still haunted him in the night.

"I am sure that the frowe Gräfin is well aware of the meaning of what she and Frowe Eva are wearing," Ritter Gottfried said sternly. "And I know that she would not permit such a thing in Frowe Eva, nor take it upon herself, without good reason."

"But!" Georg shut his mouth again beneath Gottfried's stare, though his head reeled at the knight's words, even as he realized that Margerite's hands had been hidden beneath the table for almost the whole evening.

"If there is deceit in the matter," Ritter Arnmut's softer voice broke in, "I am sure it is not meant for ourselves, but for our foes. And what better way to come into an enemy camp, than by bearing their own tokens of safe-passage?"

Georg could hardly argue with that, but he did not like it. Margerite was old and wise, yes, and might be able to risk such a deception; but such dangers were not for young women like Eva. "But why is it the women who are doing this, without so much as speaking of the matter to us."

"Because," said Ritter Gottfried, his sharp-angled face set grimly, "they know what they are doing, and we do not. It is our duty to aid them where swords and strength may serve, and perhaps where our faith may uphold theirs. But I have seen enough of the frowe Gräfin's work that I should no more question her than disturb a nun at her devotions. As for Frowe Eva, she is in the frowe Gräfin's care. And I think that you are too young to have your mind so fixed on a woman, especially one who is expected to wed another."

"You did not seem so glad of Frowe Eva earlier," Georg tossed out. In truth, he was still stinging from the way Eva had spoken lightly to Ritter Arnmut all evening, and treated Georg as though he were no more than a stock or stone while she flirted with the fair-haired knight.

Ritter Gottfried's mouth thinned again. In the flickering candlelight, his gray eyes seemed strangely unfocused, as though he were looking at something beyond Georg's head. "That is a matter between myself and God," the knight said. "And in some things, each man must look to his own affairs - though it would not be fair if I did not admit that perhaps my thoughts then were meant more for another than for Frowe Eva, whom I believe to be innocent of any ill-will."

Georg very much wanted to ask what Ritter Gottfried meant, but the knight's forbidding look was more than enough to convince him to leave the matter be. Instead, Georg helped Gottfried and Arnmut to take their armour off, and began to go over it with a handful of dried horsetail and a scouring-cloth before he could be asked. Gottfried nodded his approval, but Arnmut sat down on the bed beside the Knappe. "Come, let me help you with that," the new knight said, smiling warmly at Georg. "It is too much of a burden for one to squire two, and you are not even sworn to either of us - and you have earned your accolade as surely as I: you shall not be a Knappe much longer. And though I have been knighted, I am more than willing to clean Gottfried's armour yet, for that he is the older and a far better knight than I."

Though the dim light made it hard to tell, it almost seemed to Georg that a touch of red brightened the prominent arches of Ritter Gottfried's cheekbones. Gottfried sat down by his former squire, saying, "Well, we must ride out early enough in the morning, and we shall be done the faster if we all three set rank aside and work together. Georg, you take off your breastplate and byrnie for cleaning too: such wet weather is the very death of steel."

Margerite had half-hoped that Damiano would have taken her blow as enough reason not to travel with their company, but when she and Eva came out of the inn, the Order messenger stood smirking among the saddled horses with his hand on the bridle of a red palfrey, cheerfully impervious to Ritter Gottfried's glare as if it were no more than the snowflakes brocading his dark cloak with patterns of white.

"Greetings, Frowe Gräfin," the Italian called as though nothing had passed between them last night. "How fortunate that we should have met here, for this is no weather for a man alone to be riding in, and I may be able to guide you to better lodgings along the way."

Gottfried looked at Margerite, the shadows of the hood over his helmet making the bones of his face stand out skeletally. "Frowe Gräfin, is it truly your wish that this man travel with us? We have a long way to go, and the road through others' lands is no place to trust in a stranger."

Damiano laughed. "You cannot call me a stranger, when the Bishop of Niederwald has vouched for me. And, Herr Ritter, it is not your choice to make."

If I asked, Gottfried would see him off quickly enough, Margerite thought, catching her breath in hope. But the fur lining of her hood brushed her cheeks like Kobolt's soft paw as she shook her head slightly: if there were an adder in her chamber, best to know where it was, rather than put her hand down upon it unexpectedly. At least if Damiano travelled with them, he could not reach Nikolaus before she did and the two of them would have no time to plot against her.

"I think we must count it an honour to escort a cardinal's messenger," Margerite said uncomfortably. Gottfried stared straight at her, and she could not read the hatchet-faced knight's expression - doubt? Anger? Or was he merely trying to guess what she really wanted from the blur of her features in his sight? "Will you help me to mount, Ritter Gottfried?"

"At once, Frowe Gräfin." Gottfried led Margerite's gray gelding up to her, and Arnmut held the reins as Gottfried bent to boost Margerite up. With the body of the horse between them and Damiano, Margerite could whisper to Gottfried, hoping that he would hear her murmur even beneath the thicknesses of woolen hood and bascinet, "Trust me: he means to come to Burg Fürstensee, and I would be able to watch him rather than letting him run free."

As she swung her leg over the high pommel, arranging
skirts and cloak about herself by touch, Margerite thought
that perhaps Gottfried had not made out her words; but then
his gray-hooded head jerked in a slight nod.

Even the slow plodding through the thickening snow was
painful to Margerite's aching thighs and buttocks, and she
swore grimly to herself that whatever befell, she would do
her best hereafter to make sure that she did not neglect her
daily ride: this was the fourth time in a single year that she
had suffered the pains of long riding after letting her legs
soften away from a horse's back, and she knew that there
were several uncomfortable days and nights ahead of her.

Eva was not hampered by a child in her arms, but she
was worse off than Margerite: though she had lost her
hardening, Margerite was a horsewoman of reasonable
accomplishment, while Eva sat her dun palfrey like a sack of
meal, and if the horse had not been following the rest of the
steeds, Margerite was not sure that the girl could completely
control it. At least Father Etienne had chosen thoughtfully
when he bought their horses, for Eva's had no more spirit or
wilfulness than an ox, and would plod gently along as long
as she could sit its back.

The snow fell more heavily all that day, and Margerite
found that she was grateful for the warmth of Kobolt curled
under her cloak with Wolfram, for the cold was striking
more and more deeply into her. Even the fur-lined gloves
the Bishop had found for her did little to warm her fingers,
so that she had to keep switching hands on the reins to keep
her fingers from growing too stiff to hold them.

She found that she was more impressed than she had ever thought to be by the hardiness of the men of the Bear's Paw, for though the ones who marched on foot grumbled unceasingly, none of them slowed his pace for a moment, and now and again they would strike up a ragged marching song, their voices mostly tuneless as the scraping of iron on iron, but making up for it in loudness and spirit. Though the stiffness of riding gradually melted from Margerite's legs as that day and the next passed, the weather only grew worse, so that even Margerite could tell that they would make less than half the distance they had hoped to.

Other travellers knew enough to stay home in such weather: often they could only guess at the road, crossing the wide white stretches between the dark edges of snow-misted pine woods. There, at least, Damiano proved useful, for he seemed to know the forks and turnings well; but twice the Bear's Paw wagons mired in snow-hidden ditches and had to be pulled out, a lengthy struggle that left those who were not lending their backs to it shivering by the roadside.

At least this area was good farmland, so that the villages were not too far apart; but Margerite was so tired and cold by the time they crowded into the next small village inn that she had forgotten what day it was until Ritter Gottfried said to the innkeeper, "Tell us now where your church is, that we may go to offer our Advent prayers."

Exhausted as she was, with the blood just beginning to prickle painfully back into her numb feet, Margerite made little sense of what the knight had just said, nor did she pay attention to the innkeeper's directions until Ritter Gottfried bowed to her and said, "Frowe Gräfin, would you care to accompany us to the church? Though it is too late for us to hear the first Advent mass, nevertheless we may at least make some devotion to begin this holy season."

Margerite gulped as the realization broke through her frozen numbness: Damiano had directed her to meet with Madame du Guesclin on the first night of Advent, and now...

"I shall gladly go with you, if you will wait until I have fed Wolfram," she stammered. "Eva and Georg, no doubt you wish to come as well."

Eva looked rebellious, as though she would have far preferred to sit by the warm fire with a goblet of hot wine in her hand, but she said nothing, and Georg nodded willingly.

The village church was very cold, only a few tallow tapers burning in its darkness; the Advent altar trappings were lovingly embroidered, but the cloth was rough wool, its dyes faint and muddy. Ritter Gottfried paused at the offering-box, and though he turned his back so that Margerite could not see what he dropped in, she heard the clatter of a heavy coin on bare wood, followed by the softer clink of Arnmut's gift.

For a moment, Margerite thought of leaving the falcon-necklace - that would have bought the church and everything in it, several times over! - but in spite of the sharp pain that shot through her every time her fingertips brushed against the smooth beads in her belt-pouch, Margerite could not bring herself to cast away the jewel that had rested above Bernhardt's heart. Still, the small gold coin she dropped in would pay for fine new altarcloths, or enough candles to halo all the wooden saints that lined the walls in a bright blaze of light.

The five of them knelt silently before the altar, though the earthen floor was hard and icy against Margerite's knees even through her cloak and skirts. O Maria, O Christ, she prayed. Give me strength this night, that I may go among those who are evil and not be tainted by them. Give me wisdom against the seductions of the Devil; grant me your grace, for it is by your power alone that I may be saved. Keep me from sin, and let me lift up my eyes from darkness to light...Then Margerite shivered - Out of Darkness, Light: it was the Order's motto. Had their ways of thought crept so deeply into her mind that they tainted even her prayers? Or was it only that much of what they corrupted had once been good, as Lucifer had been the fairest of angels? O Lucifer, Star of the Morning...

Margerite knew that she knew the rest of the verse, but for a horrible instant she could not call it to her mind: she could only see the brightness of Ruprecht's eyes, and the golden hair floating like a halo about his shining face, as he had come to her bed from the ritual; and an echo of that dreadful, helpless lust she had felt under his caress twinged between her thighs.

Maria, that I should think such things upon consecrated ground! It seemed to Margerite that she could feel the throbbing heat of Ortlieb's ring on her finger, and though her glove shadowed it, she could almost see the ruby's glow through the black leather. The air of the little church suddenly seemed to stifle her, as though she breathed in bone-dust with each gasp: she could feel her muscles straining to rise, to run out where she could clear her lungs with deep swallows of icy wind. But though she shivered and cramped, Margerite forced herself to stay where she was, with sharp pains shooting up from her knees and chill sweat dewing on her forehead. She gritted her teeth: she could not think to pray, but she would not be forced from the altar.

But why should Christ allow the Light-Bearers' power within His church, unless He has forsaken you? the thought came to her, seductive in the freedom of its despair. Father Etienne gave Last Rites even to Graf Günther, and told me to pray for Kundry and Klingschor, Margerite reminded herself sternly. If they, whatever they were, were not beyond the reach of His mercy, then why should I be?

Still, she could not help breathing a sigh of relief when at last Gottfried rose from the floor and crossed himself in blessing. Lit by the guttering candles, the exaltation glowing in the young knight's gray eyes graced his bony face with surprising beauty, and a pang of envy twisted in Margerite's bowels: Why should he receive such blessing here, when I, who need it far more, can find none?

"Maria, have mercy," Margerite whispered as she, too, made the sign of the Cross over herself. A sudden shock ran up her arm, as though the red-glowing end of a hot wire had touched her finger where Ortlieb's ring rested; but it was quickly gone.

Margerite found herself lingering long over the remains of supper that night, unwilling to go to the chamber she would share with Eva - the only one in the inn; even the knights would be sleeping in the common room that night. It was not until Eva plucked at her sleeve, saying, "Come, Margerite, I think we will have no easier a ride tomorrow than we did today," that she reluctantly rose from the table. If I am to do this, I shall gain nothing from delaying, Margerite reminded herself.

Exhausted as she was, Margerite had feared, or perhaps half-hoped, that she might drift off to sleep before she could gather herself to wing away from her body. But though her limbs and back ached, and her head lay heavy on the pillow's scratchy wool, it seemed to her that she was wakening with every heartbeat. The sound of Kobolt's purr by her side thundered through her ears; Eva's soft snore and Wolfram's quiet breathing were as loud as the stormwind howling through the inn's eaves, and the wooden building creaked and groaned about her as though a host of men were hammering at its walls.

Though her eyes were closed, it seemed to Margerite that she could see the dark room lightening about her, the golden shimmer of her wardings ringing her like the stones of a keep, starred with the brilliant white of the pentagrams that kept all evil at bay in God's name. She did not dare to look at her hand for fear of what she might see; but Kobolt's golden eyes and Kriemhilt's green glowed like jewels lit by candleflame, the cats themselves no more than great black shadows in the dimness. Margerite was not sure how she did it, drawing the shining web of her soul together from her dulled flesh, but as she lifted her arms, she felt the cold wind catching wingfeathers, and when she sprang upward, the low cobwebbed roof was no longer in her path.

The tumbling rush of snowflakes around her glimmered as though the moon shone through them, a bright veil of drifting crystal; though the wind's gusts buffeted her from side to side, the falcon rose higher, her harsh shriek ringing through the wailing storm. The clouds roiled black and gray around her, mist-mountains churning with wild avalanches; streaks of moonlight silvered their ragged edges to raging rivers. The falcon shrieked again, circling up through their towering heights until she broke free; then she soared alone and serene in the pure moonlight beneath the starred sky, the cloud-ocean seething silent beneath her.

She wanted to fly higher, to keep rising and never drop back to earth, but somehow she knew that she could not. A vague thought tugged at her - something she ought to do, or have done...Her flight faltered a moment, and she sank down towards the swift-scudding gray peaks below.

West, to the Auvergne, the thought came to her. The falcon circled, skimming above the clouds like a petrel sweeping over a storm-racked sea. As she flew, it seemed to her that the band on her talon - the band of gold and ruby that bound her as surely as any jesses - began to warm and throb, pulling her onward until she suddenly knew that she must stoop. Folding her wings, she plummeted into the writhing torrents of mist, dropping from the cloud-cliffs like a stone.

The haze of snow beneath the clouds was lighter here, no more than a pale sugar-dusting across the darkness; below, the twisted branches of the great bare trees rose like white-edged claws. The falcon pulled up just above the treetops, sweeping on towards the ruddy glow shining through the woven tracery of branches, the beacon whose light echoed thrumming through her own ring.

The clearing all seethed with a faint red illumination, but the eyes of the great cat which sat on her haunches staring upwards seemed to gather that brightness into two ruby flames; and a third carmine flame burned steady and unwavering on her paw. The ivory tips of two great fangs glinted red against the sleek dark fur of the cat's jaw, and when she opened her mouth in a silent laugh, the falcon saw the cruel white spikes bloodied with red light.

So you have come, a voice said silently in her skull as she swooped down to perch on a branch, her talons sinking noiselessly into the scurf of pale crystals furring the black wood. The ruddy light-mist rose up around her; she could feel it burning slightly, as though she had flown into a cloud of steam, but she knew that if she wavered or tried to flee the cat would have her down in a single bound. My congratulations to you, Princess.

The falcon...no, her name was Margerite! She must not forget that, nor human speech, though the effort to shape words within her keen predator's mind left her dizzy. Greetings, Princess, she answered. You said I should come, and so I have.

Yes, though you have much yet to learn of using this shape by yourself, and are as likely to harm as help yourself in the doing. I see that Prince Günther's report of you was not exaggerated, nor were you ill-chosen to bear the Morning Star's seed, for you burn with power - but it was still a lucky stroke that slew your predecessor, as well as one that came close to imperiling us all. Truly our Master favours you, mother of His Son! You must come to Avignon: until I can speak with you face to face, your ignorance makes you a danger to the Order, and though you are the mother of the Child, we tolerate danger only when the gain is worth it.

This much I must tell you now, before your strength fails: beware Etienne the Exorcist! He may have aided you for his own reasons, but he is our deadly foe. I hear, Margerite thought back to the huge cat. I shall remember. See that you do. If you betray us to him in your own hurry and pride...you can guess what may befall you. You have trodden perilously close already: only your success, and the respect due you as the Child's bearer, have saved you thus far.

The cat - Madame du Guesclin - showed her bloody-glinting fangs again, then stood and stretched, powerful muscles rippling beneath her glossy dark hide and long claws biting deep into the snow. Margerite knew that the French Princess was more powerful than Ortlieb: those claws and teeth could rend her falcon-form as Kobolt dismembered a lark, tearing wing from twitching wing and dragging her guts out while her heart still beat.

Go now, Madame du Guesclin told her. I shall teach you more when we meet again, to bring you into the Council of Princes - if you prove worthy. Go!

Margerite leapt into the air, letting her falcon-wings speed her away away from the faint burning of the clearing's unclean light. The scattered snow-dust ruffled through her feathers to cool her as her pinions caught the wind beneath them, soaring upwards in a spiral towards the swift-scudding clouds.

As she dove onward through the rippling sky, the howling of the wind about her rose to a high note, like the keening of a great hunter's horn. A black wing brushed past her - the wing of a raven, floating like a huge dark leaf on the wind before her - and a cold chill stirred the roots of her feathers. Though she swept between swirling clouds, the earth a glimmer of whiteness far below, it seemed to her that she could hear distant hoofbeats clashing against a road, and the hallo, halloo! of the hunting horn.

She flew as swiftly as she could, her hurtling flight overtaking the raven and leaving it far behind. But the barking of hounds followed her, a full-voiced wild cry through the stormy heavens, and it seemed to her that the hoofbeats thundered louder along her trail through the air. She did not dare to look back, nor swerve from her course: no bird could overtake a peregrine in flight, and her trailing wingtips hissed through the bright snow like the flashing arc of a sword.

Nor did she need to scry the earth below: she could feel where her body lay, heartbeat slowing and breathing a bare flutter. Her stoop ripped the wind as she fell, slamming into her flesh with a blow that had her suddenly gasping and blinking white starbursts from her eyes.

"Margerite?" Eva said sleepily. "I heard you cry out. Are you all right?"

Margerite coughed, trying to clear her throat to answer. She was shaking hard, as cold as if the heavy woolen blankets over her had been a crust of ice. It was never like that before, she thought dizzily. Perhaps Madame du Guesclin was right, to say that I could easily harm myself by flying out as a falcon. Perhaps I should not...But even now, she knew that she could not leave the freedom of the sky behind: if she did not go by thought and will, she suspected that she would find herself flying in her dreams.

"I am all right," she croaked. But she got out of bed, wrapping her cloak about herself and standing by the fire - the coals were banked for the night, but even the little warmth they gave off was welcome.

When her shivering had eased, Margerite felt her way over to Wolfram's cradle. She knew that no other had passed her wardings to enter the room, but she could still hear the stormwind howling outside, and her mind seemed to supply the faint echoes of hounds and horsemen yet: she wanted to feel her son warm and solid against her, and to know that he was safe from whatever rode the night.

To Margerite's horror, her searching hand touched cold skin: her son had somehow managed to squirm out of his blankets. How long had he been lying there, naked in the icy night - and why had Kobolt not been there to warm him? Desperately she snatched Wolfram up, clutching him to her bosom and kneeling down by the hearth. "O Wolfram, dear Maria, please Christ..." Margerite gasped.

Wolfram squirmed in her arms, making the little gurgling noise that usually heralded more serious wails, as when she was late in giving him the breast, or would not let him grasp and pull with all his strength at the ring that hung around her neck on its thin gold chain. "Wolfram, Wolfram, thank the Virgin that you are all right!" breathed Margerite. But Wolfram began to cry with all his strength, the high ear-piercing screams of fury that usually ended only when he was red-faced and panting, too tired to shriek any longer.

Margerite cuddled her son tightly to her, rocking him and singing softly through his keening cries. Though her breasts were full, nipples beginning to ooze tiny smears of milk, Wolfram would not suck: he spat the nipple out, turning his head to the side. Kobolt leapt up on Margerite's lap as well, nuzzling his way under her cloak to rub softly against both mother and child, his deep purr vibrating through Margerite's skin. She made a half-hearted effort to push him away, but Wolfram only cried harder.

Margerite waited a long time until Wolfram had screamed himself tired. But when she had wrapped him in his blankets again, she did not put him back in his cradle. Instead she held him as she crept into her own bed, clutching him to her bosom. She did not know how close she had come to losing him...

"And you are all I have in the world, my darling," she murmured to the babe, listening to his tear-hitching breaths grow slower and smoother. "My own little one, the only love left to me..."

"Prrrp," Kobolt said reproachfully, curling himself on the pillow by Margerite's head so that the long fur of his tail just brushed against her nose. She had to smile, snaking a hand out from under the blankets to pet him reassuringly. "Yes, I love you as well, cat," she whispered to him, and his purr rumbled out in answer.

By dawn the next day, it was clear that the snow was too deep for the Bear's Paw wagons to travel, and though none was falling now, the gray clouds still hung heavy and low like featherbeds waiting to burst.

"What shall we do, Gräfin Margerite?" Paul asked, looking anxiously from Margerite to the snow-laden covers of the wains. "If we stop here, we could be here for a month. Those of us who have horses can still ride safely, but the men on foot would be slowed, and in the winter with robbers and wolves about, I don't want to leave less than twenty behind with the wagons, or they'll just look like easy pickings." There was something about the sureness with which the Bear spoke that made Margerite wonder if he had fallen upon wagons in winter himself during hard times - but that was none of her affair: she knew she could trust him.

"Your advice, Ritter Gottfried?" Margerite said crisply.

Gottfried looked at the wagons, then at the men and horses gathered about them, who stood stamping their feet in the snow and blowing little puffs of steam from noses and mouths. "It shall be hard riding, Frowe Gräfin. Yet we shall go the faster if we leave the foot-soldiers behind with the wagons; and that we must do, if we wish to reach Burg Fürstensee by Christmas."

Eva, huddled in her green-brocaded cloak, said nothing, but her blue eyes were wide beneath the soft fluff of brown fur haloing her face, and Margerite could read her pleading look as if she had spoke aloud - Margerite, you swore to do whatever was in your power to win Christoph's freedom.

"We have waited too long already for our return," Margerite stated firmly. "Those who are mounted shall ride ahead, whoever is able: the rest shall follow with the wains when they can. But let five of the men dismount and provisions and such things as we may need be loaded onto their horses, for in such weather, we have no surety that we shall always be able to reach lodgings before nightfall, and I have no wish to let cold do what swords could not."

"That is well-spoken, Gräfin Margerite!" Paul applauded. "I'll see to it myself."

By the time the gear had been loaded onto the extra pack-horses, a few soft white feathers were tumbling from the sky again. But the snow did not quench Margerite's determination to go on, and when Ritter Gottfried had helped her up and mounted his own horse, she waved the riders forward.

They passed through one village a little after mid-day, and Margerite ordered a stop there to eat, warm themselves, and rest their horses. She was glad of the chance to see to Wolfram inside near a fire, rather than having to fumble beneath her cloak, and she felt the strong temptation to stop there and stay the night; but if she faltered in her resolve now, she was not sure that she would be strong enough to keep going.

"We've been through worse in the Bear's Paw, haven't we?" Paul said staunchly as he downed his ale and raised a finger for another mug.

"Aye, we have," agreed Jochanan. "Do you remember that winter when we were camped on the Rhine..." The mercenaries' stories, grim tales of frostbite and wolves, did little to hearten Margerite, though the Bear's Paw men laughed over them. *Yet they still live in spite of that; and with God's help, we shall make it through this.*

The snow thickened in the afternoon, until Margerite could scarcely see the road before her: the whole world seemed to be a dizzying swirl of whiteness and cold. *What was it that Italian wrote about Hell? That the lowest depths were not fire, but everlasting ice, where betrayers lay locked in a frozen lake?* The throb of Ortlieb's ring on her finger seemed hot no longer, but painfully cold, like the touch of iron so frozen that it seemed to burn. *Who have I betrayed? Ruprecht, though it was a fair return for his deeds and not really by my choice... I left Christoph to his demon for Bernhardt's sake, and left Heinrich languishing, in spite of all the good he gave me; and Bernhardt, too, must believe that I betrayed him - am I dead, and this Hell already?*

"Mrow," said Kobolt, sticking his head out from under Margerite's cloak, where he lay curled about Wolfram. Painfully Margerite curved her frozen lips into a smile. No, this cannot be Hell: not with Wolfram in my arms and Kobolt, who knows neither good nor evil, beside me. Christ forgive me for such thoughts!

It was then Margerite realized that she could not see any of the other riders, nor hear either the sounds of voices or hooves crunching through the snow. The gray gelding sidestepped as her icy fingers spasmed tight on the reins in fear, and Margerite had to wrestle one-handed with her horse to calm it as Wolfram began to cry. "Paul!" she shouted, her high voice thin and lost in the snow-heavy wind. "Gottfried! Arnmut! Eva!"

Margerite almost sobbed with relief as she heard Eva's call cutting through the storm, "Margerite! Margerite, where are you?"

They shouted back and forth until at last, to Margerite's heart-shaking relief, she saw the heavily bundled shape of Eva on her dun palfrey gray through the snow, and urged her horse more quickly towards the girl.

"Thank Christ!" Eva breathed. "I feared that I was lost - I was having trouble with my horse, for she started and balked at something I could not see, and when I had her going forward again, I could not see anyone...I thought that I would die, out here in the snow..." Her shoulders began to shake.

"It is too cold to cry, Eva," Margerite said through numb lips. "The tears will only freeze on your face and make you colder...I am with you, anyway, and we have each other and two horses for warmth, and the blankets in our saddlebags, if we do not come upon any dwellings before nightfall. But let us call out again, in hopes that someone else will hear us."

The two women rode on, shouting until the breath scraped raw against their throats. Margerite's voice had dwindled to a hoarse croak by the time they heard an answer - a man's voice, though they were too far off to tell whose.

Keep shouting, Margerite urged him silently. Keep shouting so we can find you!

Ortlieb's ring throbbed once on her finger, a cold pain so intense that Margerite gasped. But the man called again, and this time she could make out words. "Keep on! I am only a little ahead of you."

Margerite and Eva nudged their tired horses into a faster walk, and at last they could make out the figure through the blowing snow, a glimpse of roan hide and black cloak against the whiteness.

"Damiano," Margerite groaned. But any company was better than none in such weather, and Damiano had carried the Order's messages all over Europe: he would be skilled at finding shelter if there were any to find, at building fires and keeping alive through harsh winter nights on the road.

"It is well that you found me, Princess," Damiano said. His face, too, was cold-pale, and when he gave her one of his jaunty smiles, Margerite could see the frozen skin of his lips cracking. But she had no time for pleasantries.

"Where are the others? Are they farther along?"

"Princess, I do not know. I thought that they were following me, for I know the turnings of the roads here even in the utter darkness of night. But when I looked back, they were gone, and so I rode on, lest I be lost as well."

If she had been close enough to strike him, Margerite would have slapped the Light-Bearer across the face: how dared he callously abandon her troop, and, for all he knew, herself and Wolfram, in such weather? But at least the men had the pack-horses with their gear, and would be in better case than the three of them if they had to stop and make camp. "Do you know where we are now?"

Damiano's gaze shifted. "Somewhat. The landmarks have changed since I was here last, and the snow is high enough to hide the road-posts. But if we ride straight on, we should come to the village of Holzenfest in not more than an hour or two."

"We should go back to look for the others," Margerite said tightly. As if in answer, Wolfram began to cry again, and her full breasts twinged painfully at the sound of his voice. But the cold was sinking deeply in, even through her cloak, and she feared what would happen if they halted for too long.

Damiano shook his head, dislodging crusts of snow from the folds of his hood. "There is no telling where they are, and if we start wandering around in search of them, we shall be lost as well. But if we get safely to Holzenfest, then perhaps you may use your Arts to find them - if you are able."

The taunt in the Italian's words was unmistakable; but Margerite knew that not only her life, but Wolfram's and Eva's, might depend on him now, so she said only, "True enough. Let us ride on, then."

They had only ridden a little way when Margerite noticed that Eva was falling behind again. The girl did not have the skill to manage her horse in the deep snow - and the dun palfrey itself was smaller and less sturdy than either Margerite's gelding or Damiano's roan. Margerite did not think that Eva could handle the horse she herself was riding, but if Eva and Damiano changed steeds, they would all be able to go a little faster.

"Damiano, I think you should trade horses with Eva."

"Why? This is my own steed, that I bought myself and have ridden for five years. Why should I trade it for a slow-footed nag?"

"I am not asking you to give it up forever, only to let Eva ride your horse until we have made it to safety, so that she will not slow us down any farther."

Damiano tossed his head in scorn as though he were wearing a feathered hat. "Let her learn to ride, or make her way behind us as best she can. It is not the way of the Order to coddle the weak - Princess."

"Damiano, get down off your horse now and let Eva take it!" Margerite snarled at him. "She is too useful to be left behind in the snow, and I want to get to Holzenfest before nightfall. Do it, now!"

Cowed, though still mumbling under his breath, Damiano reined his horse to a halt. Kriemhilt squirmed out from under Eva's cloak, hooking her claws into the thick brocade and climbing up to her mistress' shoulder as Eva clumsily dismounted. "Damiano, help her up," Margerite ordered. Damiano's shove nearly unbalanced the girl, but Eva clung to the roan's saddle and managed to right herself. The Italian mounted the dun palfrey easily, tossing a look of scorn towards Eva as she tried to settle herself in the saddle.

As Margerite had thought, they were able to set a better pace now. Through the snow and heavy clouds, it was hard to tell when day dimmed into twilight, but by the time they saw the first gray shadows of buildings through the drifting white mist, Margerite thought that the sun must be setting, and thanked God that they had reached the town at last. They could not have gone much farther: the horses' heads were hanging low, and her own steed was beginning to limp - it might have thrown a shoe, but surely there would be a blacksmith to tend it in the village.

They had passed four houses before Margerite realized that there was something wrong. Shutters banged emptily in the wind; a door to their left dangled on a single broken hinge, the snow blowing freely into the house; not a light shone, nor was there any sign that humans or beasts had ever passed through the snow-drifted streets.

"What is this, Damiano?" Margerite asked, her voice sharpened by fear.

The Italian shook his head. "I have not been here in five years. Maybe they left...or..."

Then Margerite saw the bundle of snow-crusted rags lying in one of the open doorways. The cloth was half-rotten, frozen into black folds like a dead oyster-mushroom in deep frost; but beneath the blackness glimmered...a knob of white, like the end of a bone...

"This is a plague-village!" Margerite cried out, terror striking through her like a spear of ice. Had it not been for Eva, who could not keep up even on her new mount, Margerite would have dug her heels into the horse's sides at that moment, pressing the poor beast to run, though its tired heart gave out beneath her. "Quickly, we must get away!"

She could see the naked fear on Damiano's open face, and Eva's bundled hand halting halfway through the sign of the Cross, as though the girl had just remembered that they were supposed to be Light-Bearers. But before any of them could speak, or spur on their steeds, a deep voice came from one of the doorways.

"These dead will not harm you."

Damiano whirled his head to look for the speaker. "How do you know?" he demanded belligerently. "Who are you, anyway?" The arrogant tone in his voice set Margerite's teeth on edge; she tightened her hands on the reins, ready to flee if the stranger took offense and attacked them.

Margerite heard a laugh as the man stepped outside. He was cloaked in a long coat of gray wolfskins, with the head of one, ears, face, and all, hanging over his own head as a hood: she could only see the brightness of his gray-blue eyes, the pointed tip of his nose beneath the wolf's nose, and the ruddy fairness of his short beard. He held a broad-headed spear butt-down like a staff, and two gray shapes flanked him - Wolves!

Margerite thought at first with a shudder of fear: is he a werewolf? But then she marked that the hounds' heads were broader than wolves', legs shorter and bodies heavier, and thick tails curled tightly over their backs. A great horn was slung across his chest, its wide end bound with a ring of strangely-carved silver and its tip adorned with a silver dragon's head whose stone eyes gleamed red. Yet there is no hole in the mouthpiece: how can he blow it?

"Have you forgotten me so quickly, Damiano? I thought
I had taught you better than that." Though he spoke clearly,
Margerite could not place his accent: his voice had a guttural
tinge that twisted his words into something strange and
archaic-sounding.

"Meister Stefan?" Damiano said uncertainly. "Why are
you here? I thought you were still at your castle in the
Pyrenees."

"Travelling, as you are. I mean to be at the Externsteine
for Yule - and that is all you need to know. Will you come in?
You look cold, and your horses are near to foundering; the
gray is limping already."

Margerite found herself staring at the man, unnerved. If
he were Damiano's teacher - he must be high in the Order of
Light-Bearers, and she did not know if she had the strength
to keep up her deception, for the cold had sapped both her
body and her will.

"Come into a plague-house?" Damiano asked. Meister
Stefan laughed again, a deep rich sound.

"Still thinking of your body's safety above all?" he replied.
"No wonder you have never risen any higher in your Order.
But I think you know enough to believe me when I say that
no harm shall come to you."

Wolfram began to squall, squirming in Margerite's arms
so that she could hardly hold him, and she felt a wet dribble
of milk leak from her aching nipples. Although every fibre
of her nerves trembled at the thought of stepping willingly
into a plague-house, she knew that she could not ride further
without seeing to her son. She sat caught in indecision;
then, as if disturbed by Wolfram's thrashing, Kobolt crept
out from under Margerite's cloak, leaping down into the
snow and scampering towards Meister Stefan. The hounds
pricked up their ears, standing and barking sharply at the
cat; in a heartbeat, Kobolt had hidden himself underneath
the man's wolfskin coat.

"I believe him," Margerite said. "Damiano, help me to
dismount."

Once her feet were on the ground, Margerite could see that Meister Stefan was no taller than she herself, but she could tell that he was broad-shouldered and muscular under his heavy fur coat, and he moved lightly despite the depth of the snow.

"Bring your horses in as well, that they may rest and be warm by mine," he said, and Margerite found that she was already leading her steed carefully through the doorway.

The house was in bad repair, with melted snow puddling under a couple of holes in the roof and the water-stained walls marked deeply by rot. Margerite could not help looking about fearfully for bodies, but the room was entirely clear, with only a heap of furs over a makeshift mattress of fresh pine-branches in the corner.

She had more than half expected that Meister Stefan would ride a warhorse, but the stallion munching on a large pile of hay by the wall was hardly more than a shaggy black pony, though thick-necked and deep-chested, with large intelligent eyes. The house was chilly in spite of the fire burning merrily in the hearth - it could hardly not be, with holes in the roof and cracks in the walls - but far warmer than outside.

"If you will, Herr Meister, please turn your back for a little while," Margerite said when they were all inside and the door closed. "I must feed my child."

Meister Stefan - and of what craft was he a master? Margerite wondered - threw back his wolf-hood, smiling at her as he took off his long fur coat. A sword hung at his side: there were strange marks on its silver pommel, almost like angular letters, but Margerite could not make out the writing; the pommel was adorned with a thick ring gleaming with the ruddy hue of pure gold, and a hexagonal crystal bead dangled from the top of the dark sheath.

He was dressed as any well-off man travelling by himself might be, in heavy dark blue hose and a red surcoat belted above a chainmail hauberk, with a long fighting-dagger at his side: the hilt of that was ivory, curved like a huge fang, and carved with little intertwining beasts. Meister Stefan hardly looked old enough to have been Damiano's tutor: no silver glimmered in his tangled fair hair, and if the corners of his eyes were cracked with age, the lines did not show in the firelight. His features were fine as a youth's, high cheekbones and a sharp jawline beneath his reddish beard.

Yet there was something about him that gave Margerite the sense that he was far older than he looked, and she could not help thinking of certain hints that she had read - not only spells of illusion that might give the semblance of youth and strength to the decrepit; but elixirs and practices that renewed life, even to the very Philosopher's Stone, which was said to give immortality...

"Of course," he said cheerfully. "And if you will give me leave, I shall see to your horse, for I misliked the look of that limp."

Margerite was not sure yet that she wanted him touching her steed, for there were too many ways to work mischief upon a horse. Yet he had spoken to Damiano of "your Order", which gave her hope that at least he was not a Light-Bearer - but what if he was one of their foes, and took Margerite for what she was pretending to be? But he had claimed to have taught Damiano...

"I shall do him no harm," Meister Stefan said, as if he could hear the thoughts in her mind. Margerite started. "I am a friend to horses, and even were I not, I have no reason to bear you ill will, and perhaps reason to be of good heart towards you." Again Margerite noticed his strange accent - as much in the words he spoke as in the way he shaped them; she wondered what his homeland might be.

A friend to horses - it was a peculiar thing to say. But men pray to St. Stefan to heal their wounded steeds, Margerite remembered suddenly, a cold tingle prickling down her spine. And whatever manner of man he was, Meister Stefan's own black stallion was in remarkably fine fettle for a steed that had been ridden a long way in such weather.

"I am grateful for that," Margerite said. "Please do what you can."

Meister Stefan gave her a closed-mouth smile, a look that almost made Margerite feel that something was be passing between them, though she did not know what.

Sitting on the floor with her back to the horses, Margerite could not see what Damiano's teacher was doing, but it seemed to her that she could feel the room growing warmer, almost feel a golden tide of power writhing against her. Then she heard his words clearly - but she could not make them out: when she did not listen too closely, they sounded almost like German, so that she thought she could understand a word here or there; but then the soft chant or prayer sank into strangeness again.

> *"Phol ende Wodanworun zi holza,*
> *du wart demo balderes folunsin fuoz birenkit..."*
>
> *Phol and Wodan were riding to the woods,*
> *and the foot of Balder's foal was sprained*

What is he doing? Margerite wondered. But Wolfram was sucking strongly at her breast, his little hands kneading like a suckling kitten's, and she did not dare turn her head to look.

*"Thu biguol en Wodanso he wola conda: sose benrenkisose bluotrenki, sose lidirenki: ben zi bena,bluot zu bluoda lid zi geliden,sose gelimida sin."*

*and Wodan conjured it, as well he could: Like bone-sprain, so blood-sprain, so joint-sprain: Bone to bone, blood to blood, joints to joints, so may they be glued.*

The sense of power about her flared and was gone abruptly, as though it had all been sucked in like a single breath. Margerite heard the sound of Meister Stefan dusting his hands off, speaking quietly to the horse in a tongue that sounded yet stranger to her ears, several words ending in a soft buzzing sound that she could not have put letters to. He must be a magician of some sort, Margerite thought. But what?

"Will you be my guests for the night?" Meister Stefan asked. "I have honey-mead and food to share with you, and fire and food and dry clothes are needed by those who have wandered far in the cold."

"We shall gladly be your guests," replied Margerite. "I think we should have been in ill straits had you not been here."

Margerite heard his sigh, and he said, as if to himself, "Yes: the old woman swept this village with her broom."

Margerite did not want to know what he meant by that, but Damiano at once said, "And what is that supposed to mean?"

"When the Death reached the Northlands, many saw Frowe Hölle walking there, as an old dame with rake and broom. Some villages she raked, and there a few slipped living through her tines - but elsewhere she swept, and none escaped alive."

Margerite's stomach tightened, and she felt as though her bowels were turning over in her belly. She had heard peasants' tales of the Death taking human form before, to ford a river or enter a home: but Meister Stefan's quiet certainty unsettled her, as though the plague-deaths were determined not by God's choice nor even the Devil's malice - though the Church taught that Satan could only take life at God's pleasure, to test men as he had tested Job - but by another being altogether, answerable to only its own will.

"Yet this is hardly a thing to speak of here," Meister Stefan went on. "And while you are standing, Damiano, make sure that the door is bolted and the windows shuttered tight, for Wodan's Host is riding tonight, and Christians have no business being in its path."

"I am not a Christian, old man: can you never remember that?" Damiano burst out in exasperation. "My soul is sworn to Lucifer, as are those of these women."

Meister Stefan laughed. "Whether you worship the Christian god, as Etienne does, or the Christian devil, it is all the same to me. But I see you are in one of your bad tempers. Perhaps you should have some mead: it may ease you, or at least make you more pleasant to while the night with. And you, quiet frowe who has not said so much as a word to greet me - what is amiss with you?"

"Who are you?" Eva asked, her voice soft and trembling.

"I am Meister Stefan von Hauenstein, a teacher, and at the moment a traveller, even as you are yourself," the strange man answered lightly. "And I promise that you have nothing to fear this night, though you might have had much to fear if you had not chanced upon me. Now, there are three good skins of mead in my saddlebag there, and though you are guesting here, it would please me if you would do the honour of pouring it out for us."

Margerite expected Eva to tell Meister Stefan sharply that she was a woman of noble birth and had no reason to do servant's work, but she heard Eva's heavy footfalls crossing the floor, and the gurgle of liquid flowing from a skin.

Though below her station, the dresses the Bishop had given Margerite were at least easy for her to do up herself. Wolfram, full at last, was squirming more enthusiastically, so after she had burped him, she set him down on the floor: there where Kobolt was curled beside the fire, it was warm enough. He should be crawling by now: he is old enough, Margerite thought, watching the thrashing of her son's arms and legs. She knew that she should not be worried, for some children might be crawling at six months, and others waited until eight or nine; but she could not help fearing that, healthy and lively as Wolfram seemed, he might somehow have been touched by the things that she had had to do while she was carrying him.

One of the gray hounds - not all gray, Margerite noticed: its legs were cream-coloured, and its fur darkened to a nearly black mask on its pointed face - wandered over, sniffing at Wolfram. Margerite stiffened, ready to snatch her child away from the beast; but the dog seemed friendly enough, and Meister Stefan was saying nothing.

Wolfram rolled over on his back, giggling and reaching out to grab at the thick fur and making bubbling sounds of delight. Then, to Margerite's surprise, he said clearly, "Woof! Wan' woof!"

"Yes, Wolfram, a wolf," Margerite told him proudly. "Do you want the wolf?"

"Wan' woof!" her son repeated, grasping one of the hound's dark ears in a firm grip. Obediently the dog lay down, rolling over on its side and closing its eyes as Wolfram's fingers explored its face.

"Did I hear Wolfram speak?" asked Eva, pausing with the skin of mead in one hand and Meister Stefan's - drinking horn? - in the other.

Margerite's cold-chapped lips split painfully as the smile spread across her face. "You did. And he is but a little over seven months, too!"

Damiano snorted, looking away ostentatiously as though such matters were far beneath him. He knows that the Order thinks Wolfram is important, Margerite thought, remembering the conversation she had overheard between Damiano and Nikolaus - only a few months ago? - but not why, thank the Blessed Virgin.

Forgetful of the horn Eva was filling, Meister Stefan rose from his place on the floor in a single smooth movement, reaching Margerite's side in two quick strides and crouching down to look at Wolfram. At once Wolfram let go of the dog's ear, rolling over to reach for the glittering gold-ringed pommel of Meister Stefan's sword. "So you want a wolf, do you?" the Meister said quietly to the child. "You have the adder-keen eyes of an atheling-bairn, and the grip of one born to wield a blade: I think that you shall feed a good many wolves when your time comes."

Wolfram looked up at him, bright eyes wide and round, as though he could understand what the strange man was saying, and Meister Stefan went on as though there were no one else listening, "Wolfram is your name - Wolf-Raven, that would have been once. Yes: for I see the riding of the Furious Host, the Wild Hunt, behind your eyes: the lord of the ravens' offering was there when your seed was poured forth from the eagle's flight, and your father gave you your name with the storm's rain. You..."

"Say no more!" Margerite broke in, furious with terror. Only the presence of Damiano, sitting cross-legged on the floor as Eva squirted mead into his upraised silver goblet, kept her from shouting at Meister Stefan that her son had been properly baptized, and his father had had nothing to do with it. Then, as the man's eyes met hers, she feared that she had spoken too hastily and angered him. His lips pulled back in a smile, but not a reassuring one; again she felt as though she could feel the weight of his great age pressing against her - though surely he could be no more than ten years older than Damiano or Father Etienne?

"If you would let me," Meister Stefan murmured, "I could tell you something of what lies before your son, though I know not whether it would give you liking or a worse fear. Yet knowledge is always best to have, even though it is said that the middling-wise man may be happiest - and I can see that you are one who would know, whether it bring you joy or sorrow in the end. You would have done well as my student."

"Student of what?" Margerite asked, her voice brittle, as though the words would snap under her tongue.

Meister Stefan laughed. "Why, I think you know already. I taught both Damiano, here, and your friend Etienne, as much as they could learn from me until their weirds carried them elsewhere. Etienne was ever the better student," he added with a sly glance back at the Italian, "but I have seen more of Damiano of late, while Etienne can seldom spare the time to guest with his old teacher."

"How do you know that I - have spent time with Etienne?" Margerite said cautiously.

"Should not an artist recognise his student's chisel-strokes?" Meister Stefan countered. "But you may be easy in your mind: I am neither friend nor foe to the Order of Light-Bearers. I have seen many such before, and men must do as they will. Now my question is for you: would you know more of how matters are set for your son?"

Margerite paused, a denial trembling upon her tongue. The way he had spoken of Christians - and of the Wild Hunt, that peasant-tale that...she could not help but admit it, had frightened her in the dark nights at Burg Falkenstein when the winter winds howled through the ravine behind the castle...surely, whatever he was, Meister Stefan was no Christian man, and his foretellings could not have any truth in them, if they were not prophecy granted by the will of God.

And I have gone too far already into darkness: if I cannot trust in Christ's will for Wolfram, then I may as well admit that he is...the son of Someone else, and even Etienne's assurances of his soul's freedom no more than a waste of breath.

"I would not," she replied firmly. "Rather, if we are to guest with you this night, I would know more of you. You bear a German name, but you speak as though you had been long in foreign lands, and it seems strange to me that you should know of the Order of Lightbearers, and yet be neither friend nor foe to...us." Margerite could not help glancing at Damiano, to see if the Italian had noticed the slight hitch in her speech, but if he had, he gave no sign of it.

Meister Stefan rose again, taking his filled horn from Eva's hand. "I thank you for the draught, good frowe," he said to her. "May you always have strong ale to pour out in your hall! Now see to Margerite, and then, maybe, I shall answer some questions, if you ask the right ones, or at least gladden your hearts with tales of older days. Damiano, see to the fire: it is burning low, and we need a good blaze to keep us warm in here."

Damiano's mouth twisted in what might have been an unwilling smile. "I shall tend the fire and make it wholesome," he said - a phrase Margerite hardly liked, coming as it did from a Light-Bearer's mouth; but she found that she could not summon up any mistrust for what he might do in the dwelling that Meister Stefan had claimed briefly for his own.

Margerite untied the twisted cords that held her silver goblet to her girdle, letting Eva pour some mead into her cup before the girl filled her own. Meister Stefan lifted his horn, first to Eva, then to Wolfram and Margerite - and how did he know my name? I would swear that none of us had spoken it; and he did not address me by my title, but I cannot dare to remind him of it, for I think he would only laugh at me. "Hail to you, fair frowes, and well are we met in this stead," he said formally. "May all be well between us, and may we go well from here." He tilted the dragon-tipped horn up, taking a deep swallow from its silver-bound rim. Margerite sipped at her own mead. It was not nearly so sweet as such honey-wine usually was; its taste was a surprisingly dry richness, with a faint tantalizing hint of herbs that she could not name. The mead ran fiery down her tongue, glowing in her empty stomach as if it were aqua vitae; but that was only to be expected, after a long and hungry ride in the cold.

"Will you tell us where you are from?" Margerite asked again.

"After a fashion. My folk were once called the Erulians: they fared from Norway and Sweden, down through Denmark into these lands - that was long ago! They were never great in number, and so far as I know, I am the last of that tribe. Would you know more, or how?"

"Can you see my future?" Eva asked eagerly. Margerite's mouth opened to chide her, and then closed again: she could not speak her thoughts before Damiano without betraying herself.

"Oh, yes," Meister Stefan said. He sipped again at the mead; his blue-gray eyes seemed to lose focus, and he was rocking slowly back and forth, almost as though he were drunk, though Margerite knew that even that strong draught could not have mounted to his head so swiftly. "A dark road before and behind you, and a long one...I see a greedy kinsman, grasping at your wealth and lands, but a stronger hand to hinder him; I see a dear man in fetters that you have not the strength to break. There are many wights that shall brush by you, but not touch you deeply...you shall be at the edge of the battlefield, but like many an idis before you, you shall have the might to shift swords when men are striving together. Had you been born before, I should know whose blessings to name upon you, but that matters little: the Heaven-Queen spins a bright strand for you, and golden tears shall fall after the storm is past. Would you know more, or how?"

"And what of me?" demanded Damiano.

Meister Stefan's fair head turned slowly to him: his eyes seemed filmed, unseeing, but the Italian gasped softly as that gaze fastened upon him. "Wandering, as ever; that is your weird and the duty laid on you by your Master. As before, your bravery fails when you would put your hand to the highest prizes, but as before, your cowardice serves you well, for again you shall live through what would slay stronger men. Trust less in what you think you know, Damiano, for it may yet betray you.

You would do better if you learned to hold your tongue, but your arrogance, too, may serve you, for a show of strength may save you from having to prove your worth. And if you would keep your hide whole, this warning I give you: stay away from Burg Fürstensee, for you have not the power to stand in the battle which shall rage there." Then Meister Stefan's eyes seemed to clear, and he coughed deeply, his swaying coming to a halt. "Now I have answered three questions, and it is my turn to ask. Margerite, whom do you believe the true father of your son to be?"

Margerite's breath hissed through her teeth in shock. Meister Stefan's steel-bright eyes seemed guilelessly clear, nor was he looking at her as though he expected the anger of a noblewoman whose honour had just been slandered so. "Wolfram is the son of Graf Ruprecht von Falkenstein, and trueborn heir to his father's burg and lands," she said. And this I must believe, lest my faith in God's goodness be wholly undone.

Meister Stefan looked at her for a time, but said nothing else to her. Instead he turned to Eva. "Eva, what has become of Graf Ruprecht now?"

He did not know her name before! Margerite thought.

Eva lowered her gaze, twisting the furry hem of her cloak between her hands as Kriemhilt batted soft-pawed at her fingers. Her eyes flickered sideways to Margerite, as if she were afraid to speak. Then, in a low voice, she said. "He is dead, and none knows where he is buried. And..." The words came out of her in a sudden rush, as though she had tried to dam them, but been overwhelmed by the flood. "The Tiefensee folk said that they had seen him riding on the stormwind with his hounds beside him, like Hagen von Tronje in Passau or Dietrich von Bern, and that he hunted living men as once he had hunted stags. But that was not spoken of often in Burg Falkenstein, for Margerite would not hear such tales."

Meister Stefan's lips curved slightly, as if he were a teacher whose student had repeated a lesson that he knew well already. "Damiano, what do you know of Margerite's son?"

Margerite bit her lip, tightening her fists to keep herself from moving, from striking Damiano's face before his lips could shape the blasphemous speech she feared. But Damiano said, "I know that the Imperator of the Order has made it clear that no harm must come to him, and that he is held precious in the councils of the great among us. But as for why, I have not been told: only that there is great hope vested in him."

And yet you would have left him in the snow, for your own skin's sake, Margerite thought, half-amused and half-furious as once. Your masters are not so well-served as they might have hoped for in you.

"All that is true," Meister Stefan murmured. His blued-steel eyes met Margerite's again. Of a sudden she had to brace herself: he had answered three questions, and asked three. If she asked him another...Her whole body shivered with the temptation, to ask as if she were a peasant girl creeping into a wisewoman's cottage by night - or as if she were still the maiden who had gone to Maria's Well before sunrise on Easter Sunday, hoping for a sign to show whether and whom she might marry that year - How is it with Bernhardt? Does he love me yet, or has he cut his love for me out of his heart like rotting flesh? To keep herself from speaking so, Margerite took another sip of the mead, rolling its spicy dryness over her tongue.

"A good mead, is it not?" Meister Stefan said, his voice light and amused. "There was a king of the Swedes once, who drowned in a vat of just such mead. His name was Fjölnir, as the poet Thjódhólfr of Hvíni writes:

The word of the doomed
that came to Fjölnir
was fore-gone where Fródhi dwelt:
the windless sea
of Svigdhir's spears
should overcome the prince."

"How did such a thing come to pass?" asked Eva.

"It was said that Fjölnir was the son of the god Yngvi-Freyr - a god that the North folk worshipped before the White Christ came to their lands, who brought good harvest and peace. He ruled over the Swedes and the wealth of Uppsala..."

Listening to the chantlike rise and fall of Meister Stefan's deep voice as she petted Kobolt and Wolfram alike, Margerite found that she could no longer think of questions for him, nor did the disturbing words that had been spoken have power to do more than nudge slightly at her thoughts. She wondered vaguely if there were some potion in the mead, that it should affect her so, but that was a little thing beside the fascination of the tale Meister Stefan was spinning.

After a time, as he had promised, he took some food from his saddlebags: it was only brown bread, dried meat, and cheese, such as any traveller might carry, but that did not make it any less toothsome, and when Margerite had finished her share, she felt as full and satisfied as she had ever been on rising from the Bishop's well-set table, with the memory of tantalizing flavours lingering yet on the back of her tongue.

Margerite did not know how long they sat up listening to Meister Stefan's stories: it seemed as though it must have gone on the whole night, and yet Wolfram was just beginning to grow hungry again when he stopped and said, "Well, it is time to sleep, since we must go our ways in the morning when the storm has passed. Margerite and Eva, you and the child may take my bed, such as it is: I have much yet to do tonight. As for you, Damiano, it will do you no harm to sleep on the floor, as you have done many times in the past."

Margerite had just gotten comfortable on the makeshift mattress of pine-branches - they were springy and surprisingly soft beneath the blanket that covered them, but the bed had been made for one man and his hounds, not for two women and a babe - when, drowsily, it occured to her that she had not set up a warding, as Father Etienne had warned her always to do. But she heard Meister Stefan's voice, though she was not sure whether he spoke aloud, or whether she had already slipped into sleep and was dreaming it.

"Do not fear, for you are safer here than you could ever be elsewhere. I taught Etienne to set his wards: do you think I would neglect my own, when I have guests who must be shielded for now from those who ride in the night? Sleep well, and give my greetings to Etienne when next you see him."

"I shall," Margerite murmured, or dreamed that she murmured.

Margerite awoke to bright daylight streaming in through the holes in the roof. The fire was still burning; Damiano and Eva were just beginning to stir, and the horses to shift and champ restlessly, Eva's dun snuffling about the floor for the last wisps of hay. But Meister Stefan was gone, and his horse and hounds with him.

Stiffly Margerite got up and went outside to relieve herself. In spite of the pounding ache of her full bladder, though, she stopped just beyond the door. Though the sun had not been up long, and the storm had clearly passed over before dawn, there were no tracks, not of man nor horse nor hound, in the glittering whiteness there.

"He must have left in the night," Margerite said to herself.

None of them had any wish to linger in the plague village, so they were soon on their way. A flicker of movement on the horizon caught Margerite's gaze: she shaded her eyes against the brilliance of the snow, staring over the field to where it faded into mist. There...yes, three men on horseback! She turned her steed towards them, waving hard until first one, then the other two, waved back at her, urging their horses into a stumbling trot.

As the two little groups neared each other, Margerite saw, to her relief, that it was Ritter Gottfried, Ritter Arnmut, and Georg who had found her. The two knights and the Knappe were very pale, shivering occasionally; their horses' heads hung low, and it was clear that the beasts could not have gone much further without a rest.

"Christ be thanked that we have found you!" Ritter
Gottfried croaked when they were near enough for speech.
"We have been searching all night and most of the day
yesterday, from the moment we realized that you were lost."

"Most of the men are camped a few miles back," added
Ritter Arnmut. "Paul the Bear and Jochanan and a few of
the others rode back in the other direction, thinking that you
might have doubled back towards the village where we left
the wagons. Where were you? How did you make it through
the night?"

"We found an abandoned house to shelter in," Margerite
said.

Gottfried crossed himself. "May Christ be thanked again
for His mercy! Now I swear that, should such weather come
upon us again, I shall not ride farther than an arm's span
from your side, lest I fail you once more."

Georg was staring at Eva with a curious look of anger and
relief on his long-nosed face, and he nudged his faltering
steed in to take a place right at her side. "Nor shall you
go any farther from me," he insisted, his honeyed tenor
breaking up into a squeak.

"You had nothing to fear, actually," said Damiano to the
men, with that same arrogance which annoyed Margerite
more every time she heard it. "Unlike you, I know the road
here, so the women were quite safe with me. And our horses
are in better state than yours, so if you will just tell me where
the camp is, we will go on ahead to find it, and you may
follow as you can."

A bite of cold anger rang from Gottfried's voice as he said,
"Before God, we will not! You may not understand such
things in Italy, but a German knight knows how to keep his
trust."

Damiano's backslanted brows rose in anger, and Margerite said hastily, "Indeed, we were lucky that Damiano was with us. But we shall certainly not part from you now, Ritter Gottfried. And I am more grateful than I can tell that I have faithful knights who would spend such a hard night's riding to look for me: had Eva and I not come upon Damiano, who knew the way, our lives, and that of my son, would have depended upon you alone."

Ritter Arnmut blushed, ducking his head and smiling; Gottfried bowed stiffly to Margerite from his saddle. "If we follow straight back this way, Frowe Gräfin, we shall come to the camp. And we have brought food and drink for you, for we did not know if you had any in your own saddlebags; surely you must be hungry?"

"We had both food and drink last night, but have not broken our fast yet this day," said Margerite, though in truth, she was not particularly hungry yet. Still, she smiled at the severe knight, taking the bread and the wineskin he held out to her, and began to eat as they turned their horses and began to plod back towards the camp.

# Chapter Three

In spite of the deep snow, Margerite and her riders were able to travel on without too much hindrance the next day. They were challenged several times by the men of lords who were suspicious at seeing such an armed band riding through their lands; but Margerite was quickly able to calm their fears - for what group of robbers would have a noblewoman at their head? - and some also remembered Gottfried and Arnmut, asking Gottfried if he had found the fugitive he pursued. To that, Gottfried replied only that justice had been done; and then, like as not, he would be clapped on the back and offered a goblet of Glühwein.

As Christmas drew nearer, the mood of castles and towns grew more festive: the Weihnachtsmärkten were set up in the larger settlements, wooden stalls from which folk sold all manner of things - beeswax candles and honey and mead, spiced cakes, woodcarvings and prayer beads and trinkets, wreaths and garlands of pine and bright-berried holly and pale-berried mistletoe, knives and other small bits of ironmongery, trinkets of bronze and copper and sometimes silver; whatever might brighten the swiftly darkening days for farmers and small craftsmen, it seemed, could be found there. It often warmed Margerite's heart to stop briefly at such markets for a few little pastries and a cup of hot wine, and to hear the cheerful greeting of "Fröhliche Weinachten, frowe!" as she had heard it as a girl, going two days' ride upstream with her father to just such a market; for a few moments, then, she could forget the burden she was carrying, and enjoy the warm scents of food and drink steaming in the frosty air, and the brightness of green needles and holly berries against dark wood and white snow.

At Georg's plea, they skirted his father's lands, for he did not want to give any tale of why he had run off from Burg Fürstensee until he knew how matters stood with Christoph. It was two days before Christmas when at last they came to the shores of the Fürstensee, looking over the ice-filmed water to the mountain where the great square tower rose above the lower crenellations growing out from its side and the huge ring of the castle's stone wall.

Damiano nudged his horse into a light canter, pulling the roan back as he came up beside Margerite. "Here my road leaves you," he said. "I have other things to see to, farther on."

A great wave of relief washed through Margerite, loosening all her muscles; she was hard-put not to sigh aloud. "What of Nikolaus?" she asked softly.

"I give him to you," Damiano replied, his voice equally quiet. "It is a great honour to him, to school with one of your rank. As for me, I mean to heed my old teacher's words, for I have never yet known his foreseeings to be wrong. Farewell, Frowe Gräfin." Damiano put his heels to the roan's side again, turning where the road led towards the other side of the lake.

"I'm glad enough to see the back of him," Paul declared staunchly. "So this is your new castle, Gräfin? It looks a stout and defensible place: I shouldn't like to have to besiege it."

"Christ willing, you never shall," said Margerite, looking up at Burg Fürstensee again. It seemed to her that the square tower loomed forbiddingly above the rest of the castle, its shadow darkening the stones below it, and a shiver of fear ran down her spine. It is only because I know what is there, she said to herself. But she thought she heard Jochanan murmuring what might have been a Hebrew prayer, and had to brace her courage to keep from reining her horse about.

The gates of Burg Fürstensee were closed, and a guard called out, "Halt! Who comes to this castle?"

Ritter Gottfried rode forward. "Do you not recognise us, Josef? Ritter Arnmut and I have returned; and with us are the Frowe Gräfin and Frowe Eva, as well as Christoph's Knappe Georg. The rest of these men are a guard that the Frowe Gräfin hired for safety on the way. Now open the gate at once, to greet the Frowe Gräfin as she ought to be greeted in her own castle!"

The gate swung aside, and they rode in, hooves clattering on the cobblestones of the outer bailey. The guards saluted as Margerite passed, standing sharply to attention under Gottfried's stern eye. Margerite stopped before their commander - what was his name? Ritter Ludwig.

"What news can you tell me of my husband, Herr Ritter?" Margerite asked.

Ritter Ludwig's pale blue eyes dropped beneath the rim of his bascinet, his wide mouth working silently under his square-cut sandy beard. "I fear there is little more to tell, Frowe Gräfin. For all the prayers you must have raised for him in your cloister-retreat, and for all the candles we have lit and Masses we have said in the Church here, the Graf still lies as he did before: dead, save that his heart beats and his lungs draw in air yet. Herr Christoph rules as well as he may, but he is greatly plunged in grief for his father."

"As a son should be," Margerite said slowly. "It is no little burden that has been placed on him." Ritter Ludwig's words were enough to tell her that Christoph's demon still raged in his flesh - but was still hiding its nature well enough from the Burg Fürstensee folk. And Nikolaus had, indeed, had the sense to put about the tale that she had retired to pray for her husband's health. "Where shall we find Herr Christoph at this hour?"

"He should still be at the dinner-table, Frowe Gräfin, for it is only a little past nones."

"Very well. See to quartering for these men, if you will."

Ritter Ludwig's light brows rose under his helm as he looked past Margerite and the knights to the men of the Bear's Paw Company, his heavy-mailed hand resting on the hilt of his sword. Of course he would recognise them, Margerite realized: they had fallen upon Graf Günther's men together. Well, there was nothing to do but face the matter straight on. "I hired the Bear's Paw," she said quietly, "because of the dangers of the road, and because I knew they could be trusted. They have ridden far and served me well: now we must put them up here until their fellows, whom we had to leave behind in the snow, can catch up with them. Have you anything to say to that, Ritter Ludwig?"

The knight frowned, but shook his head. "As you wish, Frowe Gräfin."

Burg Fürstensee's great hall was garlanded with Christmas greenery already, holly and ivy and pine hanging on the walls and wreathing the candlesticks on the table; the sounds of flute and harp and drum floated down from the minstrels' gallery. Margerite's mouth began to water at the delicious smells filling the air: dripping roast meat, fowl stuffed with sage and breadcrumbs and a tangy hint of citrus...it had been nearly a week since they had last guested at a castle, and riding in the cold had sharpened the edge of Margerite's hunger almost unbearably. As if of a like mind with his mother, Wolfram began to cry.

"Take that brat out of here!" Christoph shouted sharply from the high table without looking up from his plate. Nikolaus leaned over, whispering a few urgent words in his brother's ear, and at once Christoph stood, striding smoothly over towards Margerite and her companions.

He had lost weight in the past months - the blue doublet that had been cut fashionably close to his muscular body now hung on him in folds, and his rounded cheeks were pale and haggard - but he seemed as cheerful as he had ever been, so that for a moment Margerite wondered if, after all, the demon had fled of its own accord or on Nikolaus' command. She could see nothing in Christoph's eyes, no flare of Hellish light - not even an unnatural swelling or shrinking of his black pupils - and yet she mistrusted her own senses: who knew how cunning a spirit might be, when it had settled itself in human flesh for several months?

"It is well to see you again, Frowe Margerite," Christoph said jauntily, lifting Margerite's gloved hand to brush his lips over it. "I am sorry I spoke so rudely; I thought one of the servant's children had gotten into the hall. I trust you found what you were seeking in your retreat? - though Father is no better," he added, a sudden bitterness twisting his voice.

"I had hoped for more cheerful news at my homecoming," Margerite replied, raising her voice so that she could be heard over Wolfram's screams. "Christoph, forgive me, but I must tend to my babe now."

Christoph waved a hand, the long dags of his sleeves falling back from his wrist. "Go, then, and come back quickly. Frowe Eva, how glad I am to see you!" he went on, turning towards Eva and reaching out for her hand. Margerite did not stay to hear what more he might say to her, but hurried her wailing child out of the great hall and up the stair to her own chambers.

Margerite's rooms were bone-chillingly cold: undoubtedly no fire had been lit there since she left. The floor and table were thick with dust; dust clung to the leaded windowpanes so that only a few sad trickles of light streamed into the chamber, and streamers of dust-browned spiderwebs hung like dingy garlands from the ceiling. The plaster on the walls was streaked with mildew, and a few scattered heaps of old reeds lay in gnawed and moldy heaps on the floor, as though mice had been nesting in them.

Margerite had no sooner noticed that than Kobolt streaked in past her feet and under the bed; a second later, and Margerite heard a shrill squeak suddenly cut off. Though she knew full well that, if she had wanted her chambers to be readied for her, she should have sent Georg riding ahead to announce her return, she could not help her anger: had the rest of the castle been so ill-cared for while Heinrich lay in his sickbed?

When she had fed Wolfram, she stuck her head out the door and shouted for one of the servants. The maid who answered her call was an older woman, whose round face split into a grin of delight as she saw Margerite.

"Frowe Gräfin!" she said. "Thanks be to Christ that you are home at last! Burg Fürstensee has been a sad place without your noble presence, your kind voice, your..."

Margerite cut her off sharply. "I want my chambers tidied and a fire lit here at once, and Frowe Eva's as well, if they are in as sad a state as this. I must have clean linens for my bed and Wolfram's cradle, as well, and fresh rushes and scented herbs strewed upon the floor; and this had best be done by the time I have finished eating dinner."

"Yes, of course! At once, Frowe Gräfin," the serving-woman said, scuttling off quickly.

By the time Margerite carried Wolfram back into the great hall - for she would not leave him in such a cold and cheerless place as her rooms had become by choice - the others were all seated at the high table, and a solid bread-trencher was heaped with food at her own place. She unfastened her silver goblet from her girdle, and Christoph reached for the wine pitcher before him to fill it at once.

"You had good fortune in meeting Ritter Gottfried on your way back," Christoph said. "And Ritter Arnmut - shame on you, Gottfried, for knighting your Knappe where the rest of us could not join in the festivities," he added lightly. "I shall not be so stingy when Georg's time comes. Maybe that will not be too far off, either, from what you tell me of his fighting! That scar on his face seems a good badge of bravery, as well, though it makes him little prettier - eh, Georg?"

The Knappe nodded vigorously, the red shiny track of the scar down his cheek darkening with blood as he blushed. Gottfried said nothing, only looking down at his own bare trencher of bread - as strictly as he had kept the Advent abstinence on the road, he could hardly be willing to eat meat and milk now that he had come home. Monsignor Michael, sitting in his usual place a few seats down from Christoph, shook his head.

"Ritter Gottfried, you have been on a long journey, and look very thin and unwell. Since you were travelling even this day, I hereby grant you dispensation to eat freely, now and until you have gotten your strength back - and the same for all those who rode with you."

The Burg Falkenstein priest himself looked very sleek, his black beard and hair neatly oiled and combed, and not a thread out of place on his rich clerical robes: his paunch and plump cheeks suggested that he, at least, had not observed the abstinence too strenuously, nor tried to enforce it on the castle's kitchens. Margerite had to admit that, at least for now, she was glad of Monsignor Michael's lenience, though she wondered if Ritter Gottfried would object. But Gottfried, whatever he thought privately, would not argue with a priest. Slowly he pulled the remains of one of the roast chickens towards himself, carefully carving off a few thin slivers of meat to nibble at.

The musicians were singing now, a beautiful four-part harmony about spring flowers and sunlight. Margerite raised her eyebrows, for though the song was pleasant to listen to, it was hardly fit for the season. "I should like to hear something celebrating the birth of Our Lord," Margerite declared. Nikolaus raised an eyebrow at her, then smiled slyly - as if, Margerite thought, he were congratulating her on her skill at dissembling. Christoph nodded to Georg, who stood behind his knight's chair as though he had never been away, and the Knappe ran towards the stairs that led at the musician's gallery.

"A noble and pious thought, Frowe Gräfin," said
Monsignor Michael, beaming at Margerite as she selected
a juicy bite of beef - Christoph had thoughtfully carved the
food on her trencher already.

She ate it dantily, reminding herself that even had
Monsignor Michael not given their little troop dispensation,
she was still nursing and therefore as assuredly exempt from
abstinence and fast as if she were ill, or doing hard bodily
labour. The song Heinrich's musicians began next was a
familiar tune to Margerite, its words shifting back and forth
unashamedly from German to Latin,

"In dulci jubilo sing out gladly now,
Our hearts' pleasure lies in praesepio,
And sunlike glows our treasure Matris in gremio,
Alpha et O!
O Jesu parvule..."

Margerite knew that the carol had been written down by
the mystic Heinrich Suso, who claimed that an angel had
dictated it to him after a dream in which he was bidden to
join in an angelic dance. As to that, she could not speak; but
she found that the song lifted her heart. Yet, though it was
tempting to listen and forget her cares, Margerite watched
Christoph as closely as she could, alert for any sign of
distress at the singers' clear voices or the name of the Lord.
To her relief, he hardly seemed to notice what the musicians
were singing, speaking courteously to Eva instead.

"You see, Frowe Margerite, things are not in such bad
order as you feared they might be," Nikolaus said softly to
Margerite. "I and Christoph have managed everything here
very well, in spite of my father's illness and your...absence."

"I am pleased to hear it," Margerite replied. "But even
a chamber in which no one is living needs to be cleaned
regularly, lest it become a haven for vermin of all sorts, and
if fires are not lit there, the plaster will mildew and peel."

Nikolaus shrugged. "I shall have someone see to it..."

"I have already done so," Margerite cut him off. "Another time, perhaps, you shall remember, should you ever find yourself ruling your own castle."

Margerite did not miss the hard green glare in Nikolaus' eyes at those words, but she had had a bellyfull of Damiano on the road from Niederwald, and the two men had far more in common than she liked.

"And what of your quest, Gottfried?" Christoph was asking, brushing his trailing sleeve away from his plate as he rested one blue velvet elbow casually on the table. "Did you find Bertram - and what became of him?"

The breath locked up in Margerite's chest as she waited for Gottfried to answer. She was sure that the pious knight would no more lie than he would steal; yet what would befall if he told the truth?

"Yes, I found Bertram," Gottfried said. "He satisfied me that he had good reason for leaving as he did, and I found firm sureties that he bears us no ill will, nor shall he ever be a trouble or danger to Burg Fürstensee hereafter."

Christoph dabbed something invisible from the tip of his upturned nose with a napkin. "That must have been strong evidence to convince you. What was it?"

"He heard that his father had died, and he went home to claim his inheritance from his brother."

This time, Christoph guffawed. "What a lot of trouble and worry we went to over a little thing - I doubt that there was more to Bertram's inheritance than a field or two, or perhaps a one-room house! I wish my father could hear it: he would have thought this a merry jest." He lifted his goblet, taking a deep swallow. Margerite wondered how long it would take for word of Landgräfin Ortlieb's death to reach Burg Fürstensee. A long time, perhaps: the Church was keeping their part of the matter close, and Landgraf Gerhardt would hardly be eager for rumours about his wife's death and his brother's life to spread through his lands, let alone to those of others.

Ritter Gottfried looked Christoph straight in the eye and said, "Herr Christoph, Bertram was not heir to a peasant's portion, but to the rule of Niederwald." Margerite almost groaned: she might have guessed that the knight's rigid honesty would not stretch to allow lying by omission. But, after all, the Order already knows much of the truth of the matter; and in a year or two, all of the Empire shall hear about it.

Wine sprayed pale from Christoph's mouth all over the tablecloth. The servants were there at once as he choked and spluttered, wiping the table and his doublet clean as best they could; Margerite saw Ritter Arnmut, who was seated across from Christoph, discreetly brushing a few droplets from his own face.

"I never suspected you of a sense of humour before, Gottfried!" Christoph said when he had recovered himself. "Surely you cannot mean that that...shaggy fellow, that half-brigand..."

"But it is true," Margerite said. "Bertram, the Hauptmann of Burg Falkenstein's guard, was indeed Bernhardt von Niederwald, and has gone to prove his rightful claim upon those lands in law."

If Margerite had not been watching Christoph closely, she would have missed the sideways flicker of his eyes towards his brother, and the brief gesture of Nikolaus' hand in return. But the tiny movements were enough to chill her soul: however like himself Christoph appeared, Nikolaus was still the master of Burg Fürstensee - and there was only one way he could have kept that power.

"Well, well," Christoph said, refilling his goblet and sipping at it more carefully. "That is such a tale as I would hardly believe if I heard it from a travelling singer. But you speak as though you had sure knowledge, Frowe Margerite: how did that come about?"

"My way passed by the palace of Bishop Otto of Niederwald, and I guested with him for some days. Herr Bernhardt was also there, for it seems that the Bishop means to support his claim."

Christoph nodded in satisfaction; Nikolaus gave Margerite a wry sideways smile, his greenish-blue eyes glinting, and raised his own goblet slightly, as if to toast her in congratulations. "Truly, our father would have wanted to hear this tale," Nikolaus said. "To think that we sent out a knight to hunt Herr Bernhardt down, like setting a hound on a poaching peasant!"

Ritter Gottfried said nothing, but the rigid brace of his back made Margerite wonder how deeply Nikolaus' words had offended him. Swiftly she countered, "It is well that we sent a knight with both the skill and determination to find the man we thought was a fugitive, and the wisdom to judge matters rightly when he came upon his quarry." Better than you could possibly know, indeed, she thought. Ritter Arnmut's smile at her was fleetingly shy, but grateful.

"But you must have had some battles on your way, Gottfried," Christoph went on, ignoring his brother's taunt as he had always done before. "Else you would hardly have knighted your Knappe."

"Yes," Gottfried replied. "Arnmut fought well, and bravely, and earned the strokes of knighthood, which I gave to him at the Bishop's palace."

Christoph nodded. "It has always been a hard job to drag a good tale out of you, Gottfried. But congratulations, Ritter Arnmut! Will you be going home to your father's burg now?"

"And it please you, Herr Christoph," Arnmut said softly, "I should prefer to stay here in your guard, if you would have me. My father has my two brothers by his side, both of them knighted as well, and I think that I can easily be spared from Burg Eisenstein."

Again Margerite caught the sideways twitch of Christoph's eyes, and Nikolaus' faint nod. Christoph's grin was full and open, showing no hint of any difference from the cheerful knight Margerite had known before - and she was not sure whether that unsettled her more, or less, than if the mark of the demon had been easier to see upon Heinrich's elder son.

"As you will, Ritter," Christoph said, still smiling at Arnmut. "We can certainly use your strength here, and it is not easy to go from a court where one has been happy as a squire - I still recall my sadness at leaving Graf Wolfgang's castle when my term as Knappe was over, but of course I could not stay away from Burg Fürstensee."

"Thank you, Herr Christoph," Arnmut murmured. "I shall serve you well."

"I have no doubt of it," Christoph reassured him.

When Margerite came back to her chambers, they were warm and bright and clean. A plump young woman in a stained gray dress was stoking the stove, her rough hands streaked with soot. She straightened up as Margerite came in, curtseying to her.

"Does all please you, Frowe Gräfin?" she asked anxiously.

Margerite glanced over the room. The servants had done well: the spiderwebs were gone, the glass panes of the window sparkling brightly in the clear winter sunlight. The plaster had been scrubbed, and only a hint of mildew - and, Margerite noted, a faint acrid whiff of Kobolt's fresh marks - lingered beneath the scents of dried meadowsweet and applewood smoke. New candles stood in the wall-sconces and on the table, and the bedclothes looked clean and fresh and smooth, save for a few wrinkles around the nest Kobolt had hollowed out for himself, where he lay purring softly and looking pleased with himself.

"It does. What is your name, girl?"

The young woman curtsied again. "May it please you, Frowe Gräfin, I am Else, the wife of your guardsman Dankwart. If you wish it, Frowe Gräfin, I am here to tend to your chambers and yourself until you have time to find a more suitable maidservant, though I beg you to forgive me for my clumsiness, for I know little of a noblewoman's needs."

Margerite looked thoughtfully at Else. The girl was an inch or two shorter than herself, her light brown hair tied back into a severe bun that pulled hard on features meant to be soft and generous, and her wide freckled brow creased with worry as she watched her mistress. She did not look especially clever - but neither did she have the downtrodden look of a scullion; as a castle servant and the wife of a guardsman, Margerite guessed, her life would be more comfortable than the life Margerite had suffered herself in the kitchens of Schloss Niederwald. And Margerite did need a maidservant, at least until she could get Rose back: she and Eva could hardly help each other to dress here as they had done on the road.

"Such things are easily learned," Margerite said kindly. "You may begin by seeing to it that a tub of hot water is brought up for me, for I have travelled long and am much in need of a bath. The same, I am sure," she added, "can be said for Frowe Eva and the Ritters Gottfried and Arnmut: if they have not already asked, order baths for them as well. And see if Herr Jakob can find you some clothes that are more fitting to my own maid, for that stuff you are wearing is too shoddy for one of my servants."

"Yes, Frowe Gräfin!" Else said, curtseying once more before she hurried from the room.

Margerite laid Wolfram down in his cradle, wrapping him in the fresh blankets - cloths that had been hung by the fire to warm until just lately, she suspected: if Else knew little of the fastenings of fine dresses, at least she seemed to understand taking care of a babe.

"I should wait to visit Heinrich until I have bathed and dressed properly," Margerite told herself. "It would do him little honour if I came travel-stained to his bedside." But she knew that she was only putting the moment off - that, in truth, she did not want to see what several months abed, unable to move or speak, had done to that good man who was still her husband by law and oath.

And I failed to heal him - Christ forgive me if it was my love for Bernhardt that weakened my hand then!

The door to Heinrich's chamber was locked, and it was several moments before it opened. Heinrich's manservant Albrecht stood there, looking down his nose at Margerite. I should have waited until I had bathed and changed, after all, she thought. Then she reminded herself that, for all Albrecht's rich clothes and haughty air, he was still the servant and she the Gräfin.

"How is it with my husband?" Margerite asked crisply.

The old manservant's angular face softened. "Frowe Gräfin, he is no better, though the physician says that he seems no closer to death's door. I do not know if he can hear you, or if he will know you, though I have told him every day that you had retreated to a convent to pray for his recovery - a noble deed, though it seems to have booted little."

Margerite stepped in. Heinrich's chamber was sweet with the scents of frankincense and cinnamon, and though it was day, a large golden candle of beeswax burned on the little table by his bed. The blue silken coverlet drawn up over her husband's body was smooth, as though it had been pulled over a corpse. Even with the blankets shrouding Heinrich, Margerite could see how much his powerful body had shrunken in the last months: the cloth hung over wasted limbs, the chest that had been broad and strong as a bear's had sunken inwards like a wineskin from which the last drop had been drained.

His silver hair and beard were almost white now, and much thinner, a gleam of pink skull showing through the pale strands lying limp on his head; the red marks of cautery still showed on his forehead. Heinrich's slack mouth was open, a shining slug-trail of drool running down across his cheek from the corner of his lips. Though his lids were open as well, his gray eyes did not move as Margerite knelt by his bedside, laying a hand gently upon his shoulder - even through the bedclothes, she could feel his bones: he had withered nearly to a skeleton in his living death.

"Heinrich," she whispered. "Can you hear me, my husband?" Heinrich did not so much as twitch, nor did his eyes roll in his head, his stare blank and fixed as if he had never lived. Still Margerite forced herself to go on. "Heinrich, it is I, Margerite. I have returned to you. And... Ritter Gottfried accomplished the quest on which you sent him. He found Bertram, and all is well: Burg Fürstensee has nothing to fear from him. O Heinrich, I hope you can hear me, and that this news brings you some comfort! May Christ bless you and grant you mercy soon, that you come to life again, or else be freed from this earthly prison to enjoy the delights of Heaven."

And if he dies, I shall be free to marry Bernhardt...if he will still have me. But, O Maria, why should my freedom come at such a price? I would have mourned Heinrich if he fell in battle, for he was a good man; I would never have bartered these long months of his torment for my release from the vows I swore him. And little good even that will do me, if Bernhardt... if Bernhardt...

A tear fell from Margerite's eyes, then another and another, leaving a spreading dark splotch on the blue silken coverlet.

"Frowe Gräfin," Albercht said, his voice gentler than she had ever heard it. "Prayers are never wasted, though they are not always answered. And you could have done no more for the Herr Graf if you had stayed by his bedside: neither priest nor physician has been able to help him. Allow me, Frowe Gräfin..."

The tall manservant bent to offer Margerite his arm, helping her to stand. "I have watched over the Herr Graf most carefully myself," Albercht went on. "As you ordered, I have had music played for him, and books read to him, and each day I have told him all the business of the castle. And none of it has made the least difference, nor could you have."

Margerite looked gratefully up at him. She could see that the lines were graven deeper in the servant's angular face, streaks of white showing through the iron-gray of his neatly-trimmed hair and beard, as though he had been suffering with his master. A pang of guilt struck through her for letting Albrecht think that her tears were for Heinrich alone; but even were her honesty as stark and uncompromising as Ritter Gottfried's, she could not have told the old man why she had been weeping.

"Thank you," she said at last. "If...if Heinrich knows anything at all, I am sure that he is grateful for your care."

Albrecht bowed. "I live to serve the Herr Graf - and you, Frowe Gräfin."

Much troubled in mind, Margerite went back to her own chambers. There, she saw that Else had Wolfram down on the soft rug in front of the stove, laughing and tickling him with one hand as she fended Kobolt off with the other. Herr Jakob had worked quickly: Else now wore a pretty dress of green linen trimmed with a narrow band of black velvet, and a tidy blue linen coif - Margerite would not have to be ashamed of her attendant.

The maidservant leapt to her feet at once as her mistress walked in. "Forgive me, Frowe Gräfin," she gasped. "But your son was crying and squirming...I changed his cloths, but I thought he wanted to get out of the cradle, and sure enough, he stopped crying at once. I did not let the cat near him," she added hastily.

"You need not fear that Kobolt will harm my son," Margerite said. "See, they are the best of friends." Wolfram already had Kobolt's black tail grasped firmly in his little fist, tugging at it; Kobolt batted at his hand with a tufted paw, but his claws were firmly sheathed.

"I was only afraid lest it should scratch him, or try to overlay him. I never let cats near my own babes," Else added.

"That may be wise of you," conceded Margerite. "But in this case, it is not necessary, and it would break Wolfram's heart if he were to be parted from his friend."

As she spoke, Wolfram rolled over, pillowing his head on Kobolt's furry side. He ought to be crawling now, Margerite thought again.

"How many babes have you?" she asked.

The maidservant's broad face flushed, and she clapped her hand to her mouth to stifle a giggle - amazed, Margerite guessed, that the Gräfin should be asking her such a thing. "I have three now, Frowe Gräfin, and a fourth is due in five months' time, Christ and Mutter Maria willing. But do not worry: I have never been bedridden more than a day after giving birth, and I swear that it will not keep me from serving you as I ought."

Margerite knew she should leave well alone, but she could not help asking, "When did your children start to crawl?"

"Thomas was..." Else's mouth pursed as she thought. "Thomas was born just after Michaelmas, and he was crawling by Easter. Karl was born a week before St. Johannistag, and I remember that he was into everything by Christmas. And Josef, we named him after his father, he was born at Pentecost and crawling before Martinmas. Why, Frowe Gräfin?" She bit her lip then, as though she had not meant to ask.

"No reason," Margerite said slowly. Wolfram was almost eight months old now, and yet he still squirmed on the floor like a grub: she had never once seen him try to heave himself up on all fours. Could she have done him some harm by holding him in her lap as she rode for so long? Or - had Ortlieb done something to him in the few days she had kept him?

"But my sister's eldest daughter did not crawl until she was..." Else ticked her fingers off slowly, her mouth moving in thought. "Nine months and a few days. And she is a fine strong maiden of nine years now; Hildegard has her cleaning pots and sweeping the kitchen already."

Such pride, in something I thought miserable and shameful, Margerite thought. But I suppose the work does not seem as bad when set against tilling the fields and milking cows - and I hope Hildegard is kinder to her scullions than Liutbirg was!

"Babes are all different, Frowe Gräfin," Else said comfortingly. "And your noble son is strong and large and handsome."

"Ca!" Wolfram said suddenly, tugging at Kobolt's tail again. "Ma ca! Ma ca!"

Margerite laughed. "Are you saying that he is your cat, Wolfram? Actually, he is my cat, though I am sure he will not mind you claiming him."

"Ma ca!" Wolfram repeated, giving Kobolt's tail an extra pull, as if to settle the matter thus. Margerite could not help the foolishly fond smile spreading across her face as she looked down at her son.

"He is quick-witted," she said, almost as if Else were another woman of her station. Then she remembered herself, and drew her dignity back around her. "While I am waiting on my bath, it would befit you to fetch clean cloths that I may scrub and dry myself, and bath-herbs from the stillroom. Ernst will, no doubt, try to tell you what he thinks is most fitting, but what I want is lavender blossoms and dried rose-petals, if there are any."

"Yes, Frowe Gräfin," Else said, scrambling hurriedly from the room.

"Ma ca!" said Wolfram again, sinking his little fingers deep into Kobolt's black ruff. The cat closed his eyes, flicking his ears away from the baby's grasp, and purred deeply at the child's mauling.

"First you want a wolf, and now a cat," Margerite said to her son. "By the time you are grown and hold your father's castle, we shall not be able to walk in its halls for all the animals." She wondered when Wolfram would be old enough to start training a puppy of his own - that was a fitting pastime for a noble youth, and if he had inherited Ruprecht's love of the hunt, he ought to learn the nature of hounds young.

And am I mad, sitting here thinking on such things, as if this castle were as wholesome as my father's keep? Margerite thought, surprised at herself. She knew that she would have to meet with Nikolaus that night: she ought to be thinking on that, planning her strategy so that he would have no choice but to dismiss the demon that held his brother in thrall, instead of prattling to her son. Yet there had been so many things bearing down on her mind; Ortlieb's death, it seemed, had not ended their struggles, but only begun them.

"Mama!" said Wolfram, rolling away from Kobolt to grasp at Margerite's skirts. And for a moment, she could think of nothing but her son's bright eyes and golden hair; she lifted him in her arms, clasping him close to her breasts.

"Yes, Wolfram! Yes, I am your mama, and your mama loves you. O, my clever son, my clever little boy..."

After Else had undressed her for bed, Margerite said to the maidservant, "You may go to your husband for the night: if I should need anything before dawn, I am sure I can fend for myself, and a woman should be with her husband."

"You are sure, Frowe Gräfin? I mean...I have not done too badly? You are not sending me away, are you?"

"I am not," Margerite assured her. "You are to be here before dawn, to clean and stoke my stove and be sure that there is hot water for me to wash my face and a bit of watered wine and bread so that I may break my fast before dressing."

"I...thank you, Frowe Gräfin! Is there anything else I may do before I go."

"No. Go on, now."

"Thank you, Frowe Gräfin!" Else curtsied and ran light-footed from the room. Margerite smiled to herself: she knew, certainly, that servants had little enough to delight in, and little time to themselves. And more: with Else gone for the nights, she did not need to fear that the young woman would waken when the Gräfin left her chambers, or be disturbed if Nikolaus came to her door - and Margerite would be free to work as she willed. She could not have gotten rid of a more skilled or knowing maidservant so easily.

It was, perhaps, Maria's mercy that had sent her an untrained girl with husband and children, who would be glad of the leave to go at night, and not wonder at its strangeness. Else had combed Margerite's thick hair out while it was still damp, so now it lay straight and loose about her shoulders, much more comfortable than the twisted braid she had worn during her journey. She almost felt like a maiden again, or a new bride awaiting...

Margerite winced, remembering how Ruprecht had taken the pins from her coiled hair, running his hands through it in delight at its thick softness. Bernhardt had unpinned her hair as well, touching the fall of her unbound tresses as though he feared that she would vanish beneath his fingertips... would he ever touch her thus again? Margerite knew that she would never willingly lie with another man, not for any reason; if Bernhardt would not have her, she would grow old alone, with no fingers but her maid's to run through her hair.

Best not to think too much on what I cannot mend for now, Margerite told herself. But that was cold counsel, no more nourishing to her heart than gnawing on marrow-stripped bones was to a beggar's dog. Yet, whatever her sorrows, she had sworn her oath to Eva: and that, with Christ's help, she should fulfill that night if she could.

Margerite bent over Wolfram's cradle. Her son slept quietly, curled beneath his blankets as if he were in her womb again, his milk-scented breath coming soft and regular. "God be with you, and the Virgin and all the saints watch over you, my little one," she murmured. "Mama is going to make this castle safer for you."

Margerite pulled her shift off over her head, putting on her black silk robe in its place. The thin fabric slithered over her body like cool water, its smooth touch filling her with a sudden confidence. She fastened her girdle about her body, hooking the small lion-headed clasp securely - the belt of sovereignty - then put on her boots and flung her heavy cloak about her shoulders: if all went well, she and Nikolaus would be making their way through the salt caves beneath Burg Fürstensee again.

She had not forgotten how cold it was down there in summer; she could well imagine the icy chill of winter in the caverns. But this time, she said to herself fiercely, I am mistress! She picked up her gloves, though she did not put them on: if Nikolaus gave her any argument, she wanted Ortlieb's ring to be burning in his sight. Her box of magical tools she tucked under her arm; then, taking several deep breaths as though she were about to dive into a deep lake, she walked steadily out of her chamber and down the corridor to the old tower.

Nikolaus opened his door at once to Margerite's knock, bowing as she entered his room. Though she could hear the hiss and crackle of wood in his stove, he was wearing a heavy fur-lined robe, and his chamber seemed damp, with the chill of winter on it - she remembered Heinrich, or perhaps it had been Christoph, saying that the old tower was hardly fit to live in. I must not forget that Nikolaus is not weak of will, nor does he lack dedication to his Art, whatever else may be said of him.

"Princess," Nikolaus said softly. There was no familiar edge of mockery in his voice, as Margerite had half-expected, and the look on his pouchy face was one of - awe? "You are much to be congratulated, for there are few living who would dare to make challenge for the ruby ring, and fewer yet who might be able to achieve it." In spite of the cold, a thin film of sweat gleamed on his pale forehead, and it almost seemed to Margerite that she could smell an acrid whiff of fear rising from him. She did not know what to say, for Nikolaus' clear respect had thrown her wholly off-balance. "Come, sit down," Heinrich's younger son went on. "May I offer you wine?"

Margerite sat, allowing Nikolaus to fill a goblet with deep red wine. Its aroma rose rich and spicy from the cup; in spite of its chill, the first sip she took warmed Margerite deeply. Nikolaus poured his own goblet full, sitting down across from her; his pallid fingers played on the stem, twisting together as he twirled it slowly. Still Margerite did not speak, and Nikolaus began to shift uncomfortably in his seat.

"Damiano gives you his greetings," Margerite said at last.

Nikolaus breathed out in relief. "Did you meet him on the way...you must have? Why is he not here?"

"He had business elsewhere," Margerite temporized. "But he told me that I should have charge of your teaching from here on - he had reason," she added sternly, "to know that I am well capable of it, though I did not come by my rank in the usual way."

"I am sure no one could doubt that, Princess," Nikolaus said eagerly. "And I count myself honoured to learn from you. When I last heard from Monsignor Damiano, he informed me that I should soon be tested for the onyx ring - I stand ready for that testing whenever you choose."

To keep the nervous twitching of her own fingers from betraying her, Margerite interlaced her hands, pressing her palms down flat upon the table's polished surface. Remembering how unnerving Ritter Gottfried's steady stare could be, she gazed at Nikolaus without blinking until his hands began to squirm on the stem of his goblet again.

"I have reason to think," Margerite said, her voice steady, "that you have already experimented with demons - or one demon, at any rate. Is this true?"

Nikolaus swallowed hard, his plump face paling further. "It...Yes," he declared, his back straightening and his voice suddenly strong and confident. "I was successful in summoning and controlling it; it has been under my power for months, and obeys my least word even now."

"And this demon is housed in Christoph's flesh?"

"I did not think I could keep that from you, Princess," Nikolaus replied. "That is even as you say."

"I see," Margerite mused. She knew that if she stopped to think too long about it - about the horror of what Nikolaus had done to his brother, about the gibbering thing that had threatened her in the darkness of the eclipse - her will would fail her utterly. Instead, like a warrior facing a foe beyond his strength, she pressed her attack forward, because to let herself be forced back was to fall.

"Then you shall prove your control to me by summoning it forth from him again, and by sending it forth to the Hell from whence it came. As for Christoph, we shall consider how to deal with him afterwards in good time."

"I...Yes, Princess. As you say." Nikolaus bowed his head - the thick brown hair was already thinning at his crown, Margerite noticed.

"Then let us go." Margerite pushed back her chair and stood.

"Princess...we must bring Christoph with us."

"Fetch him quickly, then. Do not worry about his Knappe: say only that I have commanded this, for Georg has learned to obey my will."

"As you say, Princess." Nikolaus hurried from the room, as though he were a servant rather than a Graf's younger son. Margerite cast a longing glance at her goblet of wine, but she knew better than to drink any more of it before such a rite. Nikolaus had lost control of the demon at least once: what if it broke free again?

"Then, Christ, I give my soul into your hands," she whispered. "And may the Blessed Virgin pray for me, and pour out forgiveness for my sins. Maria, Mother - if I die this night, watch over Wolfram, as you watched over your own Son, and shield him forever from the Powers of Darkness and Hell."

It was not long before Nikolaus returned, Christoph stumbling barefoot behind him in a long nightshirt. The face of Heinrich's elder son was slack, his jaw hanging loosely and the flesh beneath it wobbling. Now Margerite saw what she had feared to see when Christoph first greeted her. His pupils had shrunk to lopsided pinpricks, one twice the size of the other, and they seemed no more than openings into an infinite blackness, as though the whole of Hell waited inside the bone-bordered compass of his skull.

"You may lead the way," Margerite said crisply - for she knew that she could not bear to have that inhuman stare turned on her as she walked down into the bowels of the earth. Nikolaus nodded, flinging a cloak about his shoulders before he picked up the candlestick on the table and gestured to Christoph. Christoph's whole body jerked as he turned to follow his brother down the oaken spiral staircase, his bare soles shuffling raspily against the wood.

Facila descendit Avernum...Margerite thought as she walked down behind them. Easy is the descent to Hell; but to turn back, that is toil, that is labour...She bit her lip so that the small pain might distract her; but when she felt the soft brush of fur against her leg, she almost shrieked aloud.

No, it is only Kobolt...I am safe with him here. The cat looked up at her, gold eyes glimmering from his shadowed black pelt. In the wildly wavering light of Nikolaus' candle, Kobolt seemed twice his natural size, his fur bristling as though he were about to challenge a mastiff for its meat, and a low growl leaked from his throat. And that, Margerite thought dizzily, is a warning. I know it is dangerous, Kobolt, but I swore an oath to Eva that I would do this, and I know no other way to redeem my pledge.

To Margerite's surprise, for she had been expecting bone-shivering iciness, the caverns that had been so cold in summertime almost seemed warm now as she followed Nikolaus' candle - and the dark shape that hulked behind him - through the stone passageways. The trails of slimy water running down the stone glimmered faintly in the candlelight, as though a huge slug had wended its way slowly through the caves; here and there, tiny salt crystals glinted like the residue of dried tears. Christoph's dragging steps grated harshly against the salt underfoot - I should have told Nikolaus to dress him and put shoes on him. His feet will be bleeding soon - and when the demon is gone, it will be Christoph who suffers the pain of it, thought Margerite. Please God, it will!

She hardly noticed the cramping in her back as she bent to get through the lower passageways, or the bite of icy water seeping in about the seams of her boots as she crossed the stream. Her nerves seemed drawn out like hot gold wires stretched thinner and thinner, as though at any moment they would snap through; she kept thinking that at any moment, the heavy shadow behind Nikolaus would turn on her, gazing at her with those Hell-deep eyes and reaching...

Demons rule men through two things: desire and fear, Margerite recited to herself, clinging to the words of the Black Book as though they were solid as prayer beads in her hand. The mage who has mastered both may rule demons; but beware the desire or fear that lurks unacknowledged in your soul!...Well, I am afraid, and I know it, Margerite thought. But I will go through with this, and if the demon turns on me, then I shall face it and trust Christ to give me strength.

Nikolaus pulled aside the black curtain that cloaked the door of his sanctuary, holding it back for the other two could pass. Instead of bending or crouching, Christoph dropped to his hands and knees, crawling in like a beast. Margerite could hear his heavy breathing echoing through the cave, and it took her a moment to steel herself enough to follow him.

"Into the triangle," Nikolaus ordered his brother. Still crawling, Christoph made his way slowly across the floor. He flinched away from the names - PRIMEUMATON, ANAPHAXTEON, TETRAGRAMMATON - written in red along the outer edges of the triangle, and his slack face twisted when his fingers touched the solid line of black paint between them.

Nikolaus opened his chest of magical implements - carefully not turning his back on Christoph, Margerite noticed - and took out his wand. His black-robed body blocked Margerite's view, so that she did not see what he did; but Christoph flung himself into the triangle and squatted there on his haunches, panting dry-mouthed with his eyes rolling in his head. Nikolaus bent down for a moment more, sealing the triangle again. Straightening, he walked over to Margerite, offering her his hand.

"I invite you into my circle, Princess Margerite," Nikolaus said. His fingers were cool and clammy on Margerite's hand, his grip loose and unsure.

She held firmly to him as he led her over the broad outer ring of deep yellow where the likeness of a snake coiled thrice, its scales a circled row of black Hebrew letters, into the inner circle with its four hexagrams about the cardinal points, to the blazing red square in the middle where the single word - Master - stood, shining black against its crimson field. The paint gleamed as though it had been freshly renewed: keeping circle and triangle whole in the dampness of the salt caverns must be an unending task.

Margerite's stomach twisted as she crossed the last of Nikolaus' barriers: she could smell a chilly rot, as though something were decaying slowly in the cool of the caves, and the sense of Nikolaus' power crawled over her skin like a swarm of wingless bees. Though Christoph was no more than two long paces from them, it seemed to Margerite that her sight lengthened as she looked at him, as though the circle had stretched to a great distance, while the two feet between circle and triangle was an uncrossable abyss, with the red letters flanking the triangle's sides blazing from the black void.

Nikolaus left the circle again and began to prepare himself for the rite, performing each step with painstaking care as Margerite watched. He had left a basin of water, undoubtedly consecrated to the purpose, there: Margerite shivered in a moment of uncontrollable sympathy when he stripped off all his clothes, standing naked in the cave's cool dampness; she could see the goosebumps rising on his pallid skin as he dipped his hands into the icy water, pouring several double handfuls over his head and letting the water run down his flabby body.

Again, she could not help feeling a fleeting moment of admiration for Nikolaus' will, that he had trained to ignore the discomfort - and even, it might be, danger - of soaking himself to the skin in the cold of the caverns. Begrudgingly she thought, Christoph did misjudge his brother grievously: whatever else may be said of Nikolaus, he is both brave and hardy. When Nikolaus seemed to feel himself sufficiently asperged, he pulled on a robe of black silk that clung to every fold of his wet body; then - not prescribed by the rite, but needful for the place where he was working - a heavy woolen robe, and a third robe of white silk above that, on which a patch was covered with fine white linen attached to a cord; Margerite knew that the Hexagram of Solomon lay beneath the linen, and Nikolaus could release the cord if he had need, to cow the spirit and force it to take the form he willed.

As he vested himself, his dank hair still dripping on his robes, Nikolaus recited the prescribed incantation, "...In the power of Lucifer, to whom the praise and the glory shall be; whose end cannot be." Margerite bit her lip at that: now, more than ever, it seemed to her that the Order had perverted what was holy, and twisted true prayers into their incantations. Carefully Nikolaus girded himself with his lionskin belt...how had he managed to get lionskin for his girdle? Margerite wondered. One could not buy such a thing in the Weihnachtsmarkt, nor even from the merchants who dealt in fine silk and Flanders brocade; yet she did not doubt that Nikolaus' belt was real lionskin, for she could see the coarse sandy-dun pelt lying thin over the dry brown hide. Damiano must have brought it to him...

She bit her lip: though she would have, Christ willing, no part in what Nikolaus was about to do, she knew better than to let her mind wander while a demon, clothed in human flesh or not, crouched in the triangle before her. Nikolaus anointed his temples and eyelids with oil, then dropped over his head a chain on which hung a round of thin silver, its graven pentacle outlined in black, with the center of the five-pointed star painted green and its angles blue.

Upon his finger he set a great disc-shaped ring. Fully invested now, Nikolaus filled a chafing-dish with charcoal, lighting it from the candle he had brought, and placed it in the circle before Margerite, sprinkling incense upon it. The pieces of gum - dark brown and honey-brown mingled, like grains of coarse sugar - began to sizzle and blacken, a pale stream of thick smoke rising up from them to fill the air with sweetness. Yet the scent did not cover the whiff of rot that Margerite smelt; rather, it seemed to make it stronger, as a bit of honey in a sauce would bring out the sharpness of verjuice.

Though Christoph's jaw still hung slack, his eyes fastened on his brother with a bright hungry eagerness that Margerite misliked. He is waiting for Nikolaus to make some slip. Christ help us if he does! she thought. A low growl at her feet replied to her; she did not dare take her gaze from the demon, but she knew that Kobolt was there, and that gave her some comfort. Nikolaus lit candles to set in the red centres of the four pentagrams around the circle, their light gleaming from the yellow points, as though the sigils themselves had blossomed into flame.

He girded his sword about his waist and took his wand in his hand; he also picked up a box of black iron wrapped about with iron wire, then strode into the circle to stand beside Margerite. Margerite's nose wrinkled as Nikolaus set the box down near the chafing-dish: she could smell a trace of sulfur and asafœdita hanging about it, foul beneath the sweet incense.

"I invoke and move thee, o spirit Azruzor!" Nikolaus cried, lifting his wand up high. "And being exalted above ye in the power of LUCIFER, I say unto thee, Obey! In the name Beralensis, Baldachiensis, Paumachia, and Apologiae Sedes; and of the mighty ones who govern, spirits, Liachidae, and ministers of the House of Death; and by the Chief Prince of the seat of Apologia in the Ninth Legion, I do invoke thee, and by invoking conjure. And being exalted above ye in the power of Lucifer, I say unto thee, Obey! in the name of him whose lure is the seduction of man, the author of death, whose power is over the Earth and to whom all unclean spirits must bow. Moreover..."

A low laugh issued from Christoph's hanging jaw; and behind the crackling sound, it seemed to Margerite that she could hear the ceaseless buzzing hum of a swarm of wasps at rotten fruit, and beyond that a myriad of faraway voices shouting and gibbering and weeping. His face writhed like wax melting in a fire, and then he spoke, his words weaving through Nikolaus' conjuration.

"I am here, O Master, and I obey you," the demon said. His voice was mushy, as though Christoph's lips had been numbed by cold; it rose and fell oddly, sometimes rising to a whining falsetto, sometimes sinking to an earth-trembling bass. "Wherefore conjure me, when I am before you already? I see that you bear the seal of Solomon the Lustful...Solomon whose dripping cock a thousand wives could not sate, once the succubus that he summoned to him had snared him with delights no earthly cunt could match, not even the one who stands beside you. Have you tasted her yet, Nikolaus? Have you been brave enough to defile your father's bed with your seed - or only sent your whining letter to the Pope of Fools, that he may give you a parchment on which he wiped his arse, for you to show off when men ask by what right you stuck your horn into your father's wife?"

Nikolaus, to his credit, did not pause even for a breath, but continued his incantation steadily. "In the ineffable name of LUCIFER, STAR OF THE MORNING, I say, Obey! whose mighty sound being exalted in power the pillars are divided, the winds of the firmament groan aloud; the fire burns not; the earth moves in earthquakes; and all things of the house of heaven and earth and the dwelling place of darkness are as earthquakes, and are in torment, and are confounded in thunder. Come forth, O Spirit Azruzor, in a moment: let thy dwelling-place be empty, apply unto us the secrets of Truth and obey my power. Come forth, visit us in peace, appear unto my eyes; be friendly: Obey the living breath! For I stir thee up in the name of the God of Truth who liveth forever, LUCIFER, SATHANAS, STAR OF THE MORNING. Obey the living breath, therefore, continually unto the end as my thoughts appear to my eyes: therefore be friendly: speaking the secrets of Truth in voice and in understanding."

Yet as he spoke, Christoph laughed; and Margerite's thoughts made sudden numb sense of the demon's twisted words - had Nikolaus applied already for an annulment of her marriage to Heinrich, in hopes of wedding her himself? Or was it only a deception? He means to shake my will, in hopes of finding a weakness in Nikolaus' circle, Margerite told herself firmly. There will be time to think on this later.

"I am here, O Master, and I obey you," Christoph repeated, his last words going off into a gale of crazed laughter. He was on all fours within the triangle now, and it seemed to Margerite that he was straining against the barrier of its lines like an untrained mastiff straining at its lead when a cat came into view. Nikolaus raised his wand, slashing it through the air as if it were the handle of a whip, and Christoph flinched back, his laughter jagged-edged with pain. Though Margerite knew that it was Azruzor who suffered at Nikolaus' hands, Nikolaus' grim smile of satisfaction unnerved her: how could he take such pleasure in tormenting the semblance of his brother?

"Now I command you in the name of LUCIFER, Lord of
all Knowledge, and in SATHANAS whom thou worshippest:
and in the seal of thy creation: and in the mighty names of
BEELZEBUB, ASHTAROTH, and LILIT, thy princes: and
in all the names of the Prince of Darkness, whose power is
supreme in the rule of Earth, sitting crowned in the dwelling
of darkness: Azruzor, I command thee to leave the body
which thou inhabitest, and to return speedily and without
delay to thy dwelling. Obey the law which I have made,
without terror or harm to the sons of men, creatures, all
things upon the surface of the Earth. Descend therefore
I say, and be thou as stewards of Time; come forth in a
moment, even as servants that hearken to the voice of the
Master; in the moment in which I invoke thee and stir thee
up and move thee in the mysteries of the secret wisdom
of the Light-Bearer. Descend unto thy dwelling place in
pleasure: let there be the mercies of LUCIFER upon thee:
be friendly in continuing; whose long continuance shall be
comforters unto all creatures. Amen."

Christoph threw back his head so that it lolled upon his
back as though his neck had broken in the violent gesture.
Still he laughed; and the mad laughter suddenly formed
words. "O fool, my Master! It was not by your leave that I
took this body, though you commanded me to it. I hold this
flesh by the leave of the Daring One, and the High Enemy
turned his face away, that no power of his might keep me
from it. Drool your constraints as you may: while I sit here,
no fire of spirit can burn me, nor can chains of adamant bind
me; and though I must obey your commands as you invoked
me first, you cannot drive me from my seat!"

Nikolaus' unhealthy pallor darkened, his knuckles
whitening on his wand as he unloosed the cord that hid the
Seal of Solomon on his outer garment and drew his sword
left-handed, wheeling it in a glittering arc through the air.
"O thou wicked and disobedient spirit Azruzor, because thou
hast rebelled..."

Christoph spat, the drool running in a shining snail-track down his chin as he flung his dreadful laughter at Nikolaus in tattered rags of words. "I have done your will and my Master's, for you conjured me in the names of the All-Unholy," he shouted, his voice echoing from the walls of the cave until what he said was lost in the buzzing vibrations of sound. Still Nikolaus continued his incantation.

"...I do by the power of these names the which no creature is able to resist, curse thee into the depth of the Bottomless Abyss, there to remain unto the Day of Doom in chains, and in fire and brimstone unquenchable, unless thou forthwith departest from the man's body which thou holdest, and returnest to that plane of Hell from whence thou camest."

"Are you deaf as well as stupid?" Christoph challenged him. "Clean the shit from your ears! I..."

"Silence!" Nikolaus' voice cracked, and Christoph fell silent at once, gazing up at him with a grin that twisted one side of his mouth halfway up his cheek and the other back nearly to his ear.

"Know this, Azruzor: if thou departest this body not now, peaceably and without harm, thou shalt be bound and tortured for all eternity, burnt even as I torture thy seal with fire now." He forced the tip of his sword under the iron wire binding the black iron box, lifting it to hang over the burning charcoal of the chafing dish.

"I conjure thee, o fire, by him who turns all creatures of good in the world to his will, and makes of them a torment, that thou torment, burn, and consume this spirit Azruzor for everlasting. I condemn thee, thou spirit Azruzor, because thou art disobedient and obeyest not my commandment, nor keepest the precepts of LUCIFER thy Master, neither wilt thou obey me nor my incantations, having thereby called thee forth, I, who am the servant of the most High and Imperial LUCIFER, SATHANAS, PRINCE OF DARKNESS, I who am dignified and fortified by his infernal power and permission. For the which thine averseness and contempt thou art guilty of great disobedience and rebellion, and therefore shall I excommunicate thee, and destroy thy name and seal, the which I have enclosed in this box; and shall burn thee in the immortal fire and bury thee in immortal oblivion; unless thou departest Christoph's body at once, returning to thy dwelling in Hell without harm or terror to man or beast or spirit."

"Burn as you like, Master," Christoph taunted him. He smiled up at Nikolaus; and to Margerite, that look was the most dreadful, for it was Christoph's own cheerful smile, but the skin of his face twitched and moved as though a horde of ants ran wildly just beneath it. "While I dwell in this flesh, you cannot touch me; and what the Lord of All has decreed, and the Foe has given his leave to, you cannot shift, not if you wore the adamant ring upon your hand, and were a mage thrice as great as the one who bears it now, or as the whoremaster Solomon himself."

"Mock me no longer!" Nikolaus snapped. "I command thee, Azruzor, to bear thyself towards me with the submission that befits a slave such as thyself. Leave off thy taunting words, and let no sign of thy nature show outwardly: return to the very semblance of my brother, that even the wisest may detect naught amiss with him!"

At once Christoph's face stopped twitching. He wiped the drool from his chin with his sleeve and heaved himself upright, standing calmly within the triangle. "Does this please you well enough, Nikolaus?" he enquired, as if he were asking Nikolaus' opinion on a newly-broached keg of wine.

"Well enough," Nikolaus replied. "I command you as before, to keep that semblance and seeming until I tell you to leave it off: so perfectly must you imitate Christoph, that even the Knappe who sleeps in his chambers may not know that aught is amiss - but remaining always subject to my will, and bearing yourself with fitting respect towards me, as a man who has come to trust in his brother's wise guidance, remembering and heeding also those signals which I had rehearsed with you before."

"As you wish, Nikolaus. Doubtless you are right," Christoph said lightly.

"Now when I free you from the triangle, go back to Christoph's room and sleep - or feign to sleep. And should Georg ask where you have been, say only that it is none of his affair."

"I shall do that," Christoph promised.

The base of the black iron box was glowing dull red now. Nikolaus slipped his sword free of the iron wire that wrapped it, holding the weapon with its tip pointed straight at his brother. Carefully he reached over the edge of his circle and touched the wall of the triangle with his wand, jerking his hand back at once.

Christoph stepped out and wandered away as though he were simply strolling through the castle. In a short while Margerite heard the distant plashing of his feet wading through the stream.

"Now praise be to LUCIFER, and to all the mighty ones of the Qlippoth, who rule beneath the earth, and whose realms are shadowed forth in all men, and in all things touched by the power of SATHANAS Our Lord! I am great in will, I am strong in magic: the powers of the Air bow to my wand, and by my sword are they abashed, to do my bidding upon the Earth and in the dwelling-place of Darkness. So it is; so be it ever; amen," Nikolaus concluded.

Margerite waited silently while Nikolaus cleaned up after himself. The hot iron box hissed and sputtered when he set it on the damp floor outside the circle to cool; the chafing-dish of coals, he left to burn down where it was, but everything else he put away in his chest. Lastly he retied the cord that held the linen panel over the parchment seal at the hem of his outer garment, then undressed and folded his robes neatly away before he put his other clothes on.

"Now you have seen that I can summon and control demons, and am strong and practiced in the rites pertaining to them," Nikolaus said formally to Margerite. "Am I not worthy of the onyx ring?"

Margerite only stared at him until his greenish eyes dropped. "I see a fool who called up what he could not put down," she replied. "It is not enough to remember a ritual, or even to know how to bandy words with the spirits of Hell: you must have the wisdom to know what is beyond your power. Maybe you can summon demons, and even control them - but until you can return them safely to Hell, you have no right to wear the onyx ring."

"But..." Nikolaus sputtered. "There is no warning in the Black Book about bringing a demon to possess the living; there was no way for me to know that magic cannot unseat such a possessor! Still, he is wholly under my control: is that not proof enough of my skill?"

"Decidedly not!" Margerite snapped, the slow welling of anguish in her soul venting itself in her angry words. "You have proven only that you are rash and foolish, and prouder than your deserts. Pride is the fortress of the magician's will," she added, remembering those words from the Black Book, "but to pride yourself beyond your strength or knowledge is idiocy. Now I say that you shall not wear the onyx ring until you have put Azruzor in his proper place, no matter how many demons you may call up and order and send back safely, nor how strong they are."

Margerite could see the jaw-muscles bulging and moving under Nikolaus' plump cheeks, as though he were gritting his teeth, but at last he forced out, "It must be as you say, Princess. I shall begin to seek that lore at once."

"See that you do so. And upon pain of the greatest suffering, make no more such attempts without my leave!"

"As you will, Princess," Nikolaus muttered, his eyes gleaming sullen green.

Before he could calm himself, Margerite struck again. "And what is the meaning of the demon saying that you had sent a letter to the Pope? What have you done?"

Nikolaus's breath hissed in through his teeth. He did not flinch back, but his inkstained hands tightened on the edge of his cloak. "Forgive me, Princess," he said steadily. "Before you won your rank - I wrote to our Bishop concerning the annulment of your marriage to my father, so that you and I might be wedded, and the lands of Falkenstein and Fürstensee held safely as one within the Order's hands. The Bishop seems a pious man, but his purple robes cloak the heart of a gambler, and he was much in need of both funds and secrecy, so..."

"I see," Margerite said, the words dry and dusty in her mouth. "How long ago was this?"

"Early in October. Though such petitions move slowly, the matter should be reaching the Pope's eyes soon. And he, too, is much in need of money since Episcopus Bertrand du Guesclin squeezed his two hundred thousand francs from the Church's treasuries: I think that the payment promised for his favour in this matter should more than suffice, since the annulment will cost the Pope nothing but a moment of his time."

Margerite had never struck any person with her closed fist, but now her fingers clenched tight over her thumb. Nikolaus' move had been a shrewd one: even should his hopes of wedding her fail, if she had borne Heinrich's child in her womb - and Nikolaus had had no way of knowing that she did not - the annulment would have declared it illegitimate in law, so that Nikolaus would have no young rival for his father's lands.

Slowly Margerite forced her hand to uncurl: she would gain nothing from hitting Nikolaus, save the knowledge that she had given way to the sin of wrath. "What cause did you give for the annulment of the marriage?" she asked. "Everyone in Fürstensee - and I dare say all our neighbors, by now; the Bishop, too, if he pays the least attention to the doings of great nobles within his episcopate - knows well that it was consummated."

"I said that you had been forced into the marriage against your will after Graf Ruprecht's death, and were made to swear without consent. That, at least, is plausible enough. I have never been certain that it was not true; else why should you have waited so long to consummate your vows?"

Margerite's head spun, and she could feel the blood dropping cold from her face. Though she had chosen to be Heinrich's bride, it was also true that it had not been willingly: she had chosen a lesser evil to protect her from a greater, as if she were drinking the burnt hairs of a mad dog to protect her from the frothing disease of its bite. She had been a fool, to mistake Nikolaus' self-centered nature for blindness. Now she could see the neat trap he had laid; and though her flight had been an accident, Nikolaus had seized upon it most cleverly, as the final chance to win what he desired. And Heinrich's brain-storm, then...

"Did you bring about your father's grievous state, or have you been using some magics to hold him to life?" Margerite asked, dimly pleased that her voice did not betray any sign of the trembling in her bowels.

"Neither, Princess," Nikolaus replied. But one corner of his full lips twitched, as though he were reining back a smug smile; and in the core of her being, Margerite was sure that he was lying to her. But what can I do? she wondered. If I were truly a Princess of the Order of Light-Bearers, I might have the cruel means to force the truth from him...but I cannot turn my hand to such work, not for this.

"We shall see," said Margerite. "And why did you not tell me of your action before this?"

"I meant to, but we had another matter to hand," Nikolaus answered, a hint of the old sarcastic bite in his voice. "Be sure, that if the demon had not spoken of it, I would have told you in any case."

"I am less than sure of that. And now you should know that I am in no way minded to marry you: had I been before, this would have changed my thoughts towards you utterly, for I would not wed a man who takes action behind my back." Margerite's words rang louder with truth than she had intended, her voice borne up by the memory of how Ruprecht had deceived her. "Burg Falkenstein is my son's when he is old enough to take it, and mine until then: I shall not brook another to rule it. These lands you seem to have well enough in hand, in spite of the grievous error you made in your brother's possession. But if you have indeed done as you said, then I must send to Avignon to assure the Pope that I married Heinrich of my own free will, without any coercion and understanding the vows I swore, and consummated the wedding likewise, and there is no cause for annulment in this case."

Nikolaus bowed his head, as if waiting for Margerite to strike him. "Princess, forgive me. I meant only to do what was best, for us and for the Order."

"Within the Order of Light-Bearers there is no forgiveness," Margerite said crisply. "You have erred; you shall repair your error, or pay the price for it."

"If you write and sign your letter, I shall send a messenger off tomorrow," Nikolaus murmured, his voice dull and exhausted. Had it not been for his crimes, Margerite might almost have pitied his weary disappointment - and pity him I should, and pray Christ's mercy on him; but not for that.

When she climbed at last into her bed, Margerite thought that she would not be able to sleep. The sight of Christoph's face twisting into the unwholesome mask of a monster, the dreadful buzzing voices that still seemed to echo faintly in her ears...she feared they would come upon her in her dreams, and worse yet in the openness of sleep than when she stood defended by her waking will.

"Kobolt, guard my sleep," she murmured. An answering, "Prrow," came from the foot of her bed; forcing her eyes open, she could see the cat's shape as a blacker shadow in the darkness, sitting bolt upright with his tail curled about his feet. Then, "Christ forgive me, that I should call on my cat to trust before Him! May God, and Christ, and the Blessed Virgin and all the saints look upon my sleep, and keep me from the terror that walks in darkness, amen."

Though she had not intended it, Margerite found that she was flying - circling high above the tower of Burg Furstensee, then arrowing suddenly north-east like a stone flung from a whirling slingshot. She gripped something in her talons; she did not know what, but she could feel it pulling her, drawn irresistibly onwards like iron to a lodestone. Beneath, she saw the road she had travelled in Merlin's wain scarred by wagon-tracks through the bone-pale reaches of snow, the barren tangles of white-laden trees furring the swelling hills, the glimmering trails of frozen streams and the sluggish movement of rivers with ice-filmed edges.

One steady, familiar light burned below: the falcon saw within as if the building's shingles were clear glass, to where Father Etienne's friend the Abbot knelt in prayer before his private altar, long gray hair flowing about his thin shoulders. But the thing in her talons drew her onwards yet - there was the white-dusted blackness of the Thuringer Wald; there, Schloss Niederwald, dark and still...and there below her, the Bishop's palace. Now the weight in her talons grew greater, until she must sink or drop it.

As the falcon plummeted, her clear sight suddenly seemed to blur: it was not the wide low sprawl of Bishop Otto's seat she saw beneath her, but a towering, black-walled castle, ringed by an unfathomably deep moat - the castle that had daunted her before, when she sought out Father Etienne in her need. Yet now, one of the upper windows glowed deep sapphire-blue; and it was to that window that the thing she held drew her, until it touched the window's brightness.

Suddenly, with no sense of passing through, Margerite stood on the floor inside. She was a falcon no longer, but a human woman; and in her hand she held a ring set with a smooth round sapphire, the candlelight reflecting golden from its polished surface, but catching a glint of dark blue from deep within. The room was ringed with books; and Father Etienne sat at a table with an illuminator's tiny-bristled brush in his hand, tracing a line of crimson through the acanthus leaves that bordered a long, finely-written scroll. He was not wearing his canon's rolled-edge hat; his head was bare, thick hair a little disheveled, as though he had been running a hand through it in distraction.

The priest set his brush carefully aside, looking up at Margerite. It almost seemed to her that she could see the pale glow about him, the silver beard-tuft on his chin and silvered wings in his dark hair gleaming as though they were in truth wrought of precious metal; his eyes burned pale blue as sunlight through water. His arched eyebrows drew inwards, noble forehead furrowing as he considered her.

"What brings you here now? Are matters already so dire in Burg Fürstensee that you need my help?" His voice was not angry, but there was a sharp edge to it - an edge of alarm, perhaps: Margerite could see his slim shoulders tightening beneath his black robe, as though his hand were ready to go to the hilt of his narrow-bladed sword.

"Nikolaus has sought an annulment of my marriage to Heinrich - and I fear that I must go to Avignon myself to keep it from being carried out," Margerite answered, surprised with herself, for that thought had not crossed her waking mind. "But I fear to go, for Madame du Guesclin commanded my presence there to no good end; I would not bear Wolfram into the dragon's mouth, yet still less would I leave him in Nikolaus' care."

Father Etienne sighed, resting his chin on his fist. The deep graving of his gold signet ring, winged hammer above rising sun, sparkled brightly; as if her eyes were still those of the falcon, Margerite could easily make out the tiny lettering of his family motto: THOUGHT BEFORE ACTION. "If I could counsel you not to go, I would," the priest said. "But you know yourself the value of your oaths: though your heart's deepest desire were to be free of Heinrich, nevertheless you swore truly to him, and a false breaking of that vow would crack the strength of all your magics, like a streak of rot eating through the heartwood of an oaken plank. Nor would it be wise for you to openly flout the Order's commands, since you have taken on yourself the burden of feigning yourself one of them. But I can yet see to your safety, as well as I may. Do not lodge yourself with Madame du Guesclin, though she offer it; instead, when you come to the gates of Avignon, go directly to the dwelling of Cardinal Jean de Grenville - I shall send him word that you are coming, and warning of the perils that you bring with you: he owes me a great favour, and shall not refuse you. I may be able to see to other guards for your safety as well, whom you may know because they will speak to you in my name." Father Etienne sighed again, his ascetic face calm as if he were pondering some abstract problem of theology. "And, Christ willing, this evil may yet be turned to good. For if all goes well, Cardinal de Grenville shall be able to contact my old friend James of Canterbury, who is at least as skilled in exorcism as I am myself: if he can travel back to Burg Fürstensee with you, then, if God will have it done, he can be the instrument by which Christoph is freed."

"Father...Nikolaus tried to command the demon to leave Christoph's body, but it would not go, though I believe there was no flaw in his performance of the Light-Bearers' rites."

Father Etienne closed his eyes a moment, a look of sadness settling over his face like an autumn cloud sinking onto a mountain's crags. "No man may be possessed by a demon without some degree of assent, though most often it is unknowing. Nor can it be done without God's leave, though men may never know why He permits such things to take place - as a test of faith, perhaps, both for the exorcist and the one possessed, who must in the end choose himself to cast out the evil that has rooted in him, and avow his trust in Christ anew.

When God gives such leave, no mortal magic is strong enough to shift a demon's power: it is only through God's grace that the exorcist is allowed to make His might manifest, and thus free the demoniac from his curse." The priest looked Margerite straight in the eyes. "But see to it that you do not let this failure shake your faith. Now you have dealt twice with this unclean spirit, and twice it has had the victory: the third time will be by far the worst, and if you are in any way daunted, it shall have power over you as well as over Christoph."

"Father, I shall pray for strength, and do you pray on my behalf as well," Margerite answered. Though she could hardly feel her own body, as though it were shaped of mist, her fear was all the keener for that: not blunted by the tremblings and sensations of flesh that dulled its edge, but spearing straight through her like a blade slicing through air. To distract herself, she seized on the first thing that came to mind. "Will you tell me, now, how it is with Bernhardt?"

"The Inquistitors arrived yester-morning," replied Father Etienne. "Father Kerlinger and two assistants - men whom I know," he added, his voice stern and grim. "As yet they have merely taken our statements and cataloguing the contents of Ortlieb's wain: it shall be some time before they come to any decision, or even call you to give testimony." He paused, brushing a thick lock of silver-strewn hair back from one ear and tilting his head as if he were listening to chimes that Margerite could not hear.

But you did not answer my question! Margerite wailed silently; as with her fear, now her frustration burned the more fiercely within her for not being clouded by living flesh. She wanted to ask again, to tell Father Etienne what she had truly meant, but the priest spoke first.

"Now you must go back: such dream-walking as you have done this night is easier than faring by choice from your body, but it is still wearying, and you have a long journey to begin tomorrow. Say, if you will, that you are going to Avignon to see to having a Papal Mass said for Heinrich's sake. Thus you may yet do more good, though you dare the powers of evil: for if Christ will, such a Mass may move His heart to grant Heinrich recovery - or release."

With Father Etienne's last words, the study vanished, and the priest with it: it seemed to Margerite for a terrifying moment that she was tumbling in a gray mist, shot through with light-streaks of red and blue and yellow. Where am I? she thought wildly. Where is my body?

Then she heard the dull crackle of a fire behind the metal walls of a stove, and a faint soft humming; and she knew that the grayness was only that of daylight through her closed lids. She opened her eyes, breathing deeply: her limbs tingled, fingers and toes thrumming strongly, as though her soul were just engaging with her body like one clock-wheel locking into its mate. The gray light through her window showed that it was only a little while after dawn; Else was testing the warmth of the bowl of water on the stove, and a tray with two fresh-browned rolls and a silver pitcher stood upon her table, just as she had commanded.

Wolfram was beginning to make the little noises that warned of a full-voiced cry to come, and Margerite swung her feet out from under the covers. She could still feel the chill of the wooden floor through the strewn reeds, but the room was nicely warmed already. Else had been not only gratifyingly punctual, but quiet in her duties; nor, to Margerite's relief, did the young woman trouble her with anything but a dropped curtsey when she saw her mistress awake.

It was only when she bent over the cradle to lift her child out that Margerite realized her right hand was still clenched tightly around something, so tightly that she had to pry her own fingers open with her left hand. As in her dream, she held a gold ring with a round blue sapphire set in it - the token Father Etienne had given her, that she might be able to reach him at need: somehow, in her dreaming, she had gotten it from the bottom of her belt-purse. Quietly she slipped it on her finger, on the hand that bore only her wedding-ring: it had clearly been sized for Etienne's slender fingers, for it was only a little too large for her.

As she suckled Wolfram, Margerite thought deeply on her dream. She did not want to go to Avignon; she had thought that it would be simple to tell Madame du Guesclin that it would be too risky to leave her duties as Gräfin anytime soon, since she had already been gone so long. But the pretext Father Etienne had given her was a sensible one, indeed obvious: if a convent retreat of prayer had done nothing for Heinrich, what was left for his bereaved wife to do but to beg the intercession of the Pope?

Nor could Margerite deny the hope that a Papal Mass might, indeed, counteract whatever spells Nikolaus had laid upon his father - and what less could she do for Heinrich, she who had sworn her wedding-vows to him without deceit, and been well-served by him in turn? Too, she had vowed to Eva that whatever power she had, she would use it to gain Christoph's freedom - not only the power of her seat among the Light-Bearers, though that had been what was in her mind then, but, by the words of her vow, all her power: and from Father Etienne, she now knew that her journey to Avignon would include the hope of finding a skilled exorcist for Christoph.

The exorcist James of Canterbury; Cardinal Jean de Grenville; Margerite whispered their names to herself beneath the soft sounds of Wolfram's sucking, fixing them firmly in her mind - though she had little fear of forgetting them: her dream was not fading with morning thought, as dreams usually did, but was set in her memory more clearly than anything she had done the day before. And I will need a witness to prove that my vows were spoken honestly: Eva is the only one I can call on for that, since Christoph is - as he is.

The Bear's Paw Company will serve to guard me one more time; I shall need Ritter Gottfried for his sight, and Ritter Arnmut will not be parted from him. I wish I could bring Georg as well - Maria, how can I leave that boy to Azruzor's service? Yet Nikolaus commanded the demon to do nothing that would rouse Georg's mistrust...thank God, he must not know of what befell Georg on the day of the eclipse...and so he should be safe enough. Eva and I will need maids, Else and - what is Eva's maid's name? Mathilde. Perhaps we can pick up Rose on the way, too, since Burg Falkenstein is along our road. Or perhaps not, since I will be dealing with the Order, and the fewer people who are close to me, the better.

"Else," Margerite said.

"Yes, Frowe Gräfin?" Else replied anxiously. "What may I do?"

"When did you say your next child is due?"

"In..." Else looked down, counting hastily on her fingers, then up again with a broad smile on her freckled face. "A little less than five months, Frowe Gräfin."

How long would it take them to reach Avignon? In such weather, Margerite thought, they would be lucky to be there in a month and a half. Three months on the road there and back, then; and Christ alone knew how long her work would take, between the Light-Bearers and waiting to see the Pope.

"I have some news that may suit you ill, but you are not to
be too distressed. It came to me in a dream last night, that
since my prayers in my retreat have not been answered yet,
I must seek help for Heinrich from a greater source. Now
I mean to go to Avignon to beg the Pope to say a Mass for
Heinrich's sake; and that winter journey will be too much
for a woman who is so close to childbirth. But you shall not
lose by it: you shall be paid as if you were still tending to me,
and you are to continue dressing as befits that station; and
your only duties shall be seeing to it that my chamber and
Eva's, are kept clean, with fires burned in them often enough
to keep mildew from rotting the plaster, and herbs and
applewood burned once a week to keep them smelling fresh
and pleasant."

The maidservant smiled bravely at Margerite, though
her lower lip quivered as if she were on the verge of tears.
"Thank you, Frowe Gräfin! You are good to me, surely far
better than I deserve. I shall say ten Aves for you each day,
that the dear Virgin may reward your kindness to a clumsy
serving-woman."

To Margerite's surprise, the thought of her servant's
prayers for her kindled a tiny warm glow in her heart - but
though she is only a peasant, and knows nothing of magic or
the higher things of the spirit, Christ loves the meek: who is
to say that He does not hear her prayers even more readily
than He hears mine? And maybe Gertrude will hear from
her seat in Heaven as well, and pray for me also: may my
kindness to Else make up for all the times I spoke sharply to
her, poor girl!

"That is well-done," Margerite said gravely. "For I have
a long and hard journey ahead of me, and I shall travel the
more surely, knowing that you are praying for me here. Now
go you quickly to fetch two sheets of parchment and pen and
ink for me, and tell Herr Jakob to give Heinrich's seal and
some wax to you: I have messages of some urgency to send."

"O, yes, Frowe Gräfin!" Else exclaimed, running from the room. Though Margerite's belly was too tight with nervousness for hunger, she poured her silver goblet full of pale watered wine and pinched off a sop of bread to dip into it, the way she had done as a young girl when her stomach sat uneasily within her. She had managed to get down half a roll before Else came back with the materials she had asked for, as well as a pot of fine sand, a rag for cleaning the quill with, a small sharp knife in case Margerite should wish to trim its tip more to her own liking, and two blue ribbons for tying the letters up with.

Margerite's first letter - she almost flinched with terror at the thought of it - was to the Pope himself: a single messenger, if nothing went amiss with him, would reach Avignon long before she did, and her letter should at least be sufficient to delay Pope Urban's decision on the annulment until she could testify herself that she had wedded Heinrich of her own will. How can I dare this? she thought, clutching her quill almost tightly enough to crack the strong white shaft.

But then she reminded herself sternly that she was a Gräfin of no little power, the frowe of two Grafs' lands, effective ruler, at least in law, of one until Heinrich either recovered and died, and regent over the other until Wolfram came of age: she might not be set as high as Ortlieb had been, the Landgräfin who was nearly equal to the consorts of any of the secular Electors of the Empire, but her rank certainly entitled her to think of approaching the Holy Father. And - Margerite could almost feel her eyes lighting as the thought came to her - she had yet another good reason to approach Urban V.

No one had thought of the matter when she asked Christoph and Eva to become co-godparents to Wolfram, for there had been so many other problems to resolve then; but Margerite thought that the role they had played there would be an impediment to their marriage, as godparents were considered as consanguineous in law. Trusting in Christ that Christoph would, at last, be freed from his demon, and being quite sure from the way Eva had wept and begged her to help, even if it meant using her feigned position in the Order of Light-Bearers, that Eva still loved and wanted to marry him, the best gift Margerite could give the couple was to approach the Pope in search of a dispensation so that they could legally join.

Thus God's purposes are worked, Margerite said to herself: the evil that the Order wills shall turn to good in this journey, and - with Christ's help, and the mercy of the Blessed Virgin - good shall come of it for all of us. She brushed her thumb over the end of the quill - it had been freshly trimmed, the narrow wedge-shaped tip sharp and hard - and dipped it into the ink. When her letter to Pope Urban V was done, Margerite scattered a dusting of fine sand over it to dry it and set it aside.

She tapped the feathered end of the quill against her chin, thinking; then she wiped the ink off its tip, and then she took the little trimming-knife Herr Jakob had thoughtfully given her maidservant and carefully pared the tip a little narrower. Then she rasped the ball of her thumb against it again, wondering if she had cut it too narrow: would a broader tip make her hand more readable? You are delaying, Margerite said to herself. This will do nicely.

She dipped the quill into the ink again, tapping it lightly on the edge of the pot to knock the swelling black drop from the end. But at the sight of the pale unmarked parchment before her, her courage failed her again. It was one thing to write a letter, even to the Pope, knowing that the matter it dealt with had likely been broached to him already, or would be soon; it was yet another to write to a man whose name she had heard only in a dream, asking aid of him on dreamt advice.

Margerite looked at her hands, trying to keep them from shaking enough to blot her writing. Ortlieb's ruby glowered deep red on the forefinger of her left hand, the black-graven words EX TENEBRAE LUX standing out sharply against the ruddy polish of the gold. On her right hand were the plain gold band Heinrich had given her at their wedding - and the cool blue gleam of Father Etienne's sapphire token: proof enough, if she needed it, that her dream had been more than a fevered answer to the horror she had witnessed that night.

*To his Eminence, Cardinal Jean de Grenville,* Margerite began, her pen stroking the flowing black lines of clear Latin smoothly over the parchment. *I, Margerite, Gräfin von Fürstensee and mother and guardian of Graf Wolfram von Falkenstein, am writing to you upon the advice of Canon Etienne de Dion...*

By the time she had finished the letter to Cardinal de Grenville, the ink was dry upon her missive to the Pope. Margerite rolled and tied it, then called for Else to light her a candle. She dripped the black sealing-wax carefully over the knot in the ribbon, then turned Heinrich's seal-ring over and pressed the image of his arms firmly into it, finally scribing in bold letters on the outside of the rolled parchment, *To His Holiness, Pope Urban V, from Gräfin Margerite von Fürstensee and Falkenstein.* When the second letter was dry, she served it in the same way, though her hand quivered a little as she wrote the name *Cardinal Jean de Grenville,* thinking even as she formed the neat letters, *If he does not exist, after all, my messenger will think me one of the world's great fools!*

Letters in hand, Margerite was on her way down the stairs to the great hall when she heard the footsteps behind her. She stopped and turned. Christoph was hastening down the staircase, his steps bouncy, smiling as though he were in the best of humours. "Good morning, Frowe Margerite," he said cheerfully. "Will you go hawking with Eva and I this day? The skies are clear, and I think the weather shall stay fair; and it shall be pleasing to have a bit of game on our table for our feast tomorrow."

Margerite stared at him: it seemed almost past belief that this was the same man she had seen grovelling within Nikolaus' triangle the night before, his face twisting and contorting as he sneered his blasphemies at his brother. *And yet I must seem to accept the demon's deception as well, lest Christoph's own life be blighted even after he is freed.*

"I shall, gladly," Margerite replied, trying to keep her own voice light lest any should pass and overhear them. "But now I have another need - steady yourself, Christoph, for I know how this matter pains you! Since the prayers in my retreat seem to have done no good, I am minded to make a pilgrimage to Avignon, there to beg the Pope to say Mass himself for my Heinrich. I shall leave on St. Stefan's Day, if the weather is not too fierce to travel, but I would send these letters ahead with a swift messenger, and I would have your advice on who among our men is best-suited to such a task."

Christoph - no, Margerite reminded herself: *remember that however much like Christoph he seems, and though he wears Christoph's flesh, it is the demon Azruzor with whom you speak...and therefore be wary* - frowned slightly in thought, pursing his small mouth. "The swiftest rider among our men is Leopold, but he sprained his ankle not two days ago, and will not be fit for such duties within less than a week. Thietmar is a good man, trustworthy and careful, whom Father often sent on his longer errands. If you wish, Frowe Margerite, I shall take your letters for him and send him on his way." Christoph held out his hand; in spite of her warnings to herself, Margerite almost found herself giving him the two rolled parchments without thought.

"I must send him myself, for I have instructions for him. Only tell me where I may find him and what he looks like."

"He should be on duty in the outer bailey at the moment. You need do no more than ask Ludwig or Gottfried, and either of them can find Thietmar and be sure that he is properly mounted and supplied for the way; they will tell you how much money to send with him, as well."

"Thank you, Christoph. When I have done that, shall I meet you at the mews?"

"Indeed you shall," he replied, grinning at her. "A bit of hawking will do you good, after three months or so of prayer."

It was Ritter Gottfried that Margerite saw first, drilling the guards in the outer bailey: even beneath full armour and padding, his thin figure could not be mistaken for any other, nor could the agile litheness with which he moved. Although the sky was blindingly clear and the snow had been shoveled from the courtyard to lie in high drifts against the outer stone wall, a thin slick of ice lay over the cobblestones.

Save for Gottfried, who stepped as lightly over the uneven slipperiness as if he were treading on fresh-mown grass, the guardsmen were clumsy as dancing bears on the ice: Margerite was not surprised to see the feet skidding out from under one of them, so that he flailed wildly against the air before he went down, landing hard on his rump. A wave of laughter went up; then Margerite heard Gottfried's strong baritone chiding the men.

"Let none laugh who has ever slipped on ice!" the knight said sternly. "This work is not for the sake of merriment, but because there is never any knowing under what conditions you must fight. Someday you may face a foe on just such slippery footing: how shall it go with you then, if you have not learned to keep your balance? Werner, I heard you braying there. Step forward, and you and I shall take a turn together - I shall even fight shieldless, to make it more fair."

The unfortunate Werner was almost a head taller than Gottfried, and twice as wide across the shoulders. His blunted blade was longer than Gottfried's, and he swung it easily, but even without the ice that made his every step an awkward shuffling dance, Margerite could tell how far he was outclassed. Hardly seeming to move, Gottfried turned Werner's first blow aside, sweeping his blade easily around the other man's parry and blocking his second strike with the quillions of his sword even as he snaked his tip past the edge of Werner's shield, setting it solidly against the guard's breastplate and pushing.

Werner's feet went out from under him as quickly as those of the guard Margerite had seen fall, and he landed more heavily, his back slamming solidly against the cobblestones and his head bouncing up: had he not worn helm and padding, Margerite judged, he might have been seriously hurt.

"In a real fight," Gottfried lectured, "I would have slashed just beneath your breastplate. Without being sure of your footing, you cannot hope to stay your enemy's blow: therefore shall you learn to stay up on the ice, which is most difficult, so that when you are ankle-deep in mud or trying to fight with loose stones slipping beneath your feet, you will know how to keep your balance. Come, Ritter Arnmut: let us show these good men how it is done." He took up his shield, and Arnmut stepped out to face him.

Margerite watched in fascination as Gottfried and his former Knappe went at each other. Arnmut was not so swift as Gottfried, but as little as Margerite knew of fighting, she could admire the smooth neatness of his strokes, and the care with which he moved his shield to turn the other knight's blade just enough so that it missed him. Ritter Gottfried must have drilled his squire on the ice before, for Arnmut kept his footing with only a little more visible difficulty than his opponent, and held out for a good while before Gottfried's blunted sword tapped his helm.

"Well-done, Ritter Arnmut," Gottfried said, slightly breathless. "You see, you men? We..."

Margerite picked her way carefully over the slick cobblestones, coughing loudly enough for Gottfried to hear even through his helm.

"Frowe Gräfin," the young knight said, bowing to Margerite. "May I be of any help to you?"

"I am looking for one Thietmar, whom Christoph assures me is a swift rider and trusty messenger, in order that he may bear two letters to Avignon for me."

Gottfried pulled off his helmet, tucking it under his arm. Despite the cold, his sharp-boned face was pink from the exercise, a few sweat-soaked wisps of dark hair plastered to his forehead and his tight-bound plait hanging limp down the back of his neck. "Ritter Arnmut, continue the drill, if you will. Thietmar, come with us."

The man who stepped out of the rank was shorter than Gottfried, square-built and stocky, wearing a plain pot-helm and well-polished breastplate over his boiled leather armour. His cheeks were clean-shaven, but a frizz of brown beard bristled along his jaw, his thick moustache bushing out to almost hide his mouth completely. He bowed to Margerite. "Frowe Gräfin, I be yers t'command." His Swabian accent was very thick, so that Margerite had a little trouble making his words out, and she wondered if he were, after all, the best man to send to a foreign country - perhaps she would be better off asking Captain Paul if there were anyone in the Bear's Paw who spoke French or Latin and could be trusted with such a mission?

"Do you speak French or Latin?" Margerite asked dubiously.

"Lit' bit a'Latin, Frowe Gräfin," Thietmar replied. "'Nough t'get 'round, anyhow. Y'send a message w'me, it gets where y'wan' it to, no question a'that. E'en read a lit' bit." He grinned gap-toothed at her.

"I can vouch that it is so, at least to the best of my knowledge, Frowe Gräfin," Gottfried added, answering the unspoken question that seemed to hang quivering in the air between them. "Herr Christoph counselled you well."

Margerite nodded. "So be it, then." She handed the two missives to Thietmar, who took them with a careful gentleness that belied his rough looks and speech. He looked at the names written on the parchments, his mouth moving as he slowly spelled them out. Then his bearded jaw dropped in astonishment. "T'Pope? Y'wan' me t'bring a message t'the Holy Father hisself?"

"There will be folk at his palace whose job it is to receive the Holy Father's letters, Thietmar," Margerite told him. "You have only to see that it gets there; I fear it is unlikely that you will be blessed with a sight of the Pope himself."

"I...I be honoured, Frowe Gräfin," Thietmar stammered. "I've ne'er been t'Avignon, but I 'spect I can find t'way easy enough."

"That is well. Ritter Gottfried, I believe I can trust you to see this man properly equipped and supplied with any monies he may need: you have my leave to order Herr Jakob to give you whatever is necessary."

"At once, Frowe Gräfin," said Gottfried.

Margerite turned to go, and then another thought came to her. "Ritter Gottfried, would you - and Ritter Arnmut, if he can be spared his duties here for the day - care to go hawking with Eva and Christoph and I? After such a journey as we have made, the two of you are surely due for a little rest and pleasure."

Gottfried's gray eyes met Margerite's, the full cold force of his intense stare fixing on her. It is only because he is short-sighted, Margerite reminded herself: I should know by now that he does not mean to seem rude. "I am always pleased to accompany you if you wish, Frowe Gräfin. But..." The young knight's armour clinked as his feet shifted, and the pink flush along his stark cheekbones deepened. "I would be more pleased if you did not ask me to carry a hawk, for...I cannot see small game moving, nor watch where the birds fly." Gottfried looked down at the icy cobblestones, and Margerite could tell that his confession had embarassed him grievously. Hawking was, after all, one of the chief pastimes that set those of noble blood apart from their inferiors; but it warmed Margerite's heart that he had trusted her enough to confide in her thus.

"You see many things that are more important," Margerite murmured softly to him. "I shall not ask you to bear a falcon if you do not wish to - but I would be most glad of your company."

"Thank you, Frowe Gräfin. As soon as I have seen to Thietmar's needs, I shall ask Ritter Ludwig to take Ritter Arnmut's place, for I believe that Arnmut will be most happy to come hawking with us."

In spite of all Margerite's troubles, as she rode out across the snowy fields with Enide's talons clasped about her leather-gloved hand and Kriemhilt and Kobolt scampering through the snowdrifts beside the riders in sudden glimpses of dark fur or flourishes of plumed tails, she felt her heart lightening. The peregrine seemed in good form, her gray-brown feathers lying sleek and neat over her lean powerful muscles. Arnmut carried Gawan, while Eva bore the other falcon Margerite had brought from her father's keep, Kriemhilt, exclaiming that though the birds were so large and frightening, she must carry the one that shared a name with her beloved cat.

Georg made do with one of the Burg Fürstensee tiercels, while Christoph had his own large goshawk - the bird he had been wont to carry even to Mass with him before his possession; and Margerite could not but notice how warily the goshawk watched her master, shifting her grip and threatening to rise and bate at any moment; while his steed stamped and pranced restlessly in the snow. It is not so easy to deceive a bird or horse as a human, is it, Azruzor? Margerite thought. To her horror, Christoph looked back to smile sweetly at her, as if the demon moving his body had heard the very thought in her head.

"Jesu preserve me," Margerite murmured under her breath. If the holy Name caused Azruzor a flash of pain, he hid it well; but at least he looked away from her. Margerite breathed deeply, the icy air burning pleasantly clean and cold in her lungs. Dressed in their best winter finery, the little silver bells on their birds' jesses jingling as they rode, the hawking party might almost have been the models for an illumination showing December's pleasures; even Gottfried wore a cloak of deep red wool edged with miniver, and a trace of silver threading picked out faint embroideries on his black velvet doublet.

Behind them rode three servants, their horses laden with food and cloths to spread upon the ground for the mid-day meal. One of them carried Wolfram, wrapped warmly in soft lambskin and a small blanket lined with fox-fur, for though there was always a serving-maid or two who was nursing her own babes and might have spared a day's milk for the Gräfin's son, Margerite would not suffer Wolfram to drink from any breast save her own.

"But you might have sent a messenger ahead to warn me that you were coming back," Christoph was saying to Eva. "The year before last, Graf Wolfgang invited us to his Weihnacht-feasting; it was always so with him and my father, that they would take turns being host each year. The war interfered last year, of course, so it is still our turn to offer a proper feast for Wolfgang and his family."

"Perhaps for Twelfth Night?" Eva suggested, just as if she were talking to Christoph in truth. "There is still plenty of time to arrange it."

Christoph sighed gustily. "Alas, Frowe Margerite has other ideas - has she not told you? She is leaving for Avignon on St. Stefan's Day."

From behind Eva, Margerite could see the girl's whole body stiffening suddenly. Had her horse been more spirited, Eva might have risked being thrown; as it was, obedient to the command it thought it had received, the little dun palfrey halted suddenly, jolting Eva hard against the pommel of her saddle. Her hand flew up; she gave a little shriek of surprise as the falcon on her wrist leapt into the air, rising high and circling in search of the game she thought Eva had cast her after.

"Eva, what is wrong?" Christoph asked, with just the right tone of slight alarm. "I had not thought that news would come as such a surprise to you."

Margerite did not know whether she imagined the faint echo of gibbering laughter in her ears then, or whether she truly heard the sound of Azruzor's mirth. *Perhaps it is blessed Maria's mercy, after all, that we must leave Burg Fürstensee again soon, though we be walking into the serpent's outstretched jaws. I do not think I could bear this too long, skittering over the truth of what speaks from Christoph's mouth like a waterbug dancing over a pond's surface in the pretense that it is solid ground, knowing that the moment it halts it will sink into a fish's mouth - if the fish does not leap to snatch it from the air.*

She shook her head to clear it of such thoughts, telling herself firmly that Christ's will would be done; Margerite had only to go on, holding staunchly to her faith. Ahead of her, Eva had managed to get her horse walking again, and Christoph was solemnly explaining Margerite's plans for her journey just as Margerite had told them to him, not a single fault of word or tone betraying whatever thoughts seethed in his demon-haunted brain.

Margerite tilted her head back, watching the falcon circling high and dark against the ice-scoured blue of the sky. *I could fly with you...no; what am I thinking, to let myself be so tempted now?*

"Have I lost her for good?" Eva asked anxiously.

"By no means," Georg assured her, tightening his grip on his horse to urge it up beside Eva's. "She will either stoop on something soon, come back to your wrist, or light in a tree. And if she goes beyond our sight, the bells on her jesses are very clear of tone: their sound will carry well in this weather."

"O, you must have done a great deal of hawking at your father's castle, to know such things," Eva said, her voice artless and clear. Though Margerite could not see Georg's face, she could well imagine the silly grin Eva's praise would bring to it. *Is she doing this to taunt Christoph?...Surely not; I think rather that she means to distract him from my journey to Avignon.*

Sure enough, Christoph answered, "It does not take a great deal of knowledge to know that a peregrine cannot soar forever, nor that good bells can be heard clearly for a distance when the air is still. But if she lights in a tree, my Knappe," he added with ominous jollity, "we may get a chance to see your skill with hunting birds - and with tree-climbing."

"Herr Christoph, if it is needed to get Frowe Eva's falcon back, you shall see that I can climb as well as my mother's pet monkey," replied Georg.

Much to Margerite's pride, though, the peregrine circled back, swooping low over them. "Halt your horse, hold out your arm and keep it steady, Eva," Margerite instructed. "If you give her a secure perch, she should come back to you."

Though Eva flinched as Kriemhilt the falcon glided in, averting her face from the wind of her wings, the bird came to light on her wrist, her talons clenching on the heavy leather glove. Margerite could not keep the smile from her face, nor could she help saying, "There, you see! That is how we trained our falcons in my father's keep."

"And the work of a skilled falconer, indeed," Christoph said, grinning at her disarmingly, so that for a moment Margerite - even she, who had seen the demon unmasked - forgot that it was not Christoph who spoke, and her cheeks flushed with pride.

By the time they stopped for their mid-day meal, the nobles waiting on their horses while the servants cleared a swath of ground, spreading the heavy cloths that would protect their betters from frost and mud and setting up perches for the birds to sit on while the humans ate, Arnmut's bag held two hares, while Margerite and Eva's falcons had each brought down a brace of doves.

"I think it must be my Knappe's turn next," said Christoph, holding up his goblet for Georg to fill with wine. "He has had no chance all day; but as for me, I fear that my Frowe Perchte is not quite in the form she ought to be - I shall have words with our falconer when we get back, for I told him yesterday that if the weather was fine, I should go hawking today. But Georg's bird looks keen and eager to fly."

"Thank you, Herr Christoph!" Georg said. The Knappe's blue eyes shone with excitement; his freckled cheeks were flushed from the fresh cold air, the scar on his face burning bright red. "I shall let that right rest upon what game we sight next, though. This is a fine tiercel, but I think he is a little small to bring down - a heron, say."

"True, and if we ride down towards the lake, there are likely to be heron there. But what of you, Gottfried? Why are you not joining in our sport?"

Christoph knows how short Gottfried's sight is, thought Margerite. This is but the demon taunting him with it. Thus she replied pleasantly before the knight was forced to speak, "Why, out of knightly courtesy, of course! Ritter Gottfried knew that with such fine birds flying as we have, we should bring in so much game as would call for another man to carry it, and generously denied himself the pleasure of flying his own hawk for that sake."

The others laughed; even Gottfried gave Margerite a small relieved smile as Christoph turned the conversation instead to talk of how they should instruct Hildegard to prepare their game for the Christmas table. The serving-men had brought a goodly number of small, richly spiced meat and cheese pastries: as she was still nursing Wolfram, Margerite could eat without guilt, though it was an Advent Wednesday, when those without dispensation were expected to fast.

Eva and Georg seemed glad enough to take advantage of the leave Father Michael had given them the day before, though Georg seemed a little uncomfortable, and once or twice Margerite caught him looking guiltily at Gottfried.

The Ritter Gottfried himself, as Margerite had expected, ate nothing, and adulterated the water in his goblet with only so much wine as was needed to keep from risking the flux. Arnmut followed Gottfried's example, but Margerite could not help noticing his occasional longing glance at the little pies whose flaky crusts crumbled beneath the others' fingers as they broke them into bite-sized pieces.

Poor Arnmut, she thought, with such a stern example to live up to: Gottfried's company must bring you great joy, if his good opinion means so much to you.

Kobolt and Kriemhilt, though they had already gotten their share of entrails from bird and hare, slunk shamelessly between the humans, sniffing and purring and nibbling, and occasionally snaking a paw out to snag a piece of pastry whenever one was left unattended for a moment.

"Hai, Gottfried," Christoph said, an amiable smile on his face. "Did I not hear Father Michael giving you a dispensation to eat properly yesterday?" He broke a piece from the pastry in his hand and popped it into his mouth, chewing with obvious delight.

"Yesterday I had been travelling," Gottfried replied stiffly. "Today I have no such cause, and therefore I fast."

Margerite reminded herself that even when wholly himself, Christoph had not been above gently baiting Gottfried a little; but there was an edge to his teasing now that she misliked greatly. Yet she waited to see whether Christoph would leave the matter be, or continue.

"And you are starving poor Ritter Arnmut, too, as if he were still your Knappe," Christoph went on. "Arnmut, has no one told you that once you are knighted, it is quite all right not to hang on every movement your former knight makes? Father Michael is always eager to perform weddings, but I do not think that even he will be willing to marry the two of you." He laughed at his own jest, and Eva giggled too, but uneasily, as though she hoped to take the sting from Christoph's words thus. Gottfried's tight expression did not change; Arnmut, though, looked down at the ground, and his fair cheeks, already pink with cold, flushed burning-red.

"Christoph, leave off," Margerite interrupted before he could say anything more. "It is greatly to Ritter Arnmut's credit that he follows Ritter Gottfried's example, and it is hardly fitting to make mock of a good man's piety."

"Come now, Frowe Margerite," Christoph replied charmingly. "Surely a little merriment cannot go amiss in such pleasant company. I only sought to remind these knights that Father Michael gave them his leave to eat well until they are completely recovered from the rigors of travel - by which time the days of abstinence will be over anyway. And it is not healthy to ride all day in the cold on an empty stomach, whether journeying or hawking. For their own sakes, I would see them eat, lest they faint and have to be carried back to the castle before the day's hunt is done."

"I shall not eat on a fast-day while I have the strength to stand," Gottfried insisted stubbornly, but Margerite's voice overrode his.

"Each man to his own conscience, Christoph. I expect the Ritters Gottfried and Arnmut know their own limits well enough, and I think you should leave the matter be now." As she spoke, she turned her left hand slightly, just enough so that the deep red ruby on her finger glowed clearly in the sharp winter sunlight. A frown crossed Christoph's face so fleetingly that Margerite almost thought she had imagined it, but then he laughed again.

"As you wish, Margerite."

To Margerite's surprise, though she knew by the heaviness of her breasts that Wolfram must be growing hungry, the child had not yet begun to cry by the time she had finished eating. She went to reclaim him from the serving-man's care, and found him sitting up in his guardian's lap, looking at the snow-covered world in bright-eyed wonder as keenly as if he, too, were seeking out a quarry to launch a hawk at. Taking her son in her arms, Margerite briefly gave the servants their instructions, waiting while they cleared and covered a patch of ground behind a cluster of trees that, even in their winter bareness, were thick enough to preserve her modesty. Eva came to help Margerite unlace the back of her bodice; she shivered as the cold air bit into the tender skin of her breast, but Wolfram's suckling soon warmed her.

"Why are you really going to Avignon?" Eva asked quietly. "Is it...business of the Order?"

Margerite told her briefly what Nikolaus had admitted to, and of her dream-speech with Father Etienne. Eva listened without a word until Margerite was done, then said, "Margerite, is there any way you can take me with you?"

"I mean to take you as a witness, and Gottfried and Arnmut to keep us safe, for the Bear's Paw can protect us on the road, but they will never be allowed into a cardinal's house. I only wish that there were some way to bring Georg as well."

Eva frowned prettily. "I can think of none, though I like leaving him with - what has possessed Christoph - no better than you do. Margerite, it almost shames me to admit it, but I think I was less uneasy when Christoph began to act strange this summer than I am now. He seems so like himself; and yet speaking with him is like picking up a egg that has rotted within: the shell is whole and smooth. No whiff of foulness as a warning, but if you shake it, you can feel the slimy matter sliding about inside, and must turn your head away at the thought of what you will smell if the shell cracks."

Margerite liked that image no better than she liked the reality, but she could not deny its truth. "Well, I mean to leave on the holy Stefan's day, so you shall not have too much longer to suffer this. And Father Etienne gave me hope that we would be able to find an exorcist who would aid us in Avignon."

Eva sighed deeply, clasping her hands in front of her generous bosom. "Christ grant that it may be so!"

When the remains of their mid-day meal had been packed away, the company rode down towards the Fürstensee, following the road around the lake's edge. There they surprised a heron splashing through the half-crystallized film of ice among the reeds; and for a brief time, Margerite's pride in her falcon overcame her misgivings again, for Enid stooped like a falling arrow, striking the heron and killing it cleanly.

By the time the shadows of the bare trees began to stretch in great dark tangles over the snow, even Christoph had managed to coax his goshawk into flight, bringing down, to Margerite's surprised pleasure, a fox in the full bright thickness of its red-and-cream winter pelt.

"Well, Frowe Margerite," Christoph said as they rose homeward, "to which of us shall the hunter's prize go? Yours, I think, was the more impressive quarry; but mine shall give a fine fur, which shall adorn a warm hood for Eva long after your heron's bones have been gnawed clean."

"Your bird's prey was the more dangerous to her, so I must yield the prize to you," Margerite answered - but her skin prickled even at this innocent speech: was the demon luring her into some trap that was too subtle for her to guess at? Even though I must face Madame du Guesclin in the flesh, and perhaps the Order's Imperator himself, she thought, I am glad that I am leaving here: I think this maze of deception wound on deception, with a spirit of the Deceiver himself at the heart of it, would drive me mad if I had to suffer it too long.

After they had delivered their game to the kitchens and Christoph had taken his leave to change clothes before the evening meal, Georg trailing behind him, Margerite took Gottfried and Arnmut aside to a quiet corner of the great hall where she was sure their speech was not likely to be overheard. She was about to tell them of her plans; but Gottfried's keen ears had heard the conversation between Christoph and Eva at the beginning of their ride, and he said at once, "Frowe Gräfin, if you mean to go on another journey, Ritter Arnmut and I would beg leave to accompany you."

"I had thought to ask you that very thing," Margerite replied. "And I am glad to know how willingly you shall go with me, for we are going into great danger - I cannot safely tell you more until we are away from here."

Gottfried nodded. "We understand. But whatever it be, we shall face it without flinching, for Christ's sake and for yours."

"I am truly blessed in my companions," Margerite said, the words catching in her throat. "So it is, then: we are to leave for Avignon on the holy Stefan's day - ourselves, Eva, and those men of the Bear's Paw who are with us. I know I may trust in you to arrange for what is needed."

"Indeed you may, Frowe Gräfin."

Though Margerite told herself she should be of easier mind now that her course was set, she could not help brooding all that evening on the frightening thought that Georg would be left in Burg Fürstensee without friends or allies to help him if Nikolaus' control should slip, or if Christoph's demon should find some sly way around his orders to hide his nature from the Knappe. But there was little she could do: Georg attended Christoph at all times, so that she could not even easily find a way to speak to him in private.

The squire had seemed cheerful enough as they hawked that day, and was no less lively as he served Christoph that evening, but until she had spoken with him, Margerite knew that she could not be sure whether Georg was truly as at ease with his knight as he seemed, or whether he, too, was treading the intricate measures of the dance of lies with the rest of them. At last, though, Georg had to excuse himself to answer a call of nature. Margerite waited just long enough that she would not seem to be rushing after him; and then she, too, left the table, catching up with Georg just as he was leaving the privy.

"I must speak with you a moment," she murmured.

Georg started, his taper splashing a few drops of hot wax on the floor. "What?...Of course, Frowe Gräfin." He had picked up the more formal habit of speech from Gottfried and Arnmut, Margerite was sure; but it was, after all, becoming in a squire speaking to his knight's noble stepmother.

Margerite led the Knappe down the hall until she was sure that no one would pass too closely to them without good warning. "Georg, how does Christoph seem to you?" she said without preamble.

"Herr Christoph seems...quite himself, actually. Frowe Gräfin, are you sure that he is still..."

"Still possessed? Did you mark his manner when he left his rooms late last night?"

Georg looked down at the modestly pointed tips of his blue shoes. "I was very tired last night," he admitted. "I went to bed when Herr Christoph did, and did not waken until dawn."

Margerite blew out a silent breath of relief, glad that the boy had not had to witness anything of what she had seen. "You may trust me: he is still possessed - indeed, I think his strangeness before was a sign that something of his own nature was still battling with the evil spirit that had seated itself in his body, whereas now the possession is complete. But what I really meant to ask you was - well, Eva and the Ritters Gottfried and Arnmut and I are going to Avignon, together with those Bear's Paw men who are here. I do not want to leave you; and yet I can think of no good cause for which I could drag you from your knight's side."

Georg's head hung low for a moment; then he straightened again. "I had hoped that Christoph was all right now," the Knappe said, his pure tenor catching in his throat and cracking as he spoke. Margerite waited silently until Georg had gotten control of himself again: the boy bore enough burdens without being forced to bear the shame of weeping in front of a woman as well.

"I know you did," Margerite said gently, just as she spoke to Wolfram when he cried. "I know you did."

Georg swallowed hard, bracing his shoulders back. "But I can stay by him now, and I will," he insisted proudly. "He is my knight, after all, to whom I am sworn, and I know his true soul is still somewhere within him."

Hearing those words, Margerite found that she had to gulp down a lump in her own throat before she could speak. "You are brave, and true," she said. "May God and Christ and the Blessed Virgin, and all the angels and saints protect you!... And if you are determined to stay, then I shall give you my strongest blessings before I go, that whatever befall, no Power of evil may harm you."

"I thank you for that," Georg replied. Looking at him standing there with the candlelight glaring faintly from his unruly red hair and the scar that sliced his thick-freckled cheek in two, Margerite realized that he was taller than she now: as she had said to Eva, the boy was indeed becoming a man. "And you shall be in my prayers as well - you and Frowe Eva, for I think I can guess something of the dangers you are daring. I wish that I could come with you to protect you as I did before, but the Ritters Gottfried and Arnmut are very good men, and I cannot flee my duty again."

Margerite glanced quickly down the corridor, lest there be anyone within sight who might take her gesture amiss. Then she stepped forward and embraced Georg tightly; and though she did not sob, she was glad of the chance to blot her wet eyes on his shoulder. And someday it shall be Wolfram whom I embrace thus, as he declares himself ready to take on a man's part and a man's danger.

# Chapter Four

ottfried went to bed not long after dark and slept for a few hours, but rose well before midnight for the Weihnacht Mass of the Angels, as did Arnmut. Though Arnmut, being knighted now, had the right to his own chamber in the soldiers' dwellings, it seemed to both of them a waste of time and trouble to move him, the more so since they would be leaving again the next morning. And - Gottfried had to admit that he would miss the reassuring sound of his companion's soft breathing in the night, and the good cheer with which Arnmut rose in the mornings, always ready to coax the banked coals in their hearth into life again to keep the dawn chill from striking too deeply into their bones as they dressed, and eager to stand on tiptoes and peer out the small window in their room to see what the weather would be like that day. Likewise, it was Arnmut who had brought in pine and holly boughs to decorate the stone chamber for Christmas. The only ornament Gottfried had ever bothered with was the wooden crucifix that hung over his bed, but the greenery gave the little room a festive air, as was right and proper for celebrating Christ's birth.

"I think there will be snow tomorrow," Arnmut said, coming down off his toes. "None is falling yet, but I can see neither moon nor stars."

Gottfried tapped hard on the thick film of ice glazing their washing-basin, pushing at the fractures until the broken shards floated free on the chill water. "That will make the road no easier on holy Stefan's Day," he said regretfully. "Still, I shall not be sorry to leave."

"It is hard to believe that Herr Christoph is truly possessed of a demon, is it not?" Arnmut mused. "He seems no different from the man we knew before."

Gottfried dipped a corner of his washcloth into the basin, closing his eyes and shivering as the cold water bit into his face. "I do not find it hard to believe at all." He had seldom had occasion to bless his bad eyesight; but yesterday it had been merciful to him, blurring the sudden twistings and shiftings of Christoph's face so that Gottfried might almost believe that he was looking upon a human being.

Arnmut was silent for a moment, considering. Then he blurted out, "Gottfried, did you...see something in him?"

"Yes," Gottfried said forbiddingly. To his relief, Arnmut did not press the matter, but took his turn at the washbasin, scrubbing his fair face until his cheeks glowed pink. As yet, though he was filling out into a well-built man, the younger knight hardly needed to shave the golden down along his jaw; Gottfried was not sure that it was not vanity that impelled himself to carefully scrape the little bristles from his face every morning, but he felt grimy and disheveled when he did not.

The two knights dressed quickly in their best clothes. As always, Gottfried felt a small pang of conscience as he hooked the button-loops over the silver buttons down the front of his quilted doublet. Though Schlangenbad was a border keep, its lands were rich and its affairs prosperous, but the deep crimson silk was finer than anything Gottfried's father could ever have bought for him; Gottfried knew nothing of the costs of fabrics, but he was sure that it had been unspeakably dear, at least by his own standards.

But Graf Heinrich had always insisted that his castle's knights be fitted out in a manner that reflected his own station when they sat down at his table: outer garments of silk or velvet and brocade, hose of soft springy wool, and the finest linen undergarments were all supplied by Burg Fürstensee to Graf Heinrich's noble-born men. Arnmut's doublet was of pale blue velvet that brought out the light of his eyes, and his woolen hose were dark blue.

The clothes had not been fashionably tight-cut when they were made, but now - when he was near enough - Gottfried could see how closely the doublet clung to the younger knight's broadening shoulders and sturdy chest, and the hose displayed Arnmut's muscular legs in a way that might have given Gottfried cause for concern, had it been deliberate: he would need new feast-garb made soon.

Wrapping heavy mantles about their shoulders, the two knights made their way out of the soldiers' quarters and over to the Burg Fürstensee church, settling themselves inside to wait their turn to make Confession to Father Michael before the midnight Mass.

Gottfried's immediate superior, Ritter Ludwig, was still waiting as well; by that, Gottfried knew that either the Gräfin or Frowe Eva was inside the confessional, for at Christmas and Easter, when all those folk who had let the stains on their souls thicken the rest of the year suddenly remembered that they must be confessed and absolved before going to Mass, such things usually went by rank.

He and Arnmut nodded to Ritter Ludwig, slipping into the pew beside the older knight; his blurred sight filled by the shimmering haloes of the church's candles and their dark gleams of blue and purple and crimson reflecting from Father Michael's prized stained-glass window, Gottfried began to meditate on what sins he had committed since his last Confession, made just before leaving Bishop Otto's palace.

The abstinence-diet and hard travel in bad weather had, by God's grace, ensured that he had not been troubled by the sin of lust, not even in those half-recalled, cloudy dreams that sometimes left the stain of shame upon his nightclothes. Wrath - Damiano, certainly, had provoked that in him a number of times; though Gottfried had usually managed to hold his temper, the sin was still in his heart. One by one, Gottfried carefully catalogued the Seven Deadly Sins, examining his soul to see where their taints might have smeared him.

Pride was ever the worst, for him: pride in his skill at arms, that he had by the gifts God had given him and the patient teaching of several good men; pride in the station in life where God had set him, as son of a noble family, knight and second commander of the guard in Graf Heinrich's own castle; pride even, sometimes, in his own obedience to the laws of Church and God, proving that there was nothing in human life that was not tainted by Adam's sin, not even the struggle to eschew sinning.

The confessional's door opened, and Frowe Eva - even at a little distance with only candlelight to see by, her size and shining crown of golden braids made her easy for Gottfried to distinguish from the Gräfin - walked out. Ritter Ludwig quickly rose to take her place.

Having gone over the Deadly Sins in his mind, Gottfried then considered the other matters that had troubled him in the last weeks. Though his conscience was not as clear concerning Jochanan as he would have liked, he had at last decided that turning a blind eye to the breach of human law was not necessarily a sin, while betraying a good man who had been his benefactor most assuredly would be.

More worrisome was the matter of Christoph - but that was beyond Gottfried's power to deal with: he could only trust in Father Etienne, into whose hands such problems were lawfully given, to arrange some aid, and pray in the meantime that God would keep the demon dwelling in the Graf's son's body from doing harm to the innocent. Lastly... His strange sight was not, Gottfried was sure, a matter of any sorcery, nor even of such high works of the spirit as Father Etienne and the Gräfin carried out.

But on that terrible night when the snow had separated Gräfin Margerite and Frowe Eva from their guard, when he and Arnmut had lashed their horses together in the lightless white storm to keep from being parted as they stumbled onwards, desperately praying that they would find the lost women alive... On that night, it had seemed to Gottfried that he had seen such phantoms as unnerved him in a way that he had not felt since he first took up sword, not even in damned Ortlieb's Danse Macabre.

In the flashes of lightning shooting blue through the snow, he had seen the white swirls gathering into the shapes of horsemen riding swiftly through the air, a great army of ghost-men whose bloody wounds showed black in the lightning-flares; he had seen the faces of the dead under their spectral helms, and some of them were men he had seen die in the summer-long battle against Graf Ruprecht's forces, cut down with swords or pierced with spears or - worst of all - their armour and flesh and limbs all shattered by the terrible blows of the Bear's Paw guns.

Gottfried had clung to his gold crucifix, praying even as he shouted the names of the Gräfin and Frowe Eva over and over again, the howling wind whirling his words into soundlessness; but it had seemed to him that he was looking upon something that no son of Adam was meant to see.

Yet he could only pray that the unholy sight had not tainted his soul: had Father Etienne been there, Gottfried could have spoken with him, but he knew full well that Father Michael would click his tongue and shake his head and warn the young knight about the dangers of hysteria and morbid imagination, and likely offer an exemption from any upcoming days of abstinence or fast-days and the suggestion that Gottfried should eat better.

God's grace flowed equally through all priests; that was a point of faith, but it did not make all priests equally knowing, or wise...Arnmut plucked lightly at Gottfried's sleeve to get his attention. Ritter Ludwig had just come out of the confessional; now it was Gottfried's own turn. After the dawn Shepherds' Mass, the Weinacht delights began.

The servants had cleared the courtyards of the outer and inner baileys, scattering sand over the slippery ice to give a better footing; a huge roaring bonfire was built up in the middle of the outer bailey, and the great trestle-tables and benches were set up for all the folk who had come up from the village - though the higher castle-folk and the knights that Christoph had invited to Burg Fürstensee for the Weihnacht feast would eat inside the great hall.

Two pigs roasted on spits over smaller fires, brown skin crackling and flames flaring high beneath them as the fat dripped onto the wood; Gottfried's stomach twisted with a pleasurable pang as he thought that the long Advent abstinence was over at last, and he would be freely able to eat the good pork, or whatever delicacies Hildegard was making in the castle's kitchens. Over another small fire hung a great iron cauldron, with a constant stream of folk passing about to let the man who tended it ladle the hot wine into their cups, and kegs of ale stood on the tables.

The snow that Arnmut had predicted was beginning to fall now, great white feathers floating slowly down, but no one paid it any heed. Outside of the circle of wet stone where the bonfire's heat had melted the ice away, some of the younger guardsmen and servants were ambushing each other with snowballs, shouting and laughing.

A pair of youths were playing shuttlecock, batting their feathered cork perilously close to the leaping flames; several others leapt and ran to strike a ball against the bailey's inner wall with their hands; while two sturdy villagers, stripped to the waist and sweating in the bonfire's heat, tried to throw each other to the ground.

Not far from the fire, but not too close, lest the heat destroy the tune of their instruments, Burg Fürstensee's musicians played and sang melodious carols in Latin and German, while other folk joined in the choruses or danced about them, cloaks flying and white clouds of breath puffing from their mouths into the frosty air as the snowflakes flecked their hoods and cloaks.

Gottfried paused for a moment to listen to the music, then added his strong baritone to the singing. "Gaudete, Christus est natus, ex Maria Virgine..." Arnmut joined in as well. His tenor was not loud, but clear and true, harmonizing beautifully above Gottfried's lower voice.

This is just as it is every year, Gottfried thought, in the space when one of the musicians was singing out the verse alone. And yet Herr Christoph - the thing that is in him - should not be able to abide this joy over Christ's birth: may I, then, take it as a sign proving yet again that God shall ever triumph, even in the flawed souls of men? He breathed deeply, letting his voice ring out loud and clear on the chorus again.

"Gaudete, Christus est natus..."

"A good Weihnachtsfest, isn't it?" a familiar voice barked behind Gottfried's ear. Paul the Bear and Jochanan waved their tarred ale jacks cheerfully at him; it was hard to tell through Jochanan's dark complexion, but a flood of red flushed the Bear's wide cheeks. For the first time since Gottfried had met them, the Free Company men had left off their armour, though their tunics and cloaks bore a number of disreputable stains.

"It is, indeed," Gottfried answered. Jochanan had saved his arm; though Paul had shown his bravery and loyalty well in the fight about Ortlieb's wain, Gottfried had learned the free soldier's true worth when Margerite went missing in the snow. Retracing their tracks from the camp after meeting up with the Gräfin, Gottfried and Arnmut had finally found him half-blind from snow-brightness, leading the horse that could no longer bear his weight - and still searching for the Gräfin and Eva, fumbling his way forward and shouting in a voice too hoarse to carry more than a few paces across the snow. The Bear was not of noble birth; but Gottfried knew some knights who would not have struggled so hard for the ladies whose favours they bore - and others in his father's castle, men who had fought brigands and Raubritter most of their days, whose manners were no more polished than Paul's.

"Eat and drink well today, for tomorrow we shall be riding through the snow again," said Jochanan. "It's not so easy a life, being Gräfin Margerite's bodyguards - but better work than we had before."

Higher pay and lower risk? Gottfried wondered. Or... morally better? How did such a man come to be lieutenant of a Free Company?

"Never a dull moment with the Gräfin," agreed Paul. "I wonder how things are going with Bertram..." He slapped himself on the forehead. "Herr Bernhardt, rather. Who would have thought it? Almost like a children's Märchen, finding out that shaggy Bertram is heir to Niederwald."

Remembering how he had mistrusted the dour Hauptmann of Burg Falkenstein's guard at first, Gottfried could only nod in agreement. God's wonders are many, he thought, and which of us can guess at the pathways He will set before us?

"Anyway," the Bear went on, "it'll be good having the two of you along - you are coming with us, aren't you?"

"As the frowe Gräfin has asked," Gottfried replied.

"And what about young Georg?" enquired Jochanan.

"Georg...cannot leave his duties as Herr Christoph's squire again so soon." Gottfried tried to keep the foreboding he felt out of his voice, but he had never had any skill at dissembling, and Jochanan's swarthy face clouded as if mirroring the knight's own expression.

Paul shook his head. "That's too bad. Georg's a good boy; if he weren't so high-born, he'd make a good man for the Bear's Paw - did I tell you I tried to hire him on the first time we met? There I was in the White Cockerel, waiting for Bertram's...Herr Bernhardt's messenger, and..." The Bear rambled happily on, punctuating his story with long swigs from his tarred ale jack. Gottfried nodded and tried to smile at the right places, but his heart was still troubled at the thought of leaving Georg alone with the thing that wore Christoph's body like an ill-fitting doublet, and he could not hide his worry.

"Is something wrong, Herr Ritter?" Jochanan asked suddenly. "Your shoulder has not begun to trouble you again, has it? Winter fasting, if it lasts long enough, often makes old wounds open and bleed."

"If you know the tale," said Gottfried softly, "then I think you can guess what troubles me. If not - this is hardly the place to speak of it."

Jochanan's dark eyes glanced swiftly about, and he nodded. "I shall do what I can," he murmured. "I have some knowledge...there are only a few things I will need..."

"Best if you spoke to the frowe Gräfin," Gottfried told him. The damp cobblestones suddenly seemed uncomfortably hard and uneven beneath the knight's sturdy boots; he shifted his feet, thinking that such matters as Jochanan seemed to be speaking of were best left to those who knew more of them. If only Father Etienne were here! he thought again.

"I shall do that, if I can find her," Jochanan promised. Gottfried looked about - if the Gräfin were outside, she was too far away for him to make her out: past five paces, faces and the cut of clothing blurred in his sight, and the Gräfin was not marked by anything so noticeable as Frowe Eva's height and golden braids, or young Georg's bright red hair.

"She is over there with Frowe Eva," Arnmut broke in, gesturing towards a small knot of women standing near the cauldron of hot wine. "Would you like me to let her know that you would speak quietly to her?"

"That would be kind," said Jochanan, and Gottfried nodded in approval: it would hardly do, after all, for the Free Soldiers to approach the Gräfin uninvited here, for all the familiarity she and they had shown each other on the road.

Like the other knights and nobles, Gottfried and Arnmut went into the great hall for the midday feast. Gloomy as the gray snow-light from outside might be, the hall was lit with enough candles to cast a soft warm glow over the long tables. Evergreen garlands hung between the wall-tapestries, filling the air with the clean scent of pine, and the fires roared defiance of the winter cold up the chimneys. The castle's musicians had come inside as well; Gottfried heard the plinking and soft flute-scales as they retuned their instruments in the balcony, and the occasional muffled curse of the lutenist as he tried to coax his strings into holding their tone in spite of the change in temperature.

Gottfried had no sooner sat down when something touched his leg. He looked down to see the Gräfin's huge black cat resting a paw on his thigh; then it sprang up, treading hard on his lap with its full unnatural weight, like a moving lump of stone. Cautiously he scratched it behind the ears, and was rewarded with a deep rumbling purr that might have risen from the bowels of the earth.

What manner of creature is this? Gottfried wondered. He remembered the cats' eyes glowing, yellow and green, as Father Etienne and the Gräfin blessed the earthen salt and shining bright behind the shadowy wings as the two - Gottfried did not know what to call them, for one could not think of a woman as a priest, but assuredly such words as witches, sorcerors, magicians could hardly apply to those whose deeds of spirit were carried out by the power of God - called upon the angel Uriel.

Is this cat, then, an angel, walking among us though we be unaware? Gottfried found that hard to believe: Kobolt had sprayed the corner of his heavy travelling cloak at some time during their first night on the road, and despite his best efforts, a hint of tomcat still lingered about it - save for the Gräfin's affection for the beast, and the way the two cats had solemnly watched the holy rite performed by Father Etienne and the Gräfin, as if they were lending whatever prayers could be prayed by cats, Gottfried would have been likelier to attribute Kobolt and his peculiarly pungent urine to the realm of demons.

As if he heard the knight's thoughts, Kobolt gave a soft chirping miaow of protest, showing the white points of his long eyeteeth; and Gottfried was suddenly, absurdly sure that he had managed to offend the cat and would not be forgiven until he had given it a share of his dinner. Perhaps this black creature is, after all, a messenger from God, who now wishes to save me from spoiling the virtue of my Advent abstinence by succumbing to gluttony at this feast.

Gottfried smiled slightly at that. Arnmut, seated beside him, raised a golden eyebrow and asked, "What are you thinking that pleases you so well?"

Gottfried repeated his last thought, and Arnmut laughed softly. "I do not think you have ever been in danger of succumbing to gluttony. But the Gräfin's cat is a beautiful creature, all the same - though I did not know you liked cats so well."

"I have never before known a cat that was fit to be a noble frowe's pet. All through my childhood, my dearest companion was an old mastiff - he was killed on my first boar-hunt, when I was eleven. I wept for him for three days, as if he had been a Christian," Gottfried confessed. "Since then, I have not had the heart to love an animal so. Or perhaps my faith is weaker than it should be, that I have not trusted enough in Him who marks each sparrow's fall." Even now, ten years later, Gottfried could feel the knot in his throat as he spoke of Etzel: there was some part of him that still strained his eyes whenever he saw a big gray mastiff at any distance, as if hoping that the hound would give the three familiar barks with which Etzel had always greeted his master, loping over to sit at Gottfried's feet and gaze adoringly into his face as Gottfried's fingers ruffled through his thick wiry fur.

"If you fear that is so," Arnmut told him, "then perhaps you should find another hound for your own. Another mastiff - or, if you cannot bear that, then perhaps while we are in France, we can get one of the great Pyrenean bear-dogs: I hear that they are handsome beasts, snow-white and powerful enough to hunt wolf or bear or boar, and they are often kept by the nobles of that country. But come, Gottfried, I did not mean to make you melancholy on a day of rejoicing!"

As if to bolster Arnmut's opinion with his own, Kobolt butted his head hard against Gottfried's chest, kneading the knight's legs hard with his paws so that his clawtips just pricked Gottfried's skin. His long black fur was remarkably pleasant to stroke, soft and glossy - Gottfried could see why those of lower birth often used cat-fur as trim where their betters would have marten or ermine.

"Mrrow!" said Kobolt warningly. Then Gottfried blinked in surprise: for a moment, it had almost seemed to him that he had felt sharp teeth sinking into a juicy piece of meat, a sharp hunger undistracted by any human concerns. I might believe that this creature, whatever he is, can know what is in my mind...but I will not believe that I can know what is in his! Gottfried said to himself. Aloud he replied, "That sorrow is ten years past. But perhaps you are right: while we are in France, I shall see what I think of their hounds."

The first course was carried into the great hall with a fanfare of trumpets, Burg Fürstensee's carver stepping proudly forward to his duty in a swirl of bright red robes as the platter of plump capons, their skins glazed golden with egg yolks and saffron and adorned with swirls of sage-crumbs, was laid upon the high table. Herr Christoph nodded to the carver - and his shape blurred in Gottfried's sight; it seemed to the young knight that he looked upon a tall black figure, its heavy-horned head bending forward as if to gore the silver-haired man whose sharp little knife was slicing through the capons so skillfully that the patterns on their skin were hardly disturbed. It seemed to Gottfried that he saw the thing's lip curling back to show him a long white fang; its red eyes glowed like sullen embers - and the red flame on the Gräfin's finger, that Gottfried had first seen burning on Ortlieb's hand, flared suddenly in answer.

"And slice Ritter Gottfried a goodly portion," Christoph's voice was saying heartily, though the demon's thin lips did not move. "See how pale he is! Abstinence is well enough for monks, but a knight should eat like a man."

Gottfried forced himself to ignore the way the black shape's outlines twisted and curled in his sight. If Christoph said that to me in jest, I would say... "Some of the Empire's noblest knights are also monks, and I have never heard that keeping holy days has weakened the sword-arms of the Teutonic Order."

Christoph's laugh, full and false, sounded from a mouth that was lengthening into the long bearded muzzle of a black goat - a goat that stood with its cloven fore-hooves on the table, displaying the unnatural length of its thin male organ standing pink against its black hide. Gottfried struggled not to blush or let his eyes flinch away, though this immodesty unsettled him far worse than the previous shape had.

"We must find you a bride soon, lest you come to believe that you are a monk in truth," Christoph's voice said. "What do you think, Frowe Margerite? Eva? What manner of woman would be best suited to our little Teutonic Knight?" The goat's narrow phallus speared rapidly in and out of its sheath, as though it were covering an invisible mate, and a drop of glistening white slime drooled slowly from the pink tip. Gottfried's ears burned with embarassment, though he knew that neither of the women - Christ be praised! - could see as he did.

"A good and pious woman of noble blood," the Gräfin answered steadily as Herr Nikolaus cut a slice of capon into neat pieces upon the bread trencher they shared, and Frowe Eva added, "I would say the same."

"What of you, Ritter Arnmut?" Christoph's voice had a clear taunting ring to it now. To Gottfried's disgust, the black goat turned its hindquarters completely around, displaying a pair of filthied human buttocks, its dark testicles dangling as a gross and bloated shadow between its bowed legs. "Surely you have not travelled with Ritter Gottfried without learning what manner of love he seeks?"

Arnmut's angry flush showed clearly through his delicate skin, and Gottfried knew that his former squire had not mistaken the sharp edge of mockery hidden beneath Christoph's light chaffing like a real blade hidden by a fragile blunting-tip on a tourney-lance. "Ritter Gottfried is not such a man as to let fancies turn him from his path," Arnmut replied. "But if he were to marry, I have no doubt that he would choose a woman as true and good as himself, and as devoted to Our Lord Jesu Christ."

Of a sudden - so quickly that Gottfried might almost have doubted all he had seen - the goat's deformed shape shimmered back into Christoph's blue-doubleted form, a smile on his lips. Yet Gottfried did not know if he was relieved to look upon the obscene vision no longer, or whether it was worse for Christoph to seem himself, knowing that the familiar stocky body and lively face were but a lie stretched thin over the foulness beneath.

"Well, let that be as it may," Christoph said. "But as for me, I know exactly what manner of woman is best suited to my liking." He turned to Eva, rising from his seat. "Frowe Eva von Bärenberg," he said formally. "Will you marry me?"

Gottfried heard Margerite's soft gasp of surprise; though Eva's face was a little blurred in his sight, he could see her blue eyes widening and her mouth falling open in shock. Behind Christoph, Georg's scarred face twitched, as if he were battling manfully against an outcry - or a gush of tears; though he seldom thought of such things, even Gottfried could hardly have failed to notice Georg's passion for Frowe Eva.

Kobolt dug his claws hard into Gottfried's leg, so that the knight almost cried out. As well my hose are dark, or the blood would ruin them, Gottfried thought absurdly, as if his mind were clutching at any straw to turn it away from what he had just heard. To keep his hand from grasping the gold crucifix at his throat, the knight forced himself to lift a slice of capon with the tip of his little eating-dagger, bringing it to the bread-trencher he and Arnmut shared and beginning to cut it methodically into pieces. Christ protect her! Gottfried prayed.

Eva covered her mouth with her hand, the black gem on her finger swirling a strand of darkness through the air as she moved it. She giggled prettily, and Gottfried saw the pink stain brightening on her cheeks.

"O, Christoph," she said modestly, "I hardly know what to say, for I am yet only a maiden. I have neither father nor mother to advise me, and my cousin Wachholt is far from here; I do not know what I can bring to Burg Fürstensee as a dowry. For myself, I would gladly say yes, but it is not fitting for a woman of my station to come to her husband with nothing. Yet I shall write to Wachholt and tell him of your proposal, that I may take on my inheritance and let myself be betrothed to you in proper fashion."

Well-done, Eva, thought Gottfried. It was dawning on him that he might have underestimated the young woman's wit; her giggles and flirting and frivolity made it easy to think of her as no more than a well-bred ornament - but he did not know that he could have thought so quickly, faced with such a cruel dilemma. Buy as much time as you may, and let us pray Christ that Father Etienne sends help for Christoph before you can no longer put off your vows - or have to deny the man you love, as well as the thing cloaked in his flesh.

"Aye, that shall be well-done," Margerite said quickly before Christoph could argue. "After all, if you wed Eva, she shall be Gräfin here someday, and you would not have folk say that your marriage was in any way unseemly. I know that you will gladly wait for her, as you love her and she you; but when two of such high birth wed, there is more to be settled than in the marriages of lesser folk."

In Gottfried's blurred sight, Christoph's tongue suddenly lolled huge and black from his mouth, flopping down to his chest and curling up in a gesture of contempt. Christ be thanked that Eva cannot see as I do! thought Gottfried. If she could, she would never let Christoph within a bowshot's range of her again; and that would be a victory for the Devil, that this evil destroy a portion of two innocent lives.

After the capons' light succulent meat - of which Gottfried,
though he felt a little foolish doing it, had given Kobolt
a fair share from his own portion; despite the pangs of
hunger in his shrunken belly, he had little appetite left now,
anyway - the servers brought out dishes of steaming brown
Mawrochen, little cones of chopped calf-lung fried and
stuffed with a filling of herbs and raisins, still strung along
their thin spits.

Beside the Mawrochen came pastries of minced venison,
also mixed with raisins and spread on coloured dough,
then rolled up into little scroll-like cylinders. Gottfried was
quite fond of both dishes, but he would not look away from
Christoph, lest the demon think that its foul seemings had
daunted him.

"Why is our knight staring at me like that?" Christoph
asked the Gräfin in a loud carrying whisper. "My sleeves
can't be dripping, since we have had no soup yet."

"But there is a bit of chicken on your doublet," replied
Margerite at once. "Let me - there!" She dabbed quickly
at Christoph's chest with the tip of her napkin. Abashed,
Gottfried turned his eyes away: through his childhood, he
had been chided for his fixed stare, but he could no more
keep from doing it than he could tell a hare from a small dog
across a wide field. Yet at least, he thought, it was the demon
who had given in first rather than himself.

Gottfried glanced at his trencher just in time to see the
clawed black paw snagging one of his Mawrochen, dragging
it off the table. Before the knight could worry about the
greasy morsel soiling his silken doublet, Kobolt leapt from
his lap, leaving Gottfried's weight-sore legs greatly eased.

The Mawrochen and pastries were followed by beautiful
hams seethed in wine and baked, with intricate designs
cleverly cut into the thick layer of browned fat over the rich
pink meat. After that came three fine white geese, their
feathered hides sewn back on and their heads tucked under
their wings as if they were merely sleeping; but when the
carver opened them, the savoury scent of roast goose wafted
out, and inside they were stuffed with a mixture of apples
and dried plums and bread dripping with juice.

Gottfried ate sparingly, lest the unaccustomed food make him ill after four weeks of fish and bread; but he was still feeling quite full when the servers at last carried in a great cake baked in the shape of a castle, surrounded by a moat of sour-cherry compote. Fine as the cake looked, Gottfried could not help his unease: the dark sweet sauce around its base, lumpy with cherries that had been restored from their dryness by long cooking, seemed to him altogether too much like a moat of blood with human pieces floating in it; and it reminded him unavoidably of the disquieting skeleton-sweet at Ortlieb's All Souls' banquet and the faintly distorted beauty of her tapestries.

I am merely over-wrought by the...thing that I see in Christoph's seat, Gottfried told himself. There is evil here, yes; but that does not mean that its touch has tainted everything within Burg Fürstensee. If I see all things as evil, it is more likely due to the beam in my own eye. Sweet wine was poured with the last course; and hot spiced wine carried about after that, as the servants took the remains of the castle and the sauce-sodden bread trenchers away to the mysterious recesses of the kitchens and cleared the hall's floor for dancing as the stately measures of a pavanne floated down from the musicians' gallery.

The older knights led their wives out onto the floor; Herr Nikolaus bowed and held his hand out to the Gräfin, and Herr Christoph did the same with Eva, and the higher castle servants followed their example. Gottfried and Arnmut were left with Ritter Ludwig's two daughters, short plump fairhaired girls of thirteen and fifteen, named Hedwig and Johanna, while Georg gravely walked over to the tall thin daughter of Ritter Friedrich von Düsterstein and said, "Please, frowe, will you do me the honour of this dance?"

The pavanne the musicians had chosen to begin with was a simple one, its steps easy for even the most inexperienced dancer to follow; and that was well, for Ritter Ludwig's elder daughter Hedwig was rather clumsy. Gottfried seldom allowed himself the pleasure of dancing, save when it was demanded by the courtesy of a noble hall, not least because he could not keep from a certain pride in his own skill and grace at the frivolous art. God had not given him his agility of body for such things, but rather that he might fight in good cause, yet he could not deny that he found it pleasant to step and whirl and leap with the music, and to feel that he was taking part in something of beauty.

But for courtesy's sake, he moderated his movements, concentrating on little Hedwig so that she would not feel ashamed or overshadowed by her partner, but rather would dance more easily with his skill making up for her lack. Still, when he saw the ease of the Gräfin's movements sweeping blurrily past the corner of his eye, Gottfried could not help looking forward to his own turn to dance with the castle's mistress.

Is there anyone here, save the married men, who is dancing with the partner he or she wishes? Gottfried wondered as he gracefully lifted Hedwig's plump hand and led her lightly down the aisle of dancers. Perhaps Herr Nikolaus is glad to be dancing with the Gräfin; elsewise, the servants outside are more free than we are. For the Gräfin would give whatever were lawful to touch her husband's hand in this dance, as Eva would to have the true Christoph beside her; if Georg had a choice, he would partner Eva rather than that poor thin spotty girl; I would choose the woman who is the best dancer...

I know not who Arnmut would have chosen, though perhaps one of Ritter Ludwig's daughters would be in his mind after all, especially if he wishes to stay at Burg Fürstensee...After the pavanne, the dancers all changed partners: though there was no law ruling the matter, everyone there knew the right order of rank, so that now Gottfried was to dance with Ritter Ludwig's wife Irmintrude.

Though short, Irmintrude was a massive woman, who Gottfried did not doubt outweighed him by more than double; but for all her size, she was surprisingly light on her feet, as though her bulk cloaked a deceptive amount of strength. Gottfried had danced with her before, and found her a pleasant partner, so long as he did not have to lift her up and whirl her about, as some dances called for.

The music that struck up now was the same tune of Gaudete that had been played earlier outside - a carol ring-dance: outside, the minstrels had led, but such dances should have a leader singing the verses in the middle as the circle of dancers sang the chorus, and Ritter Dieter called out, "Let Herr Christoph lead!"

"Aye, Herr Christoph!" Ritter Ludwig boomed in agreement.

Gottfried was too far away to make out the look on Christoph's face clearly - at least, thank Christ, he kept his own shape as he answered, "No, I am no singer! I will gladly yield my place to another." Because you fear to speak the name of Christ, Gottfried thought.

Then, to his surprise, Arnmut spoke up, saying, "Ritter Gottfried sings well; let him lead this carol."

"Let him, indeed!" other voices took up, and Gottfried found himself being pushed into the middle of the floor as the dancers formed a ring about him, singing, "Gaudete, Christus est natus ex Maria Virginae..."

"Tempus adest gratiae hoc quod optabamus," Gottfried sang: At this time of grace and longed-for blessing... "Carmina laetitae devote reddamus." Love faithfully offers songs of praise. As the dancers replied, "Gaudete, Christus est natus..." Gottfried stared straight at Christoph. Hear these words and fear, demon! the knight thought fiercely. For Christ was born to break your Master's power over men: you cannot bear His name, and must flee before His might - may you go back to Hell, to trouble Christoph no more!

As Gottfried began the next verse, the words ringing clear and loud from his mouth, it seemed to him that he could no longer hear the music. Instead, it was as if he were surrounded by a great swarm of buzzing voices, distorting his own voice in his ears so that he could only know that he was keeping tune by the feeling in his throat; and it was harder and harder for him to draw breath through the choking stench of shit and rotting blood, while his skin stung and prickled as though he wore an undershirt and hose stitched together from nettle leaves. Yet he did not falter in his singing, nor would he let the joy of the words in his heart falter.

"Deus homo factus est natura mirante," he sang: In this wonderful birth God is made man... Herr Christoph's features writhed like wax melting in the fire; it seemed that his head turned about on his neck to show Gottfried an obscene second face at its back. The blood burned in Gottfried's cheeks, but he did not miss a note of the carol: "Mundus renovatus est a Christo regnante."

The world is made new by the kingship of Christ - and you have no place here, demon: go forth to the realm of torments and sorrows that God has ordained for you in your rebellion, and trouble Christoph no more!

"Gaudete, Christus est natus," the dancers sang, their voices coming clearly again over the fading gibber of mad voices. "Ex Maria Virgine..."

Suddenly Christoph stumbled, his hands tearing free from Margerite's on one side and Eva's on the other. He pitched forward, measuring his full length on the floor at Gottfried's feet.

Can he be...? Gottfried wondered. Christ, by Your power, let it be so! He knelt by Christoph's head as the circle of dancers broke, the music staggering to a halt. "Herr Christoph, in Christ's Name, can you hear me?" Gottfried asked softly.

"Get back, get back," the castle physician, Ernst, said, waving his hands fussily at Gottfried. "Get back at once and let me see to him!"

Gottfried put his hand on Christoph's thick brown hair, though the heat pouring from the young lord's head almost scorched Gottfried's palm. "The powers of Hell shall not prevail, for Christ is King here, as in Heaven," he said.

"Pray somewhere else, for Christ's sake!" Ernst the Physician snapped at Gottfried, slapping at his hand. Gottfried's anger flared at the rude touch: from another knight, it would have been cause for challenge. He stopped his hand before it touched his sword-hilt, but Christoph was already stirring and groaning, then pushing himself up with a faint effort at his old cheerful smile.

"This is what comes of eating and drinking well at a feast, then dancing in a warm hall," he said. Gottfried's heart beat swiftly with sudden hope: was Christoph freed?

Christoph waved his hand at his guests. "I am well enough - go on, start another dance. I only need to sit a little to recover my strength, and then I shall be back among you. Gottfried, help me up."

Gottfried took Christoph's hands in his, heaving the other man to his feet. Christoph draped an arm about his shoulder, and Gottfried supported him towards a bench.

As Christoph was about to sit, his arm tightened, dragging Gottfried in closer; Gottfried felt the hot moist breath on his ear, and smelled its carrion reek, like the breath of a bear or wolf sniffing at a sleeping man to see if he might be prey.

"Come with me," Christoph whispered, and again Gottfried heard the low gibber of voices echoing the words, until they rang distorted and incomprehensible from his skull. "I will give you what you really want, what you dream about at night when you wake with wet sheets...a big cock up your tight little arse, or filling your prudish little mouth with a spurt of seed, isn't it? I can see your dreams and the thoughts you hide from yourself; I know what makes your prick stand, and why you cannot bear to be parted from pretty Arnmut for a moment."

Sickened with disappointment, horrified by the demon's obscene words, Gottfried jerked away so fast that Christoph staggered and almost fell, catching himself on the bench just in time.

"Your master is the Father of Lies, and the source of all corruption," Gottfried answered under his breath. "But Christ has power over him and over all your kind. In Christ's Name, leave this innocent man, and trouble him no more."

Christoph laughed softly. "Aye, and would the Lord of Fools give me leave to be here, if Christoph were innocent? You do not know how rotten the depths of his soul were, or why his flesh makes such a fitting home for me."

"All men are tainted by the sin of Adam," Gottfried replied steadily. "And all men are redeemed by the Blood of Jesu Christ Our Lord: where He is called on, you have no dominion."

Again Christoph laughed. "You think so? Even in Avignon, where the Pope of Idiots mouths and prances in the name of the Enemy..." He broke off suddenly, looking over Gottfried's shoulder.

"Move aside, now," Ernst said testily, bustling up close as
though he would shove Gottfried away, though he did not
quite dare to touch the knight. Saddened, Gottfried realized
that there was no more he could do: the thing that still
dwelt within Christoph's body would not show its nature for
the physician to see, and would be warier of the Christmas
singing than it had been before.

Gottfried did not have the heart to rejoin the dancing,
and the rich feast-food pressed dryly on his stomach like a
tangle of sticks and straw. Instead he slipped carefully out,
walking into the courtyard. The merriment was still in full
swing there, though the snow was falling harder, hissing into
the bonfires and gathering on the hoods and shoulders of
those who danced and played and gulped hot wine against
the chill. Pulling his own cloak tightly about him, Gottfried
managed to slip through the throng unnoticed and out
through the open gates: he felt that he could not bear to be
around other folk, with the crushing weight of his failure still
aching in his body.

But you are not an exorcist, nor even a priest, he said
to himself; and in his mind, it almost seemed to him that
his thoughts took on something of Father Etienne's dry
French-accented tone. There is no need to reproach yourself
on failing to drive out Christoph's demon, when you know
nothing of how such things are done.

Yet if my faith had been stronger, might I not have
succeeded? Or if Ernst had not broken in, when the demon
revealed itself to me through Christoph's mouth at last?

There is no way to know what might have been, Gottfried
replied to himself; and again, it almost seemed that he
could hear the comforting tones of Father Etienne's voice. It
remains only to keep faith, and trust in God to work His will
as He chooses.

Beyond Burg Fürstensee's walls, no brightness lightened the heavy gray of clouds and falling snow; Gottfried could only hear the faintest echoes of the merriment inside the courtyard now, so soft as to be almost a memory. His boots sank deep with each step; though the villagers' trampling feet had beaten down the pathway to the castle earlier, the snow had thickened again, so that Gottfried seemed to be walking on a road that had never been trodden by humans before. Against his will, his mind turned to what the demon had said to him.

But how can a spirit of darkness know my dreams, when I cannot remember them myself? the knight asked himself. Yet his thoughts trembled with uncertainty: how could he deny the demon's lies, when he could bring up no sure truth to counter them with? There was nothing unseemly in his love for Arnmut: how could two men who had endured what they had together, so that they owed life and joy to one another, not be the fastest of friends, nor dread the thought of being parted? And yet, while waking, he had never been stirred by lust for a woman: had he mistaken the worse sin for God's grace, and thought himself blessed where he had been abandoned?

A deep bark startled Gottfried from his thoughts. His head jerked up; he stared hard through the blurry curtain of falling snow, searching for the hound...did wolves bark? Gottfried had no fear of wolves, for though he was unarmoured and the cold winter was wolf-weather, his sword was by his side and he knew that wolves seldom attacked a man who stood up to them bravely.

After a few moments, Gottfried made out a large gray shape ahead of him, though he could not tell yet whether it was wolf or dog. He drew his sword carefully beneath his cloak, but made no gesture of threat - if it were a hound, it could be no peasant's guard-dog: such a beast could only have escaped somehow from the Burg Fürstensee kennels, and it was his duty to bring it safely back.

"Come!" he called softly. "Za, za, come here!"

The gray hound trotted a few steps towards Gottfried, and he saw then that it was a fine mastiff - very much like his beloved Etzel, long-legged and deep-chested, with a broad muzzle and powerful jaws. It was still too far for him to recognise, if it were one of Heinrich's hounds; but he had been gone a long time, and there was no telling what might have been added to the kennels in his absence.

"Come, come," Gottfried crooned, resheathing his sword and crouching down with outstretched hand. The mastiff came closer, gray tail wagging, but stopped just beyond arm's reach. It barked once more, then turned and began to lope away slowly, halting and looking back just at the outer edge of Gottfried's vision.

Gottfried followed the hound, calling to it. Once in a while it would stop again to let him get close, but never so close that he might grasp its collar - if it had one; he did not see the spiked links that protected a hunting hound's throat about its neck - or fasten his fingers in its thick fur.

After a time, the gray mastiff's trail wound into the woods, beneath snow-frosted dark pines and clumps of leafless trees whose bare branches were coated with a thorny fur of ice-crystals. Gottfried did not know how far he had gone, but it was growing harder for him to see through the falling snow and gray twilight; the snow-thick air was blurring his sight oddly, so that now and then it seemed to him that he saw the wooden walls and slanting thatch of a hut dark from the corners of his eye, but when he turned his head to look, he saw that he was looking at nothing but twilight trees standing where they had grown for hundreds of years, perhaps since the first days of the world.

Ahead of him, the mastiff barked joyously, and Gottfried heard a muffled voice answering it. He hastened on as quickly as he could through the knee-deep snow: the owner of such a hound must be worthy of coming to guest at Burg Fürstensee, and no one should be travelling alone in such a storm, least of all on Christmas Day.

Coming closer, Gottfried saw a small lantern's light gleaming through the snow and gathering dark, and the shadows of the dog and a cloaked figure...and a little wain, with a black shaggy pony standing head-down between its traces. Gottfried knew that he should be cautious, for there was no telling who might be travelling through the woods since Heinrich had been struck down; and indeed, it seemed to him that his chilled skin prickled with the slow crawling of half-sense danger. Yet he did not slow down, nor did he yet lay hand to sword.

"A joyous Weihnacht to you," Gottfried said as he drew closer. Now he could see the cloaked figure more clearly: shorter than himself, and bent, it seemed to be a ragged old woman. She was as ugly as any peasant-hag Gottfried had ever seen, with a long jutting hook of a nose curving down towards her long pointed chin; gray whiskers sprouted here and there along her lips, her wrinkled face was lumpy with warts and carbuncles, and shaggy tangles of gray hair hung raggedly out of the edges of her hood.

Her brown cloak was patched in so many places that it seemed to have been sewn from an hundred mismatched pieces. But the mastiff barked and frisked about her lovingly, and Gottfried reminded himself that charity was no less praiseworthy given to the ugly than to the fair.

The old woman hawked and spat violently at Gottfried's greeting. "Indeed, it is not!" her cracked voice declared. "The axle-pin of my wagon is broken, and I have a long way yet to travel before Twelfth Night. And where will I find a new axle-pin here, I ask? Are you the man to carve it for me?"

Gottfried almost replied sharply to her that he was no peasant carpenter, but a knight of noble blood. Yet he had repented of his pride that very morning; and had Christ himself scorned to do a carpenter's work?

"I may not do as well as a man who knows more of such things, old mother," Gottfried said courteously. "Yet I have a knife, and I am willing, and surely there is no shortage of wood here. If you will not scorn my poor efforts, then I shall carve you a new axle-pin as best I can."

The hag held her lantern up, looking closely at his face. "There's a good man," she muttered. "Well, here is the broken piece; see what you can do to match it."

Gottfried looked closely at the cracked pin, then asked the loan of the old woman's lantern so that he might find a piece of wood that matched it closely enough. She would not give him the light, but she held it for him as he searched through snow and fallen branches, stamping heavily along behind him.

By the time he had finished fixing the hag's wain, Gottfried's hands were so numb that he no longer felt the sting of the bad cut his slipping knife had sliced deep into the web of his shield-hand - an eating dagger meant to carve good meat in a hall was not the best tool for shaping a wagon's axle-pin. Full dark had come now, the snowflakes still drifting down to gleam white in the sphere of brightness around the old woman's lantern.

But the replacement part fit better than Gottfried had hoped. "I think you can go on safely now, old mother," said Gottfried. "But tell me, where do you mean to spend the night? If you wish, I can see to it that you are given food and a good night's lodgings at Burg Fürstensee, for I know that Gräfin Margerite would never turn away one in need, least of all in weather like this and on Weinachtstag."

The old woman cackled, tossing her head back. "I can see to my own lodgings, young man. But it is good of you to ask, all the same. Now, what will you take for your wages? Poor men want money, but you, Herr Ritter, need none; women, I might help in childbirth, but that shall do you little good."

"I helped you because it was my duty as knight and man and Christian," replied Gottfried. "I need no repayment; but if you would do something for me, then I ask only for your prayers, for I have a dangerous journey ahead of me, and a great foe even in the burg which I call home."

The hag lifted up her lantern again, staring hard at Gottfried's face as if she were as short-sighted as he. "Aye, you have the look of one who does battle with grievous enemies. For all your noble birth, I think you are no stranger to simple meals of herring and dumplings; and you have the wisdom to ask for that which few know how to value." She bent down, scuffling through the snow where the chips from his carving had fallen.

It seemed to Gottfried that it was one of those chips she picked up; then she pulled back her tattered brown cloak to reveal the full-spun distaff thrust through her belt, unwinding a length of linen thread and biting it off before she knotted it securely about the end of the chip and tied it into a long loop above. "Take this for your payment, then, and wear it with my blessing - if it is not too poor a thing for you, Herr Ritter."

Gottfried bowed his head, letting the old woman put the rough necklace she had made about his neck. "I would scorn no gift that is given with the blessing of a good heart, old mother, and I thank you greatly for it. But are you sure that you will not guest at Burg Fürstensee this night? For it is dark already, and very cold; and the village innkeeper is likely to be up at the castle with the other folk, so that there is no saying what manner of lodgings you will find."

It was hard for Gottfried to tell what the hag was thinking: the wrinkles and lumps of her face distorted every twitch of her lips into something strange, and the huge wen above her eye made it look as though she were constantly squinting. Still, he thought that there was something like astonishment on her hideous visage.

"It is not often that those I meet think on my needs so. Fear not, my good Ritter: I know where I am going, and need no guesting on the way - least of all in a castle where such evils haunt, and only the least servants know my name."

"Will you tell it to me, old mother?" Gottfried asked politely. "For myself, I am Ritter Gottfried von Schlangenbad."

"And I am known here as Perchte Iron-Nose, though you will have little luck if you ask after me. Now be on your way, as I must be on mine. Though the night has grown dark, the road is straight: follow it back, and do not turn from it for any cause, and soon you shall be back at Burg Fürstensee."

"Farewell then, Mother Perchte, until we meet once more." Gottfried helped the old woman up into her wain, and the mastiff leapt up beside her. She picked up the whip on her seat, cracking it once; her dark shaggy pony began to walk along the trail.

When the hag's lantern had faded into the distance, Gottfried turned around. He could see nothing in the darkness now, but he walked straight ahead, following the path blindly; and after a time, he saw the glow of the bonfire through the open gates of Burg Fürstensee, with the shadows of dancers black before it.

I have missed the daytime Mass, Gottfried thought in alarm. Yet - I did a deed of charity: I hope that Christ will not hold my tardiness against me for that. Numb-fingered, he touched the crucifix at his throat; though his hand was too frozen to feel it, he heard the clink of old Perchte's gift against the gold. It did not sound like wood, and when he drew nearer to the fire, he saw that the old woman had given him a wedge-shaped chip of stone with a groove scored round it beneath the knotted linen thread.

Another man, perhaps, might have taken the dirty bit of rock from his neck then - after all, Perchte was gone, and there was no risk of offending her now. But it seemed to Gottfried that he should wear it as a reminder of how close he had come to succumbing freshly to the sin of pride. And wherefore should I not bear a lady's token for the sake of charity, which is itself the love of Christ, rather than the secular love in whose name other knights carry a woman's favour? In charity and humility I won it; in charity and humility I shall wear it.

"There you are, Gottfried!" Arnmut said, his light voice warm and relieved. "I had been about to mount up and go looking for you, for Jochanan said he had seen you going out the gate, and I was afraid you had lost your way in the snowstorm." The young knight was leading his horse by the reins; Gottfried knew he could have expected no less of Arnmut, but he found that he was touched anyway.

"I stopped to help an old woman whose wain was broken," Gottfried replied. "I asked her to come back with me, but she would not - she said that her name was Perchte Iron-Nose, and she had a long way to travel yet before Twelfth Night."

It seemed to Gottfried then that Arnmut's blue eyes widened, and in the firelight, he thought he saw the pink cold-flush on the young man's cheeks fading. "Did she give you any token for your trouble?" Arnmut asked.

The question was so strange that Gottfried did not reply with the lecture he might have given, but lifted the chip of stone hanging about his neck. "This, and her blessing. But why should you ask? Surely you do not think I would have taken payment for helping an old woman in need?"

"Of course not," Arnmut answered hastily. "It is only...
no, nothing. Tales that I heard as a small child, and the
stories peasants tell in the long winter nights, nothing more.
When I was very little, my nurse used to frighten me with
stories of a hag named Perchte Iron-Nose, who would take
out my entrails and fill my belly with twigs and straw if I
were not good, or if I did not eat a good dish of herrings and
dumplings on New Year's Eve. And when our castle's roof
creaked in the snow and wind, my older brothers said it was
Perchte stamping up there, so that I would hide under my
blankets and not make a sound until morning."

"It is hardly a surprise if the woman I met were called
after such a spook, for she was remarkably ugly," said
Gottfried thoughtfully. "But I saw far worse sights earlier
this day - no, Arnmut; as you love me, do not ask about
that."

Arnmut took Gottfried's frozen hands in his own gloved
ones, then drew in his breath. "You are wounded!" he
exclaimed. "There is blood all over your hand - should you
see Ernst the Physician?"

"I would sooner trust myself to Jochanan's care again. But
I only nicked my hand with my knife, in any case; it is not
even worth bandaging."

"Well, stay here by the fire. I must put my horse back, and
then I shall get you some hot wine...You left your goblet in
the hall, but I brought it out for you." Arnmut's sweet smile
flashed fleetingly in the firelight, then the fair-haired knight
led his horse back towards the stables.

It was then Gottfried realized that the demon's lies had
done him ill after all. He could not help wondering if the
blurred faces about him were staring at himself and Arnmut,
if other folk were thinking what Christoph had spoken
aloud, about why Ritter Gottfried and his former squire were
almost never apart, and the tender care Arnmut showed
for him. Perhaps I should speak to him, lest...No: I will not
poison his mind as mine has been poisoned. As for what
others think, why should we care about it, so long as our
consciences are clean before Christ?

Gottfried walked over by the wall to scrub the blood off his hand with a palmful of snow. His fingers were prickling painfully now as the chill went from them, the deep slice between left thumb and forefinger burning as though it had just been cauterized - it was dripping blood again, Gottfried noticed, and he pressed it hard against the dark wool of his cloak to stop the bleeding before Arnmut saw and insisted that he have the cut sewn up.

"Here, drink this," Arnmut said when he came back, holding out a steaming goblet to Gottfried. "It is wine, but Jochanan gave me a little of his aqua vitae to put in it as well, and said that he would bandage your cut to be sure that it gives you no trouble tomorrow."

Gratefully Gottfried sipped at the hot drink, letting his friend lead him over to the knot of Bear's Paw men who stood laughing loudly and passing a flask around.

"Went through them like butter through a hot knife, we did," Paul was declaiming at the top of his lungs, to the sound of more raucous laughter.

"That's the other way around, Hauptmann," someone else said. Paul ignored him, blithely going on with his tale as Arnmut tapped Jochanan's shoulder.

"Here he is," Arnmut said.

Jochanan took Gottfried's hand, looking at it and shaking his head. "You were lucky you didn't slice a tendon; you could have been crippled, you know. Come with me."

The gunner led Gottfried and Arnmut to the building where the Bear's Paw had been temporarily billeted, stopping to light a few candles so they could see their way among the tangle of packs and pieces of armour. Gottfried shook his head at the untidiness - he would never have tolerated it among the men he led - but said nothing.

Jochanan had a bed to himself at the far end of the building, set at some distance from the others. Gottfried wondered at that a moment, for the Bear's Paw men had never shown any mistrust of their lieutenant on account of his religion; but then he thought that even with Jochanan's guns mostly left behind in the wains, he might not want to sleep too close to the baggage of a man whose business was making things explode fatally.

"Sit down here," Jochanan said, gesturing towards his bed before he began to rummage in one of his packs. "This will hurt."

He brought out a small silver flask, uncorking it as he held Gottfried's wounded hand tightly. Looking at the slight injury again, Gottfried had to grant that perhaps it was worth bandaging: he had not realized that the knife had gone in deeply enough to slice a good-sized flap of flesh nearly off. He gritted his teeth as Jochanan poured the stinging liquid on the wound and Arnmut asked curiously, "What are you doing?"

"This will help keep the wound from getting the rot. At least he has bled all the dirt out - Ritter Gottfried, will you let me stitch this up?"

"It is hardly worth so much trouble," Gottfried said indifferently. He was more than a little light-headed from the fortified wine Arnmut had given him...far more than a little, he realized; he was actually dizzy from it, though he had not even half-emptied the goblet. The candle-flames were beginning to spin in his sight, his ears humming with a sound like the rising drone of pipes. As if from very far away, he felt his goblet's stem slipping from his fingers, and heard the faint crash of it striking on the floor together with Arnmut's cry, "Mother of God!" Then the blackness whirled up about him, taking his thoughts altogether.

Gottfried could feel warm hands clasping one of his own in a firm, pleasant grip - am I dead? he wondered. Is this Christ, or an angel, holding on to bring me through the darkness? He tried to speak, but his mouth seemed numb, and he could make no sound.

"Gottfried," a man's light voice said urgently. "Gottfried, wake up! Please, Gottfried!"

Though it seemed as hard as rolling a great boulder off his body, Gottfried opened his eyes at last. He saw that he lay stretched out on his back with something propping his feet up and a heavy blanket over him. His doublet and shirt had been taken off, though he was still wearing hose and shoes. He could see the candlelight flickering along the shadowy thatch above him, and he still smelled the stink of a winter barracks - the candles had hardly burned down, he discovered when he turned his head; he could not have swooned for long. Arnmut was kneeling by his side, chafing Gottfried's uninjured hand between his own to warm the icy fingers; it must have been he who had spoken.

"Are you all right, Gottfried?" Arnmut enquired anxiously. "How much blood did you lose?"

"Hardly any," Gottfried told him, his voice gruff with embarassment. Was he now to be thought so weak as to faint from a small cut to his hand? he wondered.

"Can you move your arm easily?" asked Jochanan.

"It is healed entirely, and has given me no trouble."

Jochanan shook his head, his heavy features grave. "I have seen such swoons come on men who have been gravely wounded - especially when their injuries are within the body and not easily seen, as may happen if a man is struck hard enough with something heavy - and sometimes they never awaken: the heart races to exhaustion, and then falls tired and stops. I could find no bruises on you, but are you sure that nothing ill has befallen you?"

Gottfried could not say that: he still could not drive the slimy touch of the demon's whispering from his ear. He could only say, "I give you my word that I have suffered no greater hurt of body than this one little cut today."

"No greater hurt of body," Jochanan mused, rubbing at the shiny ridge of scar tissue beneath his close-cropped black beard. "That makes me think that you have taken some other hurt - an injury of the soul, perhaps?"

Gottfried found that he could not meet the Jew's dark eyes straight-on, and turned his head uncomfortably away.

"Be easy," Jochanan urged. "There is no one here who does not wish you well, Herr Ritter. But such things are better spoken than locked away in the heart, just as a wound is better opened and cleaned than sealed above and rotting below."

This man is an ally of Father Etienne, Gottfried reminded himself. And...he is a skilled healer.

Slowly, his voice sometimes faltering, Gottfried told Jochanan and Arnmut of what had befallen him in the hall. He left out only the details of what the demon had said to him: he would not foul his own mouth or their ears with such things.

"You were very brave," Jochanan said at last, "...and very foolish, to try to face down such a spirit alone and untrained."

"Aye, you were brave," agreed Arnmut, his fair face softened by his look of awe. "And...when Herr Christoph fell, I guessed...I hoped...that your prayers might have driven the demon from him. But I could not tell afterwards, for he seemed just the same as he has always been, even as he did before. And I thought you had gone to the church to pray, so I would not disturb you; I did not realize you were not there until I missed you at Mass. Gottfried, I...I am sorry if I failed you." His fingers tightened about Gottfried's hand.

"You did not fail me," Gottfried answered gently, returning Arnmut's clasp. "I was sick at heart because I had not freed Christoph, and I wanted to be alone for a little time. Had I needed help, I should have called sooner on no living man."

Jochanan took Gottfried's other hand, feeling at his wrist. "Your heart is quickening and strengthening again, so I think you are in little danger now. But I will tell you some words of wisdom: when working in the realms of spirit, at least try to find someone who knows what he's doing before you get yourself in too deeply for anyone to get you out. I know these are words of wisdom," he added, smiling, "because Rebbe Avram was a wise man, and he said them to me quite often. Now I think you should rest here while I sew your hand up and bandage you, and then you should go to your church and pray, and after that you should go to bed, because you are exhausted and we all must rise early tomorrow. Ritter Arnmut, I know I can trust you to see that Ritter Gottfried does what is best for him."

Arnmut favoured the gunner with one of his brilliantly sweet smiles. "Of course you can." Again the evil thought crept into Gottfried's mind: does Jochanan, too, think..? But he did not withdraw his right hand from Arnmut's grip: the little pinpricks of the needle piercing his skin, and the faint grating feeling of the thread drawing through it, were nothing to Gottfried, yet he was cold as if he had just come up from deep water, in spite of the heavy blanket over him, and he held to his friend's hand as if Arnmut were, in truth, the angel of deliverance he had fancied him to be in those first vague moments of awakening from his swoon.

# Chapter Five

Margerite, Eva, the two knights, and the riders from the Bear's Paw company mounted up in the frosty cold before dawn. The storm had passed; the stars glittered like chips of ice in the black sky, and the breath of riders and horses puffed white against the lantern-lit darkness. The roads were too bad for them to take a wagon, but there were a good number of heavily laden saddle-horses standing patiently in the outer bailey.

Margerite rode beside Eva, with the Ritters Gottfried and Arnmut flanking them. Five of the Bear's Paw men, including Paul, went before them; the rest rode behind. Although she knew she was riding into deeper danger at Avignon than she suffered at Burg Fürstensee, Margerite could not help the lightening of her heart as she rode out through the castle's outer gates, as though she were passing from beneath a heavy cloud. She wondered if Avignon would be like Freiburg - she had never seen a bigger city than that, but the place where the Pope and his Curia dwelt must be magnificent. The Order stands high there as well, Margerite reminded herself, but even that could not damp her tingling anticipation.

Eva seemed light-hearted as well, her smile flashing in the lantern-light. For travelling, she had braided her golden hair into a wrist-thick plait down her back, and her gloved hands held the dun palfrey's reins with more ease than before. "I am glad to be off," she said suddenly. "I had forgotten how free it feels to be on the road, and how cramping it is to be cooped up in a castle - I could almost wish that we were in Merlin's wain again."

"I would forego that gladly," Margerite answered, her voice dry. "I remember the fleas and lice and chicken-mites, and how cold and damp it was to sleep underneath the wagon in the rain."

"Aye, but..." Eva's voice trailed off, and she looked out into the darkness as if seeking words to explain what she felt. But she needed none: Margerite also remembered clearly how she and Georg had laughed and played like siblings born under the Welshman's genial eye, how Eva had delighted in the unladylike pleasures of hammer-lifting and knife-throwing and selling doubtful relics to Italian pilgrims. She was doing very well as Margerite's charge; but when her cousin sent her to the convent, he had robbed her of the most vital years of youth, that short time between childhood and taking on the burdens of a noble frowe. "Wouldn't it be funny," Eva said suddenly, "if we were to meet Merlin on the road again? He did say that he often travelled to Avignon."

"He would have said that he often travelled to the far side of the moon if he thought anyone would believe him," Margerite answered, but she could not quite make her voice as sharp as it ought to be: she had to admit that time had softened her annoyance at the Welsh rogue, leaving a certain fondness behind. And - she would not mention it to Eva, lest the girl get wrong ideas from it; but it had been Merlin's advice on using a knife, in the end, that had helped her to kill Ortlieb in their death-struggle. "Still, should we meet again, I might buy him dinner at an inn for old times' sake."

After a little time, the gray of dawn began to spread slowly over the sky, the stars fading beneath its light. Gray gave way to pale pink-gold and blue, until at last the sky was all bright with morning, and the Sun's first rays shone from the untouched white snow about them. In the clearer light, Margerite noticed that Gottfried's left hand was not gloved, but wrapped up in a swath of bandages. And he had spoken briefly with Christoph and left the hall swiftly afterwards...

"Ritter Gottfried," Margerite said bluntly, "how were you injured?"

"I sliced my hand cutting a piece of wood," Gottfried answered, frowning harshly as he stared straight into her face. Margerite would have taken that look amiss from anyone else; but the brilliance of the light on the snow blurred her own sight a little, and she could imagine how hard it made seeing for the proud young knight.

"I hope it is not serious?"

"No more than a scratch, but Ritter Arnmut and Jochanan insisted that it be sewn and wrapped so that it would not get in my way on the journey."

Margerite thought that Ritter Gottfried must have hurt himself quite badly to have agreed to any doctoring for his wound, but it was not her place to say so. Instead she gave her gray gelding a little nudge with her far leg to move him towards Gottfried's brown stallion. "I saw you speaking with...Christoph," she murmured. "What passed between you then?"

To Margerite's surprise, the knight's bony cheeks flushed fiercely and he looked down. "The demon made...an obscene suggestion to me," Ritter Gottfried mumbled, then, "I fear for Georg, who must sleep alone with him. Frowe Gräfin, is there aught we can do for the boy's protection?"

"I have already done it," Margerite assured him. "And I have made sure by...other means, that it will cause no harm nor fear to Georg, so you may be easy in your mind on that score." Then the fullness of what Gottfried had said sank into her mind. "How did the demon come to reveal itself to you? It should have been commanded..."

Looking down at his horse's neck, Gottfried told her swiftly of what had passed between the two of them when Christoph fell during the carol-dance. Margerite could not help feeling a twinge of jealousy. Without any knowledge or training, Gottfried had come closer to driving Azruzor out of his stolen dwelling than she had with all the lore she possessed; and she had failed in her own strength, whereas only Ernst's unknowing intervention had kept Gottfried from finishing the work he had begun.

But he is pure of heart and faith, and I gave up that innocence when I chose to deceive the Order, Margerite reminded herself. Then the corollary thought came to her: Ought I to offer Gottfried such teaching as I can give him? Between his sight and his strength of will, he could become a great magician.

Aloud, Margerite said soothingly, "You did very well, and you are not to blame that it happened in a crowded hall, where you could not keep on without betraying the whole matter." For she could see that Gottfried was ashamed, as if he thought his failure to exorcise the demon came from his own weakness.

"Thank you," Gottfried replied. "With God's help, it may be yet that I shall have a second chance to be the instrument by which Christ frees Christoph from his tormentor - and by God's mercy, I hope that Christoph will remember little of what was done in his shape." Two red spots burned feverishly on the high arches of his cheekbones; Margerite's mind went back to the way that Christoph had taunted Gottfried and Arnmut.

The 'obscene suggestion', and Gottfried's worry about Georg...If that is indeed Gottfried's vulnerability, Margerite thought, then he will be in grievous danger if he must face Azruzor, or any other such spirit of darkness again. It is the way of demons to tell hidden things when they will shock and harm, and if Azruzor knows that Gottfried will flinch away, then he will be able to distract him easily during an exorcism. She was surprised that she was not more horrified by the thought that Gottfried might be subject to unnatural affections; but after what she had read in the Black Book - after, Christ help her, learning of the rite by which Ortlieb had won the ring she now wore on her own hand - there was no room left for shock in her mind.

Perhaps I am becoming more of a Light-Bearer than I thought, if I can think of such things only in terms of what they will mean in a battle of spirit. For a moment, Margerite clearly saw Bernhardt as he had been - as Bertram the Free Soldier, commanding the worst of men and forced to judge their evils in similar stark terms: what would help his Company in battle, and what would have to be dealt with lest the lust for plunder or rape or slaughter endanger them after a victory. O Bernhardt, my love! If only you were here to aid me...Her eyes burned as if she had been staring at the dazzling snow for hours, and a swift-chilling trickle of water dripped down her face when she blinked.

Yet I must deal with Gottfried as best I can. If only he were easier to speak to about such things...perhaps it will come more gently to him from a woman's mouth.

"Demons have power over men through their weaknesses - most of all, those things that are unknown or denied," Margerite said. "If you mean to measure yourself against Azruzor again..."

"That is its name?" Gottfried asked fiercely.

Margerite nodded. "Its name is Azruzor, and it is a Duke of Hell, a demon of much power. Such spirits can...see into the thoughts of humans, and smell out where they are vulnerable." She thought of telling Gottfried of how the demon Damiano had summoned had appeared to her in Ruprecht's form - obeying her command, but in such a way as to distress her more than if it had shown itself in full Hellish horror.

Gottfried's angular face had gone pale, and he crossed himself. "And...are they able to tell the truth? Surely the Father of Lies can have nothing but liars in his Infernal Host?"

"They can tell the truth," said Margerite slowly. "But whenever they do, they tell it in a twisted way, whatever they think will hurt the hearer most, so that virtue becomes weakness... or the beauty of love becomes an ugly and obscene lust."

"Christ forgive me," Gottfried whispered, crossing himself again.

If I were truly a Light-Bearer, and he my pupil, Margerite thought, I should have no mercy on him now: for his own sake, I should force him to face whatever it is he fears within his soul, that he be able to armour himself against the twisted truths of Hell. And...I think Father Etienne would do the same for me. But the difference, of course, was that Father Etienne knew better what Margerite could bear than she knew of Gottfried; while the Order of Light-Bearers held that those members who lacked the strength to hold up under the harshest testing were not worth having.

"Christ forgives all men," Margerite told the knight. "And unless I am much mistaken, you have less to be forgiven for than most." Still, she could not help wondering if Gottfried and Arnmut...but if so, there was no unwillingness in the matter. The more she thought on it, the likelier it seemed to her. Azruzor, hiding his cruelty behind Christoph's habit of teasing, had said, 'Father Michael is always eager to perform weddings, but I do not think even he will be willing to marry the two of you'; and that, it seemed to her, was not too far from the mark, for Arnmut cared for Gottfried as tenderly as Ruprecht had ever cared for her while she was carrying...

His child, and no other's, Margerite said firmly to herself, cuddling Wolfram's blanket-swathed form a little closer under her cloak. Then, And what manner of example am I for Gottfried, I who seek so hard to deny what frightens me above all else? What would I do, if Azruzor bowed before Wolfram and hailed him - truly or falsely - as the Son of his Master?

"I have tried to do my best," Gottfried answered thickly.

"If Christ were not with you," Margerite told him, "how then could you have come so near to exorcising Christoph's demon by the mere singing of His holy Name? You must not doubt the strength that is in your faith; but if anything Azruzor said disturbed you more than it ought, then I would counsel you to think carefully on it. Had you been wounded in battle," she added, "would you not consider how you had gotten your hurt, and practice countering such blows so that another would not take you unawares?" Margerite was guessing now, but she could remember the men practising in Burg Falkenstein's courtyard during the siege, and the rough words of advice Bertram had shouted at them.

"That is wise counsel," Gottfried admitted. "Indeed, that was just how Ritter Ludwig taught me: by striking me with a blunt weapon, so that my bruises would show where my defense was weakest."

"If you need to speak of the matter," Margerite went on, "I am willing whenever you are ready."

"I thank you, Frowe Gräfin," Gottfried said. He looked straight ahead then, and after a little time of silence, Margerite let him be.

As they rode over the border between Heinrich's lands and Wolfram's, Margerite held her son up so that he might look about himself. "All this is your own, my Wolfram," she crooned to the babe. Wolfram gurgled happily, a tiny hand waving pink from under his blankets, as if he were already gesturing in command. Someday there would be armed men following such a wave of his arm, or perhaps noble companions watching in respect as he grandly showed off the expanse of his own lands. Margerite and her company guested with Ritter Sigmund that night. Thietmar had let the border knight know that the Frowe Gräfin would be there, and Ritter Sigmund had prepared a good feast for her: roast pork with apples, a rich stew of beef cut up in red wine, spiced with garlic and a little precious pepper, and blue trout baked with a pudding-stuffing of breadcrumbs, almond milk, and tart verjuice.

Margerite was barely able to keep from looking under the table for Kobolt, in hopes that she could catch him before he leapt up and tried to steal a trout off the platter - but perhaps he would stay away from the hall: he had stuck his head out from under her cloak and sniffed the air as soon as they came in the gate, making the chirruping mews that most often suggested that he had scented a female, then leapt down from her horse and run towards the stables. If she were lucky, he might be at his tomcat-business all night, and she would not have to apologize to Ritter Sigmund in the morning for the smell in her chamber...

"Is there any other thing you would wish, Frowe Gräfin?" the blond knight asked respectfully.

"This will do very well for me," said Margerite, looking at the various pieces of meat and fish on her stew-sodden bread trencher. "But I thank you for your care, Ritter Sigmund."

"Nothing is too good for our Gräfin and the young Graf!" Sigmund declared, wiping a few crumbs from his blond moustache with the back of his hand. "Ah, when Graf Wolfram is old enough, you should send him here for the boar-hunting. Before God and St. Hubert, I swear I have never seen such a year as this for wild boar! Scarce two weeks went past that I was not called out to see to one beast or another that was ravaging the villagers' gardens. If only Graf Ruprecht had been here...pardon me, Frowe Gräfin," the old knight said hastily, seeing the look on Margerite's face. "I did not mean to bring you sorrow by my careless words. I know that young Graf Wolfram will be just such a hunter as his father was: already his eyes have the hunter's keenness, and he looks so like to Graf Ruprecht that he might almost be his father come again."

Margerite murmured something - she did not care what she said, so long as it took Ritter Sigmund to another subject soon. Perhaps he took the hint; at any rate, he soon turned to asking if she had any news from afar. "I know that you were cloistered," he said. "But from all accounts, you had a long journey back, and you might have heard tales on the road."

Margerite told him what she knew, though that was little enough. Sigmund had heard some of the stories about the Pope's dealings with Bertrand du Guesclin and the Free Companies, and shook his head sadly. "He ought to have called for the Emperor's aid, and hung as many of them as righteous armies could not slay. Not," he added quickly, "that such men cannot be useful given the right leadership. The Bear's Paw did very well for Graf Ruprecht in our war...and I see that you still have some of them with you as guards. You could do worse than giving them a home, for I spoke often with Hauptmann Paul and that other one - what was his name? The gunner..."

"Jochanan."

"Yes, that was it. They are not like some of those other cutthroats; I suppose even a good man may fall on hard times. God's Blood, if I had the money, I'd want a troop that was armed with those Hellish guns myself."

"I would as soon see the Pope declare against them," Gottfried broke in. "Such weapons should not be used against Christians: what is the worth of a knight's life of training, if a common man can shoot him from his horse at a distance?"

"Ah, you were on the other side," Ritter Sigmund anwered genially. "And the same can be said of those longbows the English use so well, or of crossbows; it was a crossbow that slew Richard Lionheart, after all."

"Crossbows were forbidden by the Church for many years, and would God they still were!" said Gottfried.

Sigmund laughed, taking a long swallow of wine from his pewter mazer. "Men will never turn back from a useful weapon, Ritter Gottfried. As well try to put rain back into the sky... but neither you nor I can set the rules of war, so there is no use in quarrelling. Come, have some trout. You hardly seem to have eaten anything at all...or is it," he said, his voice deepening, "that you scorn to eat at the table of a man who once faced you in honourable battle?"

Margerite tensed, for such words could easily lead to swords. But Ritter Gottfried shook his head, his thin tail of dark hair swishing like a whip behind him. "Christ forfend! No: today is Saturday, consecrated to the virginity of Maria, and so I fast altogether for her sake."

"This is a new austerity, Ritter Gottfried," said Margerite. Though Arnmut sat silent, she could not help but notice the drawn look on his face, as though he were deeply worried about his friend but did not dare to speak. "And fasting may be praiseworthy, but you have ridden long and hard in the cold today: because of that, the Church does not even hold you to the Friday abstinence, let alone to fasting on that day or any other, and you certainly should not go beyond what is asked of other Christians in that regard." Especially not when you have already weakened yourself by keeping unnecessarily to the Advent abstinence for a month of hard travel in the snow; one day of feasting is not enough to build your strength up again.

But Margerite did not say that to Gottfried, for she was all too uncomfortably aware of why he was punishing his flesh: of course he would observe the day given to Maria's chastity, if he were tormented by the fear of his own desires.

"I need it for the good of my soul," said Gottfried.

"Eat, Ritter Gottfried," Margerite told him. "It will do your soul little good if you fail in your duty of guarding me because you are too weakened from fasting to swing your sword. I shall not command you against your conscience; but I must remind you of your oath of knighthood, and ask you to do what is necessary that you may be able to uphold it."

Margerite had not even finished speaking before Ritter Arnmut had lifted the last half-trout from the platter to the bread trencher he shared with Gottfried and begun to cut it up for his companion. Ritter Gottfried looked at the younger knight with a peculiar expression of discomfort on his thin face, then pulled the trencher towards himself and started cutting his own fish.

Arnmut's blue eyes widened in shock before his mouth drooped and he looked away. It was clear to Margerite that Gottfried's action had hurt him deeply, and she could not help cursing herself for making her understanding of the matter so clear. But how could they have thought that no one else knew? Or...how could Gottfried be so blind to his own feelings? Surely a man could not reach his age without understanding his own desires? And if that is so, then he and Arnmut could not have been more than friends; for Gottfried's sake, I could almost wish it were otherwise, though that be a sin.

At least Ritter Sigmund seemed cheerfully oblivious to whatever was passing between the two Burg Fürstensee knights. "The food is better here than the last time you came, isn't it? My old cook died a couple of months ago, God rest his soul, and I hired a new man from Freiburg - my cousin who lives there sent him on to me. Are you planning to pass that way on your pilgrimage to Avignon? I shall have to give you my cousin's address, for I know he would be honoured to guest you and your men. And I must say I am most honoured myself - well, everyone is impressed with your care for poor Graf Heinrich. Not many wives would try so hard to petition God on their husband's behalf."

"Graf Heinrich was...is a good man," Margerite replied, an uncomfortable worm of guilt squirming in her belly at Ritter Sigmund's praise. If he knew why...But I am not really such a hypocrite: a Papal Mass may indeed help Heinrich, and, Christ willing, this journey may aid in freeing Christoph - I know Heinrich would give whatever he could to do that, if he knew and understood what had happened.

"And you as well, Frowe Eva," Sigmund went on. "For a young noblewoman to hazard the road in such weather - that is truly worthy of praise! But tell me, how are matters between you and Herr Christoph? The last accounts I heard had you ready for betrothal. And truth to tell," he winked, "when you were here before, I was ready to swear it would not be long before you invited me to your wedding."

Eva smiled at the border knight, then veiled her lips discreetly with a tap of her napkin before she spoke. "Herr Christoph has asked me to marry him," she said. "But, alas, we must wait a little longer, for there are certain matters concerning my inheritance in Bärenberg that need to be put straight before we are wedded."

"Ah, I am sure that will go well enough," answered Sigmund reassuringly. "But let me know when the time has come for your wedding feast, for though I am old, I will be glad to dance your legs into the ground that night."

Though Ritter Sigmund might have liked to stay up drinking and talking with his guests into the early hours, Margerite put a stop to the conversation not long after the evening meal had been cleared away. They would have to rise early and ride hard to reach Burg Falkenstein before nightfall, for this winter trek was not the easy ride that she had enjoyed coming from Ruprecht's castle to Heinrich's that past spring.

Ritter Sigmund insisted on his pages bringing stirrup-cups of hot wine out to bid the riders farewell with. It was a kind gesture, and Margerite was grateful for the heat of the metal cup warming her gloves and the warmth of the drink in her belly, for she had been more than usually sluggish in getting out of her comfortable bed that morning, and had felt chilled since her feet first struck the guestroom's cold wooden floor.

Sigmund said goodbye to each of them in turn, letting Wolfram grasp his finger and tug at his beard when his turn came. Margerite could not help thinking of Bernhardt, who had never shown such affection to her child - but of course, Sigmund has been a father before, and knows how to handle babies; it is hard for a man to learn delight in children from one who is not his own. To distract herself from where those thoughts might lead, she looked at her companions. Eva was puffy-eyed and yawning, for she little liked arising before dawn.

Burg Eichenwald was out of sight behind them by the time dawn began to gray over the woods. Kobolt was still sleeping a deep and contented sleep, curled about Wolfram in Margerite's lap and purring in his dreams: Margerite thought that by the beginning of spring, Ritter Sigmund might find Burg Eichenwald suddenly over-run by black cats.

"Frowe Gräfin," Gottfried said, "I have a favour to ask of you."

"Yes, Ritter Gottfried?"

"As we left too early to hear Mass at Burg Eichenwald, would it be possible for you to ask the Burg Falkenstein priest to say Mass for us this night? I would make Confession, and receive the Sacrament...though," he added painfully, "I am hardly worthy of it."

"None of us is worthy of Christ's sacrifice, Gottfried," Margerite said, trying to make her voice as gentle as she could. "And yet He gave it to us all. You do neither God nor yourself any good by tormenting yourself over words spoken by a demon."

The flush along the sharp lines of the young knight's cheekbones showed Margerite that she had touched precisely on the source of Gottfried's pain. "Even if...there were truth in them?" he asked, his face averted from her, as though he feared to see what her own would show.

"Most especially then," Margerite replied. My poor, virtuous Gottfried, she thought. Though the knight was two or three years older than herself, she could not help the warmth of her maternal feelings towards him: Margerite would be nineteen in February, and yet he seemed so much younger than she! Dear Gottfried, what can I say to help you?

Then Margerite remembered how Father Etienne had spoken to her - was it less than a year ago? So much had happened since, that seemed hard to believe. Be wary of that snare - but, should you fail, beware even more of the trap of despair, which is only pride turned on its head: remember that all men are Fallen, and that Christ's mercy is infinite. Thinking that you are too good to ever yield to temptation is sinful pride; and should that pride be shattered, you will be sevenfold more vulnerable to the ways of the Devil.

"Gottfried," Margerite said. "I know how hard it is to find oneself flawed as are all the other children of Adam and Eve; and you are better than I ever dreamed of being. But Father Etienne told me once to beware of pride in my own virtue, and beware even more of despairing when that virtue should fail: for despair is but the reversal of pride."

Gottfried looked at her. Had she been close enough, Margerite would have reached out to embrace him as she would Wolfram, for her own heart ached with the pain she saw on his face. "I know that I can trust in Christ," the knight whispered. "But I dare not trust myself any longer, for I am not what I thought myself to be."

"That should not be so," Margerite told him. "Even Christ suffered temptation to His measure: why should you not? And as for what you are, or may be - God made you for His own purposes, whatever they may be. Shall the clay say to him that fashions it, 'What makest thou?'"

It almost seemed to Margerite that she saw the water welling up in Gottfried's hard gray eyes at those words. Yet she found herself disquieted by her own counsels: why should the clay not question its Maker? And why should a loving God burden such a man as Gottfried with what the demon had revealed to him?

She could not see Ortlieb's ring on her gloved hand, but she could feel its warmth clasping her finger, and heard, as if it were her own thoughts echoing back from the depth of years past, Why should God have given me wisdom and the desire for more, if I were meant to moulder all my life in a small keep, far from the great of the world? Why should I not use my gifts to their fullest, to win all that I was made for?

And it was by knowledge that Man fell, Margerite answered herself. Yet is knowledge not a good thing, if it is not won by doing evil? Had Gottfried been spared his knowledge now, would it not have endangered him more deeply in times to come? And I - what if I had not pressed Father Etienne, so that he told me of my Order rank and Ortlieb's ring?

"I thank you for your counsel, Frowe Gräfin," Gottfried murmured. "But...do you still want me by you? I can tell that you are greatly troubled by this. If you wish, I shall leave: Ritter Arnmut is well-able to guard you." His last words broke like wood cracking into splinters in his throat.

"I would not have you leave me," answered Margerite. "And it is nothing you have said that troubles me, but what is in my own heart."

The tight look of pain on Gottfried's angular face seemed to ease a little, and his gaze almost seemed to soften into gentleness. "If you would tell me, I will listen as best I may. I owe you no less than you have given me."

Margerite blinked, and it came to her suddenly that,
save for making Confession to Father Etienne, she had not
unburdened her heart wholly to anyone since...Not since
she had poured out all her terrors to Bernhardt before
the Marienbrunnen at Burg Falkenstein, the morning
after Gertrude's death and her own ravishment - the day
Bernhardt and she had made love. After that, there had been
some things she must keep from Bernhardt; some she must
hide from Father Etienne, and some to conceal from Eva.

Of all the folk on earth, the ascetic young Gottfried,
strict in piety and harsh in judgement, was the last person
Margerite had ever thought to find herself confiding in. And
yet I can trust him, she realized. Gottfried will never betray
me, and he sees clearly in the world where I fly as a falcon:
nothing can seem too strange to him.

"I feel...as though I have fallen into water above my head,
and am sinking instead of swimming," Margerite said. She
glanced over at Eva and Arnmut: the two of them had fallen
back behind Margerite and Gottfried, and were riding close
together and talking earnestly. The thought flashed through
her mind that perhaps it would be better for Gottfried,
after all, if Arnmut were to devote himself to Eva now, lest
someday the temptation pass his strength... but she realized
that she was grasping at a straw to distract herself. She took
a deep breath, the cold air burning down into her lungs, and
began to speak again. "While I was Ruprecht's wife..."

Once started, the words came out of Margerite in a rush,
like long-dammed water bursting through its earthen seal.
She told Gottfried about herself and Bernhardt, about how
she had taken her role as an Order Princess and her fear
that, without her knowledge or assent, she was becoming
what she pretended to be. Lastly, her voice halting and
tripping over her own words, she told him what none of her
allies, not even Father Etienne, knew: that the Light-Bearers
believed Wolfram to be Lucifer's son - and that it could be
the truth.

Margerite did not dare to look at Gottfried's face as she spoke of that: instead, she stared up at the high thin clouds feathering across the cold blue bowl of the sky. Maria, Queen of Heaven, let him be merciful to us, Margerite prayed silently when her voice fell still at last.

Gottfried drew in a long slow breath, letting it out on the frozen air in a narrow white plume. "I am ashamed to have troubled you so," he said quietly. "Your trials have been far worse than mine."

"I do not think sorrow can be weighed out on a scales," Margerite answered. "What may seem the least of things to one can be, to another...far too much to bear." Then, at last, as if in telling him her secrets she had dug out a great weight from the midden-heap of her soul and was thus able to reach a little farther beneath it for the bravery she needed, she asked him the question that had lurked in the depths of her mind since she first learned of his sight: "Gottfried - what do you see when you look at Wolfram?"

"What do you mean?" Gottfried asked, and she thought the young knight was honestly puzzled.

"I mean...I know that you see what is hidden. You saw Christoph's demon as it is..." Margerite could not go on, as though the burden of her unspoken words was far too heavy for her tongue to bear. But Gottfried's sharp-angled dark brows drew together, then lifted again as he realized what she had meant to say.

"I have never seen Wolfram as anything but a fair and bright-eyed babe," Gottfried told her. "Yet...once by his cradle I caught a fleeting glimpse of a tall man, fair-haired and with a little beard, and on his finger burned a red flame such as the one I saw on Ortlieb's hand - and on yours," he added slowly. "This was two nights before we reached Burg Fürstensee; and the man vanished before I could speak to him."

Margerite bit her lip. She had told no one, not even Father Etienne, of the apparition of Graf Günther; yet Gottfried had described him well enough.

"Who is he?"

"Do you remember Graf Günther von Hohenfels?"

"I saw him from a distance when he first came to Burg Falkenstein, but I was not close enough to see his face. Was he, too, a member of the Order?"

"One of its Princes," Margerite confirmed. "And he...is allowed from Hell sometimes, I do not know how, but at times he is able to come to Wolfram in the night."

"May Christ protect us!" Gottfried said, crossing himself. "Frowe Gräfin, do you wish me to keep guard over your son's sleep hereafter?"

A terrible, unworthy thought came to Margerite then: *Knowing what I know of Gottfried, how long can I trust my son to him?* Even before the words were fully formed in her mind, she was bitterly ashamed of them: she knew that Gottfried would chop his own sword-hand off before he would bring any harm to Wolfram, or betray her trust in him. "Yes, save that I know not how it might be done without arousing gossip. Though I would trust my soul to your honour, I know too well what others would make of it if they saw a young man in my chamber at night."

"If need be, I shall stand watch outside your door," Gottfried answered. "And perhaps that were best in Burg Falkenstein, where Graf Günther was slain..." He stopped, a look of confusion coming over his narrow face. "But Graf Günther was killed by bandits on his road home, was he not? I do not know why I said that."

"He was killed in Burg Falkenstein on the night when Wolfram was born," Margerite said bluntly. "Heinrich and the Bear's Paw saw to the rest of his men, and to disposing of the remains so that there would be no questions asked."

Margerite saw the knight's sudden comprehension brightening like dawn in his deep gray eyes. "So that was why Graf Heinrich was so anxious about Bertram leaving as he did! I thought," Gottfried added bitterly, "that I had the Graf's trust."

"It was your virtue he feared," Margerite replied. "He feared that you would think the less of him, if you heard what had taken place. But Father Etienne slew Graf Günther to keep him from carrying out a baptism of Hell; and there was no other choice left to us."

"But if you knew what he was, then why did you not bring the matter to the Church, as Ortlieb's sorceries have been brought to the notice of the Inquisition?" Gottfried asked.

Again Margerite remembered Father Etienne's words to her: this time, how he had told her of the need for secrecy in their doings. And Gottfried was as surely in need of those teachings as she had been, for she knew that he was too straightforward to realize that seeing what others could not put him in as much danger from the Inquisition as herself, with her black cat and her chest of magical tools. Just as Father Etienne had explained the matter to her then, she explained it to Gottfried now, and was gratified by his slow nod of understanding.

"So...aided by unknown allies, we do battle in secret with a host against whom we can call for no help from those whom they would conquer or destroy," Gottfried said, the corner of his thin lips quirking up wryly. "That is no easy thing; and yet what knight could turn away from such a combat?"

Now I should ask if he would learn what I can teach him, Margerite thought. But she found herself reluctant: what text, save the Black Book, did she have to give Gottfried? Much of what she knew came from that foul work - how could her teaching not be tainted? Better, she decided, if she left Gottfried's education in magic to Father Etienne: she had seen how admiringly he watched the French priest since the rite of protection they had performed in the White Cockerel before doing battle with Ortlieb. Yet was that because..? No: I see the demon's cunning now. And if its words have already overcast my mind, what must they be doing to Gottfried? Instead she said, "Bravely spoken, Ritter Gottfried. Would you bear my favour in this battle?"

Gottfried's gray eyes widened. Then he shook his head respectfully, the cold winter sunlight flashing from his open-faced bascinet. "I bear a lady's token already." He fished about beneath the chain-mail hanging down from his helmet, bringing out what looked like a grimy wedge of rough-chipped stone on a linen string. "This was given me for the sake of charity and humility: I need no other favour. And - forgive me if I misspeak, Frowe Gräfin, but it seems to me that you are more a companion-in-arms in this hidden war of ours than a lady in need of a champion."

I think I have just been paid the highest compliment Gottfried has ever given a woman in his life, Margerite thought. Aloud she said, "You do me a great honour, Ritter Gottfried. Christ willing, we shall ride to victory together."

"Christ willing, may it be so," Gottfried replied devoutly.

The thin cloud-feathers blew quickly over the heavens as they rode; the upper airs seemed to thicken and curdle through the afternoon, and by the time Burg Falkenstein crested on its peak against the horizon, Margerite could see the dark anvil-clouds billowing in. Though Wolfram should have been well-used to long riding by now, he was growing more restless, struggling and squirming in his mother's arms, and Kobolt, balancing on the saddle's high pommel with all his claws digging deep into the dark leather, was lashing his tail and glancing wildly about, his long fur rising in the cold wind as if the least stroke of a finger would strike sparks from it. Eva had dropped behind Margerite again; now she banged her heels against her palfrey's side, rocking back and forth in the saddle to urge it on a little faster. The small dun ignored her steadfastly, but Margerite halted her gray gelding with a light tug on the reins and shift of her seat, waiting for the girl to catch up with her.

"I am glad we are nearly there," Eva said, shivering dramatically and glancing up at the rising storm-clouds. "This is no place to be lost in a snowstorm."

"What do you mean by that?" Margerite asked dangerously. All afternoon, she had been trying to thrust thoughts of Ruprecht from her mind; but whenever her thoughts wandered a little, she found herself cocking her head as if to catch the sound of a far-off hunting horn on the wind.

"Why, it would be dangerous to ride blindly near a steep cliff such as the one behind the castle," Eva said, her pretty face smooth and innocent. "There are many rocks hidden under the snow on which a horse might stumble and fall, and it would be easy to ride straight over the edge at night in a raging storm - what else should I mean?"

You know full well what you mean, Margerite thought. If she had thought Eva had spoken maliciously, she would have said it aloud; but she could feel her own nerves stretched like the thin gut strings of a lute, ready to vibrate at the least gust of wind.

"I am glad we are close to Burg Falkenstein as well, anyway. Pray God, Thietmar stopped here long enough to make arrangements for us: I must confess that I will be very grateful for a warm fire, a draught of Glühwein, and a soft bed - and Berthe's cooking, even if it is no match for Liutbirg's."

Eva giggled. "I much prefer sitting at table and being served to scraping pots and eating leftovers, however finely-made they are. But I suppose it is as well that I served in that kitchen: when I am Gräfin in my own hall, I shall know what to expect of my cooks and when they are only making excuses for themselves. I wonder," she added thoughtfully, "if I will be able to hire Liutbirg's apprentice Kunigund away from Schloss Niederwald. However sharp her tongue may be, I doubt Bernhardt would be willing to let Liutbirg go, but Kunigund is young and will have learned her mistress' trade by the time I have reclaimed Burg Bärenberg for myself."

Margerite raised an eyebrow, wondering if Eva's words meant that she had, after all, given up her hopes of marrying Christoph. I could not blame her if that were so, though it would be a sad thing. "Burg Bärenberg?" she asked carefully, trying to keep her tone as light as she could. "Not Burg Fürstensee?"

"We shall see," Eva replied darkly. "It may be...well, never mind."

Margerite thought of how close to Ritter Arnmut Eva had ridden for most of the day, but forebore to say anything: Gottfried was well within earshot, and she had no wish to grind salt into his fresh-bleeding wounds.

The snow had not yet begun to fall when they reached the gates of Burg Falkenstein, but the clouds hung dark and low, and Margerite could hear the ominous rumble of far-off thunder.

"Hail and welcome, Frowe Gräfin!" one of the guardsmen shouted from the top of the gate-tower - Margerite was sure she knew his name, but she could not bring it to her mind straight off. "You men below, open the gates: our frowe is home!"

The Bear's Paw fore-riders reined their horses to the sides as the castle gates swung open, letting Margerite lead the way over the bridge across the defensive ditch. Here Ruprecht's Knappe Wolfram took his death-wound, she could not help thinking as her horse's hooves clattered on the ice-slick wood. The snow was just so thick in this courtyard as Bernhardt and I ran across it to find Paul and Jochanan, racing for Eva's life...Margerite drove down her memories, greeting the gate-guards courteously as they bowed and grinned. "Stable these horses warmly and feed them well, for they have been hard-worked of late," Margerite ordered. "Is Ritter Wilfrid within?"

"Aye, Frowe Gräfin," a guardsman said. "We got news two days ago that you would be coming, and I hope you will find that all is to your pleasure."

Margerite was surprised at how small Burg Falkenstein seemed to her now. She had remembered it as a huge castle, at least the equal of Burg Fürstensee, if not quite so grand as Schloss Niederwald. But now she saw that, though greater than the border keep in which she had grown up, Burg Falkenstein was barely two-thirds the size of Heinrich's castle, most of its tiny windows not filled with lead-edged diamonds of glass, but simply shuttered against the rain and snow. Yet Ritter Wilfrid had done well in keeping the castle Margerite had given into his charge.

Despite the bad weather, not a shingle was out of place on the roofs; the doors of the outbuildings had been freshly painted not long ago, and clean paths had been shoveled through the snow of the courtyard. The gate to the herber, too, had been either repaired or replaced lately. Margerite had to admit, indeed, that Ritter Wilfrid had kept Burg Falkenstein more carefully than Ruprecht, or even she herself, had done. I chose well in him, she thought. As soon as Margerite stepped indoors, Wolfram began to wail loudly, and none of her rocking and shushing could quiet him.

"Hush, Wolfram, hush," Margerite crooned to her babe. "You are home in your own castle now, you are home and safe, and I shall feed you soon. But please be quiet!"

Kobolt and Kriemhilt writhed purring about Margerite's legs as she ascended the stairs that led to the great hall, so that she almost had to shuffle her feet to keep from tripping over or kicking one of the cats. With each step, more memories came back to her: she almost felt that she was drowning in the past, as though she had not let time dull the events of her first year of marriage, but only ridden away as she would ride away from a pool; and now she had leapt back in again, to find the water biting as freshly cold against her skin as before, and the ground sinking away to unfathomable depths beneath her feet. She almost expected to see one of Ruprecht's great gray mastiffs trotting ahead of her - but of course the faithful hounds had gone behind their master: she had seen to their burial herself.

Ritter Wilfrid was, as the guardsman had promised, in the hall. Out of courtesy, Margerite suspected, he had left the seats that had been Ruprecht's and hers once empty, standing up from his own place at the high table to greet her as soon as she walked in.

"Frowe Gräfin!" the curly-haired knight exclaimed, bowing low. "We are honoured to have you - and the young Graf, of course - back with us."

"I shall undoubtedly be coming back more often as Graf Wolfram grows: it shall be good for him to know the lands he will rule when he comes of age," Margerite replied, raising her voice so that Ritter Wilfrid could hear her above Wolfram's wailing. "I do not mean to be discourteous, but my son is still too young to know where he is, and I must see to him at once. Are my old chambers ready for me?"

"They are indeed, Frowe Gräfin, and I called your old maidservant Rose back from Tiefensee so that she might see to your needs. Rose!" he shouted.

Gerhild's niece hurried into the room, curtseying to Margerite. "I am yours to command, Frowe Gräfin," she said breathlessly. She was still wearing one of the woolen dresses that had been Margerite's once, though she had grown a little plumper and must have let it out at the seams, and her dark hair fell down her back in a long torrent.

"I must go to my chambers now," Margerite said. "Herr Ritter, please excuse me - but I do not doubt that my companions will be grateful for your hospitality. As for myself, I would count it a kindness if you would send hot Glühwein up to me."

"Whatever you wish, Frowe Gräfin," Wilfrid said, bowing once more as Margerite and Rose left.

"I am glad to see that you are well, Frowe Gräfin," Rose said as soon as they were out of the hall. "How are matters in Burg Fürstensee?"

Margerite frowned. She had not wished to speak of it - but after all, Rose had been there when Christoph's demon revealed itself first, and borne herself bravely. "No better," she said at last.

"I am sorry to hear it, frowe. Tell me...now that you have returned from your retreat of prayer, will you want me to serve you again?"

Margerite glanced sharply at the girl, but Rose's gray-green eyes were innocently wide: though she knew that Margerite had been searching for Father Etienne, she gave no hint of having guessed at anything more - though, with Gerhild as her aunt, she must have some idea that there was more going on. But she is discreet, and was a good maid; and though I have one girl at Burg Fürstensee, I can easily use two to see to my needs.

"If you are minded to travel, I would have you with me on this journey to Avignon, and keep you at Burg Fürstensee afterwards," Margerite told her.

Rose's smile lit her triangular face, and she paused on the staircase to curtsey to Margerite again. "I would be delighted to serve you as you will, frowe."

As Ritter Wilfrid had promised, Margerite's chambers were warm and freshly strewn with rushes, the pleasant scents of lavender and rosemary and fresh linen hanging in the air. A large wooden tub stood in the middle of the room, though there was no water in it yet. "I shall see to your bath whenever you wish it, frowe," Rose said. "The Ritter's wife Gudrun said that you would be likely to want hot water after travelling three days in the snow."

"That was well-done of her. I shall share my bath with Eva." Margerite hesitated only a second over her next words: as long as Gottfried and Arnmut had slept in the same chambers and bathed together, she had no right to separate them, and she would not hurt Gottfried more by suggesting that he was morally unfit to stay with his former squire. "And see to it, as well, that the knights Gottfried and Arnmut have a bath of their own after dinner. They are accustomed to staying in the same room, as Ritter Arnmut was Ritter Gottfried's squire until just lately..."

"I think I remember Arnmut from Burg Fürstensee," Rose said with a little giggle. "Was he not the handsome squire to that knight who disliked Bertram so?"

"That is he," Margerite said uncomfortably.

"Arnmut was always very kind to me - he was the favourite of all the serving girls," she added, giggling again. "Some of them said it was a great pity he was too shy to coax into a kiss or cuddle. Not me, of course, I would never be so immodest with a man, even a handsome and well-born Knappe."

"That is well to know," Margerite said, her voice stern. "At any rate, Ritter Arnmut was knighted some two months ago...Which of the bedrooms are ready?"

"As well as your chambers, we also swept and strewed and heated Frowe Eva's old room, and...Forgive us if there is anything wrong with it, frowe," Rose added, lowering her voice. "But Ritter Wilfrid and his wife have rooms on the floor below this, where Christoph and Paul the Bear used to sleep, and his two sons are in the chamber that Father Etienne had. And...the only spare rooms are those that used to be Graf Ruprecht's. I pray that does not offend you?" the serving-maid asked anxiously.

Margerite was silent, though her thoughts raced and leapt like hares in March. Ruprecht's room...the staircase to his sanctum...but no, there is nothing left there; Jochanan blew it up, and Richard cleaned out the mess afterwards. But if Ruprecht's soul still lingers...how Mark and Brangæne mourned, the poor hounds, lying on his bed without food or drink till they died...and Gottfried, what will he see there? Even if I say nothing, he will know, just as he knew that Graf Günther was slain in Burg Falkenstein.

"I will see what else we can do," Rose offered. "I know Ritter Wilfrid and Frowe Gudrun would not mind sleeping together for a night if it is your wish that Graf Ruprecht's rooms sit unused, or we could clear the storage chamber where Graf Ruprecht's first wife once dwelt, if you would rather..."

"No," said Margerite. Her voice sounded strange and hollow in her own ears. "No, it will do. As for Paul and Jochanan, perhaps they can be housed in the tower that Jochanan lived in, if it is fit for guests. Now hurry to unlace me, for Wolfram is hungry - and afterwards, you shall tell whoever is priest here now to ready himself for a service, for Ritter Gottfried would make Confession, and we left Burg Eichenwald too early in the morning to hear Mass."

By the time Wolfram was full-fed, the shutters of Margerite's chamber were rattling alarmingly with the wind, and the thunder's soft muttering had risen to a constant deep growling. Rose had made haste to pass on Margerite's orders, so that she was back by the time Margerite was ready to have her bodice laced again. "Father Matthias is already hearing Ritter Gottfried's Confession, frowe," Rose panted. "He says that he will say Mass as soon as you are ready."

Margerite set Wolfram down on the bed, and Kobolt leapt up beside him at once, coiling his tail about his feet and staring at his mistress with unblinking golden eyes. "I shall go at once, then. Keep a close watch on Wolfram to be sure that he does not tumble from the bed - there is no cradle here, is there?"

"Frowe, we took the young Graf's cradle to Burg Fürstensee with us. But if you would rather have him in a cradle this night, and do not mind one in which a servant's babe has slept, I shall see that one is brought up, for the smith's wife has a daughter near to Wolfram's own age."

Margerite pulled the hood of her cloak closely about her face as she stepped out into the storm. The lightning was flickering almost continuously now, the wildly blowing snow flashing stark blue in its brightness. Margerite knew that it was not the icy blast of snowflakes against her face that made her shiver, though the cold struck through cloak and heavy velvet dress as if they were no more than a wisp of mist about her naked body: she knew that she was listening, even against her will, for the sound of Ruprecht's hunting horn.

What quarry would you seek in such a night, Ruprecht? Margerite wondered. Living, he had hunted stag and boar - and once, on that dreadful day when he had executed Eckhardt and all his family for the young guardsman's grandfather's poaching, he had gut-shot the old man and chased him like a deer. Do you hunt men more often now, Lord of the Wood? The clear-shovelled paths across the courtyard were almost gone now, old snow blowing over them as new snow fell.

But Margerite remembered the way to the chapel: she had gone to Mass three times a week while Father Etienne held his services, and even had it not been so - Bernhardt's chambers had been above the chapel, as befitted his post as Hauptmann of Ruprecht's guard: that way she could never forget or miss, though the night had been twice as dark and the footing three times as treacherous. Burg Falkenstein's chapel was well-lit with beeswax candles now: all the effort that had gone into cleaning it when Father Etienne took the place of poor drunken Father Hans had not been wasted.

The small building was warm and dry, and two new statues had gone up beside the lovingly restored crucifix and the image of the Virgin. One, Margerite recognised as St. Hubert at once, for his stag rested at his feet. The other... must be St. Francis of Assisi, with a bird on his outstretched palm and a wolf leaning lovingly against his leg.

Margerite smiled sadly: she could easily guess that Ritter Wilfrid had ordered the saints' statues made in memory of Ruprecht, whom he still knew only as the Graf with whom he had fought in times of war and feasted in times of peace - Ruprecht the hunter, jealous and zealous in his care for his woods and the beasts within them: what better saints to honour in his castle than the patron of hunters and the patron of animals?

Two young boys, one tow-headed and one dark-haired, were tending dutifully to the altar, their white albs gleaming against their black robes; the silver chalice and paten with which Margerite had replaced the dingy pewter vessels Ruprecht had provided shone with the brightness of constant polishing, not so much as the least fingerprint marring their mirror-perfect surfaces. Eva and Arnmut were seated comfortably together at the front of the chapel, their golden heads bent towards each others as they talked in hushed whispers. They will not be a bad match, if matters turn out thus, Margerite told herself.

Ritter Arnmut has little by way of inheritance, but Eva's will more than make up for it. Poor Gottfried, who must watch his beloved go to another and can speak no word of his love, knowing that it is both shameful and sinful! At least Bernhardt and I clasped each others' bodies once; and we always had the knowledge that someday, if Christ willed it, we might be wedded...Margerite touched Bernhardt's signet ring, still nestled between her breasts. It seemed to her that the ring burned as if it had been heated to glowing, sending a fierce pang of pain through her chest.

She knew that she had no right to wear it, since Bernhardt had given back her necklace; and yet she could not bear to put it from her, for to do so would be...to admit that he loves me no more, and will not love me again, Margerite thought. Her hand tightened against her will, crushing the heavy velvet of her dress.

Perhaps, after all, Gottfried was better off than she: at least he knew from the beginning that his love was forbidden - though sodomy was a sin of lust, Margerite was sure that Gottfried was not such a man as to desire where he had not given his heart, whether he yearned for a woman or a man - while she had come close, so close, to being able to cleave to Bernhardt...

Margerite forced her fingers to unclench, pushing away her musing as she walked slowly and deliberately down the aisle. Eva and Arnmut started when they heard her footsteps, jerking their heads upright quickly enough to make Margerite sure that there had been sweet words between them.

"Is Ritter Gottfried still making his Confession?" Margerite asked, keeping her voice low enough not to disturb the holy quiet of the chapel - though she had to raise it more than she would have liked to be heard over the constant rumbling of the thunder.

"Aye, he has been in with the priest a very long time," Eva told her. "I do not know how such a man as he can have done so much to confess in the course of four days, and most of that on the road in the snow! Surely the priest cannot be chiding him at such length over not keeping a full fast on Saturday, when most folk - even pious ones such as yourself, Margerite - do not so much as bother with abstinence."

"I fear that there is something greatly troubling him," added Arnmut. "He fell into a swoon on Christmas evening; I thought he had recovered afterwards, but since yesterday he has been silent and ill-tempered with me, as he had never been before, even when I was a raw young Knappe and made the most grievous errors in arming him. And he says that it is no fault of mine - but he will not let me do him even the smallest courtesy, and when we armed each other this morning and helped each other take our armour off this afternoon, he seemed loath to so much as touch me, or let me touch him. He has always been more modest than most, but..." The fair-haired knight glanced quickly at the stairs leading up from the chapel into the priest's chamber, then lowered his voice more, so that the altar boys could not hear it - even Margerite, no farther away than the width of Eva's body, had to bend close to hear his words over the thunder. "Frowe Gräfin, could Christoph's demon have done him some harm such as would not show at first? And is there anything you can do for him, if it is so?"

Though Margerite kept her face calm with an effort, she could feel herself cringing within like a snail drawing back from the touch of a candle-flame. She could not tell Arnmut what truly ailed his friend - not only for Gottfried's own sake, but if mistrust or loathing suddenly sprang up between the two knights, it would weaken all of them in Avignon, where they must watch each other with the greatest care. Yet the look of pleading on Arnmut's fine-chiseled face wrenched at her heart: he might have been a father begging help for his ill son, or a brother for his wounded brother. Ah, Arnmut, she thought - would you care for Gottfried so dearly, if you knew what it was that distresses him now? Or would you turn away from him in disgust, fearful for your own honour?

"I know that Ritter Gottfried's brush with Christoph's demon troubled his heart greatly," Margerite said carefully. "Even the purest of heart must expect to take some harm from dealing with such spirits of darkness; and thus, I believe, it has been with him." But what counsel can I give that will not lead to the occasion for sin, or burden Gottfried with such contrition that he fasts himself to weakness and death?

The sound of the door opening at the top of the stairs was almost lost in the thunder booming about the chapel, but Margerite saw the light of the candle in Gottfried's hand. The young knight's face was ashen-gray, and he seemed to walk down without caring where he put his feet: had Margerite not known better, she might almost have thought that Gottfried was drunk. O Gottfried, what did you tell the priest? And what did he say to you, that you seem so broken?

Gottfried set his candle down before the Virgin's feet, stumbling to sit down a careful distance from Ritter Arnmut. Father Matthias followed a few moments later: his gray-streaked brown beard, full and long as the beard of a Biblical patriarch in a painting on a church wall, covered most of his face, but his heavy-lined brow was furrowed as if in deep thought - or anger; and his deep-set black eyes glowered like coals in their sockets.

Burg Falkenstein's new priest was a tall and sturdy man, with the heavy shoulders of one who had swung sword and mace before he bowed his head for his priestly tonsure, and Margerite did not doubt that he had answered Gottfried's painful Confession with fierce zeal. Poor Gottfried! If only Father Etienne were with us...

Margerite breathed deeply as Father Matthias' bass voice rolled out through the little chapel, trying to drive from her mind, at least for the moments, all thoughts that did not lead her mind to holy things. But she could hear the wind outside, keening through the crashing thunder. I should not have left Wolfram! she thought in alarm. Not here in Burg Falkenstein, not on such a night...surely Christ would have forgiven me for missing Mass for the sake of watching over my son?

Father Matthias had chosen a passage from Proverbs as his sermon text - whether to please his Gräfin, or for some purpose of rebuke, Margerite did not know. "Who can find a virtuous woman?" he boomed. "For her price is far above rubies. The heart of her husband doth safely trust in her, so that he shall have no need of spoil. She will do him good and not evil all the days of her life..." As the priest spoke, his burning dark eyes fixed first on Margerite, then on Gottfried. "...She considereth a field, and buyeth it; with the fruit of her hands she planteth a vineyard. She girdeth her loins with strength, and strengthens her arms..." Now Father Matthias was looking at Eva and Arnmut together, but his fierce gaze soon turned back to Margerite. "Strength and honour are her clothing; and she shall rejoice in time to come. She openeth her mouth with wisdom; and in her tongue is the law of kindness."

And has it been so with me? Margerite wondered. Maria, help me to be that woman. Suddenly she remembered that it was King Solomon who wrote the book of Proverbs - Solomon the Magus, whose seal bound demons that they might not harm the children of Adam and Eve, and who had dominion over all spirits. May this be a sign of good to come! Margerite prayed earnestly. Though King Solomon is not among the blessed saints, having been born before Christ, yet he was a man dear to God, and rich in holy wisdom - King Solomon, I follow your footsteps in the paths of learning: if it be not blasphemy to ask it of one who is not a saint, I ask that you pray for me, and guide my feet on the treacherous pathways of magic.

"Her children arise up, and call her blessed; her husband also, and he praiseth her. Many daughters have done virtuously, but thou excellest them all. Favour is deceitful, and beauty is vain: but a woman that feareth the Lord, she shall be praised. Give her of the fruit of her hands; and let her own works praise her in the gates." The priest paused dramatically; and as his broad chest rose with breath, the loudest clap of thunder yet burst over them, deafening as the powder-explosion of all Jochanan's guns firing at once.

Margerite jumped; she saw Eva clutching at Arnmut's arm in fright, and even Father Matthias' eyes flickered up in startlement. Only Gottfried did not move: his gaze was fixed upon the wooden crucifix, though the look on his sharp-boned face was not rapturous contemplation, but that of a man who had just lost a leg or arm, staring at the spouting stump where his limb had been and wondering when the pain would start.

Father Matthias recovered quickly, speaking into the stunned silence, "Truly there is none who can compare with the good wife, she who struggles on her husband's behalf, but obeys him perfectly, remembering that God set Adam to lead and govern Eve, and gave Eve to Adam to be his helpmeet. She who prays for her husband, she who does good works for his soul - she is carrying out her wifely duty to perfection. But woe to the man who does not seek perfection of soul through chastity, yet who scorns to do God's will in matrimony! For his sake did God rain fire upon Sodom and Gomorrah, and for him are prepared fire and brimstone everlasting, and the gnawing of the worm that dieth not."

The priest went on in that vein for some time: praising Margerite - though there was nothing of the sycophant in his approval; it was, rather, clear that she had won Father Matthias' favour through her claims of prayer and pilgrimage for Heinrich's sake, and that made her squirm a little against the hard polished wood of the pew, for she knew how false her excuses for her travels were - and, just as obviously, flaying Gottfried with his words.

Deep in her heart, Margerite longed to stand up and tell him that he was wrong: it was she who deserved the condemnation and harsh penance he had doubtless given the young knight, and Gottfried who had earned the highest praises, mortifying his flesh with starvation and his spirit with contrition to deny his sinful desires their foothold in his soul. She could not do that; yet she knew that when the time had come for Father Matthias to offer the Body of Christ to his congregation of four, she would not be able to eat of the Eucharist with a clean conscience.

She had begun her journey to Avignon in deceit, and even Father Etienne, though he understood why she must do it, would have given her a penance for her lies - for sins committed for a good purpose, and out of great need, were still stains upon the soul. Necessity is no justification; and if I were wiser, might I not have found a better way to do what I must?

Thus, when Father Matthias lifted the silver cover from the paten, revealing the five tiny wafers, Margerite alone did not go up to kneel before the rail and receive Christ's flesh into her mouth. Looking at the backs of the other three - Arnmut and Eva fair as brother and sister, Gottfried's dark head narrow and sleek beside them - she felt a desperate twinge of loss, as if there were a great wall of glass barring her out, unseen but none the less uncrossable.

The pain ran through her chest, flaring down her left arm...and catching, burning, on Ortlieb's ruby ring, as if she had held a candle too long to the stone and the metal were taking the heat into itself to intensify into a near-unbearable circle of pain about her finger. Margerite bit her lip hard to keep from gasping at the agony, breathing deeply in through her nose and out through her mouth as she had learned to do from the Black Book. Maria, help me! she prayed. Merciful Mother...

You know that I put this ring on only for Wolfram's sake; you are also a mother, you understand how desperate I am... One by one, Eva, Arnmut, and Gottfried rose and came back to their seats, and slowly the pain in Margerite's hand eased, though her finger ached through the rest of the service: she could not help wondering if, when she were alone and could draw the ring off to look, she would find the skin blistered where the Light-Bearer gold had touched it.

Margerite and Eva, freshly bathed and dressed in clean clothes, came down to the great hall for dinner. The Weihnachten greenery was still up, garlands of pine and holly hanging between the tapestries on the wall and long loops of twisted evergreen branches dripping down from the musicians' gallery above. Ritter Wilfrid had not stinted on the good beeswax candles: their light bathed the hall in a pleasant warm glow that made the howling wind outside and the thick dripping glaze of snow on the window-panes seem very far away.

The musicians were playing a slow soft tune, singing in a language Margerite did not know - English, perhaps, or Dutch. "Lullay, thou little tiny child...Bye, bye, lully, lullay..."

Margerite took her place at the head of the high table; Ritter Wilfrid and his wife Frowe Gudrun, a short plump woman whose brown coils of braids were streaked with a few stains of gray, sat at her right, with Eva, Gottfried, and Arnmut to her left. At Margerite's request, Paul the Bear and Jochanan were also there. She might not have asked that they sit at the high table in another's castle, but Burg Falkenstein was her own, and Wolfram's: there, though Paul and Jochanan might be free soldiers of low birth, the men who had struggled so bravely for Margerite and her son should never be stinted of courtesy.

Margerite untied her silver goblet from her waist, and a servant filled it at once as Ritter Wilfrid stood and raised his own goblet. "To the young Graf Wolfram and our Frowe Gräfin!" he called out. "Thanks be to Christ that they are with us again, and may they often grace the halls of Burg Falkenstein!"

A murmur of approval answered him as the others drank. Margerite waited until they were done, then stood to return the toast. "I drink to the good Ritter Wilfrid and his frowe Gudrun, who have kept Burg Falkenstein in such fine order for its young lord," she replied. The straw-pale wine caressed Margerite's tongue with a light springtime sweetness, flowery and cool, with a faint green tang underneath; she recognised it as Falkenstein's own pressing from the first sip.

Dancing with Ruprecht at Midsummer's, beneath the high-antlered head of the stag...the sweetness of linden-blossoms on the air in the cool moonlight...Margerite pushed the thought away: she knew now that it had been more than desire that had brought Ruprecht to her in the herber that night, striving his best to sire a child at that time of power. And yet, if he had succeeded then...Matters would all have been far different; but it is well not to think too long on what might have been.

The talk turned to usual matters after that. Ritter Wilfrid spoke of how good the hunting had been that year, adding apologetically, "I do not know how long that will last, for I am not the hunter Graf Ruprecht was: he seemed to know every deer and boar in his woods, and tended them, if you will forgive the comparison, like the most careful shepherd with his flock, knowing just which beasts to take and which to let live and breed for another season. Yet I am doing my best to look after the trust you left me for the Lord of the Wood." The knight spoke Ruprecht's title with the greatest affection.

To keep herself from flinching, Margerite said quickly, "Yes, I marked that you had set statues of St. Hubert and St. Francis of Assisi in the chapel. That was well-done, to ask their blessing for the sake of Ruprecht's passion."

Ritter Wilfrid smiled. "If you mean to stay here a few days, Frowe Gräfin, we could perhaps go hunting if you like - or perhaps hawking; Graf Ruprecht always spoke with the greatest delight of your skill with birds, and I bought a pair of fine peregrines just this October. I hope," he added, "that you will not think that too extravagant, but it seemed to me that such a fine mews as Graf Ruprecht had built should not stand half-empty, and I thought that you would find them welcome upon your visits here." Though the little lines of middle age had crept onto the blond knight's eyes and forehead, his square-boned face was open as a youth's, anxious to please.

"Indeed I shall, though I fear that I cannot linger on my way to Avignon, for Heinrich is in such a state that there is no time for me to waste in gaining the Pope's prayers for him. But, Christ willing, when I come back, matters shall be better, and then I shall delight greatly in trying out these new birds."

Ritter Wilfrid seemed about to reply, but just at that moment Kobolt leapt onto the table in a swish of black fur with a huge dead rat clenched in his jaws, blood drooling from its mouth onto the linen tablecloth. Eva let out a small maidenly shriek, and Frowe Gudrun drew back with a look of horror on her plump face.

"Kobolt!" Margerite scolded, picking the tom up, rat and all. "No! Take that away!" She tossed him gently to the floor, where he crouched growling over the body. "Ritter Wilfrid, I am sorry. He has not done that..." Since he was last here, where Ruprecht did not shout at him for bringing dead things to the table, but praised his hunter's skill?

Ritter Wilfrid gave a small laugh, his face fixed in the rictus of a smile. "I had thought that there was hardly a rat left in the castle by now."

"Aye," Kai the Seneschal agreed from his place farther down the table. "Your Kobolt's black brood keep the place well-cleaned; I have not seen so much as a single rat-bite on a stable-boy or scullery maid since I told Berthe to stop drowning his kittens. But such vermin will make their way inside in weather like this, for all the cats can do."

The servants were already crowding around, sponging at the bloodstain with damp cloths. It came out easily enough: linen was always best for covering tables, for it did not stain easily even when red wine and meat juices were spilt on it. Still, there was an awkward pause where none of the diners met each others' eyes; and in that silence of conversation, beneath the warm bustling and fluttering of the servants, it seemed to Margerite that she heard the high cold note of a hunting horn sounded far beyond the castle's walls, the faint pure sound slicing down her back with the chill touch of a blade whose edge was too sharp for pain.

Her eyes flickered down to the floor beside her, though for a moment she did not know what she was looking for. Then she realized, her heart wrenching within her: she had glanced to the spot where the hounds Mark and Brangæne had sat, looking without thought to see if they, too, had heard the horn and raised their heads. It is well that I left here, Margerite thought, chilled to the marrow of her bones. Otherwise...

She could guess easily how it might have been: moving in the same paths she had trodden while Ruprecht lived, listening for his tread on the stairs and putting her hand down absently at meals to stroke the heads of hounds that were there no longer - still wedded to a ghost, and becoming more a ghost herself, day by day, as she dwelt there where every stone was still steeped in Ruprecht's memory. Or watching Wolfram grow into his father's image, in his father's castle, reaching for all those things that had been Ruprecht's, taking hound and hawk and horse as his strength grew to master them, and in the end, perhaps...

Ritter Wilfrid was speaking to her; Margerite shook off her dark thoughts, smiling graciously at him. "I am sorry, Herr Ritter," she said politely. "My thoughts were elsewhere, and I fear I did not hear all you were saying."

"It is no matter, Frowe Gräfin. I only said that the storms have been very bad this year, blowing harder and more often than I can ever remember them before. It is most brave of you," he added, "to undertake such a long journey in this weather - but are you sure it would not be wiser to wait until spring? Outlaws and wolves are at their worst in the winter snow, and after what befell Graf Günther last spring - " the knight crossed himself - "I myself would hardly dare to travel that road without three times the guards that you have brought. The band that fell upon him has never been caught, you know."

To their credit, Paul the Bear and Jochanan showed no sign of startlement at Ritter Wilfrid's words, but Gottfried's thin lips tightened and he looked aside uncomfortably - troubled, Margerite guessed, at having to be party to the lie about Graf Günther's death even by silence. Heinrich did not make the worst of choices in keeping that knowledge from you, she thought; and wondered, also, how well Gottfried would be able to hold up in the maze of deception they must both tread and weave in Avignon. But Ritter Wilfrid was looking anxiously at her, and she had to reply.

"My guard are all doughty men, in whose strength I may trust. And I trust in Christ as well, that He may bring me safely through: for if He blesses this mission, then no power of man can bring it to failure, and otherwise it is wholly vain."

The line between Wilfrid's thick blond brows deepened. "That is nobly said, Frowe Gräfin. Yet for you to ride on such a dangerous way, and take the young Graf with you...Would you not leave him in our care here, so that we may all be sure of his safety, whatever befalls?"

Of course Ritter Wilfrid was worried, Margerite realized: if she came to harm on the journey, then only Wolfram would stand between Heinrich's sons and the lands that had been Ruprecht's. Even without knowing how matters stood in Burg Fürstensee, Ritter Wilfrid had good reason to be concerned. Yes, it would be tempting, to leave Wolfram safely behind when she stepped into the jaws of the Order's greatest stronghold...

But if she did, it might not be long before someone, perhaps a new priest or knight of high repute, or a tutor bearing the best recommendations from noble friends of Ruprecht's, came to Burg Falkenstein; and that man would have a Light-Bearer's ring on his finger. And beyond that... even above the sweet pattering notes of lute and flute raining down from the musicians' gallery, Margerite could hear the howling of the stormwind, and see the cold flashes of blue lightning through the lead-webbed glass of the great hall's windows: she could not leave Wolfram here.

"That is kindly offered, and well-spoken," Margerite replied. "But I will keep my son with me, whatever betide."

Ritter Wilfrid's frown showed that he was not happy with her answer, but she was his Gräfin, and he knew better than to argue further. The servers were carrying out trays of food now. A small wild boar held pride of place, its bristles cleverly replaced by a mane of apple-slivers and its honey-glazed flanks glistening in the candlelight. It was a simple subtlety compared to those Margerite had seen in Schloss Niederwald, but that made the rich scent wafting from it no less mouth-watering.

She could hear the soft rumble of Kriemhilt purring hopefully in Eva's lap, and Ritter Gottfried had not even begun to cut Margerite's portion for her when she felt Kobolt's forepaws upon her thigh and his head butting against her elbow. Jochanan shifted uncomfortably in his seat, and Margerite bit back a sudden gasp. She did not know how closely the gunner kept the laws of his people - but she remembered Gertrude saying, Eckhardt saw him turning down a perfectly good pork sausage.

Ritter Wilfrid could not have helped but hear the murmurs about the Bear's Paw lieutenant; he must know that Jochanan was a Jew, but listening to rumours was one thing and having the matter shoved in his face at table was something else. Even as Margerite thought that, Jochanan rose from his seat, bowing to her and to Ritter Wilfrid. "If you will excuse me," he said politely, "it has come to me that I have certain matters of the Gräfin's guard to attend to. My gunpowder, in such weather..."

"Of course," Ritter Wilfrid said, and Margerite could see the relief on his broad face.

"I am honoured to have such a conscientious guardsman," Margerite added. "Go, by all means, if you must, though I hope you will return afterwards. Even if the meal is done and there is nothing but wine and pleasant conversation left in the hall, I am sure that Berthe will be glad to make up a platter of whatever food you desire."

Jochanan bowed again and departed. Margerite found herself struggling to repress a small ironic laugh: Jochanan's religion, Gottfried's struggles of soul and the tension that lay between him and Arnmut on their account, Eva's doubts about Christoph coupled with her flirtatious nature - it seemed that Paul the Bear was the only one of her close company that did not need to be watched over; and even he would have to be handled with care in Avignon, for Margerite knew full well what manner of reputation the Free Companies had left behind them. Mother Maria, do You ever feel such bemusement when You look at the men and women in Your care, motley lot that we are? Margerite wondered.

For once Maria had been a simple girl, though she had borne the redemption of mankind in her womb; did the Mother of Christ, on Her heavenly throne, think upon the unimaginable grace that had lifted her so high, to become the voice of mercy for flawed humankind before God Himself, or wonder at the many strange prayers of those who had no hope save to cast themselves into Her trust - my own not the least strange among them.

When it came time for the company to bid good night to each other, Ritter Gottfried escorted Margerite up to her room. "Frowe Gräfin, may I come in?" he asked.

Margerite glanced through the door. Rose was sitting cross-legged on the rug, playing with Wolfram and Kobolt. She would serve well enough as a chaperone - and if Margerite asked her to leave them alone for a little time, she would spread no rumours. "Indeed you may, Herr Ritter."

"How the young Graf has grown!" Rose marvelled to Margerite, looking up from her play. "Soon he will be crawling, and then you will not be able to keep him out of anything."

Margerite could not help smiling, though she could not push away the faint sense of unease that always came over her when she thought of her son's slowness to crawl. Then Wolfram sat up, reaching his arms out to her. "Mama come," he said distinctly. "Hun'ry."

"How clever he is!" Rose said in admiration as Margerite bent to lift her son up. Ritter Gottfried stood braced by the door, his thin back straight and rigid, as if awaiting an inspection, but there was a faraway look in his gray eyes that disturbed Margerite.

"Ritter Gottfried, would you wait outside for a few minutes while I feed my son?" Margerite asked, even as Wolfram repeated, "Hun'ry!" and began to cry.

Gottfried nodded sharply, turning on his heel and marching out. Rose hastened to unlace Margerite's bodice so that she could give Wolfram suck.

When Margerite called the knight back in, she noticed
at once how white his face was. But he hardly ate anything
this night, for all I could do within the bounds of courtesy,
Margerite thought: it is not to be wondered at that he is so
pale.

"Frowe Gräfin, I would speak to you alone, if I may," Ritter
Gottfried said without preamble.

Rose looked up sharply, but Margerite did not hesitate in
nodding to her. "Go down to the kitchens and fix me a posset
of hot milk and honey with a spoonful of chammomile,"
Margerite ordered. "Nor should you hasten, for I may be
some time in speaking with this good knight."

"As you wish, frowe," Rose replied, bobbing her head.

The moment the door closed behind the serving maid,
Margerite asked anxiously, "Gottfried, what have you seen?
Are we in any danger?"

Gottfried closed his eyes tightly, his lips thinning into
a single line. "Margerite, I do not know. But this burg is
crowded with shadows: where-ever I go here, it is as if
I must look upon the shades of all that has gone before.
Outside your door, and here within, I saw...the deaths of
which you had told me; and as I bathed in my chamber,
it seemed to me that two dark figures passed through the
room and into the large hunting tapestry that hangs on the
wall, and I could hear their footsteps fading beyond as if
they were walking down a staircase. Even in the chapel -
when I made Confession to Father Matthias in his rooms, I
saw an old man in a priest's robes coughing out his life; in
the chapel itself, it seemed to me that I saw you pouring a
stream of glittering water over a few fragments of bone to
wash them free of some clinging foulness."

I did not tell him of how I blessed the bones of Klingschor
and Kundry in secret! Margerite thought, amazed - no one
knew of that!

"And," Gottfried added, his strong baritone voice unsure, almost childlike for a moment, "even in the chapel, I could hear the sound of a horn blowing, as it is blowing now, though no living man could be abroad hunting in this weather. It has sounded through the evening until I thought it would drive me mad, though Arnmut could not hear it. Margerite, what is it that haunts this place?"

"Memories," Margerite said, trying to keep her voice steady. The Black Book had spoken of such talents: she could not know whether Gottfried was seeing things that had sunken into the very stones of Burg Falkenstein, or whether it was her own thoughts that cast the reflections in his mind. But God had gifted the young knight with sight beyond the usual, and his self-starvation must be sharpening his senses as well: at need, Order members would inflict just such privations on themselves, that as their fleshly ties to earth dwindled, they might grow more sensitive to the realms of the spirit. "Gottfried, if you would not be so haunted, you should eat a solid meal: that will steady you."

"I have no hunger," the knight confessed. "And besides..." The sharp points of his cheekbones reddened... "I have found that to feed one bodily appetite makes the others stronger as well, and that I would not do. Most especially," he murmured, so softly that Margerite could hardly hear it, "when I must share a single bed with Arnmut, who wraps his arms about me in his sleep because he does not know..."

Margerite put her hand on Gottfried's shoulder. She could feel the corners of his fine bones beneath the dark red silk, the thin strands of muscle corded about them like steel wires. She could think of no comfort to give him: she could not have him sleep as a guard in her room, even with Rose there to be sure there was no rumour of impropriety, for that would be a dreadful insult to Ritter Wilfrid. Yet if I had to sleep chastely beside Bernhardt...O Maria, what a cruel burden!

"And I do not think I will find it easy to sleep this night," Gottfried added. "The hunting horn - it is Graf Ruprecht's, is it not?" he said suddenly. His gray eyes widened, the candlelight glistening golden from them.

Margerite gasped, pulling her hand back sharply as though the deep red of Gottfried's silken doublet had suddenly become the dark glow of iron heating against her skin. For a dreadful moment she found herself terrified of him; the look of shock on his narrow face mirrored her own as he realized it. "Margerite, I am sorry!" he said. "I did not mean..."

Margerite breathed deeply, bringing herself back under control. "No, you only startled me. Forgive me: it is not an easy thing to realize that another can know such things." As her heartbeat slowed, she found to her surprise that her curiosity was already overcoming her shock. "Has it always been so with you?"

Gottfried frowned. "When I was very small, it seemed to me that sometimes I knew things without being told them. But when I spoke of them, my father would beat me." He frowned in concentration. "And sometimes, I think, there were words spoken of the Devil, and I was told that I must be vigilant in my prayers."

I wish that Father Etienne were here, Margerite thought. I do not know how to guide Gottfried, nor what dangers his gifts may lead him into. But the French priest was far away, and she would have to do as well as she could. And she knew that her mind had seized upon this as an escape from what they had been talking about.

"That is never bad advice," she said gently. "But as you were saying before - yes. It is Graf Ruprecht's horn that you hear in the wind. Upon his death, Father Etienne cursed him...or blessed him, I cannot say which...to hunt, as he desired to, in his woods until Judgement Day, rather than going forth to Heaven or Hell. And I was glad enough to leave Burg Falkenstein after that."

"If you fear that some harm will come to Wolfram by being here, it would be best that I stay in your chamber to guard, however it may distress Ritter Wilfrid," Gottfried told her. "I would not willingly insult such a good man as he; yet Wolfram's safety, and your own, are more important than courtesy."

"I do not think that Ruprecht would harm his own son," Margerite said, but her voice trembled as she spoke, and it seemed to her that she could hear the words Gottfried would not say: if Wolfram is, indeed, his son.

"Yet you are afraid, and I would not have it so if I can help it," replied Gottfried.

"I think there is little you can do, save ready yourself to leave tomorrow. Sleep as best you can, though I know it will not be easy. And I shall have a platter of food sent up to your room so that you may eat properly this night: that will do more for you than anything else I can do to help. You are weak with starvation as it is, and I very much doubt that one good meal will provoke any unwanted desires in you."

Gottfried flushed again to hear Margerite speaking so directly of the matter, but she went on as ruthlessly as she could. "As for Arnmut, he would not know that anything is amiss with you if you had not grown so cold towards him. He fears that Christoph's demon did you some harm, and is worse afraid that he has somehow done something to lose your friendship; as you care for him, you should not leave him thinking so."

"I care for him...very greatly, and that is the difficulty," Gottfried answered, his voice thick and muffled as though he were speaking through the folds of a heavy cloak. "But had I known, I would have insisted that he go back to his father's burg: better that we had known the sorrow of an unspoilt parting then, than..."

Again it seemed to Margerite that she heard the words Gottfried could not speak: than that Arnmut turn from me in disgust when he finds out what I am, and that his memories of our innocent comradeship be all tainted by his knowledge. And she could not deny that sorrow, not with the memory of the death-stricken look on Bernhardt's face as he unclasped her necklace from his throat and pressed it into her hand - the hand tainted by Ortlieb's ring.

"Go on as you did before," Margerite counselled the knight softly. "What is in your heart is between you and God; but it is not in Arnmut's nature to think ill of you." She thought of how she had seen Arnmut's golden head so close beside Eva's in the chapel, and how they had sprung apart like guilty lovers as she neared. For all the pain it would surely give him, would it be a kindness to assure Gottfried that his temptations were not likely to last, as if she were searing a bleeding wound with white-hot iron?

"Indeed, there will surely come a day when we must part so," Gottfried said, as though Margerite had spoken her thoughts aloud. "Though I would not have chosen Frowe Eva for him...perhaps that is but my jealousy: she is a good woman, and though her birth is far above Arnmut's, his blood is noble enough to be no shame to her."

For all the pain in his voice, Margerite found her curiosity overcoming her compassion - and she had to know what Gottfried was doing, for it might save or betray them in Avignon. "How did you come to think of Frowe Eva?" she asked carefully.

Gottfried looked surprised. "Why, did you not just speak of her and Arnmut bending their heads together in the chapel?"

"I thought it, only: I spoke no word."

"But I heard you clearly!" he protested. Then the young knight paled further, sitting abruptly down on the bed, and Margerite feared that he would swoon. "Dear Christ," he whispered. "What new torment is this?"

Margerite sat down beside him: she did not dare to put her arm about him, but she was ready to catch him if he fell. "No torment, only a gift that you do not yet know how to wield. I have...read of others who could know thoughts thus: if your sight is beyond the usual, why should your hearing not be as well?"

"I shall go to the chapel to pray," Gottfried said. He stood abruptly, then, as though the movement were too much for him, staggered and pitched forward. Margerite was not in time to catch him, but she was able to break his fall and keep his face from striking the stone floor.

The door opened and Rose came in with a steaming pitcher and a goblet on a tray, stopping to stare down at her mistress kneeling on the floor beside the knight's unconscious body. "What has happened, frowe?" the serving maiden asked. "Is he...dear Christ, he did not fall suddenly ill, did he?" The dusting of freckles on her triangular face stood out like ink-spatters in the candlelight: the Death could strike thus, without warning...

"Ritter Gottfried has been fasting long, and I believe that his rigors overcame him," answered Margerite, her voice as stern and calm as she could make it. "Help me lift him to the bed."

In truth, Margerite hardly needed Rose's help: she was no stronger than the usual run of women, but Gottfried's body seemed no heavier than the bolts of fabric she had hauled about Schloss Niederwald at Isabella's sharp commands. The young knight was breathing slowly and evenly, but his forehead was very chill and Margerite did not like his pallor. "Fetch Jochanan at once, and tell him to bring some of his aqua vitae, or whatever restoratives he may have. But go to Arnmut first and tell him to come here now."

Rose bobbed a curtsey, running from the room. It was only a few moments before Arnmut hastened in. His blond hair was disheveled, and he was wearing only a long linen nightshirt. Like all his clothes these days, it seemed a little too small for him, clinging tightly to his broad shoulders and muscular chest, and Margerite could not help thinking,

No wonder Gottfried fears the temptation of Arnmut's presence so, since his desires lie in that direction! She could almost imagine running her own hands over the new knight's well-muscled body, like stroking a magnificent horse or hound, though Arnmut did not stir her as Bernhardt did, or as Ruprecht had.

"What is wrong with Gottfried, Frowe Gräfin?" Arnmut asked anxiously, dropping to his knees beside the bed and taking one of the older knight's hands in both of his. "His fingers are cold as ice, and he looks so pale. Is he ill, or is it... something else?"

"He is faint from too much fasting, I believe," Margerite said. "Ritter Arnmut, you have tended Ritter Gottfried well before: I must put him in your charge again. However reluctant he is, you must make sure that he eats a good meal at least once a day. Otherwise, I fear that he will not make it to Avignon: imagine if we had not come safely to Burg Falkenstein this night, but were forced to camp out in the storm?"

Arnmut, too, paled. Margerite felt a little ashamed of the burden she was laying on him - on both of them, considering Gottfried's feelings - but she could think of no other way to make sure that the ascetic knight did not harm himself in his own zeal of spirit.

As Arnmut chafed one of Gottfried's hands between his own to warm it, and Margerite clasped the other, Gottfried's long black eyelashes slowly fluttered open. "Where am I?" he asked dizzily. "Arnmut?"

"Yes, yes, I am here," Arnmut reassured him, clasping the hand he held more tightly as Gottfried tried to pull it away. "You are in Burg Falkenstein with us; you only fell into a swoon - lie still and rest."

Margerite noticed that there was blood on both knights' hands, and a thick red trickle running from between the stitches that had sewn Gottfried's cut - the wound did not seem to be healing, though it had been several days. Again, as if he had heard her, Gottfried lifted his head slightly and looked at it, then dropped back as if even that slight movement had been too much for him. "It does not hurt, and it has not been long enough for it to be healed fully yet," he murmured, even as Arnmut said, "O Gottfried, I am sorry, I did not mean to hurt you."

"Lie still and be quiet," Margerite ordered Gottfried. "Jochanan will be here in a few moments." And if you can hear me, Gottfried, then say nothing and try to keep your thoughts still.

Whether Gottfried knew what she had been thinking, or was simply too exhausted and disoriented to speak, he kept his silence. It was Arnmut who spoke, saying, "Frowe Gräfin, will that hot posset do him any good?"

Margerite followed the fair knight's glance to the pitcher and goblet Rose had left on the table - milk and honey and chammomile for calming; she could think of little better for a man in Gottfried's state. "Indeed it will."

Arnmut let go of Gottfried's bleeding hand reluctantly, pouring the goblet full. Gottfried did not seem to have the strength to resist as his former squire supported his head with one hand, lifting the goblet to his lips with the other. "You heard the Frowe Gräfin, Gottfried. Drink."

Gottfried's throat moved, swallowing weakly. Margerite thought she heard him murmur, "I am ashamed to be seen like this - what is wrong with me?"

"Too little food, and one shock following hard on the heels of another," Margerite answered.

"Aye, that is surely the case," Arnmut agreed. He paused in thought, his fine-featured face very serious, and Gottfried struggled suddenly to sit up.

"We cannot possibly wait here; the Frowe Gräfin's business in Avignon is far too urgent," Gottfried insisted stubbornly. "I shall be all right: I delayed our leaving from the Bishop's palace too long, and I will not hold the Frowe Gräfin back again."

"Hush, Gottfried," Arnmut said, stroking back a few wisps of dark hair that had escaped from the tight tail at the back of Gottfried's head to straggle over his fine-boned face. "No one spoke of waiting, though I was just wondering if it might not be well. Surely a day or two, while you recover your strength..?"

"I can recover it as easily on the road," Gottfried began. The door opened and Jochanan, a scurf of snowflakes melting into the dark wool of his cloak, came in with Rose behind him. He looked at Gottfried and shook his head.

"What have you done to yourself this time?" the Bear's Paw lieutenant asked. He lifted Gottfried's bleeding hand, then laid his palm over Gottfried's heart. "When did you last eat a full meal?"

"At the Christmas feast," Gottfried answered reluctantly.

"And before that...Not since we left the Bishop's palace, did you?"

Gottfried shook his head. Jochanan picked up his hand, pointing to a stitch that had torn loose from the skin. "Open your mouth." Gottfried did: Jochanan probed his teeth with a finger, then felt along the inside of his cheek. "Are you trying to kill yourself?" he asked, his voice more harsh and angry than Margerite had ever heard it. "Your teeth are loose, and there is a sore beginning inside your mouth; the next symptom will be your old wounds opening and bleeding. You need to lie abed and eat well for a few days; you should not be travelling in the cold in this state."

"I am well enough," Gottfried protested feebly. "I was only overcome by a moment of dizziness..."

Or was he trying to kill himself, in such a way that he need not admit to himself that he was committing the final mortal sin? Margerite wondered.

"Christ forfend!" Gottfried whispered, turning his stricken gaze on her. Blood dripped from his trembling hand as he crossed himself, smeaing his forehead with a stain that was almost black against his white skin. "No, that I would never do, for there is no hope of forgiveness for suicides."

Arnmut dropped to his knees beside the bed, catching Gottfried's wounded hand in both of his own. "Gottfried, be quiet, and do not think on such things," he implored. "You are only tired and weak from austerity, and I fear that your mind is wandering."

But Gottfried looked at Jochanan, a shadow of his usual sternness crossing his face. "It is not fitting for you to speak so of Christians. I know not what the laws of your people may be, but we are commanded that the flesh shall be mortified for the spirit's sake."

Jochanan stared at him, and Margerite realized with horror that the Jew had not said anything: it was clear to her now that the knight could not tell the difference between what was spoken aloud and what was not.

"Gottfried!" she said sharply. "Say nothing more. Jochanan, of your courtesy, bind his hand and then go to the kitchen to ready your medicines - and you, Gerhild, go with him and fetch up some food. Arnmut..."

Arnmut shook his head, golden hair shimmering about his muscular shoulders. "Frowe Gräfin, I beg you, do not send me from Gottfried's side. I have taken care of him when he was worse hurt than this, and it would both grieve and dishonour me to leave him now: did he not just say that he bears me great love, and is glad of my company, even though his weakness shames him? - as it should not," the fair knight added staunchly, "stemming as it does from the rigors of his spirit."

He said nothing of the sort! Margerite thought. And thanks to the Virgin that you misunderstood him.

"But I am only a little faint," Gottfried said, very quietly.

"I wish that everyone would leave me be, for it does shame me to lie here like an invalid, though that was not what I meant." Had Margerite not been looking at his face, she would not have known that his lips had not moved as he spoke.

"Out!" she shouted, in real terror this time, for there was no telling what might be in Gottfried's mind. "You as well, Arnmut. Out!"

Arnmut rose slowly, the look in his wide blue eyes so hurt and reproachful that Margerite almost relented. Yet for Gottfried's sake, she did not dare let him stay.

"I shall be waiting outside the door, Frowe Gräfin," he said, leaving with great wounded dignity. Jochanan bent to wrap Gottfried's wound: Margerite did not know what the young knight was hearing from his mind, but he seemed to dislike it.

As soon as they were alone, Margerite found herself sitting down abruptly, tired as if she had been heaving wine-casks upstairs all evening. "Gottfried, do you have any idea what you were doing?"

"I tried to see whose lips moved as they spoke," he said faintly. "But you know I do not see well, and my eyes seem mistier than usual."

"And your own thoughts...I could hear them as well."

Gottfried crossed himself once more. "Dear Christ. Do you think Arnmut could...?"

"He did. That was why I sent him from here so abruptly."

"Thank you, Frowe Gräfin," he murmured. Though his white face paled further, the knight pushed himself up in the bed. "Is there some art you know through which I might...might keep from doing this? Elsewise I must retreat to a silent cloister, for my presence will endanger you in Avignon, and I cannot go among men like this."

Here it is, Margerite thought. I was unwilling - but he has asked for my teaching, and I cannot in conscience keep it from him.

"Christ be thanked, you do know!" Gottfried said - and again Margerite marked that his lips were not moving. "Yet why are you so reluctant?...oh, I see. I fear the Black Book as well, but if I do not dare it, I must break my oaths to you, and if your wisdom and clean soul could not overcome its taint, I do not think Father Etienne would have given it to you." Then he spoke aloud: it seemed to Margerite that she could tell the difference between the soft whisper in her mind and the cracked muttering of his worn-out voice, though she was not sure how. "Frowe Gräfin, I would learn what you can teach me, as much as your conscience allows."

"I will take you as my apprentice, in the names of Christ and Maria and Solomon the Magus," Margerite replied. "And may God and all His angels watch over us, that I never by word or thought or deed, or through my own weakness or lack of wisdom, lead you astray!"

Gottfried put his right hand in hers. His bony fingers were cold; it was like holding a bundle of winter-chilled sticks; and even had she not been watching his face, she would have known that it was the voice of his mind she heard. "I know that you never will, for you are as good a woman as was ever born, save only the Blessed Virgin herself." Aloud he said gravely, "May that be so."

Kobolt leapt upon him at that, licking away the smear of blood from his forehead and purring loudly. Gottfried suffered the cat's attentions without complaint, though Margerite knew how rough Kobolt's tongue was and how his claws pricked when he kneaded his paws against flesh.

"Jochanan will be back soon," Margerite said. "Do not speak aloud, whatever you hear from him, and try to keep your thoughts as still as possible - it were best, perhaps, if you fixed your mind on a prayer, so that if he can hear you, he will think only that you are murmuring those words as any Christian man might. This may ease somewhat when you have eaten, for food strengthens the bonds of flesh upon the spirit - and while we live in this world, that can be a needful thing, as you have seen for yourself now."

"That is so," Gottfried answered. But then he went on, and Margerite knew that he was thinking to himself. "My poor Arnmut - I am not sorry, I think, that he heard that I love him, but I fear that he will hear more if I do not learn this lesson swiftly...if he should know how I would embrace him, or that he is the desire of my heart! I would almost sooner cast my immortal soul into sin than cause him pain."

"Gottfried," said Margerite. "Pray in silence." For his thoughts now were not hers to hear, nor did she want him to know how achingly they turned her own towards Bernhardt.

At first she heard the mumbled words, "Pater noster, qui in caelis..." But that swiftly dwindled to nothing, as though his concentration on the prayer were closing whatever open door of his mind allowed his thoughts to sound through. Margerite crossed herself in reverence and thanks: here Gottfried's piety might well be the saving of him, as it should be, and she could trust that she had not done his soul any harm.

"That is well-done," Margerite told the knight after a little time. "When you have eaten, and slept somewhat, then you and I shall work more on this - but we shall have a few days here, after all, for we cannot get back on the road until you have learned to handle your gift and built your strength up a little more."

So it came about that Margerite slept on Rose's straw pallet that night, for she would not suffer Gottfried to be moved, nor did she dare let any other stay beside him. Past the rustlings of her bedding, now and again she could hear Arnmut outside the door; she had tried to get him to go on to bed, but he would not leave. She had less difficulty in getting to sleep than she might have thought. She had slept on worse as a serving maid at Schloss Niederwald, and at least her bowels were not rumbling with black bean soup and kitchen leavings - and mercifully for her, her fears for Gottfried had driven her other terrors from her thoughts, so that even the hunting-horn on the wind was faint enough for her to push from her mind.

A sudden crash of thunder woke Margerite, and a scattering of icy snowflakes on her face. She started up in her blankets, staring about wildly in the darkness. The wind had blown the candles out - she could hear it howling through the window, and the shutters banging free against the wall - and when she stood shakily, she began to shiver deeply at once from the cold. My Wolfram, I must wrap him better before I call to Rose, she thought at once. By touch, she fumbled her way over to the cradle.

Something sharp stabbed against Margerite's hand, and she bit back a small shriek. The cradle's slats were broken on one end, and Wolfram was not there. In a mad panic, she dropped to her knees, feeling fearfully about the rug: he had not cried out, if he had fallen too hard, or if one of the jagged pieces of wood had pierced his body...Something warm brushed against Margerite's fingers, and she almost cried out in relief before she realized that it was Kobolt's soft fur she felt. "Where is he?" she whispered to the cat. "Kobolt, find me my son."

Kobolt's chirping purr was almost lost in the sound of the wind wailing black through the window. He rubbed against his mistress, then walked slowly across the room, Margerite crouching as they moved to keep her hand on his back.

A flash of lightning seared blue through the snow outside, and in its brightness, Margerite saw Wolfram standing under the open window, both hands bracing his small body against the wall. His white face was turned up to the storm, his mouth open; and under the rending crack of thunder, Margerite thought she heard her son's laugh. Blinking away the after-flash from her eyelids, she hurried to him, heedless of the rugs bunching and sliding beneath her feet, and snatched him up into her arms.

Wolfram laughed again, as though his mother were playing with him, then began to squirm. "Wan' go!" he said. "Walked!"

"My precious, precious boy," Margerite crooned, holding him tightly. His hands and feet were cold, but not too icy, and she could feel his little fingers and toes wiggling. She was shivering harder, whether from terror or cold she could not say. Holding her son tightly against her, she felt about for her cloak to wrap about them both, and made her way to the door.

Arnmut's candle had burned down to a stub; the fair knight sat with his cloak pulled over his head, shadowing his features; but there was enough light for Margerite to see the drawn and worried look on his face, and she thought she might have caught the glistening track of a tear-trail. Still, he leapt to his feet almost at once.

"Frowe Gräfin!" Arnmust exclaimed. "Is all well?"

Margerite breathed deeply, forcing her voice to calmness. "Ritter Gottfried sleeps yet," she said. "But the storm blew out a window, and it is too cold in there; we must arrange other quarters. Of your courtesy, Herr Ritter..." She paused. She had been about to say, *May we sleep in the chamber that was given to you?* But something in her soul cried out against it: she felt that she had come too close to losing Wolfram that night already, and to while the night in Ruprecht's bedchamber would have seemed an invitation to...whatever had already passed so close to them. *Gottfried, why did you choose this time to batter yourself near to death with asceticism, when I need you now?*

"I did not choose it of my will," murmured the soft voice behind her. Margerite looked back to see that Gottfried had managed to relight one of the candles in the room, shielding it against the wind with his thin body and a hand cupped about the flame. "But I am here for you, Frowe Gräfin - what has come to pass? Is all well with your son?" He was shivering so violently that the candle in his hand flung golden drops of tallow about, and Arnmut ran to him at once, taking off his cloak and wrapping it about the other knight's shoulders before he took the candle from him.

"All is well, Gottfried," Arnmut said. "Get back into your bed, where it is a little warmer - or are you able to walk to our chamber if I help you?"

"I can walk by myself!" Gottfried answered. In the flickering candlelight, Margerite thought that he tried to flinch away from his friend, but Arnmut's strong arm held him firmly. Again, she thought she heard the murmur of a Paternoster beginning, and she knew that Gottfried was praying to shield his thoughts from Arnmut.

"I can see to him well enough," Margerite told Arnmut. "As I was about to say - of your courtesy, Herr Ritter, will you go to Eva's chamber and tell Rose to come here, so that she may arrange somewhere for us to spend what is left of the night?"

Wolfram began to cry then, a thin piercing wail that made Gottfried flinch and raise his hands to his ears. Reluctantly Arnmut let go of Gottfried, hastening down the corridor to Eva's room. Gottfried swayed, but kept his feet, and it seemed to Margerite that, as well as she could tell in the wavering glow from the candle-stub on the floor, his colour might be a little better than it had been.

But Wolfram's cries made it hard to think of anything but her babe; Margerite rocked him gently in her arms, holding him warm under her cloak. "What is it you want, Wolfram?" she asked in frightened bewilderment - though there was nothing strange in the crying of a child who was cold and startled.

Wolfram stopped crying and stared straight up at her. "Wan' go!" he insisted.

"Well, you are going nowhere tonight, save back into a warm bed with your Mutti," Margerite told him sternly. Still, she could not keep a faint smile from touching her lips: she thought that she would be telling her son that a great deal in the future.

And he stood! she realized: the shock had driven that from her mind. He said that he walked! Some children do that, rolling about like worms for many months until their mothers begin to fear for them, and then standing to toddle one day without ever crawling in between. But beneath that pride and relief was a more worrying thought: what had impelled Wolfram to fight his way out of his cradle and walk to the window just then?

The oilskin had blown out once before, on the stormy night of his birth. I wish we had not come to Burg Falkenstein. But how could I have passed it by? Though Gottfried was still pale the next day, he seemed much better, and did not protest when Arnmut filled his plate with a good portion of hot bread with butter, spooning cherries in honey over it.

Indeed, he ate more willingly than not, as though he had taken to heart Margerite's words about the virtue of food in dulling his unwanted gifts of thought. Wolfram was up on his feet again, toddling about and clinging to the women's skirts to keep him upright, and Rose laughed to see it.

"He will not be an easy one to keep a watch on, Frowe Gräfin," she said. "It is as well that I am going along with you."

They stayed one more night in Burg Falkenstein - a more peaceful night, Christ and Mother Maria be thanked - and then Jochanan pronounced Gottfried well enough to ride again.

"You are remarkably strong," the gunner said, shaking his head. "I would have thought that we would be here a week or more. But no matter: so long as you keep eating well, and wrap warmly against the cold, you should not slow us."

"I certainly will not," the knight answered stiffly, but made no more of the matter.

The weather had eased again when they rode out, their horse's hooves kicking up little plumes of snow that sparkled in the sunlight. It was not so bitter cold as it had been, though small gusts of wind whirled scatterings of snow from the branches now and again, and the riders had to change hands on the reins often in order to warm their fingers against their bodies.

Margerite was not surprised that Rose did not ride well; what amazed her was that the girl could ride at all, for she had thought of that too late and feared that they would end up having to leave the serving-maid behind. But Gerhild had to ride, for a midwife must often move swiftly between villages: she had taught her niece at least how not to fall out of her saddle at a trot, and how to point her horse's head in the direction it ought to go, though Margerite feared what would become of the girl if her steed ever broke into a canter.

# Chapter Six

The wind blowing over the Rhone was harsh and raw, the January sky leaden-gray, though no snow was falling, when Margerite and her band of travellers rode down the wagon-churned ribbon of mud that led into Avignon. The city was ringed by walls and towers, but the gates were open, and they passed almost unremarked into the Pope's domain.

Margerite could not help but feel disappointed at what she saw as they rode through the streets. She had expected, perhaps, something almost like a large monastery, quiet and orderly, with the sense of holiness hanging over the city streets like a breath of incense. But Avignon was more crowded and dirty than Freiburg; though there were, indeed, more priests and monks about than in other cities, there were plenty of ragged beggars and ill-clad children jostling between them, and the muddy slush in the gutters stank of rot and manure. Avignon seemed noisier than Freiburg as well, though perhaps that was only because Margerite spoke no French, so that there seemed little difference between the honking of a poultry-seller's fat white geese in the marketplace and the woman's own raucous cries to her customers.

Gottfried pulled up his horse beside a priest, leaning down and speaking courteously to him in simple, careful Latin. "I beg your pardon, Father," the knight said. "Can you direct me to the house of Cardinal Jean de Grenville?"

The priest gave Gottfried a surly glare, dark eyes glowering up from a lumpish face, but answered him in Latin that was quick and heavily accented. Gottfried had to ask him to repeat his directions several times - Margerite thought that she should have been the one to seek guidance, for her Latin was far better than the young knight's; but perhaps, after all, it would not have been seemly for a Gräfin to speak to a man, even a priest, in the street.

Still, she listened carefully - the priest was doing a lot of arm-waving, pointing to various signs and edifices that Margerite knew Gottfried would not be able to make out - and when she was reasonably sure that she knew where they were going, she said, "That will do well enough, Herr Ritter."

Gottfried thanked the priest, who grunted, standing and looking at him. Margerite realized quickly enough what the man wanted; she dug in her belt-pouch for a pfennig and nudged her horse forward to drop it into the priest's palm, saying quickly, "This for your prayers for us, Father."

The priest's thick lips twitched; the pfennig disappeared, and he turned away. Gottfried stared curiously at Margerite, but he seemed to think better of saying whatever had been in his mind - and, Christ be thanked, more regular meals and vigilant prayer had made it easier for him to keep his own thoughts hidden from others, although Margerite was never sure how much he knew of what was in her mind. As they neared the Papal palace, the houses became larger and finer. In spite of the cold and the muck of the city streets, Margerite could hardly keep herself from staring about, for even at Ortlieb's feast, she had never seen so many people in rich silks and velvets and furs.

She could not have even imagined the wealth that was here; she remembered the stories Damiano had told in Freiburg of the papal court, but she had cast more than two-thirds of that aside as the exaggeration and envy of an Order messenger. *There is little of poverty and humility here,* she thought. *But is it not fitting that the princes of the Church should show themselves as splendidly as those of the world, when their station in the eyes of God is so much the higher?And there have been many heretics who preached the way of pure renunciation and railed against the Church on that account...* Still, she could not help contrasting the glitter of gold and the soft shimmer of ermine and martin on the cloaks of those they passed with the humble austerity of Father Etienne's friend the Abbot, in whose sanctum the light of holiness burned so brightly.

The mansion of Cardinal Jean de Grenville was outside the city; they rode over the bridge of St. Benezet, a narrow span of stone upheld by a row of semi-circular arches such as Margerite could little have conceived of, with its own low chapel of St. Nicholas halfway across. Past the bridge, the companions followed the road into the countryside a little way. Although the fields were mucky with frozen mud and slush, and the tree-branches black and bare in the raw January damp, Margerite could easily imagine how rich the lands around Avignon would look in summer, warm and green and sweet with blossoms.

Wolfram looked about with bright-eyed interest - he was being surprisingly good, for since he had learned to walk, he would hardly suffer himself to be held for any length of time, and Margerite had had peace on their ride only while her son was sleeping, or when she could give him over to Rose and Eva for a time. The guards on duty at the gates of the Cardinal's mansion were dressed as richly as any of Heinrich's knights, with silken surcoats bearing the de Grenville arms over their armour and thick brocaded cloaks.

Looking at them, Margerite felt rather shabby: though her travelling-cloak was trimmed with fur and lined with silk, the wool was still dirty from long riding. She had kept her best dresses in her packs, knowing that she would need to look as well as possible in Avignon; and she knew she could do with a bath herself. But she drew herself up with as much dignity as she could when one of the guards addressed them - in Latin, thank Christ; to the best of her knowledge, none of the party spoke French.

"Who comes to the dwelling of Cardinal Jean de Grenville, and what is your errand here?"

"The Frowe Gräfin Margerite von Fürstensee und Falkenstein is come here," answered Gottfried for her. "I believe that the Cardinal knows of her arrival."

The guardsman who had addressed them - a short man with bad skin and dark hair curling out around the edges of his brightly-polished bascinet - looked down his crooked nose at them. "I shall inform the Cardinal that you are here. Wait."

"What did he say?" asked Paul. "It sounded poxy and rude to me."

Margerite was not overly impressed with the guard's courtesy either, but she did not like to say so. "All is well," she reassured the mercenary. "But I think it may be time for us to part for a little while. Is there one in your company who speaks French?"

"Might be. But we can get along well enough here; a few of the men have bits of Latin, and the Bear's Paw has served where we didn't know the language before. Folk all understand money, anyway."

Margerite gave him the purse she had counted out for this earlier. "Go and find lodgings for yourself and your troop in the city, then - but send word at once to let me know where you are, and be ready for my call if need be."

Paul took the purse, but he frowned, hesitating. "Gräfin, are you sure you want to send us away here, of all places? I don't like leaving you where there might be danger."

"Such danger as there will be...I do not think swords will be needed to ward me," Margerite answered slowly, her eyes flickering to the other guardsman. He stood silently watching them, and she could not tell from his dark eyes whether he understood a word they were saying or not. "Ritter Gottfried and Ritter Arnmut shall be beside me, and Cardinal de Grenville is a friend of Father Etienne."

"That's all right, then," Paul said with a sigh of relief. "But we'll be ready for you, Gräfin. Company - fall out!" The Bear's Paw men slowly broke away and turned back towards Avignon, leaving Margerite, Eva, their maidservant, and the two knights before the gate.

It was not long before the guardsman came bustling back. "Welcome, guests. The Cardinal awaits you within."

The travellers were relieved of their horses and baggage; another servant, a tall, slim man wearing point-toed shoes of deep blue velvet and a matching doublet, came to lead them into the Cardinal's mansion. They passed through a high-arched hall whose windows glowed with coloured panes; their guide led them up a spiral staircase of oak, and down another hall to an oaken door.

He opened the door and bowed, saying, "Your Grace, your guests are here."

The Cardinal's study was a pleasant room, warmed by a stove and two braziers, with thick deep red rugs on the floor. The shelves of one wall were lined with books; a silk-shimmering tapestry showing the Passion of Christ hid the wall opposite, and a large glass window cast its light over the Cardinal's desk. Enough chairs for their company had clearly just been brought in, arranged in a rough half-circle around the desk, and there was a glass decanter of pale red wine sitting upon it, with several glass goblets by the bottle.

Jean de Grenville was a tall gray-haired man, elegant in his red silk robes, with finely-drawn, clean-shaven features, a long aristocratic nose, and thick gray eyebrows. He rose and walked around the desk as they entered, extending his hand; Margerite knelt and brushed her lips over the large ruby of his ring, though a shock ran up her left arm as though she had taken a hard blow to the tip of the finger that bore Ortlieb's gem. The others kissed the Cardinal's ring in turn, and Margerite almost thought that she saw Eva wince slightly, though the girl hid it well.

"Greetings and welcome, frowe Gräfin," Cardinal de Grenville said warmly. He spoke good German; his accent reminded Margerite of Father Etienne's, though it was much stronger. "And the rest of you, as well - will you introduce your comrades, Gräfin?"

Margerite made the introductions, and the Cardinal nodded to each of them. "I received your letter two weeks ago, so you will find that all is in readiness for you - some wine? Yes? And what of your men? Have you left them outside?"

"They are seeking lodgings in the city," Margerite replied. "I did not wish to trouble your hospitality with seeing to soldiers, who can care for themselves well enough."

Cardinal de Grenville's thin lips curved, as if smiling at some secret jest. "As pleases you best. Come, sit down, and you shall tell me of your plans while you are here, for there was less in your letter than I should have liked to know. Etienne, as is his usual manner, sent me word that you were likely to bring danger with you, both of the flesh and perhaps of the spirit, and that you would need aid and strong guardians in this city - for the Serpent was powerful even in the holy Garden, and Avignon is far from Eden. But he seemed unwilling to tell me more, perhaps because he feared for the safety of his messenger."

Margerite looked at her companions. Father Etienne had said that the Cardinal owed him a great favour, and also that de Grenville might be able to find an exorcist for Christoph. But did he know of the Order of Light-Bearers? If he did not, and she betrayed that secret that both sides of the struggle would keep secret...

"He does not know," said Gottfried quietly, his grim stare fixed on the Cardinal. "Your Grace, you must trust in Father Etienne's counsel, for there are some matters of which we may not speak, lest it bring you into a battle which is not yours to fight."

Cardinal de Grenville frowned. "I should ask by what right Canon Etienne makes such decisions, did I not know all too well. Still, it shall be as you say. By the debt I owe Etienne, I shall give you whatever help I may, though the more you tell me, the more aid I am likely to be able to give you." He paused in thought.

"They may well be better able to guard us in this even than your own troops, if you will take no offense at my saying that, your Grace," Ritter Gottfried said.

"Gottfried!" Margerite muttered warningly - it was hardly surprising that the young knight's control had slipped, for she could tell by the way Gottfried's thin back was braced that he was exceedingly nervous at speaking so to a cardinal.

Cardinal de Grenville passed the back of his hand across his eyes in bewilderment, and a tingle of fear ran through Margerite. The Black Book counselled most carefully against showing one's power, lest it draw unwanted attention - what would the Cardinal now think of Gottfried?

"Aye," the Frenchman murmured. "These men of the Teutonic Order are also friends of Etienne, and if you will not let me help you to the fullest, then perhaps they can. They are in the city - a matter of an old land-grant under dispute - but they should be back by sunset. In the meantime, have you eaten? No? Then Pierre will show you to your chambers, and I shall have food sent up to you when you have had a little time to refresh yourselves."

Margerite was awed by the lushness of the chambers which the servant brought herself and Eva to. Even Ortlieb's own rooms had hardly been so richly furnished; standing on thick-piled velvet rugs amid silk sewn tapestries and chests with inlay of ivory and gold, Margerite felt very much the poor knight's daughter again. Rose, who followed behind clutching Wolfram tightly, was in a worse state: the maidservant's wide gray-green eyes darted everywhere, and she walked carefully around the rugs so as not to risk soiling them with her feet.

"This is fine state for us to while in," Eva declared in satisfaction, scooping up Kriemhilt as the cat made a lunge for one of the gold tassels on the long velvet curtains. "When I have had a bath and gotten into some decent clothing, I shall feel well at ease here."

"Kobolt!" Margerite said warningly - for the tomcat was backing up to the silk-covered bed and hunching slightly in a manner she knew all too well. "If you spray in here..." She stopped: she knew that there was more to Kobolt's markings than a tom leaving his seal, just as there was more to Kobolt himself than a large black cat.

As if he had never meant to do anything else, Kobolt straightened up and wandered over to a corner - one where, thank Maria, there were no tapestries and rugs within his range.

"You might have been better with a she-cat for your dear pet," Eva commented. "I fear that you will not be the most welcome of guests hereafter in many places where we have stopped. Rose, I think it were best if you made sure of water and scrubbing cloths in here at all times, since there is no telling what Kobolt will take it into his mind to mark next."

Rose stood uncertainly with Wolfram in her arms, until Margerite took the babe from her. "Go along, Rose," she ordered, for she could already smell Kobolt's musky reek beneath the faint sweet scent of incense that hung in the room.

"Down!" Wolfram said at once. Margerite let him down, holding his hand as he toddled over to the bed and began to examine the silken coverlet. When her son began to pull at the seams, she tried to gently disengage his little fingers, but he clenched his hands into fists and started to howl.

"Wolfram, Wolfram," Margerite said. "You may not tear up the Cardinal's bedclothes. See, are they not nice and soft if you just stroke them gently?"

Wolfram refused to be convinced, and it took Margerite a little while to separate him from the coverlet.

"He has grown very lively," remarked Eva. "I thought that it would not be long before it was impossible to keep him out of everything. But at least he will soon be completely weaned, and then you can give most of his care over to Rose."

"He is my son," Margerite protested. "Whether he is suckling at my breasts or no, I do not mean to leave him to another, whether that is the fashion or not."

"But you will have to anyway, when he is seven and old enough to serve as a page," Eva said reasonably. "After all, you can hardly teach a boy everything he needs to know."

"I had thought that Bernhardt..." Margerite stopped, her voice choking in her throat. Would Bernhardt really be willing to take Wolfram's small hands in his own, guiding him through sword-strokes and shield-movements? Would he have, even before - as he thinks - I betrayed him?

"Aye, and you cannot be blamed for being little willing to let Wolfram go from your sight. But you cannot keep watch over a child every moment: sooner or later you must trust his safety and his learning to others. And speaking of learning..." Eva lowered her voice so that Margerite could hardly hear it over Wolfram's half-worded protests... "can you not tell Ritter Gottfried to be more careful? If the good Cardinal were not in Etienne's debt, matters might have gone far worse for us in there."

"What have you guessed about Ritter Gottfried?" Margerite asked.

"That, were his nature other than it is, Princes of the Light-Bearers would be fighting over who had the right to take him as apprentice. There was a girl who had a gift something like his at the convent, and she was ever petted and given dainty things to eat, while I was whipped and starved." Eva's pretty face hardened for a moment, and Margerite could see the anger glowing white in her blue eyes like steel under the blacksmith's fires. "I do not know what became of her, for she was taken away before I left, but I doubt it was anything good: she was a spiteful creature, and often ill-tempered, because she misliked the things she heard about herself. And to be fair," Eva added, "though she was treated like a prize mare, the Abbess kept her carefully secluded, and would not even give her so much freedom as I had to walk about the convent: perhaps I should think more charitably of her, though it is hard."

"Charity is not a thing to be given only when it is easy," Margerite chastised Eva. She might have said more, but the door opened and Rose came back with her scrubbing things.

The dimming gray January twilight was beginning to cast a chill over the rooms through the leaded windows, and Rose had just begun to light the candles, when a knock sounded on the door. Margerite went herself to open it, for she did not know who it might be. The tall servant who had guided them in - Pierre, the Cardinal had named him - stood there.

He had changed his clothes since that afternoon: he now wore a tabard of bright red silk with the Cardinal's arms embroidered on it, and a thick gold chain about his neck. "Frowe Gräfin, the Cardinal wishes to see you and your companions in his study again. I hope you are suitably refreshed and rested from your journey now." His Latin was very clear and learned, so that Margerite had to pause carefully to choose words and grammar, lest she shame herself before him.

"We are, indeed, and I thank the Cardinal for his graciousness," Margerite answered. "Eva!"

"I am here," Eva said, coming up behind her. She had put on her finest dress, the blue silk brocade; Margerite had managed to surreptitiously let out hem and sleeves, since she did not trust Rose's stitching on such fine material, but the bodice, being too small, still pushed up Eva's bosom and displayed the white tops of her large breasts in an unseemly way.

Still, if Madame Isabella's handiwork had been any sign of such things, the dress would pass well enough for the height of French fashion, Margerite consoled herself. The Ritters Gottfried and Arnmut were already in the Cardinal's study by the time the two women got there, together with three men in the black-crossed white surcoats of the Teutonic Knights. One of the men was old, his hair and beard gleaming white, though he still looked hale enough.

The other two were, Margerite guessed, perhaps in their early thirties, one fair-haired and one dark. All three of them were above middle height, broad-shouldered and muscular of build, and all three had the hard look that Margerite had come to associate with men who had been at war long: a certain harshness of expression, and a coldness in the eyes as though they had looked too often upon the bodies of the slain.

"Frowe Gräfin and Frowe Eva," said the Cardinal, rising to greet the women. "Allow me to introduce Brother Karl, Brother Wolfgang, and Brother Helmuth of the Teutonic Order. Good knights, these two ladies are Gräfin Margerite von Fürstensee und Falkenstein, and Frowe Eva von Bärenburg."

Margerite was not sure whether she should expect the men to kiss her hand in greeting; as it was, the old man, Brother Helmuth, bowed stiffly. The two younger knights - Karl was the fair one and Wolfgang the dark - stared at her with an intensity that reminded her a little of Gottfried's, as though they were searching into her very soul. And it seemed to her as she looked at them that, beyond the blue-glass windows of their eyes, she could see a glimmer of brightness like the burning of holy candles in a church at night.

She could see in their faces how that light had seared its own mark into them, though she could not have pointed it out by any single sign: Brother Karl's ruddy face, marked by a long white scar along his jaw and down his neck where a blade must have struck under the chain-mail guarding his bascinet, was craggy and rough as any brigand's, and Brother Wolfgang's nobler features were weathered and deeply tanned, as though he had been at hard work outdoors every day of his life.

Yet there was something about them - Margerite knew that she could trust them, without question or doubt, as surely as if Father Etienne had named each and shown her paintings of their faces. So we know our own, Margerite thought. And then, Maria help me, what do they see in me, when I have so long been bearing Ortlieb's ring?

Brother Wolfgang bowed to her first, followed by Brother Karl. "Frowe Gräfin, we are honoured to meet you, for we have heard well of you and your companions from the good Father Etienne," he said. "Christ willed it that we should be in Avignon now, for the settling of an earthly matter of lands and papers, and by His grace we are here now to guard and keep you where your own soldiers cannot follow."

"Then He is much to be thanked for that!" said Margerite. "For I may well have great need of you."

Cardinal de Grenville coughed meaningfully. "It is, at the least, discourteous to speak before me in my own house of matters in which you do not mean to let me take part, save as a messenger and maker of appointments," he said, and Margerite could hear the anger roughening beneath his smooth voice, like herb-grit at the bottom of a honey-posset. "Or is it that you mean to tell me now, so that I may aid you - and protect my own, if need be?"

The Teutonic Knights looked at Margerite. She looked at Gottfried, and their eyes locked for a moment. Then it seemed to her that she heard the other voices in the room as Gottfried, the shields of his mind dropped for a moment, must hear them, a murmuring of many whispers. Gottfried's own, strongest: How can we stay in the household of an innocent man, knowing the danger that we bring with us? - Eva's: Dear St. Hildegard, are these Teutonic Knights all like Gottfried, without the sense to dissemble for five seconds together?

Brother Wolfgang's thoughts and Brother Karl's were much alike - Father Etienne did not say us yea or nay in the matter of telling him of the Order, or so much as we saw fit - but Brother Helmuth was thinking, I know little of this; such things were never mine to deal with. Perhaps now, in my old age, Christ has given me a last chance to fall in His service, if it should come to that - but I wish these young men would say what they mean: the secrecy is becoming wearisome.

The Cardinal was thinking, Now we shall see: they are close to the edge of telling me, and I am close to the edge of what I will tolerate, even for the debt I owe Etienne. And lastly Arnmut: Gottfried and the Frowe Gräfin will judge this rightly; they always do.

Mine to choose, Margerite thought. Yet still she trembled on the brink: she remembered what Father Etienne had told her, all too well - she herself wore an Order ring; what if men were set looking for such signs? And Father Etienne must have known Cardinal de Grenville for years, if he could presume on him so easily for lodgings for his friends, but he had never seen fit to tell the man of the Order.

Nor was Margerite a fool: she knew that among the great of the Church, as of the world, there must be uncounted layers and measures of trust, so that a man might be called upon to guest even a woman in peril, but still be shut away from the heart of the matter - and for whose sake, whether his own or that of others, only Father Etienne knew.

"I would not give you either discourtesy or untruth," Margerite said carefully to the Cardinal. "Therefore I shall tell you what I may, and pray you forgive me if you think there is aught I have left unsaid. Not all who dwell in Avignon, though they wear the robes of the Church, are good: you must know well enough that there is plenty of the petty ambition of the world here - and a few are foes of Christ, for the Devil lays his snares even in the Pope's own city. It chances that we have run afoul of some such, wherefore Father Etienne directed me to guest with you; as he may or may not have told you, though I did not wish to put it in my letter, he hoped that you would be able to find the exorcist James of Canterbury and convince him to return to Burg Fürstensee with us."

Jean de Grenville watched Margerite intently from behind his desk as she spoke, his chin resting in the cup of one beringed hand. His long face was calm, and Margerite could guess at no trace of his thoughts. She wished that she could look at Gottfried for counsel, but she did not dare: he was too close to letting go of his mastery of his gift altogether.

"What may I expect from these - heretics, is it? Or worse?"

"Worse, as such things may be," Margerite answered. "Have you yet heard the news from Niederwald?"

The Cardinal shook his head, his red silken skullcap shimmering in the candlelight. "There has been little news from the Holy Roman Empire of late."

"Then it may be that those within the Church who are dealing with it desire to keep it quiet until the matter is settled. But Father Etienne called the Inquisition to investigate the matter, and it was one of black sorcery."

Cardinal de Grenville crossed himself, the furrows of age on his brow deepening. "Etienne was ever involved in such matters: I suspected it when I received his message. Now say to me, what danger am I and the folk of my household in from this, and in which direction should I look to see it coming?"

"As to yourself and your household - I would say to be vigilant: I would guess that the foe will come, not with swords and fire, for they do not wish to make themselves known, but with honeyed words and perhaps clinking purses for lesser servants." Margerite paused, wondering. Damiano had sent a demon into her very bedchamber: what could the great of the Order not do, here in this city that was their Imperator's stronghold? Unless Father Etienne had somehow foreseen this, and warded the Cardinal's house on one of his many journeys through Avignon...

A deep purr broke Margerite's train of thought, and she felt the heavy warm brush of fur against her ankles as Kobolt wound reassuringly between her legs. She was not sure how to interpret that, but it comforted her nevertheless.

"And who are they?" the Cardinal pressed. "Are there names you can name for me? I am not without power in this city..."

For a moment, Margerite was sorely tempted to give him the name of Madame du Guesclin: let the Church, which was so much more powerful than she, deal with the Order Princess, and she and her son be kept in safety! But she knew there would be no safety if she did, for even if Madame du Guesclin were shackled safely in the deepest cell in Avignon - and binding her, even in prison, would not be so simple a matter as locking up Oda and Hedwig - there were all the Council of Princes to deal with, and they would hunt Margerite down as a renegade for betraying the Order's own.

"I fear that I cannot," she said. "Forgive me, Cardinal, for I have told you as much as I may. If that does not suffice, then speak the word, and we shall leave your house and find dwellings elsewhere, so that you are no longer entangled in this matter in any way."

Cardinal de Grenville frowned, looking down his long nose at Margerite as if she were a serving-maid who had clumsily spilt wine on him. "It grieves me that Etienne did not give a better report of me to his friends. Nor did I reach my station here by cowardice or by betraying those who needed my aid in the cause of Christ - even," he added, a flash of anger gleaming in his dark eyes, "those who will not give their full trust to their allies and helpers. Before God, I shall take it as the most grievous discourtesy if you leave my house now! I have taken you in as guests, in payment of an old debt, and I shall keep that trust as best I may. Advise me on how I may best aid and protect you, and that I shall do, to the fullest of my powers - and maybe another time, Etienne, or you, shall have more faith in me."

Margerite bowed her head, abashed. But she could see why Father Etienne had not told the Cardinal of the Order of Light-Bearers: he did not seem such a man as to carry out a long and secret war against the host of Satan, nor - she knew by looking at him, though she was not sure how - would he be able to undertake the manner of battles that Father Etienne fought. It was best, for himself and those around him, that Cardinal de Grenville know as little as possible, though she did not regret telling him what she had.

"You shame me, Cardinal," Margerite murmured. "As for aiding and protecting us - the chief aid we need is in the matters of which we have already spoken. Protection..." She thought of guards forced by magic to open doors in the night, of servants blinded by the pale tallow-flicker of a candle made of human fat so that they looked away from the figure walking down the Cardinal's halls and into the room where Wolfram lay sleeping. Even if Father Etienne had warded the Cardinal's mansion and all within, there was no ward that would guard against the lure of a bribe or a wheedling promise, and Margerite knew, too well, how a very little might seem like dazzling wealth to a scullion licking pots in the kitchen. "Forgive me, Cardinal, but how sure are you of your household servants? Could any of them be cajoled, or bribed..?"

The Cardinal laughed softly, but his dark eyes were cold. "Gräfin, I do not mean to mock you, but you are clearly an innocent in some ways. This is Avignon - do you think I do not know who the spies in my household are, and to whom they report, nor that I am unaware that it only takes one flick of a scrubbing-boy's wrist in the kitchen to cast a deadly powder into a capon's stuffing?"

Gottfried crossed himself, his thin face paling. Dear Maria, we are all far out of our depth here - how shall we ever come to shore, save by Your help? Margerite thought. She desperately wanted to ask if Cardinal Fleurs was one of those who spied here, but she did not dare: if word came back to him somehow that she had mentioned his name...

"I see now why Father Etienne sent us to you," she replied gravely. "Surely we are kept more safely here than we could ever have been on our own, and he chose the man who could best guide us through the mazes of this city."

The Cardinal seemed a little mollified by that; at least he waved his hand, his ruby ring glinting in the candlelight. "That is as may be," he said. "Come, now: the evening meal is prepared, and we shall speak of other matters until it is over - when, perhaps, I shall do best to retire to my own affairs and leave you alone."

After dinner, the Cardinal led his guests to his library, where, after drinking a goblet of wine and making pleasant conversation for a time, he took his leave. "You may speak safely in here, so long as you keep your voices down," he added quietly. "I shall make sure that no one has a chance to listen at the keyhole."

"I thank you for your kindness, your Eminence," Margerite replied.

As soon as the Cardinal was gone, the two younger Teutonic Knights bowed to Margerite again, their elder following half a heartbeat later. "We are honoured to be able to serve Christ through protecting you, Frowe Gräfin," Brother Wolfgang said formally. "Yet it is well for you that Father Etienne told us as much as he did, for we could not but recognise the ring you bear - a great burden, and a dangerous one: I fear that it puts your soul in worse peril than could any deeds of our foes."

"That is my fear as well." Margerite could not keep the sorrow from her voice, but their other words drew her mind away from brooding on it. "You must have seen Father Etienne since last I did. Tell me, what news have you from him - and from Bernhardt von Niederwald?"

Brother Wolfgang and Brother Karl glanced at one another. Margerite could not read the look that passed between them, but Brother Karl shook back his thick bowl-cut mass of fair hair and said, "Father Etienne is well, but expects to be occupied for some time with the Niederwald matter. The Kaiser has not formally given the Inquisition leave to act as freely as they do in other countries, and there is the delicate matter of the possible involvement of the current secular authority there: by rights, Landgraf Gerhardt should receive those whom the Church convicts, but there may be reason to examine him as well. As for Herr Bernhardt, there is still the question of the old crime of which he was accused, not to mention his actions as a free soldier with the Company of the Black Sword. He is safe within the Bishop's sanctuary, but his brother may be within rights to claim justice whenever he comes out. The whole matter, I believe, will not be settled until it goes to the Kaiser's judgement, and there is no telling how it may come out then."

"As for Father Etienne," Brother Wolfgang added, "he told us much of you and those who travel with you. Though I had expected to see one more, a red-haired squire..?"

"Georg could not leave Burg Fürstensee. It was not willingly that I left him in the charge of those who rule there, but I have taken such steps as I could to be sure of his safety of soul and body: I think no harm will come to him."

Brother Wolfgang frowned, but said nothing. It was Brother Karl who spoke next, glowering at Margerite from under heavy blond brows as though she were a recruit of whose sword-skill he was not wholly sure. "How far have you and yours advanced in the Art, Frowe Gräfin?"

Margerite did not know how to answer him. Father Etienne had never hinted that the foes of the Order had any such rankings as those they fought: she had no way to name title or degree.

Fortunately, Eva spoke up then. "I am trained only in assisting at rites, but I am well-skilled in that, so long as someone else will lead. The Frowe Gräfin has great power: I have seen her control and put down a demon that a Light-Bearer sent in hopes of catching her unawares, and that with neither circle nor triangle nor wand, but only the strength of her will. Ritter Gottfried...sees what is unseen, and also..." She flushed, her words stumbling - unwilling, Margerite guessed, to speak more about the troubled young knight to his face.

A touch of a smile softened Brother Karl's craggy face. "But he is not skilled in the Art yet, for all his gifts...are you, brother?" he said to Gottfried.

"No," Gottfried admitted, looking down shamefacedly. Nor do I know if I ought to be, for I would not have sought this out save that God led me to it: the whisper was quite clear in Margerite's mind.

"Calm yourself, brother," Brother Wolfgang ordered, his weathered features stern. "In this city, of all places, you cannot afford to show yourself so clearly, for our foe may also hear with ears keener than those of men. As you have told us, so we shall tell you. Brother Karl and I are both of high rank among those men of the Teutonic Order who defend our knights and folk most directly against the pagan sorceries of the East. Brother Helmuth knows nothing of such things - he is here only as a witness to the original grant of land which we came hither to discuss - and he does not wish to learn more: he wants only to offer aid to the cause of Christ, howsoever it may need his sword."

"That is so," the old Teutonic Knight affirmed. "I leave it those who are wiser than I to guide us through these mazes of the Devil; but as for myself, I must trust in Christ to uphold me against all sorceries and deceits, and pray that I may yet strike another blow in His defense."

"Then your faith will be strength to us all, good Brother," Margerite said.

Brother Karl swirled the red wine about in his pewter goblet - a plain and battered item, when set against the rich hangings and polished oaken carvings of the Cardinal's library, and the gilding and jewels that glittered from the covers of some of the books on his shelves. Yet it seemed to Margerite that its soft leaden sheen was brighter than careful rubbing with a cloth would allow for: she guessed that, at need, the knight's drinking-cup would serve for hallowed rites when he must travel fast or guarded and could not carry a chest of ritual tools with him.

He sipped carefully, and said, "Father Etienne told us that you slew the Light-Bearer Princess Ortlieb; and Brother Sigvrit - a man who is dear to me, for he gave me much of my training when I was new-sworn and his leg still whole - said much more of that, and other things as well." His gaze flicked to Gottfried. To Margerite's surprise, a violent flush rose over the young knight's cheekbones, and Gottfried turned his gaze away.

But Brother Sigvrit thought well of him, Margerite thought. Poor creature, it must be that he feels himself unworthy of the old man's praise, though Christ and Maria know how well he deserves it. Brother Karl must have thought something the same, for he said, "The Frowe Gräfin is fortunate in your service, Ritter Gottfried. It may please you to know that Brother Sigvrit thought it a dreadful shame that you and your companion Ritter Arnmut could not join our Order."

"I would not be fit for such an honour," Gottfried said in a muffled voice, as though he might be about to break into tears.

Brother Karl shook his fair head. "No, Brother Sigvrit has seen many young men come into the ranks of the Teutonic Knights, and his judgement is sound. Hold to that, if you should doubt yourself, for you shall need all your strength of will in the days that are to come." He stared straight into Gottfried's face, gaze fixed on Gottfried's gray eyes, and it seemed to Margerite that something was passing between them, though she could not guess what.

Gottfried straightened his back and nodded, swallowing hard; Arnmut smiled radiantly, and when the younger man patted his former knight's shoulder in reassurance, Gottfried did not flinch away from him as he had been doing over the past weeks.

"Frowe Gräfin," Brother Karl went on, "by your permission, I shall take over the instruction of this good knight for a short time, for you shall have much to do and many eyes shall be upon you, some of them the eyes of those who sleep not." A strange chill went down Margerite's back at those words; they were oddly phrased and cadenced, and she thought she could guess at what the Teutonic Knight meant. "We are safe here for, as I think you must have discerned, Father Etienne has already warded this house against just such need as ours. Yet you will need all your strength and attention for the things that you must do."

"What more has Father Etienne told you?" Margerite asked tautly, a shiver prickling over the ends of her nerves as if they lay raw to the cold January wind outside.

"That you must deal with the Light-Bearers as if you were one of their own."

No sound save the muffled crackling of the fires in the stoves and the faint sounds of coals hissing in the braziers broke the air of the Cardinal's library in the wake of Brother Karl's statement: his words seemed to ring in the silence like the cold steel of a gauntlet striking a flagstone in challenge. Brother Helmuth stared at Margerite in open astonishment, his mouth a dark hole in the whiteness of his beard; Gottfried's eyes closed a moment as if in prayer. Eva and Arnmut said nothing, but a glance passed between them. The two younger Teutonic Knights stood steadily, as if keeping guard in the darkness outside a beleaguered castle: Margerite had seen Bernhardt stand thus, his weight lightly balanced between his feet and all his muscles eased, but in readiness lest he should suddenly have to draw and strike.

"That is true," Margerite said, her higher voice clear in the stillness as the sound of a stone dropping suddenly into an unrippled pool. "I am here to meet Madame du Guesclin - and it is in her mind, if she finds me worthy, to bring me into the Council of Princes of the Order of Light-Bearers."

Deliberately she lifted her left hand so that the ruby of Ortlieb's ring glowed bloody in the candlelight. Brother Wolfgang's sword-hand clenched into a fist, as if he were struggling not to lay it to the hilt of his blade; Brother Karl crossed himself steadily. Ritter Gottfried did not move, but a shadow lay across his stark-boned face, and Margerite could see the look of deep pity in his eyes.

He knows what more there is to it, she thought, and that gave her the strength to say, "And the Order of Light-Bearers, for reasons of its own, would take my son into their care: they suffer me to keep him only because they believe me to be among their number. That is the greatest danger here: that Wolfram somehow fall into their hands."

Margerite stopped. She would not speak of the blasphemous anti-baptism that Graf Günther had desired to perform - that, for all the Order knew, he had accomplished! - nor of the fearful vision Gertrude, if it was she, had shown her old mistress. Nor, least of all, would she say any word of Wolfram's conception and her own fears for the child: when they asked why the Order desired him, she must plead ignorance, and pray that Gottfried would keep her secret as she kept his.

"That is indeed a grievous thing, that they should now cast their nets after the souls of babes!" Brother Wolfgang said, slowly uncurling his fist as Margerite lowered her ringed hand. "But how do you mean to deceive the great among the Light-Bearers without giving them what they desire?"

"I do not know," Margerite answered. "Christ and Maria help me, I do not know!"

Brother Karl's ruddy brow furrowed. "Father Etienne also mentioned your son, though he did not say why the Light-Bearers want him. Can you tell us?"

"I cannot."

The Teutonic Knight did not relent, his ruddy scarred face intent as if Margerite saw it beneath the steel rim of an open-faced helm, pursuing a foe. "It is not for his lands, for - forgive me, Frowe Gräfin - Falkenstein is hardly among the great realms of the Empire. If all they wish is a child to offer to their Master or raise in their ways, why, the streets are full of beggar-women and whores with babes that might be bought for a silver mark or less, if they were not simply given over gladly. There must be something about this child alone that they seek. Fetch him, therefore, and we shall see him for ourselves now." The tone of command in his voice was such that, unthinking, Margerite turned to fetch Wolfram. But the Ritters Gottfried and Arnmut started; Margerite could see plainly on Gottfried's face that he was about to rebuke Brother Karl sharply, and she remembered who she was.

"Brother," Margerite said coldly, "I am not a junior member of your Order, nor a serving maid, for you to speak so to me; nor does being more advanced in the Art than I, if thus you are, give you that right."

A rush of blood reddened the scar along Brother Karl's gold-bristled jaw, and Margerite could see the muscles moving in his cheeks. But Brother Wolfgang murmured, "Aye, the Gräfin speaks truly. Remember, Karl, that in this women may be of no less worth than men, though they cannot bear swords. Ask her pardon, and then, maybe, of her courtesy she will have her son brought for us to look at."

Brother Karl's blue eyes dropped, and he ground out, "I beg your pardon, Frowe Gräfin. I did not mean to offend." Then the Teutonic Knight looked straight into Margerite's face again. "But before we go further, we must settle the matter of rank and command, for in all crises there must be a leader, and there will be no time then to speak of who stands where: one must give orders, and the rest obey."

Gottfried looked from the three older knights, with their white-crossed black surcoats - the desire of his heart, Margerite thought, and the standard against which he had ever striven to measure himself - to Margerite. For a moment, Margerite felt herself quailing: how could the gaunt knight not seek to be covered by at least a corner of that mantle after which he longed so? And the Teutonic Knights were both men and warriors, while she, despite all she had done, was still a woman: how could Gottfried accept her command above theirs?

"Because I swore myself to your service, and I have seen your worth," Gottfried answered. "Frowe Gräfin, I will follow you first in whatever need be."

"And I," Ritter Arnmut declared staunchly, his beautiful face set in determination.

"I as well," agreed Eva.

The two younger Teutonic Knights looked at Margerite and Gottfried. Staring into Brother Karl's glass-clear eyes, Margerite felt as if she were straining with all her strength against a great rock. She could not have said how, nor did she know quite what was happening, but it seemed to her that she could feel herself being pushed slowly back, like a youth striving on slippery ground with a man who outweighed him by half again, though he might be the stronger.

"Trotting for hours in full armour is a painful penance," Gottfried said slowly. "Yet command does not always go to him who is most skilled with his weapons: it is best for all to be led by the one who best knows the hazards of the way, and has dealt most closely with the foe - you, Brother, have battled much that is evil, and struggled against the servants of the Light-Bearers, but the frowe Gräfin has dwelt closely with them and pried more deeply into their secrets than either you or I can guess at. Therefore give over with this testing of us: for she is both the most fitting to lead here and has the most at hazard."

Brother Wolfgang stepped back and bowed, a look of surprise on his weatherbeaten face, and Brother Karl looked aside. "Father Etienne did not warn me of this, Herr Ritter," said Brother Wolfgang. "He said only that you could see things of the spirit, though you were short-sighted in the realm of earth; he did not tell me that you could pierce even through a well-warded mind to seek its secrets."

If Margerite had not been watching Ritter Arnmut from the corner of her eye, she would not have marked the young man's faint gasp, nor the way he drew back a little from Gottfried, as though he suddenly feared to stand too near his friend. She bit the inside of her cheek, and turned her eyes aside; but she knew that, as Gottfried's commander, she must speak for him.

"Ritter Gottfried has learned his gifts of late through trial and privation," she said. "He speaks truly, however: this is my own quest and my own danger, and therefore I must lead - though I shall take the advice of those who know better than I when matters require."

Brother Wolfgang looked at Margerite searchingly, his blue eyes pale against the deep tan of his face, and it seemed to her that she felt the cool touch of his gaze upon her soul. "Then, frowe Gräfin, let me advise you as best I may," he said. "If you will, show us this child that the Light-Bearers desire, and tell us what we should know of him, that we may protect him with all our skills."

Margerite wavered. She could not tell these hard-faced knights what the Light-Bearers believed of Wolfram - what if they drew their swords to slay him? She did not know that Gottfried and Arnmut could stand against them. And if Wolfram were tainted by his conception, though Gottfried had never seen it...O Maria, help me to judge rightly!

Then Brother Karl started, staring downward. Kobolt had brushed against his ankles, and was now rubbing against his legs and purring so deeply Margerite thought it would strain the cat's throat. "What manner of creature is this?" he asked, a look of suspicion on his battered face.

"That is my Kobolt, and my friend," Margerite replied. "Though he is no hallowed being, there is no evil in him - and I believe that he likes you."

Brother Karl's hand moved towards his sword-hilt, but Brother Wolfgang restrained him with a small gesture. "No, brother. The creatures of Nature are as God made them, and no foes to us when the Enemy's will does not force them, however they may appear. And the friend of our friend is our ally."

Brother Karl grimaced dubiously, but did not flinch back when Kobolt stood to his full height and pawed at the cross of his sword-hilt. "So be it, then. Frowe Gräfin, we have asked twice: will the third time be enough?"

"It will," Margerite said, though she quailed within. What manner of guide is Kobolt? she asked herself. One who loves Wolfram, and will not see him harmed, was the answer, but it did not comfort her: the great black cat had loved Ruprecht, his fellow-hunter, as well.

In the rooms the Cardinal had given her, Rose was playing with Wolfram and Kriemhilt. They had found a ball along, the way, a pretty thing of bright red and blue stuffed cloth; now the boy, the serving maid, and the cat batted it about between themselves, and Wolfram giggled happily as he toddled after it in Kriemhilt's wake.

The tortoiseshell had almost reached the ball when Kobolt leapt straight over her back, snagging its cloth with his claws, then sinking his teeth in as if he were biting through a rat's neck and shaking it before trotting over to Wolfram and dropping it at the boy's feet.

Margerite's stomach spasmed with fear as she remembered the mouse in her son's cradle: would Wolfram try to kill his toy in turn, as if he were truly a cat? But to her relief, the child only reached to pick the ball up, then overbalanced, sitting down abruptly as he clutched the bright sphere with both hands.

"Go out, Rose, and do not come back until I call you,"
said Margerite, trying to disguise the trembling of her voice
with sternness. If Wolfram were truly marked by the night
of his conception...at least his nursemaid need not know of
it, though what might happen here in the next few minutes,
only Christ and Maria knew.

"How old is he?" Brother Wolfgang asked, staring down at
Wolfram.

"Nine months," said Margerite.

"He is well-grown and bright for his age. Yet..." Brother
Wolfgang crossed himself, not taking his fixed gaze from
Wolfram for a moment, and murmured something in Latin
that Margerite could not make out, before he crouched
to look straight into the boy's eyes. Wolfram immediately
reached out for him, small hands going to the pommel of the
Teutonic Knight's sword; Margerite did not know whether
the look that passed briefly over Brother Wolfgang's lean
weathered face was a smile or a grimace.

"There is a strong spirit in you, is there not?" the warrior-
monk said softly to Wolfram. "But that is hardly to be
wondered at, for I know something of the measure of your
mother and father. Indeed, much is now clear to me that
Father Etienne did not say. I thank Christ that He has given
me the chance to guard you: it would be ill indeed if you fell
into the hands of the Order in your tender years."

Wolfram seemed to be paying no attention to what
Brother Wolfgang had to say: his small bright face was set
in a look of utter determination as he tugged on the knight's
sword-hilt, and this time Brother Wolfgang did smile. "And
you are a warrior born, I think. A pity that you are the only
heir to your estate: you might otherwise have joined our
company when you were grown."

At those words, Margerite remembered her fears
for Wolfram: that the only way to keep him from the
Light-Bearers' clutches would be to give him over to a
better Order, his body held in austerity and his soul in
contemplation. Yet young as he was, Margerite felt that
she knew her son already - he would not be happy in the
sternness of a monk's life, even a monk of a fighting Order,
for he had been born to rule and hunt, and she could already
see the signs of Ruprecht's features beginning to show
beneath the chubbiness of his child's face.

"But he is not...touched with anything evil?" Margerite
asked anxiously. "He was in Ortlieb's hands for some days."

Brother Wolfgang frowned, disengaging Wolfram's
hands from his sword-hilt and standing up. His high brow
furrowed in concentration as he stared once more at the
child, and it almost seemed to Margerite that she could feel
the air stirring with the intensity of his gaze.

"There is...a strangeness about him, yes, though I cannot
say what. It may be as simple as your own inborn skill at the
Art, or such a gift as Ritter Gottfried displays. I do not think
that any spell lies over your son, if that is what you mean.
Though it seems to me that he has already been touched by
some Power, I cannot say that it is for evil."

Margerite thought uncomfortably of the tall shape that
she had seen by Wolfram's cradle, the likeness of Graf
Günther as he had been in life; but she did not wish to speak
of that.

"If you will let us, Frowe Gräfin," Brother Karl said
suddenly, "we may put more protections over your child.
Should the Light-Bearers fail in claiming his body, they may
essay an assault on the citadel of his soul."

Margerite bit her lip. She had not thought of such a thing
- and yet, what if she accepted the Teutonic Knight's offer,
and Madame du Guesclin were able to discern it? She did
not truly know the range of powers the Order Princess could
command, but she could guess that they outstripped her
own.

"I fear to do that until they have looked upon him," she murmured, "for reasons you may well guess - and I do not know whether I fear more not to do it. If the Light-Bearers realize how they have been thwarted, it may be that none of us will leave Avignon alive. And yet..."

"But if the...the Art will not suffice for this, what of our prayers?" asked Gottfried. "If we cannot protect Wolfram without betraying you, may it not be that Christ will lend His aid? The Light-Bearers must rely on their own powers and the gifts of their Master, but our King is a far greater one, whom we can trust to uphold us when our own wills have failed." The knight's bony face lit as he spoke, and it seemed to Margerite that his gray eyes shone in the candlelight.

O Gottfried, she thought, I am so glad that your faith has proven to sustain you, after all. Brother Wolfgang laughed suddenly. "Herr Ritter, I believe you have put us all to shame. Indeed, it is one of the greatest snares for those who practice the Art, to forget whence our power and our protection truly comes. In place of magic, therefore - since we must face some of those who are greatest among the followers of the Fallen One - let us take this babe to the Cardinal's own chapel, and put our trust in Christ, that He will prevail against both the Enemy's force and his guile."

Margerite let out a long breath, clasping her hands together to keep them from shaking. She felt as though something had narrowly passed her, and Wolfram, by... something like the brush of a dark wing, though she did not know what unholy creature could have glided through Father Etienne's wardings, nor gone by unsensed by those who were in the room with her.

The next day, Margerite sent word to Madame du Guesclin that she had arrived in Avignon, though she thought the servant who carried the message would spit when he heard the hated name, and in no way looked forward to explaining to the Cardinal why she had to visit the wife of the man who had besieged Avignon and drained the Papal coffers. The note which arrived in answer was brief: Even-tide tomorrow, at my home. Madame du G.

The Teutonic Knights, of course, could not go with Margerite, but she had Eva, Gottfried, and Arnmut, and whatever befell, she did not think that matters would come to blows so soon. She was loath to take Eva, for behind the girl's brittle gaiety, she could see the shadow of the old fear that had kept her a trembling wraith in Burg Falkenstein, but it would not do for her to come unchaperoned with two unmarried young knights - especially one as handsome as Ritter Arnmut - in her train: the Light-Bearers had enough hold on her without giving them the chance for simple blackmail.

Dusk was just falling when the four of them rode up to Madame du Guesclin's home, the first lights kindling in the windows about them to cast a warm glow over the sodden winter slush and churned mud and filth in the streets. A servant-man stood outside, heavily robed and cloaked against the biting cold.

"Be welcome here, Frowe Gräfin and your companions," he said in perfect Latin, taking the reins of their horses as they dismounted. "Madame du Guesclin is expecting you, and will be pleased at your promptness."

Margerite handed over her reins unwillingly: for all the cultured sound of the servant's voice, he had the face of a thug: the shadow of his hood deepened the pockmarks on his cheeks, and made his close-cropped black beard into a sinister half-mask about his mouth.

Or is it only my fear that makes me see him so? He is truly no more villainous looking than Brother Karl, with his scars and rough manners - if I let myself see evil where none exists, soon I will not notice when it is truly there. But the touch of his hand, when their gloved fingers brushed on the reins, sent a chill up Margerite's arm, and she could not help thinking back to Kundry and Klingschor. And if the mistress is evil, will the servant be any better? Maybe so: there were good folk at Schloss Niederwald - yet, Maria forgive me if I am wrong by it, but I do dislike trusting my horse to this man.

Another servant, a young woman this time, opened the door as Madame du Guesclin's man led the horses away. "Welcome, and enter," she said in a beautifully modulated voice. "The Maitresse awaits you in her study."

Remembering Eva's half-starved state when the girl arrived at Burg Falkenstein, Margerite could not help looking at Madame du Guesclin's serving-maid for signs of ill-treatment. But though the young woman was slender, her skin had the clear glow of good feeding, and she was well-dressed in brocade of a simple green and gold pattern over a fine white linen underdress, her hair neatly coiffed back beneath a white covering.

Margerite and her companions followed the servant-girl up a long dark flight of stairs and down a hallway, where the young woman stopped to tap on a door, saying something in French. The woman's voice that replied was deep and rich, and it seemed to Margerite that, although she spoke quietly, she could hear the great power held back behind it.

Why, she is no bigger than a child! Margerite thought as soon as the door opened. Madame du Guesclin was more than a handspan shorter than Margerite herself, and seemed shorter yet for being so heavily built, her massive bosom uplifted by a sturdy bodice of deep red velvet.

The coif upon her head was the barest wisp of white silk, her red-brown hair gleaming beneath it, and she wore red velvet shoes on her tiny feet. Margerite remembered that Bertrand du Guesclin was said to be remarkably short, as well as ugly - but he must seem like a giant beside his wife.

Then Madame du Guesclin's eyes met Margerite's, and all her surprise at the woman's stature was gone. The Order woman's blue eyes were remarkably wide and bright, set at a slight tilt in a high-cheekboned face, and the light in them reminded Margerite terribly of the shining figure that had come to her bedroom in Burg Falkenstein.

Madame du Guesclin came very close, so that she and Margerite were almost touching, and peered up into her face: if Margerite had not spent so much time with Gottfried, she might not have recognised that searching look. She must be even more nearsighted than he is - does she share his other gifts?

"Greetings, Gräfin Margerite," said the Frenchwoman. "Come and sit down; Jeanne will bring wine and cakes for us."

Margerite settled herself into a chair, as did Eva, but Gottfried and Arnmut stayed on their feet. "Please, good knights," Madame du Guesclin went on. "There is no danger in this house - I trust." She laughed.

Reluctantly Gottfried sat down, Arnmut following, though the two knights stayed very straight in their seats, and Margerite could almost see Gottfried bristling. What does he see? she wondered. Maria help us all, Gottfried, at least try not to give yourself away.

The serving maid brought in wine and a selection of small dainties on a tray, honey-cakes and small pies stuffed with meat and chicken. Wolfram was beginning to squirm in Margerite's lap, and she thought he would start crying soon, but she feared for the safety of her hostess' rugs and furniture if she let her child wander freely.

Madame du Guesclin's study was very well appointed, the honey-coloured wood of the cabinets that lined the walls finely carved with scenes that Margerite guessed must be from the great poets of Rome, showing satyrs and dryads and centaurs and such half-human creatures.

"I am pleased to meet you, Gräfin," Madame du Guesclin said. "I have heard a great deal about you; as you may know, poor Günther and I were close friends."

"Graf Günther rendered Burg Falkenstein great assistance in our time of need," Margerite replied soberly. "Surely I must count any friend of his as one of my own."

"And your companions are..?"

"Frowe Eva von Bärenberg, and the Ritters Gottfried von Schlangenbad and Arnmut von Eisenstein."

Madame du Guesclin raised her eyebrows at the first name. "Eva von Bärenberg - you were at the Convent of the Holy Cross for a time, were you not? Forgive me if I did not recognise you: it has been some time."

Margerite saw Eva flinch beneath her polite smile; she could only hope that Madame du Guesclin was too short-sighted to notice. At that moment, Wolfram let out a piercing wail, and Margerite's nose told her that he had soiled his breechclout.

"Of your courtesy, madame," Margerite said in much embarassment. "I must tend to my son."

"Come with me. Forgive us, Frowe Eva, good knights: children, alas, will seldom wait upon the needs of courtesy."

Madame du Guesclin led Margerite out and up a further flight of stairs, to a room at the top of the house. It was small, but well-furnished, a thick feather coverlet on the bed and a stove crackling warmly by the wall. Although Margerite knew that this could not be the Order Princess' sanctum, she could feel the hairs prickling on the back of her neck: she did not think she was far from the room where Madame du Guesclin performed her magics.

"Well-done, if somewhat over-swift," the little Frenchwoman remarked over Wolfram's cries. "But I wanted to ask you some questions about your companions, and this was as good an excuse as any. Can you quiet that child now?"

"He truly must be changed," Margerite admitted. "Yet perhaps the best ruse is the truthful one - have you the things I will need in the house?"

"Fortunately, one of the kitchen girls is suckling her babe. She will undoubtedly have cloths." Madame du Guesclin lifted a large silver bell from the bedside table and rang it, its piercing note clanging through the air. When Jeanne appeared, the Order Princess gave her orders swiftly, waiting for the sound of the girl's feet running down the stairs to fade before she spoke again.

"Eva von Bärenberg, I know by repute: she was one of the Abbess' girls, but I believe Graf Ruprecht had other plans for her. How did she come to be your apprentice, and by what right have you given her the onyx ring so quickly?"

"By the same right through which any of us gains it," Margerite answered boldly.

Madame du Guesclin cocked her silk-clothed head to one side, peering up into Margerite's face again. "By challenge, or by skill?"

"By skill."

"We shall see," the older woman said doubtfully. "And what of your bodyguards? How did you come by them?"

"They are both knights of Heinrich's household. They have no skill in magic, nor do they know of the Order; but they are faithful to me - and I could hardly make such a journey with no swords save those of the Bear's Paw Company to guard me, when I must visit persons of note." Margerite prayed that Madame du Guesclin would accept that answer: more than anything, she wished to keep the woman's attention away from Gottfried, for Kobolt and Kriemhilt could dissemble better than the forthright young knight.

"Persons of note, indeed," Madame du Guesclin mused. "Now tell me how it is that you are staying in the house of Jean de Grenville?"

Margerite did not dare to hesitate. Quickly she told the other of what Nikolaus had done, and her need to speak with the Pope to keep the annulment from going through. "Therefore, I thought it best to stay with one who could get me audience - and could not be linked in any way to the Order: even you have mentioned that Etienne the Exorcist is among our enemies, and he must have his own means of getting word from Avignon."

Madame du Guesclin smiled. "I am pleased to see that you have learned caution - if it is caution to lodge with the friend of a foeman. But you seem to have a great talent for cloaking your true intentions with a seeming of piety."

Those words stung Margerite deeply, for she knew all too well how accurately that described her lies about her travels. At least, to her relief, she could hear Jeanne's light swift footfalls coming up the stairs again, so that she had to say no more until Wolfram had been washed and changed.

"Now let me look at him," Madame du Guesclin said, holding out her arms for the baby. The ruby ring, twin to Margerite's own, gleamed on her plump little finger, and Margerite almost balked then: it seemed that she could feel something stirring in the air about the two of them, like the powerful coils of a great snake - such as rings the Light-Bearer circles -beginning to tighten on its prey. Yet that knowledge of danger seemed to strengthen her will, so that she was able to let the other woman take Wolfram without flinching or protesting.

As Madame du Guesclin stared into Wolfram's eyes, Margerite became aware of a low growling sound by her feet, and felt the weight of Kobolt leaning against her ankle. The cat did not hiss nor arch his back, but he was looking steadily up at Madame du Guesclin with a fixed yellow gaze that Margerite could not interpret, and suddenly let out a deep miaow that broke down almost to a roar - not a growl or the scream of challenge Margerite had heard Kobolt give when he came to a place where strange tomcats dwelt; closer to the sound he made when there was a queen in heat about. A chill prickling down her back, Margerite remembered how Madame du Guesclin had first appeared to her...O my Kobolt, I think this she-cat is somewhat beyond your reach!

Madame du Guesclin paid no attention to Kobolt, holding Wolfram so close to her face that her nose almost touched his. "I can see Prince Günther's touch here, yes..." she murmured, and Margerite's stomach knotted in foreboding: had the Light-Bearer been able to accomplish more with her son in death than in life?

But then the Frenchwoman thrust the child out, so
abruptly that Wolfram let out a high piercing cry and
Margerite hurried to snatch him from the other woman's
arms. "You did not tell me that Günther had failed!"

The words caught Margerite in the pit of the stomach
like a blow; but her gasp was as much from joy as from fear.
Even though she knew that Madame du Guesclin must be
referring to the blasphemous anti-baptism that the Order
Prince had desired for Wolfram, to have the Light-Bearer
confirming her son's freedom from taint was like a sudden
ray of sunlight bearing a shimmer of Heaven's grace.

But Madame du Guesclin was staring at her, the look in
her blue eyes more intense for her short sight, as though
that closeness distilled her gaze to the potency of a basilisk's.
Margerite straightened her back, putting her own strength
into the answering look she gave the little Frenchwoman
as she clutched Wolfram to her - and the falcon's eyes are
keener than the cat's.

In a sudden flash, almost too swift to put into words, it
seemed to her that she understood how Ortlieb had come
to deal with living folk as if they were demons within her
circle: it was ever thus with the Order, that they must strive
for mastery over one another. And with the rest of us? Did
Gottfried and I not strive so with the Teutonic Knights?
But Margerite had no room for doubt now: like a knight
charging a row of pikemen, she must break through at full
strength or fall.

"When was I to tell you such a thing? I could not report it
through Nikolaus, or Damiano; I know that neither of them
is of such a rank that he should have been told more than
how precious Wolfram is to us. I could hardly discuss such
matters with Princess Ortlieb, when she would challenge
me for my son, and I her, for the ruby ring - and her life.
Nor have we spoken in spirit more than the once, and there
was little enough time then. But for my part, I procured for
Prince Günther all the things he told me to; and what befell
when I was torn and weary from long labour and the bearing
of my first child, I still am not wholly sure."

Madame du Guesclin's blue-hot gaze seemed to sear into Margerite's soul; but now it seemed to her that her many hours of painful trial with Gottfried stood her in good stead, for it was easier to raise a wall of adamant against the thoughts of a foe than to gently guide a friend away from what he should not see. And though the Light-Bearer's power as a sorceress might outstrip Margerite's strength and that of the young knight together, Madame du Guesclin lacked Gottfried's inborn gift, and the unbearable sharpness to which over a month of harsh privation had brought it, those first days in Burg Falkenstein.

At the edge of her sight, Margerite barely noticed Kobolt's black head lifting by her knee; but she heard his plaintive cry as he sprang at Madame du Guesclin's velvet-shod foot, back hunching and tail sticking straight out as if he were trying to mount a queen. Of a sudden, Madame du Guesclin's gaze broke, and she looked down incredulously at the great black cat purring and chirping urgently against her shoe. Margerite held her breath - but the Light-Bearer Princess threw back her head with a rich rolling laugh, and bent to pick Kobolt up.

The tom was so large, and she so short, that she looked like nothing so much as a plump little girl of eight holding her first cat athwart her body like a shawl, all her majesty and awe gone in a moment. "He recognises another cat," Madame du Guesclin said, rubbing her own cheek against Kobolt's even as he purred and kneaded the red velvet of her bodice. "Yet tell me: how did you come to have an earth-spirit as your familiar? Episcopus Ruprecht reported that he had procured you one of the servants of our Master."

Margerite was almost too shocked to answer: she could tell herself only, I should have remembered better, that Kobolt cares neither for good nor evil - and would be drawn to a she-cat without any doubt! But she managed to master herself, saying, "I did not choose him, but rather it was he who came to me. What Ruprecht may have done, I do not know."

"I see," the Order Princess said, but she was smiling. "Ruprecht's strokes seem often to have gone awry. Still this may, after all, serve you better than a being which might be more clearly marked as bearing the substance of true Light, as he will often be able to go where they could not, and endure the folly of our foes as they cannot...Now," she added suddenly, "we cannot stay away too much longer, but I have found what I needed to know. It will take at least two weeks to call the Council of Princes together, and to prepare fully to do what Prince Günther could not manage. And the stars must stand in their right courses as well: know you much of astrology?"

"Far less than of many other things," Margerite answered truthfully, for she could tell that the time for a struggle of pride had passed. "Neither Ruprecht nor Nikolaus was, I think, more learned in that than must be for their works, and in preparing to meet Ortlieb, I studied the lore of spirits, not of stars. And I know that you are renowned for your skill in that Art, even among the great."

Madame du Guesclin nodded her silk-coifed head. "In all of Europe, there is none to match me. Only Flegetanis, who dwells undying yet in Egypt, may rightly claim to be my master - I see you know the name?" For Margerite could not hide her start: Nikolaus had spoken to her of the heathen Flegetanis, who had discovered the secret of the Grail in the stars, according to Wolfram von Eschenbach's master Kyot - whom Nikolaus had claimed for the Order of Light-Bearers.

The little Frenchwoman scratched behind Kobolt's ears, smiling still. "That is well. And I am pleased to see that you have learned the difference between needful pride and folly. So be it. You will come to my house every day, and I shall teach you even as we cast the horoscopes to seek out the most propitious time for sealing the Child to the service of his Father - for it is meet that the falcon should be most acquainted with the powers of the heavens. Now come." She bent over to put Kobolt on the floor, disengaging his claws from her bodice with the ease of long practice, and staying bent a moment to stroke him as he wound about her legs; nor did she hurry to brush the black hairs from her velvet dress, as many another woman would have.

If you were not a deadly foe, Margerite thought - to her surprise, almost with regret, I believe I would offer you one of the kittens of Kobolt and Kriemhilt: I think you care well for your own kind, and it must be lonely for you with your husband so often away at war. Margerite was shocked at herself for the thought; but, deeper down, it seemed to her that it was well: remembering Madame du Guesclin's kindness to her cat would make it easier to pray for her with an open heart, as Father Etienne would admonish his student to do.

It seemed to Margerite, walking trembling-legged down the long stairs, that she and Madame du Guesclin must have been closeted for more than an hour. Yet though all three of her companions were still eating polite nibbles, the tray of dainties that Jeanne had brought in hardly seemed to have been touched: Arnmut was just finishing off a small pastry, and Eva popped the last bite of a honey-cake into her mouth as the two older women came in.

"That was swift enough," Eva said approvingly. "Sometimes the young Graf will keep screaming until he has cried himself to sleep - will you not, poppet?" she asked, moving over to pat Wolfram. For a moment, her back was to Madame du Guesclin; and in that moment, Eva looked desperately down at Margerite, but Margerite could only make the vaguest of signals to her, hoping that Eva would understand that all would be explained later.

They talked of small things for some time more, or rather, Madame du Guesclin talked while the rest of them nodded and made courteous noises: she had an inexhaustible fund of information about Avignon and the more notable people in it, but her pauses for breath were hardly long enough to allow the others to speak even a word or two.

She also had the disconcerting habit of changing subjects halfway through a sentence, sometimes even halfway through a word, as though her thoughts were outrunning her speech, until Margerite was beginning to feel ready to forcibly stuff one of the little spiced meat pies into the Frenchwoman's mouth in hopes that it would at least slow her down.

In spite of that, however, and although Madame du Guesclin seemed to have cultivated a scattered and frivolous manner, her intelligence could not be mistaken: she referred casually to great works of science and philosophy, and Margerite could tell that she must be receiving news from all over Europe and beyond, for she knew more of the political happenings of the time than ever Margerite had heard discussed, even at the table of the Bishop of Niederwald.

At last, however, Madame du Guesclin rose to her feet, dislodging Kobolt from the folds of her skirt that had lain piled upon the rug. The black cat rose with a sleepy chirp, stretching and yawning so that the candlelight glinted on the white spikes of his teeth.

"You have something of a journey yet, and Avignon is less safe by night than by day," she said. "Though I do not doubt your prowess, good knights, by your leave, I shall send Louis and a few of my other guardsmen with you to bear torches and escort you safe through the city: a stranger may easily become lost in the dark here. I look forward to seeing you upon the morrow."

Though Gottfried would not have admitted it, he was almost grateful for the guidance of Madame du Guesclin's servants through the streets of Avignon. He was lost here - more so than he would have been in any wood at home, for there he knew the sounds of deer and boar and night-birds, whereas here in France, the few words he caught from those who walked quickly along the street, wrapped in thick cloaks against the sharp cold air and carrying small lanterns in their hands, were so foreign that he could not even guess whether a couple coming down the street were highborn folk on a lawful errand, or a prostitute and her evening's customer.

Ritter Arnmut rode in front of the two women; Gottfried followed behind; two servants with lanterns walked before and after each, and behind the last lantern-bearers rode one of Madame du Guesclin's men on horseback, a dark and silent figure. We are well-come out of there: Christ help us, that we must go back! Was there no other way for the Frowe Gräfin to deal with that woman? the knight wondered.

He was sure that, had there been, Gräfin Margerite would have taken it - and yet, the snippets of thought that had come to his veiled mind like the murmurs of conversation in another room left him warier of the Light-Bearer Princess than ever. Gottfried had not dared to listen too closely, yet he had clearly heard Madame du Guesclin thinking.

She has a plausible excuse for everything, yet we shall see...She deceived and slew Ortlieb: what shall she do when she finds that there are ranks among the Council of Princes, some set as high above others as Ortlieb was above she herself? As the mother of the Child...Shadows had passed in and out of the room as they spoke, half-formed and monstrous shapes; and he had seen the little woman's wide eyes flaring yellow about cat-swollen pupils in the candlelight.

It took no art to guess what form she would wear in the spirit-world where the Frowe Gräfin flew as a falcon - and though Gottfried had become fond of Kobolt and Kriemhilt, he had also marked how they played with mice between their paws: ill would be spoken of a human hunter who dealt so with his prey. At last they came to the Porte du Rhône, and there Madame du Guesclin's servants bade them farewell and turned away.

Though a few scudding clouds shadowed the stars, the Moon's light was still bright enough for them to see their way, the stones of St. Benezet's Bridge clattering icily beneath their horses' hooves as they crossed. A faint mist overhung the fields on the other side of the river, so that Gottfried could not tell whether they were already silvered by frost, or only by moonlight and damp.

The rider who had followed them with Madame du Guesclin's other servants was still behind Gottfried: he must have been given the charge of making sure that they reached Cardinal de Grenville's mansion without becoming lost on the way, though the road was easy enough to follow.

Gottfried misliked being followed so closely by a servant of their enemy, and wondered if he could turn to the man and say, "Go home now; we do not wish your company."

Ahead, Margerite and Eva were talking in low voices, but Gottfried could hear their words clearly enough. "I do remember her from the Convent of the Holy Cross," Eva was saying, and even with his short sight in the moonlight, Gottfried could see how the young noblewoman's shoulders hunched forward as if she expected a blow across them. "She came there in the spring of 'sixty-four, for...Christ help me, I fear to speak of it!"

Do you not know that one of Madame du Guesclin's men is still with us? Gottfried thought in shocked surprise. And I thought it would be I who failed in dissembling.

The knight glanced back to the black-cloaked rider who followed them. It was then he realized - were his eyes better, he might have seen it before - though the dark horse ambled as swiftly as their own steeds, he could not hear its breathing, nor did any white clouds puff from its nostrils in the frosty air.

Gottfried's gloved hand went to the hilt of his sword, tightening upon its leather wrappings, and froze there: were the Frowe Gräfin what she pretended to be, this would be the servant of an ally who rode silently behind them. Yet in a moment, the Frowe Gräfin or Frowe Eva would give themselves away to him irremediably...

Gathering all his strength, Gottfried focused his gaze as tightly as he could upon the slim blurred figure of the Gräfin, and cried out in thought as though he were shouting above the noise of a battlefield, Margerite, be silent!

Margerite shrieked aloud, her horse trying to rear and crow-hop to the side at once. To his horror, Gottfried saw the Gräfin lose her seat, coming off as the gray gelding's hooves hit the ground again. Eva was wrestling with her own mount; ahead of them, Gottfried saw the flash of Arnmut's sword, the younger knight's hair and face pale in the moonlight as he wheeled his horse to face whatever danger might be there. Of the dark rider behind them, there was no trace.

Gottfried leapt from his own steed at once - Löwen would stand until he remounted - and darted in to grab the reins of Margerite's horse before, in its fright, it could tread on the Gräfin - or on Wolfram; please Christ, he was not crushed in the fall! thought Gottfried, desperately trying to look over the dark frost-rimmed ground to see if the child had been flung free. He thought his heart would stop in his chest when he heard Wolfram's high angry wail; but Margerite lay still on the earth.

"Keep watch!" Gottfried said to Arnmut, thrusting Margerite's reins into Eva's hands - poor rider that she was, surely even she could hold another horse - and crouching down beside the Gräfin.

Margerite had fallen on her back, protecting her child with her body; her arms were still clasped lightly about Wolfram, who was beginning to squirm out of his warm wrappings, but she had had no way to break her own fall, or keep her head from striking the earth. Was her neck broken? No: Gottfried felt along the Gräfin's spine with trembling hands, and nearly wept in relief when her head moved and he saw her arms tightening on her child.

"Frowe Gräfin," Gottfried stammered. He did not know what to say, but he helped Margerite to sit up. She blinked, staring at him with eyes that were golden in the silvery moonlight as she clutched her wailing child to her breast.

"Gottfried," the Gräfin said weakly. "What happened? I thought that someone struck me a heavy blow to the skull...Were we attacked? How did they come upon us thus unawares?"

Gottfried lowered his eyes in shame, for he could not bring himself to meet her gaze. "It was I, Frowe Gräfin," he confessed, his voice nearly lost beneath Wolfram's angry cries. "We were followed by one of Madame du Guesclin's servants - I wished only to warn you, for that you and Frowe Eva were speaking so freely."

"My head feels as though I had been struck by a hammer," Margerite answered. "And I think I am not the only one."

Indeed, as Gottfried looked up, he saw Frowe Eva pressing her free hand to her white brow; and when Arnmut wheeled his horse back and said, "Gottfried, I see nothing - what is amiss?" his voice was faint as if he were wounded.

"I am sorry," Gottfried murmured.

The Gräfin held out an arm so that he might help her to her feet. "Aid me to remount now, and we shall speak more when we are safely within Cardinal de Grenville's walls." Margerite handed her screaming child to the knight and turned towards her horse; but she must have seen or guessed something of Gottfried's thoughts, for she turned swiftly back. "Gottfried, do not torment yourself with this," the Gräfin whispered to him, her delicate moonlit face close to his as a secret lover's. "Rough as you were - and how should you not be, with as little teaching as I have been able to give you? - you may yet have saved us from a greater peril."

They rode back slowly and in silence, save for Wolfram's cries. Cardinal de Grenville's gate guards looked curiously at their faces, but did not challenge them; but as soon as Brother Karl and Brother Wolfgang caught sight of the four of them, the Teutonic Knights crossed themselves, hastening forward as if to catch wounded comrades before they collapsed.

"Come to our chambers," Brother Wolfgang said quietly. "There you may tell us what befell you. Brother Helmuth is abed already, for he is old and needs a great deal of sleep these days, but I think we will not disturb him."

As soon as Gottfried stepped through the door of the chambers shared by the two military Brothers, he felt a great sense of peace settling over his soul. He could see that the luxury of the Cardinal's dwelling had been lessened as best it might be. Reeds strewed the floor instead of thick rugs, and the pitcher of hot wine steaming upon the carven oak table was a plain pewter that matched the Teutonic Knights' own goblets, dented and scratched - undoubtedly gear of their own that they preferred to the silver and gold plate of Jean de Grenville: the tray of honey-cakes beside it was silver with gilded handles, and richly wrought and engraved.

On the wall hung a large crucifix with three candles burning before it, and it seemed to Gottfried that, blurred as Christ's features were in his sight, he could nevertheless make out the keen look, both stern and kindly, that the carver had put in the Lord's eyes. *If only I might enter the Teutonic Order!* Gottfried thought longingly.

*Better, if I had entered it before ever Graf Heinrich and Graf Ruprecht went to war: then I should not know what I know now, and could turn my strength against the darkness of the world, rather than that of my own soul...*

*And yet, what would have become of the Frowe Gräfin and all her brave friends in Niederwald, had I not been there? Rather, I should thank Christ for the battles he has sent me, and pray for the strength to overcome the trials of my nature - for all men are sinners, and all fall short of the glory of God.*

*At least, though it breaks my heart, Arnmut has kept his distance since Brother Wolfgang revealed my gift...though I wish with all my soul that he did not seem to fear me now: I would give almost anything to have our friendship as it was.* Gottfried's eyes stung, and the candleflames blurred to haloes in his sight, their golden light shot through with glimmers of blue and purple and red.

Brother Karl patted him on the shoulder. "Calm your heart, brother," the Teutonic Knight said, his rough voice dropping to a murmur, so that Gottfried was not sure whether his lips were moving or not. "All roads worth travelling seem harsh and thorny at the beginning, but glory lies at their end, and joy beyond human compass: nor is there any telling when Christ will send a true companion and helpmeet to aid one along the way."

Gottfried felt his cheekbones warming, for he could not guess how much of his thought he had let slip, unguarded. But Brother Karl knows what I am: I am as sure of that as if I had made Confession to him.

"Calm your heart," Brother Karl whispered silently again, "and try to quiet your mind. I can tell that you have had a grievous shock this evening, but you do not want your companions to hear your every thought." Gottfried met the Teutonic Knight's eyes, bright against his battered face with warmth and something that might have been affection or pity, and he nodded, slowly repeating his accustomed prayers as Margerite had taught him to do.

"Eat," Brother Wolfgang was ordering the rest of them. "It is as well for you that there were honey-pastries left over in the kitchen; that will restore you after such work, for it drains the body just as if you had been doing battle in the harshest cold of winter."

For a moment, it seemed to Gottfried that he could see snow deep as a man's waist, feel frosty air so chill that blades chipped when they met and armour seemed to burn with the cold even through the sweat-soaked padding of gambesons - and the deep marrow-gnawing weariness that he knew too well, of fasting and riding hard in winter until no fire could warm the ice from his bones, and no sleep restore his strength.

Arnmut did not meet his eyes, as the younger knight had not done since yester-evening, but shyly he held one of the sweet pastries out to Gottfried.

"You must eat, if the good Brother says so," Arnmut insisted. "I do not know what happened, but you are pale as if - Christ forfend! - you lay in your shroud."

Yet, where their fingers might once have touched in friendship, Arnmut pulled his hand away as soon as Gottfried had taken the little cake, as though he feared to be burned by his senior's touch. And though Gottfried obediently took a bite of it, he could not taste the sweetness, and it seemed to stick in his throat as a dry lump.

The Gräfin told of their meeting with Madame du Guesclin. The Teutonic Knights listened carefully: Brother Karl's thick yellow eyebrows raised and drew in with his surprise and worry, but Brother Wolfgang's lean weathered face was impassive, only his keen blue eyes moving from Margerite to one or another of her companions. "And you say that your Kobolt greeted her as a friend?"

"He is a spirit of earth," Margerite said defensively, "and knew only a female cat. One cannot ask such a creature to be wise beyond the measure according to which God created him!"

"Calm yourself, Gräfin. I do not condemn your familiar spirit: I only mark that we must be wary, since he cannot lead you through this as he has led you through other troubles. But this does not explain why the four of you staggered in here as though you had been doing battle with demons, unless something took place which you have not told us yet."

"Ritter Gottfried?" said the Gräfin. Her voice was quiet, yet Gottfried could not mistake the command in it. Quickly, trying hard not to look away for shame, Gottfried explained what he had seen and what he had tried to do - and done.

Brother Wolfgang smiled ruefully, a mere lifting of one corner of his thin lips. "Often, they say, the untrained fighter may be the most dangerous, for there is no guessing what he may do who has never learned the proper ways of stroke and counterstroke. And we have seen that ourselves - is that not so, Karl?"

Brother Karl made a noise like the quiet grunt of a boar, his mouth twitching as if with a painful memory. Again, it seemed to Gottfried that he could see a tiny village beneath cruelly deep snow - a bow in the hands of a brown-cloaked peasant woman, and a knife flashing in the hands of a child as he flung himself on a full-armoured knight, stabbing unexpectedly through the opening of his bascinet so that blood spurted from the knight's half-cut throat - and Brother Karl touched the thick white scar down his neck as though it still pained him.

"Were you with our Order, Ritter Gottfried," Brother Wolfgang went on, "we would be able to put you in seclusion until you had learned what to do with your talents. Now...I fear that you may be a danger to all of us. And yet - the Frowe Gräfin must decide this, for you are her man, but I would hesitate to send you away: had Madame du Guesclin's creature followed you this far, it would have entered when the gate-guard gave all of you permission to come in, for even Father Etienne's wardings cannot stand against a free and legitimate invitation. And then matters should have gone ill for us indeed!"

"But what can I do?" Gottfried asked desperately. "Save for the mercy of Christ, I might have caused the death of the Frowe Gräfin or her son. And yet I only meant to warn her!"

"That is well indeed, for had you been trying to send more than speech..." Brother Wolfgang's voice trailed off, and he shook his head. "And I can only train you a little, for such gifts as yours are rare, and call for a teacher who has mastered them himself. The best I can say to you - if the Gräfin means to keep you by her - is: be careful, and if you must try to bespeak another, hold back your strength as well as you can. And pray to Christ, that He may guide you well, for He did not bless you so to no purpose, and there is no telling what part He means you to play."

Gottfried nodded. His hands were shaking; when he looked down at them, his thin fingers seemed insubstantial as trails of mist, his pale wrists beneath the dark silk of his sleeves no thicker or stronger than peeled willow-wands, and it seemed almost as though he were half a ghost already. Margerite was watching him, her high-boned face still white and drawn - whether from her fall, or from the blow he had unknowingly struck her, Gottfried could not tell.

She held Wolfram cradled closely in her arms; the babe had stopped crying at last, but he still squirmed fretfully now and again. Still, it seemed to Gottfried almost as though he were looking upon an image of the Virgin, aching heart-deep in the knowledge of the evil done by men, and that he himself was the first cause of her suffering.

Gottfried knelt before the Gräfin, bowing his head. "Frowe Gräfin," he said painfully. "Forgive me, for I have wronged you grievously, and only by Christ's mercy was it not worse. If you choose to send me from your service now, you are well within your rights, and I shall swear to seek out Father Etienne and abide by his advice to me, whatever it is."

"Not without me," Arnmut said, though his voice was so quiet that Gottfried did not know whether he had spoken aloud or not. Still, the younger knight's words were a glimmer of starlight through the heavy sorrow that settled over Gottfried's heart as he knelt on the hard stone and prickly rushes, waiting to hear what doom the Frowe Gräfin would speak.

Margerite was silent a long time, and Gottfried had to force himself to meditate on his prayers, lest he hear what he should not from her. Brother Wolfgang had advised that he be allowed to stay - but Brother Wolfgang was a man, and childless. And Margerite would risk much for herself that she would not for her son.

"My Gottfried," Margerite murmured, and Gottfried was quite sure that her lips did not move, "how can I send you away? I have already lost Bernhardt; I should be utterly lost without you. I have tended plenty of men that were hurt in accidents on the training-field, and it seems to me that this is little different, for whatever one can fight with, whether sword or wand or soul, must have some danger in learning its use - though I can only beg you, now that you have seen your strength, to be careful!"

Then she spoke aloud, and it seemed to Gottfried for the first time that her voice had a different resonance, like church-bells heard in the open air, rather than ringing within a cathedral's stony shell. "Herr Ritter, I shall by no means send you away, for I trust you, and you have done great service to us this night. Nor shall I bind you not to use your gifts among us, for there is no telling what may come to pass. I forgive you freely and wholly for whatever harm you did or might have done unknowingly, and pray you put it from your mind, save as a caution to keep you from using your strength too fully upon your friends. Now rise, and be at ease!"

Gottfried stood, and Margerite leaned forward to give him the kiss of peace, her lips chill and soft against his cheek. Still, when Margerite and her companions rode towards Avignon the next day, Margerite could not help glancing back at Gottfried now and again. Her head still ached a little from the echo of his blast, and Eva had complained of her headache all night - what would it have done to them if he had tried to do more than shout?

Though she knew it was unworthy of her, and that the ascetic knight would never willingly harm her, she could not help the faint tinge of fear that quickened her heart now whenever she met Gottfried's icy gaze, and had to force herself not to pull Wolfram away when he looked upon the child. And yet it is worse for him than for me, she reminded herself as they rode over St. Benezet's bridge. Even Arnmut fears Gottfried now, bravely as he tries to overcome it.

"Am I truly needed for this?" Eva asked as they passed beneath the stone arch of the Porte du Rhône. "If I am, I shall stay beside you, but if not..." Eva looked around at the crowd in the street, ermine-edged and velvet cloaks mingling with garments of rough brown wool. "After all," she added artlessly, "you did say that I was in need of new clothes, and truly, my bodices are growing so tight that I can hardly breathe."

Margerite found herself unexpectedly laughing: for all they had been through, Eva was still but sixteen. And, more grimly, while they had undressed last night, Eva had told her something of what Madame du Guesclin had visited the Convent of the Holy Cross to do: Margerite was glad enough to have an excuse, at least for a little time, not to force her ward to deal unnecessarily with the Order Princess. She unhooked a small purse of gold from her belt, passing it over to Eva.

"That is true enough: you should not be falling out of your dress when we meet with the Holy Father. Take Arnmut as your bodyguard, and go see what you can find - thank Christ, almost everyone in this city seems to speak Latin as well as French. You may as well see for some new clothes for the Ritter, too, since he has been growing nearly as swiftly as you, and Heinrich - Christ have mercy on him," Margerite added softly, "would never have allowed one of his knights to seem ill-clad. And, if you are able to do so without going into unseemly places, see if the two of you can find Paul the Bear and his men." Margerite paused, thinking. The Council of Princes would be some two weeks hence - yet if she told the Bear's Paw to be ready for that date, she had no doubt that the word would pass from the taverns through many mouths and ears, and cast more than a little suspicion upon her. "Just be sure," she finished lamely, "that we can reach them at once if we have need to. It will probably be Arnmut who must seek them out, so he must know where to find them, even if he is riding swiftly in the darkness."

"Of course. Ritter Arnmut!" Eva called, lifting her voice. The fair-haired knight turned his horse as swiftly as if he were in battle; its hooves kicked up clumps of muck, and a couple of passerbys shook their fists and cursed vilely in French, but dared no more.

"What is it, Frowe Eva?" Arnmut asked.

"Come with me. I will need your strong arm to protect me, for we have much to do today... and Ritter Gottfried and Margerite are well-able to deal with their duties," Eva added as Arnmut's beautiful face clouded with doubt. She kicked her horse into a swifter walk to ride beside the young knight, reaching out to touch his arm lightly and guide him down another street. Margerite gazed after them: Arnmut's golden hair gleamed even in the dull January sunlight, bright above his blue cloak; Eva's long golden braid was coiled up and hidden beneath her white linen coif, but - so long as her palfrey was walking quietly - she sat tall and proud as a queen upon the little steed's back, and now and again she turned to speak to Arnmut, showing the clear lines of her profile.

They are a fair couple, Margerite thought, and anyone might be excused for thinking them betrothed. As Gottfried nudged his own horse forward to ride beside her, it occurred to Margerite then that the two of them might as easily be mistaken for husband and wife. But Gottfried looked as though he had not slept well the night before, his gray eyes darkened beneath the staring ridges of his cheekbones: a watcher might easily have taken Margerite and the young knight for a pair of weary pilgrims, and thought Gottfried's thinness to be the sign of some crippling wound or disease. And for all Eva's suffering in her youth, it had not marked the girl's face, whereas Margerite thought that if she looked half as old as she felt, she must already be nearly a hag.

"That is not so," Gottfried said reassuringly. "Believe me, your trials have only made you the more fair."

Margerite started: it was in her mind to chide him for not taking more care, but she could not say truthfully that she had not wanted the comfort; and from Gottfried, at least, she need not fear courtly flattery. Instead she said, "Herr Ritter, do you know how old I am?"

Gottfried's gray eyes widened: he could not have expected such a question from her. He stammered uncomfortably, "Frowe Gräfin, I...that is, ah...no."

"I shall be nineteen come next month. Is it any wonder that I feel old before my time?"

"I had thought you older, perhaps a little older than I," Gottfried confessed, then added hurriedly, "though only because of your wisdom, and because you are so well-practiced in leadership, as many women never become."

"I have often heard it said - at least among women," Margerite added, smiling, "that women grow up more swiftly than men. You are...twenty-one, twenty-two, perhaps?"

"I shall be twenty-three in June."

"And you hold a post of great honour in Heinrich's castle, and perhaps greater here, so much as I can give. Yet you are still a virgin..." Gottfried flushed, but Margerite pressed on, "whereas I have been twice wedded, widowed, and had to tend and fear for my son since I first knew he was in my womb, more than a year past. Perhaps it would be surprising if I did not seem the older of us two."

Gottfried looked downward, and Margerite could not guess what he was thinking, though his sharp-featured face seemed both thoughtful and sad: she hoped that she had not hurt him by speaking of things that - perhaps if all went best for him - he might never know. Then he gazed about himself with the peculiarly intense look that told Margerite he was trying to make out some landmark, or perhaps force the blur of colours on a painted board above the door of a shop or inn to resolve into some clear image in his sight.

"Frowe Gräfin, if I do not mistake our way, we are nearly at Madame du Guesclin's home. And...where is your Kobolt? I thought that I saw him curled against your saddle-cantle earlier, but he is gone now."

"He comes and goes as he will," Margerite said lightly, but she could not help feeling some foreboding at the knight's words. There were spells to command elemental spirits, just as there were rites to command demons, and Kobolt had left plenty of his fur upon Madame du Guesclin's gown the evening before: could the Order subvert even her dear cat?

As before, though Margerite had said nothing to Madame du Guesclin about when she would come, the same servant was standing before the house. He seemed rather less ill-favoured by daylight, the marring of his pocked face only a faded mottling such as any man who had suffered from bad skin in his youth might show, and his neat black beard displaying a stylish cut, rather than appearing as an ominous half-mask of shadow.

"Welcome, Frowe Gräfin, good knight," he said. "My Maitresse awaits you within." He offered Margerite his arm so that she could get down without disturbing Wolfram, and took the reins of their horses again.

When Jeanne showed them into Madame du Guesclin's study, Margerite had to bite her lip to keep from gasping. Kobolt was already draped across the short woman's bosom, purring and kneading at her left shoulder, though he did lift his head to chirp a greeting when Margerite walked in.

Madame du Guesclin laughed. "Yes, he reached me perhaps a quarter of an hour before you, so that I knew you were coming. A useful creature, as well as a beautiful one - are you not, mon sieur?" she added to the cat, scratching him under the chin. "Has he kittens?"

"All over the Holy Roman Empire, and through half of France as well, or at least he shall within the next nine weeks," Margerite answered ruefully.

"I am not surprised. He is as fine a tom as I have ever seen." said the little Frenchwoman, settling more comfortably into her chair and saying something in French to Jeanne. The girl hastened gracefully to pour out wine for all of them before she left the room.

"I thank you for bringing Sieur Gottfried with you again," Madame du Guesclin went on sharply. "Why did you not tell me of his talent? He nearly destroyed one of my most useful servants last night."

"I knew nothing of it before he revealed it by chance," answered Margerite, just as tartly. "And by what right did you send one of your creatures with me without my permission? Am I not of a rank equal to your own?" She lifted her ringed hand, Ortlieb's ruby glowing balefully in the pale light from the small high window, and Kobolt leapt suddenly from Madame du Guesclin's bosom to rub about Margerite's ankles again.

Madame du Guesclin's lips pulled back to show her teeth, but her expression was not a smile. "Not yet, nor for some time to come. Even among those who wear the ruby, there are those who may command, and those who must obey. Though, if all goes well for you, you shall be admitted to the Council of Princes, still you shall be among the least there: you won Ortlieb's ring by guile and power, but you shall not take her seat there until you have fully proven your right to it."

"And how may I do that?" Margerite asked, stung by the other woman's tone.

Madame du Guesclin settled back into her chair once more. "That shall be revealed to you in good time. But we were speaking of Sieur Gottfried - sit down, man! No harm shall come to you from this."

Gottfried lowered himself reluctantly to the edge of a chair. It seemed to Margerite that she could almost see sparks crackling around him, as Kobolt's fur crackled when it was rubbed the wrong way in cold dry weather.

"Sieur Gottfried. Do you know anything of the ruby ring your Gräfin wears, or of what happened last night?"

"I saw a shadow, and it frightened me," Gottfried answered. Margerite had marked before that his Latin was somewhat rough, but now his German accent was so strong that even she was having a little trouble making out his words. Realizing what he must be doing, she almost smiled in delight: she had told him to pretend that he was no more than a simple warrior from the hinterlands of the Schwarzwald, who knew nothing of what he had done or of the Order; but if he seemed to speak Latin so badly that Madame du Guesclin could barely understand him, she would be the less able to interrogate him, and the more likely to leave his secrets unprobed. "And the Frowe Gräfin has many rings, but her ruby is the finest of them."

Madame du Guesclin sighed in exasperation. "Let us begin again. When did you see the shadow?"

"It was riding behind us. I saw it when we had passed over the Bridge of St Benezet."

"And what did you do?"

"I shouted, and it went away."

"You shouted," Madame du Guesclin mused. She clasped her hands together, her thumbs running over one another as though she were winding a piece of thread between them. "Can you tell me how you shouted?"

"Frowe?"

The Frenchwoman breathed deeply, her large bosom rising like an ocean swell beneath the green-brocaded blue of her bodice. "In what manner did you shout, Sieur Gottfried?"

"Frowe, I do not understand you."

"So." Madame du Guesclin paused for thought, then raised her powerful voice, shouting in French. Within moments, Jeanne was back in the room. The two of them conversed quickly, and the servant girl left again. "It is well," the Light-Bearer Princess said, "that I have a member of my household who is both of the Order, and who speaks German."

"I shall translate, if you like," Margerite offered, but Madame du Guesclin waved a small hand in irritation.

"No: it is best that each ask their own questions. Though you may tell me what information you got from your knight."

"Little more than you have now, I fear," Margerite said. "I noticed your servant at much the same time as Ritter Gottfried did, but he became afraid and drove it off before I could look more closely at it."

"And had you ever known him to do such things before?"

"I knew that he could see ghosts, and sometimes other things that were invisible. But it had never occurred to me that he might have any power to affect such creatures."

"One might almost think that you knew little more than your knight," Madame du Guesclin remarked.

Margerite knew that the Frenchwoman meant her words to sting, but she replied meekly, "Such things are seldom spoken of in the source from which I learned that which I have not been taught, nor did they ever come to the attention of my teachers."

Margerite did not expect the smile that curled up Madame du Guesclin's small mouth at those words. "Indeed. So you will not object if I ask you to assign me Sieur Gottfried's services for a few days, that we may learn what he is capable of and you may learn how best to use him."

Were his nature other than it is, Princes of the Light-Bearers would be fighting over who had the right to take him as apprentice, Eva had said of Gottfried. And Madame du Guesclin had not commanded, but asked...because the Order's own rules held her hand?

"Alas," Margerite said, as regretfully as she could manage, "Ritter Gottfried will not leave me alone in a strange land, and Ritter Arnmut's chief charge is not looking after me, but guarding Frowe Eva. And my Gottfried is...of sensitive nerves in many ways, and uninitiated: I will not abandon him to anything that might frighten him unduly, especially if there is any risk that it might do him harm."

Madame du Guesclin's large tilted eyes stared hard at Margerite, and it seemed to Margerite that she could almost see the tail of the great fanged cat swishing behind the little woman's brocaded skirts. "You seem very close to this knight," the Frenchwoman said, her low voice somewhere between a purr and a snarl. Margerite smiled inwardly: the thought of misdirecting the Light-Bearers so had only just occured to her, but it seemed to be working.

"And if I am, it is my right," she replied. "My Gottfried has served me well and faithfully, and we do not desire to be parted from one another."

"I see. Perhaps, if that is the case, I shall find it easier to make trial of him if you are there."

Something cold prickled up Margerite's back; at the same time, Kobolt jumped back with a hiss and Gottfried leapt from his chair with his sword drawn, thrusting out at empty air. Margerite clenched her hands, but even as she did, Gottfried lowered his blade, looking wild-eyed about the room, and Madame du Guesclin began to laugh. "Well, that is the answer to my first question," the Light-Bearer Princess said. "Put up your sword, Sieur Gottfried: the threat to your beloved was merely feigned, for that I wished to know the strength of your sight - no, wait. Give the blade here."

"I mean no disrespect, frowe," Gottfried answered. "But it is not meet that my weapon should be handled by a woman."

"That must be a surprise to you," Madame du Guesclin murmured to Margerite, with a quirking of one eyebrow. To Gottfried she said, "Very well: hold it if you wish, but I must look at it."

To his credit, Gottfried kept still while the Light-Bearer rose and came so close to his sword that her nose was almost touching the blade, though Margerite's heart beat fast and light with fear. She had seen that Gottfried's sword was blessed through long prayer, and again by Father Etienne's rites - would it give them away?

"What do you know of this blade?" Madame du Guesclin asked. Margerite thought the woman was speaking to her, but it was Gottfried who answered.

"Frowe, it was made in Köln in thirteen thirty-five, by a master smith named Johann the Smith. It was carried by my uncle Marcus until he died in thirteen forty-nine when the Death came to our lands, and given to me by my father at my knighting five years ago. It is a little shorter and lighter than most hand-and-a-half swords, so that, though I am not a large man, I can use it one-handed without difficulty, yet there is weight to it enough that it strikes mighty blows when I use it two-handed. The hilt is steel beneath the leather wrapping, which I replace whenever it becomes too stiff with blood or frayed or damaged. Though it takes a keen edge easily and well, its one fault is that when I strike edge on edge, it seems to chip more easily than most swords..."

"Silence!" Madame du Guesclin snapped. "When I wish to know such things, I shall ask. I was not speaking of the sword as a weapon of war, but of the power within it."

"Frowe, the strength of the blade comes from the blending of the steel, which was a secret of Meister Johann."

Madame du Guesclin closed her eyes in what looked, to Margerite, like utter frustration. "Never mind," she said softly. "Sieur Gottfried, kindly sheathe that now. I may safely promise you that we will soon find you a better sword, more suited to your liking and that of your mistress."

"Why would you wish to do that, frowe? It is very kind of you, but..."

The Light-Bearer Princess smiled up at Gottfried, laying her small hand upon his delicate wrist. "Because Gräfin Margerite is very dear to myself and certain of my more powerful friends, and we wish you to be able to protect her as well as you can. You do wish to protect her, do you not?"

Gottfried looked down at Madame du Guesclin's hand, as if wondering how best to reclaim his arm. "Of course I do, frowe. But I do not understand much of what you have been saying. Why should I need another sword, when I know well how to use my uncle's and it is suited to my strength?"

Madame du Guesclin let go of him, reaching up to pat his shoulder. "Everything will be made clear to you soon enough, as best as you may understand it, Sieur Gottfried," she said sweetly, as though she were talking to a confused child. Margerite was thankful that the other woman was so nearsighted: otherwise, desperate as their situation was, Madame du Guesclin could hardly have missed her struggle to keep from laughing.

The woman who entered the room next was tall and thin, simply gowned in pale blue silk with pearl-headed pins glinting from the coil of light gold-brown braids about her narrow head. She wore wire-rimmed spectacles like those Margerite had seen on Bishop Otto's secretary. Although Margerite guessed that she was quite young, perhaps only a few years older than Gottfried, she had the severe look of an old chatelaine. The Order ring that glinted on her long narrow hand was a deep amethyst - not powerful enough to win the ruby? Margerite wondered. Or merely too fastidious to carry out the appointed rite?

"Princess," she said, bowing slightly to Madame du Guesclin, then to Margerite. "I await your command." Her Latin was flawless, clearer than either Margerite's or Madame du Guesclin's, but she spoke with a trace of an accent that Margerite could not place.

"Birgitta, I need your skill in translating German. I have some questions to ask this young knight here, and his Latin is not good enough for him to understand me."

"Of course, maitresse."

Madame du Guesclin spoke in French; Birgitta listened carefully, then said to Gottfried, "When you saw this shadow that frightened you, can you remember exactly what you did? You say that you shouted: were you aware of any concentration of your mind upon it?"

Gottfried's gray eyes widened: to Margerite, he looked suddenly very young and rather afraid - as he may be: it will not be easy for him to dissemble now. "Frowe? I do not know what you mean."

Birgitta laid a long finger against her cheek in thought, considering him. "Come, now, Herr Ritter. You have the look of an intelligent young man: I think you can guess at more than you have been told. Has it ever happened before that - perhaps in battle, or at other times when you were taken unawares - you gave such a shout with all your spirit, and found that your assailant was daunted?"

Gottfried opened his mouth as if to answer, then closed it again, a look of growing worry shadowing his face. Margerite wondered if he had, indeed, used his gift unknowingly in battle before: if he had, he was such a man as to think it dishonourable. "Frowe, I was taught that there was always hope that a loud battle-cry would startle a foe, and I have seen it happen before."

Birgitta spoke in French again. Madame du Guesclin cocked her head to the side, clearly considering Gottfried carefully, then said something else. Birgitta shook her head vehemently in obvious disagreement, answering with a rapid torrent of words, then glanced sideways at Gottfried again and added something that made both women giggle. The little Frenchwoman spread her plump hands, in a gesture that Margerite could not help but read as something like, He is yours, if you want him.

"Frowe," Gottfried said desperately, "can you not tell me what you mean? Is this some matter of phantoms...such as I do betimes see; you may ask the Frowe Gräfin...or is there more to it?"

Birgitta smiled, the expression softening her severe features. "You have nothing to fear, Herr Ritter. Rather, it seems to us that you are especially talented, and should be trained in using that skill just as you are trained in using a sword, and to the same purpose, that you can better protect your Gräfin." She gave Madame du Guesclin a sharp look. "I can see that the presence of my maitresse makes you nervous, and that is understandable: she did not mean to frighten you, but she expected one of your gifts, who moreover serves such a mistress as Gräfin von Fürstensee, to be more accustomed to such things as she showed you. Now come with me, Herr Ritter, and I shall take you to a more quiet and private place where you may feel at ease."

"What do you mean to do with him?" Margerite asked sharply.

"Only to ask a few questions, and perhaps answer some, as best I may. Your handsome knight has borne up bravely, but if you have told him little, you cannot expect him to take everything in all at once."

"I must insist that you allow Birgitta a free rein in this," Madame du Guesclin added, lifting her beringed hand slightly. Margerite knew that she had just received a command: though she was little willing to obey it, she did not see how she could get out of it and still keep up her pretense of being an Order member. And Wolfram was beginning to make the little noises that presaged a full-scale wail of hunger, so that he would have to be fed soon.

"Ritter Gottfried, go along with Birgitta, and answer her questions as best you may," Margerite said, thinking, Gottfried, I do not think they will try to harm you now, and I know you can defend yourself. Forgive me for bringing you into this!

She did not know if Gottfried heard her, but he rose from his seat. The thought occured to Margerite then that Birgitta might have more in mind than questioning or testing - she, herself, would never have called Gottfried handsome: his thin body and sharp, half-starved features were not to her own liking, but perhaps she could see how his grace of movement and ascetic face might draw another woman's taste. If that is so, Episcopa, you are in for a grievous disappointment!

"As you command, Frowe Gräfin," Gottfried said stiffly.

The room to which Birgitta brought Gottfried was smaller than Madame du Guesclin's study, but better-lit, with books lining the walls. She had no stove, but coals glowed red in several braziers, so that Gottfried's winter doublet of quilted red velvet began to seem rather warm, and he could feel the sweat prickling out along his back. Sheets of parchment lay over the table; a black-tipped quill rested by an open inkwell, as though the Order Princess had called Birgitta away from writing something.

"What is it you do in this house?" Gottfried asked, hoping to delay her.

"I am learning the lore of the stars from Madame du Guesclin, and I also serve her as scribe and translator, for she must often correspond with folk in foreign lands. And there are other matters in which I am skilled of which she knows little."

"And where are you from? I do not recognise your accent."

Blurred though his sight was, Gottfried could see the tall woman's frown. "You have keen ears, Herr Ritter. I thought that I had rid myself of it altogether, at least in German. I am from Thrandheim in Norway; but my father was an Icelandic priest, a very learned man, and I gained much of my knowledge from him - do not look so shocked, Herr Ritter! Surely you know by now that priests are men like any others, whatever piety they may claim to hide it. And if you do not know it yet..." she laughed lightly... "a week or two in Avignon will make it clear to you."

There was a small silver bell on the table; Birgitta picked it up and rang it vigorously, its light ringing cutting sharply through the air. In a few moments, a servant appeared with a blue-glazed pitcher of wine, two matching goblets, and a platter of bread and cheese.

"Do have some wine, Herr Ritter," the Norwegian woman urged. "It is from the southern part of Bordeaux, and very good."

Gottfried misliked eating or drinking anything in this house, but Birgitta poured out a goblet for herself as well, though she bore his cup to him as if she were herself a servant. "Now be you welcome here, and gladly greeted, Herr Ritter - for I think you are deserving of more honour than my frowe has yet shown to you."

"Why should you think that?" Gottfried asked uncomfortably.

Birgitta paused, her glass-brightened blue eyes regarding him steadily over the azure rim of her goblet. "Madame du Guesclin is very learned and skilled, and often inclined to overlook those who do not seem to be her match in such regards. But though I lack your gift of sight, I have...certain senses; I can see how your strength flares like the Northern Lights on a clear winter night when you feel yourself threatened, as you do now. And it is also clear to me that you are not the brainless sword-swinger Madame du Guesclin believes you to be. I would be very surprised indeed if Gräfin von Fürstensee has told you nothing of our Order, or if, failing her revelation, you had not guessed much about it by now."

"I know...at least that there is something of magical art about it," Gottfried confessed. "And I had guessed that the ruby ring is a sign of high rank; while if you are a student and scribe to Madame du Guesclin, your own amethyst must show something rather lower."

Birgitta smiled, though her mouth twisted oddly at the corner, as if she had discovered the body of an insect in a fresh-bitten sweet. "That is so. Tell me, Herr Ritter, who else among the Gräfin's associates you know to be of our number."

"I believe Frowe Eva to be," Gottfried said at once: there was no danger in that revelation. "And there was a man who travelled with us from Niederwald, an Italian by the name of Damiano: he wore a ring very much like Frowe Eva's."

Birgitta was nodding slowly, her strong-boned face thoughtful. "For one as short-sighted as you, you are perceptive," she said. Then, to Gottfried's surprise, she took off her spectacles. "Try these: you may find that they help."

Gottfried held the device of wire and glass in his hand for a few moments, turning it over and looking at it. The metal was still warm from Birgitta's face, and it seemed to him vaguely improper to put it on, as if he were permitting some form of intimacy between them. But he knew there was no enchantment in the matter - Father Kunibert had worn such things, and besides, he was certain that if there were any power beyond the natural in this pair, he would know it, though he did not know how.

Slowly Gottfried raised the spectacles to his face, then gasped in surprise. The world had suddenly become clear and sharp around him, the tiniest cracks in the plaster of the walls standing out like stark slashes of ink on parchment, and the symbols scrawled over the papers on Birgitta's table so cleanly marked that, had he known anything of their meaning, he could have read them easily. But at the same time, it seemed to him that he could feel a great pressure against his eyeballs, rising slowly into pain, and he took the lenses away at once.

"Perhaps they are too strong for you, or too weak," Birgitta said, sounding rather disappointed. "I suppose you could hardly wear such things in battle, anyway...Madame, who needs them far worse than you or I, refuses out of vanity, and perhaps because," she added, her voice dropping to a conspiratorial giggle, "her husband Bertrand is the ugliest man in Europe, though she is so short-sighted that she truly believes him handsome. Well, even the mightiest in our Order may sometimes be fools when they are in love, for all their efforts to train themselves out of such feelings. But perhaps you know about that, as close as you are to Gräfin von Fürstensee."

Gottfried stared at her in shock. "I am the Frowe Gräfin's guard, and faithful man: no more!" he said. "And she is as true to her husband as living woman may be." Despite her love for Bernhardt, he thought: yet her feelings have never brought her to betray the Graf, and - praised be Christ - He does not ask that we not feel temptation, only that we not succumb to it, else I would be twice-damned already.

Birgitta's sand-brown eyebrows rose. "And yet Madame du Guesclin told me, not half an hour ago, that the Gräfin had claimed you were her lover."

Gottfried blinked. He was sure that Margerite had never said such a thing - but his Latin, though not as bad as he had pretended, was far from perfect; and he knew that when women spoke together, whatever tongue they used, sometimes they could say things that were beyond the comprehension of men. He paused, torn between his desire to defend the Gräfin's honour and the horrible fear that he had already betrayed her in some subtle plan.

The Norwegian shook her head. "Be that as it may, Ritter Gottfried. I suppose this is hardly the time for speaking on private matters, when I have been sent to ask you questions of more import. Tell me now: in your childhood, when you were angry or startled, did you ever notice those around you drawing back, perhaps with pains in their heads, or that others had trouble meeting your gaze? Or were there other things for which you were chided, because they appeared unnatural and, perhaps to the fearful, as though there might have been a touch of the Devil about you?"

Gottfried had come prepared to answer such questions, but their conversation had driven those thoughts from his mind - and he would not lie outright, even to a woman of the Light-Bearers. "I..." Mistily, as if from a dream of years ago, it seemed to him that he recalled a nursemaid - as tall as the castle's roof, she had seemed to him then, with a bun of gray hair beneath a creamy veil - drawing back from him with a sharp cry, then picking him up to shake and slap him until the tears came, shouting, "Never do that! Christ preserve us, you spawn of Satan - never do that again! Never, or I shall give you to the priest, and he shall take you away to be burned!"

But he had not known what he had done to make her so angry, save that he had been playing with something that glittered, and struck out at her when she tried to take it from him...struck out how? Gottfried wondered. He had thought he remembered a blow of his fist, but now he was not sure. Other memories were clearer, but he would not speak of those, for they dealt with things of which the Light-Bearers yet knew nothing.

"There may have been," he confessed. "If so, it was beaten out of me young." *And yet those who do not know me still turn away from my gaze, when I try to see what is in their faces. And Arnmut, my dear Arnmut...*

"I see that this has brought you little besides sadness," said Birgitta quietly. "Poor Gottfried - if I may call you by name; you may call me Birgitta, for I think we shall be working too closely to need formality between us - you have had a hard time of it. But you may rejoice now, for you have come among those who will not curse and beat you for your gifts, but cherish you."

Had Gottfried not known what he did of the Order of the Light-Bearers, tears might have come to his eyes then: it seemed to him that a great store of hidden memories pressed hard against his heart, like prisoners suddenly unshackled and storming the door of their dungeon.

Yet he remembered what he had seen in Ortlieb's wain; and he knew that Margerite had shown him truer compassion, thinking not on what he could do to further her aims, but only on the need of his heart *and Arnmut, though he does not know the taint of my soul and seems to fear me now, has been more faithful, both as squire and friend, than I could ever have asked.*

"The life of a priest's daughter in Norway was not easy either," Birgitta murmured. "My mother and I were called witches, and her kin often kicked and cursed me...She was found drowned in a well, and buried in unhallowed ground as a suicide, but to this day I do not know if she had truly grown weary of life, or if another cast her into the water with a stone about her neck."

She was close enough for Gottfried to see the tears brightening her eyes against the shadow of old grief on her face. Moved by pity, he reached out to lay his hand over hers - for Christ never taught that we should show compassion only to those who follow Him. He did not know what to say, but it seemed to him that something passed between them in that moment, and that, as with the Teutonic Knights, he could see something...a town of little peak-roofed houses with wooden shingles, and a thin girl with a long honey-brown braid in neatly-mended gray homespun spattered with mud, her eyes burning with feverish pride and her head held high as she ignored the tow-headed boys casting stones and rotten fish-heads at her back; a walled churchyard, with a strange tier-roofed church whose gables were adorned with carven dragon-heads rising above the stone fence, and outside it a grave in the mud, its bottom already dark with seeping water, and a blanket-wrapped body splashing dully down...Poor Birgitta - how can you pity me, when I was raised in a castle in honour, and beaten only by my teachers when I needed it, to get their lessons into my head? And if Vati and Mutti never understood me, at least they both live, and love me. My trials are far behind yours, and I am ashamed: how should I judge you for the path you have chosen?

Birgitta turned her palm over, clasping Gottfried's hand tightly. Her inkstained fingers were cool, soft save for the callouses of the pen.

"I did not expect this," she said huskily. Then, as if recovering herself, she cleared her throat, but did not yet let go of Gottfried's hand. "Why is it that Gräfin von Fürstensee has not initiated you into the Order yet? Even were she as proud as the greatest of them, she could hardly have missed your talents - or was there some other reason why she thought you might not be suited to it?"

The Norwegian woman was looking directly into his eyes, and Gottfried froze. Have I betrayed myself to her? he thought.

"You are like a glass filled with clear light, that cannot be cloaked for long," Birgitta replied. "Why did you so wish to hide this gift? Gottfried, why are you so afraid? You could learn all the secrets of the universe, and have power beyond your imagining - you were meant for more than being a Gräfin's guardsman, however devoted you are to her."

"I have no desire for such things," Gottfried answered thickly. "I am a simple knight, a man of the sword: I was not born to sorcery."

"Yet magic has touched you deeply already, and a strong power hangs about you even now - show me what you wear about your neck."

Gottfried let go of her hand, touching the fine gold chain hidden beneath his doublet. Now it had come to his choice: and even for Margerite's sake, he would not deny his Lord. Slowly he drew out his crucifix, letting it hang bright against the black velvet. Now Christ preserve us all! he prayed.

But Birgitta spared the crucifix barely a glance. "No, that is not it. There is something else: show me."

Gottfried had not forgotten his meeting with the old woman in the wood: he remembered her in his nightly prayers, and wore her token yet as a touchstone to keep charity and humility ever in his mind. He found himself strangely reluctant to show the chip of stone to the Order woman, or tell her the tale of how he had come by it, lest he find himself tempted to pride in his own virtue; but Birgitta did not relent.

"Gottfried, I know it is there. You need fear no harm from me: I would not hurt you..." She bit off her words quickly, but it seemed to Gottfried that he clearly heard her thinking, For by my mother's ghost, and Frigg whom she worshipped, I almost fear that I love you already, though we have known each other a scant half-hour.

Shocked by that, Gottfried unthinkingly lifted the piece of stone on its rough leather thong free to drop below his crucifix. Birgitta took off her spectacles, leaning in to look more closely at it, and drew in her breath in a low hiss. "Thórshamarr," she muttered, and then, "Hvat er hann til Kristna manna at bera? - I am sorry, Gottfried. How did you find this?"

"An old woman gave it to me as payment for fixing her wagon wheel. For that, and her prayers, were all she had to give," Gottfried told her briefly.

Surprisingly, Birgitta laughed. "It must be something of your ørlög - your fate, you would say - to receive great gifts without knowing it or understanding them. This talisman is far more precious than you think: keep it safe, for it shall protect you when you are in great need, and then, perhaps, you may find out the value of the old woman's payment for your help."

Gottfried put both crucifix and stone away quickly. Birgitta's words disturbed him somewhat; yet he would not let them distract him from the proper meaning of Mother Perchte's token - and it must surely be true in any case that a good woman's prayers could be a mighty protection at need.

"And now much is shown to me, that before was hidden," Birgitta murmured. "No wonder you have not been asked to join the Order, for your faith is as clear as everything else about you, though the one you worship so diligently has ill-treated you and is unworthy of your praise."

Uncomfortably, Gottfried remembered certain thoughts he had driven from himself in the darkness as he lay awake with Arnmut breathing softly and innocently beside him, the warmth of the young man's body as close as a lover's. But Margerite had spoken to him truly: "Shall the clay say to him who fashions it: 'What makest thou?'" Even a cracked pot, surely, had no right to curse its Maker: and the sherds might yet be useful for carrying water at need.

"That is not so," Gottfried said quietly. "As for what is in my heart - my sins are my own affair, and Christ's. But the Order of Light-Bearers would get little good of me, or I of it."

"Then why, Gottfried, since you are so staunch in your worship of the White Christ, do you serve Gräfin von Fürstensee so faithfully?"

"I swore my oath that I would do so, and I do not break an oath that I have given."

This time it was Birgitta who put her hand over Gottfried's. "Gottfried," she said, "I can yet aid you, and teach you such things as will not violate your troth, if you are willing. And that would be best for all of us, for I must either report all that I have learned from you to Madame du Guesclin - and then I do not know what she will do - or tell her that I failed, in which case I know very well what she will do." Although the tone of her last words was light, it seemed to Gottfried that he could hear the endless horror beneath them, like the ceaseless bass drone under the high skirling melody of a bagpipe; and somewhere in the middle range, the thought, and yet I would suffer it, though I am not sure why. Another wave of feeling welled up in Gottfried's heart. He could not be sure, even now, that this was not some intricate plot of the Light-Bearers to lead him by soft and winding ways into their grasp; and yet he knew that he could not in conscience abandon Birgitta now.

"I would not have you do that," Gottfried said. "If this place has the safety of your own sanctum..." Even as he spoke, it seemed to him that he could see the book-lined walls wrought about with strange and angular signs that glowed red and purple in the realms beyond light, and he knew why Birgitta had brought him here for testing.

"You know more already than you pretend," she answered quietly. "But yes: even among the Light-Bearers, there are different forms and schools of magic. I learned first from my father, who, as I told you, was an Icelander: and he was greatly wise in the runes.

Save when I summon spirits, I seldom use such circles as most others of our Order paint upon the floor: I have other ways of assuring my safety, and keeping my sanctum inviolate - even by other Light-Bearers, for the courtesy and honour we show within the Order." As Birgitta spoke, it almost seemed to Gottfried that she grew taller; that in her blue eyes he could see the brightness of the sun shining into clear deep mountains of ice, and he heard something in her voice like wind rushing through tall pines. And though she wore the Order amethyst, and must be sworn to Christ's Foe, it seemed to the knight that there was something clean about her spirit - or at least, that it was not rotted by the foulness he had felt in Ortlieb and Madame du Guesclin and Damiano.

Jeanne had just come soft-footed into Madame du Guesclin's study to kindle the evening candles when Birgitta led Gottfried back. Margerite looked sharply at the two of them. Even in the candlelight, she could see that they were both pale; she did not know the Norwegian woman well enough to judge, but it seemed to her that Gottfried looked shaken. Madame du Guesclin launched into a torrent of French that made Kobolt, sleeping curled about Wolfram on Margerite's lap, lay his ears back in surprise; Birgitta answered calmly and quietly, her eyes never wavering from those of her mistress. Finally Madame du Guesclin sniffed, resettling the saffron-coloured wisp of silk over her narrow auburn braid.

"Birgitta seems to have had little success with your young knight," the Frenchwoman said to Margerite. "She says that she can feel his strength, but that he has no way of summoning it at will, nor of controlling it - though she thinks that, if she is allowed to work with him, she may have better luck. More is known of such things in her homeland, and she has some outlandish Norwegian words for it..."

"Icelandic," Birgitta murmured, so softly that Margerite almost did not hear the contradiction.

"At any rate, you shall come back tomorrow and we shall continue teaching you the Art of astrology, while Birgitta sees what she can do with Sieur Gottfried." Madame du Guesclin cocked her head as if listening to something far away; Gottfried's eyes widened, but he said nothing. "Eva and Sieur Arnmut are at the door even now - Jeanne, go tell Louis to ready the Gräfin's horses, if he has not done so already."

"Farewell, Gottfried," Birgitta said; and it seemed to Margerite that she could hear the longing underlying the young woman's clear voice like water rushing beneath the ice of a frozen stream. "I shall look forward to seeing you on the morrow."

"And I, you," Gottfried replied, with a warmth that Margerite had seldom heard from him save when he spoke to Arnmut. Margerite did not dare to think about what that might mean - but I shall talk with him later, when it is safe.

Eva and Arnmut were both flushed pink with the cold, but seemed very pleased with themselves, Eva breaking into occasional fits of giggles. Margerite had not seen Kriemhilt come into the city with them, but the tortoiseshell cat was nestled comfortably against Eva's saddle-cantle, the gold star on her black brow very bright in the sunset's light.

"You seem to have had a fine day," Margerite said to her companion as they rode through the streets with Arnmut before and Gottfried behind. "Are you able to tell me why you are so cheerful?"

"Why should I not be?" Eva asked blithely. "I have found a dressmaker who has promised to fit me out properly for meeting the Holy Father, and had a fine day withal - Ritter Arnmut is a most pleasant companion to shop with."

"If Ritter Arnmut were not such a virtuous young man, I should wonder if you had been doing more than seeking out dressmakers," Margerite said severely, though her heart was not in it; as before, it occurred to her that Arnmut and Eva would not be the most ill-suited of couples.

She glanced back at Gottfried to see if he showed any signs of alarm - if, perhaps, Madame du Guesclin had sent something else that she could not see after them - but the young knight's sharp face was still and composed: he might have been riding entirely alone. Yet she lowered her voice carefully, "Did you speak with Paul?"

"I did. He and his men seem to have settled in very well here: we only had to visit a couple of taverns before we found them."

"I hope they were something like sober," Margerite muttered.

"Aye, well enough, though a few of them were bruised - I think they had a rough night last night, but came out of it the victors. At any rate, Paul says that they will be ready whenever you call them, and we know where to reach them now."

"Good. Maybe Cardinal de Grenville will have welcome news for us upon our return as well, for I would as soon be gone from here."

Eva peered intently into Margerite's face. "Things must not have gone as well for you: you are pale, and you have that little line between your brows that says you have been thinking too hard."

Margerite sighed. In truth - and she must admit it to herself - Madame du Guesclin's lesson had been fascinating: the woman well-deserved her reputation as one of Europe's greatest astrologers, and Margerite had found herself swiftly losing track of time and worries in the intricate charts of the stars and heavenly spheres that the little Frenchwoman had revealed to her.

She could not help wondering if it had been thus for Father Etienne when he studied with Meister Stefan - although it was hard for her to imagine that wolfskin-cloaked man with his great mead-horn and lively hounds carefully counting degrees and tracing aspects in a quiet study. "We shall talk more of that later," she replied.

When they reached Cardinal de Grenville's house, however, Pierre brought them immediately to the Cardinal's dining hall, clucking his tongue over their lateness. The first course, little squabs stuffed with a savoury mixture of minced pork, breadcrumbs, and rosemary, was already on the table; beeswax candles shone down its length, their flames glittering off the gold spoons and ivory-hilted knives - and little two-pronged forks of gold for spearing tiny dainties and sweetmeats with, such as Margerite had not seen even Ortlieb use.

The three Teutonic Knights were seated a little down from his Eminence, leaving places for Margerite and Eva at the Cardinal's right and left. Margerite could not help noticing that Brother Karl's thick fingers seemed ill at ease handling the finely wrought utensils, as though he were unsure that even guesting in such luxury did not in some way damage his vow of poverty, though his appetite seemed undiminished.

"I am glad that you have deigned to join me for the evening meal," Jean de Grenville said dryly, dabbling the tips of his long fingers in the bowl of rosewater by his place and patting them dry on his napkin. "You must have found something fascinating in the city to keep you this long."

Eva giggled. "Alas, we are none of us used to cities the size of Avignon, and it was too easy to become lost. We hope not to do it again."

The Cardinal raised a gray eyebrow. "I see. Well, prodigal children all, sit down and eat, for I have good news for you. The Holy Father shall be able to see Gräfin von Fürstensee a week from tomorrow; and you are all, of course, invited to attend his Mass this Sunday."

Margerite smiled. "That is good news indeed, and a great honour. Your Eminence, I am most indebted to you."

Cardinal de Grenville waved his hand. Margerite had to catch herself to keep from starting at the flash of the ruby on his finger - and does the Order of Light-Bearers so deliberately twist the things of the Church? Of course: God's Foe cannot create, only destroy and mock. "It is a little thing for Etienne's friends. I regret that I have yet heard no news from James of Canterbury, but the crossing of the Channel is not always an easy thing at this time of year, so perhaps that is only to be expected."

Brother Karl glanced at Brother Wolfgang, his blue eyes widening as if a frightful thought had come to him; at the same moment, Gottfried drew in his breath softly. The Cardinal gave the Teutonic Knights a mild look. "Do you know something I do not?" he asked.

"I fear it is so," replied Brother Wolfgang. "While on the road, we heard the tidings that Father James of Canterbury is dead. He fell from his horse and broke his neck, or so we were told." There was something in the knight's tone of voice that sent a prickle of wariness up Margerite's spine, as though an icy finger had touched the base of her skull: she knew there was more to it than that, but there would be time to speak of such matters later.

The Cardinal crossed himself. "Christ have mercy upon his soul," he murmured. "Father James was a good man; I shall say a Requiem Mass for him tomorrow, though I do not doubt that Christ has taken him into the Host of Heaven."

Margerite crossed herself as well, as did the others. She could not help but notice the stricken look on Eva's face; she did not need Gottfried's gift to know that the girl was thinking, What of Christoph now?

I wish I knew, Margerite thought. Truly, I wish I knew.

The news of the English exorcist's death cast a pall over the rest of the evening: Cardinal de Grenville lingered after dinner only long enough to drink a courteous goblet of wine with the rest of them, then took his leave. They gathered in the Teutonic Knights' chambers again.

"What befell you today?" Brother Wolfgang asked bluntly.

Margerite told him quickly of how matters had gone, and the lean warrior-monk nodded, his weatherbeaten face thoughtful. "Ritter Gottfried, can you tell us more of what happened? What did the Light-Bearer woman do to you?"

"She tried to show me how to..." Gottfried paused, his sharp face twisting in concentration as if he were struggling for words to express what he knew. "How to do by knowledge and choice what I did last night," he said at last.

"And did you succeed?"

"So far as she could tell, though she bade me not strike hard, lest I harm either her or myself."

"Yet," Brother Karl interrupted, "the Frowe Gräfin said that the woman had reported failing with you, at least for the time being."

Gottfried looked down at his plain black shoes - he had never, Margerite thought, been one to affect so much as three finger-widths of point on his toes. "I think that perhaps she may have something in her mind which does not altogether accord with Madame du Guesclin's plans," he said. "I am not sure what that might be; yet I thought it better not to contradict her before her mistress."

Brother Wolfgang looked searchingly at the young knight, their gazes meeting: it seemed to Margerite that she could feel the strain between them, as if they were striving with all their strength against one another. As before, it was Brother Wolfgang who looked away first. But he said softly, "You are much troubled by this, Ritter Gottfried. It were best, perhaps, if we spoke on it alone - with your leave, Frowe Gräfin," he added belatedly.

"I shall grant it, and gladly," Margerite said, her heart much relieved. Whatever had passed between Gottfried and Birgitta, it was better that Gottfried should speak of it with another man, especially if, as it had almost begun to seem to her, Christ had chosen this strange way to lead Gottfried out of the torment of his sinful desires. And her breasts were beginning to ache heavily: it was past time for her to feed Wolfram.

"When do you mean to finish weaning him?" Eva asked as they sat in their chambers with Wolfram suckling happily at Margerite's breast. "He is already chewing on everything he can put in his mouth, and surely he gets enough solid food down him: how much longer must you be bound by your son's demands?"

Margerite smiled. "As long as we both live, I suspect. But as for weaning, I was always taught that if a child does not drink its mother's milk for a full year after birth, it will be sickly in the years to follow. And it is not such a great hardship to feed my son myself. But tell me now: what were you so uplifted about this afternoon?"

"It seems a little thing now," Eva sighed, her pretty face falling into heavier lines. "And nothing to knowing that the man in whom I put such hope is dead...Ritter Arnmut and I went to several dressmakers, as I told you, and found very nice cloth for both of us - such patience with clothing is rare enough in a man, and he is a great pleasure to do such things with. But Arnmut mentioned that he had wanted to find one of the Pyrenean bear-dogs for Gottfried to ease his melancholy, and so we did. They are beautiful, Margerite - great furry white things, strong enough to chase bears from the flocks and very like bears themselves. Gottfried's is only a couple of months old but very well-trained already, so that he may let it run beside his horse or follow at his heel; and maybe it will be less painful to be in his presence if he has such a hound to distract his thoughts."

"What do you mean?" Margerite asked sharply.

"Only that he has been driving Arnmut nearly mad with his self-torments. And - Arnmut fears that Gottfried may have seen something in his mind, for which cause Gottfried will no longer bathe with him or let Arnmut help dress him, or share a bed or a plate at dinner, or any of the things that they were used to do when Arnmut was but new-knighted, and so they are both quite miserable with it."

"I am sure that Ritter Gottfried has good reason for what he does," Margerite said, her voice as stern as she could make it. "Perhaps you should tell Ritter Arnmut that it is no fault of his, but only - Ritter Gottfried has had much to come to grips with of late, and such closeness makes it no easier for him."

"I can tell him, but I do not know that he will listen," Eva replied. Her full lips trembled as though she was about to say something more, but she did not. Yet it seemed to Margerite that she could understand Arnmut's fear: had she not already unburdened her heart in full to Gottfried, she, too, would have shrunk back from his gaze, terrified at what he might come to know of her. And who did not bear some secret that he wished no other to know?

"Still, you seem to be growing quite close to that young knight," Margerite remarked lightly. "Tell me, is there something between you?"

Eva laughed, a bright sparkling sound that made Wolfram let go of his mother's nipple suddenly and giggle along with her. Margerite quickly wiped the stream of milky drool from the child's mouth, but she could not help but smile in answer to her son's mirth.

"Arnmut is a good friend, but I know now that he will never be more than a friend to me," Eva answered. "It is not so much that he is far beneath my birth - he is a very handsome boy, and charming as well - but he is far too young for me, and his heart is entirely given elsewhere. And...I do not know how Christoph may be freed, but it is he that I love, and no other. Do not think, Margerite, that because I smile easily I am untrue or lightly led aside, though maybe Christoph and I had no time to pledge ourselves before that...that thing crept into his flesh!" Eva's pretty face twisted with loathing: had she been a peasant maid, or maybe had the Cardinal's rugs been less fine, Margerite thought that she would have spat then. As it was, Kriemhilt suddenly arched her back and hissed, as though speaking the words that Eva's mouth was too fine to say.

"I did not mean it so," Margerite said. For a moment, she was tempted to tell Eva of the terrible shining spirit that had come to her in Ruprecht's shape - cloaked, maybe, in his body - and how she could not bear his touch after. But that secret, only Gottfried and Bernhardt knew - save, a treacherous part of her mind whispered, those who are highest in the Order of the Light-Bearers: they know as well, or at least they know what happened - and that was enough, perhaps more than enough.

# Chapter Seven

Each day, Margerite and Gottfried went to the house of Madame du Guesclin. Margerite did not know what Gottfried did when Birgitta took him away - he spoke of that to no one save the Teutonic Knights - but as for herself, it seemed to her that the clear knowledge of the study of the stars and planets which the Light-Bearer was teaching her, the delicate turns of Madame du Guesclin's gilded astrolabe and the precision with which it measured the fine mechanisms of the heavens that shaped the turnings of power upon the earth, were almost worth their source.

Almost: for many of the charts the two women cast together dealt with the coming weeks, and the time at which it would be most propitious to carry out the rite in which Graf Günther had failed, to dedicate Wolfram to the powers of Darkness. Yet this, too, is a weapon in my hand, Margerite reminded herself. By learning what the Light-Bearers seek, and what they fear, I will know when to ward against them and when, if it may be needed, to strike.

All the members of their company were determined to go to Confession before the Papal Mass, that they might receive Communion with the Holy Father's blessing. Surprisingly to Margerite, it was Gottfried who asked the night before, almost timidly, "Frowe Gräfin, to whom shall we confess?"

Margerite paused, open-mouthed. The Cardinal had his own chaplain, a mousy little man called Father Michel: she had assumed that they would unburden their souls to him early the next morning. Yet at Gottfried's words, a horrible suspicion had slithered into her mind: in this serpents' nest of intrigue that was the Pope's city, could even the seal of Confessional be truly trusted? She knew, all too well, that priests were merely men; that Gottfried had mentioned the matter at all suggested to her that he, through his gifts or other means, had come to realize the same here.

But if we must fear that the human ears that hear our Confession are corrupt - better, at least, that the reports go to our friend than our foes.

"It must be to Father Michel, unless you have learned some ill of him," Margerite answered. And two thoughts struggled in her breast like snakes striving against each other, so intertwined that it was hard to make out where one left off and the other began: but be discreet, for all our sakes! and whatever the nature of the priest, it is Christ who hears our sins and our penitence, and grants absolution through His servants.

"Our host spoke of spies within his household, whose presence he tolerated because he knew who they were...I very much fear that his chaplain is among them." Gottfried's voice had dropped almost to a whisper as he spoke the last words, and Margerite could see the faint tremor in his thin fingers, as though he feared that some great ill would befall him for naming Father Michel so.

"I do not doubt you, Ritter," Margerite said gently. "But can you tell me how you know?"

A tinge of pink brightened Gottfried's sharp cheekbones; yet it was Arnmut who answered the question.

"Frowe Gräfin, it was my suspicion from earlier," the fair knight told her. "And when I went to make my Confession on Wednesday..." He paused as if his will were wavering, then plunged onward. "Father Michel questioned me ceaselessly, not only on those things which might have had some faint bearing on the sins I confessed, but on other matters beyond that, in which he pretended to see the occasion for sin - and that is not, so far as I know, the duty of a priest. Unless the Church is very much different in France than in Burg Eisenstein, there is something amiss, for I was always taught that Confession was a matter of one's own conscience, not of being interrogated."

Margerite reminded herself then that, although Arnmut was very young, and it was easy to see slow-wittedness in his sweet-tempered deference to Gottfried and herself, she might have been doing herself a disservice by not being quicker to make him speak when counsel was needed. "Were you able to guess from his questions whether Father Michel might be a Light-Bearer, or a political spy?"

"My guess, Frowe Gräfin, is that he is not a Light-Bearer. He seemed...too quick to suspect unseemly things that had naught to do with our foes. And he enquired several times as to what we do when we ride into the city by daytime, and - he had questions about Kobolt and Kriemhilt that I do not think a Light-Bearer would need to ask, unless it were to throw us off our guard."

Margerite drew in her breath slowly. Among the many things of which Madame du Guesclin had quite cheerfully told her were the death of the Bishop of Cahors in thirteen-seventeen - convicted of causing the demise of the Cardinal Jacques de Via by witchcraft and waxen images, the old man had been dragged by a horse's tail through the streets of Avignon, then flayed alive and roasted to death by a slow fire. The Frenchwoman had also recounted a good deal of the conspiracy between Duke Matteo Visconti of Milan, his justice Dominie Scot, and his physician Anthony Pelacane, who had made a silver image graved with Pope John's name, the symbol of Saturn, and the name of the demon Amayon, for the purpose of killing the Holy Father.

Only because the most learned clerk Bartholomew first refused to aid in the incantations which would enable the image to do its work, then feigned acceptance and took the betraying materials to the Church, was the plot undone. "Urban does not fear sorcery as John did," Madame du Guesclin had said, "but Avignon has not forgotten what was revealed in those years. And the Order does not protect those who fall into the hands of its foes, for one who fails so greatly once may fail again."

Yet, in her worries about the Light-Bearers, Margerite had almost forgotten that the Order was not the only thing that she might have to fear in Avignon. The Inquisition's real power was slight in Germany - Kaiser Karl had given them no real authority yet - but great in France: accusations such as the one that had slain the Bishop of Cahors were but one of the many political weapons to be wielded in Avignon. What would it betide for Cardinal de Grenville, if he could be convicted of harboring a sorceress?

Not to mention the fate that would befall Margerite and her companions in such a case: such an accusation, if the Light-Bearers found her untrustworthy, might well be the simplest way of bringing Wolfram into their hands. And though Gottfried might be reluctant merely out of fear that his most secret sins might be told to another - for though he had said nothing of his work with Birgitta, Margerite thought she knew him well enough that, were there anything in it to disturb his keen conscience, she would have marked it in his bearing - she also knew that, if questioned, he would find it impossible to lie to a priest during Confession.

"Mayhap if we went severally, and hidden, to the smaller churches of Avignon..." Margerite mused. Yet who might follow them, or bribe a priest to tell what his oaths should have kept secret when they had departed? "It is a weary question. If Father Etienne were here, he could guide us; but if he were here, we should not need another Confessor."

"Why not ask the Cardinal?" Eva suggested. "Is he not himself ordained? And for Etienne's sake, even if one of you has something damming to tell of, surely we can trust him not to betray us."

Margerite looked about at the exquisite hangings of her bedchamber, the glitter of gold and silver thread from the embroidered edges of the silken coverlet and the thick plush pile of the velvet rug on which Wolfram sat with Kobolt's tail gripped firmly in his hand. *My father's income for ten years would not have bought a single one of the things that graces this room,* she thought ruefully. *And I am about to ask a Cardinal to hear our Confessions because his own chaplain is not good enough for us?*

Aloud she said, "That seems the best choice. Rose!"

The serving maid opened the door from Eva's chamber. "Frowe?"

"Go and find Pierre, and tell him..." Then Margerite remembered that, of course, Rose spoke no language other than German, and could tell the Cardinal's manservant nothing. "Just find him and bring him here."

"As you wish, frowe," Rose answered unhappily.

Margerite had to speak quite sharply to Pierre in order to get him to admit that Cardinal de Grenville was still awake, and more sharply to get the servant to agree to fetch him. The way Pierre looked down his nose at her, as though he, the overseer of the Cardinal's household in his blue silk doublet trimmed with cloth-of-gold, was of more worth than she, though she was a Gräfin and ruler in her own lands, both intimidated and angered Margerite: but by now she had more than enough experience in dealing with servants who thought themselves above her - *and should Bernhardt ever forgive me, and the two of us be wedded, I will need all that learning in Schloss Niederwald...no, I must not think on that!* Grudgingly, the tall serving-man departed at last to find his master.

Cardinal de Grenville had changed from his red silken robes to a simpler evening-robe of deep blue velvet brocaded with dark crimson, his long feet shod in dark blue velvet house-shoes from which silver embroidery glimmered. His aristocratic features showed neither pleasure nor displeasure at Margerite's summons, only a mild curiosity - but Margerite's heart quailed nervously within her, for she could not guess what feelings his carefully-schooled face might mask.

"Good even-tide, Gräfin," the Cardinal said courteously. "What brings you to wish to speak with me so late and so urgently?"

"Your Eminence," answered Margerite. "I beg you to forgive me, and to know by this that we mean no insult to either yourself or your household - but as we are going to the Holy Father's Mass tomorrow, we must make Confession, and we would ask you as a great favour to hear it yourself."

Jean de Grenville raised one thick gray eyebrow. "It is seldom that I am asked to do such duties myself these days. I have, as you know, my own chaplain: do you think him beneath you for some reason?" The tone of his voice was mild and enquiring, but its dryness had the razor-keen edge of a slim dagger slipping between two ribs.

Margerite tightened her hands, gathering her courage. It had been the Cardinal himself, after all, who had spoken of spies in his household... "Your Eminence, one of our number has already made Confession to Father Michel - and feared, from the questions he asked and the manner in which he asked them, that he might mean to report some of what he had heard elsewhere."

By the time she had finished, her heart was fluttering painfully in her chest - how dare she accuse a Cardinal's own chaplain of being a spy, and worse, of breaking the seal of Confessional? Yet the words were spoken, and she did not lower her eyes, but kept her gaze carefully fixed on de Grenville's.

The Cardinal watched her for a moment, his thin lips perfectly still and his dark eyes betraying no flicker of emotion. Margerite felt almost an irresistible urge to quail, to begin apologizing and backing down. But she would not have done so before a Prince of the Light-Bearers; and if the Cardinal ought to mistrust his own chaplain, she was doing him a favour, though it seem smeared by the grime of the insult.

Suddenly Jean de Grenville threw back his head and laughed - a deep rich rolling laugh that shocked Margerite, it was so unlike the faint dry chuckles she had heard from him before. "Ah, Gräfin," he said. "It is well to see that you are beginning to learn the ways of life here. And your German bluntness is refreshing: a French Marquise might have instructed her companions to confess only what she wanted unfriendly ears to hear, whether it was true or not. But you may put your minds at rest, for I am the only one to whom Father Michel makes his reports - no, do not look so shocked! We are all fallen, and the Church must use the weakness of human souls even as their strength, if she is to prevail on this earth. Still," he added musingly, "Father Michel is not usually so clumsy. Which of you was it that doubted him?"

Arnmut shifted from foot to foot, then murmured in a small voice and half-mangled Latin, "Me, your Eminence."

The Cardinal smiled warmly at him. "That explains much: it is often easy to forget that wit may lurk behind a fair face and sweet manner - or poor command of a language, though you seem to understand more clearly than you speak."

Suddenly de Grenville paused, his high brow furrowing as if he were listening to another speaker, though the rich tapestries on the walls muffled even the sound of their breath, and almost silenced Wolfram's little giggles as he and Kobolt played pat-paw on the thick soft rug.

"I see," the Cardinal breathed, looking straight at
Gottfried's stricken face. "Yes, good knight, I have done you
a grievous disservice by revealing this. Perhaps it were better
if you had been allowed to hold to your faith in the Church
and the Papal city - but that could well be your destruction
here. As amends, therefore, I shall hear your Confessions
myself this evening...I trust you shall find no occasion for sin
between now and tomorrow morning...and you may be sure
thereby that the seal of Confessional shall hold, and no ears
save my own - and Christ's, of course," he added, crossing
himself - "shall hear what you have to say."

"That is most kind of you," Margerite murmured.

The Cardinal waved his long-fingered hand in dismissal,
the large stone of the ring on his finger - so like Ortlieb's,
if one does not look too closely! Margerite could not help
thinking - glinting dark in the candlelight. "It is the least
recompense I can give you for a bitter lesson. Forgive me,
for I fear I have played the part of the Serpent in your Eden:
I shall pray that Our Lord transfigure this evil, too, to a
greater good."

And there, too, Margerite thought, is the difference
between the Light-Bearers and our own: they would have
counted disillusionment as a great gift, not a necessary
evil. If it is evil to injure another's trust in something
untrustworthy...is it? I do not know - but at least, I hope,
Gottfried and Arnmut are wise enough to know the
difference between Christ's perfection and the failure of His
servants on earth.

Margerite lay awake long that night, wondering if she
dared bring Wolfram to the Holy Father's Mass. The child
was far too young for Confirmation and First Communion,
of course - would merely being present do him any good? It
must, for the Pope would give his blessing to all there. And
yet, if there were any hidden taint in Wolfram, could she
risk what might befall at the touch of such holiness where
all might see it? And again, whatever else her son might
be, he was a child of less than a year: what if he soiled his
breechclouts, or began to wail in full voice because he was
uncomfortable, or bored, or hungry?

The Order of Light-Bearers would have their spies there as well: they would undoubtedly understand why Margerite and her companions must come, but would they take it ill if she brought Wolfram, when there was no need for his presence - when, indeed, it would seem at least eccentric to bring a suckling babe to such a rite? Yet, if Wolfram were lifted up to Christ's sight within the Holy Father's own chapel, and received the Pope's blessing upon his flock, might that not give him some protection against the machinations of the Light-Bearers?

But she had refused Brother Karl's offer to shield him by means of the Art...but they had prayed Christ's protection against both magic and guile...Kobolt lay heavily over Margerite's chest, purring and nuzzling his head softly against hers, as if to comfort where he could not advise; but her thoughts rolled hither and thither like a ball under the great cat's paws, and the smooth silk of her sheets felt itchy and uncomfortable as rough hemp against her skin.

Twice, it seemed to Margerite in her worried half-drowse that Kobolt lifted his head and gave a soft hiss: then she awoke fully, staring in dread into the darkness that hid Wolfram's cradle from her - afraid that she would see the tall ghost-shape of Graf Günther leaning over her son. But if the dead Order Prince were trying to get through to Wolfram, Father Etienne's wards must have held him out, for Margerite saw nothing, and after a few breaths, Kobolt lowered his head and purred softly once more.

The gray light of dawn was seeping slowly through the glassed window of Margerite's chamber when at last she thought, I cannot take the risk. I cannot betray us to the Light-Bearers, not here in their stronghold. For Cardinal Fleurs might well be at the Papal Mass - assuredly, if he knew that Margerite was coming - and she did not know what he was capable of, even under the Holy Father's eyes. The wearer of the adamant ring must be the most powerful magician in the Order, and herself and all her companions together, likely, no match for him: he stood as high in Satan's ranks as Pope Urban in Christ's.

Cardinal de Grenville must have noticed how tight Eva's dresses were growing; or perhaps he simply thought that even their best clothing was an ill reflection upon his household, for when his maidservants came in to clean the stoves and tidy the chambers, they brought with them a number of fine garments. One of the girls, a mousy brown-haired creature, ducked her head and murmured something shyly in French; the other, whose dark hair glinted with a tinge of auburn beneath the net of knotted silken cords that held it back, tossed her head and let out a little laugh before she said in good Latin, "Gräfin, our master the Cardinal bids you and Lady Eva choose whatever pleases you from among these, for he knows that you have traveled far and hard, and a noble lady cannot bring her whole wardrobe when she fares by horseback without a wain for her belongings."

"That is most gracious of him," Margerite replied soberly. "Please give him our thanks for his consideration."

Poor Rose was utterly at a loss in dressing Margerite and Eva; fortunately, the dark-haired maid remained to help, her small fingers moving cleverly and swiftly on the laces. Tired and distressed as she was, still Margerite could not help but take pleasure in the beauty of the clothes the Cardinal had provided.

For herself, Margerite selected a shift of pale green silk beneath light blue velvet figured with patterns in thread of real silver, and allowed the maid to do up her hair with fine silver wires that shone through the white silk of her coif like spiderwebs shimmering in a dawn mist. Eva chose a deep golden shift and an overdress of rose silk embroidered with gold thread - Margerite guessed that the Cardinal's servants must have spent a good length of time letting it out for her, for there were not many women as tall and well-figured as Eva.

The girl's thick golden hair was bound up like Margerite's, but in gold wire; and her coif was of the same rose-coloured silk as her gown. Margerite wore a narrow girdle of linked silver plates set with small sapphires, and Eva one of gold set with little rubies at the corners of each square: Margerite was almost ashamed to slip her little eating-knife on her belt, for the gilding of its tooled leather sheath had long since worn thin, and it seemed a shabby item against the fine clothing.

The sleeves of both dresses were so long that Margerite wondered how they would be able to eat without dragging them in their plates - would it be too uncouth to knot them up at the table? Cloaks were provided for them as well, rich dark velvet trimmed with shining white ermine-fur.

"Now I shall not be ashamed to come before the Holy Father," Eva declared, twirling around so that her skirts swirled about her, then bending to scoop up Kriemhilt and cuddle the cat against the tops of her breasts - there was still more of the creamy white flesh showing than Margerite would have chosen for her charge, but she knew that was the fashion. Kriemhilt purred lovingly, rubbing her head against the silk so that her fur ruffled up towards it. "Come, time is wearing on quickly. Let us see how the Ritters are getting along: men always complain about how long women take to dress, but if the Cardinal has treated them as kindly as he has us, I will wager you one of Kriemhilt's next litter that they are still trying to choose what to wear."

Margerite looked sharply at Eva and her cat. "Is she pregnant again?" Margerite asked bluntly.

Eva cast her eyes down, giggling. "I think if she is not, she will be soon, for the cry of a cat woke me up a little before dawn - did you not hear it? And she was rolling about the floor and writhing in a most suspicious manner. But you should look at Kobolt's nose, for if there is a scratch on it, we shall certainly know."

"Perhaps I slept better than I knew, after all," Margerite muttered. Still, she picked up her cat, holding the great black beast up and looking into his golden eyes as she touched the tip of his dark nose carefully with one finger. "I had thought you too experienced to be caught by a queen's claws," she said to the tomcat in mock reproof. "Still, Kriemhilt is not of the common run - and mayhap this will teach you to be careful which she-cats you turn your ambition towards." She had meant to speak lightly, but she could not hide the note of fear in her voice; even the French maid, though she could not have understood Margerite's words, looked up sharply.

"Is something wrong, Gräfin?" the girl asked.

"No, nothing," Margerite replied in distraction. She might have said something else, but a knock sounded on the door.

Eva's accusations of tardiness against the two knights had been unfounded, though the Cardinal had indeed dealt as well with them as with the women. Arnmut's blue silk doublet matched his eyes so perfectly that Margerite would almost have thought it had been made for him; its close fit emphasized the breadth of his strong shoulders tapering down to his slim waist, curving neatly over his hips and solidly rounded buttocks.

The dagged over-sleeves were entirely of cloth-of-gold, shining in sunrise brightness over the tight-fitting pale red of his silken undertunic, and his hose were of the same light scarlet. Gottfried, as Margerite might have expected, was dressed more soberly. He must have chosen the plainest clothes he could find from the Cardinal's bounty, though even he could hardly have avoided some luxury; his hose were black, but the simple dark blue velvet of his doublet was trimmed with ermine at hem and collar and the edges of the deep red sleeves, the gleaming-white fur casting an upward light that made his skin almost translucently pale, so that his gray eyes shone like pools of clear deep ice against the snow.

Instead of being strictly tied back in a tail, the young knight's dark shoulder-length hair fell about his face, softening the sternness of his expression. As well that Birgitta cannot see him in this; he would never be rid of her, Margerite thought, almost uncharitably, though with a tinge of surprised affection.

Yet, looking at the two knights, she could not help imagining Bernhardt in such fine garb - Bishop Otto had clothed him honourably, but Margerite had never seen him truly dressed as befitted his station. And beautiful as Ritter Arnmut is, Bernhardt would outstrip him in majesty as Vater Rhine outstrips a mountain stream - O Bernhardt, will I ever see you thus? For even if you win your birthright back...

She thought of the falcon-necklace, still lying in darkness at the bottom of her purse. It would have been a fair gem to wear with this dress, but she knew that she could not bear it: Ortlieb's ring already weighed her hand down like a shackle of molten lead. When they joined the Teutonic Knights and the Cardinal at the front door, the three warrior-monks glanced at their new finery, but said nothing: the plain black-and-white garb of their Order, after all, was more honourable than clothes that a prince or princess might not have scorned to wear. Cardinal de Grenville looked them over as well, nodding in satisfaction.

"I trust all is to your liking?...Very well, let us be off."

Margerite had seen the towers of the Papal palace rising from behind its thick walls when she rode into town each day, of course; but that was nothing to passing in through the Great Portal, the gate of Our Lady, beneath the gaze of the guards in the high round Tower of the White Cardinal and the four stone gargoyle-apes in near-human form that watched over the entryway.

They had come early for the Mass - Margerite thought perhaps because Cardinal de Grenville took a certain pleasure in showing off the Papal magnificence, pointing out the stern leaden-roofed Tour de Trouillas where Rienzi had been imprisoned, the iron cross at its summit standing black against the pale winter sky; the Tour de St. Jean, holding the chapels of St. Martial and St. John the Baptist - the Cardinal promised to bring them back when services were over, as, he said, some of the finest frescoes in the Papal palace decorated the walls within the tower of his holy namesake; and the new quarter, called Roma, which Pope Urban had added, its high-arched buildings more beautiful than any of the older edifices.

De Grenville also took them through the eastern gardens, lamenting politely that they had come in winter. Yet the neatly-clipped yew trees above the close-mown grass, though it was brown and yellow in spots beneath the frost, had their own severe beauty, set against the dark weave of leafless branches above and ice-glazed fountains below. And there, walking upon the sward, were live peacocks, their blue necks and green bodies shimmering like the finest silk as they lifted their scrawny talons with absurd pride.

Margerite stopped, transfixed: she had only seen peacocks as cured skins draped over the bodies of more succulent birds, and had secretly thought that their brilliant feathers were dyed for a more vivid effect. She drew in her breath as one of the peacocks stopped to look at the guests, then slowly lifted his tail and spread it out in a huge fan, the dark-eyed tips of the feathers shimmering as the cold breeze ruffled through them.

Beside her, she heard Eva's soft gasp, and saw that another peacock had stalked out from behind the broad trunk of a leafless oak - but this one was all white, as though it had risen, fully-formed, from the winter frost on the grass. Its tail raised, spreading pale and fragile as feathered mares'-tail clouds against an ice-blue sky: Margerite could only stare at it in amazement, all her noble dignity forgotten, and Cardinal de Grenville chuckled softly.

"There was a great menagerie here in Pope John's day," he said. "The current Holy Father cares less for strange beasts - yet the peacocks are still a fine adornment, are they not?"

Margerite would have answered, but a flicker of movement caught her eye, and she looked to see two dark shapes slinking towards the great birds with their furry bellies close to the grass. "Kobolt! Kriemhilt! No!" she said, hastening to pick up her cat. The peacocks fled; Kobolt's wide golden eyes looked reproachfully up at her, as if to ask why she had spoilt such fine sport. She shook the big cat gently. "Kobolt, you are not to hunt here. Do you understand me?"

Kobolt purred, hanging limply in her hands as if he were a small kitten in his mother's teeth. Margerite was not at all sure she trusted him to behave himself - but she could hardly carry him into the Holy Father's chapel, though she did hold him in her arms until they were well away from the temptation of the peacocks.

The Pope's great chapel was above his audience hall. They had little time to pause and look on their way through - "You will have enough time to see this later," the Cardinal murmured softly to Margerite. The chapel was more than half-full already, but Cardinal de Grenville led his guests down to a place near the front. Margerite could not help looking among the red-robed men, fearing that the clear sparkle of an adamant ring would catch her eye.

But if Cardinal Fleurs was present, either he had left off the sign of his Order rank, or else he was simply standing so that she could not see it; and none of the Princes of the Church seemed to pay any attention to Cardinal de Grenville's guests beyond the most casual glance. Margerite was so caught up in her worries that she hardly looked at the rest of the chapel until the high pure voices of the choir suddenly rang out through the large room, stilling the soft murmur of conversation.

Then she relaxed her vigilance, allowing her eyes to take in the gleams of the huge carven stone altar, the brightness of the candles shining from the wrought gold and gems of the chapel's furnishing like sunlight from a thousand tiny mirrors, the huge painting in glowing colours that adorned the walls, and the gentle illumination from the tall, stately lancet windows...

If the Cardinal's house had been luxury beyond her imagining, this was as close as Margerite could dream to the City of Heaven, with its gates and walls of precious stones shimmering in God's radiance, and the piercingly beautiful voices singing in notes that, had they not been so perfectly toned, would have struck unbearably through her skull. Hardly aware of what she was doing, Margerite turned Ortlieb's ruby inward against her palm, clenching her fist hard upon it as though to crush out a burning coal with her flesh.

Gottfried's lips were slightly parted as he stared at the huge gold crucifix hanging above the altar, his ascetic face transported with wonder and his gray eyes shining like polished stones beneath pure water. Now, more than ever, Margerite wondered what the knight saw: was the light of candles and burnished gold and jewels only a rainbow of brilliance in his blurred sight, or was the holiness of this place more clear to his eyes than it could ever be to hers?

Arnmut looked about wide-eyed, clearly overwhelmed by what he saw: surely he could never have guessed that he would someday kneel in a place so much grander even than Bishop Otto's own palace. Eva's pretty face was calm, a faint satisfied smile on her lips, though her eyes flickered slightly from side to side - looking, as Margerite had done, for Order rings? Or only comparing their borrowed finery to the clothing of those around them?

Even now, Margerite found it hard to tell with her: what was dissembling, what was the indulgent thought of the spoilt young girl she had been while her parents lived, and what she was truly feeling or guessing. And I should be composing my mind for the service - yet is my first duty, after caring for my son, not to watch over my companions? For Margerite was not at all sure that the Order of Light-Bearers could not strike at them even here, even during the Pope's Mass - O Maria, O Christ, forgive my lack of faith.

Urban V was magnificently arrayed in white brocade and cloth-of-gold, his tall mitre overshadowing his face with brightness so that it was some time before Margerite could look at the man beneath it. It seemed to her that the Pope's shoulders seemed to slump a little beneath his rich robes, that the face beneath the high Papal headdress was tired and careworn, stained dark beneath the eyes and furrowed with the wrinkles of much thought and sorrow.

It is no easy burden that Christ lays on His chief servant, though he eats off plates of gold and walks among fountains in gardens where white peacocks spread their tails, Margerite thought. Urban V was said by some to be the best Pope of the century; but he had not won that name without much toil and suffering. Christ, pity him and bless him: I think the overseer of Your vineyard labours harder than any of those who tend their single rows of vines, Margerite prayed, hoping it was not too presumptuous of her.

When the Pope spoke, his voice, though it carried well through the huge chapel, was startlingly scratchy and ordinary after the inhuman beauty of his choir. Margerite had been expecting more rolling tones, as would befit the Holy Father's majesty; but perhaps it was well to remember that, though Urban V was Christ's vice-gerent on Earth, he was still but a man. Ortlieb's ruby throbbed like an aching boil in her hand; unconsciously, Margerite closed her fist tighter, until she could feel the blood pounding against the hard gold and stone with each heartbeat.

The deacons and servers moved silently about, gold and silver thread and inset gems winking from the embroidered apparel hanging from breast and back and cuff of their albs beneath the silken glimmer of their dalmatics. At last the time came for Margerite and her companions to take their places in the line before the rail, waiting to kneel before the Holy Father and receive the Body of Christ. Margerite found that she was shivering inwardly, cold sweat dewing her forehead and sticking her silk shift to her back.

Yet even as she moved a step forward, she was thinking: if I held the wafer inside my cheek with my tongue - what power is there in a Communion wafer consecrated by the Pope himself? And do I dare to swallow? Will it stick in my throat, to mark me as a witch? Overcome by the horror of her thoughts, she could only pray, Christ, I am not worthy of this. Maria, have mercy on me.

Cardinal de Grenville had taken his Communion and moved aside; now it was Margerite's turn to settle her knees on the beautifully embroidered cushion, still warm from those who had knelt there before her, and raise her face to the Holy Father. Almost as if entranced himself, Urban lifted a wafer from the gold plate, setting it into Margerite's open mouth. With a fierce effort of will, she bit down, chewing and swallowing quickly before any other urge could move her. As she rose to return to her place, the wave of relief that swept over her left her weak-legged, almost stumbling - or is it something more?

The brightness of the Pope's chapel shimmered in her sight as though she were looking at it through rippling river-water, and she feared that she would faint before she could kneel down in the pew again. Christ give me strength, Margerite prayed once more. And perhaps her prayer was answered; or perhaps the deep slow breath she took without thinking, as her training had taught her, steadied her enough for her to make her way safely back.

When Margerite looked up to the rail again, Eva was sweeping majestically back towards her; it was Gottfried who knelt now. From behind, his thin shoulders and narrow back might have been those of a boy of twelve or fourteen; though she could not see his face, Margerite could imagine the look of rapture upon it. O Gottfried, she thought, I hope this brings you joy enough to repay in some measure what you have suffered with me!

Gottfried stumbled as he rose, steadying himself on the gilded rail as he turned. Has he been starving himself again? Margerite wondered: there was something wrong about the young knight's movements, about the way he put one hand out in front of himself as he walked slowly back towards their pew - like a blind man, Margerite thought with a stark pang of fear.

Gottfried stumbled again as his hand found the first pew, and she was suddenly certain of it. Dear Maria, what did that woman do to him? Margerite wondered hysterically. If she has harmed him, if this is her doing, then I shall - it is my right within the Order to call her out, to make her pay for the hurt she has caused him!

But Gottfried's gray eyes turned unseeing towards her, and it seemed to Margerite that she was looking into two lamps of clear rock-crystal with the Sun's light burning in their depths: she had to summon all her strength to meet that gaze. Then it seemed - she did not know how, for she put no thoughts into words, and she heard nothing from him - that she was somehow guiding him back to their row, along behind the kneeling Churchmen and dignitaries to his place, almost as if he were seeing with her eyes.

Gottfried, Margerite whispered in her mind. My Gottfried, what has befallen you? She got no answer; yet the knight turned his head towards her, meeting her gaze again, and she could not shutter her eyes against his brightness.

Soon the time will come for you to choose. The voice within Margerite's skull was like Gottfried's - not his speech, but his singing - and yet not like, as though she heard it from within an infinitely deep cavern, the sounds resonating back and forth from the stone in a harmony that shook her bones. At the same time, a bolt of searing pain shot up her left arm, so that she had to bite her tongue to keep from crying out.

Then the pain was gone, leaving only the sharp blistering burn of Ortlieb's gold upon her finger; and the light was fading from Gottfried's eyes, his sight clearing even as she looked upon him and his transfigured expression falling slowly into lines of bewilderment. His mouth worked, as though he were trying to taste the lingering flavour of the Communion wafer; he glanced up towards the railing where Arnmut was rising from his knees, and Margerite thought that she saw the glimmer of a tear-track over his sharp cheekbone.

The mid-day meal at the Cardinal's house was more sumptuous than usual, for they had all gone fasting to Communion: olives of beef sliced parchment-thin, rolled, and skewered in a delicious thick red wine sauce; partridges carefully glazed with featherings of red and gold as if they were small phoenixes, each in its own nest of meatballs encased in crisp green batter; wild-boar brawn served in slices coloured green and blue and brown which were laid out about the beast's gleaming white ribs, with the largest piece of the chopped, spiced, and almond-thickened meat molded into a passable imitation of a boar's head; a beautiful golden jelly shimmering over a sunburst of fine pointed slivers of chicken, pork and beef; and a whole suckling piglet encased in pastry which fell away at the touch of the knife, leaving the succulent herbed meat, dripping in its own savoury juices, to steam upon the table.

The Cardinal seemed in a better mood than Margerite had seen before; at one point, he remarked approvingly upon how moved she and Gottfried, in particular, had both seemed by their Communion. Gottfried shifted uncomfortably in his seat, and Margerite wished heartily then that the meal were over so that she could ask what had befallen him.

But after the meat courses came the sweets, fruits candied in fine sugar and syrups that had to be lifted to the mouth with the little two-pronged gold forks; Margerite had to take great care with those so as not to drop any of the sticky pieces on the beautiful dress the Cardinal had provided for her. She noticed that most of her companions, including Brother Karl and Brother Helmuth, were having the same trouble, but that Brother Wolfgang used the forks as if he were accustomed to them: she could not help wondering what he had forsaken to join the Teutonic Order.

After the meal, Gottfried went straight to the Cardinal's own chapel and, without a word, knelt before the altar, his lips moving in prayer. Margerite wondered if it were safe to leave him there alone - but though he had eaten sparingly at dinner, he had, at least, eaten: he would not pass out from starvation on top of spiritual exaltation, and she could hardly disturb his prayers for the sake of assuaging her own curiosity. Instead she returned to her own rooms.

"Frowe, I am glad you are back," Rose said at once when she came in. "Wolfram has been nearly too much for me: he has spent the morning crying and trying to tear up everything he could reach."

"He seems quiet enough now," Margerite answered cautiously. Indeed, her son was sitting on a rug of green and blue woven silk, bright and golden-haired and serene as an angel in a cathedral painting - chewing on something? Margerite knelt down beside him at once, prying his mouth open. The object she pulled out, in spite of her son's efforts to bite, was bedraggled and broken, its shimmering blue-green darkened with his saliva; but having seen the peacocks in the Papal gardens, she could not help but recognise it at once.

"Was Kobolt here?"

"Why, yes, frowe. He came in only a little time ago, with a few blue feathers about his mouth. It must have been a pretty bird he ate, but I suppose cats never think of such things."

Margerite closed her eyes briefly, shaking her head. "Pretend it didn't happen. No, Rose, don't ask me why."

"Bird!" Wolfram said, standing up and grabbing his mother's shoulders to support himself. His little hands were already remarkably strong, Margerite thought: he would have a good grip on a sword when he was older. "Kobolt find bird!"

"Yes, my love," Margerite said soothingly to him, though she could not help glancing about, afraid that she would see bleeding pieces of peacock on the Cardinal's precious rugs or bedclothes. "Kobolt found a bird. Someday, perhaps, you shall have such birds yourself, though I hope," she could not keep from adding in a low mutter, "that no more peacocks shall end up inside Kobolt and Kriemhilt."

As if speaking his name had summoned the cat, Kobolt came out from under the bed, purring and waving his plumed black tail, his pink tongue licking his chops. He ran to Margerite at once, putting his forepaws on her kneeling thighs and butting his head against her body as if to tell her what a fine and brave cat he was, he who had dared to attack such a huge fierce bird and brought it down to feed his mate and the kittens she was making. Margerite looked from her son to the tomcat, shaking her head: they seemed to be two of a kind, and she could not truly say whether that was good or ill.

"Rose," she said, "make sure that this wretched cat is well-fed at all times, and Kriemhilt too. I do not want them hunting in the gardens of Avignon any longer."

It was late in the evening when Gottfried came to Margerite's chambers at last. She could see the weariness on his thin face, but there was a peace there too - a peace she envied: she had spent the day thinking on the strange words that had come to her. What manner of choice was there for her to make?

She had already made her great choices some time ago, or so it seemed to her: to fight against the Order of Light-Bearers, to follow Bernhardt to Schloss Niederwald...to keep to her wedding vows with Heinrich...and to bear Ortlieb's ring? To study with Madame du Guesclin? But those were hardly choices: they had been set, it seemed to her, the moment she embarked on the difficult and dangerous path of deceiving the Light-Bearers for Wolfram's sake. And yet I could have turned away - could I? Has the Order, after all, ensnared me without my knowledge?

"Is all well with you?" Margerite enquired awkwardly, unsure how to speak to the knight now that the moment had come.

"All is well," Gottfried answered, his voice quiet. "Frowe Gräfin...Margerite, what did you see, there in the Pope's chapel?"

"You stumbled as if you were blind, turning back from the railing," Margerite told him. "And there was a great light in your eyes."

"I remember only going up and kneeling before the Holy Father. And then I was beside you again, but the taste of the Communion wafer was still sweet in my mouth - and everything in the chapel burned with light so bright that I could hardly see at all. That has faded only slowly, and I am not sure that I am myself even now: my sight seems keener, and yet those...the things I saw that were hidden from other eyes, they stand out more strongly to me now, so that even Kobolt's marks in this chamber burn with an earthen-green flame, and Father Etienne's signs flare all about the Cardinal's dwelling. And Ortlieb's ring...I can hardly bear to look upon it; I do not know how you find the strength to wear it."

Margerite stared at Gottfried in awe. If it were not blasphemous to say so, I would think that he is becoming a saint, she thought. And yet...but temptations need not be the same for all of us: it is only needful that they be mastered. But I am the greater in the Art - why do such visions not come to me?

She quashed the thought as soon as it rose from the bowels of her heart: she knew that Gottfried was far more virtuous than she, a better vessel for any Divine power - and perhaps it was for her sake that it had been granted; he remembered nothing, but she had gotten his warning, cryptic and unsettling as it was. Slowly, her tongue moving like a strip of lead in her mouth, Margerite told Gottfried what else had taken place between them.

"That I do not remember. But it may be," the knight went on, murmuring as if to himself, "that a broken pot may even serve as a lamp in times of need, though I am not worthy of such grace."

"None may judge that but Christ," Margerite rebuked him kindly. "Yet I was hoping that you would remember...that you could tell me more of what might have been meant?"

Gottfried shook his head sadly. "I fear I can only guess. We are both at the very heart of temptation - it may be that we are closer to falling victim to the Light-Bearers' snares than we know. Margerite, it would be my rede that when you have spoken with the Pope, we pack our belongings and leave Avignon as swiftly and secretly as we may. Better, maybe, to fall fighting the Order than to sink, unknowingly, deeper into their clutches: for I have seen now how they may entrap even a good soul."

His own? Margerite wondered. Or does he speak of Birgitta? - But how can he call one good who wears the amethyst ring, for which a human life must have paid?

"Because I know what brought her to that pass," Gottfried answered. "Even though she was never a Christian - and though the good brothers have counselled me sternly, that all things of heathenry must be wholly evil - in such a matter I can trust only to my own conscience and to Christ, that I not be deceived by matters beyond my understanding. Yet I would bring her out of here, if I could, but that is not my choice to make."

Is this the choice he spoke of? thought Margerite. I could... The Norwegian woman was below Gottfried's station; his father would be angry, and yet, as mistress of Burg Fürstensee and, until Wolfram was grown, Burg Falkenstein, she could give her knight such a place that there would seem no ill in such a marriage. "Do you love her?" Margerite asked.

Gottfried paused, and it seemed that he did not know what to say. But if he has never known what it is to love a woman, Margerite thought, perhaps he himself cannot tell. "You need not answer me that," she went on swiftly. "But think on it for yourself. If it is so, maybe...it may be that I can do something to aid you."

"I thank you for that," Gottfried replied, his voice stiffening; it seemed to Margerite that he was retreating from her, and she decided it would be best to press him no further.

If Madame du Guesclin had any thoughts on Margerite's attendance at the Papal Mass, she kept them to herself; nor, when Margerite told her of her appointment to bring her case before the Holy Father, did she do more than raise an eyebrow and sniff, "Well enough, that this matter is over and done with before Nikolaus can profit from his rashness and impertinence. You would do well to think on a fitting punishment for him: we reward boldness when it succeeds, but boldness that fails is a danger to us all."

Though Margerite rose early on Thursday morning, and spent some time in meditation to calm her soul, she could not entirely quiet the trepidation she felt as she walked across the Papal courtyard with Eva and the two knights beside her. She had seen enough of Avignon's corruption already - what if Nikolaus had sent a bribe that she could not overmatch? Urban V was said to be a good Pope, but his treasuries had suffered from Bertrand du Guesclin's demands: could money sway him beyond the call of justice?

The vast Salle d'Audience, that Margerite had only glanced at in passing before, was filled with people now: Papal knights in their velvet tabards with the crossed keys of St. Peter embroidered in gold thread, their heads warmed against the chill of early February by hoods of ermine and beaver; clerks in brocaded robes, nobles and dignitaries dripping with gold chains, adorned with bright-polished gems.

Yet the splendour of those who waited before the Pope was only a decoration to the hall itself. Five massive clustered columns held up the vaulted double nave, divided into several bays. The corbels of the vaulting were carved with strange and monstrous figures, wide-mouthed gargoyles and beasts both comical and fantastic. Bright frescoes painted with the intense colours of crushed gemstones and enhanced by the plentiful use of gold and silver leafing adorned the walls: the Divine Majesty Himself was enthroned in the centre, surrounded by saints and patriarchs who held scrolls inscribed in red letters, bearing their own wise words on judgement and law, righteousness and truth.

In the eastern bay sat the Judges of the Rota, the supreme tribunal of Christendom, on a horseshoe-shaped bench behind a revolving bookcase which also served as a desk - Margerite guessed that they could find and cite any of the great legal and Church authorities at once. May my case not have to go before them! she prayed: it was daunting to look at the half-ring of stern-faced old men in their red robes, for she knew that they were the final court of appeal in all cases of international and ecclesiastical law.

The north bay was magnificently painted with a huge fresco of the Last Judgement, divided into five scenes: Margerite had never seen painted faces more beautiful than those of the angels and the saints, nor any figures that struck more horror into her than the images of the writhing damned impaled on the forks of twisted devil-shapes.

The Pope himself was enthroned in full regalia, his seat raised above the heads of the petitioners. At low desks beside him were a number of Papal clerks, some writing and some running back and forth with books and scrolls; other men came and went, bringing wine and water and food on gold trays. As Cardinal de Grenville had told her to do, Margerite went to the last clerk in line.

"I am Gräfin Margerite von Fürstensee und Falkenstein," Margerite announced herself. "I believe that I am to bring my case before His Holiness this day."

The clerk glanced up at her, a look of boredom on his puffy face, then shuffled about the papers on his desk. "Yes, that is so. There will be three more before you; you may as well come back after dinner, for assuredly His Holiness shall not be done with these cases before then."

Nevertheless, Margerite and her companions waited until a Papal herald stepped forward to announce a two-hours' recess. Urban V rose from his throne; his knights formed up around him, and an aisle parted through the crowd for them.

"There are many places here where folk of quality may dine," Eva said softly to Margerite. "Shall we go? It shall be a long and hungry wait if we do no more than stand here while the Holy Father is eating."

"Let us go, then." In truth, Margerite wanted very much to seek out the Bear's Paw; but she did not know what eyes were upon her. Instead she let Eva and Arnmut lead her out through the streets of Avignon to a three-storied building whose sign showed a bunch of grapes upon an upright vine entwined by the two serpents of a physician's cadecus.

As Eva had promised, the food was very fine - pancakes filled with chopped chicken in a cream sauce scented with chervil and tarragon and thyme, scallop-edged rondels of tender peppered venison, small crusty rolls made from fine white flour, a delicious beef soup with cheese and eggs, and a flavourful light red wine. When matters are all set to rights, Margerite thought, we shall have to see about bringing in more of the wines of France...but to which castle? she wondered.

Would it be the cellars of Burg Fürstensee that she stocked so - or those of Schloss Niederwald? Even thinking about arranging the daily matters of Bernhardt's castle gave her a pleasant warm glow within, like the warmth of the first goblet of hot spiced wine after a day's ride in the cold. But like the warmth of wine, that feeling was illusory and quickly gone. How could she dream of sitting in Schloss Niederwald and ordering its supplies, when Bernhardt was still so far from gaining his patrimony - and when, worse, she did not know if he would want her beside him in the castle's great hall?

"You are very quiet, Margerite," said Eva. "Does the French cooking not please you?"

"It pleases me well enough. I was only thinking."

"I am sure you need have no fear about your case," Eva told her comfortingly, wrapping a piece of pancake neatly about its contents so that the sauce would not drip on her clothes and lifting it quickly to her mouth. She chewed and swallowed with every polite sign of delight, then went on, "After all, you have come here at the cost of considerable trouble and effort to swear that you married Graf Heinrich of your own will, and I can witness that well enough. There should be no reason for the Holy Father to insist on an annulment."

"There should be no reason, true," Margerite agreed. But if Nikolaus was able to offer a sufficient payment, or if he has allies in the Order that I do not know about, who might be whispering in the Pope's ear even now...That worry drove the other, for a little while, from her mind, just as the pain of a sharp blow could drive the constant ache of a bad tooth briefly away. Yet good as the food was, Margerite found that she had little appetite.

Margerite's was the second case called in the afternoon. The waiting had dulled her nervousness, but she still started sharply when the herald stepped before the Pope's throne and shouted, "Gräfin Margerite von Fürstensee und Falkenstein!" Swallowing hard, Margerite walked forward, her companions following her, and they knelt in turn to kiss the Holy Father's ring.

Close up, the marks of age and toil on Pope Urban's face were clearer to see than they had been in his chapel. Margerite could not guess how old he was; still vigorous, at any rate, but worn by the cares of his great office. He reached out, and one of the clerks put two papers into his hand - Margerite recognised the letter that she had written herself.

"This seems a simple enough matter," the Holy Father said, barely glancing at the parchments. His voice was already hoarse; even before he could speak or gesture, one of the Papal knights held a gilded goblet up to him so that he might wet his throat. "The claim was made that you were forced into marriage with Graf Heinrich, and made to swear to him against your will.Yet this second letter, which purports to have come from your hand, asserts that it is not so, wherefore I have delayed my judgement. Now that you are here yourself, how say you, Gräfin?"

"Your Holiness, I have come to swear before you that I married Graf Heinrich von Fürstensee of my own free will, neither forced nor compelled by any means. I would not have that marriage dissolved..." O, but I would! Margerite's heart cried. I would be free to marry Bernhardt, if he will still have me - but not at the price of forsaking Burg Fürstensee to Nikolaus, and abandoning Christoph's hope of freedom.

Gottfried glanced swiftly at her, a look of compassion softening his cold gray eyes, and Margerite knew that he had heard her thoughts. But she did not dare to pause, lest her feelings overcome her. "It was, and is, my will to be and remain Graf Heinrich's wife," Margerite finished strongly, her voice as stern as if she were pronouncing judgement upon herself - as, perhaps, she was. "I will swear to that by any oath you choose, Your Holiness, and I have brought Frowe Eva von Bärenberg as witness, for she has been my ward and constant companion, and was present herself at the wedding."

Then Margerite and Eva swore again to the truth of Margerite's words, and signed the document that one of the Papal clerks set before them.

"So be it," said Urban. He shuffled the parchments he held, glancing down again. "I see that you have two other matters to set before me as well?"

"Your Holiness, I would ask for a dispensation for my ward Eva von Bärenberg's marriage. She stood as godmother to my son Wolfram von Falkenstein; my son's godfather is Herr Christoph von Fürstensee. Now the two of them have spoken of betrothal, but because they are oath-kin..."

Pope Urban nodded. "But not kin in blood, I take it."

"No, Your Holiness."

"The wedding even of oath-kin, as you clearly know, is normally proscribed. Yet there is no other impediment to their marriage, and I see from this account that they are both pious and virtuous young people, with a proper care for the Church..." So the donation was enough, Margerite thought with a cynicism that she could not suppress. Eva was snuffling gently, dabbing gracefully at her eyes with a little silken handkerchief. The Holy Father looked down at her, and Margerite thought she saw him smile, like a grandfather granting some favour to a favourite granddaughter. "I see no reason not to grant this dispensation."

He gestured to the clerk sitting on his left, who at once began to write swiftly. "May Christ and all the saints bless your marriage, Frowe Eva, and may you and Herr Christoph live happily through the days of your life together." The Pope lifted his hand in blessing, and Eva smiled at him through her sniffles.

"Lastly, Frowe Gräfin?"

"My husband Graf Heinrich was felled by a brain-storm last summer. He lies in his bed, unable to move or speak - Your Holiness, I would beg of you to say a Mass for his sake, that he may be healed or released as Christ wills." To her own surprise, Margerite found tears thickening the words in her throat, their salt liquid prickling at her eyes like hot nettles. "I have brought a donation; I pray that this may be sufficient..." Gottfried stepped forward with the heavy bag of coins, and another clerk rose to collect it.

"It is," Pope Urban said. "Seldom in these evil days does one see such a true wife. You are to be commended, and I shall pray myself that Christ reward you justly for your fidelity."

Margerite cringed inwardly at those words; for who could say what reward she truly deserved? Yet she could only bow her head and murmur, "I thank you, Your Holiness."

"Are there any matters left which we have not dealt with, Gräfin?"

"No, Your Holiness."

Pope Urban looked down at the clerk who had been writing the dispensation. The parchment was lifted to him for his signature, and hot wax dripped so that he might press his seal upon it before handing it to Margerite. "Then I declare this case closed. Dominus vobiscum."

"Et cum spirito tuo," Margerite responded.

"Wait," the Pope said suddenly as Margerite and her companions began to walk away. "You there, sir knight - did you not take Communion from my hand last Sunday?"

Gottfried knelt swiftly before the Holy Father. "I did, Your Holiness."

"I remember noticing that you were most exceptionally moved by it. Have you ever thought of entering holy orders?"

"I have, Your Holiness. But there are other duties I must fulfill."

"Secular duties," the Pope told him quietly, "cannot take precedence over the needs of the Church and your own soul. Think well upon it, sir knight: the body of Mother Church was grievously racked by the Death, and we still have great need of good men to care for Christ's flock. That will be all. Dominus vobiscum."

"Et cum spirito tuo. I thank you, Your Holiness," Gottfried said. Margerite could hear the sadness in his voice, but he did not speak again as they made their way out of the audience hall. When they had passed out the Great Portal, however, he asked softly, "Frowe Gräfin, shall we send for the Bear's Paw now, to tell them that our business in Avignon is done?"

"I fear that it is not yet done," Margerite answered. She did not need to read Gottfried's thoughts to know how worried that answer made him. But having gone so far as she had already - after the Council of Princes, I shall know which path is the safer for Wolfram: to continue my deception, or to defy the Order and flee.

So Margerite kept on at Madame du Guesclin's house; and on the following Tuesday, the little woman looked up suddenly from the chart on which she had just traced a careful angle and said, "Tell me, Margerite, have you yet made robes suitable to your station?"

Caught by surprise, Margerite stammered, "I...that is, I have had no time, I..."

"I thought not. I shall provide you a robe for this gathering; but hereafter you must hasten to fashion your own. Do you know how to reach the mansion of Cardinal Fleurs?"

"No, Princess."

"Birgitta shall give your knight directions. You may bring one companion with you as you choose - either Eva or, if you must, Sieur Gottfried, for though properly speaking he is Birgitta's student, I gather his loyalty is to you; you may also bring your familiar, and must bring your son. You shall be at Cardinal Fleurs' mansion by no later than an hour before midnight tonight. Is that understood?"

"Yes, Princess," Margerite replied meekly. She could feel the cold lump of fear swelling in her bowels like an icy pregnancy; yet at the same time, she almost felt relieved: the time has come, and it will soon be over.

When they had returned to Cardinal de Grenville's dwellings, Margerite quickly recounted what Madame du Guesclin had said to her companions and the Teutonic Knights. Brother Wolfgang nodded grimly. "So now we shall learn whether your plan succeeded - or failed. Ritter Gottfried, it were best if you went with the Gräfin: I do not doubt Frowe Eva's skill, yet it may be that a strong sword will be needed to bring her whole from there."

But a look of horror passed over Gottfried's face like the shadow of a dark wing as he stared at the Teutonic Knight; and it seemed to Margerite that she could hear the thought echoing, as if it rang distantly from the inside of his skull: And if Margerite has truly gone over to the enemy, then you shall know it, and may do what must be done.

"Indeed, I shall have Ritter Gottfried beside me,"
Margerite said staunchly - she did not know whether it was
her trust in her knight that she wished to avow, or in herself.
"For it shall be your duty, Eva, and yours, Ritter Arnmut, to
ready the Bear's Paw by the outer gates of Avignon: there
is no telling what may befall." For if my hopes are true, my
fears unfounded, and they see it...if the Light-Bearers have
not the reason they think they have to care for Wolfram,
then I know, too well, what uses they find for innocent
children.

"Do you mean to defy the Light-Bearers in their own
chamber, then, Frowe Gräfin?" asked Brother Karl, his
scarred face splitting in a brigand's grin. "Though Brother
Wolfgang and I have not the strength to meet all the greatest
ones of the Order head-on, yet it may be that we can find a
way to be overlooked; and if we enter unsuspected, it may be
that we can come in close enough to aid you at the moment
of truth." His rough hand loosened his sword in its battered
leather sheath, as if he would draw it even then.

"I do not know what may come to pass. Yet I would be
ready for all things. Perhaps because I am a woman, I would
choose guile over force in this, but I have seen, often enough,
times when only swords would serve." Or, at need, an
eating dagger, a small voice whispered in Margerite's mind.
She pushed it away - she would never forget the horror of
Ortlieb's lifeblood gushing hot over her face to blind her, the
other woman's body collapsing heavy onto hers. But this was
no time to let herself think back on such memories, lest her
will fail beneath them.

Brother Wolfgang's lips curled into a small smile of
approval. "You have the mind of a commander, to think of
everything that may befall. Yet tell me: how shall we know if
you need rescuing?"

Margerite looked at Gottfried, holding his intense gray
gaze with her own. Slowly he nodded. "You shall know," he
said.

"And what of me?" Brother Helmuth demanded, almost querulously. Margerite had almost forgotten the old man was there: he had been sitting quietly in a chair in the corner as was his wont when his younger brethren spoke of strange matters, hardly moving except, now and then, to take a sip of watered wine from his dented pewter mug. Yet now he sat straight, his head uplifted like that of an old warhorse hearing the trumpets of a distant battlefield. "Am I no longer fit to swing my sword? Surely I shall go with you, and if I die in this, at least I shall have died fighting for Christ."

Brother Karl smiled, a strangely gentle expression on his battered face. "Brother, none would deny your right to come with us, or to do battle here. But Brother Wolfgang and I must go in under a cloak that cannot stretch out its wings to cover you - and, in truth, though you are not too old yet to fight, you have gotten somewhat past the years when you can climb walls or crouch for hours in dark corners. Rather, you shall go with Ritter Arnmut and Frowe Eva, for if it comes to fleeing Avignon, there will be strong men needed to cover the Gräfin's retreat."

Cardinal Fleurs' mansion stood a little past the outskirts of Avignon, on the other side of the Rhône. The servants who came to take their horses bore only one tiny lantern; they were all hooded and cloaked, and the white fingers that lifted the reins from Margerite's hands were skeletal and crooked, reminding her shudderingly of Kundry and Klingschor. There was not enough light for her to see Gottfried's face as he looked at them, yet it seemed to Margerite that she could feel the tension thrumming through the knight's wiry body, as though his muscles were harp-strings tuned as tightly as they could bear.

"This way," said a piercing voice from the darkness - sexlessly pure, neither alto nor tenor; Margerite could not tell whether it was a man or a woman who had spoken. But she and Gottfried followed the dark-clad figure along the yew-lined path and into the house.

Within, Cardinal Fleurs' mansion was ablaze with light, scented candles burning everywhere, shining bright from the gilded frescoes and glimmering softly from the silken and cloth-of-gold hangings. The servant who had led them in took their cloaks, and Margerite had to steel herself when she saw its face: it might almost have been a twin to Ruprecht's two servants, wrinkled and beak-nosed, with dark eyes in which a frightening, inhuman intelligence gleamed. But at least their bones are safe, charred to ashes and rinsed with holy water, Margerite comforted herself. Whatever Klingschor and Kundry were, they are beyond the Order's grasp now.

As the servant left the antechamber, Birgitta entered, treading softly. The Norwegian woman was dressed in a robe of deep purple-black, girded by a lion-skin belt about her birch-slim waist, with a sword at her side. Her golden-brown hair was no longer braided back, but flowed over her shoulders in long soft waves, and her blue eyes were wide and shining behind the glass of her spectacles, the pupils dilated as if she had been staring into the darkness. Her long white feet were bare, whispering almost silently over the elaborately patterned Eastern rugs. Two robes hung over her arm: one a red as dark as her own purple, the other plain black.

Birgitta bowed to Margerite. "Princess," she said, offering the deep red robe. "Madame du Guesclin bids you wear this."

Margerite was not sure what to do: she could not take the garment with Wolfram in her arms, and she did not wish to give him into another's hands even for a moment in this house. Birgitta, seeing her difficulty, draped the robe over a chair, then turned to Gottfried.

"This I made for you with my own hands, and I would that you wear it this night," the Norwegian told him. The candlelight in the room was bright enough for Margerite to see that it was not the usual Order silk, but seemed to be heavy-woven black linen. Gottfried stared at it for a moment - what is he seeing? Margerite wondered. And what has she done to him, that he should be willing to wear a Light-Bearer's robe?...if he does not balk now, and perhaps betray us!

"That...was kind of you," Gottfried answered. "If there is somewhere that I may undress in private..."

"It is not the way of the Order to be squeamish about such things," Birgitta rebuked him, though her voice was warm. "There shall come times when you must show your flesh freely, for it belongs to the Lord of Earth; and you have no cause to be ashamed of your body - far less, surely, than some of our members. Frowe Gräfin, I shall hold your child while you change clothes."

Margerite wanted desperately to look at Gottfried for guidance, but she found herself paralyzed by fear: she felt an appalling certainty that she could not trust him, that he had, in some way, fallen prey to the Norwegian woman's spells - or to a simpler seduction, of body or mind. Why did I not bring Eva?...Yet she, too, has been tainted by years with the Order: would she give way to the temptation to take rule here, where once she was beaten and starved and oppressed?

Margerite almost cried out at the sudden sharp pain in her thigh. Kobolt, unseen, had slunk up beside her; now he was standing on his hind legs and digging his claws into her flesh. Standing in her shadow, the cat's pupils shone green in the candlelight, and Margerite thought, What has come over me? How can I mistrust those beside whom I have risked everything? Yet even Kobolt...Did I not see him purring in Madame du Guesclin's lap this very day?

"The Princes of the Order await you, Princess," Birgitta said softly, holding out her arms for Wolfram. Reluctantly Margerite handed over her son, though he began to kick and squirm as soon as he was out of her grasp.

"Wan' Mutti!" Wolfram said. "Wan' Mutti now!"

Though Margerite knew that, to keep the semblance of her role intact, she should hasten to change clothes, she could not keep from reaching out to stroke the candlelit gold of her son's soft hair. "Hush, Wolfram, hush," she crooned. "I shall have you back in a moment."

Meanwhile, in spite of what Birgitta had said, Gottfried had gone into a corner and turned his back to change clothes. Even from behind, Margerite could see the marks of his ribs arching around from his backbone, the muscles stretched taut and ropy over the sharp-chiseled little wings of his shoulderblades. Embarassed, she turned her eyes away. Birgitta would have been clumsy enough in unlacing her gown if her arms had not been full of a squirming child; as it was, it took both of them some time and effort to get Margerite free of her clothes.

Margerite's first impulse, even though Gottfried was still standing patiently with his back turned, was to pull the dark red robe over her head as swiftly as she could; but the fine-woven material seemed to slither beneath her fingers as she picked it up, and a shudder ran through her body. Its touch reminded her...Ruprecht's shining form had bound her to the bed with silk cords...his hot silken tongue touching her most tender parts...

I bore that, and did not go mad; I can bear this, Margerite told herself sternly. Have I not worn Ortlieb's ring for these long months? Robes lent by Madame du Guesclin can surely be no worse. Gritting her teeth, she shrugged the silk robe over her shoulders, letting its hem rustle down about her ankles. At least she had brought her own belt - the lion-skin girdle of mastery, she thought; and some measure of composure returned to her as she girded it about her waist.

"Well enough," Birgitta said, giving Wolfram back to his mother. The child quieted at once, lying warm and heavy in Margerite's arms and looking trustingly up at her. "Follow me. Gottfried, I fear that you must leave that sword out here."

"It was my uncle's," Gottfried said, his sharp chin jutting in the stubborn set Margerite knew very well. "I shall not leave it by choice."

"Nevertheless. I have received my orders, and if you will follow Margerite into the Infernal Palace, you must take it off."

Gottfried frowned more deeply, and it seemed to Margerite that something was passing unheard between the knight and Birgitta. Then the Norwegian woman smiled sadly, and said something in a strange language: "Vápnom sínomscala maðr velli áfeti ganga framarr... hjalm ok brynjuskal hirða vel: gótt's til görs at taka. Gottfried, I thought you would not be willingly parted from your blade, but will you receive one from my hands for this night?"

"If I may bear it," he answered slowly.

Birgitta unbuckled her belt, sliding her sword off. It was a shorter blade than Gottfried's own - made for a woman's size and strength, Margerite had thought. But the pommel was of a strange five-lobed design, the hilt of ivory carven with writhing beasts; when she drew it to show him, Margerite saw that the length of the blade was marked with tiny pale and dark ripples, so that it seemed that a serpent ran along it as she tilted it in the candlelight.

"I think this weapon will hardly find my hand welcome," said Gottfried.

"Sólormr will welcome the hand of any brave man who keeps his oaths," Birgitta replied. "I had him from my mother - he was my only inheritance, save for my learning and my Order ring - and I would willingly give him to you."

"As a loan for this night only," Gottfried agreed, his voice almost a whisper. "Longer than that, I...could not repay as would be fitting."

Margerite was certain now that something was taking place between them that she could not hear, or understand. It seemed to her that she had seen the like of Sólormr's hilt before, though she could not remember where; but it disturbed her deeply that a Light-Bearer should offer Gottfried a weapon where he could not bear his own - the Infernal Palace! - and more, that he should accept it.

O, my Wolfram - what have I brought you to? Margerite thought as she and Gottfried walked after the violet-robed Light-Bearer. And what must I do to keep you safe? Birgitta led Margerite and Gottfried through what seemed an endless maze of candlelit corridors, their walls lined with paintings and rich tapestries.

Several times, Margerite thought she recognised Ortlieb's unmistakable handiwork: strongly coloured scenes of morality where Death or the Devil hovered, but twisted in some way that was just past naming, gloating in decay and sensuality; and it almost seemed to her then that Ortlieb's ruby tingled in answer. She is dead, but her works live on, Margerite thought. Has she any power, even now, to pursue me from the depths of Hell? Or - to follow Bernhardt, as Graf Günther follows Wolfram?

As they went further on, the hairs on the back of Margerite's neck prickled up. She knew, deep in her bowels, that something was watching her - something great and ancient, far beyond her powers of knowledge or understanding, she felt, and shivered in that icy regard. Kobolt kept pace with her, rubbing so closely against her leg that she had to walk carefully lest she trip over him; and when she glanced at Gottfried from the corner of her eye, it almost seemed to her that she could see blue sparks flashing about him like gold-fire on St. Waluburg's night, though his thin face was set in an expression of almost unearthly calm.

At last Birgitta came to a great iron-bound door. She lifted her hand and knocked thrice.

"Who comes?" a deep voice called from beyond the door.

"I, Episcopa Birgitta Thórkelsdóttir. I bring Princess Margerite von Fürstensee, together with her chosen companion Gottfried von Schlangenbad, and the One for whom this Council of Princes is gathered."

"Enter." The door swung open, and Birgitta led them in.

Margerite had to blink against the dazzlement of light within. Black candles, more than she would have thought possible, burned in rank upon rank along all the walls. In the middle of the room stood a double cube of black stone upon white, polished to a high gloss and carven all over with arcane signs and sigils. She glanced at the floor, expecting to see a circle: instead, it was paved with squares of black and white marble like a chessboard.

Then she saw that the black walls were polished to the same mirror-finish as the altar, so that the reflection from the flames of the candles formed an impenetrable circle of light about them, completed by the bar of shining steel that slid back across the door. Margerite could not see who had let them in - but Gottfried was looking at empty air as a cat might, and she understood that the door-warden was no human thing.

I am trapped here, Margerite thought. Whatever their arts, she was certain that the Teutonic Knights could not pierce through to this room. She had only Kobolt, and Gottfried - who looked terribly small and fragile in the black robe now, his thin wrists and ankles white beneath its broad sleeves and hem and his face pale in the candlelight. Margerite did not pause to count the robed men and women within the ring of flame and mirror-bright stone and steel; but half of them wore the same deep red robes as she herself, while the other half were dressed in black or dark violet. One, however, wore a garment of white silk that seemed to shimmer with faint rainbows as he moved: and from his hand glittered the clear adamant ring of the Order's Imperator. From his place behind the black altar, he beckoned to Margerite, and she came forward.

"Will you kneel to me?" Cardinal Fleurs - for it must be he - asked her: he spoke perfect German, with only a faint Provencal accent. His blue eyes glittered straight into hers, and it seemed to Margerite that she could feel the force of his will almost as a physical blow.

"I will not kneel to you, nor to any man nor spirit, save only when it is needed for deceiving our foes," Margerite answered proudly - she had read something similar in the earliest teachings of the Black Book, and could only hope that it was the right response.

Cardinal Fleurs looked at Margerite for a long time. He was a short man, no taller than she, though solidly built; his deep brown hair flowed in waves to his broad shoulders, and a wide moustache darkened his broad face, though his jaws and chin were clean-shaven. But it was his eyes that drew the gaze: their blue brilliance made all the room seem dark about him, as if only those twin azure flames burned in a lightless abyss. Her mind reeling, Margerite tried to calm herself. She had seen such brightness in human eyes only twice: once in Gottfried's at the Papal Mass...and once in Ruprecht's, as she lay bound and drugged on the bed, helpless against the dreadful spirit shining in his flesh. Yet she did not turn away - my will is a fortress of adamant, my pride the wall that cannot be breached...

"Princess Margerite," the Imperator of the Light-Bearers said thoughtfully. "Great in the Order by right of challenge, least in the Council gathered here - and mother of the child born to the Star of Morning. Episcopus Ruprecht was a flawed tool that broke in our hands, it seems; but at least once he proved useful."

Hearing Cardinal Fleurs speak thus of her dead husband, in spite of all that Ruprecht had done to her, almost made Margerite want to cry out in his defense, but she held her tongue, replying only with the neutral words, "So it seems."

"Put the Child down upon my altar, and we shall make known to you the other members of the Council."

Margerite looked at the altar - four feet high, she guessed, and two feet square - then down at the hard stone floor. "Imperator, I do not challenge you, but I think you know little of children. If I put him there, he will crawl off and harm himself. Give me leave, at least, to set him on the floor - but if he does not have a soft place to sit, do not be surprised if he tries to walk, and falls down, and cries very loudly."

Cardinal Fleurs looked at her, an expression of mild surprise on his broad face. "Set him down at the foot of the altar, then. It may prove enlightening to see what he does."

Her bowels tightening into a knot of trepidation, Margerite did as she had been commanded. Wolfram let out an indignant howl as his feet touched the cold floor, but he was pushing himself up against the twinned block of stone in a moment, his little fingers creeping over the sigils graven into its smooth surface and his small face set in concentration, as if he were trying to take apart one of his toys. The Imperator smiled, and Margerite's heart squeezed like a tightening fist in her chest.

"Stand there beside him," Cardinal Fleurs said.

One by one, the Princes of the Order came forward, each lifting a ruby-ringed hand to touch to Margerite's as they spoke their names and ranks within the Council. Madame du Guesclin, little to Margerite's surprise, stood third, only one behind the Imperator himself. Margerite recognised the fifth in rank: a grossly fat man with thick black hair and beard, she had seen him in the brighter red silk of a cardinal at the Papal Mass.

The seventh was a tall, elegant woman with the close-cropped white hair of a nun, who introduced herself as Hildegard von Waltherburg - "Abbess of the Convent of the Holy Cross," she added with a light laugh. "You may have heard of me, for I believe you have one of my former assistants. It is a pity that you did not bring little Eva with you, for I should have enjoyed seeing her again."

"Alas, I was told that I could only come with one
companion," Margerite replied. In truth, she had forgotten
that the Abbess was also a Princess of the Order: it must
have been Maria's mercy that allowed her to bring Gottfried
in Eva's place, for she would not willingly have forced the
girl to look upon her tormentor again. And how did she
travel so quickly from Passau? Margerite wondered. But
she had read of such things in the Black Book: there were
many ways by which the hosts of Hell could accomplish
swift movement, when their summoner did not fear to reveal
his power to others by doing what no mortal human could
achieve.

The Abbess looked consideringly at Gottfried, then
dismissed him with a flick of her eyes and stepped aside
to let the next Prince introduce himself. This man was
swarthy, and something about his face made Margerite
think of Jochanan, though his features were finer and his
skin darker, and the strange sword at his waist swept down
in a long curve: Margerite had heard that the Saracens used
such weapons. "Musa ibn Ahmad, Eighth of the Council of
Princes," he said, his white teeth flashing in an easy smile.
"I am delighted to see you at last, for I have heard much of
both your power and your beauty: may the Lord of Light
look well upon our meeting."

Musa kept his hand pressed against Margerite's for a
moment longer than she thought necessary, and to her
horror, it seemed to her that she felt a faint internal tingle in
answer to his touch. Perhaps he is another such as Ortlieb,
an incubus in human flesh instead of a succubus, she
thought - and if so, I must beware!

There were eleven Princes after the Imperator: Margerite
herself, then, must be the thirteenth in rank. The Black Book
had never stated whether the number of Princes was set - it
had implied, she thought, that the ruby ring could be gained
by anyone with enough power and will to win it by ritual or
challenge - but it had not mentioned that the Council had
its own ranks, either. Now I am in uncharted lands, she
thought.

Wolfram, thankfully, had left off his examination of the altar, and was toddling across the floor, intent on some exploration of his own. The members of the Council of Princes had arranged themselves according to rank in a rough half-circle about the particoloured stone, with Cardinal Fleurs standing before them - and for some reason that she could not even guess at, Margerite found herself remembering von Eschenbach's description of Parzival's half-brother: "Feirefîz in his might / was both black and white / over all his skin, save that his mouth / one-half showed with red about."

Had the Grail-poet then truly, as Nikolaus had suggested, been a member of the Order in his day - and looked upon such a sight as Margerite saw now? Yet Feirefîz had been a virtuous infidel, and had allowed his baptism for the sake of love...Margerite wrenched her mind away; such thoughts would do her little good now, when she needed all her wits about her.

"Princess Margerite," said Cardinal Fleurs - and now he spoke in Latin, so that, Margerite guessed, all there would be able to understand him. "By right of challenge, you have won the ruby ring from Princess Ortlieb. Now it is time for you to take oath and place here in the Council of Princes, before the mightiest men and women of the Order of Light-Bearers, and before Lucifer, Star of the Morning, who brings us from Darkness to Light. You swore a vow when first you set the Order's silver ring on your finger: lift your son in your arms, and repeat it now."

It seemed to Margerite then that the light of the candle-circle narrowed about her, so that she stood at the end of a long thin tunnel of fire: there was no turning back, nor any escape to either side; and yet before her was the endless dark, with Hell's light burning blue-white in the Imperator's eyes and upon his finger, and the ruby flames on the hands of those who stood behind him flaring up in answer to her own ring. She knew the oath: she had read it in horror, more than a year ago, and graven it into her mind lest Graf Günther ask her of it.

But to speak those words, and with Wolfram uplifted in her arms, as though she swore him to it as well... Yet all those gathered here, save Birgitta who had given her blade away, had swords girded at their waists: in this room, they could easily do with her as they would, for though Gottfried might strive to protect her, he was only one man against the Infernal host.

And she knew well what torments the Order of Light-Bearers prescribed for the unfaithful: it would be a long and a slow death, looking upon her own bowels staked out quivering in an unholy pentagram, and seeing the reflection of her flesh-stripped face in the dark mirror of the altar's polished stone before they finally blinded her lidless eyes.

It took all Margerite's will to clamp her sphincters tight before she soiled herself; but, as if in a trance, she reached down and picked up Wolfram, clasping him tightly to her. I am sorry, my son, she thought. I have failed you, here at the last: I trusted in my strength and wit, and they have betrayed me: I should have trusted in Christ alone.

The Princes of the Order were watching her like a ring of cats, unblinking and implacable: now Margerite must speak, but she had time for one last short prayer. Mother Maria - if You can still hear me in this place - forgive me for what I must do, and ask Your Son to judge me with mercy.

"No," said Margerite.

The single word seemed to echo from the stone walls, reverberating back and forth in one timeless moment; she saw mouths open in disbelief, and Madame du Guesclin's faint, satisfied smile. She knew all along, Margerite thought, and trapped me!

Cardinal Fleurs' mouth moved; Margerite thought she heard the words, "Take her!" But they were almost lost beneath Gottfried's cry, a burst of sound so intense that it seemed to explode in a great flower of blue light within Margerite's skull. She saw the white-robed Imperator stumble back, clasping his hands to his head; the other Princes staggered, and three of them fell, even as Gottfried leapt before Margerite and Wolfram with his sword flashing.

"Back, to the door!" the knight called, his voice ringing painfully through Margerite's bones - if he was speaking aloud; she could not tell. She obeyed him, hastening backward. A couple of the Order members were already recovering; Musa had drawn his sword, its slim crescent flashing blinding bursts of candlelight from its polished length, and was running forward to engage Gottfried. Margerite reached for the steel bar - but then it seemed to her that something gripped her in bonds of ice, freezing her limbs: she could not move, nor even cry out.

Gottfried's ripple-marked blade clashed against the Saracen's weapon, and Margerite thought that she saw sparks flying from the blow of sword on sword. With all her strength of will, she struggled to break the grip of the unseen thing that held her frozen, but she might as well have tried to bend iron shackles away from her flesh.

And one of the Order's lesser servants had run round beside her - Margerite saw the dark shimmer of violet silk, and a flash like candlelight reflecting off glass, and heard a woman's high voice screaming in an unknown tongue, "Þat kann ek it fiórða, ef mér fyrðar bera bönd at boglimom: svá ek gel, at ek ganga má, sprettr mér af fótum fiöturr, enn af höndom hapt - Áss, ópni!" Gottfried's blade slid in beneath Musa's stroke; bright blood sprayed out in a great fan over the black and white chessboard-stones, and the Saracen dropped, but Margerite could not tell whether her knight was wounded, and there were three more Order members closing in on him.

Then the steel bar screamed aside, and the door burst open. It seemed to Margerite that the Teutonic Knight's black-crossed white tabards glowed beneath their flying dark cloaks like crystals in the sunlight as they leapt through with swords drawn and helms shining, coming up to either side of Gottfried just in time to keep him from being pierced by two blades at once. "Back!" one of the warrior-monks shouted, and the three of them began to retreat to the door.

Madame du Guesclin had not lost her footing: she stood with her hand extended, her ruby ring burning and her face contorting in fury, so that Margerite could almost see the long-fanged snarl of the great cat. She shrieked something in French; Margerite heard the sharp crack of metal shattering beside her, and a cry of fierce pain. Hot drops of blood spattered her face, but she could not turn her head to see what had happened.

The Teutonic Knights guarding his back, Gottfried whirled, his borrowed sword striking snake-swift about Margerite's body, so that she would have cried out in fear if she could have. Something wailed high above the shouting and the sounds of fighting; the unseen bonds on Margerite's limbs broke as though they had never been there. "Run!" Gottfried cried to her. Margerite turned, but when she lifted her foot to cross the threshold, she found that she might as well have been trying to break through a wall of stone.

Then Kobolt's fierce fighting howl sounded at her feet, and Margerite saw the cat's black body hurtling through the open door. Something seemed to snap at his passage: she followed him through as quickly as she could. O Kobolt, she thought, you guided me through the depths of Earth once. Can you guide me through the stronghold of Hell?

But Kobolt stopped where two corridors crossed, turning his head about and yowling as if in distress. And someone had broken through to pursue her - Margerite saw the dark robe fluttering, long hair flying. Yet if I turn the wrong way, I shall be lost and alone, and Cardinal Fleurs has many servants.

Gritting her teeth in determination, she set Wolfram behind her where Kobolt could guard him and drew her dagger. Go for the throat if you can, or the belly...Again the Welshman's words came back to her, as they had when she had fought Ortlieb, though she did not know what good a knife would do against a sword.

But her pursuer slowed; and Margerite saw then that it was Birgitta. The Norwegian woman was gripping her left hand tightly with her right, but blood still flowed between her fingers; one lens of her spectacles had cracked across, and the other was missing. "Come on," Birgitta gritted between her teeth. "This way, and pray Freyr your men found your horses."

Another trap? Margerite thought. But it must have been Birgitta who opened the door, and she had no other choice, save to flee alone where she did not know the way - and the sounds of battle were growing louder behind her. She snatched up Wolfram again, ignoring his screams at such rough handling, and followed her guide at a run, back through the corridors to the antechamber where they had entered. Birgitta paused only to snatch up something - Gottfried's sword; but when she let go of her injured hand to pick it up, the blood gushed fiercely out again.

The darkness slowed them, stumbling along the path in the faint moonlight. But when they reached the gate, Birgitta spoke fiercely in French: no challenge came after that, and the two women passed outside the walls.

Margerite almost wept then, for Eva and Arnmut were standing there with the horses. "Mount, there is no time to waste!" Birgitta said. "You, take this." She thrust Gottfried's weapon awkwardly at Arnmut.

"What...is Gottfried fighting? I must go to him!"

"Mount!" Birgitta shouted. Eva clambered onto the back of her horse, holding out her arms for Wolfram so that Margerite could mount as well; and Kobolt leapt up behind his mistress, but Arnmut ran in towards Cardinal Fleurs' mansion. "Go, go on...I shall hold the horses."

"I cannot leave them!" Margerite protested.

"They are fighting to save you. Go on - would you waste the offering? Go, for your son's sake!" Birgitta's Northern accent had grown stronger, so that Margerite could barely understand her. But she could see that the tall woman was swaying on her feet, from loss of blood or from whatever power she had put forth to break the circle of light and open the door; and she could not abandon any of her rescuers just yet, for she knew what danger Birgitta must be in.

"Mount up behind me," Margerite said. "You cannot stay here."

"Have no fear for me. You must go!"

Even as Birgitta spoke, however, Margerite heard the sound of running feet from behind the walls, and shouting and the clash of weapons. Then the four men broke through the open gate, hastening for their steeds. Brother Karl was limping badly, and Brother Wolfgang's left arm dangled; a streak of dark blood stained Arnmut's pale doublet from right shoulder to left hip, and Margerite could hear the howling behind them.

In a sudden burst of speed, Gottfried outpaced the rest, running to Birgitta. With a strength surprising in his frail body, he picked her up by the waist and almost tossed her onto his horse, then slapped Margerite's steed hard on the rump before dropping back to help her injured companions. The gray gelding snorted: only Margerite's firm seat kept it from rearing back, but it charged off beneath her, and it took all her skill to keep it on the road towards Avignon.

Margerite was barely able to rein her horse to a walk when she saw the lanterns ahead of her. Wolfram's screams had steadied to a slow sobbing; now she could murmur words of comfort to him, for the horsemen were riding towards her, and she could see Paul's ruddy face in the faint flickering of the light he bore.

"Hurry back," Margerite ordered, her voice shaking. "The rest may need your help."

"What happened?" Jochanan asked, riding up beside her.

"There is no time to tell; but we must flee swiftly - as soon as we are all together: some of them may be wounded."

"Then follow me!" Brother Helmuth cried, his white moustaches bristling fiercely through the opening of his bascinet. The old Teutonic Knight drew his sword, galloping forward, and Paul called out, "Bear's Paw - forward! Dieter, Peter, Albercht, you stay here to guard the Gräfin."

Three of the horsemen broke away from the main body, ringing Margerite; the rest sped forward behind Brother Helmuth. Margerite clutched Wolfram to herself, shivering; but Kobolt rubbed up against her from behind, and it seemed to her that she could feel new strength flowing into her from his touch, calming her twitching muscles like a strong draught of chammomile and linden-blossoms.

"Wolfram, Wolfram," she murmured to her son. "Whatever happens, even if they slay us, we are free now."

Margerite soon began to shiver in the cold. She longed to tear the Order robe from her body, but that would leave her naked before the Bear's Paw men save for her least underclothes. Yet the robe only protected her modesty, and gave her no warmth against the raw icy wind blowing over the Rhône.

"Frowe Gräfin, y'look cold. Will ye take my cloak?" one of the Bear's Paw men asked.

"Thank you very much," Margerite replied. "I am in your debt."

"Nothing to't, Frowe Gräfin. Buy me a beer sometime, and we'll call't even."

The mercenary's cloak reeked of stale wine and an unwashed man's sweat, as though it had been used as garment and bedroll both for years without being cleaned, but it was warm, and Margerite clutched it gratefully about herself and her son.

Kobolt purred ecstatically at the smell, working his paws and rolling over the gray gelding's hindquarters as though he had found a bruised valerian root to chew; that distracted Margerite for a moment, but she soon turned her mind to prayer - for her comrades' safety, and for Birgitta: Maria, if she dies unshriven, know that she died in breaking the Order's chains, and freeing Wolfram and myself; do not let her be judged too harshly.

After a time - Margerite could not guess how long - she heard the sound of hooves approaching, and saw the shapes of riders dark in the faint light of Moon and stars. The Bear's Paw men drew their swords. "I'll go forward to see who they are," the man who had given her his cloak offered. "If we start fighting, run like Hell."

"You are a brave man," Margerite murmured as he pushed his horse forward into a trot. The free soldier turned to salute her, a few teeth glimmering from his grin, then nudged his steed to a canter.

Margerite watched, barely breathing, as the Bear's Paw man rode up to the troop of riders. Then he sheathed his sword and waved his arm, as if beckoning to Margerite and her two guards.

Is this a trap? she thought. He could easily have been deceived by illusion, for a short time in the moonlight?... But then she saw the glimmer of the Teutonic Knights' white tabards, the black crosses standing starkly out against the brightness; and a demon's illusion could not take that shape. She rode forward.

A quick glance and a few words in the darkness told Margerite, to her relief, that all her people were there. Birgitta still rode behind Gottfried, her arms about the knight's thin waist; Arnmut assured her that the cut across his body was shallow and had almost stopped bleeding. When Margerite asked the Teutonic Knights if they could ride on, Brother Karl snorted.

"Our wounds are little enough; I have seen men of our Order make a final lance-charge with their bowels dripping down the backs of their horses. And there is no time to wait here for healing. We came out of this too easily: I feel in my bones that there is worse to come. Therefore we must ride while we may, rather than waiting in the night for them to repair their sundered circle - not least, because they have the blood and life-strength of their own to work with now, and who knows what such sorcerors may not achieve when they feel their death-wounds on them, or afterwards?"

Graf Günther, Margerite thought. Then, What would he have become, had Father Etienne not bound him by the Last Rites?

"Then, for Christ's sake and our own, let us ride now!" said Brother Wolfgang.

Much as Margerite would have liked to ride faster, their horses were tired: they had to drop to a walk every so often, then trot, jouncing painfully along - she remembered ruefully Gottfried's remark about trotting in full armour as a harsh penance - before breaking into brief canters. It seemed to her that she should have begun to feel safer the farther they got from Avignon...but instead, an ominous feeling was creeping upon her as they rode.

The icy wind pressed harder against them; the Moon was down, and the light of the stars seemed to be dimming, as though a shadow thickened over them. As the riders slowed to a walk again, Margerite looked up: then she saw the black cloud pouring over the stars from the west, like a flood rising through a village to snuff its lanterns out one by one.

Yet they could go no faster for fear of killing the horses - Christ, protect us. Mother Maria, hide us beneath your cloak! she prayed. A blue flash of lightning flickered across the sky behind them. Kobolt dug his claws into Margerite's saddle-cantle, arching his back and hissing; her gray gelding flicked his pale ears and sidestepped nervously. Margerite had never feared storms, but now a great terror was stealing upon her.

She glanced about in the dark for a white cross, pulling her horse over; she could barely make out Brother Wolfgang's lean features. "Brother," Margerite said, "I think that we must ride as swiftly as we may now, and pray that Christ will send our steeds the strength to bear it - for I fear what will happen, if that storm comes upon us before dawn."

"I, as well," the Teutonic Knight answered, his voice low. "We must take the risk, for we may yet outride it, but whatever evil it brings will be the same whether it catches us afoot or mounted."

With those words, he spurred his horse onward, and Margerite followed, though she could hear her steed's harsh breaths beneath her - O Maria, let his heart endure! Yet the wind was growing stronger, and it seemed to her that she could hear the sound of voices moaning in it, a forsaken and terrible wailing of hatred. Her horse ran faster: it was fleeing in wild terror now, and she was just able to keep it to the road. St. Stefan, patron of horses, aid Eva's hands on the reins, Margerite prayed. Maria help us, Christ help us...

Lightning flashed again; that instant of brightness showed the bare trees black and twisted about the roadside, the frosty pastures beyond flaring blue with Hellish light. It seemed to Margerite that she heard screams drowned in the thunder, but she did not dare look back. The icy wind ripped at her borrowed cloak, its edges flapping up to batter her face like the wings of an angry hawk - They are hunting me: the horn has been blown, and the hounds are running fast on the trail.

Before Margerite could shift her grip on the garment, another gust of wind tore it suddenly from her, leaving her crouching over her horse's back in nothing but the thin silk robe. Then the storm-driven sleet struck, needles of ice battering against her as if she were naked to its sting. She covered Wolfram with her body as well as she could; she could feel Kobolt's warmth upon her lower back, but elsewhere the harsh sleet stung like a flaying-knife, as though the Order would have its prescribed revenge.

A huge flash of lightning burst down beside her, shattering the wide black trunk of a gnarled oak - the broken wood leapt up in flames, hissing angrily beneath the driving hail. Margerite's horse shied and reared; she did not know how she managed to hold Wolfram and keep to her seat - Christ preserve us, perhaps we should dismount, form a circle and ward ourselves together as best we may? But there was no time for that, though flecks of foam from her horse's mouth blew back hot upon her face; she could not pause to gather her men beneath the full force of the storm.

The wind's moaning was louder now, and it seemed to Margerite that she almost knew some of the thin chill wailing voices, the cries of the Hell-spirits. Yet she would not put names to them, lest that draw them closer to her; though she could no longer feel the reins under her frozen fingers, she clamped her knees tighter on her horse's heaving sides, and rode on.

Dark tatters, soft as mist, were beating about her now. In the next flash of lightning, Margerite saw the left sleeve of her robe blowing free, tangled with the torn flaps of silk blowing from behind her; she felt a fresh stinging on her back as the hot blood welled up from her bare flesh, and the chafing of her lion-belt against naked skin. "Take it, then!" she cried. "I do not want it!"

Then she remembered that Ortlieb's ring was still on her finger. Fumbling desperately to keep her hold on Wolfram and the reins at once, she tore it off, a burning jolt of pain shooting up her arm as though the gold had grown into her flesh.

"I renounce this ring!" Margerite shouted, casting it back into the slicing hail. "Have it back, and..." Be damned, she had been about to say, but the words stuck in her throat. "Christ's mercy upon you, as upon us all!"

The wind slackened suddenly, so that Margerite gasped in relief. Lightning still flickered blue overhead; in its fitful brightness, she could see her companions coming up behind her. Eva was still there, thank Christ, though trailing the others, with Arnmut riding beside her; Gottfried and Birgitta, the three Teutonic Knights, and the Bear's Paw men straggling behind - were there fewer of them than there had been? Or were they only strung out along the road where she could not see them in the intermittent flashes? But, Christ willing, it is over.

Suddenly a furious burst of wind hurled itself at Margerite's face like a stone. She cried out as the hail scored her face, her own blood spattering into her eyes. Her horse took off again, but it was near-spent; in the blurring bolts of lightning hammering down about them, she could see the others riding up around her.

"Hold fast, Gräfin!" Brother Wolfgang shouted, the bones of his weathered face standing out like a naked skull in the searing flashes through the darkness. "It must be almost dawn!"

Margerite opened her mouth to answer; but in that second another bolt of lightning struck down beside her. She saw the blue fire playing about Brother Wolfgang's helm, his limbs flung up in a violent spasm; she did not hear his final cry, though his mouth gaped dark and wide, but his horse convulsed and fell, flinging his body away.

"Ride!" Brother Karl shouted to Margerite as she tried to rein her wildly plunging mount in. "He is dead, and they are upon us now. Ride, as you would not fall to Hell's legions!"

Gottfried and Birgitta were ahead of her now, but the warhorse's head was down: it would not last much longer under its double burden, light and unarmoured though both riders were.

Another bolt of lightning shrieked down, blasting the road between them, so that Margerite's horse twisted its head against the reins, fighting to turn. She saw what was before her only in sudden flashes through eyes blinded half by lightning and half by darkness. In one glimmering, Gottfried had sprung from the horse; in another, blue fire wreathed his naked sword as he held it aloft. Trickles of blood scored thin black trails down his white brow and cheeks, but his eyes were open to the hail as he called out, "Strike here with all your strength - and in Christ's Name, let that be an end!"

The blackened heavens seemed to burst asunder in one single unimaginable stroke of light, tearing down through the air to the gleaming point of Gottfried's sword. The thunder was so loud that Margerite heard it, not with her deafened ears, but through her bones, a world-riving clap that left echoes shuddering through her body, and no sound at all to be heard, nor any glimmer of brightness before her blackened eyes.

There was only the warmth of Wolfram in her arms, of the horse beneath her and Kobolt against her back; the battering ache of her bruises and the stinging dribbles of blood down her naked body where the hail had struck. Her steed was no longer running: it stood stock-still, and she could feel the wet hide shivering against her bare legs.

Then gentle hands were easing her son from her grasp. Margerite thought that she let out a cry of pain between clenched teeth as rough wool covered her bleeding nakedness, but she could hear nothing. Strong arms clasped her waist, lifting her down from her horse's back, laying her carefully on the ground; hands forced her mouth open, dripping burning liquid down her throat.

Margerite blinked hard - she could feel that her left eye was swollen almost shut - and slowly the blackness of her sight began to soften to gray, with blurred figures moving before her - she was looking eastward, towards the dawn. Kobolt was lying, warm and heavy, on her chest; she could see the pale gleam of Eva's long hair, and - thank Maria, thank Christ - the girl was bending down to hold Wolfram's hand as he toddled along: the tiny figure could be nothing other than her son.

The sight of Wolfram alive and well gave Margerite strength, and she pushed herself up painfully. She could hear nothing yet, and her eyes ached with the effort to see; but she could make out a dark shape lying still on the hail-whitened ground, and two others crouched over it.

"...Gräfin?" Jochanan's voice came to her as a faint and distant whisper, though he was bending over her and speaking almost into her ear.

"Help me up," Margerite croaked. "I must see to Gottfried."

"...not have survived..." Jochanan seemed to be saying. But the gunner gave her his arm, helping her up, and painfully she walked over to where her knight lay.

Tears shone on Arnmut's fair face in the beginning daylight; his hands rested on Gottfried's chest. A great rent had been blasted in the linen robe, its edges charred away, but the knight's white skin was untouched beneath it. Birgitta knelt on the other side, her blood-crusted hands covering her face as she rocked back and forth, weeping soundlessly. The twisted shards of the broken sword glinted from the heaps of ice-stones about Gottfried's body: he could not have survived that blow, Margerite thought.

She bent down, brushing her lips against Gottfried's bloodied forehead, then reached within his robe to pull out his crucifix. Something else came with it - the chip of stone on its twisted linen string, his mysterious favour. But the stone was cracked across; and beneath its rough gray surface, Margerite saw the ruddy gleam of pure gold.

For charity, and humility, he said...The tears burned down from her own eyes: in the wavering ripples of water over her seared sight, it seemed to her that she saw Gottfried's dark eyelashes flutter, and his mouth open slightly.

"Gottfried?" Margerite whispered, her voice soundless to her own ears. "Gottfried, do you live? Can you hear me?"

Arnmut looked up, his face brightening with sudden hope. He leaned forward over Gottfried's body, so close to his face that it almost seemed that his lips would meet the other knight's. For a moment he was poised there; then Gottfried's thin hand lifted weakly, and Arnmut clasped it in both of his own, bringing it to his mouth and kissing it fervently.

"You are alive!" Arnmut said. "Christ be praised, you are alive!"

Gottfried's lips moved; his voice was no more than a whisper, but Margerite heard him clearly. "Arnmut? I cannot see..."

"I am here," Arnmut assured him.

"And I," Birgitta said, taking the fallen knight's other hand. In the growing daylight, Margerite could see that her left hand had been shattered as though one of Jochanan's gunshots had struck it; the Norwegian must have been in agony, but she showed no sign of it. "Rest now: I think we are safe, at least for a little while, for it shall be some time before the Order can gather such strength as they sent against us once more."

# Chapter Eight

Four of the Bear's Paw soldiers had been killed in the storm, along with Brother Wolfgang. The charred cloth and skin beneath the Teutonic Knight's armour left no doubt about his death, if there had ever been any, but the other men were unmarked, save that the head of one lolled loosely on a broken neck: his horse must have thrown him in its terror. Margerite saw that he wore no cloak - was this the man who had given her his garment against the cold?

"What was his name?" she asked Paul, who stood looking sadly down at the corpses of his men.

"His name was Albercht," Paul answered. Margerite remembered how he had grinned at her, riding forward to see whether the troop approaching them was friend or foe and ready to die to buy their escape - no less courageous, in his way, than Gottfried: for no man could give more than his death, whether he dared swords on the battlefield or the rage of Hell.

"A sad end for a brave man," she said, and told Paul what he had done.

"Aye, he had been with the Bear's Paw for years, and he was always beside me in the thick of battle. God rest him, he was a good companion...Do you want his boots? His feet were small enough, and you'll get frostbite if you don't put on shoes quickly."

Margerite looked at Paul in shock, and he shrugged. "Gräfin Margerite, the dead don't need their boots. If Albercht isn't walking the streets of Heaven now, he's toasting his feet in Hell. And we always said in the Company, you'll remember the man whose clothes are keeping you warm."

Margerite stared down at the dead man's face for a few moments. His dark beard had already begun to grizzle; only a few teeth showed beneath his slack lips, but she could see that he had not been so old - no older than Bernhardt, in any case.

"He wouldn't grudge them to you," Paul added. "And I'll bet you a mug of beer you can't feel your toes right now."

Margerite could not argue: she crouched down as Paul tugged the boots off Albercht's rigid feet. "Thank you, again," she said softly, looking into the unseeing hazel eyes. "May Christ remember you, and St. Martin pray for you - he gave only half a cloak to warm another, but you gave me a whole one, though we both had need of it."

Margerite did not dare delay too much longer than it took for Jochanan and herself to bind the wounds of the injured, for though the Light-Bearers' magics might be exhausted for now, they had a full measure of earthly strength yet to send forth, and her men were in no condition to battle with, say, the knights of a cardinal's household guard. Her only hope was that her foes would believe that their last mighty stroke had achieved their ends, and that, believed dead, she would be safe for a little time.

Yet they are too clever not to seek some surety of my death, Margerite thought. I underestimated them before, or overestimated myself: Maria grant that I have, at least, learned a little from that! Beneath the cloak that someone had wrapped about her, Margerite was wearing only her lion-girdle and dagger: the fury of the storm had torn everything else from her.

But she could not ride like that, and so she went to Eva, who stood talking with Rose. The servant maid on her quiet nag, further slowed by the two pack-horses she was still leading - and as a credit to her bravery, she had not let go of their lead-ropes - had been left far behind the others. And by Christ's mercy, or because she was too far from Margerite to be in danger, the storm had passed over her without hurt.

Eva was still disheveled and pale, and a few small dark bruises showed on her creamy skin, but she had clearly suffered less than Margerite - and, Margerite noticed, the onyx ring was no longer on her hand.

"I threw it into the Rhône on my way over the bridge last night," she said. "Brother Wolfgang told me that he had a foreboding of ill, and that I should ward myself as well as I could."

Margerite looked over to where the two remaining Teutonic Knights were lifting the blanket-wrapped body of their monastic brother gently to the back of his horse: it reminded her, all too clearly, of the dead-wagon following behind as they rode from the battle with Ortlieb's troops to the Bishop's palace. And how many other men shall die for me before this is all over? But she forced her mind back to the needs of the moment. "Did you pack any clothes against the chance of our flight?"

Eva smiled triumphantly. "I packed everything we could carry. And the good Cardinal - he is a fine and generous man, worthy of much praise! - told me to bring the clothes he had sent for us: he said it was the least he could do, since we would not let him aid us more directly." Even in Eva's light voice, Margerite could hear the stinging barb beneath the kindness of Cardinal de Grenville's words; but that only made her admiration of his generosity greater.

"I hope that someday we may be able to repay his kindness. Well, help me to dress, if you will - and I trust that you packed my purse where it may be easily found?"

"Do you take me for a fool?" Eva asked. "It is in my own saddlebag, along with a few spare clothes."

Before pulling anything else out, Margerite took out her falcon-necklace. The beads shone brightly in the dawn, crystal and ruby and amethyst; the gold falcon's sapphire eye glittered like blue stained-glass with a ray of sunlight striking through it. She no longer felt the piercing guilt that had stabbed her through whenever she had touched it before, only sorrow.

I made the wrong choice after all, Bernhardt - but I have paid for it now in full, I hope. Carefully she set it about her neck; then she and Eva walked behind a tangle of bare thornbushes for such cover as it could give, Kobolt and Kriemhilt scampering after them as if they had merely gone out for a pleasure-ride.

Margerite almost cried out as she tugged the cloak away from her back: the blood had dried hard, matting the wool to her flesh. Eva gasped, a hand going to her mouth. "Dear God, you look as though you were flogged with thorns! If your modesty can bear it, I shall fetch Jochanan to clean your wounds lest they fester - but I fear you will never be able to let a husband see your naked back again. At least the injuries on your face are not as likely to scar, though we shall have to make some kind of veil for you before we come among civilized folk again."

"It is no more penance than I deserve," answered Margerite. She could feel that one side of her mouth was badly swollen, as well as her eye; a large hailstone had driven her cheek against her teeth hard enough to cut the flesh, so that it hurt to speak.

Birgitta came back with Jochanan and Eva. The Norwegian's left hand was wrapped thickly in bandages, and she, too, had changed clothes. She was dressed now in a rough tunic and breeches that were too large for her, belted tightly at the waist; borrowed from one of the Bear's Paw men, Margerite thought. Birgitta stumbled over fallen branches and stones as she walked - Gottfried had never seemed to suffer so from his short sight, but then, he had never worn spectacles to sharpen his vision, either.

"I have some skill in healing," she was saying to the Bear's Paw lieutenant. "If I may aid..."

"It would be more seemly for you to do her," Jochanan agreed. Birgitta paused, blinking at him, and Margerite's swollen mouth stretched unwillingly into the ghost of a smile.

"How is it with Gottfried?" Margerite asked, though she knew the answer already: Birgitta would not have left his side if she thought that he still hovered on the brink of death.

"He is recovering his sight, and there is no doubt now that he shall live. And Ritter Arnmut is tending him. He seems very devoted," Birgitta added with a trace of sharpness - of jealousy? How was it that Gottfried won you over to our side? Margerite wondered. Was I looking at things the wrong way around, when I feared that you might seduce him to the Order?

Birgitta's touch on her back was very gentle, the Norwegian washing out the clotted gashes with a damp cloth as she murmured beneath her breath. A prickling warmth ran over Margerite's bruised skin at the soft half-chant - though the rhythms were foreign to her, there was something familiar about them, just as there had been about the carven ivory hilt of the Norwegian's sword.

Yes: Meister Stefan had chanted just so as he tended Margerite's limping horse. The hilt of his fighting-knife had been carved in a like manner, as well - and had he not said that his folk had come from Norway and Sweden into the German lands? Nor did Margerite feel anything like the touch of Light-Bearer magic in whatever Birgitta was doing... I shall have a better explanation of this hereafter, when there is time, she told herself, clenching her jaw against the burning sting of Jochanan's medicine.

Birgitta swathed Margerite's upper body in thin linen bandages while Jochanan turned his back. "I would recommend that you not wear any gown you wish to keep for a day or two yet. Some of these gashes are deep, and they may bleed a little when you ride. But there is no harm in that: it will help to clean them."

Margerite was the last to need bandaging; Rose brought Wolfram to her so that she could feed him, and then she dressed and they mounted up again.

"Should we keep to the road?" Brother Karl asked as they nudged their exhausted horses into a slow walk. "Our foes have means of gaining news other than the Black Art."

"I know no other way to go. And yet...I dislike dividing our strength, but it might be well for us to travel in separate parties. And you and Brother Helmuth would do well to hide your tabards, for of us all, you are the likeliest to draw attention here."

Brother Karl scowled fiercely, but nodded. "True enough. Who shall go with whom, then?"

Margerite thought on that for a moment. Battered as she was, dressed in her simplest riding clothes, she could easily pass for a camp-follower among the men of the Bear's Paw. So could Birgitta in her borrowed tunic and breeches, and Rose in her horse-stained and muddied servant's dress; while Eva would not look out of place riding with an escort of knights. But Birgitta, Margerite thought, would not be willing to part from Gottfried; and it was too much to ask the proud young knight to act the part of a Free Company soldier, nor would Arnmut leave his side - and she herself feared to be without him, since she could not be sure that the Light-Bearers would not be able to send something else after them.

"You brethren shall ride ahead with Eva," Margerite said slowly. "Birgitta, Gottfried, Arnmut, and I shall travel together, and the Bear's Paw must follow behind us." There: a noble frowe with her two bodyguards, a pair of poor knights with their womenfolk, and a Free Company that had come too late to ravage the French countryside with their companions - none of those would cause too much remark.

"And where are we going now?"

"To the palace of the Bishop of Niederwald," answered Margerite. "Father Etienne awaits us there, and I know no safer place, not least since the Inquisition is carrying out its investigation still."

Brother Helmuth, riding beside Brother Karl, coughed loudly. "Frowe Gräfin, I am old, and I hardly understand much of these matters with which you have been dealing. But in my youth I was a Knight Templar, and lived through the trials before we were disbanded - thank Christ, the madness of the French did not sweep through the Holy Roman Empire! Though much of my knowledge is second- or third-hand, I can give you some advice along the way, if you will listen to an old man's maunderings, and will let me travel with you."

"I shall be grateful for it," Margerite said.

Brother Karl frowned. "We are meant to go about at least in pairs when away from our Order's strongholds, that no occasion for sin arise."

Brother Helmuth chewed on the end of his long white moustache for a moment. "We are allowed to leave our squadrons when a Christian life is in peril, as the Gräfin's may be if I cannot counsel her. Brother, I know how matters may go in the investigation of heresy, and how the chance to seize wealth and power draw Inquisitors as rotten meat draws flies. And I am a Rhinelander as well.

Though more than an hundred years have passed, it is not yet forgotten what horrors Conrad von Marburg unleashed there, so that it is said still that even the king and bishops of the Rhineland feared for their lives while he was at work: the smoke of those he burned darkened the heavens, and my own nurse threatened me with his ghost when I was unruly in church as a small child. Aye, the Inquisition has been weak in Germany since, nor has Kaiser Karl given them such authority as that first man to bear the title Inquisitor haereticae pravitatis held. But it seems to me as though we are yet in battle, though our swords may be sheathed at this moment."

"It would be unseemly for me to ride alone with Frowe Eva," argued Brother Karl.

"Then let my maidservant go with her to keep watch," Margerite suggested. "And for your sake, if you will, choose a man of the Bear's Paw to accompany you."

"That would do my soul little more good: it is not meet that a brother of the Teutonic Order should keep company with a man who boasts of the sins of the flesh, as all Free Company soldiers do."

"Not all," Margerite murmured, too softly for the Teutonic Knight to hear.

Brother Karl went on, "Brother Wolfgang was given command over the two of us: now there is no saying which of us is to obey the other, for you are my senior in years and in service to the Order, but I am skilled in the Art by which, God willing, we may hope to still confound our foes. Yet I shall yield to you if you insist, Brother Helmuth; but my counsel is against us two parting."

The old man gnawed harder on his moustache, his wrinkled forehead furrowing deeply. "If you fear that our parting will bring about the occasion of sin, then I cannot command it - Perhaps, after all, we were better to travel all together, putting our trust in Christ and in the true souls of our comrades; for have we not won our way out of the lion's jaws even this past night? And though the cost was sore, we have lost a greater number of beloved brothers in battles against lesser foes. If guile is needed," he added, "for that Christ commanded us to be wise as serpents, though tender as doves - it may be that we must all play the part of brigands, insofar as we can without breaching our Rule. Brother Wolfgang might have found a better way out, for he was the wisest of us three; but my white head can come up with nothing better."

Eva frowned prettily when Margerite explained to her that she must leave off her fine clothes, but Margerite thought that she caught a glimpse of mirth in the younger woman's eyes at the thought of playing a camp-follower to a Free Company. The women changed off horses with the Bear's Paw men - camp-followers would hardly be sitting the best steeds; at least two of the fallen soldiers' horses had come back, so that there was a mount for Birgitta as well. Instead of heading directly east, the company went due north: it might help to throw the Light-Bearers off their scent for a while.

They had to stop in a town the first night, for the Teutonic Knights had Brother Wolfgang's body to bury. Brother Helmuth acted as interpreter, telling the priest in clumsy Latin that his son had been killed on the road: a few coins secured the Teutonic Knight's place in the churchyard.

As they dismounted and handed their horses to others of the Bear's Paw men to hold, Paul came over to Margerite. "Gräfin," he said, and Margerite made a quick shushing gesture. "Uh, Margerite. Forgive me, but being as you're pretending to be what you are - no one's going to believe it if you and the other frowes take a separate room. None of us will do anything we shouldn't, you have my word on it, but I don't see any way out of it."

Margerite called the other women over and briefly told them what Paul had said: she had no reason to doubt that he knew how such things went. "I shall stay with Ritter...with Gottfried myself," Margerite said, for if she had misjudged the Order's speed to recover and find her, she would be best off with him. "You others may choose as you like." Birgitta almost glared at her, but said nothing; Margerite had no doubt that she would have preferred Gottfried as her own companion - *and does she believe that we are lovers, as I suggested to Madame du Guesclin? Would I be as well to watch my back, least jealousy tempt her to do what the Light-Bearers did not, though she saved my life in their citadel of magic?*

"I shall share a sleeping-place with Paul the Bear, then," Rose said, giggling.

"And I with Arnmut," Eva added. "I know that he will take no liberties with me."

Birgitta frowned sharply, her short-sighted blue eyes flicking around at the Bear's Paw men. At last she said, "I shall share my sleeping-place with Jochanan, if I must, for he seems to me a good man, though his ways are not mine."

"And it were well," said Margerite, "if those of us whose names the Light-Bearers might know took different names for this journey. The Bear's Paw must rename itself as well, for a little time."

As in Ortlieb's castle, Margerite and Eva went by the names Gertrude and Gisela: Margerite thought that the Light-Bearer Princess had said nothing to her fellows of their presence at Schloss Niederwald, being greedy of taking Wolfram for herself. Gottfried called himself Hildebrant, and Arnmut, Wolfhart. Birgitta spoke French well enough to pass for a native, she said: she took the name Isabella, but Rose remained Rose.

The serving-girl was carrying a large wicker basket in both hands: now she gave it to Eva. "I hope you mean to deliver your gift soon, for this has been a weary burden on the road," Rose muttered.

"This very night, as may be - excuse me, I have something to tend to," Eva said to Margerite, carrying the basket away. Margerite wanted to shout at her, for this was no place for any of them to be wandering about alone, so near to Avignon, but there were a few villagers staring openly at the mercenary company with looks of mingled terror and curiosity, and Margerite knew that she should do nothing more to draw attention.

The inn was small, with but two private chambers. Margerite, Gottfried, Eva, and Arnmut shared one, while Paul, Rose, Jochanan, and Birgitta took the other: the rest of the men would sleep in the common room. Birgitta, keeping her injured hand well-hidden beneath her cloak, argued with the innkeeper for some time until she had gotten him down to a satisfactory cost for their food and lodgings. She returned to Margerite shaking her head.

"Such people!" she said. "When we came in, he nearly soiled his breeches in fear; but the moment he saw we would pay like honest folk, he tried to cheat us shamefully."

Paul had already made himself comfortable on one of the benches, sitting with his heavy arm about Rose's shoulders and shouting for ale in fractured French. Margerite heard Birgitta's faint sigh before the Norwegian woman went over to join Jochanan; she whispered something in the gunner's ear, and he put his arm around her as well. Gottfried looked appalled, and Margerite took his hand in hers, tugging him upstairs towards their chamber, with Arnmut and Eva following.

There were but two beds in the little room, and it was dark save for one small candle-stub. Margerite sank down gratefully on one of the beds, holding Wolfram in her arms. The boy had been fretful all day, as though he might have a light fever, but he was quiet enough now, and his forehead was not too warm to the touch. Kobolt and Kriemhilt leapt up beside them, rubbing against her and purring, their tails crossing as they entwined themselves about Margerite and her son.

"I much mislike this, Frowe Gräfin," Gottfried said stiffly. "If word were ever to get out that you had travelled so..."

"But none shall know save we ourselves, unless our foes manage to spy us out, and then we shall have more than rumours to fear," Margerite told him. "And now our safety depends on all of us playing our parts - even you, Herr Ritter, though I know this is little easier for you than for the Teutonic Knights themselves. At least," she added, "even if we must sleep in the one bed, I know that I need not fear for my chastity, as I would with most other men: I am grateful to have you beside me."

A stricken look passed briefly over Gottfried's face, and Margerite feared that she had hurt him where she meant only to praise. Yet he said only, "That is so. But there are two beds, and four of us, and it would be more seemly..." The knight stopped. He must have been hiding his thoughts from Margerite, but she needed no special gift to guess them: sharing a bed with Margerite might look questionable, but there would be no temptation to him, whereas Arnmut and Eva...

"No, it is well enough," said Eva swiftly. "When Margerite and I have shared a bed, she is ever complaining about how much room I take, and how I flop about like a fish in my sleep. At least, if Arnmut is troubled by such things, he will be too courteous to say so."

"I have never..." Margerite began; but thinking on it, she remembered that she might have remarked on Eva's restlessness a time or two, and, bruised and aching as she was, she could hardly bear the thought of Eva flinging her limbs about in a shared bed. Yet to put Arnmut and Eva in a single bed, when she had been so long considering what a fine couple they made...But even if Arnmut's will failed him, he would certainly never lay siege to Eva's chastity with Gottfried sleeping in the same room! Margerite thought. She shrugged. "So be it, then. Whatever passes here, none save us will know; and I know that however we are arranged, that no sin shall come of it. All I can say now is: remember that we are soldiers and camp-followers of a Free Company, and play your parts accordingly where others can see us. Now, if you will leave me of your courtesy, I must feed my son."

Eva and Arnmut glanced at each other and giggled. "But one moment more," Eva said, and Arnmut picked up the wicker basket, carrying it over to Gottfried.

"Gottfried, we found this for you in Avignon."

Gottfried looked at it disbelievingly for a moment, then set it down on the floor and crouched beside it to cautiously open the lid. Margerite heard a small bark, and at once a white bundle of fluff stood up with its paws on the edge of the basket, tipping it over. As if it knew to whom it should belong, the puppy ran to Gottfried at once, leaping up and trying to lick his face.

Even in the dim light, Margerite thought she could see the tears standing in the knight's eyes as he picked the white puppy up and held it close to his thin chest. "Thank you," he said softly. "I could have asked for nothing better."

"He is a Pyrenean bear-dog," Eva said. "When he is grown, there will be nothing that he cannot hunt and do battle with."

"Thank you," Gottfried said again, stroking the puppy's long white fur.

Once downstairs again, Margerite and Eva followed the example Rose had set by sitting close to their chosen knights. Margerite put one arm around Gottfried's thin waist: she could feel his stiffness, but after a little while, he was able to bring himself to hold her closer to him, his cloak wrapping about the two of them. Gottfried had taken off much of his armour on the road, lest its quality betray him, but he still wore his chain hauberk and breastplate, and his thin body felt cold and unyielding against Margerite's.

Yet, as she sat nestled up to him beneath his cloak, Margerite could not help dreaming for a moment of how this would be with Bernhardt - a joyous game, to pretend for a moment to be the soiled lady of a mercenary captain, with Bernhardt's strong arm about her as they drank thick ale and rough wine by the fire in an inn filled with laughter and shouts! But she knew better: there would be no joy in playing the mercenary for Bernhardt, who had dwelt in the darkness of that life so long, and to be so close to him, with Heinrich still living and their wedding-vows binding Margerite to him, would be as much torment as pleasure, knowing...

Gottfried patted Margerite's shoulder awkwardly. "There is enough to trouble us in what is, without worrying too much about what is not," he murmured softly to her. "Now remember your own words to me: the company is spending coin freely enough to show that they have just been paid after a successful venture, and we must seem to rejoice." As if to prove his own point, he picked up his mug of wine and drank a great swallow from it - but, unused to more than dainty sipping, the young knight coughed and sputtered, spraying wine over Paul and Rose across the table.

Paul laughed heartily, mopping his face with his sleeve. "Shame on you, Hildebrant, for wasting good wine! Here, I'll show you how to drink." He lifted his own mug, tilting it a little towards Margerite and Gottfried to show that it was full of ale, then raised it to his lips and drank it down in a single draught, his Adam's apple working beneath his scrubby red-gold beard. "That's the way. Go on, now!"

A small smile touched Gottfried's thin lips. "I fear I do not have the head to drink as you do," he said. "If I tried to drain my cup in one draught, I should spew up more than wine."

"Never mind. Stay with the Company, and you'll learn the skills a free soldier needs quickly enough."

Rose giggled, snuggling in a little closer to Paul. The
girl's long dark hair was disheveled, falling free about her
triangular face, and her gray-green eyes were bright; she,
at least, seemed to be enjoying her role. Margerite resolved
to have a sharp talk with her, for she remembered that the
Bear had not scrupled to make as free as he could with the
serving-maids in Burg Falkenstein - and she had no doubt
that he would keep his word to her in general, but if Rose
proved willing, that was another matter.

Eva, too, seemed to be enjoying herself more than was
seemly, sitting in Arnmut's lap with her arms twined about
his neck and their golden hair mingling. Now and again she
would kiss him on the nose or cheek and laugh, and Arnmut
seemed to like that well enough, though his eyes would
flicker guiltily towards Gottfried.

If Margerite had not remembered how Eva had spoken
of the young knight, she would have begun thinking of
preparations for a wedding then, and perhaps hoping that
it would not come so late that their first child was born
six months afterwards. Still, of all of them, she made the
likeliest mercenary's woman; if their disguise failed, it would
not be Eva who had slipped in her role.

As they stumbled up to bed that night - the two noble
couples pretending to be as drunk as most of their
companions - Margerite stopped Birgitta on the stairs. "I
have not yet thanked you," she murmured to the Norwegian.
"You saved our lives at great cost; I do not know if I can ever
repay you."

Birgitta looked steadily at her, her blue eyes gleaming in
the wavering light of the candle Margerite held. "Perhaps it
is I, rather, who should thank you. But we may speak more
on that later."

I would bring her out of here, if I could, Gottfried had said. Margerite found some comfort in that thought: for Birgitta had proved that even one high in the Order of Light-Bearers might be redeemed. And how many among them, having seen what they are, would turn away if the chance were given them? Yet the cost is heavy, and Birgitta may not have paid in full even now.

Margerite and Gottfried slept with Wolfram and the white puppy between them, Kobolt curled warmly on Margerite's chest with his tail lying over Wolfram as if to guard him. Yet the bed was hardly large enough for two, so that Margerite could hardly move without bumping into some part of the knight - and Gottfried seemed to have more sharp corners than most people, each of which dug into Margerite's bruises and cuts whenever either of them shifted position. Arnmut, Margerite thought, must be almost a saint, if he could sleep in the same bed as Gottfried and not complain. This shall be a long and weary journey, but if this deception is what is needed to keep us safe, then Maria grant we can all carry it off!

Brother Wolfgang's body was buried the next morning, the hastily-nailed box of pine lowered into the muddy hole in the small churchyard.

"A better resting place than many of us get," Brother Helmuth murmured when the village priest had finished intoning the funeral litany and the first shovelfuls of sodden earth splashed down to stain the raw white wood of the Teutonic Knight's coffin. "Often we have had to leave our dead where they fell, comforted only in the knowledge that they died for Christ and will be taken into Heaven, regardless of where their mortal clay lies."

Brother Karl nodded somberly, as did Gottfried and Arnmut; Margerite could say nothing. They did not linger by the gravesite, but made their way hastily to join the rest of their company and mount their horses. They stopped in towns as little as they could on their way, but that had to be more often than any of them would have liked: without the Bear's Paw wain, there were no tents, and Margerite feared greatly for Wolfram's health, for sleeping in damp cloaks and thin bedrolls on wet ground quickly took its toll even on the strong and hardy men of the Free Company.

When they did spend the night outdoors, they had to sleep closely huddled for warmth; and it was on one such night that Margerite asked Birgitta, "Can you tell me more of why you chose to save us?...I am grateful that you did," she added hurriedly, "and if you do not wish to speak of it, I shall understand."

"No," the Norwegian murmured. "No, you have the right to ask: for all you know, I could yet be a spy of the Order, who chose pain and risk to bring a renegade Princess to justice - perhaps with the promise of your ring as a reward."

Margerite had not thought of that. Though she was lying close enough to the other woman that their own heat warmed them both, with Wolfram and Kobolt nestled between them, a chill crept through her flesh, and she had to struggle not to draw away.

"It is not so," said Birgitta. "But then, that is what I would say, is it not?...I can only ask you to trust me, or at least trust in Gottfried's judgement." Margerite heard her deep sigh, and felt the stirring of the Norwegian's breath against her face. "So be it, then. As I told Gottfried, my father was an Icelandic priest, my mother a Norwegian...wise-woman, you might say. My father was greatly learned in the Black Art, which he practised according to the ways of his country - some of his magic was, in truth, that of the Light-Bearers; some of it came from the old ways of the Norse folk. He worshipped Óðinn - the god that you know as Wodan - as Lucifer, for he held that the two were the same primal force, the Bringer of Knowledge, condemned by a Church which wished humans to be as sheep led by a shepherd, rather than children and heirs of the gods. My mother believed that they were different beings: she prayed to the old gods, and worked the magics that had been passed down in our line from mother to daughter; but when she learned the fullness of my father's workings, she would have naught to do with him, though in taking up with him she had angered all her kin...And then she died."

Margerite could hear the old pain in Birgitta's voice, scraping against the woman's throat like a rusty nail half-hidden in splintering wood.

"But as for me, after a time, I went to my father and asked him for teaching. He it was who initiated me into the Order of the Light-Bearers, in Óðinn's name: and to and by that god I swore my oaths. Yet I have come to see that Óðinn and Lucifer are not one, nor are the elder gods demons, as the Church would have it. Hence I do not name myself oathbreaker, though the Light-Bearers may, for I am still true to the god who holds my troth. And...I do not know if I would have turned against the Order had it not been for Gottfried, and had it not come to the point where his life hung upon my choice. But I found myself chafing under their yoke: though I had reached the strength and mastery for it long since, I could not bring myself to perform the rite by which I would enter into the Council of Princes, and therefore, though I held much power in the Order, I must always be set beneath those who wore the ruby, a journeyman who would never be ranked with the masters."

And yet you wore the amethyst ring: you must have sacrificed a human being to this god, whether he is one with Lucifer or not.

The Norwegian must have felt her companion's body stiffening beneath the blankets; and maybe, even if she had no trace of Gottfried's gift, her years in the Order had quickly taught her to guess at the thoughts of others. "Aye," she murmured. "When my father felt the end of his life coming upon him - when he lay in pain, and no art could give him ease, and even the poppy syrup no longer soothed the crab eating at his belly - he chose to be given to Óðinn, and at his bidding, it was my hand that wielded the spear: the amethyst ring was my last gift from him. As to which god received him, whether it was the one-eyed Lord of the Hanged or the Light-Bearer of the Christians...that is unknown of knowledge. Even I do not know which lay nearer to his heart, for that he always claimed that they were one. But in the Order's eyes, that sufficed."

Margerite drew in a breath. The enormity of Birgitta's crime - patricide as well as human sacrifice: to a false god, or to the Devil, it hardly mattered which - was such that she could barely take it in. And yet Birgitta had said that her father had commanded the deed in his death-pain. Was it truly murder to give the mercy-stroke, or suicide to ask for it, when there was no hope of life? Margerite herself had mixed the cup to ease Ruprecht's Knappe Wolfram from this world...

Be that as it may, Birgitta is no mate for Gottfried, Margerite thought, her heart cold within her. The young knight no longer seemed quite so harsh as he had been; his own sufferings, perhaps, had taught him something of compassion. Or perhaps it was not possible to look into the minds and souls of others and not feel something for them: Gottfried had said of Birgitta's rank in the Order, I know what brought her to that pass. Yet she would have staked her soul that he had not weakened his faith in Christ thereby, but strengthened it - how, then, could he love a heathen woman, or she him?

Margerite thought that now, perhaps, like the saints of old, she should preach to Birgitta, and tell her that she had only gone from error to error, darkness to darkness: in all the tales she had read or heard, the virtuous pagans came to the way of Christ at last. And yet something stayed her tongue. What right had she, who had worn the ruby ring as a deception, to speak so to one who had truly borne the Order's chains, and broken them of her own will?

"If you would not have me by you, knowing this," Birgitta said quietly, "I shall go from you and send Eva or Rose to warm you in my stead. And if you wish, I shall leave this company tomorrow, or when you no longer have need of me to interpret for you."

"That would be an unkind return for your gift of our lives. And whatever sin you may have committed, Christ's mercy will yet forgive it, if you repent. I cannot absolve you, but Father Etienne will understand, if you choose."

"I shall not," Birgitta replied. "I keep my troth, and that is given to Óðinn. If I have done ill deeds in my search for knowledge, that is a matter of my own wyrd - my fate, you might say."

Margerite did not know what possessed her to speak as she did next: a prickling of anger at the other woman's obduracy, perhaps, or a hint of jealousy towards the ease with which Birgitta had befriended her knight, when it had taken Margerite herself such toil and labour to earn his trust. "You know that Gottfried will not have a woman who is not a Christian."

Now it was Birgitta's turn to stiffen beneath the blankets. Her voice was barely a whisper when she said, "I know. Yet I will not betray my father's god, nor the ways my mother kept. Nor would it be otherwise even if Gottfried were not so far above my own station - even if there were a hope that we might marry. It was not for his sake alone, in the end, that I turned away from the Order. Rather, he showed me what lay in my own heart, so that I could make my choice when the moment came."

Margerite heard the wistfulness in Birgitta's voice, and was not sure she believed her altogether. So she said, "I can say nothing of Gottfried's thoughts, save that he considered you to be good of soul even while you were still with the Order of Light-Bearers. But think on this: I have no little wealth and power in my own lands, and for a knight who has done as much for me as Gottfried has, there is nothing I will not do to repay, neither in friendship nor by more worldly means. If it were the true desire of his heart to wed you, and yours to be wedded to him, you would not go without dowry or possessions to bring."

Margerite heard Birgitta's sharp intake of breath; then its slow sighing outward, followed by several more deep slow breaths as though the woman were mastering her own feelings by the means taught in the Black Book - just as Margerite herself did when she had need. "I do not know whether to thank you or curse you," Birgitta told her. "For I think this knowledge is likely only to bring me more pain... but you speak from a kindly heart, and I would not scorn the offering of such a gift."

"All else is between yourself and Gottfried," Margerite said. "But if it turn out so, I shall do all I can for you."

They lay in silence for a long time, and Margerite wondered if her words had done good or evil. *Maria*, she prayed, *if I have been a fool, at least save Gottfried and Birgitta from suffering by it! But if I have spoken wisely, give Your help that the seeds I sowed this night may sprout and grow to a good harvest.*

Yet beneath those thoughts - comforting matters, if hardly small: the familiarity of marriages, dowries, the careful skirting of Gottfried's father's expectations that his son would marry a woman of noble birth to uphold his line and lands with the offer of a Gräfin's favour and gifts - Margerite felt herself troubled by something deeper. *Óðinn - the god that you know as Wodan...the leader of the Wild Hunt, the Furious Host of the dead;* she remembered Gerhild's peasant prayer as if she had heard it in her own cradle. *Against witches and unholy spirits, against Wodan's host and all his men, may Christ protect me.*

*And I let Wolfram sleep between the two of us?* Margerite thought, though she was not sure from where it had arisen, this sudden certainty that her son's soul was in as much danger as if Birgitta remained true to the Light-Bearers. In her worries over Gottfried, she had almost managed to block from her mind how Wolfram had walked first during the winter storm - how he had turned his face up to the lightning and said, "Wan' go!" *And was it that I did not dare think upon what it might mean? If Ruprecht still rides to the hunt, as men say he does...did my son see his father there?*

There had been such a storm the night Wolfram was born in that very chamber...And yet that was better than thinking on how Wolfram had gone at once to the Light-Bearers' carven altar, his little fingers smearing the mirror-polished stone as he traced the unholy signs and sigils graven into it. Meister Stefan had asked Margerite whom she believed Wolfram's father to be; had she lied, or told the truth, in her answer?

Margerite did not dare speak aloud, even to whisper, for she could not tell whether or not Birgitta slept yet. But she pulled Wolfram more closely against herself, thinking, My son, my son...was not one fear of your inheritance enough? At least I know how to fight against the Light-Bearers, though at times I may lack the strength or wit to overcome them. But have I been hiding the fear of that which I did not know how to battle from myself?

"Birgitta?" she whispered at last, softly enough not to wake her companion if the other woman slept.

"Aye." The answer came readily: the Norwegian, too, must have been lying awake in thought.

"Your god..." The words were difficult for Margerite's mouth to shape, as far from all she knew as was Iceland from the Rhine. "Is he a friend to Christ, or a foe?"

"In Norway, the priests of Christ defiled his shrines and slew his worshippers; in Iceland, the old ways were outlawed, for all Icelanders must be ruled by a single law - and we could not have stood long against King Óláfr's Tryggvason's anger, had Thórgeirr Lawspeaker chosen otherwise. How then should Óðinn be a friend to Christ? Yet I think he is no more friend to Lucifer, for the two came together to our lands, and one would be little without the other."

Margerite opened her mouth to protest that, and closed it again: for had Man never fallen, there would have been no need for Christ's sacrifice, nor the glory of Redemption. And she had always believed that pagans, whether Saracens or Lithuanians or the heathens whom the great saints of Germany had converted, worshipped only Satan in his many disguises - yet here was one who knew more of the fallen archangel's true nature than Margerite, who had stood in his very fortress on Earth, and avowed with her blood at the risk of her life that it was not so.

O, were Father Etienne here to answer my questions! Margerite thought as Kobolt stretched and purred against her body, setting his paws against the arm that held Wolfram to her and beginning to knead like a suckling kitten. But it was a long journey yet to the palace of the Bishop of Niederwald, and...

"You need not fear for your son," Birgitta said suddenly. "Among the many ways in which Óðinn differs from Lucifer is this: he does not desire the blood of the innocent, nor the tainting of the good - his offerings are the strong who fall in battle, and the wise who give themselves to him, who may stand beside him when the sons of Surtr come to break the world."

But it is not for Wolfram's life I fear with you - it is his soul. Whatever spirit it is that leads the Wild Hunt, I wish only his safety from it, not...Margerite could not quite form the thought gnawing rat-toothed at her mind, but somewhere she found the courage to ask, "Do you know why the Order of Light-Bearers wants my son?"

"I know," Birgitta answered gravely.

"And you...do you know the truth of it?"

"I know that there is much power in Wolfram, that cannot be hidden from anyone with the eyes to see it. As to whence it springs..." The blankets rustled and moved, as if the Norwegian shrugged her shoulders. "I am not sure myself, though I might guess at it. But in all the tales of heroes that I have heard - and many of them are yours as well, Dietrich and Sigvrît, Hagen and Wate - some are sons of gods, and some are closer to monster-kin. Yet greatness rises from both roots, for the gods themselves share in the blood of the giants; that likeness of might at its source is known to Christians as well, for your Lucifer was born an archangel. And even the love of a mother cannot turn a son's wyrd aside, in the end."

"You said you could guess...what would your guess be?" Margerite asked, her heart beating swiftly against Wolfram's sleeping body. Even as she asked, her conscience pricked at her: how did she come to be seeking rede from an heathen witch, when it must be forbidden to Christians to do so? Yet if she could know more...

"The wise do not speak of what they do not know. My soul tells me that there is something in Wolfram beyond the human, and that will show itself in time. But the same may be said for myself, or Gottfried - or, for that matter, you yourself: do you not fly in a falcon-hide like Freyja or Frigg? Therefore I should give you rede to not think too much on it, but cherish your son while you may, for he shall grow up swiftly enough, and you cannot keep him in your wool-basket when he is a man."

Birgitta fell silent then, and Margerite could not bring herself to ask any more questions, for the answers the Northern woman gave had only raised the troubles in her soul like dark cloud-shapes towering high upon the horizon, too vague and misty to lay names to, and yet overshadowing her with a feeling of dread. In that wise, Margerite's company travelled back towards Niederwald. Margerite's back healed quickly enough, yet, as Eva had direly predicted, the bitter scourging of the hailstones had left scars that would last the rest of her life.

Birgitta had lost the last two fingers of her left hand, and though Jochanan had managed to splint the shattered bones of the middle one so that it healed straight, she would never bend that finger again. Brother Karl still walked with a limp; and once, as Arnmut was undressing for bed, Margerite saw that a long pink scar, like a line drawn across his body from shoulder to hip, marred his white perfection - yet Christ must have been with him, for that the blade that marked him had only split his skin, rather than slicing through the muscles of his abdomen to spill his guts out on the ground.

Even when they crossed into the Holy Roman Empire, Margerite and her companions did not abandon their disguise: Margerite knew all too well how powerful the Order of Light-Bearers was within the Empire - though they are the less by two Princes here now, and perhaps more, though it is not the way of either Gottfried or the Teutonic Knights to boast of those they cut down - and the longer they kept their secret, the better their chance of reaching Father Etienne in safety.

Gottfried's white bear-dog was growing swiftly, and often he would leave it down to scamper beside the horses as they walked, or let it run a little and then call it to him - he had named it Etzel, in memory, he said, of a hound that had been dear to him in childhood, and even on the road, he seemed to be training it as well as any kennel-master. Margerite had wondered about the wisdom of travelling with a young puppy when they might have to fight or flee at any moment.

But in truth, Etzel was less trouble than Wolfram, who had suddenly taken it into his mind that there were more interesting things in the world than sitting quietly in his mother's lap as they rode: Margerite had to talk constantly to her son to keep him from trying to wriggle out of her grasp. Lent had just begun when Margerite and her company at last reached the borders of Niederwald.

There, Margerite decided that it was time to put away their disguises: she did not believe that Landgraf Gerhardt would assail the Gräfin von Fürstensee on the road, whereas, if he heard of a roving band of Free Soldiers in his lands, he would be well within his rights to send his men after them. In the inn that night, the women and the knights washed themselves and dressed properly for the first time in more than a month; though Margerite knew that there was another great trial before her now, that knowledge could not dim her relief at finally scrubbing all the grime of the journey off her skin and hair until she could almost feel her whole body glowing with cleanliness.

Birgitta had no clothes other than her borrowed tunic and breeches, now even filthier with stains and stink than they had been when she put them on, and a couple of plain dresses that they had bought along the way, but she was tall enough to wear Eva's old gowns, though it took much careful tucking and folding before the women could make one of the garments look presentable on her slender figure.

"If I recall the road correctly, we should reach the Bishop's palace late tomorrow," Margerite said to her companions as they ate. After a month of playing the Free Company woman, it almost seemed strange not to be sitting beneath Gottfried's cloak with his chainmail cold against her side, and to see Eva seated primly across from Arnmut, instead of cuddled up to him like a great cat.

"And then?" Brother Karl asked.

"And then...we shall see what happens," Margerite answered firmly. Yet beneath her confidence, she could feel her bowels gripping tight as a mass of writhing snakes. I shall see Bernhardt - and then I shall know whether there is any hope of his forgiveness. And she was not altogether sure that her courage was up to the task: better, to hold to the faintest gleam of hope in uncertainty, or to risk losing even that in sureness?

The weather had been dry for a week or so, and the road was not muddy enough to slow their horses; the Sun had just reached her height when Margerite saw the walls of the Bishop's palace rising before them. She nudged her horse up into the lead, Gottfried and Arnmut falling back to flank her.

The guard at the gate bowed as soon as he caught sight of Margerite's face. "Gräfin von Fürstensee. Your coming was not expected, but I am sure that the Bishop will wish to make you welcome, and your good knights and companions with you." He turned to his comrade on the other side of the gate, a tall youth whose face, beneath the mirror-bright polish of his helm, showed the fair wisps of a boy's first effort at a beard. "Helmbrecht, run and tell Brother Sigvrît that the Gräfin von Fürstensee and her troop have returned, and get someone out to see to their horses and show the men to their quarters."

The other guard hurried off, and Margerite led her company in. She had not forgotten the beauty of the Bishop's palace grounds, even in winter; now, with the grass springing up new and the first leaf-buds beginning to unfurl in a faint green mist over the dark branches of the great oaks that lined the walkways through the close-mown turf, they seemed all the fairer. She clutched her hand tight around Bernhardt's signet-ring, hidden beneath the blue silk of her gown where its chain tangled with the beads of her falcon-necklace.

Soon, soon, Margerite thought. Maria, grant me strength - whatever Bernhardt says to me, I shall need it. She could not help looking past the miniature Burg-shaped dovecote, its crenellations all aflutter with white wings as the birds circled in for the evening, to the little pond ringed by stone benches and rosebushes where Bernhardt had given her his pledge. The bright hips had withered and blackened with winter, and she was too far to see whether the first new shoots of growth were beginning to prick out among the thorns, or whether the rosebushes still stood stark and dead in the cold.

The young guard Helmbrecht came trotting back before the riders had reached the main courtyard before the palace, followed by several other guardsmen and, at a slower pace, Brother Sigvrît limping along heavily. The Teutonic Knight's blue eyes scanned their faces quickly, and Margerite saw him frown - he, of course, would know what it meant when three of his brothers had set out and only two returned.

Gottfried and Arnmut leapt down lightly from their horses, aiding first Margerite and Eva, then Birgitta and Rose, to dismount. "Etzel!" Gottfried called softly, and the young hound bounded up, sitting down at his master's feet and panting with his little pink tongue hanging out.

"Well-met, again," Brother Sigvrît said, his smile belying the roughness of his voice. "But before Christ, Gräfin, I hope you have brought no such trouble this time as you carried with you the last! There has been nothing but stir and confusion since - well, His Grace and Father Etienne can tell you everything."

Margerite's breath hissed out in a sigh of relief. For the last week, she had been fearing that Father Etienne would no longer be in Niederwald; yet she had not dared to fly out in search of him, for she had learned too well how such seeking made her vulnerable to the others that traversed that realm - though the mark on her breast where Ortlieb's owl-beak had pierced her had faded until its whiteness could hardly be seen against her own skin, she knew that it scarred her still.

"Brothers," the old Teutonic Knight said to his two fellows. "It is well to see you again, too - but what of Brother Wolfgang? Surely he did not go back alone?"

"He is in the arms of Christ," Brother Karl replied sadly. "I shall tell you more of that later."

Brother Sigvrît crossed himself. "God have mercy," he murmured, "Christ have mercy. Well, come you all within. His Grace will soon be sitting down for the evening meal, and I think he shall be glad to see you."

The guardsmen were leading the men of the Bear's Paw away; Birgitta, Margerite noticed, was hanging back near Rose, as though she did not know whether she were included in the invitation or not.

It will do no harm to honour her, Margerite thought. And if there is any hope that she may become Gottfried's wife, we should treat her as though she were of noble blood.

"Brother Sigvrît," Margerite said. "Before I forget my courtesy entirely, allow me to introduce to you the frowe Birgitta..." She paused in horror, realizing that she had never learned more of Birgitta than her first name and the countries of her parents.

"Birgitta Thórkelsdóttir," Birgitta filled in for her. At least, Margerite thought, her name sounded outlandish enough that her lack of any title was not so glaring; and the introduction would gain her a place at table.

"Frowe Birgitta." Brother Sigvrît gave a faint stiff bow. "Any companion of the Gräfin von Fürstensee is welcome here."

"Hungry!" Wolfram said suddenly as they began to walk towards the palace door. "Wan' food now! Put me down!"

Margerite jiggled her son in her arms to calm him, but Wolfram was having none of it. "Come, Wolfram, be quiet," she said in a soft undertone. "You shall have food very soon, lovely food, but you must be quiet now."

"No!" Wolfram insisted, screwing up his little face as though he were about to start wailing.

Margerite hesitated for a moment, but finally let him down on the ground, stooping to hold his hand as he toddled a few steps beside her. Kobolt fell in just a little ahead of them, waving his black plume of a tail in front of Wolfram's eyes for the boy to snatch at, so that Wolfram quickly fell prey to the distractions of this new game, and went along willingly enough when Margerite picked him and the cat up in a single heavy armful to pass over to Rose.

Although it was Lent, the Bishop's dining table was set as sumptuously as Margerite remembered. Finger-length eels hung in a long silver bowl of clear fish jelly; the finely molded roes of pike and carp, blended with almond-milk paste, stood in the place of cheeses; the fish themselves were beautifully gilded in many colours, red and gold, blue and silver and green, so that they shimmered on the table as though they had just been pulled living from the water.

The Bishop and his companions had just taken their places. Margerite barely glanced at Father Etienne and the three dark-robed men who sat beside him - for at Bishop Otto's other side was Bernhardt, his lips parting as his hazel eyes fixed upon her. The shock of fear ran through Margerite's whole body, and she could feel herself trembling, as she had not even when she faced Cardinal Fleurs in the heart of his sanctum. Bernhardt's mouth moved; he might have been murmuring her name, but if he were, it was drowned out by the Bishop speaking as he rose.

"Greetings again, Gräfin," Bishop Otto boomed, stretching his hand out so that Margerite might brush her lips across his amethyst ring. "You have travelled quickly: it has scarce been seven days since we sent our messenger out to you."

And how shall I explain this? Margerite thought in a corner of her mind. She was not sure what her mouth said; though she looked straight into the Bishop's ruddy face, it seemed to her that she could see nothing but Bernhardt - pale and worn, as though the last months had weighed heavily on him, but dressed in the velvets and silks that befitted his station.

His chestnut-coloured hair had grown out so that the last of the black dye could be trimmed off, leaving it curling about the back of his neck, and his brown beard was close-cropped and neatly shaped; only his hands, still rough and scarred beneath the deep blue velvet of his sleeves, seemed to show any sign of what he had been. And he was staring at her, his eyes locked upon her as though he feared that, if he blinked or wavered a moment, she would vanish as suddenly as she had appeared.

It took all Margerite's force of will to drag her awareness back to what the Bishop was saying.

"Yes, Georg has returned to his duties as Herr Christoph's Knappe," she replied. "And this good frowe, whom I believe you have not met, is Birgitta Thor..." Her tongue stumbled over the unfamiliar name; this time it was Gottfried who supplied it. "Thórkelsdóttir."

Father Etienne raised an eyebrow slightly, but his face stayed perfectly calm, and Margerite did not know whether to curse herself as a fool or not. Of course the priest would know of Birgitta - and how would he judge her, in either the allegiance she had forsaken or the one she had claimed? Yet he said nothing.

"Welcome, Frowe Birgitta," the Bishop said, extending his hand again. Margerite held her breath, but Birgitta stepped forward and bowed her head, though Margerite could not see whether her lips touched the ring or not. Of course, a Light-Bearer in Avignon must have learned how to dissemble in the face of the great men of the Church, she thought sourly, before reminding herself that that stone was hardly hers to cast.

"And allow me in turn," Bishop Otto went on, "to present to you the men who are investigating the case which you brought to my doorstep. Father Walther Kerlinger..."

The black-robed man sitting closest to the Bishop rose and bowed. He was tall and rangy of build, the broad bones of his shoulders sharp beneath the Dominican black; his sable hair was close-cropped, his face deeply chiseled. He might have been thought very handsome, save for the deep-graven lines of harshness about his mouth and the burning intensity in his dark gray eyes. His companions were less striking: Father Liutberg was of middle height, fair-complexioned and gently rounded, with a calm and compassionate expression, and Father Arnolt, socius to the pair, was a small and mousy man, his thin fingers clerk-stained with ink.

"To represent Landgraf Gerhardt, and to be sure that his rights are upheld and no unlawful charges or slanders leveled against him," continued the Bishop, "we have with us his lawyers, Herr Rudolf von Ochsenstein and Herr Manfred von Grünwald."

Gerhardt's lawyers were both, Margerite guessed, in their late twenties or early thirties, dressed in dignified robes and long coats of dark brocade with fur trim. Herr Rudolf leaned forward eagerly in his seat as he was introduced, his pale intelligent face eager as that of a hound set to the trail, but Herr Manfred only nodded calmly, his thick hands resting relaxed on the table.

A small smile played about his lips, but Margerite felt a chill as his pale eyes met hers; and young as he was, she could already see the first strands of gray dulling his ash-blond hair. This is the dangerous one, she thought. He will let his comrade run before him, but it will be he who strikes the death-blow when the hunt is ended.

"Now seat yourselves and tell me of Avignon," Bishop Otto commanded - the servants had already set places for Margerite and her companions as the introductions were going on. "You said that you had gone to speak with the Holy Father; did you succeed?"

"Indeed I did, thanks to the good offices of Cardinal de Grenville, who arranged the matter for me," Margerite answered. "The Pope will be saying Mass for my husband Heinrich: I pray that Christ will hear his plea!"

"You are a good and pious woman, to risk such arduous travel in winter for your husband's sake," the Bishop approved. "I would that such faith and dedication were more often seen among those of your station."

Margerite had little to say to that, for Bernhardt was still staring at her, and she could not read his expression. More than anything, he seemed stunned, as though a heavy mace-blow had just rung from the crown of his helm - as though he were too overcome to think, or speak, as indeed Margerite almost was herself, though she had expected to see him here.

But Bishop Otto kept talking and asking questions: how the Holy Father fared, whether she had heard Mass in the Pope's own great chapel, what news she had of this person or that. And though Margerite could not answer many of his questions, Eva had done more than shop and idle when she and Arnmut were wandering in Avignon: she had been gathering news and gossip with a skill that, Margerite thought, a professional spy might envy.

"And you will wish to know how matters have gone here," Bishop Otto said at last, dabbing neatly at the corners of his mouth with a gleaming white napkin. But Herr Rudolf coughed loudly.

"Your Grace," the lawyer said. "It were best if these witnesses were not told of the progress of the investigations so far, lest it prejudice their testimony. Herr Manfred and I will wish to take their statements at their earliest convenience, before any of the extraneous materials have been discussed."

Father Kerlinger frowned at that, turning a full glare onto the younger man. Herr Rudolf hardly seemed to notice him, continuing with his eager gaze fixed on Margerite. "Frowe Gräfin, will you and your companions be willing to tell us your role in this matter and your observations this evening, after you have had a little time to refresh yourselves?"

"We have travelled far and are weary, Herr Rudolf," Margerite answered coldly. "I am sure you would prefer to speak with us tomorrow morning."

"As you wish, Frowe Gräfin. But then I must ask you to keep to yourselves this afternoon and even-tide, and have no converse with those who are directly involved in the case, as that would lessen the weight of your testimony."

Margerite frowned, for it was coming to her how little she knew of law - no more than her own rights as Gräfin and regent for Wolfram, and the rights and duties that her father, husband, and son held in regards to those beneath them and those above them. She did not know if the lawyer were telling her the truth or not - and she did not think that she could bear it any longer, to be so close to Bernhardt; to see him so, pale and worn from the strain of the investigation that would, mayhap, determine the fate of both his lands and his own life, and not to speak with him, or know if he had forgiven her for taking on Ortlieb's ring.

"The good Father Etienne has often served as my chaplain," she said. "Would you part me from him, when I have travelled a long way and have - personal matters, that concern nothing but my soul, to speak with him about?"

Herr Manfred laughed softly. "Frowe Gräfin, if you are in need of spiritual consolation, I think you shall find no shortage of priests here in the good Bishop's palace."

"Yet," interrupted Etienne, "there is nothing in the law which would keep myself, or any of us, from speaking with the Gräfin before she has given a statement to you. Nor is she even required to do so until the Inquisition has finished their work and the case is brought to trial before the civil authorities, if that prove to be needed."

Herr Rudolf raised a thin eyebrow. "The law does not specifically require it, that is true. But there are many unusual aspects to this case - not least, the fact that the Gräfin von Fürstensee left her home and lands in secrecy, only to meet Herr Bernhardt by the most surprising chance and aid him in his assault upon the Landgräfin. For the sake of her own good name, if nothing else, surely you will wish to assist her in avoiding even the appearance of conspiracy?"

Margerite's hands tightened in her lap. The Light-Bearers fought with webs of deception and poisoned cups; she had seen her share of straightforward battle, but the lawyer's methods were something else again, like knives suddenly unsheathed in the street. They will win their case by discrediting me, if they can: no laws of chivalry bind their fighting. It angered her to give in on the first struggle - but what had she to gain by waiting?

"I am sure that Father Etienne has already explained to you how it was that I came to Schloss Niederwald under his guidance, and the grievous crime perpetrated against me by Landgräfin Ortlieb," Margerite said. "Nevertheless, if you find this detail so important as to keep me from converse with my chaplain this night, and to impose upon my weariness from travel, I suppose that I can grant your request in this instance."

"And your companions, Gräfin?" Herr Rudolf pressed.

"As they will."

After the meal, Margerite had time to clean the dust of travel off and change her clothes; she rested, playing with Wolfram for a time. It was almost sunset when one of the priests who looked after the Bishop's affairs knocked on her door, requesting her to come to the library, if she would. There, the two lawyers were waiting with a well-dressed clerk, whose sharpened quill was already poised over a sheet of parchment.

Candles burned on all the tables, their flames reflected in darkly coloured gleams from the stained glass of the windows. Margerite settled herself in the most comfortable of the chairs, pretending an ease she did not feel. Gerhardt's lawyers sat across from her, the candlelight shining from their eyes and sheening Herr Rudolf's high forehead as though a nervous sweat bedewed it.

"And so we begin, Gräfin," said Herr Rudolf, steepling his slender fingers and looking earnestly into her face. "What did you know of matters in Niederwald before you came here to meet Herr Bernhardt?"

"I did not come here for that purpose," Margerite replied. She looked at the clerk until his pale face began to flush. "You, write that down first of all, for I wish there to be no misunderstanding, neither here nor when this testimony is read out. And be sure that I shall read all that you have written before this night is out."

Herr Rudolf's mouth opened, but Herr Manfred stilled him with a slight motion of his hand. "That is prudent of you, Gräfin, though truly you have no need to mistrust us if - as we assume - your interest in this case is to see justice done. Write down the Gräfin's statement, Ludwig."

The clerk's brown head bent and he began scratching industriously on the parchment as Margerite briefly recounted the story Father Etienne had told the Bishop of Niederwald - that she, companioned by Eva and Georg, had been making a pilgrimage on foot to Fulda for Graf Heinrich's sake when they met up with Father Etienne, who had directed Eva and herself to take the part of servants for a time as a penance and a lesson in humility.

Herr Rudolf raised his eyebrows at that. "If you will forgive me, Gräfin," he said, "you do not seem like such a woman as would receive a demeaning penance of that nature easily."

Margerite was ready to snap at him, for such things were none of his affair, but thought better of it in time. "If that is so, perhaps I should have served longer in Schloss Niederwald," she answered mildly. "It was for my pride that Father Etienne set me that penance, and it would have been remiss of me not to fulfill it, when I had gone forth on pilgrimage, ready to receive whatever trials Christ should send me along the way."

"But you have not answered the question, Gräfin," Herr Manfred interrupted. "What did you know of matters in Niederwald before then?"

"I knew only what I had heard from our neighbor Graf Wolfgang von Schwarzenfels, who had once paid a visit to the court of the former Landgraf von Niederwald, and told us of Landgraf Bertrik's death. He mentioned that Landgraf Bertrik's younger son had been accused of murder, and had fled."

A gleam of teeth showed beneath Herr Rudolf's lips. "And did you then know that your guardsman was the missing murderer?"

"I knew that the matter had not been brought to trial, nor proven; Graf Wolfgang expressed his own doubts about it. But if what you mean is, did I know that my guardsman was Herr Bernhardt von Niederwald, the son of a great Landgraf - I did not know it then." And that was true enough: she had guessed, but not known until Bernhardt replied to her brief note.

"When did you know it?"

"Herr Bernhardt chose to reveal his name and state only when the time came to take arms against Landgräfin Ortlieb's soldiers in order to rescue my son, Graf Wolfram von Falkenstein."

Manfred nodded slowly, a thoughtful expression on his blunt face. "Indeed. Yet you had brought him from Burg Falkenstein to Burg Fürstensee as your own personal guard: you must have found something beyond the ordinary in him. And perhaps you were not too surprised when he left upon hearing the news that Landgraf Bertrik was dead? But we shall let that pass for the moment. How long did you serve in Schloss Niederwald, Gräfin?"

"For a little more than a month."

"And your duties were..?"

"At first I was set to kitchen work; then, because seamstresses were needed for the great feast the Landgräfin was planning and I sew with a fine hand, I was allowed to work on the costumes." Even now, Margerite could not remember those first days in the kitchen - licking the pots from hunger, her hands red and raw with the constant scrubbing, and Liutbirg's screams ringing in her ears - without a shudder.

"Did you see anything of Landgräfin Ortlieb or Graf Gerhardt at this time?"

"I aided in the Landgräfin's dressmaking. I saw Graf Gerhardt only on those occasions when I was called to help serve at table."

"And was there anything in Schloss Niederwald which seemed to you out of the ordinary?" Herr Manfred asked.

"Save that the castle seemed to me to be managed in a luxurious and wasteful way..." Margerite's voice trailed off. She could not speak of the corrupt beauty of Ortlieb's tapestries, nor of how no man who looked at the Landgräfin once could turn his eyes away from her. Except Gottfried; and now I know why he was untouched by her spells...

"Yet when your child disappeared," Herr Manfred murmured, "you seemed to think at once that the Landgräfin had taken him, and that he was in danger. Now why was this?"

"She was the only one who had left the castle that evening. Why should a woman of such standing steal a serving maid's babe, if her intentions were good? And, at any rate, I think that my suspicions were more than proven by the things that were found in her wagon."

"A wagon," Herr Rudolf countered, "that was in your possession for several days before the Bishop and Brother Sigvrît had any chance to examine it!" The young lawyer leaned forward across the table, pointing a single finger at Margerite. "Who can say that everything within belonged to the Landgräfin von Niederwald?"

Herr Manfred shook his head. "Soft, my friend. The good Canon Etienne was with the Gräfin and her companions throughout, and he has already given a statement regarding these things. There is no arguing, Gräfin, that you were afterwards proven right. Yet what we would know is: how is it that you were warned beforehand, or why did you think you had reason to fear?"

Margerite's heart beat fast. The lawyer had come to the heart of the question, the matter that she could not answer truthfully in any way. If Eva were here, she could lie barefaced, speak of whispers in the servants' quarters...but then they would demand names, and the names would go back to Landgraf Gerhardt: possible witnesses would not, Margerite was sure, still be among the living by the time the matter came to trial, and even for the truth, she would not have risked others' lives so, let alone for a plausible lie.

But thinking of Eva brought a little guile to her own mind; as the younger woman might have done, Margerite lowered her eyes, speaking in a near-whisper.

"I was afraid of the Landgräfin," she confessed, and the blush of shame warming her cheeks at those words was real. "I think all the servants in Schloss Niederwald were. And... there were no children in the castle, save my son: for all the women there, and many of them wedded, not a single one of them kept a babe by her side within the walls of Schloss Niederwald."

Herr Manfred's blunt-featured face showed no change, but Margerite thought that her answer had displeased him in some way. What is his desire? she wondered. Then it came to her: the lawyers' purpose was not to clear Ortlieb's name, for that must be impossible, but rather to save Landgraf Gerhardt from any suspicion that he might have been an accomplice in his wife's sorceries, or known of them.

Her testimony might well, if guided in the right direction, aid in protecting Gerhardt - but which direction is that? Tales of how the servants whispered about Ortlieb, with no word of Gerhardt? Or proof that even the servants knew nothing of Ortlieb's magics, so that her husband might equally well have been ignorant?

"Did you fear the Landgraf in the same way?" Herr Manfred inquired.

Margerite folded her hands in her lap, looking him in the eye. "As I said, I saw Landgraf Gerhardt only from a distance, when I served at the lower tables in his hall. I had no reason to know anything about him, whether to fear him or otherwise."

"Indeed," murmured the lawyer. "But you feared Landgräfin Ortlieb so strongly that you gathered a troop of men to attack her wagon - you hired, indeed, a Free Company to aid you. Now how did it come about that you had these men there?"

"That was a matter arranged by Herr Bernhardt, for I believe he did not think that he could simply walk into his brother's hall and demand justice," Margerite answered boldly.

"But it was easy enough for Bernhardt to hire mercenaries in order to attack his brother's wife on the road!" declared Herr Rudolf. "Now that, you must admit, is hardly the deed of an honest man or a chivalrous knight."

"On the contrary, for he acted as he did in order to save the life of an innocent child, and that from a grievous evil."

Herr Manfred smiled kindly. "Indeed, it is so. And that he did so merely on the word of a servant frightened by her mistress is indeed remarkable - or how else did you explain the matter to him, once you had mysteriously managed to find him?"

"There was no mystery in that, for Father Etienne aided us. Herr Bernhardt knew who I was, and already had reason to trust my judgement, for we had endured the siege of Burg Falkenstein together, as Gräfin and Hauptmann of the guard. And he, too, was greatly alarmed by the kidnapping of my son, for I believe that he had heard more concerning Landgräfin Ortlieb than I."

"You ought to have said so from the beginning," said Herr Rudolf. "We have already received a statement from Father Etienne. But now to the main point: did you ever - before, during, or after your service in Schloss Niederwald - hear or see anything that might have cast any discredit upon Landgraf Gerhardt, or suggest that he had any part in his wife's secret activities?"

"I heard only that the Landgraf indulged his wife greatly. As to other matters...no word was spoken about either of them in that regard by the servants."

The two lawyers looked at each other. Herr Manfred nodded, saying, "I believe that we have no more questions to ask you at this time, though undoubtedly we shall speak further later. When Ludwig has finished his scribing, you may read what he has written; then, if you please, would you do us the courtesy of sending either Frowe Eva or Ritter Gottfried in to us?"

"And, if you will, give us your word that you will say nothing of our speech to any of your companions," added Herr Rudolf. "For it would be most suspicious if you seemed to have conspired in your testimony."

Margerite stood, drawing herself up as tall as she could. "Herr Manfred, Herr Rudolf, we are not yet in a court of law, and you have no right to make such demands on me. I shall consider your words - but you shall remember my station in life, and not speak thus to me in future." She turned and strode from the library.

Margerite, Eva, and Rose had been given the same chambers in which Margerite and Eva had slept before. The room was already a little disordered, for Wolfram was playing a lively game of chase with Kobolt and Kriemhilt, toddling after the two cats and snatching at their tails. Briefly, Margerite told Eva what Gerhardt's lawyers had asked of her and her own guesses as to what they might want.

"Perhaps I shall be better able to satisfy them than you were," Eva replied, smoothing the cream-coloured silk of her headdress down over her thick coils of golden braids. "I heard more things in the kitchens, maybe, than you did among the dressmakers - and you do not need to tell me not to name any names: I know very well what happens to those who bear tales about their superiors."

A grim light glinted in her eyes for a moment, and it seemed to Margerite that she could see the stark bones of the starved waif Eva had once been beneath the pretty rounding of the young woman's features.

"I would think that you should talk to Ritter Gottfried before he goes in to speak with Gerhardt's men. Ritter Arnmut will do well enough, for he was only a squire following his knight's orders then, and no one except Ritter Gottfried ever suspects him of harbouring any intelligence behind his fair face. But deception does not come easily to our Gottfried."

The same thoughts had been going through Margerite's mind; and yet, as Eva left the room, she found herself wavering. The hour was past compline already - when did Bernhardt retire for the night? What she longed to do now was to send Rose in search of him, and then send the girl away: Rose had already proven her trustworthiness, she would leave them alone together and never say a word about it. And then...

Margerite thought of Bernhardt's lips meeting hers, even in the chastest of embraces; his hands gently unfastening the falcon-necklace, and her own clasping it about his throat with the gold and stone beads still warm from her body...

Yet he would be ill-served if she let Gottfried go in unprepared to meet with Gerhardt's lawyers. And beside the sweet dream of reconciliation, there was the other: Bernhardt's strong features twisting in loathing, or falling into the stony sorrow she had seen on his face at their parting, his broad shoulders stiffening as he turned his back to her...But whatever befalls, I have my duty to him yet.

"Bring Ritter Gottfried and Ritter Arnmut to me," Margerite ordered Rose. "And, if you can find him, Father Etienne as well."

Rose curtsied and went, and Margerite sat down, trying to compose herself amid Wolfram's gleeful shouts of "Tail!" Kriemhilt, tiring of the game, leapt into her lap; Margerite stroked her, feeling how the cat's furry body was already beginning to grow heavier with her kittens.

"And what, Frowe Kriemhilt, shall we do with this litter?" Margerite asked her. "I fear there is still much travel ahead of us, and kittens cannot run beside horses as even a young hound may do."

Kriemhilt looked up at her and purred, her green eyes glowing like jewels in the candlelight.

"At least you waited long enough not to have them upon Cardinal de Grenville's silk bedclothes. That was well-done of you, little frowe."

Wolfram lost his footing and sat down suddenly on the rug. Before he could open his mouth to cry, Kobolt was rubbing against him, brushing his tail against the child's face and batting soft-pawed at his hands, and Wolfram giggled as he patted back. Margerite sighed, looking at her son. "O, Wolfram," she said. "What manner of life have I given you? Your only close companion is a cat, and you have spent more time in my arms on horseback than you have sleeping in a cradle. Mayhap it shall make you the stronger, when you are grown to be a man; but children have little enough time for play without such things as have driven us hither and yon. At seven you shall be a page, and must learn to serve at table and attend on noble folk - maybe in Burg Fürstensee, Christ willing, but maybe somewhere else altogether - and then at fourteen you shall be a squire, and ride to the field with your knight: Christ and Maria grant that you have better luck than your namesake! And when you are old enough, you shall rule your father's lands..." Margerite broke off then, for the disturbing memories of their return to Burg Falkenstein rose up in her mind so that her voice choked in her throat - she could not tell if it was with sorrow, or with fear.

Pushing Kriemhilt off her lap, she knelt down beside Wolfram, lifting the bright-haired child in her arms. "My sweet, my love, I wish there were even one place in the world where I could trust you would be safe," she whispered, the tears prickling hot against her eyes. Not Burg Falkenstein, nor Burg Fürstensee - even here in the Bishop's palace, Damiano had summoned a demon against her: where, then, could she and Wolfram find any sure refuge?

Sunk in her dark thoughts, Margerite did not hear the door open, nor did she look up until she heard Ritter Arnmut saying politely, "Frowe Gräfin, you wished to speak to us?"

Margerite put Wolfram down carefully and rose to her feet, swallowing hard against the crackling of tears in her throat. "I would discuss the matter of your statements to Gerhardt's lawyers," she said. "Sit down - Rose, see if the Bishop's cellarer will send us up a pitcher of wine to refresh ourselves while we talk."

Gottfried and Arnmut sat. Kobolt jumped up into Gottfried's lap at once, sniffing at his fingers and purring; Gottfried stroked him with the bemused look he had whenever the black tomcat favoured the knight with his attentions, and Margerite wondered, as she often had before, what Gottfried saw when he looked at Kobolt.

As she had with Eva, Margerite detailed her conversation with Gerhardt's lawyers. Gottfried frowned as she spoke, but said nothing until she had finished.

"That is little questioning for such a weighty matter," he murmured at last. "If such a sally were made upon the battlefield, I would say that it was only a feint to draw attention from the true attack."

Margerite nodded: the knight had put into words the feeling of uneasiness that had dogged her ever since she had left the Bishop's library.

"But what, then, could they want?" she wondered.

Arnmut shifted in his chair, a tinge of pink brightening his cheeks. "Forgive me, Frowe Gräfin," he said softly. "But it almost seems to me that they might have meant some of their questions to, to..." He blushed more deeply.

"To discredit me, perhaps," Margerite finished for him. "For there shall be two matters coming before the Kaiser: whether Landgraf Gerhardt had any part in his wife's sorceries - a question to which I do not know the answer, and a difficult thing to prove even if it were true - and whether Bernhardt, perhaps by his brother's contrivance as well as Ortlieb's, was indeed guilty of the murder of which he was accused. But if shame can be brought upon Bernhardt and all those of us who have aided him, then Kaiser Karl shall be the less likely to judge in his favour."

"Aye," said Gottfried. "Yet there is nothing to discredit you, or any of us, in what we have done. And if Father Etienne's story of how you came to Schloss Niederwald was not the whole of the truth, at least there were no lies in it."

Until I claimed that I had not come to meet with Bernhardt, Margerite thought, feeling the heat rise in her own face. She could not meet Gottfried's steady gray gaze then; for Herr Manfred had, she knew, quietly accused her of being Bernhardt's leman, though he had spoken no words with which she could take issue. And once it was true...for those few months, I was able to hold to the hope, or fear, that he could have been Wolfram's father.

A faint redness coloured Gottfried's stark cheekbones, and Margerite found that she was blushing as well. Angry at herself, she lifted her head to look Gottfried in the eye. "Even without cause - and though Bernhardt and I were never alone together for a moment - it is not difficult to speak ill of a woman who leaves her husband and is, soon thereafter, aiding another man. I think Gerhardt's lawyers will seek to make much of that."

"And yet you have been chaste, and true to Graf Heinrich: that I may swear upon my soul," answered Gottfried. "As for what may be in your heart - that is not for any other to speak of, nor any save Christ to judge." Margerite heard the sorrow weighting his voice with the dull thudding of lead, and was thankful that she did not share his gift. At that moment, at least, she could not have borne to know all the knight's thoughts; it was more than enough to know that he was speaking of himself at least as much as of her.

Arnmut sat up straighter, his eyes bright in the candlelight. "Frowe Gräfin, I too may swear upon my soul that you have never behaved in anything other than a seemly fashion. And I shall gladly challenge any who speaks ill of your conduct!"

"Ritter Arnmut, Ritter Gottfried, I thank you both," Margerite said. "But I fear that even your aid may not be enough to stifle the calumnies that Gerhardt's lawyers would spread. And..."

It seemed to Margerite that the air within the room had grown suddenly stifling, and a fierce longing seized her, as it had not for some time - the longing to leap winged from her body, to seek the clean cold wind beneath her wings, and soar beneath the starlight. But at the same time, as though her soul were splitting in two, she could hear Father Etienne's voice saying faintly again, If all good folk knew of the Order of Light-Bearers, what do you think they would make of a poor knight's daughter who managed to wed first one, then a second Graf, neither of whom lived a full year after marrying her; who is knowledgeable in matters of herb-lore and astrology, and is always accompanied by a large black cat...?

She thought of how Manfred and Rudolf had pressed her as to the source of her knowledge about the danger Ortlieb offered for Wolfram; and in that moment, it seemed to her that she was certain of their strategy.

"If Gerhardt's lawyers can taint me with any of the crimes of which Ortlieb is proven guilty," Margerite said slowly, "then they will have the beginnings of a deadly case against Bernhardt. Should they have discovered that he was once a member of a Free Company, that would make him half-damned already in Kaiser Karl's eyes; if the Inquisition itself removes us from testifying on Bernhardt's behalf..."

Arnmut drew in his breath with a sharp hiss, and Gottfried's sharp-boned face paled to the white of a bleached skull, the pupils of his eyes swelling until his gray irises were almost drowned in blackness. "I fear," breathed the older knight, "that the trap is already in place."

"Why, Gottfried?" Margerite asked.

Gottfried's thin lips tightened, his brows drawing together. "I...there was something in Father Kerlinger's mind as he looked at us. I did not mean to pry," he added, his voice almost pleading, "and in truth, his mind is like a well-walled castle with only the tiniest arrow-slits showing light. But I could tell that he mistrusted us, and even Father Etienne wishes that he were not the man who had come to oversee this matter, as the two of them have little love for each other."

"And how?" enquired Father Etienne's dry voice, "did you come to learn this?"

Margerite and the two knights looked up in shock as the canon stepped into the room, closing the door softly behind him. "I knocked," Father Etienne said, "but got no answer; yet your maidservant said that you wished to see me most urgently - little surprise, considering the circumstances. But, Ritter Gottfried, I ask you again: how is it that you consider yourself able to speak on the matter of my feelings about Father Kerlinger, or his about me?" A hint of anger deepened Father Etienne's voice as he looked sternly down at the knight.

"Forgive me, Father," Gottfried whispered, staring wide-eyed up at Etienne. "I have not learned to shield myself as well as I should, perhaps, and I...you spoke very clearly, Father, so that if I had not known you would not say such a thing aloud at the Bishop's table..."

Father Etienne shook his head slowly, the rolled edges of his black canon's hat casting high-horned shadows in the candlelight. "All of you have a great deal to explain to me. Not least," he added, "the matter of why Birgitta Thórkelsdóttir is with you, when you, Margerite, are no longer wearing the ruby ring. Do you have any idea what you have brought here?"

"Birgitta has turned away from the Order, and it was she who saved our lives in our greatest peril, at the cost of much risk and pain to herself," Gottfried answered. "Whatever you may have known of her, it is no longer true."

The priest looked at Gottfried for a long time, and it seemed to Margerite that some thought was passing between them, though it was wholly shrouded from her hearing. "We shall speak on that later, Ritter Gottfried," Etienne said. "For now - I think it shall not be long before you are summoned to give Gerhardt's lawyers a statement in your turn. Remember the account you gave to the Bishop upon your arrival here, and do not stray from it; and let the same be true for you, Ritter Arnmut!"

Rose came in with a silver pitcher then; but before Margerite could command her to pour the wine, Eva entered as well, her pale blue skirt swishing about her ankles in an angry silken rustle.

"Those lawyers are as rude a pair as I have ever encountered," she declared. "Though their names claim noble blood, their manners would be more suited to a couple of drunken mule-drivers, and I think that Margerite's tomcat behaves in a more seemly fashion."

"Did they offer you insult?" Arnmut asked, leaping to his feet.

Father Etienne lifted his hand. "Hold, Ritter Arnmut," he ordered. "If Gerhardt's lawyers see that they can bait you into anger, they will do so; and that shall lead quickly to disaster. It were best if you managed to keep both your tongue and your sword still, whatever they may say. Now, Frowe Eva, what did they do to offend you?"

"They asked me all manner of impertinent questions about both Margerite and myself - they even doubted that I still possess my maidenhead." Eva flicked the silk train of her headdress back with a quick toss, her eyes flickering over the men - not least, Margerite suspected, to gauge their reaction to her words. "And they can hardly be the educated men of high birth they pose as, if they cannot tell the difference between the finest French fashions and the dress of a prostitute."

Margerite thought of how cheerfully Eva had taken to the role of a Free Company's camp follower, and had to struggle to keep the smile from her face; while Gottfried's muffled snort might or might not have been a noise of outrage.

"Did they ask you anything else, Eva?" Margerite enquired.

"They asked where we had slept on the road to Fulda, and whether I had watched you at night in Schloss Niederwald; they asked outright if I thought that either Herr Bernhardt or one of these knights might be your lover. And only then, when they believed that I was too angry to think, did they begin to question me about Ortlieb and Gerhardt." Eva smiled triumphantly. "I told them that there was not one of the servants who believed that Herr Bernhardt was guilty of the crime of which he had been accused, nor was there one who would speak of it before their masters, for their great fear of both Landgraf and Landgräfin, and I made sure that their clerk wrote down every word. And I told them that, serving in the castle, I had come to know its folk very well, and I mentioned that disappearances now would be very hard to explain when this matter came to trial - the more so, since there is so much evidence of what Ortlieb did with those who displeased her."

Father Etienne raised his eyebrows. "I would not have counselled you to speak so openly, regardless of how much truth is in what you said. Yet we may still turn this to our advantage; at the least, Manfred and Rudolf will hardly wish to raise your testimony in court unless they can contradict it - and we shall have little difficulty finding witnesses of our own, if that be so. Now, have the lawyers retired, or do they still wish to speak to Ritter Gottfried and Ritter Arnmut?"

"They told me," Eva said, looking down her nose, "to summon Ritter Gottfried. But I am sure they are capable of finding servitors here to bring their messages for them."

"Go on, Ritter Gottfried," Etienne urged. "It is not yet time to annoy Gerhardt's men needlessly, or to openly scorn them. Let them think for a little time that they have the upper hand, and they will be the easier to cast down when the hour comes."

Gottfried rose, and Arnmut followed him. "We came to Schloss Niederwald together," the fair knight said, "and I think that it will not seem too strange if we give our testimonies together, as I was Ritter Gottfried's Knappe then."

Gottfried looked gratefully at his friend; his hand moved as if he meant to touch Arnmut's shoulder, but then fell back to his side. Another thought of how Herr Manfred and Herr Rudolf might try to discredit their company came to Margerite then, but she clamped her jaw tight and breathed deeply, envisioning a great wall of sturdily mortared gray stone about herself: she would not have Gottfried see what was in her mind, for the pain it would cause him.

When the knights had left, Margerite found that she could no longer hold back the question that had been tearing at her entrails since she had ridden forth from the Bishop's palace those months ago. "How is it with Bernhardt?" she asked Father Etienne eagerly. "Does he..?" Her lips could not shape the words that she wanted to say, not with the priest's blue eyes regarding her so calmly; her heart quailed within her, and she finished lamely, "He looks as though this investigation has worn hard upon him."

The corners of Father Etienne's mouth turned down slightly, and it seemed to Margerite that she could see the tiredness in his face: his skin looked sallow in the candlelight, and the silver at his temples and in his short beard shone more whitely against his thick dark hair.

She could hear the weariness in his voice, as well, when he replied, "It is no easy thing to pursue revenge against a brother - even when that brother has done as much ill as Gerhardt has: do you wonder that Bernhardt feels his soul burdened? I think he hoped that he could win his place swiftly by means of his sword: but it is one thing to lift a blade in anger, and another to struggle slowly, with words and law and plots, towards the death of someone who was once beloved. And the only surety in this case is that it will end with death: either Gerhardt's, or Bernhardt's own." Margerite saw Etienne's slender chest rising and falling very slowly beneath his black robe, as though he were steadying himself with the same breaths that she had learned for controlling her own racing heart. "If the Light-Bearers were the only evil in this world," the priest added quietly, as if he were speaking to himself alone, "we should be blessed indeed."

What does he mean by that? Margerite wondered. Should Bernhardt, then, give over his quest; should he leave his lands to his brother's careless rule, and forget all the evil that was done to him? And yet Christ had counselled, Love your enemies, do good to them which hate you...unto him that smiteth thee on the one cheek offer also the other; and him that taketh away thy cloak, forbid not to take thy coat also. Give to every man that asketh of thee; and of him that taketh away thy goods, ask them not again.

"Yet you aid Bernhardt in this," Margerite said, and she did not know whether she was truly arguing with Father Etienne, or with her own mind.

"I could hardly abandon him," Father Etienne replied. "What one begins, one must stay with until it is ended, if need be. And Bernhardt has the right to clear his name and take his place; nor can any doubt that his folk will be better served in their souls and bodies both, should he wrest the rule of Niederwald from his brother. But as for his feelings - he may tell you himself, if he wills it. I fear that you may be here for a long time, since both Inquisitors and lawyers have many things to ask before the matter is raised to Kaiser Karl's attention; and, at any rate, it is likely to be some time before Georg receives the Inquisitorial summons and is able to obey it. If he is able to obey it."

"There was no way for me to take him with us, and not betray how matters stand in Burg Fürstensee," Margerite protested.

"I did not say that there was. But now you must tell me of what befell you in Avignon, for if you were unmasked, then Georg stands in some peril."

Margerite bit her lip, her stomach contracting painfully as though she had just drunk a great gulp of water from an icy stream. Between the shock of her escape, the dangers of the road and the constant fear of discovery, and the anxiety that had grown within her like an unwanted child as she came closer to Bernhardt, she had hardly spared a thought for Georg; she had believed him safe beneath the mantle of her protection, but if Nikolaus had learned that she had flouted the Order... "Christ forgive me," she murmured, her voice cracking as she crossed herself. "Maria forgive me, and protect that poor child."

"May it be so," Father Etienne agreed gravely. "Now, your tale."

After a moment of painful struggle with herself, Margerite began by telling Father Etienne of Gottfried's collapse at Burg Falkenstein, though she did not mention the reason why he had driven himself to such bitter austerity, nor did the canon ask. "Cardinal de Grenville received us as you asked, though he seemed rather put out that we could not tell him everything of our doings."

"I left that to your discretion, for I had no way of knowing what all your needs might be," the priest replied. "Still, it is as well that you were able to keep full knowledge of the Order of Light-Bearers from him."

"It was at his house that we met the Teutonic Knights, and there that Madame du Guesclin summoned me to her..." Margerite went swiftly on; Father Etienne raised his eyebrows slightly as she spoke of how Gottfried and Birgitta had taken up together, but did not interrupt. Calm though the French priest's face was, Margerite thought she heard his sharp intake of breath when she told of going into the Imperator's sanctum.

"And then I found that they had trapped me even as I thought to deceive them. For they wished me to swear their oath with Wolfram in my arms - and that I could not do: my only hope was a swift death for all of us. But Gottfried... cried out with all his strength, and they were stunned. And Birgitta opened the door, though her ring shattered on her hand: you may see the mark of that yet upon her. Brother Karl and Brother Wolfgang had managed to pierce the defenses of Cardinal Fleurs' house, and they came in to aid Gottfried, while Birgitta and I fled. Then we rode from Avignon as swiftly as we could, though they sent a storm against us...Brother Wolfgang was killed, and Albercht of the Bear's Paw and three other men." It seemed to Margerite that the scars on her back, full-healed though they were, stung with cold as she spoke, and the warm candlelight dimmed before her eyes in the memory of that lightning-seared blackness. "Gottfried leapt from his horse and raised his sword, calling all the storm's power against himself. The lightning struck him; the sword was shattered, and we thought him dead, yet he lived, and seems to have taken no lasting harm from it."

"And that was...a month ago, near enough?" Father Etienne asked. Margerite nodded. The priest's blue eyes widened. "It is a great wonder that any of you lived through it. Every man and woman skilled in the Art from Rome to Halogaland must have felt that storm; seldom is such power summoned from the realms beyond to our own earth, or such anger unleashed. I do not know whether you have secured your safety from the Order, at least in matters magical, hereafter - for Cardinal Fleurs is a very practical man, and if he deems you too dangerous a prey, he may turn his efforts elsewhere - or whether they shall attempt a Great Working in order to destroy you."

Margerite shivered. The Black Book had spoken of the Great Working, in which every member of the Order of Lightbearers of the rank of episcopus or above performed a part of the rite at a single appointed hour, sacrificing a human life to their dark Master in order to bring about the death of their chosen victim: she remembered the words as clearly as if the page were still before her.

This is the only sure means by which the death of the greatest may be accomplished, for Kings and Popes and mages of the highest rank all have their own protections which may not be broken by common means. But even the Imperator may not command this lightly, for if a single link in the chain is flawed, the whole shall break and all the Working be undone; and the Order shall be weakened thereafter for a time by the loss of the strength that was poured into its effort.

"Do you think they know that I still live?"

"I do not know," answered Father Etienne. "You are well-served in the warding that Ruprecht gave you; I assume you did not travel under your own name and rank..? And the Light-Bearers' power must have been strained greatly, even with the death of their own Princes within the sanctum to fuel it - I have seen Gottfried fight, and know the skills of the Teutonic Order, and I do not think that their foes came off too lightly from the encounter. Hence our foes are weakened, and may be at some trouble to cover over their losses; and they may well believe they succeeded in their effort, for that their storm found a target on which to unleash all its power. Still," he added ominously, "that will not last forever, for sooner or later they will hear news of you, through earthly means or otherwise, and know that you live yet. But there is little we can do about that now, and this place is warded as strongly as I know how, aside from its own hallowing, for I have taken great care to be sure that neither Oda nor Hedwig could send news back to their superiors - or suddenly die in their cell. You are safe, but I fear the more for Georg, for the revenge of the Light-Bearers may fall easily upon him: whatever protections you may have set upon him, his body is still in their hands."

"Then what can we do?" Margerite asked. "Is there no way that we may fetch him safe here at once? In the Black Book..." She stopped, horrified at herself. Yet the Black Book included conjurations for spirits that would appear in the form of a horse, able to bear a rider so swiftly over land and sea that one might ride from Toulouse to India in the space of an hour; and some of the Order Princes could not have reached Avignon by any natural means in the little space of time that the summons to Council had given them.

"I know that the Abbess used such spells to go swiftly from one place to another," Eva added. "I myself saw her summon a host of mounted knights, and take care to choose the red-bridled steed from among them, that she might ride safely upon the spirit's back. And if the purpose be to save a life from the Light-Bearers, how can Christ judge us harshly for resorting to such means?"

"It were well if you should beware of such thoughts, Eva," Father Etienne said, looking sternly at her. "For many a good man has been betrayed to evil in the belief that he served a greater good: that temptation is ever with all of us who practice the Art...And yet it is not only demons who may be summoned for the sake of swift travel, nor would it be a deception if Georg received his Inquisitorial summons earlier than he might otherwise have, and did not travel here by roads known to men; though he must not arrive here too early, for that would be suspicious indeed - and as Ritter Gottfried divined, Father Kerlinger and I are not the closest of friends: I do not think it was by chance that he was sent to head this investigation."

"Is he a Light-Bearer, then?" Margerite asked in horror.

Father Etienne shook his head, his thick wavy hair rippling darkly about his face. "If Walther Kerlinger knew of the Order's existence, he would call for a Crusade to hunt them down, and there would be such trials as have not been seen since the suppression of the Templars in France, save that no one would be safe from accusation. Matters in Germany would be as they were in Conrad von Marburg's day - do you know of him?"

Margerite nodded: in preparing her for the Inquisitors' questions, Brother Helmuth had spoken of the first Papal inquisitor into heresy at great length, reminding her ever that wealth and power had been no security against Conrad's zeal, but had rather drawn his eye the more swiftly, until his victim Count Heinrich of Sayn had at last been declared innocent by no less than a council including King Heinrich and the Archbishop of Mainz - and five days later, Conrad von Marburg had been assassinated on the road, and fallen unmourned.

"Conrad von Marburg knew of the Order, but none would listen to him; and that may have been as well: he weakened them in the Rhineland for a time, yet for every Light-Bearer he burned, three innocent folk went to the stake, and his memory is not blessed among those of us who fight the Order still. France had its own Malleus Haereticorum, Hammer of Heretics, Robert le Bougre; in the works of Alberic des Trois-Fontaines, it is written how he burned one hundred and eighty three Cathars in 'a holocaust, very great and pleasing to God.' Now these men were unusual among those who serve the Inquisition faithfully, but you may be sure that Father Kerlinger is another in their mold. He would bring any of us to the stake in chains just as swiftly as he would any of the Light-Bearers, and there is not the least chink of compassion in his judgement. The Inquisition's own statutes tie his hands, as they did not limit the powers of Conrad von Marburg; but he is no less fierce in his persecutions. Though Walther Kerlinger serves Christ, there are many of the Light-Bearers into whose hands I would sooner fall."

The priest's aristocratic face grew grimmer as he spoke, the candles' shadows darkening the slight hollows under his high cheekbones and the deep set of his blue eyes; and his French accent seemed stronger. "If our foes arranged his coming, they chose a risk to themselves for the sake of destroying - perhaps myself; perhaps you as well, for there is no guessing how long they have known, or suspected, that you were not truly one of them. Though it may be that Kerlinger himself hoped for the chance to do me an ill turn, if he could: he has little patience with those of us who deal with dark matters and are not ourselves appointed Inquisitors."

Margerite looked down at Wolfram, who had long since tired of his game and was now curled sleeping on the rug with Kobolt and Kriemhilt nestled against him. The child's mouth hung open, a pearl of drool bubbling at the corner of his lips; his eyelashes lay long and golden against his fair cheeks, and one chubby little hand still clutched Kobolt's black tail. O my sweetling...what manner of life did I bring you into? Margerite thought again.

"If any of your magical tools remain to you," Father Etienne went on, "I can only counsel you to ward them against discovery as best you can. Kerlinger himself might not creep into your chamber or bribe a servant - but Father Arnolt has no such compunctions. Though he may be easily overlooked, he should not be underestimated."

Margerite had to think hard for a moment to remember which was Father Arnolt...yes: the mousy little man with the ink-stained fingers, the very image of an insignificant and harmless clerk. No wonder Bernhardt looks so tired and sad. I am not sure that I did not have an easier time of it, even in the very stronghold of the Light-Bearers, than he suffers now: at least there I knew that I could trust my friends and allies, whereas here, those who should be aiding us may prove to be our greatest foes. O, if only I could go to him and comfort him this night!

"I must be about my work," Father Etienne said abruptly. "I shall not ask either of you to aid me, for the hour is growing late: it cannot be too long until matins, and there may be eyes watching us all."

Then another worry came to Margerite's mind, like a weed springing fresh from a plough-cut root. "Father, if you send a spirit to fetch Georg - will the demon that possesses Christoph not know it for what it is?"

Father Etienne's lips curled in a mirthless smile. "Yes. But there is nothing that he, or Nikolaus, can do about an Inquisitorial summons received in the full light of day, with all the folk of Burg Fürstensee to witness it; and Georg must, perforce, go with his summoner if he is required to do so. That may bring you to the notice of the Order a little earlier than you might otherwise have been: do you think it is worth the risk?"

"Of course it is!" Margerite answered at once. "Father, bring Georg out of there if you can, and if I may not aid you, at least know that you have my blessing and my prayers for you in this."

To her surprise, Father Etienne bowed his head gravely. "That is no little help, from one who has withstood what you have of late," he said. "So be it, then. Sleep as well as you may; and if Ritter Gottfried returns here this night, tell him that I would see him in my chambers as soon as he rises tomorrow - without Ritter Arnmut, if they can bear to be parted from one another so long," he added, his voice very dry.

Gottfried woke at dawn when one of the Bishop's servants came in to light the banked fire. For a few minutes, he lay drowsily in the warmth of his bed as the serving-man rustled about, tending to the stove and setting down a bowl of bread and milk for Etzel. Beside him, Arnmut was still asleep, his breath soft on Gottfried's neck - there was a second bed, but he had refused it, insisting that he was not used to sleeping alone and would not be able to rest, and nothing Gottfried could say would dissuade him.

But at least Arnmut no longer seems to fear me: we are almost as we once were, Gottfried thought. Almost: for he could not deny the morning stirring in his loins at the other young man's closeness, nor the hopeless wave of desire welling up in him as he looked at Arnmut's beautiful face, pale against the fine white linen bedclothes, and the thick golden hair tumbling over his forehead so that Gottfried longed to stroke the straying locks back. If you knew how I feel, my beloved friend, you would turn away from me in loathing. Christ strengthen me and keep me from sin!

Careful not to wake his companion, Gottfried slid out
from between the covers as soon as the servant had left the
room and dressed quickly in the gray light of dawn. His
close-fitted doublet of black velvet had grown looser on him
again, for though he had tried to eat well enough to keep
his gift from ranging beyond his control, he had also kept
the Lenten abstinence strictly on their journey; and had his
sword-belt of linked silver plates not hooked to his doublet,
it might easily have slipped down over his narrow hips. Etzel
frisked about him, wagging his tail. At Gottfried's upraised
finger, the puppy sat at once, looking up at his master with
expectant brown eyes, though he had already cleaned the
wooden bowl of bread and milk so that no scrap could be
seen.

The servant had left a pitcher of watered wine on their
table, together with a small loaf of white bread, a plate
of smoked herring, and a bowl of warm water with clean
napkins. The loaf was hot enough to steam gently when
Gottfried cut into it; though the wine had been watered
properly, gleaming pale pink in the knight's silver goblet, the
echo of its excellent flavour still came clearly to his tongue.
He had almost finished eating when he noticed the corner of
parchment sticking out from beneath the bread-platter.

Ritter Gottfried: please attend me, alone, in my chambers
as soon as you have risen. Father Etienne.

Gottfried swallowed his last mouthfuls of bread and
herring hastily, rinsing the grease from his fingers in the
silver water-bowl and wiping his hands clean on a napkin.
He looked at Arnmut once more: the youth had turned in
his sleep, flinging one arm out where Gottfried had lain as if
searching for his companion. Gottfried hated to wake him,
but if Arnmut rose to find him gone without explanation, he
would be troubled.

"Arnmut," Gottfried said softly. The fair knight murmured
something indistinguishable; his blue eyes gleamed open
a moment, then closed again as he pulled the covers more
tightly about himself. "Arnmut, wake up."

"Is it time to go already?" Arnmut murmured, his eyes still closed.

"Arnmut, I have been summoned by Father Etienne. He wants to see me by myself. You may go back to sleep; I only wished you to know, so that you would not be distressed by my absence."

"Oh. All right," Arnmut muttered muzzily. It was only a few moments before Gottfried heard his friend's breaths deepening in sleep again.

Etzel followed Gottfried down the corridor and out into the gardens - the Pyrenean bear-dog had taken quickly to housebreaking, but Gottfried knew that a puppy could only restrain himself so long. At Gottfried's word, the white hound scampered from the path, lifting his leg against the great gnarled root of an old oak tree. Gottfried crouched down, calling him back, and Etzel hurried to his master, his white brush of a tail wagging frantically. He had already learned not to leap up on Gottfried, but he leaned his head against the knight's thigh while Gottfried ruffled the thick fur behind his ears. Etzel was four months old now and growing quickly - he no longer fit into the large basket, and in another five months, he would be ready to train for hunting.

Gottfried had meant to walk about the Bishop's grounds with his dog until Etzel had done his duty, but as he straightened up again, he heard a slight cough from behind him, and turned.

"Father Etienne," Gottfried said, bowing. "I am sorry for the delay, but..." He gestured at the Pyrenean hound, and Etienne inclined his head slightly.

"Indeed. We may talk as well out here - perhaps better, since there is no way for anyone to overhear us easily. Come."

Gottfried followed the priest's tall, straight-backed figure to a pond surrounded by stone benches, sitting down beneath the spreading branches of a budding linden-tree. The sun's light through the boughs cast a tangled net of light and darkness over Father Etienne's black robes and hat, shadowing his ascetic face; a stray touch of sunlight brightened the silver tuft of beard beneath his lower lip.

Deep purple tinged the hollow flesh beneath the priest's eyes, and the tiny lines at the corners of his eyelids and upon his forehead seemed deeper than they had the night before. Father Etienne's face was sallow-gray, as though he had not slept that night, though his dark hair was neatly combed out in thick waves about his shoulders. Etzel lay down at Gottfried's feet at once, his head resting on his huge front paws.

"What did Landgraf Gerhardt's lawyers ask you last night?" Father Etienne said without preamble.

"They wished the story of how Arnmut and I had come to Schloss Niederwald; they were most interested in Bernhardt's departure from Burg Fürstensee. They also enquired as to the details of my relationship with the Gräfin, though they suggested nothing unseemly. Lastly, they asked me what I knew of Landgraf Gerhardt and what I had known of Landgräfin Ortlieb before our attack on her wain. They were more restrained than I had expected from Frowe Eva's account," he added. In truth, the lawyers had been quiet and polite, not pressing him overmuch on any point, and it had been little strain to hold himself back from seeking into their thoughts.

"Gräfin Margerite informs me that you seem to have developed certain...talents of soul, that proved helpful to you, but may put you in some danger, and Brother Karl also spoke to me about these." Father Etienne's slightly accented voice was quiet and neutral, but Gottfried could feel his heart pounding harder in the tight bonds of his ribs as the shadowed memories rose like wisps of mountain-mist in the back of his mind. I shall give you to the priest, and he shall take you away to be burned...spawn of Satan!... Yet if there was a judgement to be made upon him, Father Etienne must make it.

"I fell ill at Burg Falkenstein," Gottfried said briefly. "And for a time, I could not tell when folk were speaking aloud to me, or when my own thoughts would sound in their minds. The Gräfin showed me how to shield myself, and Birgitta taught me further, but I am still far from perfect in that skill. If there is evil in this or in aught I have done with it, I do heartily repent me for it, and beg your help."

Father Etienne took Gottfried's hands in his own, the touch of his long fingers soft and cool against Gottfried's skin. The priest's blue eyes shone brightly as he met Gottfried's gaze, and it seemed to the young knight that he could see a golden shimmering in the air about the priest, as though Father Etienne were haloed in the radiance of his own power.

"There is no evil in such gifts, save when they are used for evil purpose: the same may be said for a sword, or a pen in the hand of one who holds authority. Yet I can tell that your soul is deeply troubled, and Gräfin Margerite mentioned that your illness at Burg Falkenstein was due to bitter austerities and self-starvation. Such gifts as you bear are said to be greatly burdensome; but is it only that which weights you so grievously?"

Gottfried bowed his head. He could not lie to Father Etienne, nor could he bring himself to withdraw his hands from the French canon's clasp, though the gentle touch was beginning to stir a keen longing in his heart. But he will draw back from me in horror when I tell him, Gottfried thought.

"Ritter Gottfried," Father Etienne said, a slight snap in his dry voice. "I have heard many Confessions which I do not doubt were worse than whatever you have to tell me, and thus far Christ has lent me the strength to accept the repentance in all. Now you are not making a Confession to me, but if you are so tormented, you will do best to speak of it, that I may do my best to help you. And you are tormented," he added softly, "if this matter breaks down your control so easily that I heard your thought as if you were speaking it aloud. Will you trust me, Gottfried?"

"I will," Gottfried whispered, his voice breaking as it had not done since he was a page in his father's castle. "I spoke with Christoph on Christmas Day, and..." He could not speak aloud the foul words that it had said to him. "The demon Azruzor accused me of unnatural desires, and... it seemed to draw out what had been hidden in my heart, that even I had not known until then. I fasted to mortify my flesh and preserve myself from the sin of lust - I would have undergone minuition if I could, that the drawing of my blood lower those fiery humours which betrayed me - yet even fasting weakened me so that I could no longer carry out my duty of protecting the Gräfin. And in his innocence, Arnmut still loves me and will not be parted from me; he is sorrowful when I draw away from him, and yet to have him near is like the aching of a wound, for I know..." Gottfried lowered his eyes in shame, waiting for Father Etienne's judgement.

But Etienne clasped the knight's hands more tightly. "Look at me, Gottfried," he commanded, and Gottfried had to meet his gaze again. "There are many ways in which you are not as other men; and who can know God's will? You need not be ashamed that you love Ritter Arnmut, for such care between two knights I have seldom seen: whether he desires you or not, it is clear that his heart is given altogether to you. As for lust..." Father Etienne paused, and it seemed to Gottfried that the shadow of the linden's branches lay over his fine-chiseled features like a memory of old sorrow.

"The sin is the same, regardless of who it is that stirs you. Yet love need not be crowned by the meeting of bodies, and that which is not veiled by the needs of the flesh is the purer and more praiseworthy. Though it is also good to remember that God shaped our bodies as well as our souls: to deny that, as the Cathars did, is heresy, and there is no good in destroying your flesh out of misplaced piety. And perhaps it would be well for you to keep in mind that chastity and celibacy are not always one thing. More than that," the priest added warningly, a glint of blued steel in his eyes, "if you seek to deny your own nature to yourself, when you meet with Azruzor again, it will surely use it against you: Christ's mercy brought you forth from Burg Fürstensee before the demon had time to follow up its stroke."

Margerite had said something similar to him, Gottfried recalled. He would have drawn his hands away from Father Etienne's grasp then, but the priest held him firmly. "I know enough of the nature of demons to warn you now, Gottfried. Azruzor will seek to convince you - as he has clearly done - that everything about your love is shameful and tainted; that you yourself are too flawed to prevail over him. If you cannot accept yourself, and know that your faults are no greater nor lesser than those of any other son of Adam, then you shall fail, and perhaps the rest of us may fail with you. Do you understand me?"

"I do," Gottfried murmured. He did not know whether he had just been relieved of a great burden, or whether Father Etienne had added to it enough weight to numb him; but it seemed to him that he was breathing the cold March air more easily now, and his heart no longer fluttered so painfully against his ribs.

"You are not alone in this," Father Etienne added. "Nor is your plight unknown to those who are close to you. Brother Sigvrît guessed it at once, as did Brother Karl; Margerite would not speak of it to me, or, I think, to any other, but I would be surprised if Eva did not know. And there is not one of them who does not think well of you, or does not wish to have you among his or her closest companions. Nor, I gather, are you despised in Burg Fürstensee, though I understand it is common knowledge there that you will have nothing to do with women and gladly shared your bed with your Knappe."

A terrible heat washed over Gottfried's face, and for a moment, sinful as it was, he heartily wished that he had died beneath the Order's lightning. How could he ever look Brother Sigvrît in the face again, knowing...or return to Burg Fürstensee, afraid that every half-heard mutter or laugh unsheathed the deepest privacy of his soul to public jest?

But then, as if the memory rose from his own mind, Gottfried heard the sound of boys' clear voices shouting, Witch's brat! Priest's bastard! And it seemed to him almost as if he could feel his own back straightening with pride beneath the heavy sway of a long thick braid, even against the soft blows of hurled mud-clots and the harder sting of light stones: Birgitta had never feared to walk the streets of Thrandheim, nor given in to the mockery that surrounded her in the open light of day. If she could endure, I can as well, he thought; and that also gave him the strength to say, "But there is one woman that I love."

"Birgitta Thórkelsdóttir," Father Etienne said flatly.

"Aye. Father, I know what she was, for so I met her; but better than any, I think, I know what she is. I cannot ask her to wed me...and yet..."

"Why not?"

"Because..." Thoughts of dowry, of his father's harsh shouting, came first to Gottfried's mind; and yet Margerite had offered to see to such matters. No: it seemed to him as though Birgitta were a sister of his own blood, though long-separated and parted by many gulfs - her company was a pleasure, her mind open to his own in a way that no other was, so that he could sense her feelings within himself; nor had any other, it seemed to him, ever known his own thoughts so well.

He had seen the depths of her past: yet though there were many things there that would have made him turn away, crossing himself in horror, if he had been told by another; and though he must condemn the deeds themselves, he knew the roots from which they sprang. Thus he could not think the less of Birgitta, for she had never acted from cowardice or dishonour or wanton cruelty. He himself might not have done as well in her place - and knowing Birgitta thus, Gottfried had come to know for the first time how it was that Christ could forgive what any human mercy might spurn, for that He understood the hearts of the worst of men as well as the best, in a fullness of which Gottfried, by His grace, had been given a faint glimmering.

Though he mourned it greatly, Gottfried could not even bring himself to condemn Birgitta for her loyalty to the gods of her forebears. He wished with all his heart that she could see the light of Christ, and yet he knew what a grievous betrayal she would feel she had committed, did she turn away from the vows that she had sworn truly. He would not have her be an oathbreaker, for he knew how greatly that would lessen all that was worthy of honour and love in her soul - it was a cruel thing, that her oaths had been sworn beyond Heaven's bounds, but at least they had not been given as he had first feared.

And Birgitta was beautiful as well, fine-drawn and slender as a birch in springtime - even Gottfried could delight in looking at her, when she came close enough to him for her features to resolve in his eyes. But he did not and could not desire her: though she would never demand what he could not give, he would not offer marriage to such a woman when he must hold back a part of his own portion.

"I cannot wed her honestly," Gottfried said, "because I am...as I am." He flushed again at the words, and would have dropped his gaze once more, but Father Etienne released his hands, reaching out instead to put a finger beneath the knight's chin and tilt his face upwards.

"Then you do love her," the priest murmured softly. "For if you did not, then you would have given another reason - or be more eager to claim her. It is a great wonder to me how you could feel so about one who wore the Light-Bearers' amethyst ring, who was as staunch a foe of Christ as the worst in their Order. Yet by your compassion, it seems that she has been redeemed."

"Birgitta still follows her own gods," Gottfried replied.

This time it was Father Etienne who looked away, staring over the sun-glistening waters of the pond to the long stretches of tree-lined green beyond the budding rosebushes that ringed the little pool. Though Gottfried had not meant to pry, he saw the scene in the priest's memory as clearly as though he had been there himself: the huge study, its deep red walls lined with bookshelves; the silver astrolabe upon the table, and the boar-spear leaned carelessly by the door - and the short, broad-shouldered man whose long hair shone pale gold against his deep blue cloak, his pointed nose tilted upward as he laughed at his apprentice. *Etienne, when will you learn to believe that not all souls are for you to concern yourself with? Save talk of your Devil for your comrade Damiano, who would be his friend; you know better than to waste my time thus, when it is not a matter of the Art.*

"I may know one who can aid her, if she will go to him," Father Etienne said.

"Your own teacher?" Gottfried asked without thought.

The French priest raised his arched eyebrows. "I trust that you have learned to have more care with your gifts when you are not in the sole company of those who know of them. You have seen a little of Father Kerlinger's soul: how do you think he would see it, if you spoke the thoughts that were in his mind?"

Gottfried bowed his head, accepting the rebuke.

"But to answer your question, yes. I believe that it may have been meant for Birgitta to go at last to Meister Stefan von Hauenstein - when the time comes for her to part from you, as she must. Indeed, it would be better if she left sooner, for if she stays, there is the risk that she will draw yet more attention to us from Father Kerlinger and his companions." Father Etienne paused, his aristocratic features hardening: the look on his face would not have been misplaced beneath a helmet's steel rim, nor over the point of a sword. "And now we come to the last matter on which we must speak this morning. Ritter Gottfried, it grieves me to say this to you, for I think you will find it evil counsel, and I know that it will trouble your soul. You are not such a man as would knowingly lie even to your foes, or to the foes of Christ; how much less, then, to an anointed priest, and under oath before God? Yet Father Kerlinger shall, beyond a doubt, ask you questions which, if answered truly, would bring all of us to the stake."

Gottfried's mouth opened, and he closed it again. Last night he had guessed that Gerhardt's lawyers had already begun the delicate maneuvers of setting the Inquisition at their throats, but he had not thought further of what that would mean for him when they began to ask questions. What manner of fool, he thought bitterly, sets all the defenses for his siege before he has thought of how the troops of the foe may array themselves?

"Are you counselling me to lie, then, Father?" Gottfried asked, thinking, *I pray Christ you may have another answer, that you are only saying this to make me consider the matter more deeply!*

"I would not use you so, Ritter Gottfried," answered Father Etienne. "If I knew better counsel, I should give it to you freely." Melancholy tinged his voice like the dull clunking echo of a wooden cowbell, and the canon's sallow skin seemed to have greyed further, as though his words tired him beyond bearing.

"But there is nothing in the Art as you and the Gräfin practice it that deserves punishment, nor anything that goes against the Church - I have seldom felt such a holy blessing as you gave me on the night when we readied against Landgräfin Ortlieb's powers, and thus I should swear before Christ and all the saints," Gottfried protested.

Father Etienne shook his head, the sigh hissing from his lungs like the last breath sinking slowly from an abandoned bellows. "Christ and the saints know what we do, but here on Earth, the Church is made manifest by men. A priest's ordination does not give wisdom nor understanding, nor did God ordain that all should understand how their fellows serve Him, or even agree with one another about His will. Else there should be no heretics - and make no mistake, Herr Ritter, there are those in the church who would brand both you and I by that name as quickly as they would any Bougre or Cathar."

"Yet it cannot be right to lie...and if I am asked to swear an oath?" Gottfried asked, the fear mounting within him like cold dark water rising in a well-shaft.

"Then it must be a matter for your own conscience to decide. But perhaps you will find it easier to make your choice if I put it in terms of war, as we are surely embroiled in the greatest of all wars from life to death...We have won several battles against the Foe by a risky means; but through these maneuvers, we have been forced into a position from which we must retreat, abandoning, at least for a time, a fortress that is very precious, not only in itself but to Our Lord. Yet if we do not retreat, we will lose - our own lives, if we hold the position steadfastly and cling to the truth even when it is we who are on trial; certainly the realms of Niederwald and Fürstensee; and Christ's army will be lessened by as much as our power to act is taken away from us, whether any of us should lie and repent of imaginary crimes to exchange the pain of torture for the shame of identification as a recanted heretic, or whether we all go to dungeon or stake together. And none of our company will be able to escape this. In this battle, then, I see no strategy that will deprive our Foe of some victory: the question is, which will be of the least advantage to him?"

Gottfried remembered sitting in Ritter Ludwig's chamber as a young squire, stiffly attentive as he watched the burly knight push bone gaming-pieces about on the table to show him the strategies of battles lost and won. "And you must remember this when you are a knight, Knappe," Ritter Ludwig had said, his calloused hand tapping Gottfried lightly on the cheek to emphasize his words. "There may come a time when you are ordered to hold a position, and when at dawn the forces are so arrayed that, for your lord to have any hope, the position must be held until you and the last of your men are dead. But a day's fighting and marching can change everything: and then it may be that by dusk, though no new orders have reached you, the only way to uphold your liege is to march out and strike where you are needed. True faithfulness cannot be blind obedience, for blindness will surely betray you some day, and through you, the one to whom you have sworn."

"But to abandon a position against orders to hold it...?" Gottfried had asked, shocked at the thought; and Ritter Ludwig had tapped his squire's other cheek harder, just enough to sting.

"Did you not listen to me, Knappe? If your liege has need of it, you must stay and fight until every drop of blood in your body stains the earth. Nor may you ever take such a decision lightly into your own hands when the matter of strategy is not yours to order: in all your battles, God grant that you shall never have to face such a thing! Yet you must never forget that the possibility is there, for if you never think on it, then how shall you be able to tell when Graf Heinrich, or Christoph in his turn, needs you to make that choice?"

Ritter Ludwig must have seen the terror on his Knappe's face then, for after waiting a moment for his words to sink in, he had reached out to ruffle Gottfried's hair. "It is likeliest that you will never be in such straits," he had said reassuringly. "And you are a pious boy: it may ease your heart to pray to Christ that he will keep such a thing from happening to you - but do not forget to ask Him to grant you wisdom as well, just in case."

Over the years, Ritter Ludwig's words had returned to haunt Gottfried at times; but it was not until this day, sitting in the stillness of the Bishop's garden with the sky's blue shimmering clear and cold from the ice-edged pool before his feet and the budding twigs of the linden rustling a tracery of shadow and sunlight over his face, that he had ever felt himself facing the dread choice of which his knight had warned him, and known the full truth of Ritter Ludwig's words. God bless you now and forever, Ritter Ludwig, Gottfried thought, for you were right indeed. Had you not made me think of such a chance then, I should have been far the less able to face it now.

"I shall pray that Christ grant us a way out of this in safety and honour," Gottfried said. "...But if there is no other choice, I shall not forget what is at stake." His chest ached with the breath that sounded those words, yet he knew he could not do otherwise.

Father Etienne looked at the pool's gleaming waters, stirred to faint ripples by the light cold breeze. When he spoke again, his voice was barely a whisper, as though a great weight rested on his ribs. "It is part of the burden we who practice the Art for Christ's sake bear, and not the least part. The desire for knowledge may be a temptation; the pride of power may be a greater: with God's grace, constant vigilance may serve against those.

Yet there are times when the worst of all is this: that for the sake of good, be it ever so high, we must do evil, even of the least - and never know for certain whether it is truly the choice Christ would have us make, as He broke the laws of the Jews to aid another on the Sabbath, or whether even in our desire to serve Him, we are being seduced unknowing to the designs of His Enemy. Pray, Ritter Gottfried; do as best you can, and trust in Christ's grace: I fear there is no better counsel that any of fallen Adam's sons can give to another."

Gottfried bowed his head, but did not speak. After a time, Father Etienne excused himself and rose, but Gottfried stayed there, staring at the tiny ripples lapping at the last water-eaten rim of ice about the pool's edge. Etzel leaned his white head against his master's leg, and Gottfried stroked the Pyrenean hound absently, until his heart was composed enough that he felt he could go into the Bishop's chapel to pray without betraying his torment of soul to the keen eyes of Father Kerlinger and his assistants.

Rose had just finished dressing Margerite and Eva when the knock sounded on their door. Margerite nodded to the maidservant, and she hurried to open it. Outside stood Father Kerlinger and his two companions, with three grim-faced men in full armour behind them. Margerite could not still the pang of fear twinging through her body at the sight, even as she realized that the effect of the Inquisitors must have been carefully crafted: the full truth would be easier to pry from a frightened witness - or, if they wished to deceive her into self-betrayal, their task would be simpler if she were disordered in her mind.

"Father Kerlinger, Father Liutberg, Father Arnolt," she said graciously. "You begin your work early in the day."

Father Kerlinger looked at her, his blue eyes cold as sapphires in the winter air. "The foes of the Church never sleep, and we who guard her must be vigilant in answer. Gräfin von Fürstensee, we require your first testimony now."

Margerite was about to inform him that she would come when she was ready, but just in time, she remembered that, though his manner was not unlike that of some of the Light-Bearers, the resolute pride that had served her well in dealing with them would only harm her now. "Good Father, I am at your disposal. Would you prefer for Frowe Eva to come with me, or would you have her await you here?"

"Each must make a statement alone," Father Kerlinger replied. "Frowe Eva may await her summons."

Margerite glanced down at Wolfram, who sat on the floor playing with a little ball of feather-stuffed leather that they had picked up along the way. He was staring up at the strangers, but, to her pride, he was not crying at the sight of the tall men in their robes and armour, as another child might have - well, Wolfram had seen many strange things in his ten short months of life, and to a babe who did not know what awesome power the Inquisition wielded, Father Kerlinger and his followers were no more frightening than the rough men of the Bear's Paw, who would lift him high in the air to make him laugh or give him their dagger-sheaths to play with.

She bent down to kiss the soft top of her son's golden head, then straightened and followed the Inquisitors to the Bishop's library, the priests' three armoured bodyguards spreading out ahead and behind as if they expected her to attempt an escape. Two secretaries, dressed in the same Dominican black as the Inquistors and their socius, sat at little tables in the library, small braziers of glowing coals burning by their feet to keep their hands supple enough to write in the chill March air.

A beautiful reliquary rested on the larger table: a large silver cross twined with gold adornment, its elaborately-wrought base glistening with irregularly-cut sapphires and rubies. In the heart of the cross was mounted a sphere of clear rock crystal as big as Margerite's clenched fist, with something withered and brown - a finger, perhaps - and a sliver of white bone enclosed within. Father Kerlinger waved Margerite to a chair in front of the larger table, while he and his two companions took their places across from her.

"Gräfin Margerite von Fürstensee," the tall priest said meditatively, sitting straight-backed so that he still seemed to tower over Margerite, and fixing her with his ice-blue gaze. "Are you prepared to swear before God and Christ, on the holy relics of St. Peter of Verona?"

"I am, Father," Margerite replied. She put her hand on the rock crystal sphere, feeling its tingling chill strike through her palm - thank Christ I no longer bear Ortlieb's ring! - and swore, as the Inquisitor instructed her, to tell the truth. And Christ and Maria forgive me if I must break this oath. The secretaries shook drops of ink from the tips of their quills and bent their heads, writing industriously.

At first, Margerite had only to repeat the tale she had told, first to Bishop Otto, then to Landgraf Gerhardt's lawyers: there was nothing but truth in that, though there might be much left out. Father Liutberg nodded his fair head, making soft clucking noises at the appropriate points, but Father Kerlinger watched Margerite in unblinking silence as she spoke: had she not dealt so lately with the great among the Light-Bearers, whose power on Earth was at least a match for the priest's, she knew that she would soon have found herself stumbling over her own words.

"Tell me, Gräfin," Father Kerlinger said at last, "while you served your penance in Burg Fürstensee, did you ever see or experience aught - even the least thing, which might then have seemed innocent - that might have betrayed Landgräfin Ortlieb's heresy?"

"As a servant, I was given no chance to go to Mass, even on saints' days, nor to make Confession, nor in any other way to receive the consolation of the Church," Margerite replied at once, having been ready for the question. "We worked on Sundays as on any other day. Nor was the Friday abstinence kept in Schloss Niederwald, but meat and eggs and cheese were all upon the high table, save when such guests were there as Landgräfin Ortlieb would not offend."

"And Landgraf Gerhardt gave his assent to this?"

"He ate as heartily as any man there, Father," Margerite replied. "And his consent must have been given, for Landgräfin Ortlieb's powers of authority were surely only those that he, as Landgraf born and husband, must have allowed her."

The scribes' quills scratched a soft counterpoint as she spoke, but Father Kerlinger did not allow his thin lips the luxury of even a slight smile.

"And the Landgraf's priest - one Father Bruno, I believe? - said nothing to this."

"Father, he did not share their table: I never saw him in all the time I was there."

"Did you ever hear Landgräfin Ortlieb speak any word of impiety? Did she greet her maidservants by any salute? Were there any strange beasts that she kept by her, or that came to her chamber by night?"

To those questions, Margerite could only answer, "No," though it was a hard fight to still her face when Kerlinger asked about strange beasts, for she knew what the answer to that would be if he were to ask the same question about her.

Father Kerlinger's questioning went on in that vein for some time, but Margerite could tell him little, save for the warning against inquisitiveness that she had received from the dressmaker Bertrada, and the ominous suggestion that servants who asked too many questions might disappear.

"So," murmured Father Liutberg, his plump fingers toying with the long hem of one black sleeve. "I understand that Canon de Dion had more in mind than a penance when he sent you to work in Schloss Niederwald - what warnings did he give you?"

"Only to be careful and watchful, and to remember that the Landgräfin was a harsh mistress and I must be as perfect as I could in my humility as a servant."

The fair-haired Inquisitor smiled. "A severe penance for a woman of your birth, but it seems that you bore it well, and it is not ours to enquire into your confessor's advice. Still - how long have you known Canon de Dion?"

Margerite briefly recounted the tale of how Father Etienne had come to Burg Falkenstein at the behest of the Bishop of Augsburg in order to make peace between Ruprecht and Heinrich. "After my husband died, he stayed on, for our own priest had also died of illness during the siege - Father Hans was an old man, and sickly, and could not withstand the privations of besiegement in the winter. So Father Etienne would not leave us without spiritual counsel, and stayed until a replacement had been sent for: it was he who baptized my son, and performed the celebratory Mass when Graf Heinrich and I were wedded."

Father Arnolt had not spoken before, but now he pushed a fringe of mousy hair from his eyes and leaned forward. "The Bishop here tells us that you aided in the investigation of the Landgräfin's wain, because Canon de Dion said that he was training you as a lay assistant in exorcism. How did this come about, Gräfin? Why should a frowe as noble as yourself become involved in such a dark and perilous business?"

A prickle of danger, sharp and painful as the dig of Kobolt's claws, scratched along the back of Margerite's spine, and she wondered how much of Etienne's work was already known to these men - but it could be no secret that he was an exorcist, licensed in that duty by the Church itself.

"The Devil spares neither high nor low, nor has he any care for the modesty of women, Father," Margerite replied. "Father Etienne told me that there might be times when, for that modesty's sake, he might need a woman of strong faith and will to aid him; and for the debts I owe him and the sake of his struggles as a defender of Christ, I agreed that, if ever he needed my help and the duties of my rank and family allowed, I should give it."

"What debts do you owe Canon de Dion?" Father Arnolt pursued.

Margerite sat up straight, looking directly into the little man's brown eyes. "He brought spiritual aid and comfort to Burg Falkenstein when we were most in need; he helped me greatly in arranging the truce that ended that siege after my husband Graf Ruprecht's death, for I was but a young woman and bereaved, little able to speak for my own rights as a widowed Gräfin and the rights of the child I bore in my womb. And though the penance he gave me at Schloss Niederwald was harsh, it was well-deserved - for correcting me as was needed, I owe him my thanks as well."

"You seem well-taught, Gräfin von Fürstensee," Father Kerlinger said, his raspy deep voice drawing Margerite's attention inexorably back to him. "Now, since this is a matter of such moment, I trust you will not mind if I ask you a few routine questions in order to be sure that your understanding regarding the Church is entirely correct?"

"I will not mind," answered Margerite. But the prickle of danger strengthened, like tiny hot needles stabbing the back of her neck: Brother Helmuth had warned her that, if she herself were under suspicion, the Inquisitors would begin with the standard questions by which they had learned to root out Cathars, Beguines, and Beghards. There was no danger there for Margerite herself - but she feared where such questioning would lead.

Father Kerlinger's interrogation dealt, for the most part, with simple matters that anyone with a decent education in Christianity could answer correctly. But Margerite was glad, even so, that Rose had not been with them in Schloss Niederwald and would not soon be questioned in the same manner - she would have to have a close talk with the girl, to be sure that, if Father Kerlinger chose to ask her about her mistress, Rose could give the correct answers herself.

The priest's expression did not change, nor did the conversational tone of his voice, as he said, "And what of the black cat that follows you everywhere? Can you swear before Christ and the relics of St. Peter of Verona that it is a natural animal?"

"I can swear that, and gladly," Margerite replied - and her own voice had the ring of truth to it: for there were few things in God's creation with more right to be called natural than a Kobolt, the spirit of earth. "I do so swear, that my cat is a beast of nature, not in any way tainted by the Devil or any of his unholy servants. I have owned him for two years now, and I can swear that he is as natural an animal as any: he has sired a great many kittens, and if he were a spirit, or followed unnatural commands, my servants would have a good deal less scrubbing and washing to do."

Father Liutberg laughed softly, but Father Kerlinger's chiseled features only grew grimmer, as though he found such talk offensive. Father Arnolt raised an eyebrow, murmuring, "And yet you call it 'Kobolt'. If your pet is a natural animal - and a cat is hardly a fitting companion for a noblewoman - why should you have given it the name of a pagan demon?"

"It was a superstition at home, of which I meant only to make light, that such a spirit might take the form of a tomcat. Perhaps that was foolish of me - but I was younger then, only just wed, and did not take matters of the spirit so seriously as I ought to have. Father Etienne has chastised me for that already, for he, too, had his doubts of my cat, and blessed him with holy water to make sure that I had not, awares or unawares, allowed a servant of Christ's Foe into my care."

"Aye, Canon de Dion is zealous in such things," Father Kerlinger said flatly. "And you seem to find him, as many do, a most unusual priest."

"There are few who serve Christ with such fervor and bravery," replied Margerite. "I thank God often that He chose to send me a spiritual counsellor of such strength and wisdom."

"Has he yet led you to have dealings with demons?" the Inquisitor enquired sharply.

"Christ be praised, it has not yet happened that there has been a case of possession in which Father Etienne needed my help as an assistant in exorcism."

Father Kerlinger gave Margerite a severe look. "That is not the question I asked."

"No, Father Etienne has not led me to have dealings with demons; and of them, he has told me only such things as an exorcist's lay assistant must know, that I be prepared should the day ever come when he needs my help in doing battle with a creature of Hell."

"You aided in the investigation of the Landgräfin's wain," Father Arnolt murmured again. "Tell me, had Canon de Dion's teachings made any of the things which were found there familiar to you?"

Margerite crossed herself with a shudder that was only partially feigned: though she had tried to strengthen her mind against the memories of what they had found there, she still could not remember the three heads - and the look of horror on Gottfried's face as he realized that the boys' souls were not yet free; thanks be to Mother Maria, that Margerite did not share her knight's gift of sight! - without her stomach tightening in revulsion. "No, and I pray that I shall never again have to see or hear of such abominations: Christ be praised, now and forever, that we rescued my son from that woman in time!"

"Christ be praised, indeed," Father Liutberg said gravely. "You do understand why we must ask you these questions, do you not, frowe Gräfin?"

"I am not sure. It seems to me odd, that you should enquire so after Father Etienne and even my cat, when I understood that your purpose here was to find out how deeply the Landgräfin Ortlieb, whose evils are clear and proven, had managed to spread her corruption in her lands." Margerite drew up her back again as she spoke, a wounded tone to her voice; Father Liutberg glanced sideways at Father Kerlinger, and it was the more senior Inquisitor who spoke next.

"Heresy and sorcery, Gräfin, spread more quickly and widely than the worst of weeds. I have known many cases where one heretic would denounce another, for the sake of revenge or thinking that in so doing, he might draw suspicion from himself. Hence I have learned that all who involve themselves in such matters must be examined closely, for the virtuous have nothing to fear even when the thresher strikes every single grain in separating the wheat from the chaff. Can you swear now, and honestly, that your conscience is clean of all evil-doing?" The Inquisitor's blue eyes bit into Margerite's; and perhaps she had learned a little in her work with Gottfried, for she was suddenly certain that he meant to trap her.

"Father, I have not made Confession for a little over a month. Until I have done that and been absolved, I cannot honestly so swear - for few of Adam's children are given the grace to pass such a time without committing some sin, and I know how far short of sainthood I fall."

"Then it were well if you made your Confession and received your penance soon," Father Kerlinger said, and Margerite was not sure that she could not detect a hint of disappointment in his voice, like the faint taste of smoke in a sauce that had been set a little too close to the fire. "You may go, Gräfin, though assuredly we shall speak further with you. Inform Frowe Eva that her presence here is required."

Cold as it was, by the time Margerite stepped out into the hallway, she could feel the damp sweat sticking her silken shift to her back. Father Helmuth had warned her that Inquisitors might begin their work softly; but the sword could hiss from its sheath at any moment, and when they had read over what the diligent clerks had written down, there was no guessing what they might further construe from her answers. And Christ help Gottfried, when he is asked to swear his truth on the holy relic they have brought!

The Inquistors' questions had taken longer than Margerite
had realized; already the bells were chiming sext, though
it had been just before tierce when they came for her. She
hastened quickly towards her chambers, that she might
relieve and refresh herself before joining the others at the
Bishop's table; she did not notice who was standing in the
corridor until she almost bumped into him, reeling back so
that he must put out a hand to steady her.

"Bernhardt," Margerite whispered. Hot blood stung her
cheeks, and she could feel the salt tears prickling in her eyes
at his touch.

"Margerite," Bernhardt answered softly, dropping his
hand from her shoulder. This close, she could see indeed
how pale and worn he had grown, the lines of hardship
graven deeper about his eyes than they had been while he
served Ruprecht. He caught his lower lip between his teeth,
as though he feared to say more, but his brown-flecked
green eyes shone like a woodland pond, its shimmering
water caught in a sudden shaft of sunlight.

Margerite could have stood there thus for an eternity,
looking up into Bernhardt's face - his neat-cropped brown
beard outlining his chiseled jaw, his chestnut hair curling
about his strong features like a cunningly-wrought frame of
gleaming wood...and his gaze fixed on hers with such relief
and joy that she was ashamed to think that she could ever
have doubted his love. O, my suffering was due punishment
for not trusting you! Margerite thought in her amazement.

In truth, had the Light-Bearer disciplines not come to her
aid, she would have flung herself into his arms there and
then; she could see the faint trembling in the muscles of
his shoulders - so broad beneath the deep blue brocade of
his doublet! - and knew that he was holding himself back
likewise. But then, as if by habit, Bernhardt glanced up and
down the corridor; seeing no one, he put a silent finger to his
mouth before he lifted Margerite's left hand.

The kiss he placed on her fingers was a chaste kiss
of greeting, that no one watching - through a keyhole,
maybe, or a slightly cracked door - might have mistaken
for anything else. Yet a thrill ran up Margerite's arm at the
touch of his lips where Ortlieb's ring had rested; it seemed
to her, as it had not even after she cast the Light-Bearer's
emblem away, that her hand was clean at last, purified by
Bernhardt's blessing even as if she had washed Ortlieb's
smirch away in the waters of the Marienbrunnen.

"Greetings, Gräfin von Fürstensee," Bernhardt said
gravely, just as if nothing had ever passed privately between
the two of them. "It joys me to see you here again, and safe
after such a long journey."

"And I am glad to see you in turn, Herr Bernhardt, and
to know that you are closer to your rightful inheritance
and estate," Margerite replied. For that one moment she
would have given almost anything she possessed to have
Gottfried's gift, that she could weave the words of her
thought - Bernhardt, I love you! - into an unseen strand
to cast from the tower of her mind to that of Bernhardt's,
and hear his reply in turn. But, covering her thoughts with
words, it seemed to Margerite that she had spoken ill, for the
corner of Bernhardt's eye twitched as though he were trying
to hide a wince.

"As God wills, and the course of justice moves. That
course is slower and less sure than I had hoped - though
maybe swifter and more sure than I had feared. Yet it will
be some months before the Inquisition has finished their
investigations; they are, as Father Etienne assures me, slow
but exceedingly thorough. And Gerhardt is slow to send his
castle folk to answer their questions, though he cannot delay
too long, for fear of confirming their suspicions."

I wonder how much your brother did know? Margerite
thought. She had begun to wonder about Ruprecht inside
of three months...but that was in a smaller castle, and he
had not bound her mind or heart by any spell. Except that I
loved him, and would not think ill of him...Did Gerhardt love
Ortlieb so?

"But we shall speak more of this later, when Father Etienne may explain matters better than I can," Bernhardt went on. "I believe the Bishop's table is being set even now, and it is not fitting for us to stand talking in a hallway like guardsman and serving-maid." The corner of his lip quirked into a half-smile, and it seemed to Margerite that she saw a faint gleam of humour in his hazel eyes - a light that sparked an answering glow in her heart.

"We shall speak later, then," Margerite agreed, inclining her head towards him. "Good day to you, Herr Bernhardt."

Bernhardt bowed, then turned and walked away.

And it must be thus between us while Heinrich lives, Margerite thought, the exultation of her heart chilling to despair as quickly as a cloud might cut off the warm light of the sun. Yet I cannot wish Heinrich ill...I would have him hale again, and no longer a breathing corpse in his bed... but until he is gone, Bernhardt and I can be no more to each other than Landgraf von Niederwald, if all goes well, and Gräfin von Fürstensee. O Mother Maria, I can feel my heart creaking beneath this burden: strengthen it now, lest it break!

Although two hours of praying had calmed Gottfried's mind so that he felt he could face the company at the Bishop's table, he found that he had almost no appetite. He sat beside Birgitta, carefully cutting her fish for her - her shattered left hand made it difficult for her to slice her own food, and a noblewoman at table should be given that service by courtesy in any case; Gottfried had not failed to mark how Margerite had introduced the Norwegian. Birgitta would be given all honour as my wife, if only...He wondered how much longer she would be there, if Father Etienne had spoken to her yet.

If so, the Northern woman showed no sign: she sat calmly, lifting each morsel to her lips as daintily as any high-born maiden and dabbing her fingertips on her linen napkin after each bite. Yet it seemed to Gottfried that, beneath the mask of quiet on her sharp-boned face, he could sense something from her - some turmoil that she was walling away from him, for he could not catch her thoughts as he was used to doing. He did not know then why he dared to speak silently to her, but he could not help himself.

O Birgitta, Gottfried thought, why are you so silent? What troubles you?

Birgitta turned her head, and her eyes met his: so near, near enough that Gottfried could see the faint silver-white flecks in her blue irises, it seemed to Gottfried that no veils parted them then. He could feel her sorrow as if it were his own, aching in his thin chest with each breath, and yet beneath it her heart quivered with eagerness, like a mastiff straining at the lead as it caught the blood-scent of a wounded boar, and he knew that she would leave very soon, even before he heard the words, By this even-tide - beloved.

Deliberately Gottfried caught the soft inner part of his lip between his teeth, biting down until blood flooded his mouth as though he had been knocked down on the tilting yard. But that pain was familiar, and quelled the tears rising to his eyes, for he had been taught in early childhood not to weep at any hurt to his body; and he was able to go on cutting Birgitta's food for her as if nothing had taken place.

Yet, when the last of the scented sugar-and-rosewater sweets had been eaten and Bishop Otto rose from table to signal that the meal was over, Gottfried accompanied Birgitta to her chamber, Arnmut trailing a little behind, as though unsure of whether he was wanted or not.

"A moment," Gottfried said to Birgitta, and dropped back. The light through the stained-glass windows of the corridor dappled Arnmut's golden hair and fair skin with brilliant colours, like an illumination painted with crushed gemstones. How can my heart be so torn? Gottfried wondered. But he had long since learned, as well, not to think too closely about what he might want, or have.

"Arnmut, I believe that Birgitta will be leaving today, and I would have a few moments in private to bid her farewell, if I may."

Arnmut's mouth opened in surprise. He closed it again, then said in a small voice, "But... but why? I thought that she...that you and she..."

Gottfried shut his eyes, for he could not bear to look on Arnmut's face in that moment. I have not told you half of what I should have - dear Christ, what price honesty? Opening his eyes again, he saw his former squire's expression changing, from shocked surprise to something gentler - compassion, it might be, or understanding, if the two were not one and the same.

"Gottfried, you need tell me nothing you do not want to," Arnmut murmured. "I trust in your judgement, as I have since I first swore myself as your Knappe...I shall be waiting in our chambers," he added, his voice stronger; then he bowed to Birgitta. "Farewell, frowe Birgitta, if this must be farewell. You are a brave woman, and good, and it has been an honour to travel with you. Nor shall I ever forget all you have done for us."

Birgitta smiled sadly. "Farewell, Ritter Arnmut. I stayed as long as I might have. Now take care of Ritter Gottfried, for my soul tells me that he will have need of a staunch friend in the days that are to come."

"Always, frowe," Arnmut answered, his voice thick as though he, too, were fighting back a rush of feeling; and Gottfried had to struggle not to reach out to him, to glance, even once, into the open and light-filled windows of his mind.

"I hope," Birgitta said, as she closed the door of her chamber behind Gottfried, "that this will not appear too unseemly to the priests here - but be that as it may: they can do me no more harm, and I think they will not judge you too harshly for consorting with me."

Gottfried did not know how to answer that. Standing here in Birgitta's chamber - though he could see nothing of her in it, save for the small bag that stood neatly packed by the door - he felt awkward and tongue-tied, as he had not even when he had first met her. Yet she has heard my thoughts, he reminded himself. So perhaps, after all, I can speak them aloud to her without fear. "I shall miss you."

"And I, you," Birgitta answered warmly. "I would stay with you, if I could...even now, I..." Her voice trailed off, her fingers twisting in the end of her long honey-brown braid, and she looked suddenly away from him, her high cheekbones flushing pink.

"I would have you stay, if I could," Gottfried said. "And yet I have nothing to offer, and we..."

"We are too far apart, I know," Birgitta said sadly. "I would that we had both been born in an earlier day, when we might have sought the same goal. Or that...no: without your faith, you would not be the man you are, just as I would not be the woman I am if I were to turn from my troth. Yet even that..." She sighed, dropping her braid and straightening her back. "Best for both of us if I go now, lest staying together bring us more sorrow than parting."

Gottfried could not deny the wisdom in her words, though they wrenched at his heart like a pair of cold iron pliers. So this is love for a woman, he thought distantly - not like what I feel for Arnmut; yet closer, maybe, than it seems.

"Aye," Birgitta murmured. "Because I love you, I would not hurt you any further - and I have my own road to travel, that must lead me far from you."

"But how can you go alone?" Gottfried protested. "You must know the dangers for a woman travelling by herself, and the Light-Bearers are your foes now. Stay a little, until we can send you on more safely."

Birgitta shook her head.

"Will you at least let me detail some of the men from the Bear's Paw to accompany you?"

She shook her head again. "I have no fear of the perils of the road, Gottfried. No unfriendly eyes will see me passing, nor need I be afraid of winter-hungry wolves or outlaws. And - I have seen the stronghold to which I am going, and know that I shall arrive there unharmed: I have enough of spae-sight to be sure of it."

Gottfried could think of nothing else to say: he could no longer deny their parting, any more than he could look at a rocky crag dropping off before his feet and say, The precipice is not there, I may ride my horse onwards. His thoughts fled for refuge to the one matter he had been meaning to mention, save that there had been no time nor privacy. "I broke your sword. I am sorry; I do not know how I can repay you, for I know how dear to you it was."

Birgitta smiled, her braid swinging behind her. "You saved my life with it, and those of all who were with us. Few weapons have a better end. And it may be, as well, that where I am going, I shall find a smith to reforge it: other blades have been broken, and come forth the greater for being shattered and remade. Do not let that trouble your heart, my Gottfried." She paused: in Gottfried's blurred sight, only her face was clear, grave and pale as a delicate carving of birchwood. "And the favour you bore shattered as well. Gottfried, you bore that for charity and humility - though I do not think you understand what it was you carried. But you have no lady's favour now: will you bear mine, until that day comes when you desire another's?"

"I will."

Birgitta bent down, rummaging in her bag. The scarf she pulled out was deep blue, its loose-woven linen rough beneath Gottfried's fingers - other knights carried sleeves or scarves of fine silk, embroidered with patient care; but he would not have exchanged this for any of them. He looped the favour carefully over his belt, tying it into place.

"Now give me a kiss of farewell, if you will, for I do not know if or when we shall meet again," Birgitta said. Though her voice was clear, it seemed to Gottfried that he could hear the weeping behind it, like the crystal sound of a tiny waterfall running just beyond sight in the woods.

Gottfried stepped forward, embracing Birgitta for the first time. Her body felt fragile as a small bird's in his grasp, and yet he could feel the wiry strength in her slenderness. Their lips touched, warm and soft; Gottfried tasted the faint tang of salt in the kiss, and felt the wetness on his face, though he did not know from which of their eyes the tear had dropped.

"Farewell," he said.

The days of Lent passed with consuming slowness for Margerite. Though she was warm and well-fed, treated with exquisite courtesy and friendliness by Bishop Otto, she could not help feeling as she had during the siege of Burg Falkenstein: the constant grinding sense of being encircled by her enemies, of eyes watching by day and night for the least show of weakness...

She had not been able to speak to Bernhardt except for a few courteous words exchanged in the corridors or at table; Father Etienne had counselled both of them separately not to try to meet, in the gardens or elsewhere, as for them to be seen together would strengthen the weapon in the hands of Gerhardt's lawyers. Margerite's eyes would meet Bernhardt's across the table, but one must always glance quickly away, and if there were messages between them, they had to go through Father Etienne, which meant that Margerite could say nothing of what was in her heart.

Even the Bishop's cook, after a time, could hardly make the endless fish-meals palatable to Margerite, whether he cut the meat of carp and pike into neatly scalloped rondels beneath a sauce of cream of almonds made piquant with verjuice and the first tiny shoots of scallions, or soaked lampreys in a wine that, even at Burg Fürstensee, Margerite would have saved for noble guests; and under the eyes of the Inquisition, Margerite could not bring herself to claim the exemption from abstinence that, as a nursing mother, she would almost surely have been granted.

Besides, it wore on her that, every few days, she must lie before the relic of Saint Peter of Verona: accepting the full Lenten abstinence, she thought, might aid in cleansing some of the sin from her soul. By Good Friday, Margerite's fine dresses hung on her like a sack, and her breasts had nearly gone dry, so that Wolfram suckled them for comfort more than nourishment, and threw back his head with a howl when he found that there was no milk there for him.

"There is a little man who will be glad of Lent's end," declared Rose as Margerite rocked her son and crooned to him. "There, young Graf, soon you will have fine meat to eat, now that you are old enough, and will forget that milk comes from your mother's breasts - not that any man ever really forgets that," she added in a low undertone. "Speaking of milk, I see that Kriemhilt's teats are bulging. I wonder, will she give us her kittens on Easter Day?"

Margerite looked over at the cat who lay on her side on the bed, easing her swollen belly. "She may well," Margerite said. Wolfram was still crying; she stood, meaning to pace the floor with him until he calmed, but a wave of dizzy faintness swept over her, so that she had to sit down again at once.

Rose swept the child from her arms. "Frowe, are you well? You are suddenly pale - I told you that you should have asked for a dispensation from the Lenten abstinence."

"I am well enough," Margerite said distantly. The dizziness was already draining from her head, but when she tried to rise again, she found that she could not muster the strength to stand. *Dear Maria help me - is this the Order's doing? Have they managed to seep through Father Etienne's defenses like water through the foundations of a castle, to drain my life-strength thus?*

"Stay here and rest, frowe," Rose ordered her, with a hint of sharpness in her voice that echoed the tones of her aunt the midwife. "I shall go to the infirmary: they have milk and cheese there for those who are ailing - that is where I have been getting Wolfram's food. And if those black-robed priests do not like it, then they may go to the Devil! I think it is as much their fault that you are so ill as the fault of the Lenten diet."

"You must not speak so about priests, Rose," Margerite chided her serving-maid - though more gently than she had meant to: the questions of the Inquisitors had worn hard upon her in the last month, and she could not deny the truth of what Rose had said.

"I am as respectful as I ought to be of priests who act as they should," the girl replied, her small mouth set sullenly. "But Father Arnolt offered me money last night to let him search your bags... at least I think he did; he was most careful in what he said, but it seemed clear to me that there was some sort of reward in the matter."

"Why did you not tell me of this at once, Rose?" Margerite asked, startled.

Rose frowned, brushing back a stray wisp of dark hair that had escaped from her braid. "I was not sure what he meant at first...it was only with some thinking on it that I became certain. I pray your forgiveness, frowe. I did not let him in, anyway," she added with more assurance.

Margerite sighed. Her head was spinning, and she hardly felt that she had the strength to lift a hand - was this dreadful news, that the Inquisitor was pursuing her so, or did it mean that Father Kerlinger and his companions had given up, at last, on their hope that one of Margerite's company would betray them under questioning, and had turned to other means as their last resort?

"When you have had some proper food, I shall look for Father Etienne," Rose told her. She set Wolfram down on the rug where Kobolt slept with his plumed tail curled about his nose, ignoring the child's cry as she swept out of the chamber. Wearily, Margerite picked up her knitting: she had been able to occupy her hands at least, if not her mind, in making a new shirt for Wolfram, letting the quiet click of her four needles and the softness of the loose-spun wool beneath her fingers bring her such soothing as they could. Now she had only to cast off the neck, and her son would have a fresh white garment for Easter...

Rose had not been gone long when a knock sounded on the door. Margerite put her knitting aside and pushed herself up out of her chair, walking slowly over to open it.

"Herr Bernhardt!" she said, hardly noticing the dizzy spinning of her head for the sudden pounding of blood in her heart, but mindful, still, that there might be others listening or watching beyond her notice. "What brings you here?"

Bernhardt bowed gravely to her. "Gräfin, your maidservant informed me that you were feeling unwell, and suggested that you might be cheered by a little company. Since Frowe Eva is enjoying the sunlight in the Bishop's garden, and your two knights are occupied in their Good Friday devotions, I thought that I would come to greet you."

Margerite was torn between anger and delight; it seemed to her that she knew perfectly well what was in Rose's mind. *The little wretch thinks that I have been pining for my lover..!* But there was an uncomfortable amount of truth in it: Margerite knew that the long month of questioning and waiting would have been far easier to bear had it not been for Bernhardt, so near and yet untouchable, with no chance to speak save the formal words of courtesy exchanged at table or passing in the corridors of the Bishop's palace.

"Your company is indeed welcome, Herr Bernhardt. Do come in."

Bernhardt left the door open behind him - a wise precaution, though Margerite regretted it; in her weakness, she desired nothing more than to fling her arms about his broad shoulders, to feel his strength holding her up. Sitting down, he glanced at Wolfram, now happily playing with Kobolt as Kriemhilt watched through slitted green eyes from the bed. "Your son is well-grown for his age," Bernhardt commented - was there a little warmth in his voice? Margerite did not know whether she heard it, or only wished it. "And he has taken no harm from travelling so long?" Now, Margerite was sure she heard the undertones in his words clearly, and she answered as truthfully as she might.

"Nothing seems to have marked him," she said, though her voice was not as sure as she would have liked.

"That is well." Bernhardt's eyes found her face for a moment, then flicked away, his scarred hands tightening about each other in his lap. Margerite realized suddenly that he was uneasy, as she had never seen him; it came to her that she hardly knew Herr Bernhardt, son of the Landgraf of Niederwald. *And if he comes to his rightful place, can things ever be as they were between us?* she wondered.

Even if Heinrich...Margerite thrust the thought away. But it seemed to her that, with the fear of the Inquisition or Gerhardt's lawyers listening, that there was nothing of which they could speak: that the hidden matters they had shared rose like a sheer castle wall between them, blocking out all the common things that might pass between a man and a woman.

"It must have been a weary wait for you here," Margerite said at last.

Bernhardt nodded. She could see the circles beneath his eyes, translucent blue against the ash-dusted gray of his pallor, and she felt ashamed that she had borne her single month of interrogation as badly as she had. "Aye, such matters move slowly. At least I have been able to try my skills at arms with the Bishop's guard, and for all Brother Sigvrit's injuries, he is as wise a sword-master as any of the men in my father's Schloss, so that I have learned well from him and...would be ready to fight, if it came to that. But that is most unlikely, for Gerhardt will hardly lay siege to the Bishop's palace. Though I understand," he added, lowering his voice, "that Father Kerlinger and his companions mean to go to Schloss Niederwald after they have finished here, and that Ortlieb's handmaidens..." He stopped suddenly. Margerite guessed that her face had betrayed her thoughts. Yet it would be cowardly not to know all of what I have done, she told herself sternly.

"Have they spoken?"

"The Bishop has told me none of the details, save that he gave permission for their full interrogation," Bernhardt answered reluctantly, the harsh lines biting deeper into his face as he spoke. "I do not think he has been informed of what they have said, if they have spoken at all."

Margerite thought of what she had heard concerning the means of interrogation which the Inquisition was authorized to use: water, fire, the cruel dislocation of limbs. She did not know which Father Kerlinger might exercise - Maria be thanked, the Inquisitors had not yet reached the point of speaking to her of such things, which Brother Helmuth had warned her would be the next step after the questions designed to root out heretics.

And whatever is done to Oda and Hedwig, it is likely less than what they inflicted on Ortlieb's victims; and far less than the pains of Hell that they must face, if they do not recant...Yet how can a soul be saved, that repents only from fear of pain? And if such means were used in magic, even for the best of ends, I have seen enough that I would fear the Devil's snares there.

"But I am sorry for troubling you with such things, Gräfin," Bernhardt said, and Margerite could see the pain in his expression. "It is a great sadness to me that a noble frowe such as yourself should have been drawn into these matters, though I should have failed without your help." Beneath the formal words, his hazel eyes shone open and vulnerable, and it seemed to Margerite that she could feel the full weight of what he would say - that he loved her, that he would have spared her all that she had borne, if he could have.

"By God's will and the Virgin's mercy, I am glad to have aided you," Margerite answered. "And I pray that it not be too much longer until all is resolved."

Bernhardt sighed. "Amen to that. Tell me, how much longer do you think it will be until Christoph's Knappe arrives?"

Margerite's belly tightened suddenly at his words: of course, he would not know what Father Etienne had done. Nor did she think that the priest had told him much of what had befallen her; Father Etienne had hinted darkly that Bernhardt was more closely watched than the rest of them, since much of Gerhardt's hope would rest, in the end, on discrediting his brother.

"It is a long ride to Burg Fürstensee, and the roads are muddy this time of year. Still, a single courier travelling swiftly...If, Christ willing, no delays befall them, I hope it will not be too much longer." I hope that Father Etienne's messenger reached Georg in time to save him from Christoph's demon; God grant that it got there before the Order sent news to Nikolaus!

"And when they are done with him, you shall be returning to Burg Fürstensee, and to your husband?" Bernhardt's tone was perfect, the polite and casual enquiry of a nobleman to a wedded woman: it was Margerite that had to fight for control, reminding herself, He grew up in a great court, learning to school himself as a ruler must; I must not forget that polished manners may be as much a mask as his wild beard and gruff Free Soldier's manner were. Nor, after these long months of deception, should I take it amiss that he is yet more skilled in that art than I!

"I shall indeed, and hope to find that he is better than he was when I left: surely the Holy Father's prayers will have done him some good, in soul at least! I regret that I have had to be gone so long, but Herr Christoph is surely holding Burg Fürstensee's lands well in his father's place."

"Surely he is: I believe he is a most capable young man." But Bernhardt, his back to the door, frowned in despite of his words, his eyes closing in a wince of pain for a moment. He feels it deeply, that his own cause has cost Christoph these further months of torment.

O Maria, if only we could take counsel freely together! Margerite thought. And her heart beat counterpoint beneath it, beat with the longing that was the true meat beneath the deceptive sauce of courteous words and the shape of the matters that - grievous and painful as they might be, of more real import, maybe, than the feelings they disguised - she and Bernhardt were speaking of because they could not so much as clasp hand to hand, let alone give voice to what they had spoken of in the Bishop's garden four months ago.

"And I hope truly that all will be well in Burg Fürstensee," he went on. "For your sake and that of Graf Heinrich's - I have ever counted him a good and honourable man, even when I had to do battle against him - and, if you will forgive me for saying it, because I believe I shall need your help once more when I come before Kaiser Karl to present my case."

Margerite sighed, the tension that had been humming along her nerves all flowing out with that single breath. Though what he had said might be entirely true and proper, she, and perhaps only she, could hear the plea underlying his voice: Bernhardt might need the aid of the Gräfin von Fürstensee, but it was the woman Margerite he desperately wanted by his side when the time came for him to know what judgement Karl IV would give on his life.

"You may be assured that nothing shall keep me from giving it, for surely it is my duty as a Christian and a subject of the Holy Roman Empire to be sure that the truth is spoken in this matter, and that Kaiser Karl knows all that he must know to declare a just decision. Herr Bernhardt, though I was not there for the beginning of this matter between yourself and your brother, I know how ill Schloss Niederwald was ruled: by Maria and Christ, you have my word that I shall support you!"

As she spoke - for though the door was open, she had heard no footsteps in the corridor, and from where she was seated, she knew that none could watch them without her seeing - Margerite lifted the hidden ring on its chain from between her breasts and, greatly daring, pressed it to her lips a moment as if to put its seal upon her last words.

Bernhardt smiled, the weariness falling from his face as Lazarus' gray grave-shroud must have fallen away to show the bright skin of a living man beneath, and Margerite's heart squeezed tight with painful joy. She could not offer him the falcon-necklace again, for it would be as good as a confession to Gerhardt's lawyers for Bernhardt to carry her favour in this silent battle; but Margerite, too, was in the lists where words were wielded in place of lances, and it was enough that she bore his token.

Bernhardt lingered for a little while after Rose came back with a pitcher of milk and a plate of soft white cheese and egg-bread for her mistress, speaking of polite nothings as if to assure any unseen listeners that he had no fear of discovery there; and by the time he took his leave, Margerite realized that she had nearly finished the food her maidservant had brought and was beginning to feel heavy and a little sleepy in her fullness.

"I wonder," Rose said thoughtfully, "if the Bishop's household is too grand to colour eggs for him to bless on Holy Saturday. I shall see if I can find some, and also paints, for surely we could do with that blessing more than ever now."

"Yes, that is so," Margerite agreed. "And perhaps you can do that same service for the Ritters Gottfried and Arnmut: Gottfried will not think of it for himself, and it is good to remember that there is more to serving Christ than prayers and austerities." And all of us need the touch of resurrection, for this weary round of questions and lies has weighted our souls with the darkness of sin as surely as any stone sarcophagus-lid weighs upon the dead.

Eva came back with Rose: the serving maid carried a tray of little paint-pots and brushes, but the young noblewoman cradled a large bowl of hard-boiled eggs. Eva had grown a little thinner on the Lenten diet, though it suited her well, her slimmer waist making her rounded breasts and hips stand out more prominently; she had certainly not wasted away as Margerite had.

In her light green silks, with her long golden hair flowing free down her back, her cheeks pink from the day's sunlight, Eva might have been playing the part of the May Queen in a great castle's counterpart to the village festivities where Margerite had once sat on a throne entwined with greenery, crowned with flowers.

If we were at Burg Fürstensee now, and Christoph freed, he would surely be dressed as King Summer...For a moment, Margerite thought longingly of her father's little fortress, of the young man-at-arms who tilted at the straw figure of Winter with a green branch, knocking the long-bearded doll into a pond and declaring the death of all cold and sadness, before sprinkling everyone's festive finery with a whirl of bright droplets from his leafy lance.

If the villagers of Burg Falkenstein had done likewise, Margerite had not seen it, lying in bed with her new-born babe in her arms this last May-Day, and this year...At least we have eggs to celebrate Easter with; and next year, mayhap at Schloss Niederwald...

"A fair day at last," Eva said cheerfully. "Margerite, we should go outside for our painting, for the light and air will do you good. But it is well that I chanced upon Rose in her searching, for in the end we had to go and beg Father Etienne's help - did you know that he illuminates his own pages? He whisked away the parchment he was working on before I could read it, but the painting was most beautiful. We were in great luck there, as well, for he had his colours already mixed. And things must be going well for us, after all, for he seemed in a fair mood and even gave me a little gold leaf for our eggs."

"That was very kind. We should share it with the knights, though."

"O, no, Arnmut was with us, for Rose met him in the infirmary where he had gone for the same purpose, and Father Etienne gave him some of his own. So we shall have someone to test our skills at painting against, but I have always held that women have the neater hands. And I mean for us to win the victory here: it would be shameful if such a dour knight as Gottfried could paint prettier eggs than you and I. But let Rose fetch us a little table for the garden, for truly, we should not waste the spring sunlight while we have it."

Margerite yielded quickly enough to her friend's importunings, and it was not long before they were seated on one of the stone benches beside a pool, eggs and paint-pots arranged on a small table before them. Rose sat nearby, watching Wolfram toddle about on the fresh grass; Kobolt crouched by the water's edge, the tip of his tail twitching as he looked into the depths - after a little fish, or perhaps a frog - and Kriemhilt curled up in the sunlight.

The first points of pink were just piercing through the tips of the little green rosebuds springing out from their unfurling leaves; the white flowers of strawberries starred the velvety green of the lawns, and Margerite could hear the distant call of a cuckoo through the cooing of the Bishop's white doves. For a moment, she almost felt guilty at the warm spring of peace and happiness welling up within her - yet, she reminded herself, though Good Friday was a day of mourning, it would be impious not to rejoice at the coming of Easter and the surety of the Resurrection.

When she took Father Etienne's brush in her hand, Margerite felt a slight welcoming tingle through her fingers, growing stronger as she dipped the tip into the rich thick blue the priest had mixed. Of course, Etienne would not waste the precious pigments ground from lapis and ruby without some blessing: he had given them a greater gift than Eva, perhaps, knew.

"Be careful of what you paint or write with these," Margerite said softly.

Eva nodded, her face darkening a moment. "I was taught to scribe for the Abbess, and not with such ink as Father Etienne uses." Then she smiled, her white teeth glinting like the edge of a blade in the sunlight. "But Arnmut has told me that I need never fear her again. It was she who gave him his scar, for he was slow to lift his sword against a woman - yet he achieved my vengeance afterwards."

"Vengeance belongs to the Lord, and this is no time to let such things burden your soul," Margerite chided her, though, knowing how Eva had been tormented in the Convent of the Holy Cross, she could put little sternness into her voice. "Remember her in your prayers, or at least ask for the strength to do so."

Eva sniffed slightly, but said nothing to that, bending her golden head over the egg and brush in her hand.

When the blue coat had dried on her first egg, Margerite touched the brush into the bright ruby-red, tracing the shape of a shield. The gilding of the stag's head and mantling would come last; the leaping silver fish, she painted in pure white. And beneath the arms, in shining black ink, she drew the letters of the von Niederwald motto as carefully as she could. A boast it might be, but one that was fulfilled so far, and at the same time a prayer and a distillation of all her hopes, for both Bernhardt and herself: the single word, UNCONQUERED.

"By the grace and will of God, ADONAI ELOHIM," Margerite whispered softly as she blew upon the egg to dry the precious pigments - fire's red, water's blue, the white of air and black of earth, and her own spirit breathing upon them. "Maker of Heaven and Earth, Redeemer of Men: may it be as I have written, and all set to rights."

Setting that egg aside, Margerite picked up another, turning it over in her hand and staring at the pale pinkish-brown surface. A stray thought came to her then: folk painted eggs for those they loved, but how long might it have been since the stern Father Kerlinger was given such a gift on Easter Day? And she had prayed hard for herself, for her companions and for Heinrich and Christoph, and even for the souls of her foes in the Order of Light-Bearers; but it had never crossed her mind to ask Christ's grace for the Inquisitors.

Again, the colour she chose as a background was blue - the blue of Maria's robes, for that mercy that saw and understood the hearts of men with a mother's love. Upon that, she painted a five-petalled rose in white. Though she could feel the power in Father Etienne's pigments and brushes as surely as in the chalice and paten from which he served Mass, she knew that it would be wrong to try to use it to compel Father Kerlinger against his will. But though the Inquisitor's mind might be harsh and narrow, suspicious of all that he did not understand, yet he, in his own way, did the best he could for Christ and the Church.

Therefore, Margerite wrote carefully upon the egg: CHRIST GUIDE YOU IN WISDOM; MAY HIS JUDGEMENT BE MANIFEST THROUGH YOUR WORK. The tiny letters wound about the egg like the Hebrew names of God entwining the circle in Margerite's sanctum beneath Burg Fürstensee - she could not suppress a pang of memory, hoping that Nikolaus had not desecrated the place she had hallowed with her prayers and her magic - and as she murmured the words to give them life, turning the egg carefully in her hands, it seemed to her that she could feel a touch of heat glowing from the painted shell, as though it had just been lifted fresh from beneath the hen.

Eva was still working on her first egg, the bright hue of the ground-ruby pigment shining in lines of fire against the whitened shell. A twisted manlike demon-shape, bound in chains with flames leaping about it, and above, a man's head with a line carefully marked around it where she would gild a halo of blessing. Margerite recognised the rounded face, the little uptilt at the end of the nose...

What better time to pray for Christoph's freedom than at Easter, when the Devil's power was broken and mankind freed from Adam's bondage? Margerite thought; then, with a prickling of alarm, But to whom does Eva mean to give this egg? Still, she said nothing, for she could see the dark widening of the pupils in Eva's blue eyes and the slowing rhythm of her breath in the rise and fall of the young woman's large breasts beneath their drapery of green silk: Eva was in a trance of magic as surely as Margerite herself had been, and Margerite knew better than to break it by a careless word, but instead closed her eyes, feeling the warmth of the sun on her lids even as the image of Eva's painting still burned beneath them. Christ and Maria, grant her prayer; may **HE** who rules the angels and has dominion over all, against Whom all Satan's wiles and forces could not prevail, drive Azruzor back to Hell!

When the women rose to carry their painted eggs back to their chamber so that they could finish them with the gold leaf Father Etienne had so kindly given Eva - for the least breath of wind would have cast the infinitely fragile wisps of gold all over the Bishop's garden - Margerite found that her legs were trembling beneath her; she was glad that Rose was carrying Wolfram, for she did not think she could bear the child's weight. Inside, only the sternest application of will kept her hands steady enough to touch a dry brush to the edge of a gold fragment until the shivering gleaming tissue clung so that she could carefully lift it and lay it upon the tacky yellowish slug-trails of gesso.

As each egg was completed, it seemed to Margerite that she could almost hear a sound like the fading echo of a bell-stroke, one laying silently upon another until the table was covered with bright eggs and her bones shook with the silent harmony. She had not realized how much of a strain it had been, to keep herself from doing any trace of magic in the Bishop's palace. Now, though she hardly had the strength left to sit upright in her chair, the vast contentment of her soul wrapped her in warmth. Impious as the likeness might be, she knew that it would feel like this to sleep in Bernhardt's arms after making love.

"Christ be praised," Eva breathed, and as their eyes met, Margerite knew that her friend felt the power of their working as surely as she herself. Later there would be time for doubt, to wonder if they had dreamed the feeling, or if their foes could yet counter what they had done: now Margerite was utterly sure that they would prevail.

Then Eva giggled, a relievingly natural sound. "Now I shall be surprised if Gottfried and Arnmut have painted anything so beautiful. I think the honours shall belong to us on Easter Sunday. Rose, I am hungry and thirsty now - go fetch some wine, and bread and herring if the kitchens have nothing better for a fast-day afternoon. Stronger souls may go without food altogether this day, but such painting is work enough for women."

Margerite awoke before dawn on Easter Sunday. Lying beneath the warm bedclothes in the dark, she could hear the soft sounds of Rose's feet whispering over the thick rugs - then something else, a soft mew and a deep purr. By the stove, a taper flared to light, its flame glancing bright from Rose's wide cheekbones and pointed chin.

The purr rose to a slightly louder miaow, followed by little wet chewing noises. Margerite sat up. Halfway down Eva's bed, Kriemhilt was curled about three little dark shapes, and the candlelight glistened off the last of the deep red afterbirth disappearing between her teeth; the cat's birthing-blood stained the fine linen of the bedcovers. Kobolt sat beside her with his tail coiled about his paws, watching with an air of fierce pride.

"Oh, Kriemhilt," Margerite sighed. "Eva, wake up!"

Eva opened her eyes sleepily as Rose lit the rest of the candles, then pulled herself carefully out of bed and knelt down beside the cat. "Kriemhilt, love, let me see them," she crooned. "What beautiful kittens they are - have you more in there? Yes, they are perfect, lovely little cats." She kept murmuring nonsense as she picked up each kitten in turn, looking beneath their tiny tails. "One boy and two girls, I think...Is that another coming?"

Though Margerite dreaded the apologies she would have
to make for the ruining of the Bishop's bedclothes, she could
not help smiling. But the dawn-tide Mass would soon begin,
so, regretfully, she had to tell Eva to leave the cat to her
birthing.

"That is a good sign for this Easter, is it not?" Eva asked
as Rose helped her into the deep golden shift and rose silk
overdress that Cardinal de Grenville had given her. "Even
our cats know that it is time for new life."

Margerite was about to answer in kind, but something
stopped her: she could not help feeling that not all things
that were brought to light must be good. And we have
secrets enough that are best concealed...She thrust the
thought away, turning her eyes instead to the bits of gold
leaf glittering from the bowl of painted eggs on the table.
Yesterday the Bishop had blessed them, beaming down
on her as though he were truly pleased to see that she and
Eva were taking such joy in the Easter customs; today, they
would be given out at his table - and then we shall see what
virtue is truly in them.

Margerite washed her hands and face in the bowl of warm
rose-scented water that her serving maid had provided
them. Though she did not speak aloud, the words of
cleansing went through her mind like flickers of blue flame,
and it seemed to her that she could feel the incantations
full-shaped even in the fragmentary phrases. I exorcise thee,
O Creature of Water...Asperges me, Domine, hyssopo, et
mundabor...She could feel the familiar Easter excitement
rising in her, the surety that the time of darkness and
sorrow was over, that the sun would soon ascend in glorious
brightness just as Christ had ascended from the dank stone
of His tomb.

So thinking, she wiped Wolfram's face with a damp linen towel. He let out an indignant squeal at the first touch of the water, but soon quieted, staring wide-eyed up at his mother. "The winter storms are over, my little son," Margerite murmured to him, a strange relief spreading through her at her own words. "The night is over, the day is come, and you are still here and safe in spite of all."

Carefully she dressed her child in his new shirt, the white wool gleaming against his pale skin and his golden hair shining bright above it. Wolfram's little fingers plucked hopefully at the hem as if he meant to unravel the garment, but she had cast it on tightly with a stitch that was very much like braiding, proof, at least for a while, against her son's inquisitive tugging.

The great chapel of the Bishop's palace was nearly full when Margerite and Eva entered it, the dawn light shining clear through the stained-glass Crucifixion above the white-draped altar so that the blood from Christ's wounded hands and feet glowed like rubies and a ray of gold streamed through the halo about His thorn-crowned head as if to show God's blessing made manifest on that holy morning.

Great white lilies adorned the niches of the church; the candles burning all about the walls glowed softly beneath the brightness of the windows. Gottfried and Arnmut were already in their places in the front row, next to Father Etienne and the priests of the Inquisition. Like the women, the two knights were dressed in the finery they had worn to the Papal Mass in Avignon; and as she knelt on the padded rail beside Gottfried, it seemed to Margerite that she could hear the faint sound of singing as though she were listening to a hymn uplifted in the distance.

Wolfram squirmed in her arms, getting one hand free and pointing up to the stained-glass window. "Pre'y!" he said. "Light!"

"Yes, my sweet, but you must be quiet now," Margerite whispered to him. "Hush, and be good." She did not know, in truth, whether it had been wise to bring her son - but after all that had passed, she could not bear it if he did not receive the Easter blessing. And would to Christ it were only the darkness that I feared for him; but there is, there must be, some knowledge in his soul that this light is different from the light of the Order...

A hush fell over the chapel for a moment. Then, in the silence, the clear boys' voices rang out from the choir, their harmony shivering through stone and coloured glass as they sang the words that were silent all through the mourning-time of Lent.

"Alleluia, alleluia..." Margerite caught her breath, her heart uplifted and pierced at once by the beauty of the renewed Easter rejoicing and her misgivings gone in a single moment: her soul was clean from last night's Confession, as it had not been for too long, and it seemed to her that she could feel the high pure sound of the singing, the sweet scent of the incense, shining through her body as though she were a clear pane of crystal in the light of the rising Sun.

As Margerite entered the Bishop's dining hall at midday, her mouth began to water at once: she could smell the rich scents of roast meat, of pastries made with eggs and milk, and her stomach tightened with a dizzying craving for all those good foods that the Lenten abstinence had denied her. Rose trailed behind, setting the basket of painted eggs on the table in front of her; a similar basket stood by Gottfried's place, and to Margerite's surprise, the young knight actually smiled shyly at her as she sat down beside him.

"I made this one for you," Gottfried said, handing her an egg. Margerite drew in her breath as she looked at it. Nearsighted as Gottfried was, and unpracticed at so many things away from the field of arms, she had expected his painting to be clumsy.

But the egg he had made for her showed the Virgin holding Her Son, done as finely as any illumination Margerite had ever seen; some of the detail-work on the faces of mother and child was so delicate that her own eyes could hardly take it in - and, in startlement, she realized that Gottfried's golden-haired Christ-Child looked very like Wolfram. Though the knight's spoken Latin might be imperfect, his writing was both precise and beautiful: between Maria's twining five-petaled roses, he had neatly scribed the words AVE MARIA, GRATIA PLENA.

"Thank you," Margerite said. And she knew, and was sure Gottfried understood, what she was thanking him for: the gift itself, but more, the prayer behind it - his prayer and his avowal of trust, that Wolfram was yet untouched by the Powers of Darkness which had assailed the child so greatly in his short life.

In their turn, Margerite and Eva began to give out their eggs as more of the Bishop's household and guests took their places. Margerite glanced covertly at the ones Eva was handing over, but she could not see the first one the girl had painted, and wondered again what Eva had done with it, or meant to do.

Bernhardt received his egg as though she had given him a precious jewel, turning it over in his hands and staring at it in wonder. "This is as fair a gift as I could have asked," he murmured. "I fear that I did not think to paint one for you, for my mind has been less on such joyous things than, perhaps, it should have been."

Margerite laid her hand on the place where his ring nestled hidden between her breasts, and a faint smile touched Bernhardt's lips. "May this day bring resurrection of all our hopes," he said quietly.

At last, screwing up her courage, Margerite took the egg she had decorated for Father Kerlinger, approaching the grim-faced Inquisitor as he made his way to his seat. "Happy Easter, Father," she said, holding it out to him. "May Christ bless you on this joyous day."

Father Kerlinger's dark brows went up as he regarded the painted egg in Margerite's hand, and it seemed to her that his stern mask of age softened with the widening of his steely blue eyes. He took it from her uncertainly, as though he were receiving a goblet of wine that he did not wholly trust to bear no poison in its depths, his thin lips pressing together as he and read the words that she had written upon it.

"A noble thought," he said at last. "Few of those whom I have questioned - even so informally as I have questioned you - would think to pray so."

"Even the best among us may be aided by prayer, Father," Margerite replied boldly. "And Christ has called you to a task of difficulty and danger. Why, then, should I not have remembered you on the day of His victory?"

For the first time, Margerite saw the Inquisitor smile, and his pale azure eyes warmed upon her. "That is well-said, Gräfin. As you bless, may you be blessed."

And, Margerite thought in surprise, if I had begun by thinking of you more as an ally, if one in whom I could not confide most of what I know, instead of an enemy whom chance had put in Christ's host beside me, might this past month have gone better for all of us? Or was it only through the use of the Art to invoke Christ's will more clearly, that your heart softens where it was hard before?

The first dishes the Bishop's servants brought about were small omelets, tinted green with tansy-juice; the tart flavour brought the juices to flowing faster in Margerite's mouth, whetting her appetite for the next course. After the omelets, the serving-men carried in four great platters on which whole roasted roe-deer nestled in beds of thin fresh onion-shoots, the velvet of their new-springing prick-horns covered in gleaming gold leaf; with them came bowls of a rich ruddy-brown sauce.

It took Margerite some effort to sit still as the Bishop's carver sliced the steaming meat free from haunch and loin and back, but she managed to wait politely as the silver trays were carried about and Gottfried cut her portion into dainty pieces for her. The tender meat almost seemed to melt away to nothing in her mouth as she chewed, and she had to remind herself that there would be a good many more courses to come, lest she risk disgracing herself by eating too gluttonously at first.

Still, Margerite was not the only diner who had more care for the Easter meat than for conversation at that meal; even Bishop Otto, who normally talked as expansively as he ate, was almost silent in his attention to the feast. The roe-deer were followed by young squabs, their dark flesh sweetened with a stuffing of figs, and each bird surrounded by an honour-guard of four little wine-seethed thrushes; then uncased sausages of ground pork cooked with eggs and cheese and basted with a sweet, spicy batter to be carried golden-brown and hot about the table.

After that came a cook's jest of which Margerite had heard, but which she had never seen: yolk-gilded capons done up as pilgrims, each bearing a roast lamprey as a staff. Glazed suckling piglets garlanded with primroses were borne in next, and then dishes of saffron-yellow pudding with fresh violet-petals scattered across their golden surfaces, and pastries made with eggs and milk and cheese. By the time the servants carried about the platters of thin sweet wafers dusted with a heavy snow of ground white sugar, Margerite felt replete as she had not been since leaving Avignon, comfortably heavy and satisfied.

The Bishop dipped his fingers in his bowl of scented water to wash the lingering stickiness of the sweet wafers from them, then dabbed his chin with his napkin. He seemed about to speak when the door opened and two men in armour, grimy and disheveled from long travel, walked in.

At first Margerite did not recognise the young man who staggered to his knees before the Bishop to press his lips to the amethyst ring: his face was pinched and gray, the copper of his helm-matted hair tarnished dark by grease and dirt. Then, looking closer, she saw the scar twisting Georg's homely features; his honeyed tenor voice was rough with exhaustion, but still unmistakable.

"Your Grace, I beg your forgiveness for coming before you so, but we have ridden hard because there is a matter that can wait no longer, and I know not where to seek help, if it be not at your hands."

Bishop Otto's wide brow furrowed alarmingly as he stared down at the youth. "You are... yes, Georg von Schwarzenfels. Rise, and tell me what brings you here in such a state on this holy Easter Sunday."

Georg's back straightened as he stood, but Margerite could see that he was beginning to sway from tiredness. "Your Grace, if I may, I would speak privily with yourself, Father Etienne, and the Gräfin von Fürstensee, for it may be that this is a matter not best known to all."

Christoph, Margerite thought with horrid certainty, even as the Bishop nodded and rose from his seat. "Come with me. Etienne, Gräfin, if you would?"

Bishop Otto led the three of them through the halls to a chamber Margerite had not seen before, a room with large windows of clear glass to give a good light for reading or writing. There were several wooden chests about the walls, and a sheaf of parchments was stacked neatly on the table beside two books with gilt-embossed covers.

"Now, young Georg," the Bishop said, seating himself behind the table and lacing his fingers together. "What have you to say?"

"Your Grace, Herr Christoph von Fürstensee, the knight
to whom I am sworn as Knappe, is possessed by a demon,"
Georg answered bluntly. Margerite pressed her lips together,
but did not dare to speak; surely Georg would not have the
sense to betray what knowledge they had, how long it had
been...

Bishop Otto frowned darkly, his thick raven eyebrows
drawing together until they nearly met above his nose.
"That is a most grievous charge, and scarce one that is easy
to credit: you did well not to speak it in the dining hall. But
what makes you think that this is so?"

Margerite thought that she herself would have needed to
steel her spine against the Bishop's blue glare; she expected
Georg to quail, but instead he sat straighter, meeting Otto's
gaze full-on.

"A month and two weeks ago, Herr Christoph began
to rave and curse at those around him, and spoke such
blasphemies to Father Michael as drove that priest from
his hall. Most folk thought it was ill-temper in wine, for he
had drunk deeply and been out of sorts all day. But when
everyone save the servants had left, I stood beside him as
a Knappe ought, and there was a stench of brimstone and
decay about him that put me in fear. Then he struck me
when I did not fill his cup quickly enough, and his hand
left a blister upon my cheek. I prayed in my heart then,
being afraid, and he knocked me down again with a blow
that flung me halfway across the hall. After that, it seemed
as though he came to himself again; yet he was taken by
another such fit that Sunday as soon as he heard the bell
ringing in our chapel, and shouted orders that the clapper
be cut from it. And..." Georg lowered his eyes for a moment;
Margerite saw the muscles in his cheeks working, pulling on
the long scar that slashed the side of his face.

"The night before your messenger came, he did a violence to me that no man should do to another, and injured me much against my will. Therefore I should have left in search of your aid that same day, though I am grateful that the Inquisition's summons came so that I should not seem renegade to my oath, even when the vow had been broken so grievously on his part - or rather, by the creature of Hell that dwells within him, for I do not believe that what took place was by any will of Herr Christoph's own."

Bishop Otto sat motionless for a time, even as Margerite's own heart raged against her. This was by my fault - O Christ, O Maria, why did I let you stay in Burg Fürstensee? I should have known that my arts would not be strong enough to protect you against all bodily harm. She wanted to go to Georg, to embrace him, but her guilt fettered her in sharp-edged chains; she remembered, all too clearly, how it was to be thus defiled - and how much worse for Georg, to have suffered it as he had!

"Etienne," the Bishop said, his mellow deep voice strained as though there were a small bone caught in his throat. "This is not a matter in which I can make a judgement; I must trust in your advice again."

Father Etienne's finely-chiseled lips had gone white as Georg spoke, and his long fingers clenched; he, too, Margerite guessed, must be thinking that he might have done something to prevent what had happened, if only he had known - or if he had chosen differently before, when it came to a question of deciding between Christoph and Bernhardt.

"My advice," he answered tightly, "is that I and my assistants must ride for Burg Fürstensee as swiftly as we may: too much time has passed already. Your Grace, I shall need your aid in convincing the good Fathers of the Inquisition that they have had long enough to question the Gräfin and her companions, and that they may not linger over Georg as they have with these others."

Bishop Otto's eyes squinted shut for a moment; his florid face seemed to sag, an unhealthy undertone of gray stealing across it. "Etienne, what evils have been loosed in this world of late? Are not the sins of men enough, that these... incomprehensible abominations should take place as well? I could almost curse the day when you came to seek into matters at Schloss Niederwald, did I not know that you were but the physician who must open the festering wound in order to cure it. Yet until you brought Ortlieb's wain to me, I would not have believed in such things." The Bishop passed the back of his hand across his broad clammy brow, then let his head droop down. "And to hear of this on Easter, of all days! Is the world truly coming to an end, as we feared during the Death?"

"None may know the hour God has appointed for that," Father Etienne answered. "Nor would I have wished this upon you; but Christ knows what each soul must bear. Yet now I must ask you again: Your Grace, will you give me the help I need?"

"I will give it."

"Gräfin Margerite and I shall tend to Georg, then, and leave you to deal with Father Kerlinger and his companions. I trust we may command your servants as we need, that we may ride out tomorrow?"

"As you will," Bishop Otto said wearily.

A chamber was arranged for Georg swiftly enough, a wooden tub brought in and the Bishop's servants commanded to heat water for his bath. Though Margerite dreaded what more Georg would have to say - he would be within his rights, she thought painfully, to curse them all - she knew that she could not refuse to listen: if they were to face Azruzor again, she would have to know all that had taken place. Father Etienne poured out a measure of aqua vitae for the young man; Georg drank it gratefully, and though he shuddered at the strength of the draught, Margerite could see a little colour returning to his face under the travel-grime. He turned to Margerite.

"Does Eva live yet?" he asked, his sweet voice husky. "It... the demon told me that Nikolaus was no longer bound by your orders, for the Light-Bearers had full leave to slay you and all with you, excepting only your son, if they could take him."

"She lives, and is well," Margerite assured him. "But you...O Georg, I am sorry!"

"It was my choice to stay with my knight," Georg answered. His face was set in a look of grimness such as Margerite had not seen upon it before, furrows of determination graven deep about his wide mouth. He was, she realized, no longer the boy he had been, but a man in his own right - as he had just proven by taking the decision to reveal Christoph's possession upon himself. "And I suffered but a short time, whereas Herr Christoph has been bound by that... that thing for more than three-quarters of a year now."

Father Etienne grimaced slightly. "It were better if I had not believed that another could do my duty there while I dealt with matters here. Now I shall make that good, as best I may. I would not cause you more pain by choice, Georg - but if we are to free Herr Christoph, I must know all that has taken place, and be aware of how much harm his demon has done."

Looking steadily into the priest's eyes, Georg said, "It is my belief that Nikolaus means to convince the folk of Burg Fürstensee that his brother has gone mad, so that when Graf Heinrich finally dies, he may take rule there unopposed. As I told the Bishop, Christoph raves and blasphemes, and his seeming fits were coming ever more quickly on the heels of one another. Before I left, I saw to it that Ritter Ludwig set a guard about Graf Heinrich's bed, for it would have surprised me little if Nikolaus directed his demon at last to slay the Graf, that Christoph and Graf Heinrich be removed from lordship together."

"That was well-done of you," approved Father Etienne.

Margerite said, "Georg, I owe you a great debt, that I do not know how I can repay, for it seems to me that you have likely saved the lives of my husband and stepson, and preserved Burg Fürstensee. But if we win through here..."

Georg shook his head. "Margerite, you can repay me with your aid in exorcising Christoph. Then I shall have fulfilled my duty as Knappe, and when Azruzor is thrust back into Hell, that shall be a fit revenge for what I have suffered at his hands as well. After that...I shall no longer stay at Burg Fürstensee after my knighting, but return to Schwarzenfels." There was a coldness in his sweet voice as he spoke, like honey poured over snow. Margerite remembered how Christoph's demon had spoken to her: she, prepared in her mind by the Black Book, had been little disturbed by its obscenities - but Gottfried had been driven nearly to his death by Azruzor's words.

"Georg," Margerite said gently, "what did the demon tell you?"

Georg's homely scarred face contorted suddenly into the mask of a snarling gargoyle. "Things that I would have given almost anything in the world not to know!" he answered fiercely. "I have soiled myself thus far for Christoph's sake, but I shall be glad beyond telling to be free of - those I had trusted with my life and soul." His voice cracked, and a single drop of water oozed from his eye, creeping slowly down his dirty cheek until it caught the smooth track of his scar.

"Let us have it out now," Father Etienne said, his voice stern. Georg shook his head, glaring up at the priest.

Father Etienne regarded him for a time, his highboned features cool and distant. "If you believe all that the demon said to you, then you shall be of less than no use in what we must do. Should that be so, you were better to stay here until you have recovered."

"It is my right to be there for the exorcism," Georg insisted.

"Not if your mind has already been broken by whatever lies or twisted truths Azruzor may have given you," Etienne told him implacably. "You have borne a greater burden than any of the rest, and it is not to be wondered at if you have fallen beneath it."

"I have not fallen!"

"Yet you would condemn companions who have fought and bled beside you on your enemy's word? I had thought that a Knappe would at least have learned a little more of strategy than that."

Georg drew in a deep, sobbing breath, wiping his eyes with his hand and smearing muddy tears across his face. "I was alone there, and, dear Christ, it was so hard to bear." The young man's voice shook, and Margerite could see the trembling of his hands; then the words poured out of him in a great gush, like a gout of pus spurting from a green-swollen wound.

"He said of you that this was all a game of politics to you, that you had chosen to aid Herr Bernhardt and let Christoph languish because you would have the ear of the Landgraf of Niederwald - that we were no more than pawns on your chessboard. Herr Bernhardt was a mercenary of the Order; I do not know how, but it seemed to me that the demon showed me how he had burnt women and children alive in their houses, laughed with his comrades at the death-throes of a priest kicking on the end of a spear, raped and tortured and robbed the dead. He told me of the filthy rites in which Eva had taken part, and warned me that she was a slut, that she had lately shared her bed with Arnmut. And he said that I was lucky to have escaped from Gottfried's clutches, that if he had not had Arnmut as a Knappe to...to abuse, that he would surely have done worse to me than Azruzor himself did. And that I know was not a lie, for I had heard others speaking of them. And..." Georg stopped, his scar flaming bright with the rush of blood to his cheeks.

"Go on," Margerite said, the words dropping like stones from her tongue. "What did he say of me?"

Georg dropped his gaze, and when he spoke again, his voice was muffled. "He told me about Wolfram."

Margerite breathed deeply. The Easter feast roiled heavy in her belly now, and for a moment she feared that she would spew it up.

"And how much of this do you truly believe?" Father Etienne pressed.

"I...forgive me, Father, but I do not know...When I was by myself, I believed it all; it was as though I was in a dark dream, where I could not remember anything clearly. I know that some of it is true: I know that the Order of Light-Bearers forced Eva to evil things, and that Herr Bernhardt was a Free Soldier - and that Gottfried and Arnmut have an, an unnatural relationship."

"Georg, did you not share a chamber with those good knights all the way from Niederwald to Fürstensee?" Margerite reminded him. "And in that time, I would wager that you did not see Ritter Gottfried so much as look lustfully at either yourself or Ritter Arnmut, let alone do anything in the least improper."

"No; he was always careful to turn his back from modesty even when one of us was using the chamber pot," Georg admitted. "Had it not been for Azruzor, I would have said that the tales were all lies, but...I was afraid, and after what the demon did to me..."

"It was not only once, was it?" Father Etienne asked softly.

Georg shook his head.

"You need not be ashamed, for there are few who could have withstood such torments as long as you have. I will not tell you to put the demon's words from your mind altogether, for he will only renew your doubts when you face him. Rather, you must sort out for yourself what is truth and what falsehood - and what is truth besmeared with words that make foulness out of what might be fair."

"It is true," Margerite added, "that Eva slept in the same bed as Arnmut on our way from Avignon, just as Gottfried and I shared a single bed, for it was necessary to disguise ourselves in order to escape the Light-Bearers' fury. But all four of us were in the same chamber, so I can swear to you that perfect chastity was kept by all, and the worst impropriety there was Ritter Gottfried's sharp elbow digging into my side."

Georg looked at her wide-eyed, hiccuping out a little surprised laugh before his face froze again. "And...Wolfram? Is what Azruzor told me true?"

Margerite's tongue froze in her mouth. She had not confessed this last thing to Etienne; she half-wanted to leap up, to flee in terror before the dread words could be spoken, yet she felt herself fettered to her seat. But, to her great relief, it was the French priest who answered, his voice firm and quiet.

"Wolfram is a child like any other. If the Order of Light-Bearers suffers delusions about him, that is no fault of his, or of Margerite's. None can be damned in the womb save by the sin of Adam, nor is any human being - or spirit; remember that the host of Hell were angels once - created without the capacity for both good and evil, though our foes would have us believe that it is not so, in order to lead us away from forgiveness and into despair."

Margerite knew that Father Etienne was speaking to her as much as to Georg, and she could have wept with gratitude, the more so when Georg shook his matted head.

"I have been weak, and a fool," the young man murmured.

"Not so," Etienne told him. "You have fought long and well against a foe beyond your power to overcome; and had we not sent rescue, you would still have freed yourself to seek out the aid that was needed. Such deeds call for both strength and wisdom, and there are many men who bear the belt of knighthood that would not have done as well as you have."

The Bishop's servants were bringing in buckets of hot water for Georg's bath now, and Etienne rose gracefully from his seat. "Wash, and rest a little. I shall see that food is sent to you, and then there are a few more things that we must speak of before you give your testimony to the Inquisition - pray Christ, the Bishop will manage to impress upon them that they must be done with you quickly!"

# Chapter Nine

When Margerite rose the next morning, she found a sheaf of parchments resting upon the table in her room. On top of it was a note, written in a careful and angular hand.

Gräfin von Fürstensee: here are the accounts of the testimony given by yourself and Eva von Bärenberg. Each of you should read them to ensure their accuracy and affix your signatures. If you have no further questions or statements to make, then our need of you is at an end and you are free to return to Burg Fürstensee. May Christ speed you and stand by you in your duties there. - Walther Kerlinger.

"Eva, awaken," Margerite called. Eva turned over, muttering something into her pillow; she had been awake late the night before, nibbling on meat and cheese pastries and cooing over Kriemhilt and her kittens - five now, little dark rat-tailed creatures sleeping comfortably beneath the warm drape of their mother's gold-dusted black tail.

Margerite had not been able to bring herself to tell Eva the details that Georg had recounted about his ordeal, for that was his to speak of or be silent about as he chose himself, but she guessed that Eva knew at least some of what might have come to pass from her own experiences with the Light-Bearers, and that there had been more in her mind than the pleasures of eating meat at last after Lent and playing with her cats. Still, the sooner she awoke, the sooner they could prepare to depart; and so Margerite called to her again, until at last Eva rubbed the sleep from her eyes and sat up on the side of her bed.

Margerite read the testimony carefully, lest some cunning turn of transcription should have made her betray herself in it. But what the Inquisitorial secretary had written was clear and straightforward, though, to her surprise, he had left out entirely the enquiries that showed suspicion of Margerite herself, save for a full rendition of how she had come to be serving at Schloss Niederwald.

Although the room was still cool with morning, Margerite found when she passed her hand over her brow in relief that a fine dew of sweat had dampened her skin - but, it seemed, she had been cleared in the minds of the Inquisitors. Nevertheless, she read what had been written a second time to make sure, and she noticed that Eva did as well.

"And there is another danger come through," Eva said with a sigh. "None too soon, either."

"Aye, but I fear there is worse ahead." For I failed to drive Azruzor from his stolen flesh twice, and what power over me will that give him when we meet again? Father Etienne warned me that the third time would be the worst...Even the strongest cannot overcome evil without taking some scathe from it, and my soul is already marked...

Eva set her jaw firmly. "I have no doubt that we shall conquer. Now I shall set Rose to packing our belongings, if you will take these back to Father Kerlinger, and see to it that our menfolk are prepared to leave as well: if we hasten, we can be gone before midday."

Georg was just coming out of the Bishop's library as Margerite reached it. Now that he was bathed and rested, Margerite could see the marks of his ordeal more clearly on him. His nose was set more askew, as though the blow of a fist had broken it, but its length and the stubborn jut of his chin no longer looked incongruous on his young face, the features that had once seemed mismatched grown into a look of grim strength, underscored by the pink scar ripping down from the knob of his cheekbone.

Georg's bright red hair had not been trimmed or cut for some time, straggling long about his shoulders, and Margerite could see the first red-gold glimmer of stubble upon his cheeks: though he had been a youthful fifteen, he looked older than Gottfried now, with the first lines already furrowing his forehead and tracing fine about his eyes. Such a change, in less than four months! Margerite thought.

"I have given and signed my testimony, and the good Fathers assure me that they are finished with the rest of you as well," Georg said briefly. "Are the men of the Bear's Paw still with us?"

Margerite nodded.

"Then, by your leave, I shall tell them to make ready."

Margerite nodded again, her eyes stinging. There was something in the Knappe's blunt curtness that reminded her of Bernhardt as she had first known him, his mistrust of her barely covered over by the requirements of his post - and the agony of his soul shrouded little more thickly by his rough Free Soldier's manner. "Yes, tell them to be ready to travel with all speed," she said. Georg bowed briefly and hastened away.

The Inquisitors were waiting in their accustomed places, but Father Kerlinger rose and bowed to Margerite, his rawboned frame clumsy in the courtesy. "Good morning, Gräfin. I trust you found the transcription accurate?"

"I did indeed, Father, as did Frowe Eva."

"That is well. You may, perhaps, wish to know that your accounts have been corroborated by several of the servants from Schloss Niederwald."

Margerite raised an eyebrow. She had not known that any of the Schloss Niederwald folk had yet been interrogated - but even a Landgraf, she supposed, could not refuse to let his servants answer an Inquisitorial summons. "I am little surprised, for I answered as truthfully as I could, but it is kind of you to tell me."

The priest made a small gesture of negation. "It seems that you have, indeed, done a great service to Christ, albeit in a most irregular manner - as is," he added, his dark brows drawing close over his piercing blue eyes, "typical for Canon de Dion. But I understand that you are going home to great peril, and I would give you my blessing."

"I will receive it most gratefully, Father," Margerite replied. She knelt before Father Kerlinger; the touch of his hand was rough and warm on her head as he blessed her.

"I shall pray for you in this endeavor. Be careful of Canon de Dion, for I am not yet entirely convinced that all his methods are truly within the scope of the Church. But perhaps, after all, you do not need my warning, for you seem both intelligent and well-taught in matters of piety." The corner of his thin mouth quirked. "It is a pity that God saw fit to make you a woman, for otherwise you might have done well in the Inquisition. Godspeed, Gräfin."

As the company mounted their horses by the gate, it seemed to Margerite that she felt a strange sense of doubling: the oak trees lined along the pathways rustled green with spring leaves, the first flowers shone around the bright water of the pools, and yet she could not shake the memory of mounting up, just so, before leafless trees and icy water - Is it only that I am leaving Bernhardt one more time? she wondered.

But the falcon-necklace gleamed at her throat now, her protection still against the seeking eyes of the Order of Light-Bearers, and no longer weighted by the sorrow of its return; beside her, Father Etienne sat comfortably upon his great black steed, and it seemed to her that she could feel the unseen power of his presence wrapping about them, yet another fortress wall to keep her foes away.

"May I aid you to mount, Gräfin?" Bernhardt asked, striding towards her. Margerite did not bother to hide her smile of delight as his hands went about her waist, lifting her to the saddle with gentle strength. But the glimmer of happiness fled swiftly, for a dark furrow creased his brow, and she could see the worry in his brown-flecked green eyes. "I take it ill," he said softly, "that I may not be with you in this. You have faced too many dangers without me already, and too often it has been for my sake; I would come with you, if I could."

"Pray to Mother Maria for me, and for us all," Margerite replied. She thought then to assure Bernhardt that she would be well-protected by the knights and soldiers who would be with her - but she could not say that, for it would sound as though she did not need him. "I shall be the stronger in this for knowing that your thoughts are with me."

"My thoughts, and all my heart," Bernhardt murmured, his lips barely moving, so that it seemed to Margerite as though he spoke with his mind as much as with his breath. "But at least we shall be together in the last battle, if Christ bring us both safely through what lies between now and then."

"Let it be so...I shall send word as soon as I can, and do you the same."

Bernhardt bowed his head before Margerite, clasping her hand in both of his own. His lips brushed over her riding-gloved fingers, sending a delicious shudder through her body at the faint warmth. *O Maria, I am not made of stone, and it has been so long...* "Fare you well and safely, until we meet again."

As they set out, it hardly seemed to Margerite a fit day for beginning such an undertaking as they were travelling towards. The April air was deceptively warm, only a soft breeze stirring the green shoots of grain in the fields; Etzel gambolled by the hooves of Gottfried's horse, as white and furry - and nearly as large - as the sheep grazing by the road with their young lambs frisking beside them. Wolfram was in a lively humour, pointing at everything they passed and shouting out names or giggling with delight; Kobolt lay draped before her saddle-cantle, while Kriemhilt and her five kittens rode in the basket that Gottfried's Pyrenean bear-hound had outgrown.

Behind her, Margerite could hear the men of the Bear's Paw talking and laughing as they rode; once Paul's unmistakable voice shouted, "Are you trying to tell me there's an hundred countries in the world?", and another man replied, "Pay up, he's won the bet!"

But Georg rode at the fore of their company, flanked by Gottfried and Arnmut; though all the men, save for Father Etienne, were fully armoured - Landgraf Gerhardt would surely not attack them now, with their comings and goings known to the Bishop and the Inquisition, but none of them would count themselves safe on the road - Margerite could see how stiff the Knappe's back was, and tell that Gottfried was keeping a wide distance from him.

*Because of what Georg is thinking about him?* Margerite wondered. *Or can he see something that I do not: has Georg been marked by the demon? I had hoped that my wardings would protect him from that, at least, if I could not save him from bodily harm.* Father Etienne, too, seemed troubled; at least, he was staring cooly into the distance, letting his reins hang slack in his hand and guiding his black horse with only the slightest pressure of his knees, as though his thoughts were altogether elsewhere. After a time, his silence began to weigh on Margerite's ears more heavily than another's words, and she said softly, "Father, what are you thinking on?"

Etienne turned his head towards her. The rolled brim of his canon's hat cast a shadow across his face; only his pale blue eyes gleamed from its shade. "Upon whom I should have with me when we exorcise Christoph. You and Gottfried, at the least, must be there, since you have both faced it already and failed to drive it forth; but that will make the task the harder. As for Georg - he did not try to master the demon, but it has grievously wounded him, so that he must overcome it as well. But I shall not deceive you: I am not at all sure that our strength will be equal to the task of casting it out."

Margerite drew her breath in sharply, tightening her arms without thought around Wolfram so that he squealed in protest. "Why not?"

"Because if one of us falters, then it may well have the victory. We could drive it from Christoph's flesh, only to have it house in any of you that it has marked. And again, for Christoph to be freed, he must truly will his own freedom - and I do not know for certain what it was that led him to give his first consent, nor how long he was vulnerable to it. But that is often a matter that an exorcist must have faith in overcoming. What worries me more is the failed attempts that have already been made, for you cannot imagine how much stronger that will make the demon against both yourself and Gottfried. Further, there are dangers of both body and soul to all of us who take part in the exorcism, and to Christoph most of all. He may never be as he was before, and there is no saying what harm may be done to the rest of us in the struggle."

"Are you trying to frighten me, Father?" Margerite asked quietly. "I assure you, I am aware..."

The little muscles of Father Etienne's square jaw tightened beneath his close-cropped beard. "You are not! Margerite, you have a great deal of inborn ability, and you have developed a respectable skill in using it; God's grace was truly with you in bringing you forth from the Order's stronghold...but you do not yet know what it is to face a demon unconstrained by any will but its Master's.

The Order of Light-Bearers, for all their evil, are human; thus far, Christoph's demon has been bound to some degree by Nikolaus' magic, but when the exorcism begins, all that will cease, and you will see it in its naked damnation. You have met Father Thomas, and he is one of the fortunate. His body was broken in his last struggle with a creature of Hell, but his soul does not seem to have been seared in the way that often happens.

I have known other exorcists who lost the use of a sense, or their joy in life - or faith and hope, until their hearts grew weary of beating and their lungs of breathing." A gray cast seemed to creep beneath the French priest's sallow skin as he spoke, his aristocratic features hardening until he seemed remote as a mountain dimly glimpsed through a distant haze of rain.

Margerite swallowed hard, trying to clear the gummy thickness from her mouth. "But what can we do?"

"Pray and cleanse our souls as best we can. And speak with Georg." Father Etienne's blue eyes flickered to the three men riding in front of them. "Of all of us, he is in the most danger. I spoke with him long last night, but Azruzor's poison has lodged deeply within him. Ritter Gottfried might aid by means of his gifts, but I do not know how Georg can be brought to trust him again, for it may be that the demon chose what harm to do him for the very purpose of breaking our fellowship. While Gottfried, I think, is not yet reconciled with himself..."

The priest sighed. "And though it seemed to me at the time that I made the right choice, no man truly has the wisdom to weigh one evil in the scales against another. I, too, have a failure against this demon to consider, and the fate of my friend James of Canterbury, just at the time when he was needed to aid, is much on my mind. Therefore, Margerite, I would appreciate it if you would keep your silence for a little time and let me think."

An angry retort came to Margerite's lips - she had said but a few words, after all, while Father Etienne had been talking a great deal - but she swallowed it down. Though nothing had been spoken of the matter, she knew that she was no longer in command of their company, and it little behooved her to go against the wishes of the one man who might be able to guide them out of this desperate crevasse.

Their company stopped at the same inn in Würfenstein where they had stayed before, and were greeted gladly by the balding innkeeper. "Will the same chambers suit you, noble frowes, good knights?" he asked. "I see you have fewer men-at-arms this time; there is enough space down here for all of them to bed."

"That will do well enough," answered Margerite, but she could see Georg glancing sideways at Gottfried with a momentary scowl on his face. Gottfried did not wince, but his thin body stiffened as though he were bracing against a heavy blow. "And if there is another room for our priest..."

"Of course, Gräfin!"

Margerite breathed an inward sigh of relief; she could think of no safer place for Georg, wounded of spirit and vulnerable as he was, than beside Father Etienne. If there may be any healing, to keep him from tearing our company apart, she thought, marking how Georg sat at a little distance from the rest of them when they were all settled down at the table, and did not so much as offer to cut Eva's meat for her. She had been afraid that Gottfried would go off his food again, but though he ate with his usual sparingness, he seemed willing enough to take his share of the good veal in cream sauce that the innkeeper had served up for them.

At least he is steadying himself for what we must face, as a knight should, Margerite thought, and saw the Ritter's faint nod at that. The further days along the road were no more comfortable. Georg's dark moodiness seemed to spread through the rest of the company like ink spilt into water; he spoke little, and when he did, his words were short and harsh.

It was little surprise that Etzel kept his distance from the young man, for Margerite was sure that the white bear-dog could scent Georg's hostility to his master easily enough, but she found herself more disturbed by Kobolt's sudden wariness - she could not put a name to it, but Georg's bitter words and pinched face seemed to give off something like a whiff of disturbing perfume.

With the good weather holding, their band had made excellent time by Saturday evening. "Tomorrow," said Father Etienne as they settled down for their supper in a small inn called the Laughing Horse, "we shall not travel, but rather shall spend the day in prayer and purification."

Georg's mouth dropped open, then snapped shut in sudden fury. "How can we waste a day like that? Do you mean to halt every Sunday, when we have such urgent work to do?"

Father Etienne's eyes flicked about, and he held up a hand to quiet the Knappe. "Soft, Georg. It will help little if we try to charge in without preparing our own souls as we must."

"What good will a few prayers muttered from so far away do?" Georg asked, his voice caught painfully between leaden misery and brittle-edged anger. Suddenly, the hair stood up on the back of Margerite's neck; she heard Kobolt's soft hiss by her feet, and Etzel's quiet growl by Gottfried's, even as Father Etienne slowly rose, his black-robed shape dauntingly tall in the shadows of the inn's candle-flames.

"Georg, Margerite, Eva, Gottfried," he said - quietly, but with a sharp snap of command in his voice that brooked no argument; his eyes seemed to gather in the meager candlelight like goblets of pale sapphire glass, shining down dauntingly at them. "Come with me now."

Margerite and Gottfried stood up at once, but Georg froze in his seat, the scar along his cheek darkening to virulent purple as the rest of his face paled. "I have said nothing wrong," he mumbled.

Father Etienne shook his head. "I wished to wait for this until...but never mind: it must be done now. Georg, you shall come along, willingly or not: I do not wish a brawl here, but if need be, I shall not hesitate to ask these knights, and so many of the Bear's Paw men as may be needed, to bring you."

Georg's wide eyes glanced from Gottfried to Arnmut. It seemed to Margerite as though she could smell the acrid scent of his fear, sharp as soured wine - and that something else that had been disturbing her, much stronger now.

"Georg," she murmured gently, "do not abandon your trust now, when it is most needed. It may be that we have failed you before, but it is our duty to make amends for that; and you must be sure of it in your heart, elsewise why would you have determined to seek us out for aid? Surely you know that we are not your foes, but the foes of that which has harmed you - and, I fear, is carrying out its work in you yet."

"No," Georg panted. "No, I am free of it - it is far away, it cannot touch me now..."

"Look at me, Georg," ordered Father Etienne. But the Knappe squeezed his eyes tightly shut, his head jerking convulsively away from the priest's gaze.

Gottfried's hand moved, a single quick gesture to Arnmut. In the next moment, the two knights were grasping Georg firmly, lifting him from his seat with his arms held behind his back.

"Up to my chamber, quickly," directed Etienne. "Matters are worse with him than I feared."

By the time Gottfried and Arnmut had dragged their struggling burden into the little room, a steady stream of curses was vomiting from Georg's mouth; but Etienne put his hand on the young man's sweat-matted red hair.

"Be still," he commanded, and abruptly Georg was, hanging limply between his two captors and glaring up at the priest. "Now, Georg, you must choose: choose between clinging to anger and despair, or opening your soul once more to Christ's mercy and trusting in Him again."

"Where was He when I needed His aid?" Georg asked bitterly. "I endured Azruzor's torments by myself, and my prayers did no good - no, nor the Gräfin's spells, either. And you have taken me as though I were an enemy, when I did no more than to ask why we should linger on the road; how have I earned this mistreatment?"

"You have not earned it, no more than one who is ill has earned the foulness of his medicine's taste." the priest replied. "And yet he must still take the draught if he is to heal. I knew that this time would come; I had hoped that it could be dealt with more gently, with the aid of our friend the Abbot, yet our strength here must suffice to root out the demon's touch on your soul."

"Others here have been more deeply touched by evil than I!" Georg protested. "It was not I who wore a Light-Bearer's ring, nor have I ever willingly taken part in their rites. Nor am I..." He broke off his words then, as if some remnant of courtesy still barred his tongue, but Margerite saw Gottfried's face whiten, the knight's gray eyes wide and dark in the shadowy room.

"This is no place nor time to turn against your friends, Georg," Father Etienne chided. "Can you remember nothing of their good?"

It seemed a simple question, almost rhetorical - but tears oozed from Georg's eyes, bright tendrils of tangled hair whipping back and forth over his face as he shook his head violently. "I...I cannot remember," he whispered, the words straining from his throat as though it were a reed-pipe half-blocked with mud. "I think...there must have been some reason, but I, I cannot..."

It seemed to Margerite that, even as Georg spoke, she could feel a dark veil drifting across her own soul, warping the shapes of her friends in her eyes. Eva, standing silently behind Georg, looked suddenly fat and dumpy, her rich golden hair washing out to a miserable mouse-brown and her low-cut dress showing the overblown breasts of a cheap whore; well-proportioned and handsome as he was, Arnmut's face took on a cast of brutish stupidity, like a long-beaten ox. Gottfried's features sharpened to wolfish ravenousness, and Father Etienne's remote composure seemed unbearably cruel, a light of stern malice in his pale gaze.

The room stank of foulness, a stench that seemed to underly everything, tainting the last taste of cheese pie in Margerite's mouth as though it had been cooked beside a festering dungheap. Her stomach roiled with nausea and fear; she wanted to run to Wolfram, to protect him, as Rose in her innocence could not, against whatever evil was in the minds of her companions, but even as she thought on him, she could not recall any trace of the childish beauty of his face - only the soul-searing light in Ruprecht's eyes as he had bound her.

"Christ preserve us from such delusions!" murmured Gottfried. As he spoke, the moment of horror passed from Margerite's sight, but she could see its shadow still lurking in Georg's eyes, like a dusting of dark powder across his glass-blue irises.

"Christ preserve us, indeed," Father Etienne agreed gravely. "Hold him firmly, for I must make ready."

Silently, the priest opened the chest in which he kept his ritual tools, bringing forth cup and brazier, salt and holy water, dagger and censer and wand and candle. Georg stared at him in fear; having seen, as it were, through his eyes for that brief moment, Margerite could understand his terror, but think of nothing she could do to calm him.

Mother Maria, lend Your help, she prayed silently, even as Etienne's flint clinked from steel and he spoke the first words of prayer, "I exorcise thee, O Creature of Fire...so that every kind of Phantasm may retire from thee and be unable to harm or deceive in any way..." The priest's candle-wick glowed to a burning ember, then, beneath his breath, leapt up suddenly, shedding its clear golden radiance throughout the room. But Georg closed his eyes, turning his face away.

"He sees it as clearly as I do, but he thinks it to be a creature of demonkind," Gottfried said. Georg's head rolled on his shoulders, so that he could stare up at the knight without facing Father Etienne's candle.

"How can you know that?" he asked wildly. "I said nothing...I...What are you doing to me?"

Margerite heard the breath sigh soft from the canon's lungs, and it seemed to her that she could feel some of the strain that trembled in the air easing, even as Father Etienne lit the coals in his censer and sprinkled incense upon it.

"I exorcise thee, O Creature of Air...Let all malignity and hindrance be cast forth from thee, and drive forth all the deceits of the Enemy, all the impurities and uncleanness of the Spirits of the World of Phantasm..."

Georg shivered, cowering, and Margerite thought of what Father Etienne had said of the lasting harm that demons could do to the minds of those who strove against him, even those who gained the victory in the end. Dear Maria, to live like that..! Kobolt chirped, rubbing against Margerite's skirts; for a moment his touch seemed sticky, as though her bare leg had brushed against the slimy skin of a newt, but then she felt the reassuring warmth flowing from him, even as the trails of smoke from Father Etienne's censer wove blue-gray trails through the candlelight.

Georg's pupils had shrunk to pin-pricks; now and again he tossed his limbs, but he seemed to have lost all his strength; Gottfried and Arnmut held him easily. "What are you doing to me?" Georg moaned again. Father Etienne went on calmly with his work, not pausing a breath in his prayers; but Eva came about to face Georg, though he flinched away from her touch.

"None here will hurt you," she murmured to him. "Will you not trust me, at least - knowing that I can do you no harm?"

Georg closed his eyes, as though he could not bear to look upon her, while Father Etienne intoned the words of blessing above the little bowl of glittering white salt, then raised his wand, walking about the room and tracing shapes in the air - figures of protection, holy names; Margerite recognised some of them, but not all.

"All of you," Georg whispered. "There was not one of you who is what I thought him to be, not one...everything I thought good is befouled, destroyed..."

Father Etienne went to each of them in turn, sprinkling a few drops of holy water upon their heads and making the sign of the Cross. As the water touched Margerite, it seemed to her that she could feel a cleanness and peace spreading out from it. Lastly, he blessed Georg, then carefully lifted the gold crucifix from about his own neck, laying it on Georg's chest and saying, "Now, in the name of Our Lord Jesu Christ: if any evil spirit has taken up dwelling here in the body of Christ's servant Georg, let it no longer be concealed, but make itself clearly known, doing no violence to those gathered here and obeying me in all things, though I am an unworthy servant of God."

Margerite realized that she was holding her breath, fearing what might happen; but the Knappe did not begin to moan or thrash at the holy symbol's touch. After a little time, Father Etienne nodded in what might have been relief.

"You are injured, but you still hold the citadel of your soul," he said to Georg. "And do not think that Margerite's wardings were without power, for they barred the way to the worst of the Foe's siege-engines: without that aid, you should long since have been possessed yourself.Yet, without further assistance, you shall not be able to hold out much longer; and you yourself must call for it, by Christ's mercy and His compassion. Else I can do nothing to help you, for you yourself are preparing the Foe's way in."

Georg's head came up at that, his wide mouth twisting into a snarl. "Why should Christ bother with me now?" he asked, his sweet voice jagged-edged and ugly. "He abandoned men to the Death, and now to these worse things that have come after it; I expect no help from Him."

At Georg's words, Margerite felt the tears falling from her eyes, their mineral taste sharp in her mouth as the waters of the faraway Marienbrunnen. "Mother Maria, help us," she prayed, her lips barely moving. "Holy Maria, Mother of God, pray for us sinners, now and at the hour of our death..." It seemed to her that she could feel the stifling dark pressure outside their little ring of brightness, starting to ooze in like black water through cracking stone; she expected that at any moment, Father Etienne would raise his wand or sword and speak a mighty incantation to strengthen their walls to impregnability. Yet the priest only stood there with his crucifix in his hand, staring down at Georg.

It was then that Margerite heard Gottfried's voice - hardly more than a singing resonance in her skull, as though she leaned her ear against the stone of a chapel resounding to a choir's full-voiced hymn. "None of us is ever wholly abandoned by Him, save according to our own choice. But each of us who has touched the one who wronged you has taken some harm: will you listen to me, Georg?"

"Mother Maria, give pity here, as You wept for Your son," Margerite whispered. "I failed Georg, but I pray You will not." Even as she prayed, it seemed to her that she heard Birgitta's voice saying, "Cherish your son while you may, for he shall grow up swiftly enough, and you cannot keep him in your wool-basket when he is a man...Even the love of a mother cannot turn a son's wyrd aside, in the end." She found that she was weeping so hard she could not speak, for it seemed to her that Georg's tormented features blurred into Ruprecht's finer-cut face, into Wolfram's...She had come closer to the Knappe, though she did not remember moving, so that her tears splashed down on his upturned face where he sagged between the two knights.

"None of us is without break or stain, but he lies who avows that is all," Gottfried was saying, and beneath the echoing soundlessness of his words, it seemed to Margerite that she could feel something more - a thread of pain drawn from her own heart, shining with the hurtful glitter of precious beads in the winter cold; a fiery whiplash across her back...no, not hers, but Eva's, and a taste of foulness in her mouth that she did not know how to spit out... the bite of fear sharpened by love, the despair of seeing an armoured back turning away in loathing; and Margerite did not know whether that was her own terror or Gottfried's... the acid-limned memory of a man's contorted face, the silent screaming of a soul trapped behind the clear glass of its own eyes, somehow mingled with the early lines of age on Georg's skin and the bitter knowledge of failed wisdom, failed trust...and distantly, the sight of blood cooling on a swordblade, its clotting darkness splashed brighter red from two sharp cuts searing, guilt-sliced, across her wrists; she had seen Bernhardt's scars...

Yet she could feel the pure water running across her face as well, washing her eyes warm and clear, trickling down over and around her body to soothe the ripping agony between her torn buttocks; and it seemed to her that she could scent roses fresh through the sweet frankincense as the last of the fetid stink decayed and was gone into clean earth. Georg's voice broke into harsh sobbing. Margerite could not make out what he was saying, but after a moment he found his footing on the floor, his breastplate grating on Gottfried's as he turned in the knight's arms to embrace him.

"Forgive me, that I doubted you, all of you...May Christ forgive me," Georg said through his tears at last. Margerite drew in a deep breath, wiping her own wet cheeks.

"Be assured that He does, as do we all," answered Father Etienne, and the rest of them murmured assent, taking it in turns, each by each, to clasp Georg briefly in their arms. "And forgive us as well, for Christ is beyond all error, but we failed you in our ways."

"Freely and gladly," said Georg. "Yet I see now that there is little that needs it. I had forgotten what Ortlieb was, though she showed it to me herself; and I feel again that there is hope for Christoph."

"May it be so," said Eva, a smile breaking over her tear-stained face. "O, Georg, faithful Knappe, will you bear my favour in this battle, until Christoph is free and I can give it to him?"

Georg bowed shakily. "That I shall gladly do, noble frowe." He staggered, and Gottfried moved in to catch him, helping him over to the bed where he sat down hard, Kobolt leaping up to rub against him and purr.

"Rest to strengthen your body, and prayer to strengthen your soul," Father Etienne advised. "We have won the first skirmish, as it seems, but we shall need all the time we have yet to make ready."

And this is why he did not summon steeds to bear all of us more swiftly, as he sent one to rescue Georg, Margerite thought. I would not have had the wisdom - and would have ended with Georg, as well as Christoph, within the grasp of the Foe.

"And do not think," the priest went on, his blue eyes hooded in the candlelight, "that this strategy that has served once will serve again, for that would be a sure trap. This night we have seen the spoor of our foe, and struggled heart with heart; in Burg Fürstensee, we shall see it again. Then neither skill nor strength, gift nor Art may prevail, but only be the means of betrayal, for the moment any one of us sets his own power against that of the demon, then we are lost." Etienne's gaze lingered on each of them in turn, and Margerite shivered as she imagined what they had felt, the short searing vision of each other's pains and failures and fears, tainted by the full blackness of damnation - the blackness of which Georg's despair had been but a thin shadow. "Tomorrow I shall begin to instruct you in the rites, for this night has proven to me what I suspected: for your own sakes, this cannot be my battle."

The air went out of Margerite in a sudden rush, her stomach clenching beneath the blow of fear. She struggled to calm herself, to speak as cooly as she had in her terror before the Imperator of the Light-Bearers. "If you are not to lead the exorcism, then who is?"

Father Etienne stared at her, the silvered wings of hair at his temple glittering blurred in her sight, as though something within her could not bear to look full at him while he pronounced his judgement. "You must, Margerite, with Gottfried as your chief assistant. And even now, I can tell you that only by Christ's grace can you prevail."

"But I am no priest, nor is Gottfried!" Margerite protested. "Surely only a priest can perform an exorcism?"

"By the rules of the Church, indeed. Yet - as you know, not all consecrations given by Christ are those of the Church; Father Kerlinger would hold this a great heresy, and indeed I should say it to few, for fear of the danger to their souls. Each of you has received a certain blessing already, and been called to battle directly against the power of Lucifer on earth, in a way that not many of the priesthood are. Yes, you are unworthy of this trial; but even as I am, no more and no less. And if it is needed, I shall be there to lend the Church's authority."

St. Walpurga's Eve passed while they were still on the road; it seemed incredible to Margerite, that no more than a year had gone by since she had given birth to Wolfram, only two since she had wedded Ruprecht. She wished with all her heart that she could look back on that wedding-day with joy, remembering the flowers and dancing, her delight and amazement at the towers of Burg Falkenstein; but the happiness of the young girl she had been seemed irretrievably tainted now by what she knew, by the memory of the gleaming amethyst on Ruprecht's finger even when he had lifted his hand to unbind and stroke her hair that night. And the one time she had lain in Bernhardt's arms, shaking with horror at what she had just seen and felt; and the weariness of Burg Falkenstein's siege...

O, that I had married such a boy as Ritter Wolfhart,
though he dwelt in a smaller fortress than my father's; I
should have been innocent still, rejoicing in children and,
Christ willing, a living husband. What joy have I had from
dressing in silks and velvets, or from men bowing and
calling me Frowe Gräfin?

Kobolt chirped in an offended manner, nudging Margerite
above the saddle-cantle, and at the same moment, Wolfram
began wailing in her arms, and she had to smile unwillingly.
She wished peace for Wolfram, but she would not have
traded him for a moment of it: better to have her heart
drawn by rack and tong in fear for him every day, than
never to have his chubby little fingers curling about hers on
the reins as she did now, or to have felt her heart's blood
transforming by bodily alchemy into the milk that he had
suckled from her breasts.

Yet, as the days of their travel wore on, Margerite marked
that they were all speaking less and less. She thought
that her companions were sunken in thought as she was
- remembering the days of their lives; recalling old sins,
perhaps, that might turn to fang them in the foot like a snake
crawling from a white-worn skull, or slowly questioning, as
she did, the worth of what they had endured. When words
were spoken among them, it was chiefly Father Etienne
drilling them on the rites and principles of exorcism: the
prayers that must be made, how a demon's logic must not be
argued with, whatever it said, nor must the exorcist think to
face it by his own strength.

Margerite found that hardest to grasp, for it went against
everything that had protected her before in dealing with
spirits of evil, when her unshakeable will had sustained
her; but the canon was firm, and implacable in giving her
penance for her pride. Gottfried, Father Etienne warned
strenuously against the heroism that had led him to dare the
Light-Bearers' storm for the sake of his comrades, and once
Margerite heard the priest quietly reminding her knight
that he could expect the demon to call out every sin he had
committed, of deed or thought.

Margerite did not know what Father Etienne said to Arnmut or Eva: they would be there only to restrain Christoph should he grow violent, but still the demon would do its best to harm them if it could. It was a little past two weeks into May when their band rode up to the castle of Georg's father, Graf Wolfgang von Schwarzenfels. Burg Schwarzenfels was well-named, for it stood high upon a dark crag in the middle of wide fields: no foe's army would come creeping upon it, and the banners of the knights riding out to meet the oncomers waved brightly in the wind.

"Halt, and name yourselves!" Graf Wolfgang's foremost knight shouted as he lowered his lance-tip, his voice muffled by the chain-mail hooked across his face beneath his gleaming bascinet. "Where are you going?"

"My father's men were not so suspicious before," Georg murmured to Margerite. "If you will, Gräfin, let me speak."

Margerite nodded, and Georg pulled off his helm, riding forward so that the Schwarzenfels knight could get a good look at him. "It is I, Georg!" he called to them. "And you should know me well, Ritter Thietmar, though it has been some months since we met last. With me is the Gräfin von Fürstensee; does my father not wish to make us welcome this night?"

The Ritter raised his lance again, riding to meet Georg. "You shall indeed be welcome here, for we had feared greatly since word came that you had been summoned by the Inquisition - and more word followed of how matters were at Burg Fürstensee. But it is no courtesy of mine to tell you such things: your brother Herr Konrad is within, and there will be time enough for you to speak with your father when he returns this even-tide."

The great hall in Burg Schwarzenfels was, perhaps, not so large as that at Burg Fürstensee, but it was more finely furnished: a keen eye with a thought to the season had chosen the tapestries of springtime riding and flower-gathering that ringed the walls with the same pale greens, golds, and whites blossoming in the gardens outside, and the polished tables bore no scattered marks from daggers and puppy-teeth as had those of Heinrich's hall.

Gräfin Anna sat placidly embroidering, but at the sight of Georg, the plump woman threw down her work and ran over to her son, hugging him with such enthusiasm that hairpins dropped from her green silk coif and it slithered askew on her red braids.

"Georg! Thank Maria, thank Christ, you are safe! My son, we had feared for you so!" she sobbed.

Georg closed his eyes, returning his mother's embrace. "I am safe, Mother," he reassured her. "I will not say all is well, for Ritter Thietmar's words make me think it is not; but as you see, I am here and whole."

Still clinging to her son, Gräfin Anna shouted for servants to bring refreshment for their guests, "And tell Konrad to leave his hounds and come here at once, for his brother is home!" She disengaged from Georg, dabbing at her eyes with the trailing blue silk of her sleeve. "Forgive me, Margerite, if I seemed slow to greet you - you poor thing, have you heard no news? Sit down, you and your knights and the good Father, there will be wine in a moment, and something for young Wolfram - is he weaned yet? My, how he has grown! - Did you come by yourselves? No, you could not have on such a long journey, surely you have some guardsmen?"

"They are outside by the stables, Mother. I have given orders for them to be seen to already."

As Georg spoke, a tall, broad-shouldered young man in a close-fitting doublet of somewhat dusty red velvet came in. His strong-featured likeness to Georg and Graf Wolfgang was clear to see, though his hair was dark and he wore a bushy moustache; Margerite remembered that Konrad was the second son, the tournament champion.

Konrad did not quite fling himself on Georg as their mother had done, but he moved with hasty grace to embrace his brother, as if to reassure himself that Georg was, indeed, back in the flesh. "It is well to see you again, Georg." He turned, bowing deeply to Margerite and Eva, with a polite nod of acknowledgement to Wolfram, cradled in Rose's arms. "And to meet you at last, Gräfin von Fürstensee, and the young Graf von Falkenstein. As for you, Frowe Eva, your beauty is far-famed, but surely even less in the telling than in the seeing. Ritter Gottfried, Knappe - no, Ritter now; forgive me - Arnmut, and..."

"Canon Etienne de Dion," Father Etienne supplied.

"Welcome, all of you, to Burg Schwarzenfels, and be welcome to stay as long as it pleases you. Though my father is out hunting, he should return by sunset; in the meantime, I am honoured to greet you." But Konrad's face seemed shadowed by more than the faint stubble-marks of a dark beard over his long jaw, and it seemed to Margerite that she could see the watchful tension in the heavy muscles of his shoulders, as though he held the weight of a lance poised for lowering.

It shall do us no good to delay this knowledge, she thought, and took a deep breath. "Herr Konrad, we are honoured by your welcome, and thank you for your hospitality. Now I would not be so rude as to speak of troublesome matters before we have so much as shared a drop of your wine, save that..."

"You need not be, for here it is," Konrad answered quickly; and indeed, the servants were already coming about with pitchers, so that Margerite had to fumble hastily to unloose her silver goblet from the cord that tied it at her girdle. Though unwatered, the sweet green-gold wine was weaker than those served in France, or at the Bishop's table; it reminded her, with a faint pang of homesickness, of the wines from her father's own vineyards.

When each of the guests had drunk, and host and hostess had pledged them in turn, Konrad settled back with a frown. "Now, Gräfin, have you heard no word of how matters have gone in Burg Fürstensee since you departed to ask prayers for your husband in Avignon?"

"Georg said that Christoph had been...ill," Margerite replied carefully, with a sideways glance at the Knappe, who sat rigid and tight-jawed in his chair.

"I fear that I must tell you worse than that. Not long after Georg's departure - and I am sure there is a story of some interest there, that my brother should be summoned as far as Niederwald by the Inquisition! - Herr Christoph is said to have run mad. As we have heard it, though I sorrow to grieve your heart with this, he made an attack on his own father; had it not been for Ritter Ludwig chancing to be nearby, and hearing the shouts of the servants, Graf Heinrich would have been slain in his bed by his own heir. Herr Nikolaus, or so we are told, has his brother locked up now to keep him from hurting himself or another, and has called in physicians from Freiburg, but there is no news that anything has availed. Graf Heinrich, it is said, lives yet, but he is no better than he was, and in the last message we received from Herr Nikolaus, he did not expect his father's life to be much longer, for he has rapidly been showing signs of failing. Now this is a sad homecoming, frowe, and I would ask you to forgive me for being the bearer of such news."

As we expected, Margerite thought sorrowfully - Thank Christ that Georg, hurt and troubled as he was, had the wit to ask Ritter Ludwig to guard Heinrich, that Christoph might not be freed only to discover such deeds on his conscience. It will be bad enough...But this was no time to think of such things.

"It is often a friend's duty to bring word to a friend, whether that word be good or ill," she said. "And I know that Heinrich counted all your family dear to his heart; better to hear from you than another...By the grace of God, as it happens, Father Etienne is a skilled physician; it may be that he can achieve what Nikolaus' healers could not."

"We shall pray for that most fervently," Gräfin Anna said, putting her goblet down and clasping her plump freckled hands tightly together. "Young Christoph was dear to us, as well..."

"My closest friend, when he was a squire here, though he is a few years older than I," Konrad broke in. "I know not what could have brought this illness about, for he was ever steady of mind."

"Herr Christoph was struck on the head at Burg Falkenstein, falling from a horse," answered Father Etienne. "It is my guess that his troubles now may stem from that wound, and if that is so, there is hope for his healing."

Margerite glanced sharply at the canon, but, as usual, Father Etienne's calm ascetic features showed no hint of whether he might be dissembling for Christoph's sake, or whether Christoph's injury might have led to his vulnerability...and Christoph had complained of headaches, touching his skull where he had been wounded...That was better than to believe that he had consented in any way to his possession, but she did not know if she dared hope for it. Yet Konrad's lips flickered in a faint smile of hope under his wide moustache, and Anna clasped her hands more tightly together.

"If that is so, Canon, it is the best news that has come to us in a long time!" Konrad said. "Tell me, is there any help we can give you?"

"Only prayer," Father Etienne replied.

Then Margerite noticed the gray cast over Gottfried's angular features, and the flicker of his hand as he finished crossing himself. She could not ask him what was wrong, but he spoke instead. "What of Ritter Ludwig?" he asked. "Did he - was he harmed in the fight?"

Konrad drew in his breath through clenched teeth. "Ritter Gottfried, I am sorry. I had forgotten that you were his Knappe. As we heard the tale, Ritter Ludwig would not let Christoph harm Graf Heinrich, but in his own turn he would not risk harming Herr Christoph, and so he was wounded, and died of fever a couple of days later...true to his oaths; he was a good knight."

Christ forgive me, that our last farewells were so brief! Pray for me, Ludwig, I should have thanked you better for all you taught me, Gottfried's silent voice whispered. Aloud, he said, "None could have done better than he, but would God I had been there to aid! And I was his second, though I pray the Herr Graf would not have begrudged me to the frowe Gräfin...Is it Ritter Dieter who commands the Burg Fürstensee guard now?"

Konrad tugged thoughtfully at one end of his moustache. "I am not sure. I thought I had heard something about his return to his family, an ailing elder brother or such. Herr Nikolaus will be glad to see you, in any case, for I gather that Christoph's...illness, especially after Ludwig's death, had much disheartened the folk of Burg Fürstensee."

"Indeed," murmured Gottfried. "Herr Konrad, Gräfin Anna, I thank you for the courtesy you have shown, but I would go now to your chapel if I may."

"Be free of this burg as if it were your own," Konrad told him, and Anna nodded assent, pushing her coif back into place on her coiled red braids. As if he were still Gottfried's Knappe, Arnmut followed the older knight out silently.

As promised, Graf Wolfgang came back a little before sunset, his huntsmen carrying the heavy body of a boar behind him. Though clearly delighted at Georg's safe return, he greeted their company with the same regretful welcome as Konrad had shown, but he, too, cheered at the news that there might be hope for Christoph's healing.

Margerite left it to Father Etienne to explain why Georg had received the Inquisitorial summons; she had thought that he would keep his usual close-mouthed counsel, but to her surprise, he recounted it in the same near-fullness that they had first given the Bishop of Niederwald. But when the matter goes to trial before Kaiser Karl, she reminded herself, everyone in the Holy Roman Empire shall hear of it, and it may be that no ally shall be wasted then. Graf Wolfgang listened incredulously at first, but by the end of the tale, he had broken into a full smile.

"I never thought that Bernhardt was guilty, you know," he said. "And if the woman was a witch - well, that explains everything, does it not?"

Margerite little liked agreeing with him, for the memory of the clammy sweat that had lain upon her brow and back as she had answered the questions of the Inquisition was still as close to her as the silken touch of her shift; but she could not doubt that it was true in this case. So she smiled, and said something, leaving Graf Wolfgang's other questions to Father Etienne, until Gräfin Anna enquired, "Will you stay with us for a few days so that Herr Nikolaus has a chance to make ready for your homecoming, or do you mean to go on tomorrow? We can send a messenger out now, if you like."

"Word has gone ahead of us already, thank you," replied Margerite. At least, she thought with a shiver, word that, as the demon told Georg, I am no longer counted among the host of the Light-Bearers, but as their enemy, to be slain if they can.

Then she thought on what the news might mean, that both the remaining castle knights of Burg Fürstensee were gone: the guard disoriented, with only Nikolaus to listen to, and he with a completely free rein throughout the castle...Danger of our souls and our lives both.

Gottfried nodded slightly as Margerite met his gray gaze, and she knew that he had thought on the matter already; Ritter Ludwig would have taught his Knappe not to lose his sense from grief. He nodded again, to the thought crossing her mind; she heard his voice in the stillness.

Better if we leave Wolfram behind. There is no telling when, or whom, we shall have to fight; but he shall be safe here.

Margerite thought about the three days of woodland road before them; thought of Nikolaus wandering free in the castle as they strove with Azruzor for Christoph's soul - for she could see no way to restrain him without accusation - and what if, in the crisis, they failed at last and left the demon free?

"There is one boon I would ask of you, though," Margerite said. "Would you be willing to take the care of my son Wolfram? But for a few days, all going well," she added hastily. "Yet, if Christoph has proven dangerous in his madness..."

"Most gladly, my dear," answered Gräfin Anna at once. "And very wise of you, too, though I wish it did not have to be so. Still, who knows but that he may come back here as a page or squire in happier times: young as he is, let us think of it like that."

They were barely out of sight of Burg Schwarzenfels the next day when Gottfried reined his horse in, trotting back to Margerite as Georg and Arnmut continued before.

"Is something amiss, Herr Ritter?" Margerite asked quietly.

"I think it will be well now to inform the men of the Bear's Paw that we may be facing battle soon. And, if you will forgive me, Frowe Gräfin..." Gottfried swallowed hard... "I have already told Jochanan of Herr Christoph, for he aided in healing me when, when I was in my first dismay from the demon. I would have him know fully what we face now, not least because there is no telling what more Nikolaus may have done since we were last in Burg Falkenstein. As for his commander Paul, if I recall correctly his words from when we first met, he has faced dark things before."

"Aye, that is so," said Father Etienne's dry baritone from behind them. "Jochanan would not be my first choice as a defender in the Art - no, Ritter Gottfried, not because he is a Jew, but because he is only half-trained in the Qabala and clumsy with words besides. Yet I have seen him and Paul the Bear fight most valiantly; and someone must be ready to command a defense of swords while we struggle against Christoph's demon. Do not look so surprised, Herr Ritter: I, too, was listening last night, and know what it means that the last of Graf Heinrich's guard commanders was sent away."

"One more time, is that it, Gräfin?" said Paul, grinning in the red-gold scurf of his beard when Margerite, Father Etienne, and Gottfried had explained their thoughts to him and Jochanan. "You know we're always ready to charge right into Hell behind you - begging your pardon," he added, with a swift glance at Gottfried.

"It may not be so far from that as Christian men should wish," said Gottfried; Margerite had not been watching him closely enough to know if he spoke those words, or only thought them, but the Bear ignored him cheerfully.

"There's a few of our lads should be there yet, and Jochanan's guns if the fighting goes outdoors, though I don't think you want us to use them in the castle. Tell me, Herr Ritter, how many of your guardsmen do you think you can trust?"

Gottfried frowned. "Before, I would have said every one of them. But Nikolaus would not have arranged for Ritter Dieter to leave without some reason, and he has arranged things so that he seems Graf Heinrich's rightful successor now - if I knew nothing of the truth, even I might follow him against a late-wedded Gräfin backed by a Free Company. Georg shall be better able to tell us how matters stand."

"Ill, I fear," Georg answered quietly when he had ridden back and the same question had been asked of him. "Nikolaus could not have chosen a more sure means to do his will: many of the men have forgotten the worm who lurked among his books, and remember only that Nikolaus first seemed his brother's right-hand man, then the lord who was cool-headed when Herr Christoph showed his first fits. The knights had known him longer and more closely, and were less sure of him, so that they, I think, would have listened to Ritter Gottfried. But among the others - there were also senior guardsmen who seemed less themselves than they had been."

Gottfried crossed himself. "Do you mean that they suffer from the same ill as Herr Christoph?"

"I have no way of knowing such things. But it seemed more to me as though they dreamed, or were drugged with poppy syrup."

Margerite thought of how woodenly Herr Jakob had moved and spoken beneath Nikolaus' spell - how many could Nikolaus hold at one time? And perhaps I have erred in thinking of him merely as a lesser magician, who could not achieve the Light-Bearers' onyx ring: had he not dared overmuch in his early pride, he might wear the amethyst now.

"So," said Gottfried grimly, "the Bear's Paw shall face... you have some forty men left, have you, Paul?"

Paul's fingers moved on the reins, but it was Jochanan who said, "Thirty-two, with our last wounded who died in the battle with Ortlieb and those who fell by Avignon."

"Outnumbered perhaps two to one, then, and perhaps with other things to face as well, unless Father Etienne can do something to even the odds."

The priest's arched brows drew together. "Something, yes. Blessings before we reach Burg Fürstensee, for those men and weapons that are fit to receive them; if Nikolaus has truly spelled some of his men, I may be able to loosen the bonds on their minds. But if Nikolaus thinks to use force of arms, then you shall have no easy time of it."

"That's a double ration of beer afterwards, then." Paul grinned again. "But we've been through worse. And this time, at least," he added beneath his breath, "we'll have swords in our hands, and be able to fight our foes, instead of galloping into rout as soon as battle is joined." Jochanan muttered something in agreement.

"But how if they hear of our coming and bar the castle against us?" asked Jochanan. "What recourse have we then?"

Margerite tilted her head back, looking up at the wide blue bowl of the sky; and it seemed to her that, though she gazed from the ground, a hint of the falcon's keenness came to her eyes, and she was sure of her speech. "That shall not happen, I think. Nikolaus owes me a debt of shame in his pride, and will seize this moment for the sake of his standing within the Order. I have no doubt that he shall let us in, but what happens after that is in Christ's hands." *And o, I wish that Bernhardt were here beside me: now, of all times, as we prepare to battle rightly, I would have his strength to lean on! ...Mother Maria, who knows how the heart needs mercy, grant that we shall see each other again...*

Nikolaus rode out at the head of a detachment of heavily armoured guardsmen to meet Margerite and her company on the road that wound up from the shores of the Fürstensee. Margerite did not recognise him at first, for he, too, was fully armed and armoured, the sunlight shining bright from his breastplate and shoulder-pauldrons and glinting in ripples from the long chainmail shirt beneath his plates.

Beside her, Eva drew in a shocked breath, for mounted and in armour, Nikolaus looked more like his brother than they had ever guessed. The difference was only something in the way he sat his horse, as though his limbs were unused to the weight of armour, and his gauntleted hands were clumsier on the reins than Christoph's; and as he grew closer, Margerite could see the glint of green in his eyes above the chain-mail hooked across the front of his bascinet.

"Greetings, Margerite!" Nikolaus called out as the two bands halted an hundred feet apart. "Frowe Gräfin, you have been long away."

Margerite nudged her horse into a walk, moving up to the knights and the Knappe who blocked the path before her. "Fall back, and let me pass," she said quietly. "I must speak to him."

"Frowe Gräfin, that is not wise..." Gottfried began, but Margerite cut him off. "Do not argue with me! He must know how matters stand here - and I do not wish to give him pretext for battle."

Reluctantly Gottfried laid the rein against his warhorse's neck, and the dark brown steed sidled sideways so that Margerite had room to pass. Briskly she rode out in front of her band.

"Nikolaus, I have indeed been long away. Now this is a sad homecoming, for I am told by Graf Wolfgang that my husband is no better, and that matters go ill with Christoph as well." And keep that in mind: if anything happens to us, you have a strong neighbor on your borders who will want to know why. "It grieves me that I was gone so long to so little avail, when I had hoped that my prayers in Avignon might be a help to Heinrich - yet now I am home again and have, perhaps, brought some healing for Christoph."

The veil of chain-mail served Nikolaus well, for Margerite could not see enough of his face to judge his expression, but his gaze flicked past her to the rest of the party. "What manner of healing?"

"With me rides Canon Etienne de Dion: he is a skilled physician as well as a learned scholar and priest, and believes that he knows the remedy for Christoph's madness."

"Then I greet you and your company with all joy!" Nikolaus said. "Come, Margerite, ride in beside me. Had I known you were coming," he added, "I should have dressed more fitly to meet you, but I was just out drilling the men when I heard word that you were riding in."

Margerite turned and gestured to Gottfried, Arnmut, and Georg. "For honour's sake, your brother's faithful Knappe and these two good knights of Burg Fürstensee shall ride with us, as well as our guests, Frowe Eva and Father Etienne."

As she rode through the outer gates of Burg Fürstensee, Margerite felt a peculiar tingle over her body, as though she had passed swiftly through a sheet of falling water. Curled before her, Kobolt suddenly stiffened, driving his claws into the high saddle-pommel, and a low growl trickled from his throat. This is a place where evil walks freely, barely bound even by evil will, Margerite thought.

It seemed to her that she could hear Gottfried murmuring a Paternoster over and over again, and she wondered what he saw - if something darker than the shadow of a small swift-moving cloud lay over the gray stone of the chapel in the outer bailey, if, within the inner bailey, a glimmer of scales showed among the rustling green leaves and pink-tinged white roses of the herber. The old square tower at the southeast corner seemed to rise higher than it had before, looming ominously above the L-shape of the newer keep. Gottfried surreptitiously crossed himself, and Arnmut did likewise.

"The daymeal should be ready to serve," Nikolaus told Margerite. "Will you and your companions come to the table?"

Margerite little liked the thought of eating there, for all it was still her husband's castle by law, but she could not refuse. Thankfully, it was Gottfried who spoke for her. "We all fast this day, for we shall all have a part to play in the healing of Herr Christoph, and Father Etienne says that God's aid shall be much needed."

Nikolaus' eyebrows raised, his forehead wrinkling in the shadow of his bascinet's rim. "Then far be it from me to interfere, if there is hope that you can indeed help my brother. But what can you do to aid a physician, Ritter? Though you are undoubtedly pious, I had never heard that you were skilled beyond the battlefield." He swung himself down from the back of his dun warhorse, landing with a soft grunt as his feet took the full weight of armour and body together.

Father Etienne looked down at Nikolaus from the back of his own black steed, his high-boned face severe. "When dealing with one who is disordered in his wits, Herr Nikolaus, especially one who is such a fighter as Herr Christoph, then it is well to have strong men there to hold him so that he cannot injure himself or another in his madness - as, I am told, he has done already."

"Aye. Poor Ritter Ludwig - he was a grievous loss to Burg Fürstensee, and I mourn him greatly."

At those words, Gottfried stiffened, and it seemed to Margerite that she knew his thought. *You lying scum! I should...no, Christ forgive my anger: I am not worthy of this task, when a few words can so provoke the sin of wrath in me. Mea culpa, mea maxima culpa...* The knight leapt smoothly from his horse, dropping the reins to ground-hitch the brown stallion, and came over to help Margerite dismount. She could still feel the tension quivering through Gottfried's wire-strong hands, and the skin was drawn tight over the angular bones of his face, but she heard no more of his thoughts.

Nikolaus took off his helmet. Though his brown hair was rucked up beneath it, there was no sign that he had been sweating: if he had truly been drilling his men, as he claimed, his hair would have been matted and dripping. A warning? Margerite wondered. Or did we escape, by chance...or by Father Etienne's magics...a trap that had been laid for us?

"Well, if I cannot offer you food, is there anything else that you desire? Or would you go at once to see to Christoph? Believe me, if there is anything which you require for your work that Burg Fürstensee can supply, it is yours." Nikolaus' blue-green eyes did not waver as he spoke, his plump-cheeked face as honest and open as that of any peasant behind his ox; and it seemed to Margerite that she could hear the ring of sincerity in his voice.

Is this how he means to hinder us? Margerite thought. By feigning to offer help? But...the Order ring on his hand was still plain gold: if Nikolaus had not won the onyx by now, it could only be because Margerite's judgement yet stood, though she was no longer a Princess of the Light-Bearers. No wonder we are being greeted so well - for if we succeed, Azruzor will be driven back to Hell, and nothing then will stand in the way of Nikolaus' advancement.

"Now, Margerite," Nikolaus went on, "how much do you owe your soldiery? I do not grudge them a couple of meals and a night's rest, for they seem to have served you well, but I would as soon have them gone: you know Father had no love for the Free Companies."

"Paul and his men have served me faithfully and well, indeed. Later, we shall talk of what they are owed - but it is in my mind that, if they are willing to give up their wandering lives, Burg Fürstensee could do with more experienced and loyal troops. And you yourself saw, nearly two years ago, what Jochanan's guns could do: I can assure you from my own experience that such weapons are better to have on one's own side." And you may take that as a threat, or a warning, if you like!

Nikolaus shrugged, his mail jingling against the polished breast- and shoulder-plates. "As you wish. We shall speak more on that matter later, in any case. Now, what do you need for your day's work?"

"A chamber in which we may prepare ourselves, and speech with Father Michael," replied Father Etienne. "That shall suffice for now."

It was nearly sunset when the six who would perform the exorcism gathered before Christoph's door. Each of them had confessed and been absolved; Father Etienne had performed a Mass and asked for God's help, then blessed them with the fullness of his powers. They were all dressed in white robes, save for Etienne, who wore his canonical surplice and purple stole, and each held a large candle with holy Names of God written carefully upon its wax.

The men had swords and daggers belted at their waists, but Father Etienne had charged Arnmut and Georg most strictly not to draw their weapons unless there was need - "and that order," he had said, "you may take from either myself, Margerite, or Ritter Gottfried; but if Ritter Gottfried or I draws blade, do not hesitate." Behind them were Paul the Bear, Jochanan, and ten picked men of the Bear's Paw. Nikolaus had argued first that no large guard was needed; when Father Etienne reminded him that there was no guessing the strength or cunning of a madman, he had said that the castle guardsmen would suffice.

But Gottfried had told him flatly that, with Ritter Ludwig dead and Ritter Dieter gone, there were no other fighters in Burg Fürstensee save himself and, perhaps, Arnmut to compare to the leaders of the Bear's Paw, or to Christoph himself; and to that, remembering that Gottfried had been second in command of the castle guard, Nikolaus had to reluctantly acquiesce - though he insisted on adding another ten of his own men to the watch on Christoph's door, and Gottfried could hardly protest that.

"Christ be with us all," said Father Etienne, signing the Cross above their heads. "Let us begin."

The first thing that struck Margerite as she stepped into the outer room of Christoph's suite was the stench: a decaying fecal odour, heavy with the foul sweetness of rotten corpses. Dear Maria, has Christoph been let to rot in his own dung? she wondered. But this room was clean, so far as she could tell from the light of their candles - clean and empty: the furniture, save for the stove, had been taken away, and no tapestries hung upon the stone walls, nor did any rug hide the well-scrubbed floorboards.

The lock clicked shut behind them: Nikolaus had given the key to Father Etienne, though with ill grace. Margerite wished that Kobolt were beside her, his fur brushing warm against her leg; but Father Etienne had told her that under no circumstances might she allow her familiar to approach this fight, lest the temptation to use his strength - and her own - against the demon become too great for her. The stink grew stronger as they approached the door to Christoph's bedroom.

Margerite's heart pounded painfully in her chest, but she could hardly bear to take a breath, for it seemed as though even to draw that fouled air into her body soiled her; already the clean lightness that she had felt after her Confession was gone, as though her soul were a fresh-washed piece of white linen growing sodden and filthy even as it was used to wipe away a stain. Christ is with me: His will be done, Margerite reminded herself, and stepped through the door, her candle held out before her.

At first Margerite hardly recognised the naked man shackled to the bedpost by one ankle. Christoph had grown almost painfully thin, as though he had not eaten in the last month; his ribs stood out above the wasted skin-folds of his belly, and the heavy bones of his shoulders and arms showed bloodless-white through the skin drawn tight over them. His face was covered in a brown scurf of beard, and his hair was a tangled mat of grease.

The bedclothes were clean, but torn and scattered, and, as in the outer room of the suite, all the other furniture except the stove had been taken away, as had the tapestries and rugs. A yellowish stain down one wall, with shards of crockery beneath it, showed where Christoph had flung a bowl of food away.

Yet, when he looked up and saw Margerite, Christoph sat down docilely, covering his privates with his hands. "Margerite!" he croaked, with the relief of a prisoner seeing the bearer of his ransom. "I am so glad you came. Nikolaus said I was mad, and he chained me up - I feared that he would kill me, but even he would not lift his hand to a brother. And, in truth, I was not myself for a time, but my soul has cleared now. Have you come to free me?" He gazed hopefully up at her: though the rounding of his cheeks had sunken so that the wide low bones showed through, his tip-tilted nose and plaintive expression were those of a little boy.

For a moment, and even though she knew better, Margerite found herself wondering if Azruzor had indeed departed Christoph's body. It sounded so like him, if wretched and weakened by his long confinement - and who would have fared better, shackled in his own bedroom by a mistrusted brother, with his clothes and all his dignity taken from him? But Father Etienne had warned her about the deceits of demons, and so she nodded to Gottfried, Arnmut, and Georg. "Tie him," she said.

"Margerite! Why?" Christoph pleaded, his voice aching with the pain of betrayal. "Have you come to kill me at last, after this month in the dark?" But he did not resist as the three men bound his wasted limbs, fastening his hands and his free foot securely to the bed; Gottfried, averting his face modestly, drew a flap of the shredded blanket to cover Christoph's groin.

"No, Christoph, we have come to free you," Margerite said. Father Etienne handed her his leaden phial, and she made the sign of the Cross, sprinkling holy water over herself and each of the others. As the holy water touched Christoph's naked body, he jerked, shivering violently, but made no other sign. At Father Etienne's nod, Margerite took a crucifix from his bag and laid it upon Christoph's sunken breastbone, its gilding glittering against his mold-white skin.

Margerite knelt before the bed and began to recite the litanies of the saints in a clear voice, though the fecal stench in the room seemed to grow stronger with each breath she took, so that she was almost choking on it by the time she said, "Do not remember, O Lord, our sins or those of our forefathers." The answer of the others, "And do not punish us for our offences," came to her as if from far away, its echoes twisting oddly in the bare room. But as she began the silent Paternoster, it seemed to her that she could hear Gottfried reciting it with her, solid as the thrumming of a lyre's lowest strings beneath her own voice as she spoke the last words aloud, "And lead us not into temptation," to which the others answered, "And deliver us from evil."

"Save this man your servant," Margerite recited, and her companions chorused, "Because he hopes in you, My God."

"Be a tower of strength for him, O Lord."

"In the face of the Enemy."

"Let the Enemy have no victory over him."

"And let the Son of Iniquity not succeed in injuring him."

"Send him help from the Holy Place, Lord."

"And give him Heavenly protection."

"Lord, hear my prayer."

"And let my cry reach you."

"May the Lord be with you."

"And with your spirit."

"Let us pray."

But as Margerite spoke the last words and drew breath to begin the first prayer, a torrent of sobbing laughter ripped out of Christoph's throat. "Margerite!" he shouted. "Do you think that you are a priest now? Leave this travesty be, and let me go - or would you be another Pope Joan, defiling the Papal throne with the blood of childbirth? By what right do you do this?"

His question struck to the soft chink of doubt in Margerite's heart, and she flinched, the words of the exorcism fading from her mind. But she answered, "I am a servant of God, as are you, Christoph, and the right to drive out that spirit which torments you is given me by the lawful representative of Holy Church, Canon Etienne de Dion. Yet it is only as an instrument of Christ that I do so, and it is His strength that shall prevail here, not mine."

Even as she spoke, she could feel her fluttering heart calm, and began the next prayer. "God, it is an attribute of Yours to have mercy and to forgive...Holy Lord! All-powerful Father! Eternal God! Father of Our Lord Jesus Christ! You who destined that recalcitrant and apostate Tyrant to the fires of Hell; You who sent Your only Son into this world in order that He might crush the Roaring Lion: look speedily and snatch from damnation and from this Devil of our times this man who was created in Your image and likeness."

Christoph screamed, his howls deafening Margerite's ears to her own voice; the blessed candles burned steadily, but beyond the golden haloes of their flames, and all about the room, it seemed to her that she could see a shifting flicker of red light. "Throw Your terror, Lord, over the Beast who is destroying what belongs to You. Give faith to Your servants against this most Evil Serpent, to fight most bravely. So that the Serpent not hold in contempt those who hope in You..."

"Contempt?" Christoph shouted. "Contempt! I have
seen what you are, all of you. What makes you think that
anyone will listen to you? A witch pretending to be a priest
- a sodomite pretending to be pious - a frightened boy
pretending to be brave - a scullery maid pretending to be a
lady - and a priest who preaches that it is right to lie when
circumstances make it advisable! Why should you not be
held in contempt by every Power in the world, yes, and every
person too?"

"Let Your powerful strength force the Serpent to let go
of Your servant," Margerite prayed, "so that it no longer
possess him whom You deigned to make in Your image and
to redeem by Your Son, Who lives and reigns with You in the
unity of the Holy Spirit, as God, for ever and ever."

"Amen," the others replied.

As Margerite gripped the crucifix about her throat
with her left hand, readying herself to address the demon
directly, a bolt of pain shot up her arm from the finger where
Ortlieb's ring had rested, so that she gasped a mouthful of
foul air and staggered a moment, reeling and choking. "I cast
it away," she murmured, her lips barely moving about the
low monotone of her breath. "I am absolved of my sins, and
forgiven, as Christ has forgiveness for all."

The pain did not ease; it seemed as though she clasped the
blade of a glowing dagger in her hand, but she did not let
go. She had failed there before, when the demon's touch on
her Order ring had distracted her, but that would not suffice
now, any more than she could compel it to loose its hold on
Christoph's body by the simple means of the Art that had
almost succeeded against it at first.

"Unclean spirit! Whoever you are, and all your companions who possess this servant of God. By the mysteries of the Incarnation, the Sufferings and Death, the Resurrection, and the Ascension of Our Lord Jesu Christ; by the sending of the Holy Spirit; and by the Coming of Our Lord into Last Judgement, I command you: tell me, with some sign, the day and the hour of your damnation. Obey me in everything, although I am an unworthy servant of God. Do no damage to this creature, or to my assistants, or to any of their goods."

Christoph laughed hysterically, his back arching into a high bow against the ropes that dragged his limbs agonizingly backwards. Only his forehead and his heels still rested on the bed, and his red-crowned penis jutted out like the jagged stub of a broken branch. "Is this what you want of me? You were my Master's stove - yes, he stoked you to a fine heat, dribbling out wetness between your legs as a creamy sauce for the dish he would cook in you, swelling your belly until you brought forth his pride. Still sealed to him, whether you know it or not, and the Master is jealous: no man's profited from getting his cock up you since, have they?"

Margerite's face burned with shame at the demon's obscene words, but she had been ready for them, and answered calmly. "Who are you? By the power of Our Lord Jesu Christ, tell me your name and number."

"You know my name already, witch. Did you not stand in Nikolaus' sanctum, and aid his feeble attempts to drive me from my rightful home? Twice you have failed against me, and this third time you are in my power." Margerite could not see Christoph's face, for the cruel bowing of his neck hid it, but his body jerked, his heels drumming against the bed with a clatter of chain from his shackled ankle.

"I am in the power of Christ alone, Who protects all those who trust in Him. Tell me your name, and how many of you habit unlawfully within the body of Christ's servant Christoph."

"Azruzor!" Christoph shrieked. "I am Azruzor, and I am alone, yet not alone, for where I am, we are, all the host of Hell without number. You are more than outnumbered, you are overwhelmed, drowning in us, with each breath you take, you take in the power of the Prince of Air and Darkness."

As he spoke, Margerite heard the unholy sound that she had heard before on the day of the eclipse, those countless voices buzzing and humming about her in a nonsensical babble, twisted as the gibbering of an idiot child tearing the legs from a captured squirrel.

"You can never escape, and you know it...can you not feel the ruby ring burning on your hand still, Princess? From the moment you put on the silver, you were one of us, accepting the vows worked into the metal - yes, you saw the trap, and still you walked into it, thinking you were too clever, too cunning, for its jaws to close on you. And Etienne let you do it...whom do you think he really works for, cloaking himself in the robes of the Church while he lies to it and flouts it at every turn?"

Do not dispute with the spirit, Father Etienne had warned Margerite. They are subtle beyond man's knowing, even when their crudity most disgusts you.

"Christ died to free all of us - even myself, flawed as I may be, and certainly Christoph whom you torment. Now, Azruzor, how many of you are there? Who are you? What is your power? Why do you hold this person whom Jesu Christ saved? In the name of Jesu Christ I ask it, and you will answer!"

Suddenly Christoph slumped like a dead thing, the joints of his shoulders cracking as the strained ropes went slack. The crucifix had fallen from his chest; Gottfried scooped it out of the tattered bedclothes, laying it upon him again. As the image of Christ touched him, Christoph began to throw himself from side to side, frothing like a mad dog and shrieking.

"Don't touch me! Don't touch me! You, unclean, your cock reeking of the shit you would love to sheathe it in...how many mornings have you lain in bed a little after you woke up, feeling Arnmut's innocent dawntime hardness against you, and hoping it would press just a little further? You ran from me when I told you what you wanted, but you're ready to beg for it now, aren't you? And everyone knows your shame: do you think Georg is the only man in this castle who won't share a room with you?"

Margerite saw Gottfried flinch, as though each word struck him like a hammer-blow, but he answered steadily, "I am clean, for I have been Confessed and absolved. Nor is it set for any man, that he should place the judgements of men above those of Christ. Before Christ, I am indeed unworthy, yet His mercy is endless, for He knows both the evil and the good in our souls, and from what wellsprings they rise. And you have no power against His grace, neither in your lies nor in your truths." As Gottfried spoke, he held the crucifix firmly against Christoph's chest. The knight's thin fingers trembled from the tightness of his grip, and the cords of his shoulder muscles stood out sharply beneath his white robe, as though he were striving against something that outmatched his strength.

Christoph's head rolled to the side, and he spat out a gush of foul steaming matter that splashed over Gottfried's hands and robes. Gottfried drew his breath in with a sharp hiss, as though the yellow-brown vomit burned him fearfully, but he did not let go.

"Etienne!" Christoph shouted. "Why are you standing back? Does the great exorcist fear me, that he sends women and youths to do his job? Have you gone soft in your age, you who have matched your will against so many of my Master's kingdom?"

Father Etienne did not answer, though his jaw tightened beneath his silver-shot beard and his deep-set eyes seemed to glow from the hollows beneath his arched brows. He merely put the phial of holy water into Margerite's right hand again, as if warning her to be ready. Even as the lead, warm from the priest's grasp, touched her skin, the great bed began to shake, its carven posts clattering loudly against the floorboards.

Margerite unstoppered the phial, dipping her fingers in and casting a scattering of holy water over both Christoph and the bed. Christoph shrieked, and the bed suddenly stood still as it had been before.

"What do you do, Azruzor?" Margerite pressed. "What is your purpose, and why do you torment this creature of God, Christoph?"

"Creature of the Foe?" Christoph's mouth mocked. "Creature of my Master, proud in his place, his cock bursting with lust whenever Eva bent down to show her big white teats bursting out of her whorish bodices, and heedless of the prating of priests. Do you think the Daring One sends us to the innocent? This body is mine by rights." His skin was stretched very tightly over the wide bones of his face, drawing his lips back into an unnatural grimace; his cheekbones and forehead shone like polished ivory, and his gray-green eyes bulged so far from their sockets that they seemed lidless as a reptile's.

Margerite felt the pain of that stretching in her own head, as though a knotted rope were drawing tight about her temples; she could feel the pressure building behind her eyes, her aching eardrums bulging with it as though they would burst from within. Still, though each breath of stinking air sent a jolt of agony through her skull, Margerite replied, "You have no rights here, for you are defeated by Christ's sacrifice. Christoph is a sinner, like all men, and like all men, he is redeemed by Jesu Christ, and made free from the Devil's tyranny.

Now tell me, in Christ's name, what is your purpose, and why do you torment Christoph?" She was pointing her forefinger at the demon, as though she held her own wand, and it seemed to her that she could feel the current sweeping through her, painful as a stream of knives cutting her unworthy flesh, perhaps, but powerful almost beyond her bearing.

"I was summoned!" Christoph raved. "Summoned by hate, summoned by the tainted bond of brother for brother, the love of Cain for Abel. You know that bond well, for you serve it; your lover, with whom you betrayed poor Ruprecht, is striving even now for his own brother's death. And all of you - all of you! - helped him. By that right, you cannot drive me out: you have done no penance for that sin, and your hands stand ready to commit it once more, not reluctantly, but with eagerness. Can you dispute that?"

Margerite remembered the grayness of Bernhardt's worn face, and her own doubt when Father Etienne had spoken of what must come to pass in their case against Gerhardt. A sinking feeling came over her, her entrails knotting like worms; and it seemed to her that she hung alone in a dreadful abyss. The candle-flames were only the faintest points of light against the darkness, fading quickly from her sight; she was shivering with cold, and yet her bones ached with the searing pain of fires in her flesh. The demon's words rang about her brain, breaking into fragments of babble, shattering into countless voices that cried out in mocking laughter and despair. The sin of Cain...Cain...Cain...

Strong hands closed on her arms: Margerite blinked through the mist, and saw that Arnmut and Eva were holding her up. With a supreme effort, she whispered, "Lord, hear my prayer."

Her companions answered raggedly, "And let my cry reach you," but, save for Gottfried, their voices were mere shivers through the demonic howling about her.

"May the Lord be with you," Margerite forced herself to say, though she could not hear her own voice.

"And with your spirit."

"All-powerful God!" Margerite prayed. "Word of God,
the Father! Christ Jesu! God and Lord of all creation!
You gave power to Your apostles to pass through dangers
unharmed. Among Your commands to do wondrous things,
You said: Drive out Evil Spirit. By Your strength, Satan
fell like lightning from Heaven. With fear and trembling, I
pray and supplicate Your Holy Name. Pardon all the sins of
Your unworthy servant. Give me constant faith and power;
so that, armed with the power of Your holy strength, I can
attack this cruel Evil Spirit in confidence and security.
Through You, Jesu Christ, Our Lord God, Who will come to
judge the living and the dead and the world by fire."

As she prayed, Margerite felt new strength come into her
trembling limbs, so that her own feet could support her
again; the flames of the blessed candles brightened against
the darkness, and when her companions chorused the final,
"Amen," she heard them clearly. Still, she could feel the
pressure within the room, as though some great creature
moved just above their heads; Father Etienne and Eva, the
tallest of them, were stooping slightly as though to stay
below the darkened air where the candlelight no longer
reached.

Margerite breathed in deeply, though it was like drawing
a clot of flux-sodden wool into her lungs, and said, "Azruzor,
I command you in the name of Jesu Christ! Tell me by what
means you entered the body of God's servant Christoph,
and why you remain to torment him. By the power of the
Most High - ADONAI ELOHIM, YOD HE VAU HE - you
are commanded to reveal these secrets unto me! Not by my
will, but by that of Christ whom I serve," Margerite added
just in time, for Father Etienne had warned her most strictly
against falling into the habits of the Art, if she should use
those powers and formulae she had learned. At her last
words, Christoph screeched in frustration, like a hunting cat
that had just missed its prey. Froth bubbled from his vomit-
stained mouth, and he gurgled, "Why? Why should I tell
you?"

"Because God, who cast your master Lucifer down from Heaven, rules this world and all the worlds unseen. Even in Hell, Satan has no dominion save as God allows it; now, by the power of Him who cast the rebel angels down into the fiery pit, you shall answer my questions. By what means did you enter the body of God's servant Christoph, and why do you remain to torment him?"

The buzzing voices rose up again, and it seemed to Margerite that she could feel them swarming inside her skin, like wasps making a wound in the sweet flesh of a bruised pear. She strove to keep her mind free of the poisonous sensation, concentrating on the clouded-glass eyes glaring greyish from Christoph's sunken-cheeked, straggle-bearded face as she repeated, "By the power of the Most High, you are commanded! Speak, Azruzor: in the name of Jesu Christ I command it!"

Christoph broke wind with a long ripping sound. A dark puddle soaked slowly through the bedclothes beneath him - dark as blood in the candlelight, as though his bowels had torn free; Margerite could hardly smell the fresh shit above the feculent odour emanating from his body.

"Nikolaus called me!" he shouted. "He called me with his arts, with the aid of Günther's ghost! He called me and bound me; but still I could not have entered, if not for the break in the bonepan, the crack in the white wall of the brain through which any dark wind can blow, the hole in the pillar through which the Unseen becomes real."

Christoph's head rolled on his neck like the head of a throat-cut sheep, his milky gaze sweeping over each of them in turn. "And each of you has opened that way in yourselves. Margerite, through what hole do you fly out of your flesh as a falcon? Etienne, it was no follower of the Great Fool that taught you your arts: he knew that when you grip a spirit, the spirit grips you as well, and you have been scarred by my kin many times. Eva, how often have you seen a demon glaring from living eyes - or from the eyes of the dead? - and crawled before it in fear, willing to lose your soul, if it meant that you would not be beaten again? Georg, I know your crack...the crack of your arse, the hole into which I plunged, anointing you to open the way for Unholy Spirit. And you, Gottfried...you see what I am, more clearly than any of these. You look with the eyes of a spirit, the earth clouded before you, but what is real seeming bright in your sight - even now, you hear my thoughts, you feel me against you...did you not know that you are open to me, as if you bent before me with your legs spread? I could have any of you, at any time..."

"No," Margerite said firmly. "All who are here are under the protection of Our Lord Jesu Christ, as is Christoph, whom you have no right to torment. You may have entered through hate and weakness, but Christ's love overcomes all hate, and His strength helps all men in their weakness. Christoph is baptized, saved, and forgiven: you do not have the freedom of his body or his soul. Now, by Christ Jesu our Saviour, you shall tell me why you remain to torment him."

Christoph began to writhe and thrash dreadfully, so fiercely Margerite began to fear that, struggling against ropes and shackle, he would tear his own limbs from their sockets. But Gottfried held the crucifix firmly to his chest, though the young knight's pale face twisted with pain and he shook his head over and over again, as though to deny whatever the demon was saying in the silence of his thoughts. At Margerite's nod, Eva, Georg, Arnmut, and Father Etienne moved in to take hold of Christoph's arms and legs; wasted as he was, the possessed man struggled so hard that each of them could do no more than hold down one limb.

"Freedom!" Azruzor screamed, his body flopping from side to side against the grips that held him. "Freedom, yes... you poor slaves, you know nothing of it. Starving yourselves to please an indifferent Will, tearing yourselves apart for nothing - no chains could be as heavy as the ones you take on willingly. I give Christoph freedom to say what he always wanted to say, do what he always wanted to do - o, he saw his father lying helpless in bed and he could not bear the shame; in his heart he wanted to give the mercy stroke. Just as he wanted to sate his lust on Eva, to grab her breasts and fling her down - to curse Father Michael for his whining, to beat his clumsy Knappe until the blood flowed - that was all Christoph, I only gave him a way, and give him a way, for all the sins that were in his heart to take wing from out of his will like birds from a crumbling pie-shell. And which of you will trust him now? Will you bed with Christoph, Eva, knowing where his prick has been? Knowing that I was the truth of his desire for you?"

"You were not, and are not, and I love him!" Eva answered, her hands tightening on Christoph's left wrist hard enough to whiten the wasted flesh beneath her fingers.

"Yet you will always see me within his eyes, and know it! I may retreat, but you can never drive me out, for I am that sin that creeps within the heart, that only the paltry thread of words and law hold back. I stay because I can, because it is my nature. For I am power, I am freedom, the right to say, I will not serve - I shall do what I will, and no law shall hold me."

"You are neither power nor freedom!" Margerite replied. "Your Master is powerless before Christ, and you and all who serve him are slaves, sinking ever deeper with each act of rebellion against God. Nowhere in Hell is freedom to be found: Hell is a petty tyranny of fear, like that I have seen among its servants on Earth."

Margerite made the sign of the Cross and rounded the bed, placing her right hand on Christoph's forehead. She could feel the feverish heat beating up from the damp dirty skin, the oily sweat trickling around her fingers. Only with a great effort of will could she keep from pulling her hand away and wiping it on her robe: she had gutted animals at the hunt, their entrails warm and slimy to her touch, and nursed her sister and mother as their bodies ran with the stinking effluvia of the Death, but she had never touched anything so foul as Christoph's unclean flesh. "Behold the Cross of the Lord," she intoned. "Depart, Enemies!"

"Jesu, with ancient strength, with noble power, is conqueror," her assistants chorused.

"Lord, hear my prayer."

"And let my cries reach you."

"May the Lord be with you."

"And with your spirit."

"Let us pray: God, Father of Our Lord Jesu Christ, I invoke your Holy Name and suppliantly request you. Deign to give me strength against this and every other unclean spirit which is tormenting this creature of yours. Through the same Lord Jesus."

"Amen."

"Get your hands off me!" Christoph spat. His lips rucked back far enough to show the rims of bleeding gums in crimson half-circles about the whiteness of his teeth; his eyes rolled about like glass beads in his head. His skin was still stretched unnaturally over the skull, shining with his sweat as though he had been anointed with oil, and Margerite felt a painful shock thrumming up her arm from where she touched him, like the shock of a hard blow running up the bone. "Sow! Whore! You lay with Heinrich to save the life of our Master's son; you would have lain with the lowest leper begging on the street if you had to. And yet he kindled your lust all the same - what a pleasant wifely duty, to take pleasure from a man you did not love. And how kind of you, to protect our Master's property."

"I have kept my vows to Heinrich," Margerite answered. "Nor is your Master mine; nor does my son belong to him. As for you: I exorcise you, Most Unclean Spirit Azruzor! Invading Enemy! All Spirits! Every one of you! In the name of Our Lord Jesu Christ - " she made the sign of the Cross - "be uprooted and expelled from this Creature of God." Margerite made the sign of the Cross again. "He Who commands you is He Who ordered you to be thrown down from the highest Heaven into the depths of Hell. He Who commands you is He Who dominated the sea, the wind, and the storms. Hear, therefore, and fear, Satan! Enemy of the Faith! Enemy of the human race! Source of death! Robber of life! Twister of justice! Root of evil! Warp of vices! Seducer of men! Traitor of nations! Inciter of jealousy! Originator of greed! Cause of discord! Creator of agony! Why do you stay and resist, when you know that Christ our Lord has destroyed your plan? Fear Him Who was prefigured in Isaac, in Joseph, and in the Paschal Lamb; Who was crucified as a man, and rose from death."

"Rose from death?" Christoph jeered. "There is no end to death; death is triumphant. All of you - you have seen how little prayers avail when the black boils rise hot in living flesh, when the sick cry and groan and twist their limbs about, and can find no mercy. Which of you has seen that, and not heard the Enemy and all his works cursed? No surplice could save a priest then, when the coughs of the dying sprayed the miasma of sickness into the air. No fasting, nor good works, nor any virgin's purity availed, nor any physician's skills: death took them all, from peasant to king, and their bones lie stinking beneath the earth, never to rise again. And you shall all die - you, Eva, your heart shall fail when you have grown so fat that your feet can hardly carry your weight!

Etienne, one day you shall meet a foe too fearsome for you to overcome, and your bones shall lie unburied in the dark wood. For you, Georg, a fall from your horse; one day, Margerite, the fever shall thicken in your lungs, and you shall drown in your own waters on dry land. As for you, Gottfried, for you the worst fate of all is set: you shall outlive all of them, everyone you love, and die in a doomed battle in a foreign land, striving to protect a woman who, in the end, shall be burned as a witch - and know that if you were not so old, with hardly the strength left in your withered bones to lift a sword, you might have lived through the fight to save her from that fate!"

"You are a liar, and your master the Father of Lies," Margerite said, though her voice rang hollow in her ears. She had seen such deaths as the demon predicted for her, and as he had spoken, it seemed that she could feel it in her flesh - even now, her lungs felt clogged with congestion, her face hot and head light with fever. Another deception?... but if the day comes that it is proved true, and I despair in the memory of the demon's words, then that too shall be a victory for Hell. "But even if you spoke truth, all men must die; yet Christ is the conqueror of death. He awaits us, and He shall resurrect the dead when His time comes - and then, Azruzor and all evil spirits, you shall tremble, and there shall be no fleeing His judgement! Retire, therefore, in the name of the Father, and of the Son, and of the Holy Spirit."

As she spoke each Name, Margerite made the sign of the Cross on Christoph's forehead, though he spat up at her and his spittle, striking her face and neck, seemed to sear like drops of molten iron. "Let the sorceries that brought you here melt as wax before the flame of Our Lord, for against His will and His might they have no dominion, and know that the sin of Cain, like all the sins of men, is redeemed by the suffering of Christ upon the Cross. Give way to the Holy Spirit, because of this sign of the Holy Cross of Our Lord Jesu Christ, Who lives and reigns as God with the Father and the same Holy Spirit, for ever and ever."

"Amen," Margerite's companions chorused. It seemed to Margerite that she could hear their voices with a glasslike clarity through the low constant muttering about them: Eva's, rough with unshed tears; Georg's sweet tenor; Father Etienne's soft French accent; Gottfried's strong baritone; and Arnmut's higher voice, chiming like a quiet bell. And it has not yet spoken to Arnmut - God grant him strength; he is the one of us who has not been truly tried in such matters.

Even as Margerite thought that, Christoph let out a low mirthless chuckle that ripped jagged up the back of her spine. "Little Arnmut, did you think I had forgotten you? O, you have given my Master as much pleasure as any other here, for all the evil they have done. How sweet it was, to watch Gottfried suffering and starving himself, fearing what you would think if you knew his inmost soul - as you feared his knowledge of you! Even better than watching the two of you writhe together in a bed of damnation; for a thought is as good as a deed to my Lord, and seeing you hurt each other by turning away, even as you sinned in your hearts... damned if you do and damned if you don't; what a fine pair of dancers you make for us."

Arnmut gasped, his grip on Christoph's leg slackening. At once the foot tore through his grasp, slamming out against his chest to knock him across the room. His back struck the wall; he slid down, collapsing in a heap on the floor, and Christoph laughed again. "If you loved him as much as he loves you, Gottfried, you would go to see whether he is alive or dead."

"Christ...protects him," Gottfried grunted, the low coughing grunt of a man with a fatal gut-wound. The muscles of his thin forearms and the cords of his neck stood out sharply as he strove to keep the crucifix in place on Christoph's chest, and beads of sweat shone golden on his sharp-featured face, like sun-glimmering dew along the edge of a sword. "From your words, and your blows, and all the evil you do - Christ protects him, and us all."

"Lord, hear my prayer!" Margerite cried: she knew that she could not let the exorcism waver, even for a moment - even were Arnmut's life in the balance.

"And let my cry reach you," the others answered, though Gottfried's voice was barely a whisper.

"May the Lord be with you."

"And with your spirit."

"Let us pray: God, Creator and Defender of the human race, You who made man in Your own image. Look on this, Your servant Christoph, who is assaulted by the cunning of the unclean spirit Azruzor. The primeval adversary, the ancient enemy of Earth, surrounds him with the horror of fear, paralyzes his mind with darkness, strikes him with terror, agitates him with shaking and trembling. Repel, O Lord, the power of Evil Spirit Azruzor! Dissolve the fallacies of its plots! May the unholy temptor take flight. May your servant be protected in soul and body by the sign of Your Name." Margerite made the sign of the Cross on Christoph's forehead again, and he began to fling himself about, kicking fiercely with his one free leg.

Yet she continued with the rite, making three signs of the Cross above the crucifix on Christoph's chest as she said, "Preserve what is within this person. Rule his feelings. Strengthen his heart. Let the efforts of the Enemy power be dispelled from his soul, Lord, because of the invocation of Your holy Name. Grant the grace that he who has inspired terror up to this, now be put to flight and retire defeated, so that this man, Your servant, be able to worship you with a firm heart and a sincere mind. Through Christ Our Lord."

"Amen," the others chorused. And, a heartbeat after, Margerite heard the faint, "Amen", from Arnmut, who pushed himself up and limped slowly back to take his place by Christoph's befouled bed, grasping the flailing leg with all his strength.

Christoph's limbs went slack; the taut-stretched skin of his face softened, and his snarl eased into a quiet smile. He began to hum, a quiet, almost peaceful, half-tune. But the darkness of the air above the candlelight was deepening, pressing down heavily upon the exorcists, and it seemed to Margerite that she could not escape that humming as it rose around her like a rising river of sound, pressing against her so thickly that it seemed as though she were drowning. She could not shut the tune out: a simple, wandering song, and quiet as it was, it seemed to her that through it she could hear a ceaseless shriek of despair like a pipe-drone, never pausing for breath nor rest, but growing louder inside her skull.

This, she knew, was what lay beneath all the blasphemies and obscenities: those were the gaudy distractions of the wind that might tear at the leaves of the soul and shake its branches until it cried out in pain, even uproot the weaker; but this was the worm gnawing at the root, the despair of naked damnation that must, in time, bring down even the strongest will. Wings of darkness flashed across her sight; the blessed candles' glimmer was pale and faint as the illusory glow of fox-fire in the woods at night. The words of the rite of exorcism had gone out of her mind.

"Our Father," Margerite whispered. "Our Father..." but she could go no farther. It seemed to her that she could feel the choking fluids in her lungs again, pressing cold against her failing heart - and worse, the coldness of spirit creeping over her. She was alone, utterly alone; the candlelight barely touched the human shells standing empty about her, and upon the bed lay a corpse, its flesh half-rotted away to show the white bones of arms and legs, the dark-etched lines of its ribcage and the shining white skull where wet eyes rolled still in the sockets.

She did not know whether she was looking down on
Mutti's body, or perhaps her little sister's - naked, wasted
by the Death and rotting already before the merciful end;
her shoulders shook with dry sobs, but she could not shed
a single tear. And this is the end, the end of all lives and
all things, something whispered to Margerite, even as she
coughed a wet gout of liquid from her filling lungs. God does
not care; the dead lie dead, alone beneath the cold earth
or heaped into stinking pits; the great seal themselves into
boxes of stone, where their bones float in the decaying melt
of their flesh, even beneath the effigies of their pride.

Despair weighed upon her heart like a headstone; and still
the voice whispered, *The indifferent sun may rise, but here
all clocks are stopped.* Her hand fell. It seemed to her that
she stood naked, only the cold hanging clammy as a wet
garment to shroud her body; with each flutter of her heart,
she could feel some human impulse passing, and the voice
that whispered to her echoed like her own voice within her
head. Love? The need to quench your body's wants; you
went to Bernhardt when you no longer desired Ruprecht.

Friendship? Others to use to your ends, as you used
Gottfried at the risk of his soul, taught Eva to serve you
even as she served the Abbess, though you tricked her into
willingness. Mother-love? You would keep Wolfram as a
pet, to cherish and play with - but what shall you do, when
he shows he has a will of his own? Is it not your heart's
desire, to keep him in your wool-basket forever? Trust, and
faithfulness? Only the knowledge that another will do your
will. Forgiveness? A few prattling words; easy to pray for
the dead, when it soothes your own soul, but what do you
do for the sake of your living enemies? Nor are any of your
companions better than yourself: they scrabble, as you do,
for power over others. Sometimes your desires run together,
and then you exchange tokens or fine words or promises, but
it is always the same.

You are alone, in the end, still alone, with no one to hear the cry of your heart. Listen: this is your own cry. And the sound rose to a high wail, an agony that shivered through Margerite's bones, beat at her like the hail of the Order's storm that had torn her flesh and scarred her back. Yet Margerite stood firm, for she knew that this, too, was part of the demon's struggle with her. She could not remember the words of any prayer, but she could remember the spring breaking free from a clogged pipe, the stone face of the Virgin stained by earth and moss; and the water running over Bernhardt's cheeks like a sudden flood of tears, the sign of forgiveness, and healing for a battered soul.

Maria, have mercy, she prayed. Give us hope and strength, blessed Mother, for our own cannot prevail; pray for us, and for Christoph, as I am sure his own mother does in Heaven. Then it seemed to her that she heard another voice, faint and shaking through the ceaseless wailing that ripped at her ears - a young man's voice, high and clear, and a deeper one rising beneath it. "Salve, Regina..."

"Hail, Holy Queen," Margerite breathed, blinking hard to clear her sight as Eva chimed in, an octave above Arnmut and Gottfried. "Mother of Mercy - hail, our life, our sweetness, and our hope..."

A sudden rush of strength seemed to fill her, and she made the sign of the Cross over Christoph's forehead again.

"I enjoin you under penalty, Ancient Serpent! In the Name of the Judge of the Living and the Dead! In the Name of Our Creator! In the Name of the Creator of the World! In the name of Him Who has power to send you into Hell! Depart from this servant of God, Christoph, who has had recourse to the Church. Cease to inspire your terror in him. I again enjoin you solemnly, not because of myself who am weak, but because of the strength of the Holy Spirit: that you go out from this servant of God, Christoph, whom the All-Powerful God made in His own image. Surrender, not to me, but to the minister of Christ. His power forces you. He defeated you by His Cross. Fear the strength of Him Who led the souls of the dead to the light of salvation from the darkness of waiting. May the body of this man - " she signed the Cross over Christoph's rapidly rising and sinking chest - "be a source of fear for you. May the image of God - " she signed the Cross on his forehead - "be a source of fear for you. God the Father commands you! God the Son commands you! God the Holy Spirit commands you! The faith of the Holy Apostles, Peter and Paul, and the other saints commands you! The blood of Martyrs commands you! The purity of the Confessors commands you! The pious and holy intercession of all the Saints commands you! Get out! Offender! Get out! Seducer! Full of guile and falseness! Enemy of virtue! Persecutor of the Innocents! Give way, most despicable being! Give way, most impious! Give way to Christ in Whom you did not find any of your own doings! He destroyed your kingdom. He bound you up in defeat. He broke your strength. He threw you out into the exterior darkness where destruction was prepared for you and your followers."

Christoph's head snapped back, and he let out three sharp doglike barks, then a high, eerie howl. His body whipped from side to side, as though a great invisible whip were lashing him, and Margerite could see the welts rising red against his white skin. "In the name of Jesu!" Margerite shouted. "Azruzor, you and all unclean spirits are commanded to leave this creature of God, Christoph! Go you forth, leaving him whole and entire. Depart from this person; depart from the Church of God!" She signed the Cross, first over Christoph, then over each of her assistants. "Fear and take flight at the name of Our Lord whom the Powers of Hell fear..."

"I go!" Christoph shrieked, a high unearthly sound that Margerite had never heard from a man's throat, not on the battlefield nor among those writhing in the throes of the Death. "I go! But beware our revenge, for we shall have it! I have marked you, all of you. Though I cannot stay here..."

The shriek rose and rose to a wordless scream, shaking through Margerite's bones, shivering the floorboards beneath her feet so that she could see the bedposts trembling. Then, suddenly, it was cut off, and Christoph lay panting and trembling on the bed, blinking like one who had woken after the breaking of a great fever. He opened his mouth as if to speak, but only a dull croak came out.

"It is gone," Father Etienne murmured. "Christoph, will you profess your faith?"

"I...will," Christoph whispered. Quickly Gottfried drew the covers over him with one hand to protect his modesty, though the knight's other hand stayed firmly holding the crucifix on Christoph's chest as Father Etienne intoned the Athanasian Creed, followed by Christoph's rough whisper.

Margerite then recited the prescribed psalms, and at last, laying her hand on Christoph's heart, said, "We pray You, all-powerful God, that Evil Spirit, Azruzor, have no more power over this servant of yours Christoph, but that it flee and not come back. Let the goodness and the peace of Our Lord Jesu Christ enter him at Your bidding, Lord. For through Jesu we have been saved. And let us not fear any ill, because the Lord is with us, He Who lives and reigns as God with You in the unity of the Holy Spirit, for ever and ever."

"Amen," chorused the others, and Christoph smiled weakly, repeating, "Amen," as Eva sponged his dripping brow with the hem of her white linen sleeve and Georg bent to untie the ropes holding his limbs to the bed.

"Have we the key to this?" Georg asked, and Margerite's heart missed a beat. If Christoph remained shackled at Nikolaus' will...now that the demon was gone, Nikolaus would find his brother more useful dead than alive...

Eva's mouth shaped into a shaky grin. "I have not forgotten all the skills I learned in the Convent of the Holy Cross, where I had to steal food in silence to keep myself alive - nor did Father Etienne forget that I knew that craft: he told me where to find the key. Nikolaus may not even have missed it yet." Margerite had not noticed the string about the girl's neck, but Eva drew out a rusty key from between her breasts, bending to unlock the shackle herself.

Christoph drew his leg free with a thankful sigh: the iron had galled his flesh deeply, so that trickles of pus and blood ran down from the wound - he would have the shameful scar of a criminal or galley-slave for life, but his boots would hide it from the eyes of men, and Eva, who knew from what bondage he had gotten it, would not care.

Even now, Margerite could feel no exaltation: only a quiet exhausted peace, though the blessed stillness, no longer filled with the gabble of Hellish voices just beneath her hearing, seemed to ring like a great silent churchbell about her. The smell of Christoph's voiding was still strong in the empty room, as was the sharp odour of the vomit that stained his chest and Gottfried's robe, but those stinks seemed natural, even sweet, as the smell of rain-damp earth after the feculent reek of the demon's presence.

Margerite's white linen robe was sodden-wet; Arnmut's golden hair stuck out in dripping spikes, as though he had just taken his helm off after battle, and Georg wiped his gray face on his sleeve; while Eva's quiet tears of joy flowed into the drops of sweat trailing down the pale curves of her cheeks. Likewise, Margerite could see how Father Etienne's hands shook as he took chalice and paten from his bag, preparing for a Mass of thanksgiving - there was no altar, but the knights and Knappe were ready to hold the holy implements. Margerite sank gratefully to her knees, for her legs shook too hard to hold her up much longer, and even the bruising hardness of the bare floorboards against her kneecaps felt comforting in its solid reality.

"Father," Christoph croaked, "If you are about to say Mass, I would make Confession first."

Father Etienne smiled, the look of fragile joy on his exhausted face thin and transparent as pale light shining through a stained-glass window. "That is well. The rest of you, step outside - but in Christ's Name, be wary, and do not go far from here! You are all worn from this battle, and if Nikolaus thinks as I expect..."

"He will wish to take and slay us quickly, while the deed may still be blamed on Christoph's madness," Gottfried finished. "All of you, remember to eat and drink nothing unless one of us has brought it straight from the kitchen, or drawn the water from the well with our own hands, for Nikolaus has already thought of poison." He crossed himself, his thin lips twitching with loathing.

Margerite shuddered, remembering how swift Gottfried had been to tell Nikolaus that they were all fasting. Still, she was grateful for the warning - but she almost wished that Gottfried had not reminded her, for suddenly she could feel the sand grating in her throat each time she spoke, and there was barely enough water in her mouth to moisten her tongue for speech.

Gray light was already sifting faint through the window: their battle with the demon had lasted all night, and she had gone empty and thirsty, save for a swallow of Communion wine and a bite of the Host, since awakening the morning before. Her bones ached with weariness; her lids slid gritty across her eyes whenever she blinked, and suddenly she yawned hugely - O Maria, for a cup of watered wine and a little loaf of white bread, and then a warm bed to sleep in!

"Not yet," Gottfried said softly. "I hear...I am not sure what, for it is far and blurred, but I do not think we can rest yet." Unexpectedly, the knight clasped Margerite's hand in both of his, his thin fingers hard as ivory against her flesh. I am better used to such privation than you; take you such of my strength as you can use. As Gottfried whispered silently to her, it seemed to Margerite that she felt something flowing between them - like a stream of warmth, it seemed, yet it refreshed her as if she had ducked her head into a bucket of icy well-water, as she had sometimes done in the drowsy heat of summer at her father's little Burg.

"Enough," she murmured, pulling her hand away. "You, too, may need to fight." And with the battle against Azruzor done, I shall have Kobolt's help again.

Even as Margerite thought that, she heard a faint miaow from the outer room, and the brush of tufted paws over the floorboards as her cat ran towards her, leaping into her arms in a single bound. She grunted softly under the impact of his weight - though Wolfram was large for a year-old child, Kobolt was still a little heavier - but she clung tightly to the tom's solid warm body, letting his rough tongue lick the sweat from her face as they all, save Father Etienne and Christoph, moved out of the bedroom.

Arnmut, Margerite noticed, was limping badly and could not stand quite straight. Gottfried spoke before she could, saying, "Arnmut, how badly are you hurt?"

The fair-haired knight moistened his tongue with his lips. "Only bruised and sore, I think. I should not have weakened - I am sorry."

"No, you need not be!" Gottfried insisted. "You did not give in, even against the demon's worst assault, and it was you who began the Salve Regina in the last darkness, to remind us all of Maria's mercy." Margerite thought of the egg that Gottfried had painted for her, that beautiful miniature of Maria holding the Christ-Child, that she kept swaddled carefully in wool in her saddlebags - had that, she wondered, been in some way part of the prayer that had saved them from the last despair, or at least paved the way for it? "But at least let Margerite see to your injuries, for she knows something of healing - or, better, I shall call in Jochanan."

"Is it safe to...?" Arnmut started, but even as he spoke, the lock clicked and the door swung open. Kobolt raised his head from Margerite's shoulder, white spiky teeth glinting against his pink mouth as he hissed.

Dear Christ, of course the seneschal has his own keys for every room in the castle! Margerite thought, even as the three men ranged themselves in a half-circle about herself and Eva, hands hovering close to their sword-hilts.

Herr Jakob's half-bald head poked in, his bright eyes glancing about them. "How goes it?" he asked breathlessly, staring at their exhausted faces and Gottfried's vomit-fouled robe. "Is Herr Christoph healed?"

"Father Etienne is still with him," Margerite answered, guarding her words. Then, angrily, "But why did you open the door? I gave strict orders that no one should enter."

"Frowe Gräfin, forgive me," the old senseschal said. "But the Herr Graf, your husband - he has taken a sudden turn for the worse. Ernst the Physician fears that the Herr Graf will not live out the hour, and I thought you would want... and then I heard your voices, and thought perhaps..."

Margerite glanced at Gottfried. The young knight's gaze was fixed on Herr Jakob's face, but after a moment, he shook his head, and Margerite heard his silent voice, Something veils all his thoughts - I cannot pierce them so swiftly.

I would be a fool to go, when we know that Nikolaus has meant all along to trap and slay us, Margerite thought. Yet... with Azruzor gone, it may well be that the evil working that held Heinrich as he was has broken as well. And if I do not heed, and he dies without a chance to see my face, I shall bear that guilt all my life.

"Send for Father Michael at once, if you have not already done so," she said briskly. "Arnmut, Georg, Eva - you stay here, for Father Etienne and Christoph may yet have need of you. Gottfried, come with me: if, God willing, Heinrich can hear in his last moments, it may comfort him to know how you kept faith, and assured the safety of his sons from what he feared."

Outside in the corridor, the men of the Bear's Paw stood to one side of the door, the Burg Fürstensee guardsmen to the other. Paul grinned with relief, whacking Jochanan on the shoulder. "By God, I told you the Gräfin would be all right. Those were some horrible noises out of there, though: we thought sure you'd got a whole herd of madmen in with Herr Christoph."

Jochanan nodded soberly. In the faint morning light through the windows and the guttering flames of the burnt-down torches, Margerite could see the touch of grayness beneath his swarthy complexion: Father Etienne had called the gunner half-trained, but he must have sensed something...still, Margerite could feel her mouth twisting into a painful smile, for what Paul the Bear had said was all too close to the truth. Only the sudden prick of Kobolt's claws in her shoulder shocked down the hysterical laughter bubbling up within her before more than a shrill giggle could burst out. She drew a deep breath, then another, thankful for the clean taste of the torch-smoked air in her lungs.

"All is not over yet," she said, hoping that those words would stay Nikolaus' hand. "Keep your guard, for there may still be need of you."

"You can count on us, Gräfin!" Paul assured her. "But I'll be charging you for a new jerkin soon - see what your cat did to it?" All the leather that showed beneath the free soldier's battered breastplate was torn to shreds: Kobolt must have been pawing frantically at him all night.

"And that you shall have," promised Margerite. "But now I must go to my husband: let me through." She set Kobolt down, but the black cat wove closely about her feet as she walked the short distance down the corridor, almost as if he were trying to trip her up. This must be a trap, she thought. And yet...

Heinrich lay unmoving in his bed, his lids transparent as egg-white over his blue eyes. The little veins showed through the thin crinkled parchment of his skin, tracing his forehead with sparse-drawn, unreadable signs; Margerite thought that he was already dead, and her heart tightened upon its blood. Have I come too late? she wondered. Father Michael, hurry! Then she saw the faint flutter of the Graf's withered lips as his breath sighed in and out: Heinrich lived yet, but she had not been lied to, for it seemed to her that she could feel his life sinking, its faint remaining shimmer like the last glaze of mud in a cattle-pond drunk dry.

Weary as she was, Margerite hastened to her husband's bedside, and Gottfried followed at a more respectable distance, standing straight and respectful as though he were coming before his Graf in the great hall to make his report at last. The scents of fresh lady's bedstraw and meadowsweet rose up beneath their feet, mingling with the soft perfume of roses and spikenard. Though day had come, the dawn light brightening through Heinrich's window, the beeswax candles that burned upon the dark oaken tables and chests had been freshly replaced within the hour.

The embroidered scarlet coverlet was clean, and the fine linen sheets fresh with lavender, just as they had been the night Margerite came to her wedding bed: Nikolaus, Margerite guessed, had been careful to see that everyone in Burg Fürstensee knew how well his father had been tended. Margerite knelt by Heinrich's bed, reaching beneath the covers to bring out his withered hand and clasp it in her own.

Though only a few wasted strings of flesh clung to them, she could feel the solidity of his heavy bones still, the strength of the foundation enduring when all that had been built upon it was gone. He wore no rings now, for they would have slipped from his fingers, but his nightshirt was of fine dark silk, and a golden chain glittered beneath his thin gray beard.

"The Herr Graf wakes," Gottfried murmured to her. "And he knows you are here."

Margerite bent over Heinrich, and it seemed to her that his eyelids trembled, like the barest shivering of breeze through his spiderweb lashes. "Heinrich, my husband. Forgive me, that I was gone so long...that I could do nothing to help you..." The tears rose aching in her dry throat, like blood drawn by the painful scratching of her voice.

Heinrich's white lips moved a little, and a faint sound breathed from his throat, though there were no words to it.

"Yes, Herr Graf, Herr Christoph is safe now," Gottfried answered. "The frowe Gräfin brought him freedom, and healing."

One side of Heinrich's slack mouth twitched, as though he were struggling against his body with all his might in the effort to smile; then his lips fell lax again, the breath rattling hoarse in and out of his lungs.

"It is I, your Ritter Gottfried," the knight told his lord. "I did not fail you: I found Bertram, and you may be sure that he shall never trouble nor do ill to Burg Fürstensee."

Heinrich's translucent eyelids fluttered down, then cracked open again, a pearly sliver of eye gleaming clear between the frail lashes. The crumpled skin of his throat shook under the neatly-brushed strands of his gray beard, and he wheezed, so soft and indistinct that Margerite could hardly make it out. "Mar...rite."

"I am here, my husband!" Margerite said gladly. *May he, after all, recover? But then...no, I shall not think on it: Christ grant him healing, now that Nikolaus' spells are broken!*

"Thsss...." Margerite could not tell whether Heinrich's bony fingers tightened, just a little, on her own.

"He thanks you," Gottfried said. "For..." and in the gray light from the window, it was easy to see the blush tinging his knife-edged cheekbones... "for your wedding night, that last precious gift to an old man, and bids you know that what happened was no fault of your own. And...he hopes that you shall wed again, for you are young and have Burg Falkenstein to tend for Wolfram many years yet, but he prays you remember him with kindness."

"Always, Heinrich," Margerite said, her tears falling freely. She would not have chosen to wed him, had there been another way - but he had treated her with such kindness and honour that she could not help loving him: not with passion, true, but with the affection and respect such a good man deserved. "You shall always be dear to my heart."

The corner of his mouth struggled upwards again. "Thn... iss well."

Heinrich did not speak again; and when Margerite glanced up at Gottfried, she saw that the young knight's eyes were closed, his sharp face set in a harsh mask of concentration. She waited, clinging to Heinrich's cold hand as though she could warm all his body through it.

A knock sounded on the door, and Gottfried hastened to open it. Herr Jakob bustled in, Nikolaus behind him. Heinrich's youngest son was half-armoured, his chain-mail shirt and breastplate sagging over his heavy body and his plump cheeks framed by the dark gleam of an open-faced bascinet - as though he were wary, but not over-ready for a fight.

As the old man's eyes fell upon Margerite, they widened, his mouth opening in a shriek. "Murder!" he cried. "The Gräfin is murdering the Graf!"

Nikolaus and Gottfried drew their swords even as Herr Jakob sprang forward at Margerite, knobby hands stretched out to grab her. Margerite tried to leap up, but her feet caught in the hem of her robe so that she stumbled backward, and the seneschal caught one flailing wrist, pulling her close: in spite of his age and sedentary post, Herr Jakob's limbs had not wholly lost the strength of a fighting man, and Margerite could not break free of his grip.

She could hear the shouting in the corridor, and the clashing of blades, and the shape of the trap sprang out clear in her mind: Herr Jakob would swear, no doubt, and believe that he had seen her holding a pillow over Heinrich's face... The old seneschal screamed again, his grasp slacking for a heartbeat as he glanced down at the great black cat clinging to his leg with teeth and claws.

Margerite balled her free hand into a clumsy fist, striking, not at Herr Jakob's face, but at the swollen joints of the arthritic hand clamped on her wrist. He let go of her with a cry, clutching his arm tight to his body in agony as he tried to kick Kobolt free from his leg. Gottfried's blade flickered past Nikolaus', shrieking a deep glittering scratch across his breastplate.

It seemed to Margerite, light-headed from exhaustion and shock, that she watched with a sort of double vision - one man unarmoured, swift and graceful, but knowing a single blow would kill him; one armoured, heavier and slower, but able to withstand his foe's strokes...Bernhardt and Ruprecht had fought so, and in the end it had been the armour that decided...

Yet Nikolaus was not Bernhardt; even Margerite could tell that he was hard-pressed to defend himself, backing towards the door as he called for his men. And twice already, she thought Gottfried might have slain him - the knight must be holding his hand for some reason, loath, perhaps, to kill Heinrich's son before the Graf's fading eyes. She thought of the cry that had stunned the Light-Bearers in their citadel: had Gottfried forgotten that beneath the long-drilled reflexes of sword clashing on sword, or was it only that he counted it dishonourable in a battle of blades?

Twisting his body desperately, Nikolaus managed to deflect the two-handed blow that would have driven the tip of Gottfried's sword deep enough to shatter the chain-mail over his shoulder; the same momentum turned him sideways, so that Gottfried's next stroke only rang from his breastplate, and then he was beyond reach.

Herr Jakob was just straightening, his lips pressed white with pain. Gottfried leapt backward, his eyes meeting the old man's in a single searing glance. Margerite held her breath, for all the knight's humanity seemed to have burned away in his fighting: the angular bones of his face shone pure as a naked sword-blade, his dark hair whipping about his face in tendrils of shadowed flame; and the brightness of his gray eyes scarred her sight like lightning. He has come newly forth from the Refiner's fire, Margerite thought in her frightened awe. Thus would St. Michael look, wielding his lance at last against the ancient dragon; and, caught in that terrible gaze, Herr Jakob crumpled and sank slowly to the floor.

Gottfried had no name for the fierce exaltation that filled him. It seemed to him that all the things of earth about him were lost in the mist of his sight, bed and tables no more than vague gray phantom-shapes; Margerite's white skin glimmered pale, but Herr Jakob was all shrouded in darkness. He saw the old man's body sink down, and turned again towards the sounds of fighting, hastening out into the corridor where the men of the Bear's Paw struggled to keep the Burg Fürstensee guardsmen from Heinrich's door.

Their bodies were no more than blurred ghosts in his vision, but he saw the gold-white glitter of sword-edges sweeping clear through the air, and the red shimmer of blood leaping where they bit. Nikolaus stood behind his men, sword uplifted: he had grown tall, and a veil of purple-black light shifted about him, even as more guardsmen came thundering and panting down the corridor to aid him. And the misty air roiled, coiling into serpent-shapes that snaked cold tails down about arms, misshapen ghost-heads lowering to sink fangs in: no blood sprang from their icy touch, but it faltered the limbs, froze the heart...

The other men were moving slowly, so slowly that, as Gottfried leapt in to join the fight, he had time to strike thrice at the things curdling out of the air for each time he sank his blade into human flesh, and to aim his blows, not to kill - for even in this ecstasy, he knew that Burg Fürstensee's guardsmen did not deserve death, thinking that they defended their lord - but to pierce shoulders and legs, to halt those who raised swords against him without slaying. His sword seemed weightless in his hand, his limbs light as the rushing of wind, and the dull eyes that met his own flinched away in fear.

Jochanan's dark face glistened with sweat as he swung his falchion desperately about him. Gottfried saw the ceaseless low mutter of Hebrew prayers hissing through the gunner's clenched teeth as a thin blue flame - he must guess what he faced. Paul the Bear battled sturdily; it seemed to Gottfried that he could see the faint glimmer of the Free Soldier's breastplate and helm, proof against the unseen foes that gnawed at the spirits of his men. Arnmut and Georg held the door to Christoph's suite, each defending the other as best they could without shields, but a half-mask of blood covered Arnmut's face like a rent veil of crimson silk.

Then, suddenly, Georg was gone, wrenched bodily away by a thin white-robed figure that grasped the sword from his hand. Among all the blurred shadows fighting in the hallway, Christoph's face was clear to Gottfried's sight, alive with rage and a deep, deep bitter grief.

"Away!" Christoph shouted hoarsely at the guardsmen, and Gottfried saw their strokes falter into defense, their ghostly outlines wavering with unsureness. "Back, and let me through - I command you!" He swung his sword about him in wide sweeping strokes, clearing a path: no one, even now, dared strike at him. "Nikolaus, now you must answer with your body for what you have done!"

Nikolaus' dark silhouette stiffened; he half-turned away, as though he meant to flee...then turned back: in the tiny corner of his mind that was not caught up in the rushing glory of the fight, Gottfried thought, Of course, he cannot prove himself a coward now! And Christoph is weak...But Christoph's very bones seemed to burn with light, with the force of his furious will, so long chained by the demon, now bursting free with a strength beyond the strength of his wasted flesh.

"You are mad still," Nikolaus answered, his voice booming hollowly in Gottfried's ears. "Put down your sword! I do not wish to fight you. Men, disarm him!"

But Paul was shouting, more loudly, "Let him through, God damn it! He has the right - Bear's Paw, guard!" Only four of the Bear's Paw still stood, but between their renewed attack and Christoph's blade whirling as he staggered towards his brother, the guardsmen could not or did not dare try to take Christoph. Gottfried's sword sang through the air, cutting his way through those men who stood before Nikolaus: only two could fight abreast in the corridor, and Nikolaus had not thought to command that his soldiers bring polearms.

Then the way was clear, the guardsmen reeling bleeding back. Nikolaus walked forward steadily to meet his brother, sword held in both hands with the tip pointed at Christoph's throat. His mailed bulk gleamed dark and solid before the ragged hermit-thin man who challenged him, and the mist-worms converged, wreathing Christoph's head in darkness. Gottfried heard Nikolaus' thought: Christoph is weak - his footing is uncertain, he does not have the strength to avoid the bodies of the dead on the floor.

A few blows to drive him back, and it will be all over. Anyway, I am mailed and he is not, and I have my spirits to aid me. Still Gottfried knew that Nikolaus underestimated his foe. Even now, he could see the precise skill with which Christoph cleared his way, and Nikolaus had gotten little better since his brother could call a kill on him five times of five on the sparring ground.

Gottfried could have slain the younger lord easily before, if he had not hoped to take him alive, talk to him. But it had gone past that now, for Gottfried could feel the dark things that Nikolaus had summoned chewing at the walls of the world, the pressure of the Light-Bearer's thickening magics aching in his head, and he knew that if Nikolaus were taken and lived, he would unbind his creatures from spite.

And Christoph has a right to revenge, if any does... save that Nikolaus is his brother. In that instant, even as Christoph's blade cut in towards the open face of Nikolaus' bascinet and the torch-flames bent and curled beneath the dark wind rising hard in the passageway, Gottfried knew what he must do. His own sword rose, stopping Christoph's edge in a jarring two-handed block that rang through his bones to his shoulders. He did not hesitate a second, but swung on with all the strength of back and hips twisting into the blow.

Nikolaus saw the stroke coming; moved his weapon too late, so that it was but halfway up when Gottfried's sword drove perfectly into the tiny crack between helm-rim and gorget, yanking down the face-opening of his chainmail coif and rolling it under as the blade's edge sliced past it and through the soft tissues of Nikolaus' neck until it bit to stick deep in yielding bone. The dark shimmer that had played about the Light-Bearer faded as he dropped, the roiling mists above thinning and tattering into harmless streamers.

Only by long habit did Gottfried wrench his sword loose from the falling body and bring it up again. He was just in time to block Christoph's next stroke, and his next.

"Christoph!" Gottfried shouted, and did not know whether he cried aloud or not. "Christoph, stop! The fight is over!"

Christoph's blade was back; he held it frozen for a moment, as though he were gathering all his strength for one more blow. Then, slowly, the tip of the sword sagged down.

"Why did you get in the way, Gottfried?" Christoph asked, his voice cracking as though he were about to burst into tears. "After all these months...and he was my brother. He was my brother! It was my right."

Gottfried breathed deeply, the dizzy exaltation falling away from him as his sight cleared, colour and depth filtering slowly back into the world - now, blurred as they were, he could see the tattered leather of the Bear's jerkin and the dark iron of Jochanan's breastplate as they leaned, panting, against the wall; the blue and red tabards of the Burg Fürstensee guardsmen who stood warily with their weapons down, looking from the Bear's Paw men to Christoph. "Your right? Maybe. But have you not had enough of the Evil One's work, that you are so eager to stain your forehead with Cain's mark?"

Christoph let his sword-point drop to the ground, wiping his face wearily with his left hand. "Aye," he muttered. "You are right. But, dear Christ, I was helpless in...its grip for so long, and between what it did with my body, and to have Nikolaus ordering me about when no one was there to see, delighting so in his power over me...a thousand, ten thousand times I wished to kill him, and though it laughed and cheered me on, the hope of revenge almost seemed worth it..."

"Your tormentor is gone," Gottfried told him firmly. "And by God's grace, I was able to help you; for there is no guessing whether such a deed might have drawn the evil spirit back to your soul."

Christoph crossed himself. Suddenly his sword clanged down: he swayed and began to fall, but Gottfried was there to catch him, bearing him up. Christoph's arm came around Gottfried's shoulders, clinging tightly. "You men," he rasped as Gottfried supported him past the astonished soldiers. "Let it be known that Nikolaus is dead for the sake of his own deeds; let there be no more fighting within these walls. As for me, I am free of the poison that disordered my wits, but I am weary...Obey the orders of the frowe Gräfin, as is fitting, and know that I now put Ritter Gottfried in command over Burg Fürstensee's guard."

Gottfried would have helped Christoph in to his own bed, but Christoph shook his head vehemently. "No," he croaked. "I cannot bear it, to go back in there now. Take me to my father. If there be no better place for me, I will sleep on the rug like an hound, and be faithful at last to his trust which I failed."

Georg came up to take Christoph's other arm about his shoulder, and between them they walked the young lord to Heinrich's rooms, with Arnmut limping close behind as if to catch Christoph should he fail - though in truth, Heinrich's son was so wasted that Gottfried could have carried him easily without help, even exhausted from the exorcism and the battle as he was. The blood was already drying dark on Arnmut's face and robe; but looking more closely, a pang of fear gripped Gottfried, for he could see the bone gleaming white through the gash along his friend's hairline. Still, the wound had nearly stopped bleeding, and Arnmut's step and hands were steady enough.

Margerite stood by Heinrich's door; Herr Jakob still lay in a crumpled heap by the Graf's bed. What did I do to him? Gottfried wondered. Even now, the memory was fading, as if he had just awoken from a dream.

"How stand matters with my father?" Christoph asked as Georg and Gottfried eased him down into a chair.

"He is failing fast," Margerite answered sadly. "Arnmut, call for - no, you are wounded."

"Not badly, frowe Gräfin," Arnmut assured her, dried blood flaking away from his sweet smile. "Shall I fetch Father Etienne?"

"Aye, for I will not be surprised if the sounds of battle have frightened Monsignor Michael away - if he was summoned at all."

Father Etienne was already kneeling in the hallway, giving the Last Rites to a young man in a bloodied blue and red tabard. Beside him, Jochanan had set his falchion aside and was stitching a flap of flesh back into place on the shoulder of a bare-chested Bear's Paw soldier, and Paul crouched down with his hand pressed hard against another mercenary's thigh to keep the life-blood from spurting out of the great vessels.

Nikolaus' corpse sprawled disregarded on the floor, his breastplate enameled darkly in the great gush of blood from his near-severed neck. Bad as his eyesight was, Gottfried thought he saw the surviving Burg Fürstensee guardsmen turning their faces from it; but, more certainly, he heard the whisper of their thoughts, vague and confused as those of men startled out of sleep. What came over me?...like a dream, I thought Herr Christoph...Someone said the Gräfin had, but surely...fighting, but I can't remember why...must have been...not myself, but I don't know...

Bespelled, indeed, Gottfried thought grimly. Praise Christ for His protection, that we had not other cases of possession to deal with, and that Nikolaus' evil magic all seems to have died with him. But there was no time to waste: he turned to one of the guardsmen who had come late, and stepped aside without engaging - looking up into the broad freckled face, Gottfried remembered that the man's name was Werner, and that he was strong and capable, but not overly graceful or bright.

"Werner, go at once to fetch Monsignor Michael, for the Graf has need of him - and so, I fear, may some of these others. And when Monsignor Michael is on his way, call for Ernst the Physician and tell him to bring up a good supply of bandages."

"Yes, Herr Ritter!" Werner answered at once, his bewildered expression clearing to a look of relief. The big guardsman set off at a run, his heavy feet pounding along the corridor. Father Etienne was still shriving the fallen; Gottfried and Arnmut glanced at each other, but neither of them would interrupt the priest at his duty.

"Monsignor Michael shall be here quickly enough, in any case," Gottfried told the other knight. "Have you any other wounds?"

"I think not." Arnmut touched the gash on his head gingerly, wincing as his fingers met the torn flesh, then looked at his hand. "Yes, it has stopped bleeding. They were well-spent, those long hours you made me defend myself with a wooden sword and no armour to protect my ribs: I think every bruise you gave me then saved me from a wound now. And Georg acquitted himself equally by my side, though Herr Christoph took him by surprise. But who could have thought that the Graf would be strong enough to walk, let alone fight, after his ordeal?"

It seemed to Gottfried that Arnmut was talking faster than usual, pouring out a torrent of words to stave off - who knew what? Time to think of such things later, he thought.

Arnmut's head came up, his blue eyes shining pale from the reddish-black crust of blood, and Gottfried felt the shock of his gaze as though he had laid his hand upon the shuddering iron rim of a man-high churchbell to still it. Not knowing what to say, he took refuge in the familiar needs of battle's aftermath. "If you are truly hale enough, you might help Jochanan with the wounded as best you can," Gottfried said gently. "Or - until or unless Herr Christoph commands otherwise, and I doubt he shall, you are my second here. When your injury has been seen to, it would be well for us to summon the rest of the guardsmen to the great hall, that we may be sure order is altogether restored in this castle."

At Christoph's dry-throated request, Georg hurried off to fetch some watered wine. Heinrich still breathed, but the rise and fall of the coverlet over his chest could hardly be seen, and Margerite clenched her fists anxiously. What is keeping you, Etienne? she wondered acerbicly. But of course, she had seen the bitter fighting outside: there would be others who were closer yet to death than Heinrich, with the blood of battle fresh on their souls as on their bodies, and she could not expect Father Etienne to walk past them.

By the bedside, Herr Jakob stirred, pushing himself up slowly. Margerite tensed, ready to run or defend herself, but the old man only stared blearily about. "Frowe Gräfin?" he said tentatively. "What happened? Is the Graf...?"

"Not yet dead," Margerite said, not bothering to keep the harshness from her roughened voice. "But why...?" She stopped: if Herr Jakob did not remember, and he might well not, there was no sense in telling him of the accusation he had shouted.

"I do not know what came over me, frowe Gräfin," the seneschal apologized, dusting off his dark velvet robe. "The world spun around me, and everything went black. Perhaps I am too old to sit up all night," he added with a ghost of a grin. "And I have not felt myself of late, not since Herr Christoph became ill."

I am guilty enough yet, since I did nothing to free you before; but Christ be praised, I think it is done now! Margerite thought. Aloud she said, "Then sit and rest yourself. There was - a misunderstanding, and fighting outside, but it is over. Nikolaus is dead, but as you see, Christoph is here, and well."

Herr Jakob hastened to Christoph's chair. He tried to lower himself on creaky knees, but Christoph waved a pale hand. "No, you need not kneel before me. Just as Frowe Margerite says, I am well now. And I would that whatever harsh words I spoke in my illness were forgotten. As you shall forget them, if you are my friend," he added, the snap of command clear even through the huskiness of his battered voice.

"Of course, Herr Christoph. I think none of us..." The old man passed his veiny hand over his eyes, blinking. "It seems as though a dream of evil has passed, though I do not know why. Forgive an old man's ramblings, my lord."

"Rest, and do not think too much on it," Christoph ordered, just as Georg came back in with a silver pitcher and a ring of goblets on a tray, Monsignor Michael trailing behind him. The priest was as sleek as ever, his shoulder-length black hair curled and glossy black beard neatly combed, but the pouches of flesh sagging purple beneath his brown eyes were new, and an unhealthy pallor moulded his plump cheeks, as though he had not slept well for some time. Margerite had never, in truth, suspected the castle's priest of great spiritual awareness, but the oppression within Burg Fürstensee had clearly weighed upon him.

Margerite held to her husband's hand as Monsignor Michael pronounced the Last Rites over his Graf - touching holy water to Heinrich's lips in earnest of the final Confession he could not speak, and anointing his wrinkled forehead with a gleaming film of blessed oil. Christoph, too, tottered over to the bedside, leaning down when the priest had finished.

"Farewell, Father," he whispered. "I shall keep Burg Fürstensee well for you, and all the folk within. And, God and Eva willing, it shall not be too long before the new Graf von Fürstensee has his own Gräfin."

Heinrich's eyes turned upwards, a single blue glint showing beneath the withered lids. One corner of his mouth struggled to move, almost smiling. Then his lips fell slack; his breath rattled out, and no gasp wheezed in to follow it, as though he had been clinging to life with all his strength only for the sake of his son's farewell.

Exhausted as she was, the next hour passed in a vague daze for Margerite. A few fragments were clear in her mind - the bells of the Burg Fürstensee chapel, their clappers hastily replaced, tolling out the deep death-notes as the shrouded bodies were borne out of the castle; Christoph, herself, and Gottfried standing in the great hall, with Georg, Eva, and Arnmut beside them, and Father Etienne's hoarse voice recounting what had happened, or as much of the truth as might be told; gathering in Christoph's bare bedroom again, circling with flame and censer, holy water and salt, to cleanse it of whatever last trace of evil might still linger within those walls...And, finally, the Mass of thanksgiving, the sweet taste of the Host upon her tongue, and then her maidservant Else's hands helping her to strip the sweat-stinking linen robe off and wipe her body with clean cloths before she stumbled into bed, Kobolt purring on the pillow beside her.

Gottfried and Arnmut walked out of the castle together. The sunlight outside was so brilliant that Gottfried had to blink, his blurred sight all dazed with brightness, and Arnmut limped slowly in pace with him as they went to get Etzel out of the kennels. The great white bear-dog frisked about in his freedom, barking happily before he sat down at Gottfried's feet with his head cocked, brown eyes looking up expectantly. Gottfried crouched to rub his ears, saying, "Good hound, good hound," and Etzel licked his master's face.

Gottfried's exhaustion struck him in a great wave then, unstringing his sinews so that he began to shake. Only now that it was over, his limbs covered with clean doublet and hose instead of the fouled and bloodied robe and the sun warm on his dark head, did he realize how terrified he had been through the black hours of the exorcism, the brief nerve-snapping wait for Nikolaus to spring his trap; and afterwards, wondering if any of the Burg Fürstensee folk, deluded not by spells and spirits, but by plausible lies and the actions they had seen, would challenge Christoph over the deaths of his father and brother...

Gottfried embraced Etzel tightly, clinging to the hound's powerful furry body for a moment until his shivering stopped; and he did not protest when Arnmut put out a hand to help him up.

"Time to rest now, I think," Arnmut said.

Then, unexpectedly, he dropped his eyes, a flush coming to his pale cheeks, and Gottfried needed no gift of the mind to know his thoughts. There was but a single large bed in their chamber in the soldiers' quarters, and Arnmut had not slept on the pallet since his knighting, but now...if they both...It hurt Gottfried to speak as he did, as though he were tearing the words bloody from his entrails, but in honour he could say nothing else. "If you wish, I shall go back to the castle. I know the Gräfin and Herr Christoph will not begrudge me Ritter Ludwig's chamber, if no other is sleeping there now."

Arnmut looked at him, blue eyes wide in his stricken face. The gash at the edge of his hair stood out black against his white skin. Though Jochanan had stitched it neatly, it was likely to scar; and yet Gottfried thought the mark did not mar Arnmut's looks, but only set off the fineness of his features and shining gold of his hair the more brightly. "Would you leave me, then, Gottfried?" he asked quietly. "Or have me leave, since you command the guard here?... My father will have a place for me at Burg Eisenstein."

The sickening fear clenched cold tongs in Gottfried's belly. He did not dare speak his thought aloud, both for what it would mean, and for the foolishness of its sound, like the prating of a half-skilled Minnesinger - May Christ forgive me, Arnmut, I would sooner have been slain, save that we would have been parted thus! But, worn as Gottfried was from the night and the battle, with his every nerve rasped nakedly raw, his painful-won and imperfect control betrayed him. Arnmut's mouth trembled into a smile, and he whispered, "I, as well."

As if helping a weary companion - and perhaps he was, for Gottfried found the courtyard's cobbles growing unsteady under his feet - Arnmut's sturdy arm tightened about Gottfried's waist, and they made their way towards their chamber.

# Chapter Ten

It was late in the afternoon when Margerite rose from her bed again. She washed herself hastily with cloths and warm water, telling Else to have a bath readied for her later that night, and to see that food was brought to the great hall for herself and her companions. Heinrich lay in state upon his bed, hands folded across his breast, two silver marks laid upon his eyes to close the lids, and a scarf of white silk tying up his jaw to keep it from falling slack to his chest. His body had been clothed in a silver-embroidered robe of rich blue velvet and miniver, and a chain of linked silver rondels had been draped about his neck.

Lying there so, he seemed more peaceful than he had been in his illness: save for the round silver coins staring unwinking up from beneath his gray brows, he might have fallen into a natural sleep. A pallet had been brought in for Christoph - it seemed strange, to see the fine linens and crimson coverlet decking the simple servant's bedding, but Margerite was glad that he had not returned to sleep in the site of his bondage. Christoph rested quietly, a faint snore issuing from his open mouth. Before falling asleep, he must have called for Albrecht's help in washing and shaving himself, for his sunken cheeks were beardless and clean, and even with his brown hair spread out across the pillow, Margerite could see that its straggles had been neatly trimmed.

Kobolt followed her in, scampering over to Christoph with a little chirp, then sniffing at his ear and licking it. Christoph moaned softly and turned over, tugging the blankets partway over his head, and Margerite picked the cat up, whispering, "Hush, Kobolt. I am sure Christoph will be glad to see you later, but he needs his sleep."

Heinrich's old manservant Albrecht sat in a chair, watching quietly. His gray eyes were swollen and red-rimmed, as though he had been weeping, but his voice was clear as he said quietly, "Graf Christoph seems well, frowe Gräfin."

"It is good that you have been watching over him, though I believe he is healed, as much as may be in such a short time."

Albrecht's long face tightened, as if in pain. "That young Nikolaus should have fed his brother slow poison! And so intent he was to show his care, calling in physicians from Freiburg...Tell me, frowe Gräfin: do you believe that Graf Heinrich's ill could have come from the same source?"

Margerite could hear the rending grief in his voice, like a leg-wound tearing at its stitches with each step. And here too, she thought, there are two truths: but should I burden the old man with guilt when he could have done nothing - far less than I?

"I know of no poison that could have caused a brainstorm such as Heinrich suffered. I am no physician - but Father Etienne could think of none either. It was ill chance that set temptation before Nikolaus, not any deed of men." And Margerite wondered how the Light-Bearers had found Nikolaus, how they had known he would be apt to their teachings...but that, now, she might never know: Nikolaus would keep the secret in his grave, and Damiano would answer no more questions for her.

"Ill chance, indeed," Albrecht answered heavily, but Margerite heard the worst of the pain draining from his voice like pus streaming free of a broken abcess: he would heal. "Well, Gräfin, what am I to do now?"

"Serve Graf Christoph as you served Graf Heinrich," Margerite answered. "Heinrich's body, and Nikolaus', must soon be borne to lie in the chapel: then Christoph, I think, shall want fresh linens on this bed. And there will be a funeral soon; he shall need fitting clothes, and some of those resewn for him, for he has lost much weight and he will not wish to look as though he is wearing another's finery. As for Christoph's old rooms, let them be cleaned thoroughly, so that there is no stain of his illness left anywhere. I myself, with Father Etienne's aid, shall see to Nikolaus' chambers. Aye, it is beneath my dignity," she added, for the old man's mouth had opened in protest. "And doubtless beneath the good canon's: yet if Nikolaus was dealing in such poisons, there is no telling what more he may have left behind, and I will not have any of our castle folk endangered - or offered temptations of their own."

"That is both wise and good of you, frowe Gräfin." Albrecht bowed his gray head, not meeting Margerite's eyes. "I must confess that I doubted you for long. A young wife and an old man...and then you left of a sudden, and returned but briefly before departing again... forgive me my thoughts, but fallen Man is often inclined to see the worst, and I had been with Heinrich many years, since we were both young. Men's tongues will wag, as well, and cleave to scandal before virtue; yet now I see, as I trust all do, where the true serpent in our garden lay. Will you forgive me my misgivings, frowe Gräfin? At least I spoke no word against you."

"I will forgive them gladly, for such loyalty as you gave my Heinrich is a rare gift, and I did little that would have soothed your doubts. If there were others who did speak words against me - what is done is done, and Christ has delivered Burg Fürstensee from its bondage: I pray that no evil may linger in men's hearts here. But as for me, I do not know how much longer I shall dwell here. Burg Fürstensee and all its lands belong to Christoph now, and Eva's heart is yet true to him, so that there shall soon be another Gräfin von Fürstensee."

"That is joyful news in the midst of sorrow!" Albrecht answered, smiling crookedly. "But what of you, frowe Gräfin? Where shall you go, if not here?"

"My son Wolfram has his own lands," Margerite said, though her heart quailed within her at the thought of going back to Burg Falkenstein. Yet she could not keep Wolfram from what was his forever: even if she were to marry Bernhardt, she would bear him other children, Maria blessing them, and Wolfram would not be heir to Niederwald. Though at least he would be safe in his childhood - but I cannot speak of that yet. "It were well if he grew up knowing his folk, lord in his own castle, so much as a boy may be."

The old manservant nodded gravely. "It were well, indeed. I shall see to those things you have mentioned, frowe Gräfin. I believe that Father Michael is already readying the chapel to receive the dead."

Margerite bent to softly kiss Heinrich's cold brow, and then walked down to the great hall. She had been, she saw, the last to awaken: bread and cheeses were already set out on the table with pitchers of wine. As the sharp scent of the cheese reached her, her stomach twisted with a pang of hunger and an unladylike rumbling; the little bread she had eaten that morning was by no means enough to relieve the terrible drain of fasting followed by the night's exorcism, and her very bones felt hollow.

She took her place beside Father Etienne; Eva sat to the right of the empty chair that was now Christoph's. Georg, Gottfried, and Arnmut were on the other side of the table. It struck Margerite, as she looked at the two knights, that there was something different about Gottfried. It was little evident in his appearance, for his dark hair was pulled back in the usual severe tail, and he wore a doublet of plain black velvet with no brightness about it save his gold crucifix and the sword-belt of narrow silver plates about his thin hips.

Yet it seemed to Margerite that there was a new peace in his sharp face, like a rocky beach lapped by the first gentle summer waves after the long battering of harsh winter storms. Arnmut's blue eyes were wide, almost dazed, but she could not mistake the happiness lighting his angelic features.

Margerite turned her mind from wondering what had passed between them: if every rumour about them were made true at last, that was not her right to know. But it seemed to her that the two of them must be freed from the heart-suffering the demon had mocked, and she regretted that she could not wish them joy, save as Gottfried might know what was in her thoughts.

Margerite greeted her friends as politely as she might before she spread a generous slather of fresh white cheese on a piece of soft white bread. The faintly salty creaminess melted into her mouth, and she washed it down with a sip of sweet light wine. She almost thought she could feel the strength flowing back into her body with each bite, and only determined will kept her from cramming the lot into her mouth as quickly as she could, like a beggar child trying to devour a crust before a bigger waif took it away.

"Frowe Gräfin," said Georg courteously, "do you think Graf Heinrich's funeral can wait long enough for my parents to attend? He was much beloved by them, and they would, I think, wish the chance to say their last farewells to him."

Margerite thought a moment. Three days - perhaps as little as a day and a half for a hardy and skilled rider on a fast horse such as Thietmar - to reach Burg Eisenstein; then at least three days for Graf Wolfgang and Gräfin Anna to ready themselves and come to Burg Fürstensee - no, longer than that: Anna would have her maidservants and her wain. And the weather was warm with summer, so that even in the coolest part of the castle, the old tower, dead flesh would breed maggots all too quickly.

"I fear that Heinrich must be laid to rest before they will be able to get here. But I shall send to them at once: at least they can kneel for a Requiem Mass for him, and drink to his deeds and memory at a feast afterwards." And I think there will be a more joyful reason for them to be here when the day comes, for Christoph must know well now that you have earned a Ritter's spurs, Margerite thought, concealing her smile behind another mouthful of bread and cheese.

But for half a heartbeat, an answering grin glinted on Gottfried's thin face like the fin of a fish flicking silver from dark water: he, too, knew how well Georg deserved the knightly accolade. Father Etienne's face, however, was still grim, and his pale sapphire eyes looked out over the length of the hall. The musicians' gallery above the far end was silent: today, Margerite thought, there would be no music unless she or Christoph commanded it.

"What of Nikolaus?" the canon asked. "Do you mean to hold his funeral together with his father's - or to hold it at all?" His dry baritone voice sounded neutral, as though the question were nothing to him, but Margerite thought she knew Etienne de Dion, and the burdens that weighed on him, well enough by now to guess when he was hiding the strains of his soul.

"Father, I had thought to take your advice," she hedged, but quailed beneath the look he turned on her. "...in truth, I had not thought beyond that, for which Christ forgive me. Did you shrive him at the end?"

"I anointed his body, at least. It was a grievous blow Ritter Gottfried struck him - but well-struck, as much as any stroke can be that slays a man. And it is not mine to guess what Nikolaus would have said, had he lived to give or withhold consent for his Last Rites; but we may always hope that it might have been his will to repent, and that Christ shall judge him with mercy."

Margerite thought to herself that it was unlikely Nikolaus would have repented at his death: she had felt the thickening air as the fight raged, the thunderstorm-prickle of the hairs along her arms and at the back of her neck. And more, she had seen something of his defiant pride and the force of his will: he would not have bowed at the end. Father Etienne had performed the proper rite, and who was she to say how Christ might judge Nikolaus? - yet it seemed ill to her that the body of him who had betrayed his father and brother so grievously should lie beside Heinrich in the little crypt beneath Burg Fürstensee's chapel, and it was hard to find it in her heart to wish Nikolaus upon consecrated ground, for his very bones almost seemed a blasphemy to her.

"Christ may judge Nikolaus on the Last Day, but it is Christoph's right to pronounce judgement here in Burg Fürstensee," Eva spoke up unexpectedly. "If he decrees a traitor's unhallowed grave for the brother who used him so ill, that is no more than earthly justice should have."

"Yet having right and what is right may differ," murmured Gottfried. "And I do not think Christoph's rage will deafen him to our counsel."

The scar along Georg's cheek darkened as he sat up straighter, his long chin jutting out angrily. "For myself, I would see Nikolaus' body burned and his ashes scattered where they might never more do harm. You saw the results of his deeds at the end: I lived with them for months, and Christoph suffered worse for longer."

"I would say the same," Eva agreed, and it was no maidenly blush that flushed her rounded cheeks and brightened her eyes, but the high colour of fierce anger. "And if Nikolaus' body is not disposed of as that of a traitor should be, without honour or blessing, that would be much the same as denying the right of the judgement by which he was slain."

Margerite could not argue that point, and even Etienne nodded slowly. "We shall speak more of this when Graf Christoph has roused himself," the priest said. "For now, Nikolaus lies in the chapel with the other dead."

And perhaps, Margerite thought, if I trust in the power of Christ, Nikolaus' presence shall not pollute God's house, but rather the holiness of consecrated ground shall prevent any other evil from entering the flesh that did Lucifer's will in life. As the sun was setting, Christoph came slowly into the great hall. He walked carefully, like a brittle-boned old man.

The black-on-scarlet brocade of his tunic hung about his body in folds; the silver-sheathed tip of his belt dangled near his knees, and he held his right hand curled so that the gold signet ring would not slip from fingers grown too thin for its solid circle. But there was a little more colour in his face than there had been, and he did not falter as he came to seat himself in the Graf's high chair of carven oak, nor did his hands shake as he drew his eating-dagger to cut some bread and cheese for himself.

"I do not know how to thank all of you properly," he said without preamble. "Yet there are some few things I may do... Georg, I swear that no knight has ever been more faithfully served by his Knappe, and I know you have distinguished yourself in battle as well. I shall send to your parents, that they shall attend your knighting here as soon as they may."

Georg's smile was not the radiant delight that Margerite remembered, but a quieter look of satisfaction - and his mouth crooked at the end with sorrow, as though the price for his desire had, after all, been higher than he would have willingly paid. Yet he bowed his head, and said, "I thank you, Herr Christoph - Graf Christoph."

"Please forgive me for all that befell you...that would not have, had you not been so loyal to me. I do not know how I can ever make good for your sufferings, but you have my oath that, should you ever be in need of aught I can fulfill, it is yours."

"I know that you never meant me ill, nor would have harmed me," Georg answered, his honeyed tenor cracking slightly, as though the tears were catching in his throat. "You need no forgiveness, for you bore worse than I."

"Yet I shall hold by my oath. Ritter Gottfried, you shall command the guard of Burg Fürstensee as long as you desire it, with Ritter Arnmut as your second. But should it be your wish to hold lands and a castle of your own, that, too, may be arranged, for the two of you are now the foremost of my knights."

Gottfried looked at Arnmut. Though no word was spoken between them, Arnmut smiled at his companion, and Gottfried said to Christoph, "Herr Graf, we shall hold the post you give us here while we may. But that shall not be forever, for it may not be too much longer before we must accompany the frowe Gräfin to Bohemia, to give her testimony before the Kaiser."

Christoph's eyebrows lowered, the look in his gray-green eyes distant, as though he were trying to make out the words of a far-off muttering in his memory. "There was something... about Bertram, was it not? There is much that I remember only in pieces, and I do not know if it is not better so. Nevertheless, I shall be grateful for your aid, and the places of commander and second shall still be yours when you come back, if you want them." He turned to Father Etienne. "Father, I do not know how best I can repay you. But you have only to speak, and any gift I may give is yours."

The priest's gold seal ring glinted as he steepled his long fingers, looking into Christoph's face. Margerite wondered if he would ask for Nikolaus' burial in holy ground; but she was little surprised when he said, "Give me, then, all that is in Nikolaus' chambers, to do with as I see fit."

"It is yours, and welcome!" Christoph said heartily. "Command my servants as you will, for there is nothing there that I would have, or would see again by choice." The new Graf looked at Margerite. "And you, Margerite - what would you wish? Burg Falkenstein is still yours, and your son's; I can hardly offer you a castle as fine, or lands as wide. But it was you who led the rite that freed me, and took the worst danger upon yourself. How can I ever show my gratitude for such help?"

Margerite found herself suddenly tongue-tied: Christoph had no power to give what she truly longed for, and nothing more would come to her mind. Kobolt lay quietly in her lap; she stroked him, and he purred in contentment. But then she bethought herself of what was to come when they made their way to the Kaiser's court - to Burg Karlstein in Bohemia; Gottfried had spoken with such sureness that she could not doubt it.

"If you may leave Burg Fürstensee in trusted hands," she said slowly, "then, when the time comes, I would ask you to come before the Kaiser with us, to speak in support of Bernhardt von Niederwald - whom you knew as Bertram, Hauptmann of Ruprecht's guard. For I think he shall need all the friends he can find then, and those who can tell the Kaiser what manner of man he is."

"There is much for you to tell me yet," Christoph remarked. "But whatever help I can give, I shall...And you, Eva," he said at last, turning to the woman beside him. "What may I offer you?"

Eva tilted her golden head to the side so that she was looking up into Christoph's eyes, and laid her soft white hand over his pale one. "You know what you may offer me," she murmured. "You may or may not remember what was said at Christmas, when I would not pledge myself. But it is you who speaks now, and my answer will be very different, if you ask."

Christoph closed his fingers about hers, lifting her hand in both of his. "Eva - will you marry me?"

Eva's bowed lips parted in a sweet radiant smile, and Margerite could see the tears brightening her blue eyes in the sunset's fading light through the high windows and the growing glow of the candles the servants were beginning to carry about. "O, yes, Christoph," she breathed.

Christoph slipped the signet from his own finger, setting it gently onto Eva's. "Then let the banns of our betrothal be posted: our wedding shall take place on the day that you set for it." He leaned over to her, and they kissed.

After a little time, when Christoph had eaten, Father Etienne said to him, "Herr Graf, what do you mean to do with your brother's body?" His dry voice was more gentle than when he had spoken to Margerite, but Christoph flinched back, his gray-green eyes widening like a child threatened by a master's hand.

"Father, I...I had not thought," he stammered. "Surely it were better if you and Margerite made that choice?"

Father Etienne's pale sapphire gaze did not waver; he seemed about to speak, but, unexpectedly, Gottfried answered first. "Herr Graf, it was your choice that Nikolaus be slain, and mine to slay him. Though at first I would have taken your brother alive, that he have a chance to repent of his evil deeds, by the end of the fight it was needful - if you ask me in a few days, when you have gained more of your strength back, I shall tell you why. Nevertheless, it seems to me that the decision must fall to us, for we took his life into our hands."

Christoph sat back in his chair, staring astounded at Gottfried. His bony fingers curled tight about the silver stem of his goblet, and when he spoke, it seemed to Margerite that she could hear a spark of temper in his voice, though it was fitful as a flame sputtering from a damp candlewick. "Herr Ritter, you take much upon yourself to speak thus!"

Gottfried did not reply to that, only stared steadily at Christoph until the young Graf looked away. Beads of sweat shone on Christoph's broad forehead, and he wiped them away with the back of his hand, pushing the damp spikes of his thick brown fringe to the side. "Yet you are the foremost of my knights, as I have just said, and...you seem to have learned much in your travels. What advice would you give me now?"

"Bury Nikolaus in hallowed ground, and let Father Etienne perform the funeral rites for him. I do not know if you yourself were better counselled not to watch, for the evil that he did you was beyond measure and there is no telling what such a farewell would stir in your soul; but rather, I would say that you should go to the chapel and pray Christ's mercy upon him, and for the grace and blessing that you, too, may be able to forgive his crimes against you someday. Though such forgiveness might test the soul of a saint, one who asks Christ for such a thing with all of his true heart surely shall not be denied." Gottfried spoke quietly, as he usually did, but it seemed to Margerite that she could hear a deeper resonance than usual in his baritone voice, as though he were utterly certain of things other humans could only guess at, and his harsh-angled face was as calm as if he had just come from prayer.

Unexpectedly, Christoph gave his knight a pale ghost of a smile. "Are you sure, my Gottfried, that you have not turned priest while you were away?" But there was no sting in the words, and Margerite was glad to hear even a feeble jest from his lips. "But if I were wounded in body, I should trust you to help me from the field, and now...I shall abide by your choice in this matter. Father Etienne, will you consent to say the funeral Mass for Nikolaus?"

"I gave the Last Rites to his body, for he was past consent or denial, and could not be denied that last least chance of his soul's repentance," the priest answered. "I will say his funeral Mass as well: justice must be done on earth, that evil not rule unhindered, but now there is none who can pass judgement upon your brother save Christ."

To Margerite's surprise, Gottfried insisted on taking a
hand in digging Nikolaus' grave, the sun hot on his sweat-
darkened back as he struggled with the unaccustomed
shovel. She stood beside the knight as he dug, and Etzel
sat at her feet with his white head cocked to the side and
his long pink tongue lolling out, panting in the summery
warmth. When Gottfried at last climbed out of the waist-
deep pit, his hair falling in straggles about his earth-smeared
face, Etzel nosed anxiously at his hands, and Margerite saw
that sticky tatters of dirt-caked skin hung from his blistered
palms.

"Leave the grave-digger to finish, Gottfried," Margerite
said. "Your hands need ointment and bandages, else it will
be some time before you can hold a sword again. And such
work is not for a Ritter."

"What pride is it, that can slay a man and yet not dig his
grave?" Gottfried replied. Beneath the dirt, his skin was
chalk-white, his gray eyes wide in their dark hollows. "I have
killed before at need: I do not know why this death troubles
me so much more than the others, and yet I am uneasy in
my soul...Perhaps it is because I never spoke with Nikolaus
while he lived, nor did any of the things that I might have
done to turn him from his end."

Nor I, thought Margerite. For I was already deep in my
masquerade...And yet, because of that, I knew Nikolaus, and
knew... "There is nothing, I think, that you could have done.
He did not trust you, nor would he have listened to you. I
know that you were already marked as a foe in his mind, for
he warned me to be wary of you. I have more of such guilt
to bear than you do - and, before Christ, I swear that I could
not have turned him from his evil either, unless a miracle
had been vouchsafed me."

Then it seemed to her that, though Gottfried's thoughts were not sounding in her head, that she knew what was within his mind. "Gottfried, Nikolaus was nothing like Birgitta. For though it was not a Christian act, when she gave her father his end, it was done swiftly, and with love, to spare him the longer pains of death - whereas Nikolaus chose Heinrich's long suffering, and spoke to me of how the choice of his death must be made according to cold plans. You were the instrument through which the chance of mercy was granted, but Birgitta herself decided to leave the Light-Bearers: Nikolaus would not have turned thus."

Gottfried sighed. "Aye. And yet..."

"If you feel that you must do penance, then it were better done upon your knees, praying for Nikolaus' soul, than by striving thus at work of which you know nothing and for which you are not suited. Come now, and let me see to your hands before they become infected, for I may need them to wield lance and sword for me soon enough."

Still, as she stood by the raw dark wound of the grave in the green grass of the churchyard, watching Gottfried and Arnmut lower Nikolaus' plain coffin of white pine down on ropes, Margerite could not help thinking about the man she had known - the man Nikolaus could have been.

Would Heinrich and Christoph have looked differently upon him, had they seen him unflinchingly soaking himself with ice-chill water in the cold of the salt caves, or if they had known how fearlessly he struggled for mastery with beings that might have frozen their own bowels in terror? They had spoken contemptuously of packing him off to the Church, and never guessed what strength he might have within - and yet they might not have heeded it.

Even Gottfried's piety had been a matter for affectionate jest, and much of the affection, Margerite thought, had come from the young knight's skill on the battlefield.

Christ forgive you, Nikolaus, that for all your power of will, you were not able to overcome the first test set for you. You were better off, had you not been born Heinrich's son.

"Ashes to ashes," Father Etienne murmured, "and dust to dust."

Christoph was not there, nor Eva nor Georg; but Margerite bent down to take up a clod in her hand, the damp earth scattering black across the rough-hewn pale wood of the coffin's lid. Justice, as the French priest had said, had been done on earth: the casket's wood would rot in time, and the worms have their way with Nikolaus' flesh until his very bones had crumbled to dust. And he was not the only one of those here who has done evil, knowingly and unknowingly: Christ, I pray you have mercy on his soul, as I hope you will have mercy on all of us when we are come ourselves to this; blessed Maria, pray for us, now and at the hours of our deaths.

As she prayed, Margerite felt her lungs tightening, and coughed softly to relieve them. There was nothing there - no fluid filling her chest to press against her heart, only clean and empty air - but she knew that, though the demon Nikolaus had called was gone, the shadow of its prophecy would be with her through her life. Christ, she prayed again, have mercy on us all! There was a great deal of work to be done in the next days.

To his credit, indeed, Nikolaus had kept his father's castle and lands in good order; but Herr Jakob had fallen ill with a feverish flux, as though the enslavement of his will had taken a grievous toll on his body as well, so that Margerite had to struggle through pages and pages of the old man's crabbed handwriting without help. Christoph was not able to stay up for more than a couple of hours at a time, though Eva fussed over him and tended him as though they were already wedded - and if, as the demon had threatened, she saw any lingering memory of its taint in his gray-green eyes, there was no telling it from the way she would sit on the cushioned chair beside him and gaze into his face.

Georg, too, served his knight as faithfully as any Knappe could, giving Christoph his shoulder to lean on when the young Graf wearied and fetching him possets and meat pastries from the kitchen whenever Eva bade him see that Christoph ate. But the most gruelling work was done at night, when Margerite, Father Etienne, and Gottfried slowly cleared out Nikolaus' rooms.

Margerite could not keep from feeling a certain grudging respect at all her stepson had managed to do under the constraints of life at Burg Fürstensee: Ruprecht, lord of his own castle, with the sanctum he himself had constructed for his own needs and the aid of Kundry and Klingschor, had not, so far as Margerite known, kept such a store of sigils and talismans, nor had he had spirits bound into rings and wands thus for his use - though Ruprecht had been an alchemist, rather than an aspiring spirit-ruler, and Margerite yet knew too little of that art to judge, save that the falcon-necklace he had made for her was clearly a master's work.

Still, by the nature of his work, Nikolaus' chambers were perilous in the cleansing, and it was slowed still further by the need to explain everything to Gottfried as they went alone, for Margerite had not forgotten that she had sworn to teach him, and Father Etienne assented to that, saying sternly to the young knight, "There may come a time when your gifts and strength - yes, and even the purity of your heart - are not enough: you shall need knowledge of the foe as well, for you may be assured that they have not forgotten you."

They buried Heinrich three days after his death. Father Michael performed the funeral rites, his rich mellow voice rolling out through the Burg Fürstensee chapel and the brilliant sunlight through the stained glass casting a play of shining colours over Heinrich's face, as though to reflect the light of Heaven's gemstone gates upon him. The church was filled so that a child could not have squeezed in, and many of Heinrich's farming-folk waited in the courtyard outside, thick necks bowed in respect: he had been loved.

Ritter Dieter had come back, and there were a few of Heinrich's other knights in attendance as well, including Gottfried's father, Ritter Günther von Schlangenbad, and his elder brother, Ritter Karolan - tall men both, heavy-built, blunt-featured, and slow-footed, resembling Gottfried only in the harshness of their expressions; Margerite could not help wondering how such seed could have produced Gottfried's delicate bones and agile grace, strange as a cat springing from a mastiff's loins, but she was glad that he had found his place with her.

Heinrich, forgive me, Margerite prayed, staring up at the deep cobalt-blue glass of the Virgin's robe and the rich gold of the Christ-Child's light-burning halo as Father Michael intoned the ritual words over her husband's body. I shall always remember you with love, for you were a good man, and kind to me. You saved me from the clutches of the Light-Bearers when I had need of help, and I thank you for the blessing you gave me on your deathbed. If you knew who Bernhardt truly is, I think you would - pray you will - approve, and hope you will not feel yourself betrayed, that I had given my heart to him before ever I met you.

Margerite had been surprised to find out that Nikolaus had, in secret, set a stone-carver working on his father's effigy some months before Heinrich's death: she wondered if he had come, in spite of his self-discipline, to feel some guilt at the sight of his father lying helpless in bed for so long, or whether his action had been one more strand in the deception he had tried to create, the image of a dutiful son and a good lord. And yet that deception itself turned to good: Burg Fürstensee was kept well in order, and the Graf's lands thrived in his care. Nikolaus might have made no bad ruler - but in time, would children have begun to go missing around the Fürstensee? Or the darkness that Margerite had felt upon stepping within the castle's walls to spread out, tainting the villages one by one as a drop of sour milk would spread to curdle a full pot?

Best to thank Christ for how much was saved, Margerite thought, as Gottfried, Arnmut, Georg, Dieter, Günther, and Karolan lifted the pall upon which Heinrich lay, bearing it down the narrow staircase into the candlelit crypt where the lidless sarcophagus gaped beside a closed one bearing the figure of a long-gowned woman with an elaborate headdress - Heinrich's first wife, her plump face composed in a look of patient serenity, as though she had been content to wait through the years for her husband's company.

The knights carefully lowered the body of their Graf into the box of stone. Margerite closed her eyes a moment, for she could not help remembering the image that had come to her in the exorcism, of bones within just such coffins floating in the liquid decay of flesh; and a brief shock of soul-chilling despair ran through her veins even as her throat twisted in a pang of nausea. The body is only dust, to return to dust; the soul is God's, Margerite reminded herself sternly. And Christ has already taken Heinrich to himself: this I must believe, or give the demon a victory after its defeat.

"Ashes to ashes," Father Michael murmured. "Dust to dust." Heinrich's knights gathered about the lid with its carven stone effigy, heaving it up with soft grunts and letting it down over their Graf's body.

The stonecarver had done well: Heinrich's proud nose, the curls of his beard and his brawny shoulders and chest, all stood out clear and recognisable, though gray beneath the flickering candles - his image would last long after all who stood here were themselves gone to earth. "Requisiat in pace."

Coming back up into the church, Margerite had to blink against the painful brightness of the stained-glass window, the light stinging tears into her eyes. And that was no unseemly thing, that she should weep at Heinrich's funeral; but though she was in truth sad, she also felt herself greatly lightened, as though a single breath would suffice to fling her falcon-winging into the sky. For I am a widow again, and free, now, to marry as I will.

Perhaps it was that sense of lightness, as she lay in bed that night with Kobolt purring by her side and the gold pendant of the falcon-necklace warm between her breasts, that impelled Margerite to begin the deep breathing, the release of her curled fingers and tense feet, that would lead to letting her body drop away and her wings unfurling from her sides. For a moment she wavered - she had been safe from her foes thus far, but she knew that she would be in greater peril in the air. Yet her company had dealt them a mighty blow at Avignon, and she had walked earthbound so long...

Even as she thought that, Margerite was rising, wings beating hard to bear her up from the ground. The wooden floors, the shingles of Burg Fürstensee's roof - they melted away like mist from her sight as she circled upward, launching herself out over the lake that glimmered with moonlight like black silk rippling beneath the sun. The wind rushed through her feathers, whelming her thoughts like strong cold wine; below, she could see the white blossoms of wild cherry trees gleaming through the dark pine-branches, the fleece of new lambs pale as pearls on the shadowed grass where they slept beside their mothers.

The falcon shrieked in harsh triumph and defiance - for what could catch her in the air? Save if an eagle stooped from above to take her unawares, she was safe on the wing; her speed made her more than a match for even the greatest of birds. Margerite skimmed northwards, hill and wood and meadow unfolding like a thick-brocaded tapestry beneath her. The fresh spring air sang keen and cool to her sharpened senses; the moonlight seemed to shimmer about Burg Schwarzenfels' gray walls where it rose on its craggy black rock.

There she swerved from her course, circling the watchtowers and turrets above the thick stone wall and wheeling down the road to the rich pavilions and campfires to settle upon the earth outside the half-open door of one pavilion - some swift flicker of brightness within had drawn her eye unnoticed, perhaps, or maybe it was only that unerring sense by which she had found what she sought before. Rose lay snoring on a small bed, her long curly hair spread out in a dark sunburst over her pillow, and beside her was Wolfram's cradle.

Margerite had never looked upon her son in her flights before, whether because he had always been beside her or whether she had not dared, she did not know. Yet now the falcon stared with eyes keener than the woman's, looking up at the finely-carved cradle where the infant Graf von Falkenstein rested. Wolfram slept on his side beneath blue-embroidered blankets, his little hand curled loosely about a wooden top, as though even in his slumber he would not let go of his toy. His white skin seemed to shine in the darkness like parchment veiling a candle-flame, his fine gold hair bright as day.

In their seven and a half months of marriage, Margerite had never seen Ruprecht asleep; but she could see his face clearly in their son's, the fine line of his jaw and straight nose, the arch of his golden eyebrows and his noble forehead, and her falcon-heart beat hard enough, it seemed, to stir the small feathers along the curve of her breast. Be all things well with you, my little son, and may they stay so always! Margerite said silently to Wolfram.

She spread her wings again, ready to leap upward - but then Wolfram's blue eyes opened, and he lifted his head to look through the slats at her, pushing himself up on the side of the cradle. The painted top fell unnoticed from his hand, landing silently on the rug and rolling lopsided about its own axis.

"Pre' bird!" he said. "Want bird! Rose, want bird!"

Margerite's heart clenched, the grip of her claws loosening on the earth. If Wolfram could see her - what else had he seen, in the burning sanctum of the Light-Bearers or as they fled the storm? Or at Burg Falkenstein, when he walked for the first time to stare out into the whirling snow? He should never go there again - but, dear Maria, how can I keep him from his own land?

Though the falcon's call was harsh, the noise she made now was softer, a murmuring call to her young. And she had spoken in bird-form before, to those who could hear her... "My dear Wolfram, hush, for it is your own Mutti. Mutti loves you, my Wolfi; hush, and be good."

Wolfram's face screwed up, and he wailed piercingly, "Mutti! Mutti, come here!"

As the boy shrieked, Rose rolled out of her bed, half-tripping over the hem of her white shift as she staggered blindly in the darkness. "St. Gertrude help us!" she said. "Wolfram, what is wrong with you?" She lifted the boy up in her arms, but he kept crying, "Mutti, come here!"

"Ach, young Graf, you have only had a dream," the serving girl murmured, cradling Wolfram against her white-clad bosom. "You will see your Mutti soon enough, Christ and all his saints willing, but she is not here now."

"Is!" Wolfram insisted. "Mutti here!"

Her arms full of the child, Rose could barely move one hand to make a token sign of the Cross over herself. "If Christ is good, that is not so," she murmured to herself, then, louder, "There, there, Wolfram. You have only been dreaming."

"Mutti here! Mutti bird," Wolfram said stubbornly, his chin setting just as Ruprecht's had when he announced the beginning of his war with Heinrich. Margerite knew she could not linger any longer...and, as she struggled into the air again, she thanked Maria that Wolfram was too young to say what he had seen: Rose would think no more than she had said, that the boy had dreamed of his mother, and missed her, as any child might.

658

But those worries sloughed away like dried mud falling in flakes from the hide of a galloping horse as Margerite winged more swiftly onwards, keen and sure in her flight as an arrow from a skilled bowman's hand. It did not seem long to her before she saw the great oak trees that lined the lanes about the palace of the Bishop of Niederwald; the white doves had settled into their Burg for the night, but the white roses shone pale about the moon-rippled pond where she and Bernhardt had pledged themselves.

Few lights glimmered within, as late as the hour was - and that was natural; yet it seemed to her that she could feel a hollowness about the Bishop's palace, that it was as empty as a snail-shell from which the snail's flesh had long since withered. Bernhardt is not here, she thought. They must have begun the journey already - if we do not make haste, we shall reach the Kaiser too late! She knew what she needed, but it did not still the longing in her heart; she tilted her wings, circling, and sped above the road that led eastward, until she saw the wagons encamped by the walls of a large abbey.

There, too, nearly all the windows were dark, save for the light burning in the chapel - and one other, where the falcon saw candlelight shining within. She folded her wings and dropped as if she were stooping upon a rabbit, pulling up sharply to settle herself upon the sill. Bernhardt sat inside, the candle's flame glimmering from the golden embroidery on his deep red doublet, bringing out the heavy ridges of brow and cheekbones and pooling the hazel glint of his eyes in shadow. Across the table from him sat Bishop Otto, the great amethyst on his finger shining cool purple as he waved his hand.

"It shall be as Christ wills," the Bishop said. "He has led you this far, through many perils; do you think He will abandon you now? Be sure, I sent my swiftest rider to inform the Gräfin that the time has come, and I do not think she will fail you. She is, indeed, a remarkable woman," he added. "Even Father Kerlinger speaks well of her, and I had never thought to see such a thing."

"She is remarkable indeed," Bernhardt said. Though Margerite could tell that he was trying to keep his voice as calm as his face, the falcon heard more keenly; the mingled love and longing in it cut as keenly as a single high note bowed upon a viol, shaking through her high-wrought nerves. "Yet I do not think all her wisdom can speed horses and wagons more swiftly on their way than they are able to go: I would not have her come to Burg Karlstein, only to find that the matter is done with, and I..."

"Speak no ill!" the Bishop said, his fleshy face suddenly set in grave earnest. "This is a time when only faith can help you, for if you let yourself fall prey to doubts, you will be the less able to speak when it is needed. And you know, better than I, that whether Kaiser Karl restores your lands to you shall depend almost wholly on whether he believes you are telling the truth."

"Aye," said Bernhardt sighing. "And so it is as it was those years ago: no witnesses, no answers - unless Gerhardt is put to the question, and I do not think that likely - and only my bare word between myself and death, save that now it is the word of a proven murderer and a Free Soldier."

"If you slew your guards to escape an unjust condemnation, that is not murder," Otto argued. "And how is the Kaiser to know of your past, save you tell him? Gerhardt surely does not know what you did after you left Niederwald, for if he had known, I doubt that you would breathe today."

Bernhardt opened his mouth, but then fell silent. Of course, he could not speak of the Light-Bearers to the Bishop; yet Margerite knew as well as he whom he had pretended to serve in his long quest. The Order had failed to gain their revenge by magic, but they had one weapon yet to hand, and a harder one, perhaps, against which to struggle.

"O, my love, be sure I will not fail you," Margerite said without thought. But neither of the two men heard her, sitting grim and silent as they contemplated the battle ahead of them.

Margerite rose at first light; Else dressed her quickly, and she hastened down to the soldiers' barracks, Kobolt pouncing behind her. Gottfried and Arnmut were just coming out of their room; Etzel padded quietly on his master's other side, great white-plumed tail wagging as he saw Margerite. Again, Margerite marked the light in the two knights' faces, the almost disbelieving happiness in Arnmut's eyes as he glanced sideways at his friend. She wished that she could have left them in peace for at least a few more days, but there was no time to waste.

"Frowe Gräfin," Gottfried said, bowing to her. "Is there something you would have us do?"

"It is time to ready the guard for travel, for we must set out for Burg Karlstein as soon as we may," Margerite answered. "This time, we cannot ride as swiftly as before, for I must travel and arrive as befits my station; yet I would make all the haste possible, that we not reach the Kaiser too late. And choose those men who will guard us well, for there is no guessing what foes we may meet on the road: I have no doubt that the Landgraf von Niederwald knows very well who his enemies are by now."

"Be sure we shall not fail you, Frowe Gräfin," Gottfried replied, and the two knights bowed to Margerite again. Their formality woke a pang of regret in her breast - she had not realized how good it had been to have them calling her by name, friends and comrades-in-arms - but it could not be otherwise here, between the Gräfin and the commanders of Burg Fürstensee's guard.

"And what of the Bear's Paw?" Arnmut asked suddenly. "Frowe Gräfin, would you have them with us, or is it time for us to say our farewells to them?"

Margerite blinked. In truth, she had not thought on the matter at all: it seemed so natural to have Paul and Jochanan close, and she had come to rely upon them so greatly, that the thought of having to engage them again or pay them off had never occurred to her. And Heinrich would never have thought of hiring on Free Soldiers as part of his castle guard...but I am still Gräfin here, and Christoph gave Gottfried and Arnmut command.

"What are your thoughts?" she said. "Ritter Gottfried, Ritter Arnmut - would you have the Bear's Paw stay with us?"

"If they will stay, there are few men I would rather have by my side than Jochanan and Hauptmann Paul," Gottfried answered at once. "Though their manners may be rough and I would not ask too closely about their past, I believe they are as faithful as my good hound." He patted Etzel, who sat down at once and thumped his tail on the floor. "If I have any doubts, it is only the question of whether they would choose to settle, or would rather go on as they have been, without any master save whoever has hired them for a battle."

"I think they will stay," Arnmut murmured. "I spoke with the Bear more than once on our travels, and more than once he said that he was beginning to grow old for sleeping on the ground and not knowing where his next beer was coming from...I, too, would gladly have them with us here."

"Then I shall ask them if they would be Free Soldiers no longer, but become my guardsmen for life," Margerite said. "But in any case, I think Paul will not refuse to lead his men to Burg Karlstein with us."

Christoph and Eva, too, had risen early; the two of them were sitting in the great hall, with their heads close together. Christoph already looked stronger, good food and wholesome rest strengthening his weakened body. But is he well enough to make such a journey? I think that I must release him from his promise to me, for even travelling in a wagon will be a strain for him.

"Good morning, Margerite," Christoph said brightly. "Will you join us? There will be food soon, for I am still following your advice and breaking my fast with something more solid than bread. And you look as though you had been up all night."

Margerite sat down beside them. "That is not so. But I did receive a message before dawn. Bernhardt has set off already on his journey to Burg Karlstein, and we must make haste to ready ourselves for travel."

"So soon? Is the messenger still here?"

"No," Margerite answered. "Nor is there any letter for you to see - but I have no doubt that the summons is genuine."

Eva laid a hand on Christoph's blue velvet sleeve. "But Christoph cannot travel so soon. He will need time to rest yet - Margerite, will you free him from his oath?" She closed her hand possessively, as if to cling to her husband-to-be.

No oaths were ever sworn between us, Margerite thought, looking at the determined set of Eva's small chin and rosebud mouth, and the blue eyes staring straight into her own. She was as my squire for a time, but now she is not; she is a grown woman, and ready to fight me for Christoph's good. Is it always so between women, that what men mark with ceremony and vows, we know only in our hearts?

"I must do so, for, Christoph, you are truly not well enough for travelling. Perhaps if you can send a letter of support with us..."

"No." Christoph sat up straight, turning to face Margerite full-on. "As I swore, I will do. And it will do me good to be out in the fresh air: how can I recover my strength cooped up within castle walls? I shall ride when I can, and I shall wager my best stallion against a copper pfennig that I will be horsed and strong enough to wield a lance as well as ever I have by the time we reach Burg Karlstein!"

Margerite smiled, for now Christoph truly sounded like himself. But Eva's golden brows drew together, and she clasped Christoph's hand in her own. "My Christoph, this is not wise of you. Margerite is willing enough for you to stay behind until you are better, and I..."

"If witnesses are needed, you shall surely be one of the first among them," Christoph answered her. He disengaged his hand, lifting it up to stroke a finger gently along the curve of Eva's cheek. "My Eva, would you be parted from me again so soon? Be sure, I shall let you tend me, as I did when I was wounded in Burg Falkenstein."

"And it was no easy thing to keep you from trying to lift your shield before your arm was fully mended," Eva broke in tartly. But Margerite could see the corners of her mouth twitching, as though she were struggling to hold back a smile of satisfaction. "Love, if you promise to truly abide by my advice, and that of Margerite and Father Etienne, then I suppose you may come with us...I would not leave you so soon, either," she whispered.

Christoph sighed, closing his eyes. Then his lids sprang open again, and he looked at Margerite. "But what of Georg's knighting? Least of all would I break my oath to him, who has suffered most for me. And it would be cruel if his family were not there to witness it, but Burg Schwarzenfels is straight to the north, and we must go eastward to Bohemia."

"Graf Wolfgang is already upon the road," Margerite reassured him. "It will be two days, at least, before we are ready to depart, however much haste we make: there will be time for Georg to receive the strokes of knighthood, and sit beside his father at the celebratory feast."

Christoph's eyes narrowed. "How do you come to know so much, Margerite?" he asked, a low burr of distrust in his voice. "Surely another messenger did not come from Wolfgang this morning before dawn?"

He has known only suffering from the Art, Margerite reminded herself, and wondered, also, if Azruzor had left him with the memory of herself standing beside Nikolaus in the circle as he tried to compel the demon to leave. "Christoph, I ask you in the names of Christ and Maria to trust me, for I can swear honestly before them that I have never wished you ill, nor done you ill, save as I was too weak to free you before. But for that, I think, I have made such amends as I can...Will you believe me?"

"Believe her," Eva whispered on Christoph's other side. "I, too, can swear to the truth of what she says."

The air sighed slowly from Christoph's lungs, and at last he nodded. "There will be time on the road, I suppose, for you to explain everything to me. Do you know when Wolfgang and his family shall be here?"

"I would guess that it should be no more than two days. I will see to the arrangements for Georg's feast, if you like."

Christoph grinned. "If you are not offended, Margerite, I should like Eva to see to it - with your help, of course. She shall soon be the Gräfin von Fürstensee, and ought to get used to ruling within the castle."

He is himself again, Margerite thought, and growing quickly into his place as Heinrich's successor. And, so thinking, she said, "Herr Graf, the commanders of your guard and I were discussing the Bear's Paw. Ritter Gottfried and Ritter Arnmut both wish to hire them permanently as guardsmen, and I am of a like mind: does that meet with your approval?"

Christoph frowned in thought. "My father would not have approved. But I notice that they fought for me when my own men defended my brother - yes, I know: our guardsmen were deluded through no fault of their own. Still, I shall not swiftly forget the sight of men in Burg Fürstensee tabards lifting their swords for Nikolaus' sake. And if Gottfried, who was ever as staunchly set against the Free Companies as any man might be, speaks for them, then I shall not refuse. You!" he said to one of the servants who had begun to carry trays of food in. "Go to Paul the Bear, and tell him and Jochanan that we would see them now."

It was not long before the leaders of the Bear's Paw came into the great hall. Paul's thin red-gold hair was still rucked up in sleepy spikes, and Jochanan was rubbing his eyes; they looked as though they had dressed hastily, for the lacings of the Bear's leather jerkin were only half-tied, and Jochanan's dark tunic hung askew.

"Yes, Herr Graf?" Paul said. "What do you want of us?"

Christoph leaned forward in his seat. "Gräfin Margerite, Ritter Gottfried, and Ritter Arnmut wish to know if you will take the post of guardsmen here at Burg Fürstensee," he told them bluntly.

Paul and Jochanan looked at each other. Jochanan shrugged, spreading his hands as if to say that it was up to the Hauptmann, and Paul shuffled his feet uncomfortably. "Herr Christoph... sorry, Herr Graf...uh, I can't say yet. I need to talk to the lads first. Some of them might want to go...what kind of pay are you offering?"

Taken aback, Christoph stared at the two mercenaries. Margerite guessed that he had no more idea of what free soldiers should cost than she, as Ruprecht's new bride, had had two years ago. "Perhaps, Herr Graf, that is a matter that your commanders and I should deal with," she interposed swiftly. Then, to Paul, "It is easier and usually less dangerous duty than hiring out for battles, of course, but then, there is less chance for plunder. And you will have quarters supplied, and a beer ration - a normal beer ration," she added, remembering the first accounting she had seen from the Bear's Paw in Freiburg - "as well as food."

Paul's small blue eyes shifted from side to side, and she could see the flush rising in his unshaven cheeks. "Well, Gräfin Margerite, we'd like to stay with you while you need us. But... the lads are my troops, and I don't want to ask them to serve under a different commander. Tell you the truth, I'm not sure how much I'd like that myself...Let us think about it, all right?"

Margerite smiled gently at him. "As you will. But I shall need to hire you once more, in any case, for we shall be leaving for Bohemia in perhaps three days' time, and I would have you with us."

The Bear's broad face cleared, and he grinned. "That's a sure thing, Gräfin. You can count on us, can't she, Jochanan?"

"Of course," the gunner answered.

Margerite would have liked to ask them to sit and eat, for the scents of thyme and lamb were rising savoury from the bowls of sizzling sausages on the high table, mingling temptingly with the smell of fresh white bread and meat pastries.

That would not have been seemly; but again, she found herself almost missing those days when they travelled as equals on the road, Gräfin and knights and Free Soldiers. "Then go and ready your men; but consider our offer, for we shall ask you again when we come back from Burg Karlstein."

"Are you sure you want those men among our guard?" Christoph asked when Paul and Jochanan had left. "They are doughty warriors, as I saw well enough for myself when Father was fighting Ruprecht, but they hardly seem like ones in whose loyalty I could trust."

"I have trusted them with my life, and more, many times," Margerite said sharply. "And if there is trouble on the way, you shall see their worth for yourself."

"So be it, then," Christoph said, drawing his ivory-handled eating dagger and beginning to cut a sausage into small pieces for Eva as Kriemhilt leapt into her lap with a soft chirp.

"O, my little darling!" Eva exclaimed, petting her. "You need food for your children, don't you?...Christoph, cut those a bit smaller for my cat, for she has five little ones to feed."

Christoph laughed, his worried look gone in a heartbeat. "This castle shall soon have more cats than others have mice," he protested lightly, but he took a piece of sausage between his fingers and held it out for Kriemhilt to eat in dainty nibbles. "She has very pretty manners, doesn't she?"

"O, yes, she is a perfect little frowe," answered Eva, scratching behind the tortoiseshell queen's dark furry ears as Kriemhilt purred gratefully. "And I would far rather have cats than mice - what became of her first litter? I have not seen them."

Christoph frowned, tilting his head as if listening to a faraway music. "I do not know...I cannot remember clearly. I think...they all got away, for they went into the stones, where I... where it could not..."

"Do not think on that!" Eva said in alarm. "Hush, my
Christoph: forget that I mentioned it. It is better for you
to leave such things be. Now cheer yourself, for our guests
are not likely to sleep much longer, and if Ritter Gottfried
is not too busy with his duties, Karolan and Günther would
like to find out if he can unseat either of them on the tilting
field, for it has been long since either of them has seen their
kinsman fight."

"That will be a sight worth seeing," Christoph agreed. "I
wish that I were fit to take part."

"It will not be long, my love," Eva promised him. "But eat
now, and you will be stronger the more quickly."

I am not needed here any longer, Margerite thought,
watching the two of them together. The thought brought
her a faint echo of that same sorrow and relief she had
felt yesterday at Heinrich's funeral. And Burg Fürstensee
had never really been her home, not so much as Burg
Falkenstein...but where would she go at last, to find rest and
refuge for herself and her son?

That question shall be answered soon enough, Christ and
Maria willing, Margerite told herself, picking up a bit of
sausage and popping it into her mouth. At her feet, Kobolt
miaowed in protest, crouching down on his haunches to
leap, and she quickly dropped a piece down for him before
he jumped up on the table to take it for himself.

As Margerite had predicted, Graf Wolfgang and his family
arrived just before sunset two days later. They embraced
Christoph with delight, enquiring after his health and
exclaiming in shock when they heard of Nikolaus' betrayal.
Graf Wolfgang shook his dark head, whistling low through
his teeth.

"I would never have said it before, out of respect to your
kin, but I always thought there was something wrong about
that boy," Wolfgang told the new Graf. "I never suspected
that he would go so far, though...I should have come to visit:
I blame myself that I did not."

"It is as well," Christoph answered uncomfortably.
"And there was nothing you could do, not when the best
physicians from Freiburg could not tell. But that is over, and
I would rather not speak of it now."

Gräfin Anna patted him on the shoulder, her round face
motherly and concerned. "Of course not, my dear. Sit down
now, you look tired, and we shall speak of happier things - I
think there is a ring I recognise on Frowe Eva's finger?"

As their guests congratulated Christoph and Eva heartily
on their betrothal, Margerite went to Rose, taking Wolfram
from the serving maid's arms. Her son laughed brightly,
grabbing at his mother's linen coif and pulling it askew on
her coiled braids. "Mutti fly!" he cried.

"Hush, Wolfram," Margerite said in alarm. She had hoped
he would have forgotten what had passed in the night.

"Mutti fly," he insisted. "Mutti bird."

"Silly child, silly little Wolfram," Margerite told him
fondly, though her heart quailed within her. She could not
deny the knowledge of what would seek him out in time:
how could she disarm him of the ability to recognise the
dangers about him, as Gottfried's parents had tried, in their
ignorance, to disarm him? And yet a child could hardly learn
discretion, or know what manner of things were never to
be spoken of before others: no one would listen to a baby's
speech, but how would it be when Wolfram was old enough
to string together complete sentences, and yet too young to
learn how to keep silence when it was needed? I shall ask
Father Etienne and Gottfried for their aid, Margerite told
herself.

Thanks be to Maria that we shall be safe for a little time
yet!

"Aye, frowe, but he is stubborn," Rose agreed, smiling.
"He had an odd dream two nights ago; I found him standing
up in his cradle, and saying the same thing over and over,
and since then he has been watching the sky. He must have
missed you dreadfully."

"There is no telling what a child will fancy," Margerite said. "But you are back with me now, my little Wolfi, and you need not worry any longer."

"Mutti fly?" Wolfram asked doubtfully. Margerite cuddled him, rocking him back and forth as she carried him to her place at the table.

Georg kept his vigil in the Burg Fürstensee chapel that night, and at dawn they all gathered to see him take the oath of knighthood, the rising sun bright on his shoulder-length red hair and his white velvet doublet. The young man's scarred face was grave and thoughtful as he spoke his vow, and his honeyed tenor voice crackled with fierce fervor when he swore to defend the weak and helpless.

I would have saved him from it if I could have, Margerite thought: yet I think all Georg has gone through will make him a better knight in the end. For he knows himself what it is to be helpless against a stronger man: he has suffered terror and ravishment as those who ride brightly from castle to tourney or war seldom do, and when he lifts his sword, it will be to protect those who need his aid from those who do the Devil's work on earth.

Christoph was recovering his strength quickly: he stood straight and proud before his kneeling Knappe, and his sword's weight hardly seemed to drag at his arm as he tapped Georg's shoulders with the flat of the blade. There was little force behind the buffet he gave the young man; but the Graf did not stagger when he stretched out his hand to help the new Ritter to his feet - nor, if Georg flinched when Christoph embraced him with the kiss of brotherhood, was Margerite able to see it.

Gräfin Anna girded Georg's swordbelt about his waist, giving her son a loud kiss, and each of the knights present embraced him in turn. Konrad's powerful hug lifted his brother off his feet, and the tourney champion boomed out, "Well, little brother, now that you are a knight, you must break a lance with me after Mass! And if you can unseat me, I shall give you my own warhorse and retire forever from fighting in tournaments."

"Done!" said Georg. Margerite tried not to grit her teeth with impatience: she knew that their wagons would not be fully loaded and ready to leave until morning the next day, but the men's frivolity still grated against her nerves, knowing as she did that Bernhardt was already on the way to Burg Karlstein, while she lingered here. Yet I should not grudge Georg his day: thanks to the Bear's Paw, even making Burg Fürstensee ready for guests and feasting has hardly slowed us in preparing to go.

Ritter Konrad was in no danger of losing his warhorse to Georg; but though he dumped his brother easily on the grass three times, he praised the new knight's improvement. "You are placing your lance well now, and you have gotten faster, though you have some way to go yet," he said when he had lifted his greathelm off. Konrad's dark hair was already ruffled and matted with sweat, his strong-boned face red from the heat of helm and armour in the summer sun, but he was not even breathing hard. "Walk about a little to work off the stiffness from your fall while I ride against Ritter Gottfried; then I shall show you a few more tricks. Ritter Gottfried, are you ready?"

"I am," said Gottfried, his voice muffled within his helm. "Will you make such an offer to me as you made to Georg?"

"Indeed not!" Konrad laughed. "You were already quite good when I tilted against you last, and I have no doubt that you have gotten better since."

As the two knights mounted up and trotted their horses to opposite ends of the tilting field, Christoph leaned close to Eva and said, "Now this shall be a bout to watch! The lance is Gottfried's best weapon; he is handicapped a little by his weight, for one so light is more easily unseated, but then, his horse can move all the faster for it. He is almost always the first to strike a blow; still, a champion such as Konrad knows many ways to turn the thrust. And Konrad has proper tilting harness as well - you see how the left side of his helm is plated with no breath-holes, and the left side of his armour is thicker than the right. Now watch..."

Gottfried's brown stallion and Konrad's gray were gaining speed now, thundering into a full gallop. Though the lances were rebated, with blunt crowns instead of sharp war-tips, Margerite found herself holding her breath: even tourney-tilting was so dangerous that, until Pope John had lifted the ban earlier in the century, those who died in tournament were declared suicides and denied burial in consecrated ground.

As Christoph had said, Gottfried's lance struck home a heartbeat before Konrad's, and the bigger knight tilted his shield skillfully: he swayed beneath the impact as the wooden pole shattered, though he kept the crown of his own lance on target. Margerite's eyes were not well-trained enough to see quite what happened then, but it seemed to her that Gottfried turned sideways, and Konrad's lance slid past his shield without breaking.

"By Christ, they're good!" Christoph breathed. "Did you see that, Eva?" He went on explaining enthusiastically as the horses slowed and Arnmut carried a fresh lance out to Gottfried. Most of what he said made little sense to Margerite, and she doubted it was much more comprehensible to Eva; but Eva nodded and murmured as though she were fascinated by everything her betrothed was saying.

The second pass was closer still. Both lances shattered, and both knights rocked hard in their saddles; Margerite saw that Gottfried was nearly flung clear, only a stunningly graceful twist of his body keeping him in his seat.

"Now they have each other's measure," Christoph said. "This pass will be the true one: watch closely."

Again the horses began to pick up speed, their big hooves tearing divots of turf from the field. At the last moment, the tip of Gottfried's lance dipped, impacting squarely on Konrad's shield: the two lances broke with a thunderous crack, and Gottfried flew sideways from his saddle. Konrad was nearly knocked off as well, clinging to his horse's neck with much less grace than his opponent had shown, but he managed to haul himself back up and get his steed under control.

Gottfried's horse stopped perhaps two hundred feet away, as his master sat up slowly. Konrad slid from his saddle, hastening to Gottfried's side and offering him a hand.

"Well-fought!" Margerite heard Konrad saying as the two knights walked back together, greathelms under their arms. "With a bit of proper training and a little more weight on your bones, you could be a tourney champion yourself. You very nearly had me off there, and were you as heavy as I, I am not sure I would have unseated you. If you come to Köln this summer..."

The tilting went on for some time more. Gottfried was not unhorsed again; Arnmut and Georg also gave good accounts of themselves, to Margerite's pride. As for Christoph, Margerite had been afraid that he would take it ill to watch and not ride himself, but even watching the informal tournament seemed to have quite restored his spirits: he spent more time walking about than sitting down, and cheered loudly when he was not explaining the finer detail of the mock combats to Eva.

It was, rather, Margerite who found herself saddened. She could not help thinking of Bernhardt...of how it would be to hear his lance booming against another knight's shield, of seeing him lift his weapon to salute her openly before he lowered it and urged his horse on to a full gallop - her silken kerchief tied about his arm, perhaps, that all might know he fought for her...Bernhardt has fought for me in real battle, she reminded herself.

Such tilting may be pleasant to watch, and calls for bravery; men have died in it before, and yet it is still gilding on parchment, with no solid metal beneath it. But though it might be frivolous, Margerite could not help wondering how Bernhardt would acquit himself against Gottfried, or Konrad. She knew that he was a strong fighter, well-trained and skilled from defending his life in more battles than most knights saw in their lives. And yet it must have been nearly a decade since he last ran a formal tilt: how different would that be from the brutal struggle of war?

Still, that will not matter until the Kaiser has given his judgement: if it goes well, there shall be plenty of time for Bernhardt to tilt with his knights, and if not... Maria help us, such things shall not matter.

When Konrad had run the last pass, skillfully unseating Gottfried's father, he doffed his helm and came over to kneel before Margerite. "Now, frowe Gräfin, since I have been undefeated this day, I would ask a boon of you."

"What would you have?" Margerite said, looking down from her chair at Konrad's sweat-soaked face. His strong features were very serious, and she was sure that this would be no little thing - but though the day's tilting was hardly a proper tourney, she felt it would be difficult to refuse him.

"Let me travel to Burg Karlstein with you. My father should stay in his lands; but I am free to go, and our family would lend its support to yourself and Herr Bernhardt. And besides - " Ritter Konrad grinned suddenly, a look that reminded her very much of Georg - "it may be that I shall have a chance to show my skill before Kaiser Karl while we are there; for my elder brother Hugo is in the Imperial guard, and though I may not be his match yet, I think I am doing well enough not to be ashamed before the Kaiser's eyes. Will you grant me this, frowe Gräfin?"

Margerite's first impulse was to agree gratefully. But Georg had made a brave offer likewise, and been ill-repaid: how could she drag a second of Graf Wolfgang's sons into the perils they faced with a clean conscience? Bad enough that Georg, as a witness to the battle with Ortlieb, would have to go along: Konrad knew nothing of the foes that might assail them, nor, champion though he was, would he have any defense against the subtler arts of their enemies - even so much as a whisper of what had befallen his brother in Christoph's service: such words at a chosen time could tear their company disastrously asunder.

Margerite was about to say no when she heard a soft chirping purr, and Kobolt darted out from behind her chair to arch his back and rub against the skirt-hoops of Konrad's armour. The knight's eyes flickered down, and his mouth tightened - in anger, Margerite thought at first; but then she saw the faint wrinkling at the corners of Konrad's eyes, and realized that he was fighting to suppress a smile. She reminded herself sternly that Kobolt's judgement was not that of a human, for he had taken to Ruprecht and Madame du Guesclin, as well as to Gottfried; but if there were any cause to doubt Konrad's heart, it must be well-hidden indeed to escape not only her gaze, but those of Gottfried and Father Etienne.

"I will grant it," Margerite said.

Konrad bowed his head, taking her hand and kissing it courteously. "I shall defend and serve you well until you are safely home again, frowe Gräfin."

"I thank you greatly, Herr Ritter, and in turn shall do all for your sake that I may," Margerite replied - though his words left her wondering, as she had before: But where shall I be safely home?

Their company left just after dawn the next day - Margerite, Christoph, Eva, Georg, Konrad, Gottfried, Arnmut, Father Etienne, and some eighty men-at-arms, including those men of the Bear's Paw who were hale enough to march and fight. At Gottfried's advice, Christoph had left Burg Fürstensee in Ritter Dieter's hands. Father Etienne had also spent a full evening with Herr Jakob, and pronounced him fit to carry out the duties of a seneschal by himself, assuring Margerite quietly that he had taken such steps as would make certain that Herr Jakob was no longer vulnerable to such Light-Bearer magics as Nikolaus had worked on him.

Rose, Else, and Eva's maidservant Mathilde came along as well, and old Albrecht insisted on accompanying them to tend Christoph; but Margerite had drawn the line at allowing Ernst's presence on their journey, telling the physician that Father Etienne was well able to see to the Graf's health.

Margerite started on horseback, but Wolfram, she quickly found, was growing too large and lively for her to ride easily with her son in her lap, so that it was not long before she gave up and got into the wagon where Christoph rode. At once Wolfram toddled over to the basket where Kriemhilt slept curled around her kittens; one green eye slitted open, and the cat let out a warning "mrrow" when he reached for her tail.

"This is not how I had dreamed of setting out to see the Kaiser," Christoph said ruefully. "I had always thought that I would be horsed and armoured, ready to offer him my service in battle, not riding in a wain as an invalid."

"Still, you shall do him service, and I believe that you have a wager with me as to the condition you shall be in when we reach Burg Karlstein."

"That is so." Christoph grinned. "And I am feeling better every day, so I think my best stallion is safe. But you say I shall do Kaiser Karl service: how may I do that, when I know so little of what has befallen?"

Margerite looked ahead to where Father Etienne rode beside Gottfried and Arnmut. The sunlight shone brightly from the two knights' bascinets, glinting in ripples from the chainmail on their arms and picking out the gilded thread that outlined the crossed red swords on their blue tabards in lines of fire, but the canon's black rolled hat and cassock seemed to suck in the light; the only brightness about him was the fine glint of silver strands through the thick wavy brown hair hanging about his shoulders - and were there more white hairs on Father Etienne's head than there had been before they drove out Azruzor?

Etienne, one day you shall meet a foe too fearsome for you to overcome, and your bones shall lie unburied in the dark wood...Margerite crossed herself at the memory of the demon's words. If she were a wanderer, with no safe place to call home - how much more so Father Etienne? At least she had her son, her love for Bernhardt, and her hope that her journey might come to end; the priest had only the Art, his faith, and his place in the long secret war, and Azruzor's prophecy was all too plausible.

But she also remembered Brother Helmuth's words at Brother Wolfgang's graveside: Often we have had to leave our dead where they fell, comforted only in the knowledge that they died for Christ and will be taken into Heaven, regardless of where their mortal clay lies. I need not add to Etienne's burden by asking him to make this choice, Margerite told herself. Christoph was looking at her curiously, little lines of worry worming into the skin of his forehead and the corners of his eyes.

"What is wrong, Margerite? You must tell me sooner or later, you know."

"I was thinking of something else for a moment," Margerite confessed to him. "If you are ready to hear, then, I shall tell you. For you have the right to know, after all, and if someday our foe returns to Burg Fürstensee, Eva should not have to defend it alone." Kobolt crept into her lap, purring, and as she stroked the black tomcat's soft fur, Margerite noticed that her hand was trembling, but she forced herself to continue steadily. "The tale begins... for me it began when a messenger came to my father's keep two years past, but perhaps it truly started earlier, when the daughter of a poor knight of Niederwald made her way to the Landgraf's Schloss - or when Lucifer said, Non serviam, and was cast flaming from Heaven..."

Margerite told Christoph of all that had befallen, save for how Ruprecht had fathered Wolfram. He listened quietly, until she spoke of the salt caves beneath Burg Fürstensee, and then he drew in his breath. "I knew that the caves were there: there was a time, very long ago, when the Fürstensee folk mined there, and an old saying that Burg Fürstensee was built on salt. We had always thought that meant the money to build it came from selling the stuff that we collected at the mouths of the salt springs, and that they had simply weakened over the years...

I wonder how many people old Graf Walther had to silence?" he added thoughtfully. "Or whether it would be wiser to open up the caves for mining again, or to keep that back door in case of need?"

Margerite thought of her sanctum - still whole and undisturbed: she had stepped into it for a few moments before she, Etienne, and Gottfried had undertaken the cleansing of Nikolaus'. Even though Nikolaus had known she was no longer an Order member, he had left it alone - by the strength of the Light-Bearers' honour? Or because he could not cross her wards? If the salt caves were opened, she would have to scrape away the paint, free the power she had built there, and know that miners' rough boots would tread where she had once chanted in her holy sanctuary.

But, if she left Burg Fürstensee, she would have no right to speak in that decision: Christoph was Graf, and the castle and all beneath it were his. "That is for you - and Eva - to choose," she said sadly. "But we found the way out only by the help of Kobolt and Kriemhilt..."

Christoph said nothing more until Margerite told him of Gottfried's gifts. He nodded when she mentioned that the knight could see what others could not; she found herself reluctant to speak of his ability to read thoughts, for she knew how frightening it could be to know that another could see what was hidden in one's mind, but if Gottfried stayed at Burg Fürstensee as the first of Christoph's knights, the Graf would need to know all his talents. Margerite tried to skim over how Gottfried had come to his full strength, but Christoph shook his head sadly.

"I remember what it said to him through my mouth. Believe me, Margerite, I should have cut my tongue out before speaking thus to such a good knight! I heard it taunting him, and could do nothing."

"That is over now," Margerite answered swiftly. "You have made amends as best you could - and Christ and Maria may be thanked, that the evil the demon willed turned at the last to good, for if Gottfried had never been forced to his gifts' awakening, we should not have escaped in Avignon..."

"I have never heard such a tale," Christoph said at last when Margerite had finished. "And save for what I endured myself, I should not have believed it - I like it little, that there are such powers in this world against which a man's sword is useless. If I could have met it face to face, matters should have gone differently."

"Maybe. But that is the way of things: this earth is but a part of God's creation, and would be the least part, save only for Christ's humility in descending to redeem it."

Christoph's lips pressed together. "Still, that one as weak as Nikolaus should have overcome me so easily..."

"Nikolaus was not weak!" Margerite answered sharply. "That was your great error, Christoph: you underestimated him and mocked him, and never saw his strength. If you had known before what you should have learned by now, you might have had a man of wisdom and courage, and skilled in the Art as well, by your side, instead of a bitter foe. There is nothing you can do for your brother now, save pray for his soul - and look for your own part in his downfall. For he sprang from the same loins as yourself: it may be that you shall have a son like him, who cares more for books than the tilting field, and then what shall you do?"

Christoph shook his head slowly, looking past Margerite at the silvery ripples of wind over the burgeoning green wheatfields. "I do not know. I only wished to make a man of my little brother - how did I make him a monster?"

"Nikolaus made his own choice. Yet you aided in driving him to it, as, Christ rest him, did Heinrich. Do not blame yourself too much, but do not excuse yourself from blame either. I know this is a bitter lesson, but would you have the bitterness without even the learning?"

"You have changed too, Margerite," Christoph murmured. "Almost, you remind me of Father Etienne...I shall think hard on what you have said, and mayhap I shall know what to do if I sire a son who is more like Nikolaus than myself, and make amends to my brother's soul thus. But other matters are closer. We cannot go to the Kaiser with this tale in its fullness: what do you wish me to say to him?"

"I wish you to speak for Bernhardt. You fought against him, and saw how he kept to the rules of war; you saw, as well, how faithfully he served me in Burg Falkenstein. Let it be known that Fürstensee will defend the rights of Bernhardt von Niederwald, however his defense is needed: that shall suffice, for your part."

The journey to Burg Karlstein was smooth - almost too smooth; yet Margerite found that, now and again, she would feel a prickling on the back of her neck and look nervously about her, and as they crossed into Bohemia, Gottfried seemed to grow ever more high-strung, so that he would start when Arnmut laid a hand on his arm, or if he were spoken to unexpectedly - or sometimes at nothing at all, though he never said why.

Father Etienne, in contrast, seemed to become graver and more quiet, yet it seemed to Margerite that she could feel his attention and his power spreading about their company like a deep pool glinting with sudden sparkles of gold. She herself longed to fly out as a falcon at night, to spy out the land with eyes keener than those of her body, eyes that might see where their foes lurked. But she did not have to ask Etienne in order to know how unwise that was: though her necklace might hide her from the Light-Bearers' scrying, her falcon-shape would draw their notice like a beacon-fire on a night-blackened hilltop.

For the most part, they guested in castles along the way:
the Graf von Fürstensee and the infant Graf von Falkenstein
were welcomed willingly by their peers and the lesser keep-
knights. Sometimes they stopped in abbeys; it was rare
that they had to find a guesthouse, or camp along the road.
Margerite was not surprised by how many of the rulers and
abbots they visited knew Father Etienne: the priest had been
travelling in his strange work for twenty-odd years, after
all. What shocked her was how swiftly the news of Ortlieb's
death had gone before them, the scattered flotsam of truth
borne up on a swelling wave of rumour.

To Margerite's relief, her part in slaying the Landgräfin
von Niederwald had almost been lost as the tale grew: it was
said that the Devil had appeared on a great black horse to
bear Ortlieb away, or that she had burst into flame and fled
when the priest who was with Bernhardt von Niederwald
sprinkled holy water upon her. Her wagon, it was said, had
been stacked high with the bones of murdered children, and
servants at Schloss Niederwald had recounted how their
mistress had bathed in the blood of virgin maidens to keep
her skin white and soft.

Rumour had it that Bernhardt, in his exile, had fought
with the White Company; that he had taken the tabard of
the Teutonic Knights and battled against the heathens in the
East; that he had dwelt in a charcoal-burner's hut, toiling
patiently like a peasant as he awaited his day for return;
and that the Virgin herself had appeared, with the Christ-
Child in her arms, to ride beside him when he went to face
the sorceress Ortlieb at last. There was no arguing with
such stories: Margerite and her companions only listened
in amazement, though Margerite, at least, found herself
secretly glad that most of the tales painted Bernhardt as a
hero.

At last they came within sight of Burg Karlstein, the square towers of the Kaiser's castle standing high upon a steep grayish chalk-crag and the roof-spires pointing proudly upwards. The black Imperial eagle on its golden banner and the Luxemburger lion, silver on red, fluttered bright against the blue sky, announcing that Kaiser Karl was in residence. About the crag's foot swept the river Beronka, glittering in the sunlight where it rushed beneath the thick summer-leaved trees.

Even from the distance, Margerite could see the thickness of the crenellated walls and the clean sharp edges of the light reddish stones, the towers' peaked gray roofs lifting each above the next as the hill rose beneath them. Unlike most castles, where towers and wings were added generation upon generation and often haphazardly, Burg Karlstein was so perfectly constructed that its massive parts might almost have grown from the living rock like a nest of great pale crystals.

Only the Kaiser's power and wealth could have raised such a castle in a scant few years: but this was Karl's own seat, and though Bohemia was far from the Rhine, Burg Karlstein - by the Kaiser's will - was the heart of the Holy Roman Empire. Christoph turned his horse, trotting back to the wagon where Margerite rode with Eva, their serving-maids, and Wolfram.

"Well, Margerite, I am as hale as I promised I would be!" he said, grinning cheerfully at her. The Graf von Fürstensee had thrived on the road: his broad breastplate, dagger- and sword-chains jingling from their anchoring points on his chest, fit him well again, as did the padded doublet of blue fustian beneath it, and his cheekbones no longer glared from his face. "I believe you owe me a copper pfennig."

"Gladly paid," Margerite replied, fishing in her purse and tossing the little coin to him.

Christoph snapped it out of the air with a single flick of his hand, still grinning in delight, then rode back to his place behind the two standard-bearers. Arnmut carried the Fürstensee banner; Margerite, having none of the Falkenstein men with her, had prevailed upon Jochanan to bear her son's standard - the white eagle's head upon its red field which Wolfram had inherited from Ruprecht: they would be recognised, for they had sent swift riders ahead to announce their approach. As they drew closer, upraised trumpets glittered gold from the thick walls of Burg Karlstein, and Margerite heard the high fanfare drifting through the warm summer air.

The path up to Burg Karlstein was steep enough that Margerite could hear the horses that drew her wain blowing hard as they neared the gates. Besieging the Kaiser's castle - pray God it was never tried! - would be no easy task: Karl had chosen his site and built his fortress to last until the next millennium, or longer, if Christ did not return in judgement first. The castle's massive gates were open, but a troop of knights stood at attention there, the sunlight sparking from their brass-edged armour and the gilded Imperial arms impressed on the leather coverings of their shields; their open-faced helms were crested with bright feathers, Imperial gold and black or Luxemburger silver and red.

Another fanfare sounded as Arnmut and Jochanan reached the gate, stepping aside to let Margerite's wagon pull up beside Christoph. Margerite lifted her son in her arms as the most ornately armoured of the Kaiser's guard came forward.

"Graf von Fürstensee, Graf and Gräfin von Falkenstein," he called out in a strong voice. "I welcome you to Burg Karlstein in the Kaiser's name. You and your men may enter."

The horses raised their heads, stepping in proudly. Margerite had seen peasant's houses that were not as broad in their widest point as the thickness of Burg Karlstein's walls; the highest of the castle's square towers loomed mountainous above the courtyard. Servants in the Kaiser's livery were hastening at once to take the reins of the men's horses.

A tall blond knight in a doublet of red velvet brocade embroidered with the silver fork-tailed Luxemburger lion came to the front of the wagon; Margerite saw his blue eyes flicker from herself to Eva, as if he wondered for a second which of them were the Gräfin von Falkenstein, but he must have remembered then that the Graf von Falkenstein was yet an infant, for he bowed to Margerite.

"Gräfin, allow me to assist you," he said courteously. Margerite passed Wolfram to Rose and gave the Kaiser's knight her hand, letting him support her weight as she dismounted from the wagon. He aided Eva likewise, then said, "Gräfin, Frowe Eva, we received your messenger in good time, and chambers have been readied for you. The bells shall soon ring sext, and the noonday dinner be served after that - alas, the Kaiser shall not be in attendance this day, but it is his will that his guests be invited to eat in his hall. Unless, of course," the knight added politely, "you are so wearied from your travelling that you would sooner rest for a time."

"We shall gladly accept the invitation," Margerite replied.

Forbidding as Burg Karlstein might be from the outside, the Kaiser's seat was so dazzling within that it took all Margerite's willpower not to stop and stare at the painted frescoes and gold-leafed molding in the halls.

Karl IV had called the greatest artists in his realm together
to adorn his castle: the walls shone with intense colours,
the blue of powdered lapis, the green of crushed emeralds
and malachite, and the true clear red of rubies, interspersed
lavishly with glistening gold and silver.

Only the Papal palace in Avignon, Margerite thought,
might be its equal - and perhaps not even that; but she
was a Gräfin and the mother of a Graf, and she would not
gawk like a peasant. The tall knight led them along the
passages quickly, up a coiling spiral of stairs, and on to their
chambers.

"If you wish, I shall return to escort you to dinner," he
offered.

Margerite smiled, holding her hand out for him to kiss.
"That would be kind of you."

As the guest-chambers of Cardinal de Grenville had
been, those of Burg Karlstein were better appointed than
Heinrich's rooms in his own castle. Margerite thought
that surely by now, she should be used to such splendour
- but she found herself too uneasy to sit, or even move to
lay Wolfram on the white silken bedclothes. She breathed
deeply, trying to gather her feeling of distress to a clear point
so that she could face and name it: what was amiss here?

Something creaked faintly behind her, and Margerite
whirled so swiftly that Wolfram began to cry in her arms.
The heavy square-carved oaken door was swinging slowly
ajar - then she saw the black paw curling clawed around its
edge, followed by a black head pushing its way in.

As soon as he had forced the door widely enough, Kobolt
leapt in and onto the bed in two great bounds, growling
and clawing at the coverlet, then biting into it and kicking
violently with his back legs. Rose cried out and started
forward to pull the cat away; but Margerite saw the writhing
of something beneath the white silk, and commanded,
"Rose, stop!"

Suddenly Margerite felt a snap, a brief flare, and then nothing - like a dry willow wand breaking and tossed into the heart of a hot fire. Kobolt lay quiet on the ravaged bed, purring in triumph, and she sighed in deep relief.

"The Kaiser's coverlet, frowe!" Rose wailed in horror, looking at the gashes Kobolt's claws had left in the thick silk. "What can we do? What will he do to us for ruining it?"

Half-dizzy with relief, Margerite laughed. "Rose, I do not think Kaiser Karl concerns himself with the bedclothes in his guest-chambers. And if his servants ask questions, I shall be the one to answer them." But her legs were trembling as she laid Wolfram on the bed beside the great black cat.

She had known for days that the Light-Bearers must be readying their reception for her at Burg Karlstein - was it luck, that she had gotten past the first trap so easily, or was that no more than a gauntlet cast at her in challenge? A warning of honour, or a gesture of contempt, perhaps, depending on the measure of those who waited inside the Kaiser's castle: she knew now that among the Order, there were those who were capable of either.

"Be quiet for a little time, Rose," Margerite ordered her servant, sitting down on the bed beside her son and beginning the deep breaths that would calm and still her mind, free her senses to feel whether there was any other danger lurking in her room.

Though it was full daylight, the Kaiser's banquet hall blazed with candles, their flames reflecting tiny everywhere from gold and silver and polished gems, so that it was as bright inside the castle as outside. The walls were painted with images of Kaiser Karl's forefathers, from ancient white-bearded Noah and several Biblical patriarchs, to the antique gods, thunderbolt-wielding Jupiter and dark Saturn, and their heroic descendants Ilus and Priam, to Karl the Great crowned and throned in a place of pride, followed by the lines of the Frankish kings and Luxemburger rulers. The tablecloths were embroidered silk, the goblets jewel-studded gold; the voices of a choir and the sweet thrumming of their instruments rose high above the talk.

Margerite had to blink against the splendour, for it seemed to it that her mind could not take it all in; but in her arms, Wolfram laughed and stretched out his hands as if to embrace the whole hall - she had not dared leave her son with only Rose and Else, not even with Kobolt to guard him as well.

"Graf von Fürstensee, Gräfin von Falkenstein, Frowe Eva, Herr Konrad, Herr Georg, I believe that your places are this way," said the Kaiser's knight. They followed him along - they were not, of course, at the high table: that would be reserved for nobles above their own station, but they were well-seated along the right bench, above the saltcellar in the shape of a gilded swan with winking ruby eyes.

Margerite was more than grateful for Cardinal de Grenville's gifts to them: in her blue silk embroidered with silver threads, and Eva's rose wrought with gold, they were as well-dressed as most of the women there; nor were Gottfried in his dark ermine-trimmed doublet and Arnmut in his blue silk with cloth-of-gold sleeves any less noble in appearance. Christoph might have looked a little shabbier in contrast, for the red-on-blue brocade of his doublet was a little worn in places, and the golden silk of his dagged sleeves was plain, but the heavy chain of silver rondels set with emeralds that draped his heavy shoulders proclaimed his rank clearly enough.

Georg's red hair flamed above the white velvet doublet he had worn for his knighting, green silken sleeves flaring out from its fur-trimmed armholes; Konrad's black velvet overgarment, buttoned with huge silver clasps, was fitted so tightly to his muscular chest and slim hips that Margerite almost wondered how he could breathe in it, and his pale yellow sleeve-pennants trailed nearly to his knees.

As for Father Etienne, he had clothed himself more finely that day than Margerite had ever seen him dress: a robe of deep red velvet with small gold-threaded starbursts, girded with a belt on which similar gold starbursts glittered from the black leather, draped his slim figure; though he still wore his canon's hat, the horns of its rolled corners shadowing his face with priestly dignity, his large gold crucifix hung, not on its usual simple chain, but on a massive collar of gold squares set with oval stones of a clear dark red. None of them, Margerite thought, would need to be ashamed here at the Kaiser's court.

Then Margerite saw Bishop Otto's purple vestments, and beside him - her heart leapt like a salmon in her breast - Bernhardt, his hazel eyes fixed upon her and his lips parted in joyous disbelief as he rose from his seat to greet her. She shifted Wolfram to her left hip, holding her right hand out for Bernhardt to kiss, and a shiver ran through her body as his soft mouth and close-cropped brown beard brushed her skin.

"Gräfin von Fürstensee," Bernhardt said warmly, straightening and looking down into her eyes. "Mother Maria be thanked, that you arrived so swiftly! I did not think you would be here for at least two weeks yet, if not longer. And by then it should have been too late, for the Kaiser's counsellors have bidden him hear this case soon - aided, I think," he added softly, "by those who are no friend to us: Gerhardt sits at Kaiser Karl's high table as Landgraf von Niederwald."

Margerite glanced involuntarily towards the head of the hall. Bernhardt's brother, the Landgraf's narrow gold coronet on his thinning brown hair, sat there indeed, leaning towards a man in a gem-studded doublet of particoloured red and gold velvet. Although neither of them was looking at her, Margerite felt the warning prickle lifting the small hairs at the back of her neck.

"There is more yet to tell," Bernhardt went on. "But come, sit down by me and we shall speak further. Herr Christoph, greetings! It is good to see you looking so well."

Christoph swallowed audibly, a fleeting look of angry shame flashing on his face before he could master it. "Herr... Bernhardt, my title is Graf von Fürstensee now. My father died a few days before we set out."

Bernhardt's powerful chest rose in a deep breath beneath the dark blue silk of his long tunic. "It grieves me to hear that," he said. "Graf Heinrich was a fine man: I found him strong and honourable in war, and he was accounted a good ruler in peace. The Gräfin had told me of his illness, and I prayed for his recovery. May Christ receive his soul."

Margerite did not miss the glimmer of suspicion in Christoph's gray-green eyes, but the young Graf held his tongue. Yet when you have come to know Bernhardt, Christoph, she thought, you will know that every word he spoke was true - however it might have rent his heart.

"And you, Georg," Bernhardt said. "I see that you are belted and spurred now - my congratulations for a well-deserved accolade!"

Georg nodded, a smile twisting crookedly onto his scarred face. "Thank you, Herr Bernhardt. Have you met my brother, Herr Konrad?"

"Herr Konrad von Schwarzenfels," Bernhardt said, bowing to the other knight. "I have not met you, I believe, but your father guested with us once at Schloss Niederwald, and I have heard of your fame as a tourney champion. It is an honour to meet you."

"Likewise, Herr Bernhardt," Konrad replied. "I have come in my father's stead to offer Burg Schwarzenfels' support to you. Such deeds as those of which I have heard are deserving of honour, though I understand from Gräfin Margerite and my brother that the stories have changed a trifle in the telling."

Bernhardt's mouth tightened, and though he did not look
up towards the high table again, Margerite could see the
tenseness gathering in the heavy muscles of his shoulders.
"That is so, and in more way than one. But I thank you
greatly for your offer of help, for I may well need it. Ritter
Gottfried, Ritter Arnmut, Frowe Eva, Father Etienne - it is a
great joy to see you again, and I pray that matters here turn
out as well as they did when last you were beside me."

Bernhardt continued speaking courteously as they
took their places at the table and greeted Bishop Otto. To
Margerite's relief, fine gilded goblets had been set out for
them; her silver vessel had been one of the finest possessions
of Ritter Martin's daughter, but it had picked up a few small
dents in the course of her travels, and she would have been
ashamed to put it on the table. But if I become Landgräfin
von Niederwald...no, best not to think of such things yet, lest
God punish me for my pride.

The servers were bearing the first course around now,
their platters heaped high with glittering thrushes gilded
with what Margerite thought might be real gold leaf. She had
seen Liutberg's apprentices applying a tissue of metal gilding
similarly to small birds before Ortlieb's All-Souls' feast,
but she was not certain of how to eat them until she saw
Bernhardt picking one up neatly and biting into it without
showing any concern. And if the gold is pure, it can do our
bodies no harm.

Still, she hesitated: that serving-woman there, with her
hair neatly coifed in white linen and her eyes discreetly
lowered - Margerite could not see whether any of her rings
were engraved; could she have sprinkled something upon
the golden thrushes that she was tonging onto Eva's plate?
Or the cellarer's assistants, treading silently around the table
in their long-pointed, silver-buttoned shoes to fill the guests'
goblets with wine: might one of them be an initiated Light-
Bearer, or under the thrall of the Order - simply in its pay,
perhaps?

Mother Maria help me, I would sooner be eating coarse pea-bread and stockfish in Merlin's wagon than have to look with fear at the Kaiser's board! she thought, and absently caught Wolfram's small hands in her own as he reached out to grab one of the gold birds on her plate. Margerite did not think it was by chance that Gottfried leaned a little over the table to look at her then. But there was no more to his severe gray stare, she thought, than his struggle to make out her features; his dark silky hair, unbound and combed out to fall about his shoulders, shimmered as he nodded to her and delicately began to eat one of the thrushes.

She heard the knight's voice as clearly as if he had spoken aloud: I am watching: thus far, we need not fear what is set before us. And I do not think our enemies are so foolish as to try poisoning us at Kaiser Karl's table. As Margerite turned back towards Bernhardt, she saw a little smile, as of some private mirth, on his lips. "What is it?" she asked, for she knew that, even as Herr Bernhardt von Niederwald with all his courtly graces remembered, Bernhardt did not smile without reason.

"A small thing only," Bernhardt answered, turning another gold thrush over in his strong scarred fingers. "May all our enemies' strokes go so astray...I had not been here longer than a day when I was informed that you were flaunting Ritter Gottfried as your lover in Avignon."

Margerite was glad that the white silk of her coif hid her ears, for she could feel them flaming red beneath the silver-threaded coils of her braids. She did not know whether to laugh or be furious; but she merely said, "I hope you did not believe this," and bit deliberately into one of her thrushes.

Bernhardt's smile widened, and Margerite felt her heart fluttering beneath her ribs - dear Christ, they had shared so little laughter in their love! "Neither of you nor of Ritter Gottfried, for I know you, and I was more than shocked to see him wearing Frowe Birgitta's favour."

Then the mirth fell from Bernhardt's face like a glass mask dropping to shatter on the floor, and he added grimly, "But it troubles me that those who bear us no love should have chosen such a means to drive a wedge between us, for it leads me to wonder what more has been whispered, and into which ears."

Suddenly the delicately-flavoured flesh of the small bird seemed tasteless and dry in Margerite's mouth, the shreds of fine gilding tickling her tongue unpleasantly, so that she had to wash it down her throat with a good swallow of spicy white wine. "Yet the Kaiser is said to be a pious man, and a great stumbling-block to those who are not likewise," she said hopefully, wondering which of them she was trying to convince. "...Did Father Kerlinger come with you?"

"Yes. You do not see him here because he has no taste for such finery of food as the Kaiser's kitchens serve. He hopes, I believe, that this case will open the door for the Inquisition to act more freely in the Empire, so that his aid shall be valuable beyond measure." Yet there was a look of sadness on Bernhardt's face as he spoke, his thick brown brows drawn together and the hollows of his cheeks shadowed beneath the strong arching bones: was he, perhaps, picturing Gerhardt given to torture by water or fire or strappado? Even Christoph in his extremity had only sought Nikolaus' death...Margerite was glad that she could not know what her beloved was thinking.

The servers brought around the second course, suckling piglets roasted to a glistening brown and stuffed with a mixture of fine cheese and breadcrumbs. As he cut the pork into small pieces for Margerite and himself, Bernhardt told Margerite more of how matters had gone thus far. He had been received with courtesy, but far less than that due him as the son of Landgraf Bertrik von Niederwald; he did not elaborate, but Margerite knew that he should have been sitting at the Kaiser's high table.

As to whether it was Kaiser Karl's own choice to hear the case quickly, or whether the Emperor's secretaries had scheduled it, Bernhardt did not know, but he was sure that it had been the hope of those who favoured Gerhardt that Margerite and Father Etienne would not appear at Burg Karlstein in time to speak.

"In truth," he murmured, "I had almost begun to give up hope myself, for I knew that you could not leave your battle once you had joined it, and did not know how long it might take you to deal with matters at Burg Fürstensee. And when I was told that our audience would take place in a week's time, I nearly gave way altogether to despair, for I knew there was no way for Bishop Otto's messenger to reach you in time, save if Maria sent an angel to speed his horses on the road...How did you know when to set out? Or should I ask?"

Margerite looked into Bernhardt's eyes; she could almost have drowned in the green-flecked brown of their depths, as though her soul were pouring into him through their locked gazes. She swallowed hard, tasting the rich echo of succulent pork and cheese in the back of her mouth. "Best to praise Mother Maria that we did know," she replied. "I am sorry that you had to fear we would not, but there was no way to send word to you."

"Still, you are here, and I am abashed at my lack of trust," he said warmly. "But to come so far, and think that I saw the blade of defeat descending upon me in the last moment..."

The pain scraped raw in Bernhardt's voice: though his chestnut hair was neatly dressed and curled about his shoulders like a proper nobleman's, and though he was clothed in the finery befitting the son of a Landgraf, his hand rested upturned on the table and Margerite could see the slick white scar upon his wrist where the blue silk of his sleeve had fallen back - he would bear that mark of his deepest despair to the end of his days, even as her own back would always be scarred by the hailstones that had gouged her skin as she fled naked from Avignon.

"Let us trust yet in Maria and in Christ, who have brought us so far, and pray that they aid the Kaiser's judgement. Surely they will not forsake us now," Margerite told him gently. But her words brought another thought to her mind: she remembered the Easter egg she had painted for Father Kerlinger. That had worked its prayer or magic upon him, as Eva's, it might be, had set in motion the freeing of Christoph - could she touch Kaiser Karl's mind likewise? She had her tools of the Art with her...Later, Margerite whispered to herself, popping a pinch of cheese stuffing into Wolfram's mouth before he could begin to complain of neglect. "You said that the audience had been set for a week's time," she went on, more briskly. "How long ago was that?"

"Three days: it is this coming Monday that the Kaiser will hear the case. And now that you are here, I am glad of it: we must bear ourselves as well as we can until then, and I think it shall seem a long time. The more so because...I did not lie to Graf Christoph, and this night I shall pray for Graf Heinrich's soul, and his forgiveness." Bernhardt looked into Margerite's eyes, and though he did not so much as brush her fingers with his own, a deep tingle of warmth spread outwards from her heart through her body, her womb tightening with desire. "Yet now, if you are still willing, I would redeem my pledge to you."

Margerite touched Bernhardt's signet ring, a hard lump hidden beneath the glitter of the falcon-necklace on her breast. "And I would redeem mine," she murmured. "Whatever befalls, I shall be with you."

# Chapter Eleven

lthough the thick walls of Burg Karlstein kept the castle's rooms cool, they did not keep out the muggy heaviness of the summer air, so that Margerite found herself tossing uncomfortably on her bed that night. It seemed to her that she could feel the prickling nervousness of a thunderstorm building about the crag, and when she stroked Kobolt to calm herself, tiny blue sparks crackled in the cat's black fur. She had warded her chambers and Eva's as best she might; she knew that Gottfried was protecting himself and Arnmut, and Father Etienne had assured her quietly that he would see to Georg, Konrad, and Christoph - and the faint reek of Kobolt's familiar musk told her that the tomcat had added his own strength to the barriers about her room.

They would not try a direct assault, not here, Margerite told herself. One shriek would bring the guards running; and the Light-Bearers must know that if they are to win the victory here, their means must have no stink of sorcery about them. Yet, though she knew that she was in all likelihood safer here than she had been anywhere for the past two years, Margerite could not still the tension thrumming through her limbs. Save when she forced herself to lie quietly, she found her muscles twitching, her body twisting in the soft sheets as though she squirmed beneath the skilled hands of a lover.

Her mouth curved wryly at the thought: except for that once with Heinrich, she had not lain with a man for almost two years, since she and Bernhardt had embraced at the Marienbrunnen. But she could remember how he had caressed her breasts, his weapon-calloused hands gentle upon her aching nipples; how he had stroked her shivering flanks, soothing her bone-deep terror away, and let her come to him when she was ready, easing herself onto his shaft as they lay side by side until his warmth had wholly filled her...

Margerite found that she was pressing her thighs hard together as she thought of Bernhardt, as though to hold the memory of his lovemaking tightly within herself like seed that might yet sire a child. And though this is lust, she thought, it is not unfaithfulness: for though it is secret yet, Bernhardt and I are betrothed. Margerite crossed her arms over her breasts, holding herself tightly lest some sound escape her: she had waited so long for this, so long, and was not sure she had ever truly believed that the time would come.

But the battle is not over, she reminded herself. The Kaiser could still declare Bernhardt outlaw, if the wrong words turn him against us; he could even demand his life, and to whom then would we be able to appeal? The thought chilled Margerite like a bucket of snowmelt sluicing over her head and down her back - or maybe it was the sweat chilling on her body, for she had thrown the torn coverlet to the floor and strewn her sheets about without noticing. She reached down and pulled the bedclothes back over herself, lying on her back with her arms crossed upon her chest and trying to breathe herself into calmness.

Would I use the Art to save Bernhardt, if it tainted his victory? Margerite asked herself. But she knew the answer: if it came to a question of his life, she would use any means that came to her hand. And she feared for him, feared deeply: she knew, somewhere within her, that he had not come to terms with the things he had done between Ortlieb's first betrayal and the day he and she had restored Maria's shrine in the woods. For Bernhardt was a just man - and justice, meted in full, could yet demand the Free Soldier's life.

The longing for someone to speak to ached deep in Margerite's bones now, bitter as the arthritic bite of old age: yet if they had needed care in Bishop Otto's palace, how much more so here? She could not go wandering down the corridors of Burg Karlstein so late at night - she was not even sure where Father Etienne had been lodged, or Gottfried. And, if she were truthful to herself, Margerite had to admit that she did not want to reveal all that troubled her to either of the men: the advice they would give her might be what was best for her soul, but she did not think it would unbind the knots cutting into her heart.

Rose and Else would not understand, and should not know. As for Eva, Margerite knew exactly what the younger woman would say: she would tell Margerite to do everything in her power for the man she loved, and trust that what Bernhardt did not know would do him no harm. But that did not satisfy her either, for Bernhardt had been manipulated by one sorceress already, and it seemed to her that if she used the Art for him against his will, whether he knew it or not, she would still become as Ortlieb had been to him.

*Yet I would do it to save his life...ah, Maria, forgive me!*

In that moment, Margerite found herself longing for the company of Birgitta, for the Norwegian woman's cool, honest counsel - a feeling strange as the food-cravings of pregnancy, for she had hardly ever been other than uncomfortable in the former Light-Bearer's presence. But neither Etienne nor Gottfried, she thought, could understand a woman's heart in such a matter; while Eva's advice would be little different from that Kriemhilt would have given, could the tortoiseshell cat speak of how she would defend her kittens and mate. *Perhaps Birgitta and I were more alike than I could see, both caught somewhere between Heaven and earth, between flesh and spirit: Christ forgive me for wanting a heathen woman's redes, but I would welcome her now!*

Yet Birgitta was long gone, and Gottfried had never said where, if she had told him, though he wore her favour yet. Even if Margerite dared to fly out and seek her in falcon-shape, she would not know which way to go. She reached out for Kobolt, hoping at least for the comfort of his warmth and soft chirping purr, but the cat had left the bed: even in a Kaiser's castle, Margerite guessed, there must be a few mice to hunt. Clutching the bedclothes tightly to herself, Margerite rolled over on her stomach, but it was a long time before she slept.

It seemed to Margerite then that she was outside, the cool wind blowing her hair back and rushing like a river through the pines about her. Above, a square forbidding tower loomed black against the stars; the faint moonlight showed a valley sweeping far below, and the sharp shadows of mountains about the crag on which she stood. Kobolt rubbed against her legs, letting out a little cry as though he were calling to another cat, and she saw the glow of a lantern in the darkness, bobbing between the trees: someone was walking up a winding path towards her.

"Where am I?" she said aloud.

"In the Pyrenees," a woman's low voice answered her. Now Margerite could see the gleam of white linen beneath a dark cloak, the glimmer of lamp-lit eyes under a peaked shadow. Even as she thought she recognised who was speaking to her, Birgitta tossed her hood back, and Margerite saw her mutilated half-hand upon the lantern.

"What am I doing here?" Margerite asked.

"You are dreaming, as am I. The landvættr who follows you, your Kobolt, came to me and bade me follow, and so I walked out to look for you: I did not think that you could come so close to Meister Stefan's keep. But why have you sought me out, Margerite?"

"I did not mean to - I was only thinking of you, and wishing...a foolish thing, really."

Birgitta shook her head, her ash-blond hair falling pale about her dark-cloaked shoulders. "So powerful, and yet you cannot rule your heart. But which of us can, in truth? Ask as quickly as you may, and I will answer: but you must not stay out too long."

Margerite opened her mouth to speak of Bernhardt, but the question that came out was, "Why did you leave Gottfried?"

"Because I would not have had him be other than he is, nor would he have had me be other than I am. And that is the truest thing I know of love: would you know more, or how?" The Norwegian woman's pale face and long hair seemed to shimmer in the darkness, her white shift shining under her heavy cloak: it seemed to Margerite, though she could not say why, that it would be perilous to look upon her too long, as old women's tales warned against looking at the elves that flashed bright over the hills at Easter dawn.

"My question is answered," Margerite said, turning her face away. "Thank you."

"Then go to your home again and sleep well: you have a battle yet to fight. Tell Gottfried that my heart is with him yet, and may your god uphold you well." Birgitta turned and walked away. Margerite saw no gate or door opening in the castle's black wall: but one moment the Norwegian woman was there, her lantern casting a faint halo about her dark silhouette, and in the next heartbeat, she was gone.

"Come, Kobolt, guide me home," Margerite murmured, and opened her eyes to the darkness, and the sounds of her serving women and Wolfram breathing quietly in their sleep. Her cat was curled beside her head, his tail draped across her cheek as if it were a plait of her own hair. She was not sure how, but she felt strangely eased, the turmoil in her heart stilled at last.

"I would not have had him be other than he is, nor would he have had me be other than I am," Margerite murmured softly to herself, fixing the Norwegian's words in her mind as the dream began to fade.

She had spoken to Bernhardt before of how they each had their own battles to fight: it would not have aided her, if he had cut Christoph down with his sword when the demon in Christoph's flesh threatened her most direly, but only have put her in greater and more lasting danger. Likewise, she knew now, she could do no more than witness for Bernhardt: if he could not move Kaiser Karl to judge in his favour by the truth of his own case, his victory would be no more than theft, and his self-judgement harsher than the headsman's sword.

Maria, grant me strength: let me allow Bernhardt his own fight. A little before tierce on Monday morning, Margerite and her companions came to the Kaiser's reception hall. Like all the rooms in Burg Karlstein, it was magnificently painted: the Kaiser's arms were set upon the southern wall, the black eagle proud upon its gold-leaf field, and the inscriptions SPQR and Roma caput mundi regit orbis frena rotundi were painted above the images of the great Roman emperors in their purple togas and gilded crowns: Julius Caesar, Augustus, Vespasian, Constantine, and others whose names Margerite did not recognise stood together with such notables as Cicero and Tacitus, looking down as if to advise their successor, Kaiser Karl IV, on the business of Empire.

Two great beams, carved, painted, and glittering with gold leaf, upheld the ceiling, which likewise bore panelling of richly carved and painted woodwork, as did the walls; and a brightly painted triumphal arch led out to the eastern turret and the Kaiser's own chapel. The benches' backs bore a pattern of deep-carved oak leaves interspersed with gold acorns; here and there, the carver had added the figure of a squirrel or a small bird, their eyes set with tiny gems. Karl's gilded throne was raised on a high dais: its back was carved with the Imperial arms on a tall panel above where the Kaiser's head would be, its arms ending in the heads of lions with manes of pure gold and sapphire eyes.

Beneath the dais to the left was a long table: there the Kaiser's secretaries sat in their embroidered tabards, gold rings gleaming on their fingers as they sharpened their quills and shuffled through the stacks of parchment before them. Two heralds in gleaming surcoats stood on either side of the throne dais, gold trumpets dangling loosely in their hands: they stared straight ahead, bracing themselves stiffly at attention. Margerite had thought that the Kaiser's judgement hall would be as full as the Pope's had been, but the long rows of benches were almost empty.

She wondered if Kaiser Karl had ordered the court's privacy - perhaps, because he was unwilling to spread the dark tale of Ortlieb's crimes further and give them full crediblity? Bernhardt was already there, sitting on the left side of the room with Bishop Otto; the three Inquisitors and their secretary had placed themselves a little apart from the claimants, their plain dark robes like a spill of black ink upon a scroll's illumination.

In contrast, Gerhardt, sitting on the right side with his two lawyers and a few men whom Margerite did not recognise - supporters of his, no doubt; and high nobles, from their clothing - was dressed so richly that Margerite wondered how he could bear up beneath the weight of gold on his body. His deep blue doublet bore the arms of Niederwald: the stag's head surmounting the shield, the full-faced helm in its antlers and the mantling around the shield were embroidered in solid gold thread, as was the motto UNCONQUERED; the leaping fish was done in silver thread, and rubies winked from the red field. Above that, Gerhardt wore a heavy chain of gold plates set with irregularly-cut sapphires and emeralds; but its weight seemed to bow his shoulders, and the matching belt about his hips drooped beneath his slight potbelly; every so often he would reach up to adjust the golden coronet slipping on his mousy brown hair, the knee-length dags of his red silk sleeves falling back to show the thick gold bracelets on his wrists.

Large rubies glowed from the gold buttons fastening his pointed blue shoes, and his dark red hose were embroidered all over with figures in gold thread. His goatee had been neatly combed and oiled, but Margerite could see the pouches of darkness beneath his eyes and the deep wrinkles graving his broad forehead. Bernhardt was not so bejeweled, but in contrast to his brother's ostentation, he presented a picture of sober dignity.

His deep blue tunic of heavy velvet reached below his knees in front and back, its ermine trim tracing the mid-thigh slits at the sides; his over-sleeves were the same plain dark blue as the tunic, and the tighter under-sleeves were pure white silk. The close crop of Bernhardt's beard marked out the strong line of his jaw and chin where Gerhardt's little goatee weakened the von Niederwald features; though Bernhardt wore no coronet, his wavy brown hair was brushed back over his proud brow, curling about his stern face like a frame of carven walnut.

Margerite and her companions went to join Bernhardt. Wolfram's weight was already beginning to wear upon her arms, but she had not left him since coming to Burg Karlstein - and he was the Graf von Falkenstein: infant though he was, his presence would lend more strength to their case. She had fed Wolfram well before court, and played with him until his little head was drooping from exhaustion; she could only hope that he would sleep quietly. Though, in spite of everything she knew, she still felt foolish speaking to a cat as if he were a man, she had lifted Kobolt in her arms and, looking straight into his golden eyes, told him that he must not follow her to the Kaiser's court.

Bernhardt looked down at Margerite as she seated herself next to him. His quiet smile barely touched the lined corners of his eyes, and the fear that had slumbered uneasily in her heart moved within her again. "So it is time for me to receive the Kaiser's justice," he murmured to her. "...Pray to Mother Maria that there is mercy within it as well."

For you, my love? Margerite wondered. Or for your brother? But she nodded, longing desperately to lay her comforting hand upon his. Soon, she told herself. Soon.

As if at a signal she had not seen or heard, the heralds lifted their trumpets, the melodious blast of the fanfare echoing through the Kaiser's judgement hall. "Rise, for His Imperial Majesty Karl IV, Kaiser of the Holy Roman Empire, King of Bohemia!" they sang out together. The assembled company stood.

First through the triumphal arch were the Kaiser's bodyguard, twelve tall, powerfully built men in full armour. Their open-faced helms were crested with panaches of gold and black feathers; the Kaiser's eagle, embossed in black enamel, glistened dark upon their gilded breastplates, and they held drawn swords point-up in their hands. Their boots boomed off the floor as they marched in perfect step to arrange themselves on the dais about Karl's throne, turning their swords as a single man so that the tips just touched the floor.

Behind them came the Kaiser himself; and all knelt as he passed. Karl IV was shorter than his guards, a man of medium height and spare build, with long dark hair hanging to his shoulders beneath his crown and cap. He wore long robes of white brocaded with gold over an undertunic of bright red silk: in his hands, he held the gold Imperial orb with its jeweled cross on top and a sceptre of gold and ivory, and St. Wenzel's crown rested on his head.

The great emblem of the Kaiser's God-given power bore four high trefoils of gold adorned with pearls; it was surmounted by an arching cross-band with ruby-tipped arms and a great pale blue sapphire gleaming at its heart. Another huge sapphire, polished but unshaped, shone in the centre of the wide gold band ringing Karl's head, surrounded by plane-cut amethysts and cairngorms; the crown rested on a white silk cap that shone with pearls and fine white embroidery like pale filigree, its double peak arching up beneath the high cross-band.

Yet it was not the splendour of Karl IV's regalia that drew Margerite's gaze: rather, she found herself staring at the Kaiser's huge lustrous black eyes, gazing intensely from the sunken hollows beneath the rounded dark vaulting of his brows. Karl's cheeks were slightly hollowed as well, his nose long and straight and his mobile lips set off by his pointed black beard - not the face of an Emperor, as Margerite had imagined it, but one so fraught with power and deep thought that she would almost have knelt before him had he been dressed in simple blue wool.

Behind the Kaiser walked a well-dressed man in a long cloak of red silk lined with white fur, carrying a cushion with the Imperial arms embroidered upon it, and another man in elaborate priestly regalia, his alb shimmering with gold thread and pearls, who bore a large pearl-encrusted reliquary cross of pure ruddy gold. Two pages came after them, boys perhaps seven or eight years old who wore smaller versions of the heralds' surcoats with the Kaiser's arms embroidered in black upon cloth-of-gold, and long-sleeved tunics of black silk.

The taller of the youths, a dark-haired, curly-headed boy, carried a gilded pitcher; the shorter, whose brownish-blond hair fell straight about his plump face, bore a magnificent goblet, its bowl a thin agate shell swirling with translucent browns and reds, yellows and oranges, and its rim and foot of finely wrought gold. Twelve more guards followed as the cushion-bearer placed his burden in front of the dais and the pages took their places by the Kaiser's seat.

"Rise, and be seated," Karl IV said, settling himself upon his throne. His voice was clear and mellow, but Margerite could hear the faint snap behind it, like the bite of well-aged apple wine. "We, Karl IV, Kaiser of the Holy Roman Empire and King of Bohemia, declare this court to be open, by the grace and beneath the blessing of Christ." Then he leaned forward, his great dark eyes suddenly burning like coals smouldering to red heat.

"Landgraf Gerhardt von Niederwald, Herr Bernhardt von Niederwald, we are ready to hear your case! Be assured that we have already read the documents which all of you have submitted, and we are grievously angered that such things should come to pass in the house of one of our great nobles, and bring such shame upon our realm. We await your explanations. Landgraf Gerhardt, you may come before us."

Gerhardt rose slowly, bowing and walking with great dignity to kneel on the cushion at the foot of the dais, the long points of his red silk oversleeves trailing on the floor like the drooping wings of a slain bird. He thinks that he is walking to his death, Margerite realized suddenly, and is determined to meet it resolutely. He is Bernhardt's brother, after all...Somewhere in the back of her mind, she heard a soft whisper - the murmur of a Pater Noster, its words slipping smooth and familiar as polished stone beads beneath the fingers: again, she was thankful that she did not share the burden of Gottfried's gift, for it would have been intolerable to hear Gerhardt's thoughts.

The Kaiser sat staring down at Gerhardt for some time, until the Landgraf von Niederwald began to shift uncomfortably. Then he spoke again. "Landgraf Gerhardt von Niederwald. Swear upon this reliquary - in which are enshrined a drop of the sweat shed by Christ on the way to His Crucifixion, two thorns from His crown, and a fragment of the True Cross - that you will answer me fully and with the truth."

The reliquary-bearer stepped closer to Gerhardt, lowering the pearled cross; Gerhardt kissed it and took the oath.

"In their account," said Kaiser Karl, "your lawyers urged us to take no notice of the crimes of your wife, claiming that you were wholly ignorant of her deeds for the eight years of your marriage. We find that unlikely, to say the least. We understand that you refused the summons of the Inquisition - as was, to be sure, your right, since Father Kerlinger's only authority within the Empire is that given him by the Church. Nevertheless, you shall answer our questions now. How was it that Landgräfin Ortlieb could commit kidnap and gruesome murder within the confines of your own castle, not once only, but at least three times over in the course of less than half a year, while you yourself remained unaware of her doings, as, according to the Inquisitorial testimony, did all your servants?"

The gold plates of the chain draped over Gerhardt's shoulders and back flashed as he straightened his neck to look up at Kaiser Karl. "Your Majesty, if I knew enough to guess at how she had done it, I might have known enough to learn of what was happening, and deal with her as was needed. My wife's grievous crimes are yet a mystery to me, save that I know she was aided by her women Hedwig and Oda, who have been in the custody of the Inquisition since Ortlieb was murdered: it may be that Father Kerlinger can answer the question of how these cruel things were done better than I, who knew nothing of them at the time, and know now only what I have been told."

It seemed to Margerite that the great odd-shaped sapphire on the Kaiser's brow drew in the room's light to distill it into a searing brilliance, burning from the rich ruddy gold like a star caught in pale blue glass. "Do you claim," Karl asked mildly, "that you were enchanted by Ortlieb's spells?"

"I make no such claim, your Majesty. But I loved her - and maybe I was blind: I let her command my servants as she would, and rule Schloss Niederwald as she would, for I believed that there was no evil in her, but only such beauty as would delight the eyes of angels." Gerhardt's voice shook as he spoke, and his collar of plates shimmered with the trembling of his shoulders, as though he were near to tears.

Beside Margerite, Bernhardt's hands clenched tight into fists, the muscles of his jaw bunching beneath his beard: Margerite could not tell whether from anger, or from pain... He, too, had such a memory of Ortlieb. She forced herself to loosen her hard grip on her sleeping son, lest Wolfram awake and begin to cry.

The Kaiser's frown did not ease. "So you say that you are a fool, and because of this, though not by your direct leave, black sorcery and murder were allowed in your own castle."

"It must be so, your Majesty," Gerhardt answered in a muffled tone, his shoulders shaking harder. "Yet it is no crime to be deceived: I, too, was Ortlieb's victim."

One corner of Karl's mouth lifted in a sardonic, humourless smile. "'The woman beguiled me, and I did eat?' Yet a woman's deeds are her husband's responsibility: it was not Eve's Fall that tainted the human race with sin, but Adam's. And it was by your authority, it seems, that your guards turned away in blindness from your wife's comings and goings at night; by your will that she, a poor knight's daughter, was granted the freedom to do as she would beyond all right and law. Do you deny this?"

"I cannot deny it, your Majesty."

Kaiser Karl looked down at his Landgraf for a long moment. "Landgraf Gerhardt von Niederwald, you may return to your seat. Gräfin Margerite von Fürstensee und Falkenstein, you may come before us."

Startled, Margerite's grasp tightened reflexively on her son. Wolfram's eyes sprang open, and he let out a plaintive wail. "Hush, my sweet Wolfi, hush," she whispered urgently. "Eva, can you..?"

Eva took Wolfram quickly from her arms, crooning to him in a soft murmur and rocking him. Remembering just in time how Father Etienne had instructed her to approach the Imperial presence, she curtsied deeply before walking up to the cushion, curtseying again before she knelt. The priest bearing the reliquary lowered it to her: she touched her lips to the cold metal and smooth pearls, and said, "I do swear before Christ, Whose holy relics are enshrined here, that I shall answer your Majesty's questions fully and truthfully."

"That is well," the Kaiser told her. "Look at me, Gräfin."

Margerite lifted her head. The full force of Karl's intense dark gaze struck her like a blow inside her skull - a blow such as she had not felt since Gottfried, crying out in silent startlement, had knocked her from her horse. Her tongue clove to the roof of her mouth, and she could feel her limbs trembling beneath the Kaiser's regard.

"By your admission and that of your comrades, you are guilty of the slaying of Landgräfin Ortlieb von Niederwald, and charged with her murder by Landgraf Gerhardt von Niederwald. How do you plead to that?" Karl asked her bluntly.

"I did slay her, your Majesty. But I had pursued her to save my son's life - and it was she who drew the knife first."

"So the accounts of those who were there all say. What is not fully clear to us is how you knew of the danger. We have read in the documents of this case that you, as penance, served as a simple maid in Schloss Niederwald. And what we would know is this: how is it that you alone, when all the other servants of that castle professed ignorance, were aware of the great peril in which the young Graf von Falkenstein stood?"

Margerite drew a deep breath, forcing her shuddering muscles to unlock. To the Inquisition, she had concealed the truth, though it meant a false oath upon the reliquary of Peter of Verona. But an Inquisitorial saint was one thing, and the relics of the Crucifixion were another: it would cost her her soul, if she were to lie before Christ's sufferings. And...Kaiser Karl's dark eyes bored into her own like augers, St. Wenzel's sapphire burning blue in the centre of his forehead. She was sure, though she could not have said how, that he would know if she failed in the great oath she had just sworn.

"Your Majesty, I knew that Landgräfin Ortlieb was a black sorceress before ever I came to Schloss Niederwald. I knew that she had tormented and betrayed Herr Bernhardt von Niederwald by means of her magics: though my penance was a true one, it was also the case that Canon Etienne de Dion had come to Niederwald in order to conduct his own investigation into the Landgräfin's doings. For as you have said, your Majesty, the Inquisition's power in your lands is limited to the authority of the Church, but it is Canon Etienne's duty, as exorcist and bearer of his special office, to seek into such matters where-ever he is needed." By the time she had finished speaking, Margerite's voice had sunk to a dry croak, and she could hardly hear her own words over the painful thudding of her heart.

Kaiser Karl regarded her thoughtfully, long fingers playing upon the jeweled orb cupped in his hand. Beneath the sparse darkness of his moustache, his mouth was stern as he said, "And did you mean your son as bait for her?"

"Your Majesty, I tried to conceal him from her as best I could: I would have stood and fought within her own castle to keep Landgräfin Ortlieb from taking him. But he was less than half a year old, and unweaned: I could not leave him when I went to Schloss Niederwald, for in our secrecy, there was no way to find a nursemaid. And, for the sake of his noble line, I would not have had my Wolfram nourished upon a lesser woman's blood."

"I see. You may return to your seat, Gräfin. Canon Etienne de Dion, you may come before me."

Margerite backed away, curtseying as she went. Wolfram, thank Maria, had quieted, and she received him gratefully into her arms again as Father Etienne doffed his canon's hat, made his bows, and sank gracefully to his knees before the Kaiser's throne. He kissed the reliquary, saying, "I do swear before Christ, Whose holy relics are enshrined here, that I shall answer your Majesty's questions truthfully and as fully as my oaths of priesthood permit."

The Kaiser frowned, but said, "We may ask you for nothing more. Tell us, Canon de Dion, by what authority you made the investigations of which the Gräfin von Fürstensee und Falkenstein has spoken."

Father Etienne reached into his belt-pouch, pulling out a small rolled parchment tied with a ribbon from which a lead seal hung. "By the authority of Holy Church," he replied, his French-accented voice clear in the quiet room. "Pope Innocent VI granted me the special office of Defensor Hominum; that office was renewed by Pope Urban V upon his accession, that I might serve Christ by guarding His flock with all of the powers vested in me, and in ways beyond the scope of most priests - or the Holy Inquisition."

Kaiser Karl raised a dark eyebrow, then nodded to one of his heralds, who took the little scroll from Father Etienne's hand. Slipping the ribbon off, the Emperor unrolled the parchment, looking at it for a time, then carefully rolled it again and replaced its binding. "An unusual office, indeed, but it seems a legitimate one. Canon de Dion, in the course of your... investigations at Schloss Niederwald, did you come across anything which might have led you to believe that Landgraf Gerhardt von Niederwald had any part in the heresies, blasphemies, sorceries, or other crimes of his wife?"

"Your Majesty, the Landgraf's part in the Landgräfin's heresies, blasphemies, and sorceries was, so far as may be proven, no more than what has already been spoken: that of turning a blind eye to the evil within his own house. I had no opportunity to examine Schloss Niederwald for evidence of his complicity, as I deemed it unsafe to force my investigations on the Landgraf's own seat after the Landgräfin's death, but I, too, can attest to his servants' claims that they knew nothing of dark arts practiced by Landgraf Gerhardt. However, it is suspected by some that both he and the Landgräfin Ortlieb may have had a hand in arranging the murder of which Herr Bernhardt von Niederwald was accused nine years ago."

"Is there any evidence for this?"

"Your Majesty, to the best of my knowledge, there are only two living who may know any portion of the truth: Herr Bernhardt von Niederwald, who protests his innocence, and Landgraf Gerhardt von Niederwald. If, indeed, there is more to the rumours than the simple convenience of a death by which the likelier heir was condemned and his kinsman gained both the heir's title and the woman of surpassing beauty who had been his brother's."

"We shall deal with this matter when we have finished with the one at hand," the Kaiser said. "Canon Etienne de Dion, you may retire." He stared out over the room, a long, considering gaze. "All of the witnesses here, I believe, have read and signed their testimonies. Is there anyone who has anything more to add concerning the trial of Landgraf Gerhardt von Niederwald?"

Margerite waited, her lower lip between her teeth. In the silence, Wolfram drew breath and let out a sudden cry. Horrified, she clamped her hand over her son's mouth, but it was too late.

Kaiser Karl looked down at Margerite and Wolfram. His mouth curved into a smile, and she could see the faint crinkles of amusement at the corners of his dark eyes - Karl's beloved son Wenzel, she remembered suddenly, was but five years old. "Although we are informed that the Graf von Falkenstein was a witness to many of these events," the Kaiser said mildly, "we believe that he does not necessarily mean us to take that statement into account. Gräfin, we understand your fear of parting from a child who has suffered so much peril - even within our own stronghold - but perhaps you shall be reassured if he is put into the care of our own son's nursemaids for the remaining duration of this court?"

A blush warmed Margerite's cheeks: Kaiser Karl clearly knew how closely she had watched Wolfram since arriving at Burg Karlstein - but she could hardly tell him that she did not trust the women who cared for his precious heir. "Your Majesty, I, and Graf Wolfram von Falkenstein, are most honoured," she replied.

The Kaiser nodded to two of his knights, who sheathed their swords and came forward to her. One of them lifted Wolfram from her arms - his homely face was so close to Margerite's that she could see the little patch of white-blond stubble that his razor had missed on his left cheek, and smell the faint scent of sugared spices on his breath. Margerite expected Wolfram to start screaming again, but instead he quieted, bright eyes staring at the man's feathered helm-crest and little hands going out to tug at the chain linking his gold-hilted dagger to his breastplate. Margerite looked quickly at the knights' hands, but their gauntlets covered their fingers up to the first joint: she could not see if either of them was wearing any rings.

All is well, Gottfried said silently to her.

"Be good, Wolfi," Margerite murmured to her son, but she could not help feeling disquieted - not only at their parting, but because the Kaiser, though he had seemed close to closing the court, wanted the child taken away: what more did he mean to do?

The knights left with Wolfram, their step more gentle than it had been when they marched in. Kaiser Karl waited until the door had closed behind them to speak again. "We ask once more: is there anyone here who has anything to add concerning the trial of Landgraf Gerhardt von Niederwald, or any word to speak before we pronounce judgement on Landgräfin Ortlieb von Niederwald, Hedwig von Rabenwald, Oda von Schwarzenstein, Landgraf Gerhardt von Niederwald, and Gräfin Margerite von Fürstensee und Falkenstein?"

Margerite heard nothing but her own breath and her thumping heartbeat, until the Kaiser raised his scepter and the heralds lifted their trumpets to their lips, blowing another fanfare. "Then we, Karl IV, Kaiser of the Holy Roman Empire and King of Bohemia, pronounce our judgement thusly. Gräfin Margerite von Fürstensee and Falkenstein, you are exonerated of the murder of Landgräfin Ortlieb von Niederwald: it is our judgement that you acted rightly, in defense of your son's life and soul. Let the body of Landgräfin Ortlieb von Niederwald be exhumed and burnt, and her ashes scattered to the winds. If Hedwig von Rabenwald and Oda von Schwarzenstein will not repent of their heresies, blasphemies, and black sorceries, let them be burnt before the eyes of the folk of Niederwald. If either of them will repent, let her be imprisoned as a penitent for life under the care of the Church: for their part in the Landgräfin Ortlieb's crimes, they shall never walk free again. Father Walther Kerlinger, we believe that we have no further need of yourself and your companions in this court. You may leave now, if you so desire, but we shall grant your request for a private discussion some short while hence: you shall be informed of our further wishes in this matter later."

Karl breathed deeply, pointing his sceptre at Gerhardt as the three black-robed priests rose, bowed, and backed out of the Imperial presence. "Landgraf Gerhardt von Niederwald, we find that no malice can be proven against you in this instance, but you are nevertheless guilty of gross misrule. For the shame and evil which you have permitted in a great house of this our Empire, we do hereby strip you of your title and place, and decree that if you are found to have no kinsman suitable for rule, the lands of Niederwald are to be deemed possessions of the Holy Roman Empire and shall be distributed as we see fit. You may keep that castle which belonged to your wife by right of inheritance, but we further decree that Canon Etienne de Dion shall first examine it and destroy whatever he finds there that is unclean; and that from its revenues, you shall pay for ten years each of Masses for the souls of the three youths whom your wife kidnapped and murdered. Before Christ and His holy relics, our judgement in this matter is spoken: let no man henceforth presume to dispute it." Karl lowered his scepter, staring at Gerhardt until he bowed his head.

I think we have won a victory, Margerite thought. Or... something on the road to a victory. But Gerhardt's defeat will do us little good if the Kaiser decides to judge Bernhardt for his years in the Black Sword, and his hate for such bands of soldiers is well known.

"We shall now hear the case of Herr Bernhardt von Niederwald," the Kaiser declared. He raised an eyebrow at the dark-haired page, who gracefully poured a pink stream of watered wine into the agate goblet held by the shorter boy; the cup-bearer lifted his charge to Karl's lips so that the Emperor might wet his throat, then both of them stepped aside again. "Herr Bernhardt von Niederwald, you may come before us."

Bernhardt rose and gave the Kaiser a courtly bow, striding forward to kneel before him. His voice was strong and sure as he took the oath upon the relics of Christ, though Margerite, watching, found her chest so tight with nervousness that she could barely drag air into her own lungs.

"Herr Bernhardt von Niederwald, I would have you tell me what befell on the night of the murder of Herr Konstantin von Adelsberg."

"There were many guests in Schloss Niederwald, for my cousin Elisabeth had just been wedded. I left the feast early in the evening, for I had an assignation with Ortlieb: I had meant to ask her hand in marriage, but we could not wait so long and - I was sure that I was the only man who had ever lain with her. I went to her chamber, and in the middle of our congress... she began to chant, and asked me to chant words unknown to me." Bernhardt's voice had dropped so that Margerite had to strain to hear him, and her heart choked: she could imagine the shame, if she had been forced to speak before the Kaiser - and him - of how Ruprecht had taken her last. My poor, dear Bernhardt: I wish you could have been spared this!

"And then it seemed to me that I saw her eyes changing, like an owl's, and the shadow of wings about her. I fled in terror, wrapping myself in a cloak. In my own chambers, I drank a cup of wine, and when I was calmer, I thought that it had been no more than a passing dizziness. I went back to her room, to apologise and to get my clothes. They were there, but she was not, and my sword was gone from its sheath. I feared greatly what she might do, thinking herself abandoned and betrayed by me, as it seemed, in the very moment when she gave herself over to me. And so I hastened outside, not knowing where she might have gone, but looking for her through the gardens. Then, away from the torches on the paths, I heard a cry, and ran to it. There at my feet lay Konstantin. I reached down to him, and found that my sword was through his chest. I pulled it out, his blood pouring over my hands...and then the guards were there. I swore my innocence by every oath, but my father would not even hear me, and Gerhardt swore that he himself had been speaking with Ortlieb all that night."

"And do you swear, before us and upon the holy relics of Christ, that you did not commit that murder?" the Kaiser asked quietly.

"I do so swear," Bernhardt replied.

"Yet, being sure of your innocence, you slew two good knights to make your escape. How, being locked in and unarmed, did you manage this, and why did you do it?"

"Your Majesty, I was beset in my cell at night by a thing that I could not name, save to call it a demon. I broke the lock in my terror, and wrested the sword from Jürgen's hand, lest it pursue me. But he struck at me with his dagger, and Erich attacked me as well. From the age of seven, like all youths of noble birth, I had learned to follow stroke with counterstroke: with blades raised against me, and already so maddened by fear that I had the strength to wrench an iron lock awry, I had no time to think of what I was doing until it was too late. Then I fled: I should have faced death, knowing it unjust at first, and then justified, but I could not bear to be locked in again at the mercy of that creature of Hell."

Kaiser Karl crossed himself with the hand that held his sceptre. "If you speak the truth indeed, then Christ preserve us all! Canon de Dion - no, stay where you are. We charge you to tell us now: is this tale possible?"

"Your Majesty, I fear that it is all too possible," Father Etienne answered. "Among the possessions of the late Ortlieb were several items used only for the summoning of demons. I believe that Herr Bernhardt is telling the truth."

The Kaiser gestured to his cup-bearer, and the page lifted the gold-bound agate goblet to his master's lips once more. Margerite saw Karl's throat move beneath his short dark beard, and could not help wondering if he were wishing for something stronger. *I would wager you have never heard such a case before; and if Christ is merciful, you shall never have to judge such matters again!* she thought.

Thus refreshed, Kaiser Karl lifted his eyes, looking at Gerhardt. "Herr Gerhardt von Niederwald, come before us. No," he said sharply to Bernhardt, who had begun to rise, "We did not give you leave to retire."

Gerhardt knelt awkwardly on the floor beside his brother, and, at the Kaiser's nod to the relic-bearer, kissed the reliquary and repeated his oath once more.

"Herr Gerhardt von Niederwald, what do you have to say of Herr Konstantin's murder?"

"Your Majesty," Gerhardt answered, a tinge of eagerness enlivening his broken voice, "Bernhardt has not told you the truth, nor has he told you all that passed. He left the feast early, indeed - because he and Herr Konstantin had quarrelled over Ortlieb, a fierce dispute that nearly came to swordplay there."

The Kaiser raised an eyebrow. "Herr Bernhardt?"

"It is true that Herr Konstantin and I had quarrelled. He had spoken of Ortlieb as no knight should speak of a lady, and I told him that if I heard such words from his mouth again, there would be swords drawn between us...She said afterwards," Bernhardt added softly, "that she would reward me properly for defending her honour."

"Yet Ortlieb was with me all that evening," Gerhardt broke in. "I swore that before our father: I swear it again to you, your Majesty."

Kaiser Karl stared down at the two of them, his dark brows drawn closely and his lips pressed tight. "So it is one oath against the other," he mused. "One of you is lying to us - nor is he lying to our Imperial Majesty alone, but he is flouting the suffering of Our Lord. We shall see how this proceeds. Herr Gerhardt von Niederwald, you may retire. Herr Bernhardt von Niederwald, remain where you are, and continue your tale. What did you do after you had fled, and why?"

"I had nowhere to go," Bernhardt went on as his brother backed away from the Kaiser's throne-dais, "and nothing but the clothes on my back and the sword in my hand. My face was known to the great houses of the Empire, and news of the accusation against me would spread swiftly: I had no skill but the sword - and I knew fully how I had been betrayed. I lived by eating what I could find in the woods and stealing food, now and then, from storehouses when I could do so without risking being seen. When my beard hid my face, I dyed it and my hair black with walnut-hulls, and I joined the Company of the Black Sword."

"A Free Company." The Kaiser's mouth twisted as though he had just tasted meat that had turned rotten beneath the cover of a sweet sauce. "May we take it that this company was no better than any of the other bands of mercenaries that have ravaged and damaged the lands of ourself and our brother rulers over these past years?"

"Your Majesty, that is so. I regret what I did in my time with the Black Sword, and do penance for it yet."

"It is not our prerogative, nor is it our purpose, to judge your soul!" Kaiser Karl snapped. "How long were you with the Company of the Black Sword, and what rank did you hold there?"

"Five years, your Majesty. I rose from common soldier to second in command. Then we were employed privily by Graf Günther von Hohenfels, after which he recommended me to Graf Ruprecht von Falkenstein, who was in need of a Hauptmann for his guard, his former commander having died when the Death returned."

"And you, in turn, recommended the Bear's Paw Company to Graf Ruprecht to assist him in his war with Graf Heinrich von Fürstensee - a war verging on feud, which we declared illegal in our Golden Bull, and initiated by Graf Ruprecht to the detriment of one of our most loyal nobles. Further, this was done at a time when the Free Companies were declared both illegal by ourself and excommunicate by his Holiness, Pope Urban V."

Margerite saw Bernhardt's back stiffen, but he said only, "Yes, your Majesty."

Bernhardt! Margerite thought. Say something more to defend yourself - it was Ruprecht who ordered you to hire mercenaries, and you chose the Bear's Paw because they were the least evil of the Free Companies! But she knew that Bernhardt was too proud to speak so: he had humbled himself as far as he could, even before the Kaiser with, it might be, his own life at stake.

"You hired this same Free Company in Niederwald last year, where they had remained rather than accept the absolution of their sins and embark upon Crusade in Hungary."

"That is so, your Majesty. But little good came of that gathering of free soldiers: it may be said, as well, that the Bear's Paw had no part in the rape of Avignon."

The Kaiser's sallow face darkened, and Margerite quailed at his glare, though it was not directed at her. "Herr Bernhardt von Niederwald, we did not ask for your judgement in that matter!" Karl sat back in his throne, breathing deeply and allowing his page to offer him several sips of watered wine. O, Bernhardt, Margerite thought as her heart sank, did you never learn that it is ill-done to remind a powerful man of his grievous failures?

When Karl continued, his voice was calm as ice thickening upon a pool. "For what purpose did you hire the Bear's Paw in Niederwald?"

"Upon learning of my father's death, I knew that it was time for me to return: to challenge my brother's rule, and call to your Majesty for judgement. But I knew also that if I entered Schloss Niederwald without a strong troop at my back, I would be seized and slain before ever I had the chance to appeal to anyone."

The Kaiser's lustrous eyes blinked slowly, the gems in his crown flashing red and blue, purple and dark as he moved his head from side to side. "And with such a tale of your deeds as you have related, you thought that we would strip your brother of his inheritance and set you in his place as one of the foremost nobles of our Empire?"

"Your Majesty," Bernhardt replied proudly, "I did not presume to guess at what you might do. But I knew that it was time for me to reveal that I lived; to speak, for all to hear, of the thing for which I was first unjustly condemned; and, if I might, to break Ortlieb's hold upon Niederwald, for I could no longer live in peace, knowing that she held full rule there. I would have my name cleared of that false accusation: if my deeds afterwards have blackened it, then that is as may be. But at least I have done one worthy thing in my travails, for my father's folk need suffer no longer from the evils done by Landgräfin Ortlieb."

"Herr Bernhardt von Niederwald, you may retire." Karl's penetrating gaze scanned the room, settling at last on Margerite. "Gräfin Margerite von Fürstensee und Falkenstein, come forward."

As before, Margerite curtsied, knelt, and swore to her truth upon the pearled reliquary. She waited with bated breath, sure that the Kaiser would ask her about Ruprecht and his hiring of the Bear's Paw, and eager to answer.

Karl leaned forward, his dark eyes suddenly smouldering with fury. "Gräfin, how did you dare to bring a Free Company here - here, to our own Imperial seat? Did you think that we are blind and deaf, not to know what manner of men come with each supplicant before our court?"

Mother Maria, help me now! Margerite prayed. To her surprise, her own voice was even, without the least tremor of fear or uncertainty, as she said, "The men of the Bear's Paw are no longer free soldiers. They are my own men, who have guarded and aided me in many times of need since Ruprecht first hired them: I am thankful to Herr Bernhardt, that when my husband commanded him to find a band of mercenaries, it was those who were most honourable for whom he searched, rather than for lawless men steeped in the evil of their ravaging deeds."

"No longer free soldiers, you say," the Kaiser murmured. "That can be answered easily enough." He looked at the taller of his pages. "Johann, see to the summoning of Hauptmann Paul and his lieutenant Jochanan. Be sure that they are disarmed and well-guarded when they come before us."

"Yes, your Majesty!" the dark-haired page piped, giving his gold pitcher to the well-dressed man who had brought in the kneeling-cushion and running from the room.

If it had not been for Margerite's Light-Bearer training, she knew that her face would have showed her fear then: there was no guessing what the Bear would say before the Kaiser. Why did I speak thus? she wondered. Dear Maria, what manner of fool am I, to hazard all on Paul's choice?

"We have heard other things of you as well, Gräfin," said Karl. "Chief among them, that you left your husband, Graf Heinrich von Fürstensee, in order to travel secretly to Herr Bernhardt's side, and that you are indeed his leman, in breach of law and oath. How do you answer this?"

"I swear that I have been altogether true to Graf Heinrich, and never lain with any man save him since the death of my first husband Graf Ruprecht," Margerite answered steadily. "Nor have I allowed so much as the occasion of sin, but, because I knew what suspicion might lie upon me and for the sake of both my honour and that of Graf Heinrich, have taken great care that Herr Bernhardt and I never met in private but that there was at least one other person of good repute there: for the most part, either Father Etienne or Frowe Eva. They will attest to this under oath, as may Herr Gottfried, Herr Arnmut, and Herr Georg, all of whom, your Majesty, are present here."

The Kaiser looked past Margerite, considering her companions for a moment. Then he nodded. "We shall prove the worth of your testimonies presently. For now, I shall hear what more you have to say regarding Herr Bernhardt, if there is any more."

Sweat slicked Margerite's palms unpleasantly, but even had she been so ill-bred as to wipe them on her dress, she would not have dared to move beneath Karl's penetrating gaze. "Your Majesty," she said, "Herr Bernhardt is a good man, who has wholly renounced whatever crimes he may have committed in the Company of the Black Sword, and sought through great pain and peril of his soul to atone for his sins by the freeing of Niederwald and the submission of himself to your judgement. I have known him for two years now, and know that in that time he has not acted other than as befitted a knight and a ruler of noble birth. Should you search the length and breadth of the Empire, you would find few better men, nor men more loyal: the Devil, through his handmaiden Ortlieb, won a great victory when Herr Bernhardt von Niederwald was driven from his father's lands.

I came here, not only to give my testimony and receive your judgement, but, as my son's regent until he comes of age, to offer Falkenstein's support of Herr Bernhardt. Though I may no longer speak for Fürstensee, as the rule there has now passed to Graf Heinrich's son, Graf Christoph is here with me to offer that same support, as is Herr Konrad von Schwarzenfels, who has come in the stead of his father, Graf Wolfgang von Schwarzenfels. We pray your Majesty to heed this, and to consider the words of your loyal subjects in your judgement of Herr Bernhardt von Niederwald."

"Is this so?" Karl asked, his eyes meeting those of Konrad and Christoph in turn.

"It is," Konrad answered strongly, his booming voice echoing from the painted walls. "I shall vouch for Herr Bernhardt, with my oath and my sword and my life."

"I, as well," Christoph added. Margerite's heart swelled warmly within her at their words, her throat tightening. Christoph had known Bernhardt only as Ruprecht's Hauptmann Bertram, and Konrad knew him not at all, yet they trusted - herself? Georg? Or Eva, or Gottfried and Arnmut, or Father Etienne; perhaps, all of that little company that had made their way through the darkness to Kaiser Karl's Imperial seat. But Christoph was still speaking. "Your Majesty, I fought against Herr Bernhardt in Graf Ruprecht's war, and I can offer proof that he is no lawless ravager. When Graf Ruprecht destroyed the first of our villages, among those peasants who came to my father for shelter was a young girl. She said that, when the settlement was plundered, Ruprecht's Hauptmann drove off a soldier who meant to rape her by feigning that he wanted her for himself; but he only kept her in safety, and when she asked how she could thank him, he told her to light a candle to Maria for him, and pray for his soul. However his worth may have been hidden, even then, that was the deed of a true Ritter. Nor do I think that a man who had conducted himself worse in a Free Company would have passed by the opportunity to take such prey when his lord allowed it to him again."

The Kaiser nodded. "I have heard your words, and shall consider them. Be sure, however, that I also know these nobles who came to this court to lend that same support to Herr Gerhardt von Niederwald. Gräfin, have you any more to say?"

"No, your Majesty."

"Then you may retire."

As Margerite sat back down, the doors behind them at the far end of the hall opened. The page Johann ran light-footed to take his place on the Kaiser's dais again; behind him marched six guards, herding Paul and Jochanan forward. Though Margerite had seen to it at Burg Fürstensee that the Bear's Paw members were clothed for their journey as befitted a Gräfin's guardsmen, in tunics and trousers of good blue fustian and linen, the mercenaries, staring about themselves in confusion and awe, still looked as misplaced in Karl's glorious hall as if they had been yanked straight from an alehouse brawl to stand before the glowing chalcedony gate of Heaven.

Paul's thinning red-gold hair stood up in rumpled wisps; the Kaiser's knights must have taken even his iron-bound leather cap from him. Jochanan's swarthy skin shone with sweat, and belatedly, Margerite thought of how many laws the Jew had broken by taking up arms and fighting beside Christians, and that, moreover, in a Free Company. If their foes had bothered to tell Karl about Jochanan, or if the Kaiser's own sources had informed him...Mother Maria, whatever befalls, may I not have brought that good man to his death!

Kaiser Karl watched the two free soldiers intently as they made their way towards his throne. One knight put a hand on each man's shoulder when they had approached near enough: the mercenaries stopped, looking confused. "Bow," the guard who was nearest Jochanan whispered out of the corner of his mouth. The gunner managed a creditable obesiance, but Margerite had seen dancing bears bow less clumsily than Paul.

Their guards marched them up to the Kaiser's dais, the one who had prompted them before hissing, "Kneel," to them. Suddenly a horrible thought struck Margerite: could Jochanan kiss a Christian reliquary, or would he refuse to do reverence to the sign under which his clan had been persecuted so terribly during the first years of the Death? And to defy the Kaiser on such a matter, in his own court... Christ forgive me, I have doomed him after all - Gottfried! she thought desperately. Can you hear me? Can you do anything?

Margerite heard nothing in the silence, but it seemed to her that, for just a heartbeat, Karl's penetrating gaze went blank and empty. Then his nostrils thinned as he looked down his long nose at the two soldiers. He waved the reliquary-priest aside, murmuring, "That will not be necessary here." More loudly, the Kaiser said, "Paul, called the Bear, and Jochanan, called the Gunner. You are here to answer one question. Are you still the leaders of the Free Company known as the Bear's Paw, or are you now the guardsmen of Gräfin Margerite von Fürstensee und Falkenstein?"

Although the kneeling cushion lay on a thick rug, Paul shuffled as though the floor was uncomfortably hard on his knees. "Uh...your Highness..."

Margerite clearly heard Jochanan's whisper, "Your Majesty."

"Shit...sorry! Your Majesty. Uh..." Sitting behind them as she was, Margerite could not see whether Paul looked sideways at his comrade, but she distinctly heard him whisper, "Jochanan, help me out here! What do I say?"

"Your Majesty," the Jew said firmly. "I carried the Gräfin's standard - the Falkenstein standard, that is - when we came here. I am Gräfin Margerite's man."

"I am, too," said Paul. Loud as his voice was, Margerite could not mistake the bewilderment in it - and, perhaps, the hint of pride behind that. "Your Majesty."

Kaiser Karl contemplated the two men kneeling before him, his stern, hollow-cheeked face showing no hint of his thoughts. At last he permitted himself a small smile. "That is well. Gräfin," he added in a dryly rueful tone, "it seems that you have been more successful than either we ourselves or His Holiness in this matter of reforming the Free Companies. Paul and Jochanan, you may retire: sit behind the Gräfin. Guards, you have my leave to depart."

Jochanan grabbed Paul's arm before the Bear could turn his back on the Emperor, and the two of them stumbled backwards. Margerite had to bite her lip to keep from laughing, and she could see that the Kaiser's two pages were struggling equally hard to suppress their giggles.

Karl tapped the butt of his scepter on the arm of his throne. "I have heard your testimonies, but the first question still remains: that of the murder of Herr Konstantin. Is there any person here who can offer me more than an unsupported - and conflicting - oath?"

In the utter quiet, Margerite realized that she was chewing at her fingernails, a childish fault that had been beaten out of her so long ago she had forgotten that she had ever done it. Embarassed, she forced herself to fold her hands in her lap and wait. Surely, after all this, there would be an answer: Father Etienne would produce a witness, perhaps, or some vital, lost proof of Bernhardt's innocence...some evidence from Ortlieb's wagon, a confession from one of her women...

The stillness of the hall seemed to hum in Margerite's ears. Her heart, she thought irrationally, should have been fluttering like a butterfly captured in cupped hands, but the silence between each hammering beat in her chest seemed to stretch unbearably.

Then Bernhardt rose to his feet, bowing to the Kaiser and walking forward to kneel before his throne.

"Your Majesty. As I swore my oath on Christ's relics, I will trust in Him to uphold my case: He saw what there was no other to witness. In this trust, I will place my soul, my life and all my hopes to the test. Your Majesty, if you will name a champion who is willing to duel me in single combat until one is slain or has yielded, I shall prove with my body the truth of my oath, that God's judgement be manifest where the judgement of men cannot pierce: and if He does not grant me victory in proof of my right to rule Niederwald, then let my life be forfeit."

Margerite gasped silently. Bernhardt was an excellent fighter, yes - but the Kaiser's guards were picked from the mightiest warriors in the Empire: if Konrad, champion that he was, would admit himself to be less than a match for his elder brother, what chance would Bernhardt, who had not run a tilt in at least nine years, have against one of Karl's own chosen knights?

Kaiser Karl frowned. "It mislikes us greatly, that arms should serve thus in place of law. Yet as you say, Herr Bernhardt, it seems that there is none who may judge this matter save God, and it is too grievous to turn aside from. If you are guilty of Herr Konstantin's murder, you deserve death; if you are innocent, then it seems that we can hardly deprive you a second time of your patrimony." He leaned back, sipping from the agate goblet when his page offered it and looking at the twelve knights arranged about the throne dais.

For a moment, his dark gaze lighted on one, then passed on - Margerite realized that the long-jawed face inside the glittering helm-rim bore a close resemblance to both Konrad and Georg: he must be their elder brother Hugo, who of course could not fight the man to whom his brother had sworn their family's support. "Ritter Wilhelm," he said at last, looking at the tallest of his guardsmen. "Will you take up the challenge given by Herr Bernhardt von Niederwald?"

"Aye, your Majesty. I will take it up gladly, for I do not believe that any man who fled from judgement to fight in a Free Company has the right to rule lands within the Holy Roman Empire. Moreover, Herr Gerhardt von Niederwald is known to me, and however his wife may have deceived him, I am willing to prove with my body the truth of Herr Gerhardt's oath against the falsehood of his brother's." A shiver trickled down Margerite's spine as Ritter Wilhelm spoke. His voice was low and flat, the voice of a dangerously angry man; she thought of Gerhardt sitting at the Kaiser's high table, and had no doubt that Kaiser Karl had chosen his champion in full knowledge of how the knight's loyalties lay.

"Then so be it. And because we would have this matter resolved as swiftly as possible, the two of you shall meet upon the field this afternoon on the stroke of nones, and may Christ give victory to him who is in the right." Karl lifted his sceptre. "We now declare this court in abeyance, until the justice of God is made manifest by trial of arms. Thus we, Karl IV, Kaiser of the Holy Roman Empire, King of Bohemia, have spoken." The Kaiser stood to the sound of a final fanfare from the trumpets; his audience stood as well, kneeling as he walked down from the dais and, preceded and followed by his bodyguard and attendants, departed through the triumphal arch.

As soon as Kaiser Karl was gone, Gerhardt and his supporters stalked out without so much as a glance at Bernhardt's side of the room. But Margerite turned to Bernhardt: for now the matter was for God to decide, and the judgement of men no longer hung over them. Bernhardt bent his head, taking her hot damp hands between his cool dry ones and raising them to his lips, and she almost thought she would swoon at his touch. Carefully, he reached for the chain concealed beneath the gemstone beads of her falcon-necklace, drawing his signet-ring up from its hiding place like a bright fish, and lifted it over her head.

"Let our pledge be known now," Bernhardt said. "Margerite, will you marry me?"

"Bernhardt, I will." Margerite stretched her hand out, and he slipped the heavy gold ring onto her finger, its weight warm and comforting.

Then, at last, Bernhardt's strong arms went about her again, and she turned her face upwards to receive his soft passionate kiss upon her lips. As their mouths touched, Margerite's knees trembled violently beneath her, her legs too weak to uphold her any longer, but Bernhardt held her firmly in his embrace. She clung to him like a drowning swimmer to a sturdy oak, a thrill of pleasure tightening her belly like a distant echo of their old lovemaking as his hardness pressed against her.

Margerite wanted desperately to tear away the layers of silk and velvet that veiled them from each other, to cleave to Bernhardt as if they were in truth one flesh; and yet she thought she could not have borne for the moment of their kiss to end. At last the sound of applause and cheering broke her reverie.

Paul and Jochanan were clapping furiously, and Paul shouted, "Congratulations, Bernhardt! Well-done!" Margerite's face burned with delighted embarassment, as though she and Bernhardt had been making love in truth; she breathed deeply, trying to steady her legs as Bernhardt reluctantly unfolded his arms from about her. Their other companions were grinning; even Father Etienne smiled, though Gottfried, blushing darkly, had averted his gaze from their embrace. *I hope you are not so shy with Arnmut,* Margerite thought, laughing in dizzy excitement.

"My congratulations to both of you," Father Etienne said. "You have done well." Margerite nodded in reply to his benison: the priest was not speaking of their betrothal, she knew, but as Confessor to both of them, he knew how long they had struggled against each other's temptation.

But that is over: only a little time now, and we shall be wedded. Margerite would have pulled the warmth of that thought around her in her moment of joy, unshadowed by fear and doubt, but she had learned the harsh lessons of the Art, and added unwillingly to herself, If Bernhardt lives.

The rest of their comrades congratulated them as well, the men embracing Bernhardt and thumping him on the back, while Eva pulled Margerite into her powerful arms for a hug that nearly cracked her ribs - dear Maria, she will bear strong children! Margerite thought.

"When do you mean to set the wedding?" Christoph asked. If he bore any rancour to Margerite for this, so soon after Heinrich's death, it did not show in his face or his voice: he seemed as cheerful as the rest of them.

"I shall not presume to guess at God's judgement," Bernhardt answered soberly. "Yet... there is no harm in speaking of it, I suppose: if He does not grant me victory, then our plans shall matter little in any case. If Christ wills it, Margerite and I shall return to Schloss Niederwald when our time here is done, and we shall be wedded there - with, I hope, all of you to witness."

"Then, if the Landgraf von Niederwald gives us leave, we shall celebrate two weddings there!" Christoph said. "For Eva and I have waited long enough, and are not minded to delay matters any further - are we, beloved?"

Eva tilted her head to the side, smiling at her betrothed. "I will gladly say my vows whenever and where-ever you wish, Christoph," she murmured. Margerite almost laughed at the meek sweetness in her voice: she would have wagered almost anything that the idea of a double wedding had come from Eva in the first place.

The sound of church bells echoed faintly through the thick walls of the audience hall, chiming sext. The Kaiser's table would soon be set, and Margerite found that her belly was roiling with hunger: she had been too nervous earlier to swallow more than a bite or two of soft white bread, and even that had almost stuck in her throat. But she had Wolfram to think of yet, for even though Wenzel's nursemaids and guards had charge of him, she misliked leaving him alone.

"We shall speak further at table," she said. "But I must go to fetch my son."

Margerite got lost more than once in her search for the Imperial nursery, but there were plenty of servants about to direct her way. When she got there at last, she saw six knights standing outside the door.

"How may we aid you, noble frowe?" one of the guards asked as she walked up to them.

"I am the Gräfin von Falkenstein, and I have come for my son Wolfram, Graf von Falkenstein. Is he within?"

The knights glanced at each other, then at Margerite, their gazes sliding over her as if they were feeling along her dress for hidden daggers. One of them nodded; another spoke.

"Frowe Gräfin, if you speak of the fair babe who was brought here earlier this morning, he is indeed. I shall ask permission for you to enter."

He opened the door and went in, returning a moment later. "You may go in, frowe Gräfin."

Wenzel's nursery was furnished as lavishly as any chamber in Burg Karlstein, though instead of paintings and gilding, the walls were warmed with thick tapestries, and children's toys were scattered all over the precious rugs. Wolfram was standing up, the hilt of a small wooden sword clutched in both his chubby fists and a fierce intent look on his little face; relieved to see her son still there, it was a moment before Margerite noticed who else was in the room. It took her a second to recognise the Kaiser: he had taken off crown and cap, leaving his dark head bare, and was crouching on the floor, his gold-brocaded robes pooled about him as he patted the fair-haired boy sobbing on his shoulder.

"He hit me!" the boy was crying.

"You were playing at swords, were you not?" Karl asked reasonably. "And Graf Wolfram is little more than a year old: you cannot expect him to know that you are my son. Now hush, for the Prince of Bohemia should not cry when he is bruised. Pick that up again, and go another round with Graf Wolfram - but remember that he is much younger than you." He looked sternly at the boy. "If you strike him too hard out of anger, I promise that you shall regret it, and that with great swiftness. Do you understand me, Wenzel?"

"Yes," the young prince answered, wiping his eyes. He was a pretty child, Margerite saw, though his soft milkwater fairness was surprising in contrast to his father's dark hair and strongly marked features. As Wenzel bent to pick up the toy sword and buckler from the rug, Kaiser Karl looked up at Margerite.

"Greetings again, Gräfin," he said. "It seems that your son has managed to bruise mine... No!" Karl laughed as Margerite began to stammer an apology. "That was well-done for a child so young; I think it caught Wenzel by surprise, and mayhap he has learned not to underestimate an opponent smaller than himself." The Kaiser turned back to the children. "Now, boys, you may lay on again."

Margerite watched in amazement as the two boys fought. Wenzel began to circle his opponent, but Karl clicked his tongue sharply. "Graf Wolfram is too young for footwork, Wenzel: face him straight-on." Even as he spoke, Wolfram launched a two-handed blow that cracked off Wenzel's little buckler; the larger boy struck back, but Wolfram just managed to get his sword up in time to block, and poked Wenzel in the stomach with its tip. Wenzel fell backwards from surprise even as Wolfram lost his precarious balance, both of them sprawling on the floor and beginning to howl.

"Amazing," the Kaiser said, raising his voice above the children's complaints with a father's practiced ease. "I never would have thought that an infant of Graf Wolfram's age could so much as hold a sword, much less fight as if he had already begun knightly training. I think he shall be a true champion when he is grown - hush, Wenzel. Graf Wolfram did not hit you hard enough for you to cry about it."

Wenzel pouted, but sat up and wiped his face with his green silk sleeve. Margerite suppressed a cringe: except for feasts and such occasions, she would not have put such stuff on a child, but she supposed the Kaiser could afford it. But dear Maria, the cost when the Prince of Bohemia starts climbing trees and splashing into mud puddles!

"I look forward," Karl went on, "to seeing what Graf Wolfram becomes when he is older. If you like, Gräfin, you may leave him with Wenzel for the rest of your stay here."

"I thank you very much for your kindness, your Majesty, but I am accustomed to having Wolfram close by me."

The Kaiser quirked a dark eyebrow, but said only, "Well, as you please. Perhaps you will bring him back here to visit Wenzel again before you depart?"

"I shall be glad to do that, your Majesty."

"Hit him," Wolfram said with great satisfaction, smiling up at Margerite as she carried him out of the Imperial nursery.

"Yes, you did, my love," Margerite replied proudly. "And the Kaiser says that you shall be a champion when you are grown." Perhaps, after all, Wolfram's travels had done him no harm: Margerite remembered how the men of the Bear's Paw had let him play with their sheathed daggers, poking lightly at him as he waved the bound weapons in the air and praising him greatly when he managed to tap one of them. Arnmut, too, had joined in the game sometimes, and once, to his embarassment, she had even caught Gottfried at it - it was in no way unnatural, she assured herself, that a child raised thus should take to weapon-play as easily as he had learned to walk.

The first course, tiny boiled larks' eggs suspended in a clear golden wine-jelly, had already been served when Margerite and Wolfram took their place beside Bernhardt in the Kaiser's hall, and the men were talking intently.

"Still," Christoph was saying, "it surprises me that the Kaiser should have stripped Gerhardt of his lands and rank so easily."

"No surprise at all," Father Etienne answered, his ascetic face grim. "Nothing could be proven - but there was more than reason to think that Gerhardt knew what his wife was, if he did not take part in her deeds himself. And Kaiser Karl, though pious and just, is also a practical man: he knew how sharply his revenues from Niederwald had dropped in what should have been a rich year, and you are much mistaken if you think that he did not have plenty of reports from other sources on how badly Gerhardt and Ortlieb managed their realm. I suspect that he was more than pleased at a good excuse to remove Gerhardt.

And," the priest added, "I think that matters have worked very much to the Kaiser's advantage. Should Bernhardt be victorious, he will have a competent ruler for Niederwald against whose right no one can argue, but over whom he yet has a hold, since the shadow of the Black Sword can never be fully erased and Kaiser Karl has the resources to bring as much - or as little - of the past to light as he pleases. Whereas, if Bernhardt falls this afternoon, Niederwald shall revert without challenge to Karl himself: whatever the outcome, it shall profit the Empire."

"That is harsh counsel," muttered Konrad, prodding a lark's egg out of its jelly and chasing it about his golden plate with the point of his knife. "Christ grant our victory! - Herr Bernhardt, are you truly intent on fighting this duel yourself, rather than allowing me to champion you?"

"It is my right that must be proven, and I shall not let any other bear the challenge in my stead," Bernhardt replied staunchly.

Konrad shook his head, frowning under his dark moustache. "How long is it since you last ran a tilting course?"

"Some nine years, perhaps, but I have seen much battle since."

"Aye, and much of it as a foot-soldier. I do not mean to doubt you, Herr Bernhardt, and I know that God upholds the right...but my brother Hugo has mentioned Ritter Wilhelm to me before. He is a fierce man, without mercy, and perhaps the best of the Kaiser's guard; which is to say, the best in the Holy Roman Empire. I would guess my own chances against him as less than even - but, if I may speak honestly and without insulting you, Herr Bernhardt, though I have not seen you fight, it is likeliest that you have no chance of winning unless you are indeed granted a miracle."

Bernhardt's mouth tightened, his brows drawing in; but Gottfried spoke before he could. "That is true, Herr Konrad. I have seen Herr Bernhardt fight several times now, chiefly in war, but also in a smaller engagement. He is very good, yet, as you say, he is less practiced with the lance, and his chief opponents have not been other knights. Still, this duel is not to prove who is the better man, but rather, to let God show His judgement to us. I have full faith that He shall not fail us: even so, the First Crusade took Jerusalem against all odds."

Konrad looked at the smaller knight. "I wish I could share your faith, Ritter Gottfried."

"I, as well," Georg said unexpectedly. "For I have seen that God does not always step in to save those whose cause is right, when their strength on earth is the weaker: else there would be no need for us to swear the oath of knighthood. And I have learned, too, that there is a difference between faith and blind foolishness - Bernhardt, will you not let my brother champion you?"

"I will not," Bernhardt answered, his voice harsh. But then he smiled, unclenching his fist from the hilt of his eating dagger. "Though I do thank you for the offer. Yet remember: this is not a tourney, where the first unhorsing ends the bout, but a battle to death or yielding. If I am unhorsed before Ritter Wilhelm, I have had more experience than most knights ever get in facing a man on horseback from the ground." His tone had roughened again, and for a fleeting moment, Margerite saw the grim hardness of the mercenary in Bernhardt's face. "Unless his lance pierces me - and I think I am still skilled enough to avoid that - the duel is likely to be finished on foot. Though Ritter Wilhelm may still be better with a sword than I, the difference shall not be nearly so great then. Believe me, I knew well what I was doing when I asked the Kaiser to choose a defender for Gerhardt's oath, although I did not guess that he would find a man who truly wished to take up my brother's cause so easily."

Father Etienne arched an eyebrow. "Your brother was not the only person in this castle with the chance to spread tales, as you must be aware. But the Kaiser knows his own men well, and plays them cleverly. I do not think it was by chance that both Ritter Hugo and Ritter Wilhelm stood by his side this morning: had it been you who needed one, you should have had no lack of champions."

As the servers came about to clear the table and bring the second course, Bernhardt stood. "Though I have made my Confession already, a time of prayer shall serve me better this afternoon than a heavy meal in my stomach. If you will excuse me..."

"I shall come to pray with you, if I may," Margerite said.

Bernhardt touched her hand, looking gravely down at her. "Of course - my betrothed."

They had heard Mass in the Chapel of the Holy Cross the day before; but now Bernhardt and Margerite made their way to the Marienkirche on the second floor of the castle's middle tower. This chapel was not so wildly ornamented as the other - the Chapel of the Holy Cross, at the top of the largest tower in Burg Karlstein, had seemed to be a single huge reliquary, the walls gleaming with ruddy gold and precious stones, and the polished gilding of the high-vaulted ceiling, wrought with patterns of rosettes between the arching ribbed beams, reflecting back the light of the candles that lined the lower walls a thousand thousand times.

But the ceiling of the Marienkirche was flat-beamed, painted with the bright intense blue that came only from powdered lapis, with the haloed figures of gold-haired angels lined in neat row upon row to look down at those who entered, and gilded stars winking between them. In a large peaked niche above the altar stood the statue of the Virgin with her Son upon her knee, a curtain of pale blue and gold brocade drawn behind them, and the niche's walls were painted with the pure blue and glittering gold stars of the Queen of Heaven.

Above to the right was an elaborately-carved reliquary cabinet, and a row of lesser niches lined the wall to either side: hung across them was a great tapestry made from alternating panels showing the displayed Imperial eagle, black upon white, and rampant gold-crowned Luxemburger lions with their twisting forked tails, silver upon red. The walls were painted dazzlingly: the scenes on the eastern wall were serene, knights and rulers and saints; but Margerite shivered as she looked upon the western one, for there the Apocalypse was shown forth in its full horror.

Tinges of green and black cast a lurid light over the serene heaven-blue: the red mask of a thunder-demon glared from a darkened, bolt-shattered cloud, and beside it the proud roofs and towers of a city toppled as the earth heaved beneath it. The spears of angels, narrow searing streaks of light, lanced from above; beneath, demons jeered and ranted and shook their fists in rage - and it seemed to Margerite that the painter had known more than a man should, for as she looked upon their leering, twisted countenances, she saw the expression of mirthless laughter and idiot blaspheming delight that Christoph's face had veiled thinly with flesh at his exorcism.

She crossed herself, and she and Bernhardt went forward to kneel upon the stone rails between the carven benches. The painted countenance of the Marienkircher Virgin was joyful: it seemed to Margerite that the sculptor had caught Maria in a moment of happiness, as though she had forgotten the sorrows that lay in store for her Son, and was thinking only of the delight of holding her child in her lap. Margerite lifted Wolfram a little higher, as though to show him to the Virgin, and he laughed, waving his hands in the air. But beside her, Bernhardt's hazel eyes filled with tears, and he bowed his head: he must be wondering, even now, if his sins had after all made him unfit to take the rule of Niederwald.

Mother Maria, Margerite prayed, You know what manner of man Bernhardt is - You know that he did not forsake You, even in his blackest despair, and prayed to You from the deepest parts of his soul. Bid mercy of Your Son for us, for He is just...Her eyes flickered sideways to the lurid brilliance of the Apocalypse on the western wall...but He offers forgiveness to the worst of men.

Mother Maria, Queen of Heaven, Who has aided us so long; as Bernhardt restored You to Your place at the Marienbrunnen, will you restore him to his own? We are in Your hands now, and in Christ's: as You strengthened my soul, that the demon Azruzor be overcome, I pray You to strengthen Bernhardt's heart and arm, that what our Foe did those years ago now be undone, and Bernhardt full-healed at last.

Although the strain of holding Wolfram's weight up quickly began to ache in Margerite's arms and shoulders, and the cold stone of the kneelers was bruising-hard against her legs, she did not cease her prayers until she heard the footsteps behind her, and lifted her head to see Georg in full armour, a chainmail coif dimming his red hair and a tilting-helm under his arm.

"It is time to make ready," the new knight said softly. "Herr Bernhardt, may I be your second on the field?" Though Georg's scarred face was quietly intense, Margerite, thankfully, saw no sign of the bitterness that had marred him before. O Bernhardt, say yes! she thought.

"I should need no second," answered Bernhardt. "But for the honour you do me, and your friendship, I shall be pleased to have you." In spite of his long kneeling, he stood easily; Margerite, numb-kneed and unbalanced by Wolfram's weight, got up more clumsily, and Bernhardt stretched out a hand to steady her.

"My lady," he murmured, "as you have prayed for me, will you give me a token of your favour to bear on the field this day?"

"O, gladly!" At first Margerite thought of her falcon-necklace, but that was a thing of the Art: it had no place in a holy battle such as Bernhardt was about to fight. Her sleeves were fastened tight to her underdress...She reached into her belt-pouch, her hand closing on the little beads that rolled like polished grains beneath her fingers, and drew out the garnet strand of her rosary. "Bear this for my sake, and for Mother Maria's," she said to Bernhardt.

He closed his hand about hers, bringing her fingers up to his lips for a chaste, sweet kiss before he took the rosary and looped it about his own neck.

Konrad had offered Bernhardt his tilting armour, for they were close to a size, but Bernhardt had refused it: as he said, he was likely to finish the fight on the ground, and the half-reinforced armour would only make him clumsy. Bernhardt already had a shield bearing the Niederwald arms: Margerite guessed that Bishop Otto had arranged it for him before their departure for Burg Karlstein. Konrad also had a number of instructions for Bernhardt - how Ritter Wilhelm held his shield, what his favourite movements were, how his right leg had been wounded last year and was ever so slightly weaker than the left - and other such things as meant a great deal to fighting men.

Gottfried and Arnmut had been praying as well, though they had gone to the Chapel of the Holy Cross; but Christoph, Eva, and the two von Schwarzenfels knights had been busy seeing to it that Bernhardt had everything that he would need, from a greathelm down to the blue and silver pennants hanging proudly from his lances. Gottfried offered to lend Bernhardt his own warhorse, but Konrad shook his head.

"Your Löwen is a noble steed, but he is used to a light rider - it would make little difference in most fights, but in such a joust as this, the least things may be important. Hugo says that you may use his horse, and I will also gladly offer mine, though I advise you to take his, not because I am a niggard, but because his steed was given him by the Kaiser and is the better of the two."

As Georg and Konrad helped Bernhardt into his armour, Margerite wondered where Father Etienne was. Still praying? Or had he gone off to arrange something else altogether? He would not interfere in the course of the fight, no more than she would - less so, something whispered in the back of her mind - but was he, perhaps, making sure by his own means that no one else would? For, perceptive as the Kaiser was, even he could be deceived, and if he were led to grant Niederwald to the wrong person, then the Light-Bearers would have lost little by Ortlieb's death. Mother Maria, uphold Bernhardt, for he fights for us all!

The afternoon sunlight shone dazzlingly on the meadow beneath Burg Karlstein where the duel would take place. Word had spread quickly in the few hours since the Kaiser had held his court: as Margerite walked down the road from the castle beside Bernhardt, she saw the profusion of spectators like a mosaic of countless precious gems spread out below, the armour of Karl's knights glinting like pieces of silver set between the ruby and sapphire and emerald, amethyst and white chalcedony and topaz of the nobles' richly-coloured clothes, and the roped-off dueling field was green as a long strip of malachite.

Kobolt scampered ahead of Margerite, stopping now and again to look back at her with a little chirping purr as though he were urging them onward. Jochanan carried the Falkenstein banner once more, and Arnmut, that of Fürstensee. Bernhardt had brought the Niederwald standard beneath which he had fought at Ortlieb's wain; Georg bore it proudly forward, and the silver fish seemed to leap upon its blue field as the breeze caught the heavy fabric.

Many of the court who had come to watch the duel were
sitting on rugs, nibbling at dainties and sipping wine; there
were several small pavilions set up to shield the ladies' fair
skin from the sun, and the voices of minstrels rose above
the gentle strumming of harps and lyres and the odd little
long-necked string instrument called the Bohemian bird.
Margerite's heart clenched with a sudden surge of anger:
had Bernhardt come through such great travails, only for his
last trial to be an hour's pleasant diversion for bored nobles?
Soon two men shall be fighting, perhaps dying, upon this
field, and the fate of Niederwald shall rest upon the combat -
and this might as well be a tourney in France!

These court members, in their silks and gold…how many
of them knew what it was to flee through the night in terror
of their lives, or to sleep on a straw pallet filled with lice and
bedbugs? Which of these giggling women with their little
lapdogs in jeweled collars could stand before the very gaze of
a demon; which of these men might have the bravery to go
back, as Bernhardt had, to a home become the very mouth of
Hell?

And yet, Margerite thought, her anger fading as swiftly
as it had roused, I pray that such times may never come
to any of them. It seemed to her then that the world about
her doubled in her sight: she could still see the pavilions
and field and thronging folk, but they seemed tiny to her
gaze, as though she were looking down at them from the
top of Burg Karlstein. And the green meadow was no more
than a thin glaze of enamel above an unfathomable abyss of
darkness; and the blue sky was but a water-shimmer below
the swirling, burning myriad of stars.

How fragile this earth is, Margerite thought in wonder,
to seem to us the most real part of being! And yet it is
compassed wholly by the realms of spirit, by such things as
few men could bear to see face to face, for either beauty or
horror. But we who know - it is our duty to guard this frail
world, and hold it unbroken for those who dwell here. She
took Bernhardt's gauntleted hand in her own; she knew he
could not feel her tightening her grasp through the metal,
but he looked down to meet her eyes.

"Defensor Hominum," she whispered: Defender of
Men. It was Father Etienne's office, but also her own - and
Bernhardt's: for today with his sword, if Christ willed, he
would close off another of the many avenues by which the
hungry, clamouring darkness strove to breach the walls God
had raised to protect His Creation.

Bernhardt shook his head. "I am not worthy..." he
murmured, and Margerite did not know whether he spoke to
her, or to Maria.

"You are my champion," she said gently. "If you were not
worthy of this battle, you would not stand here now to fight
it."

He paused a moment, looking out over the long bare strip
of green grass marked off by the fluttering lines of pennants.
Ritter Wilhelm stood at one end, one squire checking the
tightness of his armour-straps and another fitting the last
pieces of barding on his red warhorse. At the other end were
Gottfried, with Etzel sitting at his feet; Konrad, holding the
reins of a magnificent grey stallion whose hide gleamed with
the same glossy sheen as the polished plates of the armour
that covered his neck, breast, and hindquarters; and Father
Etienne.

Directly across the list-field was a pavilion of white silk,
from the roof of which the Imperial banner fluttered. Karl,
crowned and sceptered, was already sitting upon his throne
there, surrounded by his retinue of heralds, pages, and
knights, with little Wenzel seated on a smaller throne beside
him to the right. A man wearing the robes of an Archbishop
and holding a crozier sat to the Kaiser's left, and by him
were two priests with censer and holy water sprinkler.

"I pray Christ you are right. I know that the oath for which
I fight is true, but my sins..."

"Are forgiven and absolved long since," Margerite
answered firmly.

Bernhardt nodded, and together they walked down to
their end of the list, Christoph and Eva and Paul following
them with the standard-bearers, Rose carrying Wolfram
behind them and Kobolt and Kriemhilt running ahead.

The Kaiser's heralds raised their trumpets, the notes of
their fanfare shivering across the field. Margerite saw Karl
lift his sceptre, and a herald stepped forward. "Hearken unto
the words of his Imperial Majesty and King of Bohemia, Karl
IV!" the herald shouted, his high tenor clear through the
warm afternoon air. "Let Herr Bernhardt von Niederwald
and Ritter Wilhelm von Holzenheim come before his
Majesty!"

Margerite clasped Bernhardt's hand one last time before
he turned to walk down the field and kneel before the Kaiser.
Karl's voice did not carry well, but the herald repeated
each phrase loudly so that all gathered there could hear the
Imperial words.

"Herr Bernhardt von Niederwald, Ritter Wilhelm von
Holzenheim! You have come here to prove Christ's will
with your bodies on the field of battle! Now, before God and
before ourself, we would ask you to swear again, on these
holy relics of Christ's Crucifixion, to that which each of you
will defend!"

"Your Majesty," Bernhardt stated strongly, "I do swear
on these holy relics, with Christ as my witness, that I am
altogether innocent in the murder of Herr Konstantin von
Adelsberg, of which I was falsely accused."

"Your Majesty,"Ritter Wilhelm called out, "I do swear
on these holy relics, with Christ as my witness, that Herr
Bernhardt von Niederwald lies; that he is false, recreant,
and an unrepentant murderer, and was justly accused of his
crime by his noble brother, Herr Gerhardt von Niederwald;
and this shall I prove upon his body with lance and sword, if
he still dare to meet me in the field."

"If you dare to meet me, Ritter Wilhelm, I shall prove upon your body that the oath you have sworn is false!" Bernhardt shouted. The Kaiser lifted his sceptre again, and said something that Margerite could not make out, for the herald did not repeat it, but the two men kneeling before him quieted.

"Archbishop Johannes Ocko von Vlasim!" Karl said, the herald calling his words out once more. "Come forward to bless these knights, and to pray that the will of God be done this day."

The Archbishop rose from his seat, making the sign of the Cross over the heads of the two kneeling men. Margerite could not hear what he was saying clearly, but she saw Johannes Ocko's assistant cense the two combatants, the clouds of incense smoke swirling almost solid white in the sunlight. The Archbishop bowed his head in prayer for a time, then blessed the combatants and sprinkled their coifed heads with holy water.

"Christ's will be done," the Kaiser said. "Amen! Herr Bernhardt, Ritter Wilhelm, mount your steeds: you may begin upon my signal."

There were still a few drops of holy water caught glittering in Bernhardt's chestnut hair like crystals strung on copper wire when he had reached his horse. Before he put his great helm on, Margerite embraced him. The sweet moistness of Bernhardt's mouth had a faint salty taste: Margerite realized that it was the taste of her own tears in the kiss. "I love you," she whispered to him, then, remembering that they no longer had to conceal themselves, said more loudly, "I love you!"

"And I love you, Margerite." Bernhardt held her to him gently, as though he feared to break her body on the plates of his armour. Though Margerite could not touch his flesh through it, it almost seemed to her that she could feel his heart beating beneath his steel breastplate. He put his bascinet on and they kissed once more through the helm's open face: then Georg lowered the greathelm over Bernhardt's head and strapped it on, and he mounted up, taking lance and shield from Georg's hand.

At the other end of the lists, Ritter Wilhelm sat ready on his steed, shield balanced at his side and lance held lightly in his hand. Bernhardt raised his weapon in salute, but the other man did not return the gesture.

The Kaiser spoke; the herald shouted, "Herr Bernhardt von Niederwald! Ritter Wilhelm von Holzenheim! Are you ready!"

"I am!" Bernhardt called back, his voice muffled by his helm; Margerite could not hear Ritter Wilhelm's answer at all, but the herald shouted, "Begin!"

The two horses surged forward, the plates of steel on their necks and flanks flashing in the sun, and the spikes on their narrow nose-plates glinting wickedly. Margerite could almost feel the ground shake beneath the pounding of their great hooves, and her fists knotted tightly in her skirt - she did not know how any man could survive the stroke of a lance with such power behind it.

It seemed only a few heartbeats before the keen tips lowered to strike. As they met, Ritter Wilhelm lifted his lance slightly, aiming for Bernhardt's head. Bernhardt threw up his shield, ducking down, and Margerite gasped in relief as Ritter Wilhelm's point ripped along it; but though Bernhardt's tip struck its mark, his dodging had cost the blow its force, and his foe did not so much as waver in his saddle.

Then the horses were past each other, recovering from the familiar stumble of impact. The two riders circled widely, urging their horses up into a canter as they rounded the corners at their own ends of the field.

"Well-done, Bernhardt!" Margerite called when he rode by her. Though she doubted he could hear her beneath the thick metal and padding of his greathelm, her companions added their cheers as his horse's hooves flew from canter to gallop.

This time, Ritter Wilhelm's lance-tip barely glanced off the edge of Bernhardt's shield. Instead of punching in beneath his breastplate, it shrieked off the metal guarding his right side; but he turned Bernhardt's lance with almost contemptuous ease, trotting past to the roaring cheers of the crowd as his foe reeled in his saddle.

"Christ, he's good!" Christoph whispered, adding quickly, "But I had not thought that Bernhardt could joust so well: two passes against the Kaiser's champion is an honourable show for any knight."

Margerite glanced sideways at Gottfried, hoping, perhaps, for some reassurance. But Gottfried was leaning forward, grasping the pennanted rope that marked off the field, his face drawn and tight as if he were trying to see something past his eyes' reach - he was not looking at Bernhardt.

"What is it, Gottfried?" Margerite asked in alarm. Even as she spoke, she heard Etzel's low, rumbling growl, and Kobolt gave a queer little cry. Instinctively she moved to snatch Wolfram out of Rose's arms, even as the horses broke into their third charge down the field. The riders met with a thunderous crack; a lance-head spun glittering into the air... Bernhardt flew from the saddle, and Margerite cried out involuntarily as his body landed on the grass with a heavy thump.

To her shock, Ritter Wilhelm, broken lance-stump in hand, wheeled his steed; the red horse reared, striking out with both forehooves at the fallen knight. But Bernhardt rolled away and up in a single swift motion - "He told me I must learn to rise quickly when unhorsed," Georg breathed - scooping his lance from the ground and aiming it, not at the man, but at the warhorse.

Who is that? Gottfried's silent voice cried urgently within Margerite's skull. It seemed to her then that her gaze shattered into pieces: she could see Ritter Wilhelm trotting his horse in a wide arc, keeping out of Bernhardt's reach as he drew his own sword; at the same time, she was looking down the list at Gerhardt, who stood by the pennanted ropes with his hands clenched into fists by his sides, mouth open and eyes staring - and she also saw the green mist of the field lined with vaguely manlike blurs of colour; but thin shining bolts of Hell-black light were surging into one from all around, like an inverted sunburst, and the black flame issuing from the indistinct paleness of its face was searingly clear and sharp. Blue and red and flashing gold - Gerhardt was still wearing the Niederwald doublet over red hose; the two figures, seen and half-seen, merged into each other, and Father Etienne grasped her shoulder.

"Ward yourself, Margerite!" the priest hissed, even as Ritter Wilhelm kicked his horse into a full gallop and bore down on Bernhardt. Kobolt yowled, Kriemhilt screeching a teeth-rattling harmony above; a black thunderclap of pain burst through Margerite's skull.

She staggered, crying out, but through her darkened eyes, she could still see Ritter Wilhelm swerving his steed past Bernhardt's lance-tip, Bernhardt drawing the weapon back and jabbing viciously up to catch the horse beneath its neck-plates. The spurt of blood shone clear as sunlight through ruby glass; the roan stallion reared, spraying a bright red fountain out over Bernhardt as it kicked convulsively at the air and toppled with the lance still buried in its throat.

Eva wrested Wolfram from Margerite's arms as the second thunderclap exploded in her head, an agony so shattering that she reeled back and would have fallen if Father Etienne had not caught her. Light flashed blue from the edges of Gottfried's blade as he stepped before her; a halo of brightness limned the two armoured figures closing, sword to sword, on the field, but Margerite could no longer see which was which - she thought it was Bernhardt who struck the first blow, but then remembered that he had lost his shield when he fell.

Each heartbeat pounded a sharp spike through her skull; summoning up all her strength, she clutched the pain to her like a fistful of nettles, flinging it away as hard as she could, and her sight cleared a little. Now, looking past Gottfried, Margerite could see Ritter Wilhelm raining furious hammer-blows on his foe. Gripping his sword with one hand on the hilt and one on the pommel, Bernhardt was fending the other off as best he could; but Ritter Wilhelm's shield protected its owner from Bernhardt's strokes.

Behind the waist-high line of pennants, Gerhardt's hands were moving, his eyes blasted holes of darkness in his pale face. At Margerite's feet, Kobolt cried his warning; she heard Jochanan muttering in Hebrew behind her. She had no wand, no tools of power, but she pointed her right forefinger - the Wand is my Will! - holding her left hand palm-out as if it were a knight's shield.

In the next second, something struck the heel of Margerite's left palm, a tremendous concussion shivering through the bones of that arm and driving her elbow bruising-deep into her side as she leaned forward to meet it. Her gaze fixed on Gerhardt - though he was an hundred yards away, she could see him as clearly as if they stood chest to chest. His skin was a flimsy veil of white muslin over the dark flame writhing within him, a black light so intense that it burned Margerite's eyes like the unbearable white fire of the sun.

A shout went up from the crowd. Bernhardt was staggering, his right arm hanging limp against his side, and Ritter Wilhelm's sword lifted again.

You! Margerite thought in angry recognition - not to the man Gerhardt, that hollow shell, but to the power scorching within him, thwarted before, but ravenous for revenge...the darkness rising, even now, to strike out once more through his mouth with the blow that would consume her; the Light-Bearers' perfect vengeance, slaying her in despair as she saw Bernhardt fall.

"No!" she cried aloud as Bernhardt dropped to his knees, that single word searing across the field like a pure spear of brightness. Gerhardt's mouth stretched wider, impossibly wide; he stumbled back, toppling to the earth.

And in that instant, Bernhardt's bent legs straightened to drive him upwards beneath Ritter Wilhelm's shield, the full force of his body behind his sword-point as it slid between two of the plates covering the knight's abdomen, shattering the chain-mail beneath and piercing Ritter Wilhelm's body to the spine. Gerhardt's defender dropped like a puppet with cut strings, his sword falling from his hand as he sprawled loosely on the ground in a welter of blood, and the Archbishop hastened out with his assistants to lift the fallen man's helm from his head.

Margerite leaned back against Father Etienne, breathing hard through her open mouth as Gottfried sheathed his sword and came back to help support her. Her left arm was numb to the elbow; she felt odd, as though she were floating half a handspan off the ground.

"Help me...out to him," she gasped. Paul cut the rope that barred the list-field, its pennants fluttering to the ground, and, with Father Etienne holding her left arm and Gottfried holding her right, she made her way painfully across the trampled grass to Bernhardt.

Bernhardt stood with his head lowered, leaning one-handed on his sword. His breath hissed stertoriously through the holes in his faceplate, and Margerite could see that he was swaying on his feet as Georg ran around to help him doff the greathelm and the bascinet beneath it. Bernhardt's face shone red with heat and exhaustion, his dripping hair almost black with sweat and standing up in a wild mess when he shook his arming cap and chainmail coif off.

"How badly are you wounded?" Georg asked anxiously. "Your arm..."

"Broken, I suspect, but not bleeding." Bernhardt's voice was tight with pain, but he waved the red-haired knight away with his left hand when Georg would have started unstrapping his greaves. "No, they will hold it in place until Jochanan can see to it. Margerite..."

Margerite let go of her two supporters, tottering the few steps to him; and she and Bernhardt clung shaking to each other. She almost did not hear the fanfare, though the trumpeters were less than thirty feet from her: it seemed that there was nothing in the world except Bernhardt's armour against her body - sun-hot and sticky with blood, but dearer than any touch she had ever known - the welcome sound of his harsh panting in her ears, the warm smells of fighting-sweat and blood, and, gladdest of all, Bernhardt's hazel eyes shining down at her and his trembling smile as he bent to kiss her.

"Hear ye the Kaiser's word!" the herald cried. Belatedly, Margerite and Bernhardt looked over at Karl's pavilion.

Kaiser Karl had risen from his throne; the rope was down, and he was walking onto the field with his retinue about him. Margerite and Bernhardt knelt down, as did their companions.

"Herr Bernhardt von Niederwald," the Kaiser said. "By the grace of God, you have proven your innocence and the truth of your oath. And behold, Christ's judgement is manifest, for your brother, who swore falsely to him, lies dead without a wound!" He gestured towards the spot where the crowd had drawn back from the fallen body. Gerhardt lay on his stomach with the utter stillness of the dead, his arms flung out to the sides and his chin digging into the earth. This close, Margerite could see the burnt-out, wasted look of him, like the fragile bark shell of a heart-charred tree: she wondered if, even if he had succeeded in killing her, he could have survived the wildfire power that had roared through him. "Now, before all those gathered here, we, Karl IV, do grant you, Bernhardt, the lands of Niederwald and confirm you in your patrimony as Landgraf von Niederwald, and we shall hear your oath upon that office."

Though Bernhardt had to lift his right hand with his left in order to put both within the Kaiser's grasp, and paleness shocked across his face as he moved his broken arm, his voice was strong as he swore to serve and faithfully obey his lawful ruler. Karl, in turn, swore his protection and care to Bernhardt, then bent down to speak quietly to him, waving the herald to silence.

"How bad is your arm, Landgraf?"

"It will hold, your Majesty."

"That is well. Rise, Landgraf Bernhardt von Niederwald, and you, Gräfin Margerite von Fürstensee und Falkenstein." The Kaiser looked quickly at Father Etienne, Gottfried, and Georg, then nodded to his herald. "Command the presence of Graf Christoph von Fürstensee, Graf Wolfram von Falkenstein, Frowe Eva von Bärenburg, Ritter Konrad von Schwarzenfels, Ritter Arnmut von Eisenstein, Paul called the Bear, and Jochanan called the Gunner."

As the herald shouted out the names Karl had listed, Margerite saw that Kaiser Karl was smiling in his beard. He is well-pleased, she thought. But why should he not be, since no one now can doubt Bernhardt's right to be Landgraf von Niederwald?...Yet what more can he mean to do?

"Rise, all of you," Karl commanded when their companions had come forward and knelt. "Niederwald is now ruled by its rightful Landgraf, but we are given to understand that it is still lacking a Landgräfin. As we have just seen to the rectification of the former matter, it seems meet to us that we should deal with the latter as well. Gräfin Margerite von Fürstensee und Falkenstein, are you willing, before God, our Majesty, and these gathered witnesses, to take Landgraf Bernhardt von Niederwald as your lawfully wedded husband?"

Margerite's mouth dropped open. She had never expected...she had dreamed, sometimes when she allowed herself such fancies, of a wedding feast in Schloss Niederwald...At her feet, Kobolt purred luxuriously, winding about her ankles.

"I am, your Majesty," Margerite said, amazed that she could get more than a squeak out of her throat.

"Landgraf Bernhardt von Niederwald, are you willing, before God, our Majesty, and these gathered witnesses, to take Gräfin Margerite von Fürstensee und Falkenstein as your lawfully wedded wife?"

"I am, your Majesty," Bernhardt answered firmly.

The Kaiser lifted Bernhardt's right hand with infinite gentleness, placing Margerite's into it. "We now declare you man and wife, in the sight of God and the law of the Holy Roman Empire, and may Christ bless your marriage until the end of your days. So we, Kaiser Karl IV, have spoken: let no man henceforth presume to dispute it."

Bernhardt turned to Margerite, wrapping his good arm about her shoulders and drawing her in. Their lips met: she did not know if it was his sweat, or her own, or both, that salted their kiss. But as Margerite gazed up into the shadowy green-flecked depths of her husband's eyes, she saw that the pain of Bernhardt's broken arm was but a little thing to the deep and healing joy welling up in his soul at last, pouring into her own heart's brimming basin until her tears spilled over with delight.

*the end*

## EPILOGUE: SCHLOSS NIEDERWALD, 1372

Wolfram trotted down the stairs, his new bow swinging in his hand and a little quiver of arrows slung over his back. Yesterday had been his seventh birthday, and he had gotten all manner of presents. Ritter Gottfried, the commander of Schloss Niederwald's guard, and his second-in-command Ritter Arnmut, had given Wolfram the white Pyrenean puppy that followed at his feet; he had not decided what to name it yet, so he had been calling it Puppy. He had gotten a sparrowhawk from his mother, and the bow and arrows were a present from Paul the Bear. Jochanan had given him a little toy handgun mounted on a long stick, with which he had pretended to shoot at his little sister Katharina until she began to cry. Kobolt had not forgotten Wolfram's birthday either: to his nurse's horror, the great black cat had woken him by dropping a fresh-killed dove on his pillow.

But the best present of all had come from Landgraf Bernhardt: a real dagger of Köln steel, with a rondel-pommel and quillions just like a knight's sword. Wolfram's nurse had forbidden him to cut at tables or chairs with it, but he had secretly made his mark on his bedpost, and been gratified by how easily the sharp edge shaved the wood away. Now, however, it was time for Wolfram to try his bow properly. Lothar the gamekeeper had told Wolfram before that dawn and dusk were the best time for hunting: deer bedded down during the day, and birds slept at night, but most creatures moved in the little spaces of time between light and darkness.

Wolfram could hear Liutbirg's high screech as he came through the great hall to the door of the kitchens. "You can tell by touching it, you idiot! What kind of cook's apprentice doesn't know when an oven is hot enough for bread? God rot your bowels, I'll stuff your head in next time, maybe that will teach you what it should feel like!" In spite of the shrieking, a wave of delicious smells engulfed Wolfram as he stepped into the kitchens, and Puppy stopped to sniff the air, little white head cocked to the side and pink tongue hanging out. Kobolt ran ahead, crouching in preparation to leap up onto the table where one of Liutbirg's apprentices was chopping sausage-meat fine.

"Come on," Wolfram said impatiently to the hound and the cat. "We have things to do this morning." He slapped his thigh; Puppy followed him, but Kobolt would not be diverted from his course, jumping up to snatch a slice of meat from the very hand of the girl cutting it. She shrieked, and Liutbirg screamed more loudly, raising her ladle.

"Out! Out! You limb of Satan, get out of my kitchen, and take those filthy animals with you. Out, I say, or you'll feel the weight of my hand!"

Wolfram prudently hurried along, Puppy running beside him. He knew the old shrew would hit him: she had done it before, whenever she caught him creeping in to taste the sweets she mixed for the Landgraf's table. Once he had asked his mother why, when he had to be polite and address people by their titles, Liutbirg was allowed to yell and curse; to which Margerite had laughed and said that a cook who rivaled the Kaiser's own was allowed many things that others were not.

Kobolt caught up with them again as Wolfram hurried down the stairs to the back door, his stolen meat in his teeth. "There are better things to hunt this morning," Wolfram told the cat sternly, but Kobolt seemed not at all abashed.

The air outside was cool and fresh, the dawn's gray slowly paling from the sky. Wolfram passed by the gate to the kitchen garden - there would be nothing in there except sparrows - and went on to the larger gate that led into Schloss Niederwald's formal gardens. The guard on duty there winked at him as he passed, and he grinned back.

Wolfram slowed as he walked between the narrow black turrets of close-cropped yews, taking an arrow from his quiver and setting it lightly to the string. He could hear the chirping of small birds above the musical play of the fountains: there was a thrush standing on the edge of a stone basin, dipping his bill into the water, but Wolfram was after bigger game.

Two peacocks strutted on the long strip of greensward ahead of him, their shimmering tails dragging on the ground. He lifted his bow, sighted along the arrow...then remembered that Mutti had told him most specifically not to shoot her peacocks. "I lose enough of them to Kobolt as it is," she had sighed. "I have told him and told him to leave them alone, but he will not remember - well, I suppose he is a cat, after all." It had seemed a strange thing to say: what else would Kobolt be?

Even now, the tomcat was running ahead in a smooth scurry of black fur, his thick plumed tail feathering out behind him like a lance-pennant in the wind. The startled peacocks squawked, fluttering up from the ground to the low branches of the nearest trees where they perched with their long tails trailing, haughty little eyes glaring down at the hunting cat. Kobolt's teeth clicked rapidly as he hunched down, then leapt to seize a tailfeather in his teeth.

The offended peacock shrieked as the cat dropped down with its feather, taking wing to a higher branch; but Kobolt trotted proudly back with the long eye-tipped plume in his mouth. Wolfram took it from him, stroking the tom's wide soft head: he knew that, if Kobolt had wanted to, he could as easily have closed his teeth in the peacock's throat. He let Puppy sniff the long peacock-feather, then stuck it through his belt and went on.

There was a small lake at the bottom of the formal gardens, where Mutti and Landgraf Bernhardt would sometimes go out in a boat with their friends in the summertime. Part of it was edged with reeds, and Wolfram carefully crept around in that direction, for that was usually where the ducks and geese were, though the proud Niederwald swans were floating in the middle of the lake, shining white against the gray water. Sometimes wild herons would settle there as well, stalking through the shallows on their long legs, their narrow bills jerkily prodding the water for fish.

The mud sucked at his shoes as he moved in closer, soaking cold and clammy through the leather: he should, he thought, have taken them off, for Nurse would have something to say about that, but he would have gotten his red hose muddy anyway. Kobolt stayed back on dry ground, washing a paw fastidiously with his pink tongue. His golden-eyed stare seemed to say something about the stupidity of a young Graf who would get his feet wet on purpose, but Wolfram ignored him. Puppy, however, splashed gleefully after his master. "Shhh!" Wolfram hissed.

Suddenly there was a great flapping of wings through the rushes as the startled waterfowl rose, quacking hysterically. Wolfram drew his bow, taking aim, but he had been a little too slow: by the time he fired, the duck he had aimed at was already out of range, and the arrow fell short, splashing into the water. I shall have a stronger bow in time, he thought. He pulled another arrow from his quiver, setting it in the bow as the flock of fowl settled slowly towards the other end of the lake.

Wolfram waited quietly as the dawn-gray sky brightened towards blue. He knew, though he was not sure how, that there would be something else for him to shoot - if he were patient, if he did not move or speak. His hands relaxed on the bow, his breathing grew deep and even; only his eyes moved, keenly alert as he watched for the least stirring of reeds, flickering back towards the ducks and geese floating at the other end of the lake to see if any of them would rise again.

Then he heard the unmistakable slap of webbed feet against water: one of the swans was running over the lake, beating its great white wings furiously to launch it into the air. It stretched out its long neck as it left the surface, soaring powerfully in a low arc towards Wolfram's hiding place. Wolfram drew his bow, his eyes following the arrow-tip to its target even as he released the string. The arrow sank deep into the swan's snowy-feathered breast. and the smooth beating of its wide wings broke into a furious, convulsive struggle as it dropped, crushing the reeds beneath it.

Wolfram ran out at once, splashing loudly through the knee-deep water to claim his prize. The swan was so heavy that he could barely lift it, hugging its arrow-pierced breast to his own; its head hung limp over his shoulder, a little blood drooling from the corner of its beak. Triumphantly he lugged it back to the shore where Puppy and Kobolt waited for him, panting from the effort, and let it down upon the grass.

The swan's black eyes were already dulled with death, and its feathers were wet and muddy where it had fallen. Wolfram stretched its wings out to look at them - their span was twice that of his own arms - then plucked a handful of dew-wet grass and started to wipe off the worst of the mud, for he wanted his prize to look its best when he carried it back to the castle. He was able to get it fairly clean, though Puppy kept trying to lick the blood from around the arrow and Kobolt was able to snatch a mouthful of feathers from the swan's neck before Wolfram pushed him away.

Mine, Wolfram thought proudly, smiling to himself. He had made a perfect shot - he thought of the swan's struggling fall, and knew it would have been unbearable if it had kept thrashing in the water in pain. And then he would have had to run back to the castle for help, because Mutti had made him promise never to go too near the swans, which could break a grown man's arm with a blow of their powerful wings. But I knew I could shoot it cleanly, and I did!

Wolfram picked his swan up again, toiling up the long gentle slope towards the castle. It was not long before his arms and legs began to ache with effort from his burden: he stopped, squatting to put the swan down, and began to think if there were any better way to move it. The gate-guard was too far away to hear and - he pushed Puppy's curious wet nose away from the pinkish stain of blood on the swan's white breastfeathers - if he left his prey unguarded, Puppy and Kobolt between them would chew it to bits; but if he dragged the swan, it would get all dirty again. Perhaps if he spread the wings out, and wrapped his arms around under them, like so...

"Good morning, Graf Wolfram. I see you have found a use for your bow already."

Wolfram looked up in surprise. Ritter Gottfried was walking lightly towards him, his own huge white Pyrenean hound Etzel - Puppy's sire - following at his heels. The knight was not wearing any armour this morning, though his sword and dagger hung from the belt of silver plates about his hips: he was dressed in a plain doublet of deep red velvet over black hose, his dark hair pulled back in its usual simple tail, and the only adornments he bore were the small gold crucifix at his throat and the scarf of blue linen that was always knotted about his swordbelt.

"Yes, Herr Ritter," Wolfram answered politely. "I killed it with one shot." He liked Ritter Gottfried, but he was a little afraid of the stern-faced knight as well. He often suspected that Ritter Gottfried could tell exactly what he was thinking, and though Gottfried would play at wooden swords with him, correcting his moves and praising him when he managed to land a good blow, he seldom smiled or laughed: his friend Ritter Arnmut was much more fun to play with.

"That is skillfully done," Gottfried commented. "It is a heavy bird; would you care for some help bearing it home?"

Wolfram had been about to ask, but the knight's words fanned a spark of stubborn pride in his heart - and something else, a memory vanishing from his grasp like a wisp of fog. "I killed it, and I will bring it back."

Gottfried merely nodded. "I shall carry your bow if you like, then." Wolfram handed it over gladly, for it had been hard to keep his grip on both the weapon and the swan, and pushed himself to his feet with his burden in his arms.

"Skillfully shot, as I said," the knight went on as they walked slowly up towards the castle. "But, Wolfram, you should know that this is no season for shooting swans. They are nesting now, and it is ill to deprive young things of their mother when they cannot fend for themselves."

Wolfram thought about that for a moment. It was easy for him to imagine hungry little birds crying in their nests; and the thought, somehow, seemed mixed up with something of his own Mutti...Mutti's blue eyes looking at him from the sharp-beaked head of a falcon; her voice saying, Mutti loves you, Wolfram, hush and be good; and he had cried, for she was gone and he was alone with only Rose to look after him...The swan's body was cooling in his arms, and an immense guilt chilled him like cold water soaking through his clothes: had he killed a mother like his own?

"I didn't think about that," Wolfram snuffled. "I'm sorry."

Ritter Gottfried's gray eyes stared intently down at him, that penetrating gaze that always made Wolfram nervous, as if the knight were looking straight into his head. "Yes, I see that you are...Your father was a hunter, too," he added unexpectedly. "But he always took the greatest care in which beasts he chose to slay, and when, that it might be the better for the ones he spared: God gave Adam dominion over all the beasts of the earth in order that he might tend them according to their needs, even the creatures of the wild. Remember that, Wolfram, when next you draw your bow."

"I will. I promise it!" Wolfram said.

Ritter Gottfried patted his shoulder awkwardly. "That is well. But I did not come looking for you to talk to you of swans, nor of hunting, though it is strange that...well, never mind. Come, let us sit down."

Obediently Wolfram followed the knight to a stone bench by one of the fountains, easing his feather burden down and stretching out his sore arms. Puppy flopped down, a panting lump of muddy white fluff, on the grass; Etzel sat by his master, his big head resting on Gottfried's thigh.

Ritter Gottfried was silent for a moment, staring at the pale stone figure of the young maiden who ceaselessly poured water from her jug into a basin garlanded by gray stone roses - Wolfram had often wondered if it was magic, that the jug never emptied, however long she poured, nor did the basin at her feet ever overflow.

"You are seven now," the knight said at last. Wolfram nodded, wondering why Ritter Gottfried had bothered to say so - had he not given Puppy to Wolfram for his birthday yesterday? "And seven, so the Church tells us, is the age of reason. More to the point, perhaps, it is also the age at which it is time for you to take up the duties of a page, here or in some other castle. Now we spoke of this last night after you had gone to bed..." and by we, Wolfram knew that he meant Mutti and Landgraf Bernhardt and Ritter Arnmut and himself: it was those four who most often held counsel in Schloss Niederwald, for reasons that Wolfram could only dimly guess at, though he knew that it had something to do with something that had happened when he was very young, before Bernhardt had become Landgraf and married Mutti. "And your Mutti decided that it would be best for me to talk to you about it."

"Why?" Wolfram asked, staring straight back into Ritter Gottfried's deep gray eyes. The knight did not look away from him, as adults often did when he met their gazes directly, but said steadily, "Because there are things, many of which took place before you were born, that still touch deeply on both your Mutti and Landgraf Bernhardt. She feared that neither of them could advise you best: as a Graf, you shall learn that no one's counsel is uncoloured by the wishes and fears of their hearts, but you are too young for such things yet. In short, Wolfram, you have several choices before you. Graf Christoph von Fürstensee has offered to take you as a page, if you are willing, as has Graf Wolfgang von Schwarzenfels - Georg's father; you will remember Ritter Georg, at least from his visits here?"

Wolfram nodded. The red-haired knight had put him up on a pony's back, leading him about by the reins, but shaking his head with a grin when Wolfram had demanded to go faster.

"Landgraf Friedrich von Thuringia, to whom Landgraf Bernhardt was squired in his youth, has also offered to take you as a page, as has the Margraf of Meissen: both of them are great and noble men, and you have visited their castles, so you should know what awaits you there. Then again, you may do your service to Landgraf Bernhardt here in Schloss Niederwald. Your mother would prefer for you to stay here with her, for in your infancy she went through many trials to keep you safe, and she fears that there are those who may still mean to do you harm."

"What sort of harm?" Wolfram asked eagerly. It seemed to him that he could remember swords flashing within a ring of fiery light, a block of black and white stone carved with patterns that were almost familiar - the thought frightened him, but thrilled him too, though he could not say why. "Will they come to fight me?"

"Not harm to your body, Wolfram, but harm to your soul. Forgive me if I cannot tell you more, but you are too young yet to understand. If Margerite had her way," he whispered softly, "you would stay here in Schloss Niederwald forever and never know about the Order, or about your father."

"What about my father?" Wolfram demanded. "Who is the Order?"

Ritter Gottfried's eyes widened in shock, his knife-edged cheekbones whitening as the blood drained from them. "Christ forgive me! Wolfram," he said, staring intently into the boy's face, "I did not speak, and you did not hear me."

For a moment it seemed to Wolfram as though he were pushing against a great stone block, trying to move it aside...then his strength failed; a cloud veiled his sight, and something hummed vaguely in his ears. He blinked and shook his head, trying to remember what Gottfried had last said...Forgive me if I cannot tell you more, but you are too young to understand.

"What am I too young to understand?" Wolfram asked.

"The perils in which you may yet stand. However, I believe that they will come to you sooner or later, regardless of how carefully you are kept. When you are older, you shall know more. At any rate, there is yet another choice before you. You are, as you know, the Graf von Falkenstein, with castles and lands that you have not seen since you were an infant."

"I remember the storm," Wolfram said. "I got out of my cradle, and I walked to the window. The snow and wind were coming in."

Ritter Gottfried passed his hand across his brow, a faraway look on his face for a moment, as if he, too, were trying to remember something. "Yes...Yes, they were. Amazing, that you should still be able to call to mind something that happened when you were so young." The knight looked greatly troubled, and Wolfram wanted to ask him what was wrong - if it had been Mutti or Ritter Arnmut, he might have, but he did not dare to pry into Ritter Gottfried's thoughts.

"Your own folk, I believe, would think well of it if you came home, to grow up in the lands you are to rule rather than returning to them as a stranger ten years hence. Many others have said as much, and no doubt you will hear it often before you make your choice. But now I have a question for you. Have you ever - perhaps when you were just awakening, or just going to sleep - seen a man standing by your bed, who may have disappeared when you looked closely at him?"

"O, yes!" Wolfram answered. "He is tall and thin, with fair hair and a little pointed beard. Is he an angel? Nurse tells me that angels watch over me while I am sleeping."

Ritter Gottfried frowned. "No, he is no angel. I would not put you in terror needlessly, but it may be that he is your most dire enemy. Should you see him, close your eyes and say your prayers until he goes away. If he speaks to you, do not listen to anything he says, but come to tell your Mutti and myself directly, even if your nurse says that you should be in bed...I fear that his strength will be greater at Burg Falkenstein. If you decide that you must go there, Ritter Arnmut and I shall go with you, though for my own part, there are few castles on earth in which I would care less to dwell."

"Why is that? Is it haunted?" Wolfram enquired hopefully.

Gottfried stared severely at him until he dropped his eyes. "You will be better off someplace else, either staying here or going to another castle. Graf Christoph and Gräfin Eva have a daughter who is the same age as your sister, whom I do not doubt you will find pleasant company."

"Katharina is no fun," Wolfram declared. "She cried when I pointed my gun at her."

"A proper knight, Graf Wolfram, does not threaten women, least of all with terrible weapons of war - even in play. And unless I am much mistaken, you will find that Gräfin Eva's daughter does not cry so easily as your gentle little sister. Or, if you are more minded to hone your skills at fighting than to play with other children, I understand that Herr Hugo has recently come home to aid his father in the rule of the Schwarzenfels lands. He was in the Kaiser's guard for several years, as is his brother Herr Konrad now; and Herr Konrad was a tourney champion just as Herr Georg is now, which should show you the worth of the Burg Schwarzenfels armsmasters. Neither here, nor in the castles of the Landgraf of Thuringia or the Margraf of Meissen, shall you find a better man than Herr Hugo to train you with sword and lance."

Gottfried rose gracefully from his seat. "But there is time yet for you to think on all of these matters, and we should get your swan to the castle and cleaned before its bowels spoil the meat. I think, as well," the knight murmured as Wolfram heaved the swan up in his arms again, "that there may come another choice for you before too long: there is something in the air this morning such as I have not felt for years, though I do not know what it may be."

Gottfried said nothing more on that subject, but Wolfram had a great deal to ponder on as he carried his booty up towards Schloss Niederwald. He had thought to go in by the back gate, since that way was shorter, but Ritter Gottfried suggested that, if he wished to bear his prey in triumph, that it would be better to go in through the front door and thus to the great hall. "For your mother and Landgraf Bernhardt are undoubtedly breaking their fast by now, and I am sure they will wish to see what you have done."

The stained glass window of Schloss Niederwald's triangular entrance hall cast a pool of coloured light upon the flagstones. Wolfram's feet tingled as he walked through it, as though he were treading through flames that did not scorch him; it was as good as sitting in the chapel on a sunny day, ignoring Father Bruno's drone and squinting his eyes to stare up at the new window that Mutti and Landgraf Bernhardt had put in until the ruby and amethyst panes burning about Maria's glowing blue cloak and the shining white and gold of the Christ-Child in her arms all blurred into a brilliant wheel of colour stronger and more beautiful than any gemstones.

It was a hard climb up the stairs to the great hall with the swan: the huge bird seemed to grow heavier with every step as it slowly stiffened and cooled in his arms. Wolfram was panting hard by the time Gottfried nodded to the guard, who flung the door wide so that they might enter. Mutti and Landgraf Bernhardt were in their usual places at the head table, Katharina sitting primly beside Bernhardt in her little blue gown and pearled silk coif like a tidy miniature of her mother and nibbling on a little loaf of bread.

Suddenly eager to show them his swan, Wolfram no longer felt its weight as he bore it proudly forward with Puppy romping about his feet. "Mutti, look!" Wolfram called out. "I shot a swan, all by myself!"

Mutti smiled at him, her blue eyes warm as a caress. "Well-done, Wolfram! Set it on the table so we may see."

Wolfram's heart swelled with happiness as he heaved the great bird onto the table before his mother. One trailing wingtip struck her golden goblet, and she was just in time to save it from splashing wine all over the pale blue and green brocade of her gown, but she was laughing as she moved the cup aside. She touched the arrow in the swan's breast gently with a fingertip. "That was a single shot, I think," Mutti said. "You will grow to be a great hunter." Yet she had stopped laughing, and a faint mist veiled her blue eyes as she spoke, as though the words reminded her of something. My father? Wolfram wondered. No one ever speaks of him, save that Ritter Gottfried told me this morning he was a hunter.

"Aye, he will," said Landgraf Bernhardt, and for a moment his bearded face seemed grim, but then he, too, smiled. "That was well-shot indeed, Wolfram. I think you have earned the right to go with us when next we ride out after roedeer."

Katharina was looking at the swan, her blue eyes wide. "You killed it! Wolfi, it was a pretty bird. Why?"

Wolfram thought of the swan's young again, and almost hung his head with guilt, but he remembered that he was too old to be abashed by his little sister, and he could not bring the swan back to life. "We will have swan for dinner tonight," he said.

"I don't like swan," Katharina declared, pressing her mouth into a thin line of disapproval. "It's tough."

Mutti laughed. "So it is, Katharina, but would you deny your brother the right to eat what he has slain?" She gestured to one of the servants. "Take this swan to the kitchen, and tell Liutbirg to see what she can do with it. And be sure that it is carefully skinned and the hide cured for refeathering. If Jochanan has any flammable spirits, then perhaps, Wolfram, you shall see your swan breathing fire tonight."

Wolfram clapped his hands: sometimes when there were special guests, a swan or boar's head would be carried about the hall with blue flames coming from its mouth, and that delighted him more than any other subtlety. Still, he gazed sadly after the swan as the serving-man bore it off towards the kitchens.

"And you're dirty, too, Wolfi," Katharina criticized. "Nurse will be furious with you."

Wolfram glanced down at his tunic. The gold and green brocade was wet and a little dirty from the swan's feathers, with a stain of blood upon his chest where he had embraced his prey, and he could not see the colour of his shoes or his hose below the knees for the mud. Somewhere along the way, he had lost Kobolt's peacock feather too.

"Wolfram, Wolfram," Mutti sighed, and shook her head. "Next time you want to hunt waterfowl, tell Rose so that you can be properly dressed, and bring one of the huntsmen with a water-dog to retrieve your game for you. You must not wear fine clothes when you are likely to ruin them, for you know nothing of the means by which they are bought. Now go put on something clean, for you are not fit to sit at the table, and then you may break your fast, if you did not manage to steal something from the kitchen on your way out."

"Kobolt did. I didn't."

Mutti and Bernhardt both laughed at that, the Landgraf's mouth twisting up into a crooked grin. "Yes, I remember Liutbirg's ladle well enough myself. I have seen knights fighting on the field with less fury than our cook defending her kitchen...well, go on, Wolfram."

Remembering his manners - for Mutti insisted that a young Graf should always be courteous, even with his family - Wolfram bowed to the two of them and sketched another bow to his sister, then reclaimed his bow from Gottfried's hands and turned to go.

At that moment, a faint trumpet-blast wafted in from the walls outside. Mutti looked at Bernhardt, raising a curved eyebrow enquiringly.

The Landgraf shook his head. "I have not heard news of any guests coming. Gottfried?"

"No, Landgraf. I shall go see what is afoot."

The knight hastened from the hall. Wolfram, seeing his chance, slunk back into a shadowed corner. This was exciting: could it be one of the enemies Ritter Gottfried had spoken of?

"Father Etienne, perhaps?" Mutti was saying. "He sometimes arrives without sending word. And if he is travelling quietly, he may need our help."

Bernhardt crossed himself. "I pray it is not so, though of course if he does we shall give him whatever he needs. Are you well enough to aid him? I heard you coughing last night."

"I am well," Mutti said firmly, making Wolfram even more curious. Mutti and Bernhardt spoke of Father Etienne, sometimes, as though he ranked equally with the Kaiser himself - but what could Mutti help the priest with, that she would have to be in good health for? And Bernhardt had spoken to her almost as if she were a knight about to be called for a dangerous adventure...

Ritter Arnmut ran light-footed into the hall, his chainmail jingling and his cheeks pink beneath his open-faced bascinet. He bowed to the couple at the high table. "Landgraf, Landgräfin," he said. "There is a party of messengers from Kaiser Karl here, some twelve mounted knights. I have invited them in; their horses are being stabled, and they shall come before you shortly."

"That is well, Herr Ritter," Landgraf Bernhardt replied. "Did they tell you what your business is?"

"No, Landgraf. Herr Konrad is among them, however."

Bernhardt and Mutti both smiled - in relief, Wolfram thought. "Fetch Ritter Gottfried back in," Mutti ordered. "We would have the two of you here to hear their message, for we do not know what counsel we shall need upon it."

By the time the Kaiser's messengers entered Schloss Niederwald's hall, both Gottfried and Arnmut had taken their places at the high table, and the servants had spread out plates and refreshments. The smell of sausages and meat pastries made Wolfram's mouth water, and he wished that, like Kobolt, he could jump up on the table to snatch whatever took his fancy, but he knew that it was a sufficient stroke of luck that Mutti and Bernhardt had forgotten he was still there. Beside him, smelling the food, Puppy whined, and Wolfram crouched down to pet him, whispering, "Hush, be quiet, or they will make us go away."

Kaiser Karl's men were all dressed in fine armour beneath tabards embroidered with the Imperial eagle, the peaks of their bascinets crested with gold and black feathers - something Wolfram had never seen before, for he was used to crests sculpted with animals or heraldic devices. One of them, a tall, strong-featured man with a heavy black moustache, looked familiar; and it was he who stepped forward to bow before the Landgraf and Landgräfin.

"Be welcome in our hall, Herr Konrad," Bernhardt said. "What word do you bring from our Kaiser? The swords of Niederwald are, as always, at his service."

Herr Konrad smiled broadly. "Landgraf, the arms our Kaiser seeks are too small yet to wield a sword. We are sent to ask after the Landgräfin's son, Graf Wolfram von Falkenstein."

Wolfram could contain himself no longer. Forgetting his muddy dishevelement, he jumped to his feet, running out to the middle of the hall. "Herr Konrad, I am here!" he piped. "What does the Kaiser want of me?"

The Kaiser's knight stared down at him in amazement, and Wolfram was suddenly conscious of how he looked, dirty and foot-soaked from his morning's hunting. His cheeks flared, but he remembered not to shuffle his feet or hang his head like a peasant. "Graf Wolfram von Falkenstein, you have grown greatly since last I saw you," Herr Konrad said. "It is my pleasure to tell you that his Imperial Majesty, Karl IV, seeks to know whether you have already taken up the duties of a page elsewhere, or whether you would consent to serve in his household until you are of an age to become a squire."

Wolfram drew in a deep breath. His Mutti was smiling, but he could see the way the corners of her lips trembled, as if she were about to burst into tears. Katharina stared wide-eyed at him, her mouth open in shocked astonishment. Ritter Arnmut smiled too, a look of unmingled delight on his face; but Ritter Gottfried was only watching him quietly with that peculiar intense look, as though his gaze would pierce Wolfram's skull. Only Bernhardt was not looking at him. Instead, the Landgraf inclined his head towards Mutti, as if to say that it was a matter for her.

Then Ritter Gottfried, too, glanced at Mutti, and it seemed to Wolfram as if he could see something like a glimmer of light flashing between them, like an afterimage of sunlight bright behind blinking eyelids. Mutti nodded her coifed head, sighing softly. "Wolfram," she said. "You have reached the age of reason, and I know Ritter Gottfried has spoken to you of your choices: to stay and serve here, or to go elsewhere as a page...or to return to your own castle, Burg Falkenstein. Now it seems that another choice has been offered you, and one of great honour. If need be, we shall discuss each of these further before a final decision is made; but I should like to know your will in the matter, if it be that you have given it any thought yet."

Wolfram thought quickly. Burg Falkenstein sounded interesting, and it was his - he remembered looking out the window at the storm, and it almost seemed to him as though, remembering, he could hear the faint echo of a hunting horn again, as if it were calling him on. Yet something in what Ritter Gottfried had said had daunted him: facing the thought of returning to Burg Falkenstein was like trying to swing a knight's full-weight sword as it wobbled and drooped in his small hands. Not yet, but someday, he thought.

As to the other places that had been offered him, they all seemed equally unreal and dreamlike. Though their family had been Landgraf Friedrich's guests only this last Christmas, he could not even call that castle to his mind. But he remembered Kaiser Karl, the man in gold and white robes whose huge dark eyes had watched him play at swords with Wenzel - Mutti said he had been too young to remember anything, but it was clear in his mind. Wolfram had felt safe beneath the Kaiser's gaze, as though he were in the arms of a father strong enough to lift the world. And... again, he did not know how to put words to what he felt now, yet he was quite sure it was real.

The hunting horn of Burg Falkenstein, clear through the wailing of the storm...somewhere, the unbroken circle of candlelight shimmering before his gaze; the carved stone, black and white, its polished surface with the hauntingly familiar sigils smooth beneath his fingers...and Kaiser Karl's reassuring voice, gold brocade shining on white silk and white pearls gleaming on a cross of gold, a cross that Mutti had knelt before and lovingly kissed. For a moment, it seemed to Wolfram as though he stood teetering on a mountain's peak: a step in one direction would plunge him down upon the darkened crags below; another would set his track on the sunlit path before him, and the wind blew cold about him as if to lift him from his feet. And they all drew him, tugging at his heartstrings like three musicians quarrelling over a lyre. But the choice was his own: and he thought that this would not be his last chance to make it.

"I would be Kaiser Karl's page," Wolfram said.

He heard his Mutti's sigh of relief, and she dropped her hand from her mouth, as though she had been biting her fingernails the way Katharina did. "If that is what you wish, Wolfram, then I can think of no place of greater honour for you - can anyone here?"

Bernhardt shook his head, and even Ritter Gottfried gave her one of his rare quiet smiles. Mutti gestured to one of the servants, who ran to the kitchens to return with a pitcher of wine; goblets were filled for the Kaiser's knights, and Mutti rose to her feet. "Then I give you Graf Wolfram von Falkenstein, Kaiser Karl's newest page. Wolfram, may you serve the Kaiser well, and Maria and Christ be with you ever!"

The goblets lifted; the toast was drunk. Tasting the sweetness of the wine, Wolfram knew that he could not be happier. I chose the right one, he thought proudly. I hope I can do it when the time comes again!

# Historical Notes

This story takes place chiefly in 1365-66. The Black Death (not known by that name at the time: usually referred to as either the Death or the plague) had returned to Europe for a second, less devastating but still virulent, attack in 1361. Most of the primary characters are too young to remember the first outbreak in 1348 clearly, and so it is usually the second outbreak of which they are speaking. The realms of Niederwald, Fürstensee, and Falkenstein are fictional, though Bernhardt's neighbors the Margraf of Meissen (Saxony) and Friedrich, Landgraf of Thuringia, are real. In this period, the Holy Roman Empire was rather fragmented, and so such realms could have conceivably existed.

Burg Karlstein, one of the great architectural monuments of the fourteenth century, stands yet as Karl IV built it, 30 kilometers from Prague. Many of the impressive interior decorations are still in reasonably good condition; the extreme lavishness of the Castle's decor, particularly the gold and precious stones ornamenting the walls in the Chapel of the Holy Cross, was described in sources of the time. Both St. Wenzel's crown and Karl's agate goblet - originally a Roman bowl, made into a goblet by the addition of the gold band and foot in the Middle Ages - still survive.

The Order of the Light-Bearers is fictional. However, the fourteenth century was both the age of heresy and the beginning of the Rennaissance. The Order is chiefly based on a combination of ideas of the time concerning heretical beliefs, such as those expressed in the trial of the Knights Templar in the earlier part of the century, and conspiracies of a later date, such as the Bavarian Illuminati. Had the Illuminati been, as some conspiracy historians have suggested, born from earlier organizations, they might have been very like the Order of the Light-Bearers as they are presented in these books.

The magic practised by the characters in this trilogy is generally consistent with mediaeval belief. The Satanism of the Order of the Light-Bearers is more appropriate to the late mediaeval/Renaissance imagination than to reality: it has its origin in the trials of the Templars, the alleged theology of the Cathars, and similar sources, with specific rituals altered from books of dubious origin (particularly the Key of Solomon and the Goetia) to be appropriate for Satanists - or, more accurately, Gnostics worshipping Lucifer as the source of knowledge.

Father Etienne and Margerite are representatives of the traditional practise of mediaeval magic, in which the magician chiefly uses the power of God and various angels to compel spirits or forces; the rituals of the Light-Bearers are counter-improvisations on this theme, and should not be tried at home. The practice of summoning spirits to carry the magician swiftly from place to place was apparently a favourite among mediaeval sorcerors: in some Scandinavian folk-stories, the magician calls the Devil whom he tricks into giving him a ride, but grimoires of this period and slightly later include instructions for calling up non-demonic spirits for transport purposes as well.

The organization of the Light-Bearers is roughly an inversion of that of the Church, though the concealed hierarchy of the Council of Princes is unique to the Order, in which power and position are all-important. Birgitta's deceased father represents a typical figure of Icelandic folklore, the sorceror-priest. In the introduction to his translation of an Icelandic galdrabók (grimoire), Stephen Flowers observes that the rebellious and intellectual Satan may have been more attractive to the Óðinnic tradition than the God of the Catholic church, and it is this viewpoint which we have maintained for the late Father Thórkell.

Modern followers of the Norse religion, however, generally
repudiate the mediaeval confusion of the Heathen god
with the Christian devil, an awareness to which Birgitta
herself comes at last. The Icelandic spell by which she
opens the Light-Bearer's barred door is a verse from the
Eddic poem Hávamál, in which Óðinn recounts a list of
the magical songs he knows: it translates as, "I know that
fourth (magical spell), if there are bonds on my limbs: so I
chant, that I may walk, the fetters spring off my feet, and the
shackles off my hands."

Her exclamation upon seeing Gottfried's favour from
Perchte is also in Icelandic: "Thórr's Hammer - what is that
for Christian men to bear?" Likewise, her remark on the
subject of Gottfried's sword is in Icelandic: the first portion,
"One should never step a foot away from his weapons on
the field," is the advice of Óðinn from the same poem as the
spell, while the second part, roughly, "One should guard
helm and byrnie well: it is good to have them to hand,"
are the words of King Hákon the Good upon entering
Valhall, according to Eyvindr skáldaspillir's memorial poem
Hákonarmál.

The charm with which Meister Stefan heals the horse is an
Old High German charm known as the "Zweite Merseburger
Zauberspruch". Variants of it are known throughout the
Indo-European version, including a few Christian versions
in which Christ appears as the master magician; the Zweite
Merseburger Zauberspruch, however, calls on Wodan.
Another figure of folklore met in this book is Mother
Perchte: variations of the repairing-the-wain story appear
throughout Germany. Usually the helpful man is a peasant,
who is given a handful of wood-chips for his trouble; he
casts them away, thinking them worthless, but one of them
sticks in his boot or clothing, and when he gets home he
finds that it has turned to pure gold.

The item which Perchte gives Gottfried is a miniature flint
votive axe from the Stone Age: such axes, both full-sized and
miniatures, were known in Germanic folklore as "thunder-
stones" and often hung in a house to protect it from
lightning. Birgitta's identification of it as "Thórr's Hammer"
is quite accurate: the axe of the Stone Age thunder-god may
have directly evolved into the symbol of Thórr's Hammer,
worn by Norse Heathens as an answer to the Christian cross,
and a connection between the apotropaic stone axes and
the god Thórr was perceived in Scandinavia up nearly to the
present day. The "herring and dumplings" Perchte mentions
were her traditional foods; they are also, of course, proper
food for the abstinences Gottfried observes so strenuously.

The ritual of exorcism carried out by Margerite and her
companions is based on the actual Catholic rites of exorcism,
as published by the late Father Malachi in his book Hostage
to the Devil. Much of the general description of possession
and the process of exorcism is also based loosely on the
descriptions of the cases in this book: the reader is assured
that the means of demonic expression as we have rendered
them are actually toned down considerably from the
distressing details given by Father Malachi. We have also
taken a considerable liberty in making Margerite the chief
executor of the exorcism: the Church restricts this very
dangerous and problematical activity to qualified priests.

Although the primary characters and their realms are
products of my own imaginations, as are such notables as
Cardinal Jean de Grenville and Cardinal Fleurs, Urban V
and Karl IV are both real historical figures. In the middle of
what Barbara Tuchman called "the calamitous fourteenth
century", Pope Urban and Kaiser Karl stand out as two of
the genuinely good political figures of the day. The influence
of both is present throughout the trilogy, most especially in
their heroic attempts to either destroy or clean up the Free
Companies ravaging Europe. Unfortunately, these efforts
were either largely fruitless or actually backfired.

When the Papal excommunication and Imperial sanctions
failed to work in 1364, Urban and Karl tried the counter-
means of offering the Free Companies absolution if they
would just go to fight on various southern and eastern
crusades, notably Granada and Hungary. A large band
of Free Companies under the command of Bertrand du
Guesclin surrounded Avignon and demanded 200,000
francs; Bertrand refused to accept monies raised from the
laity, insisting that the payment must come from the Papal
treasury.

Meanwhile, another large group under Arnaut de Cervole
gathered in Lorraine on the way to Hungary, but the citizens
rose against them; the people of Strasbourg refused to
let them cross the bridge over the Rhine, and Kaiser Karl
was forced to come with his own army to bar the way.
Bertrand du Guesclin, when not leading gatherings of
Free Companies, was one of the most important military
leaders in France. He can best be described as the Middle
Ages' foremost anti-knight: a Breton born of poor nobility,
notable for the success of his decidedly unchivalric tactics
and the ruthless effectiveness of his bloody-minded
Breton followers, contemptuous of the Church and of the
impractical knightly ideals in general.

Bertrand du Guesclin was also known as the ugliest
man in France, being flat-nosed, dark-skinned, short and
heavy; Cuvelier's poetic rendition of his life describes his
parents' disgust for their gruesome-looking son, and he
was described as an "hog in armour" (Tuchman, A Distant
Mirror, p. 226). Madame du Guesclin was, indeed, famed
for her astrological and occult skills; her description is
fanciful, but given Bertrand's appearance, we thought it not
unreasonable to portray her as both short of stature and very
near-sighted. The account of Papal Avignon, particularly
the Papal palace in 1365, is as accurate as we could make
it, down to the white peacocks on the Pope's lawn. Avignon
in the fourteenth century was, indeed, a hotbed of occult
activity of various types, from the perfectly acceptable
science of astrology to criminal attempts to do murder by
means of images, as described here.

Following the brief, devastating career of the proto-Inquisitor Conrad von Marburg, the Inquisition did not have a free hand in Germany until 1369, when Karl IV issued an edict extending the fullest possible authority to the Inquisitorial papal delegates, for reasons not generally clear. The Dominican priest Walther Kerlinger was the Inquisition's principal delegate in the Empire under Karl. Their chief charge was the investigation of the Beghards and Beguines (the same heresy; Beghards were members of its male religious community, Beguines were female), a possibly Luciferian or Gnostic sect which also had some connection with the flagellants (officially suppressed from 1349 onward).

The Inquisitorial methods were generally as described, with burning a last resort for those who refused, even under torture, to confess and repent their heresies (in this period, primarily deliberate martyrs such as Cathars and members of other alternate sects). As mentioned here, the Templars in Germany escaped the persecutions suffered by their Order in France. The Teutonic Knights, who at this time had conquered Prussia and were generally engaged in campaigns to the East, are most often portrayed in historical and historical/fantasy novels as bloody-minded villains; although there is undoubtedly a certain basis for this, it was our pleasure to present a different side of that warrior Order here.

Trotting for hours in full armour was an actual penance of the Teutonic Knights, and a fairly harsh one: the rising trot (English posting) was not developed until the seventeen-hundreds, and an armoured sitting trot would swiftly become extremely painful (for normal use, the mediaeval horse had a very smooth gait between a walk and a trot which was known as the pace or amble, similar to the Icelandic horse's tölt). The intense austerities practiced by Gottfried were not uncommon in the Middle Ages as a response to a perceived need for penance. Technically, abstinence was supposed to be practiced on Wednesdays, Fridays, and Saturdays, but the Friday abstinence was the most notable of the three.

Exemptions from the regular weekday abstinence and the longer periods such as Advent and Lent were extremely common, for reasons including physical labour, travelling, pregnancy, nursing, sickness, and having a soft priest who would let his lord get away with it.

In the Middle Ages, the expression of affection between men was generally far more open than it is today: a knight could speak of his love for a male friend without raising any eyebrows. The very close relationship between Gottfried and his former squire Arnmut - like that of Prince Philip and Richard Coeur-de-Lion, who likewise shared a single bed while Richard was visiting Philip after the signing of peace between Philip and Henry II in 1187 - though quite sufficient to arouse varying degrees of suspicion among their associates, was by no means as obviously sexual as such closeness would seem to the modern observer.

Trial by combat was rarer than it is usually portrayed as being. It was chiefly employed in extremely grievous cases such as this, where no other means to determine the truth could be found, as the last resort of justice. Wolfram's delay in crawling and sudden ability to walk are not too uncommon; his early verbal development and co-ordination, and the level of mental and verbal acuity displayed by both himself and his sister Katharina at the ages of, respectively, seven and five are unusual, but by no means impossible.

Children in the Middle Ages were generally dressed and to some degree treated as small adults, not least because they were expected to be responsible adults much earlier than they are now (Margerite was chatelaine of her father's castle at fifteen, and is nineteen when she marries Bernhardt - as a comparison, Joan of Arc was burned at the age of nineteen); child prodigies of all types were no rarer in the mediaeval period than they are today, and possibly more common, given the early training and encouragement in certain skills, particularly among the nobility.

The Christmas songs in Burg Fürstensee, In dulce jubilo and Gaudete, were both popular mediaeval carols; the composition of the mixed language In dulce jubilo, by the mystic Heinrich Suso, pre-dated the events here by only a few years. Carols led by one singer with a chorus joining in, usually as accompaniments to ring-dances, were a favourite entertainment of the Middle Ages. The English song sung in Burg Falkenstein, the "Canterbury Carol", is also mediaeval.

Although heraldry was well-established by the fourteenth century, a certain amount of variation still occurred. In particular, the double-headed eagle which became the emblem of the Holy Roman Empire alternated with a single-headed eagle. Karl IV seems to have preferred the latter form: in his portrait from the votive tablet of Johannes Ocko von Vlasim, the shield by the Kaiser's feet shows the single-headed version, as does the armourial hanging in Burg Karlstein's Marienkirche. Gold and white seem to have been variously used for the field: the armourial hanging has the black eagle on a white background, as does one of the shields in the Ocko votive tablet, but the shield by Karl's feet shows it on gold.

The Great Pyrenees breed, a huge white furry dog bred to keep bears and wolves from the flocks of French shepherds, already existed and was reasonably popular among French nobles in the Middle Ages; with the resurgence of native predators in the wilder parts of France, the Great Pyrenees is also experiencing a resurgence in its traditional duties. Meister Stefan's dogs are Norwegian Elkhounds, a breed which has not changed significantly in any particular since the Stone Age. Kobolt and Kriemhilt, though earth-elementals in actuality, are based in their feline form on the Norwegian Forest Cat, a breed which probably also existed in the Middle Ages, being thought to have descended from long-haired cats brought back to Scandinavia by Viking travellers in the East. A full-grown Forest Cat tom (they may reach 25 pounds) is quite capable of bringing down a peacock: the authors have lost fowl of their own this way.

The general sense of time was based on ecclesiastical hours: matins (between midnight and two in the morning), laudes (dawn), prime (about 6 A.M.), tierce (about 9 A.M.), sext (about noon), nones (about 3 P.M.), vespers (about 5 P.M.), and compline (between 6 and 8 P.M.) - the precise times, of course, depending on the season of the year. Gear-operated clocks were used in the fourteenth century, but generally appeared as tower-clocks in urban areas.

Those who are familiar with the works of Richard Wagner may recognise Wolfram's shooting of the swan from the first appearance of Parsifal in the opera of the same name.

# Glossary

aventail - a throat-protector of chain-mail worn with a bascinet.

bascinet - an open-faced helmet with a conical top, sometimes worn under a greathelm.

Frowe - Lady. The masculine equivalent, fro, had probably been lost before the conversion of the Germanic peoples; hence the modern Frau and Herr (the latter from the Old High German herro, implying age and wisdom). Herr is used here roughly as "lord".

fustian - a type of relatively inexpensive fabric, usually wool, with a raised nap, similar to velveteen.

Graf - specifically, "Count", but in practise, a Graf could be anything from a local lord with three knights to the prince of a very large area. Ruprecht and Heinrich are on the lower end of the title's implications.

Gräfin - the feminine equivalent to Graf.

greathelm - the typical knight's helmet of the Middle Ages, covering head and neck. It offered better protection than the open-faced bascinet, but also restricted the vision, head-movement, and breathing of the wearer. Modern re-enactors have been known to refer to helmets of this type as "sweat-buckets", and for good reason.

Landgraf/gräfin - a title similar to Graf, but suggesting a realm of very significant size.

Knappe - squire. Young men of noble birth would be squired to a knight, and would expect to be knighted

either on the battlefield after a significant deed, or in the
general course of proper service.
Ritter - knight. "Ritter Gottfried" would be equivalent to
the English "Sir Gottfried".

Óðinn - the Old Norse name of the god also known as
Wodan or Wotan in Germany. He is the Germanic god
who is most often associated with magic, particularly the
magic of runes and incantations.

panache - a crest of feathers, most popular in eastern
Europe at this time.

rondel - a flat circle.

Verjuice - a sharp flavouring made from unripe grapes
or sometimes crabapples, used in much the same way as
lemon juice is commonly used nowadays.

Melodi Lammond-Grundy grew up in California and went to college at the University of Southern Mississippi. She spent some years in Colorado, then moved to San Francisco, where she was, for a time, a member of the well-known household and writers' community. She has been in the pagan/heathen community since the 1990s and has degrees in both history and anthropology.

In her spiritual life, she has studied spae-craft, a form of trance-based native Germanic divination. A spákona is the diviner, not the art of divination. which she learned from Diana Paxson.

She still practices divination and psychic readings to this day, lending herself to speak about current events. Her writing skills were first shown in several online publications, followed by co-authoring the Falcon Dream Trilogy. Melodi was one of the first authors to come on-board at Three Little Sisters, and we are pleased to be able to present both her non-fiction work and her upcoming Atlantis novel.

From his humble beginnings, Stephan Grundy/Kveldulf Gundarsson would make his mark on the world by writing on the rarest and obscure myths breathing new life into them, for a new generation of readers. His fictional works written under Stephan Grundy focused on mythology and history and were met with international success. Along with his fictional works, under the pen name Kveldulf Gundarsson he stamped his mark on Germanic Paganism (also known as heathenry) and Germanic Culture.

He is an Elder in the organization The Troth where he has dedicated a majority of his life influencing major changes in the organization, including the development of anti-racist and anti-sexist ideals. He has fought for equality in transgendered communities, as well as fighting for the acceptance of Loki. Gundarsson has shaped heathenry through his numerous academic and fictional works as well as his extensive articles, thesis papers, and his creation and sustainment of the lore program within The Troth. His hobbies included wood-working, jewelry making, and gardening as well as historical re-enactment. He is currently attending medical school in Ireland supported by his loving wife Melodi where they maintain a local hof called The Tribe of Thor

# The Three Little Sisters

The Three Little Sisters is an indie publisher that puts authors first. We specalize in the strange and unusual. From titles about pagan and heathen spirituality to traditional fiction and non-fiction we bring books to life.

https://the3littlesisters.com

www.ingramcontent.com/pod-product-compliance
Lightning Source LLC
Chambersburg PA
CBHW040509170726
48295CB00012B/142